THE YEAR'S BEST

science fiction

fifteenth annual collection

ALSO BY GARDNER DOZOIS

ANTHOLOGIES

A Day in the Life
Another World
Best Science Fiction Stories of the
  Year #6–10
The Best of Isaac Asimov's Science
  Fiction Magazine
Time-Travellers from Isaac Asimov's
  Science Fiction Magazine
Transcendental Tales from Isaac
  Asimov's Science Fiction Magazine
Isaac Asimov's Aliens
Isaac Asimov's Mars
Isaac Asimov's SF Lite
Isaac Asimov's War
Isaac Asimov's Planet Earth
  (with Sheila Williams)
Isaac Asimov's Robots
  (with Sheila Williams)
Isaac Asimov's Cyberdreams
  (with Sheila Williams)
Isaac Asimov's Skin Deep
  (with Sheila Williams)
Isaac Asimov's Ghosts
  (with Sheila Williams)
Isaac Asimov's Vampires
  (with Sheila Willilams)
Isaac Asimov's Moons
  (with Sheila Williams)
Isaac Asimov's Christmas
  (with Sheila Williams)
The Year's Best Science Fiction, #1–14
Future Earths: Under African Skies
  (with Mike Resnick)

Future Earths: Under South
  American Skies
  (with Mike Resnick)
Future Power
  (with Jack Dann)
Aliens! (with Jack Dann)
Unicorns! (with Jack Dann)
Magicats! (with Jack Dann)
Magicats 2 (with Jack Dann)
Bestiary! (with Jack Dann)
Mermaids! (with Jack Dann)
Sorcerers! (with Jack Dann)
Demons! (with Jack Dann)
Dogtales! (with Jack Dann)
Ripper! (with Susan Casper)
Seaserpents! (with Jack Dann)
Dinosaurs! (with Jack Dann)
Little People! (with Jack Dann)
Dragons! (with Jack Dann)
Horses! (with Jack Dann)
Unicorns 2 (with Jack Dann)
Invaders! (with Jack Dann)
Angels! (with Jack Dann)
Dinosaurs II (with Jack Dann)
Hackers (with Jack Dann)
Timegates (with Jack Dann)
Clones (with Jack Dann)
Modern Classics of Science Fiction
Modern Classic Short Novels of
  Science Fiction
Modern Classics of Fantasy
Killing Me Softly
Dying For It

FICTION

Strangers
The Visible Man (collection)
Nightmare Blue
  (with George Alec Effinger)
Slow Dancing Through Time
  (with Jack Dann, Michael Swanwick, Susan Casper, and Jack C.
  Haldeman II)
The Peacemaker
Geodesic Dreams (collection)

NONFICTION

The Fiction of James Tiptree, Jr.

THE YEAR'S BEST

science fiction

fifteenth annual collection

edited by **Gardner Dozois**

ST. MARTIN'S GRIFFIN ✹ NEW YORK

In memory of
my mother
Dorothy G. Dozois
and my father
Raymond G. Dozois

Rest in Peace

ISBN 0-312-19033-6

First St. Martin's Griffin Edition: June 1998

10 9 8 7 6 5 4 3 2 1

acknowledgment is made for permission to print the following material:

"Beauty in the Night," by Robert Silverberg. Copyright © 1997 by Agberg Ltd. First published in *Science Fiction Age*, September 1997. Reprinted by permission of the author.

"Second Skin," by Paul J. McAuley. Copyright © 1997 by Paul J. McAuley. First published in *Asimov's Science Fiction*, April 1997. Reprinted by permission of the author.

"Steamship Soldier on the Information Front," by Nancy Kress. Copyright © 1997 by Nancy Kress. First published in *Future Histories*, edited by Stephen McClelland, Horizon House (UK) 1997.

"Reasons to be Cheerful," by Greg Egan. Copyright © 1997 by Interzone. First published in *Interzone*, April 1997. Reprinted by permission of the author.

"Moon Six," by Stephen Baxter. Copyright © 1997 by Stephen Baxter. First published in *Science Fiction Age*, March 1997. Reprinted by permission of the author and the author's agent, The Maggie Noach Agency.

"We Will Drink a Fish Together . . . ," by Bill Johnson. Copyright © 1997 by Dell Magazines. First published in *Asimov's Science Fiction*, May 1997. Reprinted by permission of the author and the author's agent, Gay Haldeman.

"Escape Route," by Peter F. Hamilton. Copyright © 1997 by Interzone. First published in *Interzone*, July 1997. Reprinted by permission of the author.

"Itsy Bitsy Spider," by James Patrick Kelly. Copyright © 1997 by Dell Magazines. First published in *Asimov's Science Fiction*, June 1997. Reprinted by permission of the author.

"A Spy in Europa," by Alastair Reynolds. Copyright © 1997 by Interzone. First published in *Interzone*, June 1997. Reprinted by permission of the author.

"The Undiscovered," by William Sanders. Copyright © 1997 by Dell Magazines. First published in *Asimov's Science Fiction*, March 1997. Reprinted by permission of the author.

"Echoes," by Alan Brennert. Copyright © 1997 by Mercury Press, Inc. First published in *The Magazine of Fantasy & Science Fiction*, May 1997. Reprinted by permission of the author.

"Getting to Know You," by David Marusek. Copyright © 1997 by David Marusek. First published in *Future Histories*, edited by Stephen McClelland, Horizon House (UK) 1997.

"Balinese Dancer," by Gwyneth Jones. Copyright © 1997 by Dell Magazines. First published in *Asimov's Science Fiction*, September 1997. Reprinted by permission of the author.

"Marrow," by Robert Reed. Copyright © 1997 by Robert Reed. First published in *Science Fiction Age*, July 1997. Reprinted by permission of the author.

contents

acknowledgments

The editor would like to thank the following people for their help and support: first and foremost, Susan Casper, for doing much of the thankless scut work involved in producing this anthology; Michael Swanwick, Ellen Datlow, Virginia Kidd, Vaughne Lee Hansen, Sheila Williams, Jared Goldman, David Pringle, Jonathan Strahan, Charles C. Ryan, Nancy Kress, David G. Hartwell, Jack Dann, Janeen Webb, Warren Lapine, Ed McFadden, Tom Piccirilli, Dave Truesdale, Lawrence Person, Dwight Brown, Liz Holliday, Darrell Schweitzer, Corin See, and special thanks to my own editor, Gordon Van Gelder.

Thanks are also due to Charles N. Brown, whose magazine *Locus* (Locus Publications, P.O. Box 13305, Oakland, CA 94661, $43.00 for a one-year subscription [twelve issues] via second class; credit card orders [510] 339-9198) was used as a reference source throughout the Summation, and to Andrew Porter, whose magazine *Science Fiction Chronicle* (Science Fiction Chronicle, P.O. Box 022730, Brooklyn, NY 11202-0056, $35.00 for a one-year subscription [twelve issues]; $42.00 first class) was also used as a reference source throughout.

Doomsayers continued to predict the imminent demise of science fiction throughout 1997, some of them even seeming to look forward to it with gloomy, headshaking, I-told-you-so-but-you-wouldn't-listen-to-*me* relish; but, although there were cutbacks—some of them serious ones—it seems to me that the actual numbers and the actual real-world situation do not justify these sorts of gloomy predications. To modify the words of Mark Twain, the Death of Science Fiction has been greatly exaggerated.

The big, dramatic, catastrophic recession/bust/slump that genre insiders have been predicting for more than a decade now in fact did *not* happen in 1997. In spite of cutbacks and even some failing or faltering imprints (and new imprints, some of them quite major, were being added even as old ones disappeared), science fiction and the related fields of fantasy and horror remain large and various genres, with almost a thousand "books of interest" to the three fields published in 1997, according to the newsmagazine *Locus*, and science fiction and fantasy books were still making a lot of money for a lot of different publishers (although the market is changing and evolving, with mass-market titles declining and trade paperback titles on the rise). Artistically and creatively, the field has never been in better shape, with an enormous and enormously varied number of top authors producing an amazing spectrum of first-rate work, ranging all the way from the hardest of hard science fiction through wild baroque Space Opera and sociological near-future speculation to fantasy of a dozen different sorts, with uncountable hybrids of all those sorts of stories (and with other genres as well, including the historical novel, the mystery, and even the Western novel!) filling in the interstices. In terms of there being first-class work of many different sorts available to be read, *this* is the Golden Age, nor are we out of it!

As usual, there were many contradictory omens out there to be read, and it is entirely possible to read the very same signs and make either pessimistic or optimistic predictions about the future, depending on what evidence you look at and what weight you arbitrarily decide to give it.

There were certainly plenty of Bad Omens around to look at. Original books declined by nearly 100 titles in 1997 compared to 1996, which, in turn, had had 130 fewer original books than 1995, a drop of over 17 percent in two years; the magazine market was still precarious; and mass-market continued to shrink. HarperCollins cancelled 106 books, about 7 percent of the 1,600 trade books they published last year; TSR Inc. fell deeply in debt and was sold to Wizards of the Coast Inc.; Wired Books, the publishing arm of *Wired* magazine, was reported to have lost $35 million dollars, scuttling their plans to launch an imprint of SF titles (or at least putting it on hold); and there were cutbacks elsewhere as well. You could read these omens and draw quite a gloomy picture of the future, and many commentators did just that.

On the other hand, while mass-market continued to shrink, trade paperbacks and hardcovers were growing more frequent, and while some companies were struggling financially and/or contracting, Avon, under the direction of Lou Aronica, is launching an ambitious new genre line called Eos (replacing the old AvoNova imprint), HarperPrism is increasing the number of titles it produces, and Simon & Schuster UK is launching another ambitious new SF line, Earthlight, under the editorship of John Jerrold. Jim Turner was dismissed from his long-held job at Arkham House last year, but bounced back by launching a new small-press imprint of his own, Golden Gryphon Press, and Stephe Pagel also launched a new small-press imprint, Meisha Merlin Publishing. You can draw a different set of conclusions from *these* facts, and forecast a quite different sort of future.

Then there are things that can be viewed as *either* positive or negative, depending on which spin you put on it. Random House UK sold its SF/fantasy imprint, Legend, to Little, Brown UK, publisher of the Orbit SF line; Legend will be absorbed into Orbit, under the editorial direction of Tim Holman, with Colin Murray staying on as editorial consultant and Lisa Rogers joining the editorial team. The downbeat take on this is that there's now one genre line where there once were two, but since the Legend backlist will be reissued as Orbit books, it's quite possible that the end result of this will be that *more* genre titles will eventually see print than they did before. Similarly, although TSR Inc. died as an independent entity, the absorption of its output into Wizards of the Coast Inc. may eventually result in more overall titles being published in that area as well. And you'll notice that even really severe cutbacks, on an almost unprecedented level, still leaves HarperCollins a very large company even *after* the cuts (and most of those cuts weren't SF titles anyway).

Then there were other developments whose ultimate ramifications are impossible as yet to predict at all, one way or the other.

We got a break from the usual game of Editorial Musical Chairs in 1997, a year in which there were few if any significant changes, as far as which editor was working where. Once again, however, there were some major changes at the very top levels of publishing houses, the consequences of which—which could prove to be either positive or negative—may take years to work themselves out. Elaine Koster left Penguin Putnam, where she was president and publisher of Dutton, Plume, and Signet, to become a literary agent. Clare Ferraro, former senior VP and publisher of Ballantine, took over as president of Dutton and Plume, but not Signet. David Shanks, the president of Putnam and Berkley, took on the additional job of president of Signet. Judith M. Curr, former senior VP and editor-in chief, will become publisher at Signet. Harold Evans, president and publisher of Random House, resigned to become editorial director and vice-chairman of Mort Zuckerman's Publication Group. He was replaced by Ann Godoff, former executive VP, who also retained her former title of editor-in-chief of Randon House. Random House executive VP Jane Friedman became president and CEO of HarperCollins, replacing Anthea Disney, who became chairman of Rupert Murdoch's News America. And HarperCollins (UK) deputy managing director Malcolm Edwards moved to Orion to become managing director and publisher.

So I'm not willing to read memorial services over the grave of the genre just yet. Science fiction has plenty of problems, sure, from the decline of the midlist (which has driven many authors into writing media novels in order to survive) to the general unavailability of backlist titles as opposed to the way it was in the Old Days, from the way new authors can find their careers deadlocked by the refusal of chain-store buyers to order books from anyone whose first few titles didn't do geometrically increasing business (a system that, if it had been in place back then, would have insured that you'd never have heard of writers such as Isaac Asimov, Robert Heinlein, and Frank Herbert, all of whom built a following slowly over a number of years) to the alarming tendency of some publishers to think that they can assure "sure sales" by publishing *nothing but* media tie-in novels (apparently realizing that just publishing media novels is not a *sure* enough sure-thing, some publishers have now progressed to publishing media tie-in novels by *media celebrities*). What's next? How about media tie-in novels by *famous serial killers?* I can see it now: *Star Trek Bloodbath,* by Charles Manson—but science fiction also has a lot of vitality and staying power, and, for all its problems, it's far from down for the count yet.

As I've said here before, even if a deeper recession is ahead (and I'm not at all sure that it is), I find it unlikely that any recession will be capable of reducing SF to pre-1974 levels of readership or sales, unless it's a recession so big that most of the publishing industry at large collapses with it. And as Gordon Van Gelder recently said, in an editorial in *The Magazine of Fantasy & Science Fiction,* commenting on a critic's lament that there's nothing but crap to be found on the shelves in the SF sections of bookstores: "Back in 1960, he wouldn't have been so distressed by the SF section of the story because *it didn't exist back then.* Remember please that SF specialty shops like A Change of Hobbit in L.A. and The SF Shop in New York were founded in the 1970s because SF could be so hard to find. . . . Personally, I think there's more good SF getting published nowadays than most people have time to read, there are plenty of interesting new writers coming into the field, and lots of the field's veterans are producing top-flight work. So what's this talk about SF dying?" I also wholeheartedly agree with Warren Lapine, who, in an editorial in the Spring 1998 issue of *Absolute Magnitude,* said: "It's time that everyone in Science Fiction got off their collective asses and stopped whining about the future. Are you worried about magazines? Then subscribe to a couple of them. Are you worried about books? Then buy a few of them." I was in an on-line real-time conference a couple of weeks ago, talking—typing?—to a woman who said that she was extremely worried that all of the science fiction magazines were going to die, and who then went on to add that she goes down to Borders bookstore every month, faithfully reads all the science fiction magazines while having coffee and croissants, and then *puts them all back on the shelf* and leaves the store! And I thought to myself in amazement, Lady, you're part of the problem, not part of the solution. *Next time*, skip the croissants, take out your wallet, and actually *buy* the goddamned magazines *before* you read them! Similarly, don't wait for that novel you've been wanting to read to hit the used–book store, buy it *now*, while the royalties will not only do the author some good, but will actually help to keep the entire mechanism of the science fiction publishing industry in operation.

Of course, none of this may be enough. Gordon and Warren and I may all be whistling past the graveyard. Only time will tell.

But my own prediction is that science fiction as a viable genre will survive at least well into the next century—and perhaps for considerably longer than that.

It was another bad year in the magazine market, although some of the turbulence caused by the recent chaos in the domestic distribution network—when bigger distributors abruptly swallowed up the small independent distributors—has quieted a bit, with things settling down (for the moment, at least) to somewhere closer to a rest state. The print magazines that survived the storm are working on adopting various bailing strategies to deal with the water they shipped (adjusting their "draw," for instance—sending fewer issues to newsstands that habitually sell less, so that fewer issues overall need to be printed and distributed in order to sell one issue, increasing the magazine's efficiency, and thereby lowering costs, and so increasing profitability), and nervously eyeing the new storm clouds—in the form of new hikes in paper costs coming up next year.

To move from the world of overheated metaphor to the world of cold figures, all the science fiction magazines suffered further drops in their circulation figures in 1997. About the only cheerful thing that can be said about this fact is that it was not as precipitous a drop as had been registered the year before, when the distribution network problems really began to bite deep, and that a few of the magazines are actually beginning to creep *up* again, although minusculely, in newsstand sales. Still, *Asimov's Science Fiction*, *Analog Science Fiction & Fact*, *The Magazine of Fantasy & Science Fiction*, and *Science Fiction Age* all registered the lowest circulation figures in their respective histories. Even the fantasy magazine *Realms of Fantasy*, the only magazine to show a *gain* in circulation in 1996, was down some, although only by a measly 0.5 percent. *Asimov's* lost about 3,700 in subscriptions but gained about 360 in newsstand sales, for a 7.4-percent loss in overall circulation. *Analog* lost about 6,230 in subscriptions and another 38 in newsstand sales, for a 10.5-percent loss in overall circulation. *The Magazine of Fantasy & Science Fiction* lost about 6,730 in subscriptions but gained about 800 newsstand sales, for a 13.0-percent loss in overall circulation. *Science Fiction Age* lost about 4,590 in subscriptions and about another 2,220 in newsstand sales, for a 14.0-percent loss in overall circulation. *Realms of Fantasy* lost about 151 in subscriptions and about another 100 in newsstand sales, for a barely perceptible 0.5-percent loss in overall circulation—basically, they're holding steady.

This is probably not as dire as it looks. For instance, one of the traditional advantages that has always helped the digest magazines to survive is that they're so *cheap* to produce in the first place that you don't have to sell very many of them to make a profit. I'm willing to bet that most of these magazines are *still* profitable, in spite of declining circulation.

Still, it's hard to deny that things are dicier these days than they were ten years ago, especially in the area of newsstand sales. There are so few distributors left now that it's a buyer's market, and the distributors know that very well. The few surviving distributors often charge much-higher fees for carrying titles or ask for greatly increased "discounts," both higher than many SF magazines can easily afford to pay; some distributors also set "subscription caps," refusing to even handle magazines with a circulation below a certain set figure, usually a higher circulation figure than that of most genre magazines. Many newsstand managers have also become pickier, sometimes refusing to display magazines that fall below a certain circulation figure—again, a figure usually higher than that of most genre magazines. The result of all this is that it's harder to find genre magazines on newsstands, with some carrying a lot fewer copies of each title than before, and many newsstands not carrying them at all.

This is not as serious as it looks either, in the short-term, anyway. Most SF magazines are subscription-driven, and always have been, with newsstand sales a considerably lower percentage of overall sales than subscription sales, so they could get by without newsstand sales if they had to—for a while. Declining newsstand sales hurt magazines the most by cutting them off from attracting new readers, casual newsstand browsers who might pick up the magazine and read it on a whim, but who, with luck, might like what they see enough to eventually become new subscribers; without a constant flow of new subscribers, a magazine's circulation will continually dwindle as natural attrition eliminates a percentage of the old subscribers, until eventually the magazine becomes inviable. So one of the biggest problems facing magazines these days is to find ways to attract new subscribers even *without* a strong presence on the newsstand. One way to do this may be with a greatly increased presence on the Internet, which, if things go well, might enable the magazines to get around the newsstand bottleneck and attract the attention of potential new subscribers to their product even without much traditional newsstand display. I expect that this will become an increasingly important outlet in days to come and may be what saves the magazines in the long term—if anything can.

At the beginning of 1998, Penny Press announced that all of their fiction magazines, *Asimov's Science Fiction*, *Analog Science Fiction & Fact*, *Ellery Queen Mystery Magazine*, and *Alfred Hitchcock's Mystery Magazine*, will change size, starting with the June 1998 issue. The new format will add a little over an inch in height and about a quarter inch in width to each issue of *Asimov's* or *Analog*; the page count will drop from 160 pages to 144 pages for regular issues, and from 288 pages to 240 for double issues, although the larger pages will allow *Asimov's* and *Analog* to use about 10 percent more material per issue. The hope is that the increase in size will increase the visibility of the magazines on the newsstands (where, at the moment, digest-sized titles tend to get lost because other, larger magazines are shuffled in front of them), and increase their attractiveness as a product to distributors, who seem to favor larger-format magazines over digest-sized magazines these days. This marks the end of an era; for almost fifty years now, there have always been at least three digest-sized SF magazines on the newsstands (although *which* three changed as time went by), but now *The Magazine of Fantasy & Science Fiction* stands alone as the only true digest magazine left in the genre.

The other significant change for *Asimov's* and *Analog* was the establishment in early 1998 of Internet Web sites for both magazines; *Asimov's*'s site is at http://www.asimovs.com, and *Analog*'s is at http://www.analogsf.com, both sites sponsored by SF Site. Both sites feature story excerpts, book reviews, essays, and other similar features; and live interviews, "chats," and other on-line-only features are planned for the near future. More significantly, perhaps, you can *subscribe* to both magazines electronically, on-line, by giving a credit card number and clicking a few buttons, and this feature is already bringing in new subscribers, particularly from other parts of the world where interested readers have formerly found it difficult to subscribe because of the difficulty of obtaining American currency and because of other logistical problems (*Asimov's*, for instance, has already picked up new subscribers from France, Russia, Ireland, Italy, and even the United Arab Emirates).

The Magazine of Fantasy & Science Fiction completed its first year under new editor Gordon Van Gelder, although most of the material that appeared there this year was probably part of the extensive inventory left behind by former editor Kristine Kathryn Rusch. A favorite literary parlor game this year was to try to pick out which stories in the magazine had been bought by Gordon and which by Kris, with even one of the *Locus* columnists joining in with speculations as to what inferences about "new directions" for the magazine you could draw from the stuff in the June issue, the first one with Gordon's name on the masthead. Gordon merely smiles like a Cheshire cat and refuses to answer these questions, but I suspect that *most* of the speculations to date have been wrong. It'll be interesting to see how the magazine does change in coming months, and in which directions, as Kris's inventory finally runs out. Gordon has brought new science columnists Pat Murphy and Paul Doherty in to supplement Gregory Benford, and the book reviews seem to be rotating on an irregular basis among Robert K. J. Killheffer, Michelle West, Elizabeth Hand, and Douglas E. Winter, with a review column by Charles de Lint also in most issues, occasionally a review column by Gordon himself, and Paul Di Filippo (who is doing critical columns for *Asimov's*, *F&SF*, and *Science Fiction Age* all at the same time, which may be a genre first!) contributing quirky metafictional literarily oriented comic pieces from time to time. *F&SF* changed its Web site; the new one at www.fsfmag.com had not gone up in time for me to report on it for this book.

The British magazine *Interzone* completed its seventh full year as a monthly publication. Circulation went down very slightly this year, but remained more or less the same as last year—disappointingly, no major gains, but at least no catastrophic drops either. *Interzone* is one of the most reliable places to find first-rate fiction in the entire magazine market, with the literary quality of the stories consistently high, and it's one of the magazines that you really should subscribe to, especially as it is almost impossible to find *Interzone* on newsstands or in bookstores on the American side of the Atlantic. To miss it is to miss some of the best stuff available anywhere today. *Interzone* also has a Web site (http://www.riviera.demon.co.uk/interzon.htm), although there's not really much there—you *can* subscribe to the magazine there, though, which is perhaps the salient point.

Science Fiction Age successfully completed their fifth full year of publication. Although overall circulation of *Science Fiction Age* dropped again in 1997, by a substantial 14 percent, the magazine seems in general to be successful and profitable, with editor Scott Edelman attributing the drop in circulation to readers switching subscriptions to *Science Fiction Age*'s companion magazines, *Realms of Fantasy* and the media magazine *Sci-Fi Entertainment*, as well as to the newly purchased media magazine *Sci-Fi Universe* (both media magazines are also edited by Edelman). As Edelman points out, this gives Sovereign Media four successful genre titles where before they had only one (*Science Fiction Age* itself, the first magazine published by Sovereign), and that that is worth siphoning off some of the original magazine's subscription base. (It's a good argument, but one that will look a little thin if *Science Fiction Age*'s circulation continues to drop in the future.) Artistically, *Science Fiction Age* had its best year yet, publishing some very strong stories, and for the second year in a row was a more reliable source for good core science fiction overall than was *The Magazine of Fantasy & Science Fiction*, which still published more fantasy and soft horror stories this year than they did good SF stories.

Tomorrow Speculative Fiction is now an "on-line electronic magazine" called *Tomorrow SF*, and is reviewed below. *Aboriginal Science Fiction*, reported to be dead in 1995, came back to life in 1996; it managed only one issue in 1997, but published another one just after the beginning of the year in 1998.

Realms of Fantasy is a companion magazine to *Science Fiction Age*, a slick, large-size, full-color magazine very similar in format to its older sister, except devoted to fantasy rather than science fiction. They completed their third full year of publication in 1997. Under the editorship of Shawna McCarthy, *Realms of Fantasy* has quickly established itself as by far the best of the all-fantasy magazines (the other, the much longer-established *Marion Zimmer Bradley's Fantasy Magazine*—in its tenth year of publication in 1997—comes nowhere near it in terms of literary quality or consistency); in fact, the best stories from *Realms of Fantasy* are rivaled for craft and sophistication only by the best of the fantasy stories published by *The Magazine of Fantasy & Science Fiction* and *Asimov's Science Fiction*. *Worlds of Fantasy and Horror*, a magazine that publishes both fantasy and mild horror, had fallen into silence, publishing no issue in 1997, and was being said to likely be dead, but in early 1998 it was announced that DNA Publications, who also publish the SF fiction semiprozine *Absolute Magnitude* (see below), will be reviving the magazine under its original title—which it lost when its license lapsed—*Weird Tales*; Darrell Schweitzer and George Scithers will stay on as the magazine's editors.

A promising newcomer to the magazine market is a full-size, full-color British magazine called *Odyssey*, which published one practice issue and one real issue in 1997. This is a nice-looking magazine, although the interior layout is a touch chaotic and confusing; and it ran some good stuff by Brian Stableford, Jeff

Hecht, and others, although in my opinion they should concentrate on actual science fiction and stay away from the gaming fiction, horror, and fantasy (which tends to be weak here, as it also is in *Interzone*). They also need to forge an identity for themselves other than "not *Interzone*," a positive, strong identity and flavor of their own. At the moment, the magazine could go in any of a half-dozen directions, and it's hard to tell in which of them it's more likely to go. If it goes in the right direction, though, it could be a quite valuable addition to the magazine scene, and I wish them well.

It was also announced early in 1998 that *Amazing Stories*, reported to have died back in 1994, will rise yet again from the grave, something it has done several times in its seventy-year-plus existence. This time *Amazing Stories* will be brought out in a full-size, full-color format by Wizards of the Coast Inc., who recently bought TSR Inc., *Amazing*'s former owner. The new version will feature media fiction as well as more traditional science fiction, with several *Star Trek* stories in each issue, and will be edited by the editor of the former incarnation, Kim Mohan. It's scheduled to be launched at the 1998 Worldcon in Baltimore.

We should mention in passing that short SF and fantasy also appeared in many magazines outside genre boundaries, as usual, from *Alfred Hitchcock's Mystery Magazine* to *Playboy*.

(Subscription addresses follow for those magazines hardest to find on the newsstands: *The Magazine of Fantasy & Science Fiction*, Mercury Press, Inc., 143 Cream Hill Road, West Cornwall, CT 06796, annual subscription $25.97 in U.S.; *Asimov's Science Fiction*, Dell Magazines, P.O. Box 54625, Boulder, CO 80323-4625, $33.97 for annual subscription in U.S.; *Interzone*, 217 Preston Drove, Brighton BN1 6FL, United Kingdom, $60.00 for an airmail one year, twelve issues, subscription; *Analog*, Dell Magazines, P.O. Box 54625, Boulder, CO 80323, $33.97 for annual subscription in U.S.; *Aboriginal Science Fiction*, P.O. Box 2449, Woburn, MA 01888-0849, $21.50 for four issues; *Marion Zimmer Bradley's Fantasy Magazine*, P.O. Box 249, Berkeley, CA 94701, $16 for four issues in U.S.; *Odyssey*, Partizan Press 816-816, Leigh-on-Sea, Essex SS9 3NH, United Kingdom, $35 for a five-issue subscription, $75 for a twelve-issue subscription.)

The promise of "on-line electronic publication" remained largely unfulfilled in 1997—there aren't really that many good, professional-level science fiction stories being published on-line at the moment, although I did find two stories I liked this year that were published only as phosphor dots on an "on-line magazine," one from *Omni Online* and one from *Eidolon: SF Online*, that we're bringing to you in print form for the first time anywhere in this anthology. But this whole area is growing so *fast*, with changes coming so rapidly and new Web sites springing up so rapidly, that the potential here is enormous, and I can't help but feel that this market will end up being a very significant one before we're too many years into the next century. The SF community on the Web, in particular, is growing and expanding with dizzying speed, growing even as you watch it, and is not only getting larger, but is also (perhaps more importantly) growing more *interconnected*, forging links from site to site, with traffic moving easily between them, growing toward becoming a real community—and a community with no physical boundaries, since it's just as easy to click yourself to a site on the other side of the Atlantic or on the other side of the world as it is to click to one next door. This growth and evolution of a tightly interconected on-line SF community is a development that may prove to have significant consequences in the not-too-distant future. So even though this whole area at the moment probably produces less worthwhile fiction annually than a couple of good anthologies or a few good issues of a top-level professional print magazine, it's worth keeping an eye on this developing market, and even taking a closer look at it.

As has been true for a couple of years now, your best bet for finding good on-line-only science fiction, stories published only in electronic format, would be to go to *Omni Online* (http://www.omnimag.com), where the stories are selected by veteran editor Ellen Datlow, longtime fiction editor of the now-defunct print version of *Omni*. To date, *Omni Online* "publishes" the best fiction I've been able to find on the Web, including this year's strong stories by Simon Ings, Brian Stableford, Paul Park, Michael Bishop, Michael Kandel, and others, but it seemed to publish fewer stories this year than last; and with the recent death of *Omni* founder Kathy Keeton, a strong supporter of the *Omni Online* concept, some insiders have speculated that perhaps General Media is losing interest in the *Omni* site and that it may be in danger of being closed down. This conjecture has been officially denied, though, and I hope that the *Omni* site stays up and running, as, at the moment, it is the most reliable place I know of on the Internet to find professional-level SF, fantasy, and horror. (There's other stuff there as well: nonfiction pieces, interviews, reviews, a place where you can "walk" through a virtual representation of the Titanic, and so on, and they also do regularly scheduled live interactive interviews or "chats" with various prominent authors.)

A new innovation there this year are "round-robin" stories, written by four authors in collaboration, each writing a section in turn, and cycling in that fashion until the story is done. "Round-robin" stories rarely hold up well against "real" stories, since usually some of the pieces don't really match very well, and these don't either, but they're fun and much better-executed than stories of this sort usually are. Authors who participated in the round-robins this year included Pat Cadigan, Maureen F. McHugh, Terry Bisson, James Patrick Kelly, Pat Murphy, Jonathan Lethem, and others, so at the very least, they offered you a rare opportunity to watch top creative talents at play.

The only other "on-line magazine" that really rivals *Omni Online* as a fairly reliable place in which to find good professional-level SF is *Tomorrow SF* (http://www.tomorrowsf.com), edited by veteran editor Algis Budrys, the on-line reincarnation of another former print magazine, *Tomorrow Speculative Fiction*. This is also a very interesting and worthwhile site, although the fiction here is not quite as strongly to my taste as that of the *Omni* site, something that was true of their respective print incarnations as well. Still, the stuff here is always solidly professional, and they published ("posted?" "promulgated?") good work this year by Kandis Elliot, Michael H. Payne, Robert Reed, Paul Janvier, K. D. Wentworth, and others. *Tomorrow SF* is also engaged in an experiment that, if successful, could have profound implications for the whole electronic publishing area. Starting last year, they "published" the first three on-line issues of *Tomorrow SF* for free; then, this year, they have begun charging a "subscription fee" for access to the Web site, hoping that the audience will have been hooked enough by the free samples that they will continue to want the stuff enough to actually *pay* for it. The wise money is betting that this will not work, the argument being that so much stuff is available to be read for free on the Internet—oceans and oceans of it, in fact—that nobody is going to pay to access a site; they'll just click to a site where they can read something for free instead. I'm not entirely convinced by this argument, however. It's true that there are oceans and oceans of free fiction available on the Internet, but most of it is dreadful, slush-pile quality at best, and if Budrys has sufficiently convinced a large-enough proportion of the audience that he can winnow out the chaff and find the Good Stuff for them, they may well be willing to pay so that they don't have to wade through all the crap themselves. This has been the function of the editor from the beginning of the print fiction industry after all, and people buy print magazines for the very same reason: because of the implicit promise that the editor has gone out into the wilderness of prose and hunted down and bagged and brought back for them tasty morsels of fiction they'll enjoy consuming, and I don't see why this wouldn't work for an on-line magazine as well. The question then becomes, *has* Budrys succeeded in so convincing a large-enough portion of the potential audience to actually keep him in business? The jury's still out on that question so far. But if *Tomorrow SF* can succeed in getting readers in significant numbers to pay to access the site, it could have a big effect on the shape of genre publishing on-line.

Another interesting experiment on which the jury's still out is taking place at *Mind's Eye Fiction* (http://www.tale.com/genres.htm), where you can read the first half of stories for free, but if you want to read the *second* half of the story, you have to *pay* for the privilege, which you can do by setting up an electronic account on-line and then clicking a few buttons. The fees are small, less than fifty cents per story in most cases, and although the wise money is sneering at this concept as well, I think that this setup could actually work if they got some Bigger Name authors involved in the project. At the moment, most of the writers you can access here are writers who don't have large reputations or avid followings (who are willing to take a chance on a screwy concept like this because they have little to lose), and that may make it harder for this experiment to succeed as fully as it otherwise might.

The quality of the fiction falls off quickly after these sites, although there are a few new contenders this year. Most of these sites are still in their infancy, however, and not working entirely up to speed as yet; most are also associated with existent print magazines. *Eidolon: SF Online* (http://www.midnight.com.au/ eidolon/) offers information about back issues of *Eidolon* magazine and about Eidolon authors and about the Australian professional scene in general, as well as reprint stories from previous issues, available to be read on-line or downloaded. They are also promising to publish a good amount of original on-line-only fiction in the future, though at the moment the only such story available is one by Sean Williams and Simon Brown—and that one was good enough to make it into this anthology. *Aurealis*, the other Australian semiprozine, also has a site (http://www.aurealis.hl.net) with similar kinds of features available, although so far they've announced no plans for original fiction. I've already mentioned the *Asimov's* (http://asimovs.com/) and *Analog* (http://analogsf.com/) sites. Both sites are currently running teaser excerpts from stories coming up in forthcoming issues, as well as book reviews, critical essays, and so forth, and I plan to start running a certain amount of original on-line-only fiction on the *Asimov's* site as soon as I can arrange to do so, as well as live interactive author interviews and chats. Another interesting site is the British *Infinity Plus* (http://www.users. zetnet.co.uk/iplus/), which features a large selection of reprint stories, most by British authors, as well as extensive biographical and bibliographical information, book reviews, critical essays, and so forth. They too promise to begin running a good deal of original on-line-only fiction in the near future, and (as far as I can tell, anyway; it would be helpful, with this and other sites, if they'd label more clearly what's a reprint and what *isn't*) already have some excerpts from as yet unpublished novels. *Terra Incognita* (http://www.netaxs.com/~incognit), *Century* (http://www.supranet.net/century/) and the two Canadian semiprozines *On Spec* (http://www.icomm.ca/onspec/) and *TransVersions* (http://www.astro.psu.edu/ users/harlow/transversions/) also have Web sites, although not terribly active ones. *Talebones* (http://www.nventure.com/talebones) is another interesting site, although oriented toward horror and dark fantasy rather than SF. Longer-established sites that are worth keeping an eye on, although the quality of the fiction can be uneven, include *InterText* (http://www.etext.org/Zines/InterText/), and *E-Scape* (http://www.interink.com/escape.html).

If none of these sites has satisfied you, you can find *lots* of other genre "electronic magazines" by accessing http://www.yahoo.com/arts/humanities/literature/ genres/science_fiction_fantasy_horror/magazines/, but I hope you're extremely patient and have a strong stomach, since many of these sites are extremely bad—in fact, there's more amateur-level, slush-pile quality fiction out there on the Internet than you could wade through in a year of determined reading.

While you're on-line, don't forget to check out some of the genre-related sites that *don't* publish fiction. *Science Fiction Weekly* (http://www.scifiweekly.com), which has been around long enough to be venerable by on-line standards, is a good place to start, a lively general-interest site, with SF-related news, reviews of other SF sites of interest, and lots of media, gaming, and book reviews (including an occasional column by John Clute), as well as links to many genre-related sites. Also valuable as a home-away-from-home for genre readers is SFF NET (http//www.sff.net), which features dozens of home pages for SF writers, genre-oriented "live chats," and, among other lists of data, the *Locus* Magazine Index 1984–1996, which is an extremely valuable research tool; you can also link to the Science Fiction Writers of America page from here, where valuable research data and reading lists are to be found as well, or you can link directly to the SFFWA Web page at http://www.sfwa.org/sfw.

There are some new contenders in this area this year as well. The newszine *Locus* now has an on-line version up and running, *Locus Online* (http:// www.locusmag.com), and it's quickly become one of my most frequent stops on the Internet, in part because of the rapidity with which breaking news gets posted there, and for the other reviews and features, but mostly to browse Mark Kelly's comments about recent short fiction, which are similar to the contents of his column in the print *Locus*, but with some additional perspectives not available in the print edition. Another ambitious new site, which has quickly become one of my favorite destinations while Web-surfing, is *SF Site* (www.sfsite.com/), which, in addition to hosting the *Asimov's* and *Analog* sites, and having lots of links to other genre-related sites of interest, also features extensive review sections, and is perhaps more oriented toward print literature (as opposed to media and gaming stuff) than is *Science Fiction Weekly*. *SF Site* has also just started carrying a short-fiction review column by Dave Truesdale of the print semiprozine *Tangent*, which is one of the few places on-line other than *Locus Online* where you can find genre short fiction being reviewed on a regularly scheduled basis. And for a refreshingly iconoclastic and often funny slant on genre-oriented news, from multiple Hugo-winner David Langford, check out the on-line version of his fanzine *Ansible* (http://www.dcs.gla.ac.uk/ansible/). Many of the criticalzines also have Web sites, including *The New York Review of Science Fiction* (http://eebs.english.vt.edu/olp/nyrsf/nyrsf.html), *Nova Express* (http://www.delphi.com/sflit/novaexpress/index.html), *Speculations* (http://www. speculations.com/), *SF Eye* (http://www.empathy.com/eyeball/sfeye.html), and *Tangent* (http://www.sff.net/tangent/), but most of these sites are fairly inactive.

Many Bulletin Board Services, such as *GEnie*, *Delphi* (which also now has a Web site, http://www.delphi.com/sflit/), *Compuserve*, and *AOL*, have large on-line communities of SF writers and fans, with *GEnie* having perhaps the largest and most active such community. Most of these services also feature regularly scheduled live interactive real-time "chats" or conferences, as does SFF NET— the SF-oriented chat on *Delphi*, the one with which I'm most familiar, and which gives you the opportunity to schmooze with well-known professional SF writers in a relaxed and informal atmosphere. It starts every Wednesday at about 10:00 P.M. EST.

It was a bad year in the semiprozine market, particularly in the fiction semiprozines, although even as old titles falter, new titles appear on the horizon to replace them—or *try* to anyway. Some of the proposed new titles look promising, but the odds are greatly against any new magazine succeeding in the current market and under the current distribution system, I fear, particularly an under-capitalized magazine, and that description fits most semiprozines. Those long odds don't seem to discourage people enough to stop them from trying though.

There was no issue of *Century* published in 1997, just as they didn't publish their last three scheduled issues in 1996; and although the editor was claiming as recently as a couple of weeks ago that *Century* would eventually rise again from the ashes, he was assuring me of exactly the same thing at the end of 1996, so at this point I'm skeptical. *Century* was the most promising fiction semiprozine launch of the '90s, but for the moment, I'm afraid that I have to consider it dead; they'll have to Show Me that I'm wrong by actually *publishing* an issue before I change my mind, and even then I'd think they'd have to show they can publish on something approaching a regular schedule before they'd entirely regain the trust of their subscribers. I'm going to continue to list their subscription address here, in case you want to take a chance on them, but at this point in time I can't in good faith recommend that you subscribe, since there's at least a decent chance you'll never see anything in return for the money. There was also no issue of *Crank!*, another eclectic and literarily sophisticated fiction semiprozine, published this year, although one is promised for early in 1998; let's hope they can hold it together and not follow *Century* into the black hole that seems to claim most ambitious fiction semiprozines these days.

The two fiction semiprozines that seem closest to making it up into the ranks of the professional magazines, and which do get some nationwide distribution on the newsstands, are *Absolute Magnitude: The Magazine of Science Fiction Adventures* and *Pirate Writings: Tales of Fantasy, Mystery & Science Fiction*. These are both slick, professional-looking, full-size magazines with full-color covers, both of them—especially *Absolute Magnitude*, which often has very spiffy covers—frequently looking *better* than any of the professional magazines, including *Science Fiction Age*. What's on the *inside* is a lot more uneven, however, and the fiction in both magazines ranges from good to awful, with little overall consistency of quality; neither magazine had a particularly good year in 1997 in fact—both being easily outstripped in the quality of the fiction they published even by much-less prominent semiprozines such as *Terra Incognita* and *Tales of the Unanticipated*—although there were interesting stories by Barry B. Longyear, William F. Wu, and others in *Absolute Magnitude* and interesting stories by Paul Di Filippo, Don D'Ammassa, and others in *Pirate Writings*.

Absolute Magnitude seems to have had a slight edge in overall quality over *Pirate Writings* this year, although other years it has been the other way around. *Pirate Writings* does get more variety by publishing mystery and generalized adventure stories as well as science fiction, but they also make the mistake of devoting a section of the magazine to "short-short" stories, almost all of which have been dreadful (there are very few good "short-short" stories published in any given year, and so far *Pirate Writings* has not managed to find any of them—not really surprising, since often there are none published at all). The nonfiction is also uneven in both magazines, but *Absolute Magnitude* has an edge here because Allen Steele's regular column is solid and interesting; *Pirate Writings*, on the other hand, *loses* points for publishing the "Surreal World" column, which really should be called "Credulous World" instead, as it reverentally trots out one old woo-woo chestnut—like the Philadelphia Experiment or the Men in Black—after another: there's already too much of this crap floating around in the SF readership, and I don't like to see it encouraged. Both magazines could stand to improve the quality of their book reviews.

Both magazines continued to struggle with their production schedules this year, with *Pirate Writings* managing three issues out of their scheduled four and *Absolute Magnitude* managing two out of their scheduled four. *Absolute Magnitude* also went through internal upheavals this year, with the rest of the business partners involved in the magazine pulling out of the partnership, leaving

Warren Lapine as both editor and sole publisher. Lapine swears that the magazine will continue, though, and I tend to believe him, especially as Lapine has recently expanded his empire to include *Dreams of Decadence,* an all-vampire fiction magazine, and is in the process of reviving *Weird Tales.* I wish both of these magazines well, and they deserve to survive and prosper, but they also need to work harder to improve, especially in the area of making the quality of their fiction more consistant.

The three longest-established fiction semiprozines now are two Australian magazines, *Aurealis* and *Eidolon,* and a Canadian magazine, *On Spec. Eidolon* was strong again in 1997—not quite as strong as it had been in 1996, but strong enough to prove itself the best of the three magazines once again this year, publishing strong fiction by Dirk Strasser, Simon Brown, Sean Williams, Rosaleen Love, Russell Blackford, and others, and publishing a collaboration by Sean Williams and Simon Brown on their *Eidolon Online* site that was one of the year's best stories. Perhaps this is a reflection of the recent boom in Australian science fiction, where they appear to be enjoying an upsurge of creative energy and artistic excitement. *Aurealis* also had a good year, publishing strong fiction by Peter Friend, Rick Kennett, Michael Pryor, and others. As opposed to the Australian magazines, the Canadian magazine *On Spec* seems to have gone into a bit of a slump for the last couple of years, and little of really exceptional quality appeared there in 1997, although they did publish interesting work by Derryl Murphy, Steven R. Laker, Ursula Pflug, and others. The idea that Canadian science fiction *should* be gray, depressing, dystopian, and set in the near-future, that these somehow are defining national characteristics, looks like it's growing toward codification in recent years, but it seems like a curiously self-limiting set of indicators to choose, and much of the Canadian stuff seems pale and bloodless when contrasted to the more vigorous and exuberant (although sometimes rawer) Australians. Perhaps part of the problem is that *On Spec* is edited by a collective, rather than by a single editor who could impose his or her personality powerfully on the magazine. Still, *On Spec* has published a lot of interesting stuff over the years and has helped to find and develop a lot of new writers, so it is worth your support. All three of these magazines have been around long enough to be considered fairly stable and reliable, as such things are judged in the semiprozine market, and all have good track records for delivering interesting and unusual fiction, so they're good bets for your subscription money; odds are they they *will* all be around and producing issues next year. *Eidolon* and *Aurealis* managed only two issues out of a scheduled four this year, while the more-reliably-published *On Spec* brought out all four of its scheduled issues.

Of the other fiction semiprozines, the most interesting of the American newcomers was probably *Terra Incognita,* which published some of the best stuff to be found in the semiprozine market this year, including good, high-end professional-level stories by Timons Esaias, Terry McGarry, Brian Stableford, and others, including a couple that made my shortlist of stuff to consider for this anthology. On the other hand, they only managed to produce one issue in 1997, so they'll have to increase their reliability before they really become a contender, and their self-imposed restriction of publishing only stories that take place on

Earth still strikes me as being too limiting—seems to me that to survive and prosper, a magazine must publish any really first-rate fiction it can find, whether it's set on Earth or Mars or inside a black hole or *wherever*. Still, *Terra Incongnita* is a very promising magazine, well worth keeping an eye on. Good professional-quality work was also being published this year in the long-established *Tales of the Unanticipated,*which managed two issues this year, featuring strong work by R. Neube, Stephen Dedman, Martha A. Hood, Gerard Daniel Hourarner, Neil Gaiman, H. Courreges Le Blanc, Robert J. Levy, and others.

Also worth checking out, although not quite at the level of the above two magazines yet, is a promising new Canadian magazine called *TransVersions*, which seems to be publishing livelier stuff than *On Spec* has managed of late. *Non-Stop Science Fiction Magazine* (somewhat clumsily subtitled *Ultra Dystopias of Future & Fantasy Utopias*) reappeared in a new, somewhat smaller (although still larger than digest-sized) format this year, and managed one issue out of a scheduled four. *Non-Stop* is still a brash, swaggering, boastful magazine, proud of its in-your-face arrogance, that doesn't quite live up to the self-congratulatory claims it makes for itself, although there is some interesting stuff here, and at least the magazine can't be accused of being dull or stuffy. There's worthwhile fiction (although no actual science fiction) here by Barry N. Malzberg and Paul Di Filippo, but, as was true the last time they published an issue, the nonfiction here is considerably more interesting than the fiction, including an interview with Vernor Vinge (listed as "Vernon" Vinge on the contents page) and intriguing essays by Paul Di Filippo and Charles Platt. In England, *The Third Alternative* seems to be one of the most prominent semiprozines at the moment, and *Back Brain Recluse* is still going strong, although both of these magazines tend toward literary surrealism and horror rather than core science fiction, and may be too far out on the edge for some readers. A confusingly named Irish semiprozine called *Albedo 1* (which leads to issues being listed as, say, *Albedo 1* #14) is very crudely printed and ameteurish-looking compared to the above magazines and also leans toward literary surrealism; but it also published some interesting professional-level work this year by Brain Stableford, Ian McDonald, and others. *Space & Time*, which tends more toward fantasy, in spite of its title, had one issue this year (with interesting work by Bill Eakin, Don D'Ammassa, Don Webb, Sue Storm, and others), as did *Xizquil*. *Adventures of Sword & Sorcery* continued to publish, up to issue four now (featuring, I notice, a story from the ubiquitous Stephen Baxter!), but I didn't see it. If there were issues of *Plot Magazine* or *The Thirteenth Moon Magazine* out this year, I didn't see them. *Keen Science Fiction* officially died, and I believe that *Argonaut Science Fiction* and *Next Phase* are also dead.

Promised for next year is a SF fiction semiprozine called *Age of Wonder*, which is already announcing that its premiere issue will feature stories by Gregory Benford and Stephen Baxter—sounds pretty promising.

I don't follow the horror semiprozine market much any more, in fact I try to keep them away from my door with crucifixes and holy water, but *Talebones: Fiction on the Dark Edge* still seems to be a lively little magazine, and it's broadening out to include a fair amount of science fiction in its editorial mix as well as fantasy and horror, a development I welcome. It published interesting stuff by Amy Sterling Casil, Leslie What, and others this year. The highly respected *Cemetery Dance* seems to be back in full swing again after a long hiatus caused by the ill-health of the editor. I suspect that there were issues of *Aberrations* out this year, but, if so, I didn't see them. *The Urbanite* published two issues, featuring work somewhere on the borderline of horror and surrealism. I saw no issues of *Deathrealm* or *Grue* this year, although I didn't look for them exhaustively, either.

Turning to the critical magazines, Charles N. Brown's *Locus* and Andy Porter's *SF Chronicle*, as always, remain your best bet among that subclass of semiprozines known as "newszines," and are your best resource if you're looking for publishing news and/or an overview of what's happening in the genre. (*SF Chronicle* seems back on track again, after missing several issues last year due to health problems on the part of editor and publisher Andy Porter, and it's a good to see them back.) *The New York Review of Science Fiction*, edited by David G. Hartwell, completed its ninth full year of publication, once again not only publishing its scheduled twelves issues but publishing them all on time; that it can do this year after year in a field where most other criticalzines are lucky if they can manage to bring out one issue out of four is something of a small miracle and may lead some other semiprozine editors to wonder if Hartwell has signed a pact with the devil. The reliability of its publishing schedule is not all that *The New York Review of Science Fiction* has going for it, not by any means. It has always been eclectic and interesting, but in the last year or two I've been finding it more interesting than ever before, publishing not only the usual reviews and critical articles but playful bits of metafiction by Michael Swanwick, "Read This" lists of recommended books by various authors, and fascinating items such as Avram Davidson's exchange of letters with Philip K. Dick.

Once again, there was only one issue of Steve Brown's *SF Eye* and of Lawrence Person's *Nova Express* in 1997, something that's been true for several years in a row now—both magazines are insightful, intriguing, and entertaining, when you can find them, but take their publishing schedule with a large grain of salt; perhaps *Nova Express* should follow *SF Eye*'s lead and stop claiming to be a quarterly publication. It's already hard to imagine how the field would get by without David A. Truesdale's *Tangent*, which has become such an institution in the genre after only a few years that it seems like it has always been around. In a field where almost no short fiction gets reviewed, with the emphasis in almost every other review source on novels, *Tangent* performs an invaluable service for the genre by providing a place where interested readers can find reviews of most of the year's short fiction—something that can be found almost nowhere else except for Mark Kelly's review column in *Locus*. *Tangent* is also doing yeoman service for the field by becoming deeply involved in helping to assemble a recommended reading list for the yearly Sturgeon Award, and although the quality of the criticism here is still uneven, the coverage is remarkably complete, reviewing stories from obscure sources that probably never get reviewed anywhere else, including very minor semiprozines and on-line "electronic magazines." Truesdale's energy and fannish cheerfulness have made *Tangent* popular enough that I would not be at all surprised to see a Hugo win in the magazine's future.

This year Dave has expanded his empire into the Virtual World as well, contributing a short-fiction review column for SF.Site that's one of the few places on-line where short fiction is regularly reviewed, other than the reprint of Mark Kelly's column on Locus Online. *Speculations,* which features writing-advice articles as well as extensive sections of market reports and market news, is a useful resource for young or would-be authors, although the general reading public may be less interested.

(*Locus,* The Newspaper of the Science Fiction Field, Locus Publications, Inc., P.O. Box 13305, Oakland, California 94661, $53.00 for a one-year first-class subscription, 12 issues; *Science Fiction Chronicle,* P.O. Box 022730, Brooklyn, N.Y. 11202-0056, $42.00 for one-year first-class subscription, 12 issues; *The New York Review of Science Fiction,* Dragon Press, P.O. Box 78, Pleasantville, NY, 10570, $31.00 per year, 12 issues; *SF Eye,* P.O. Box 18539, Asheville, NC 28814, $12.50 for one year; *Nova Express,* White Car Publications, P.O. Box 27231, Austin, Texas 78755-2231, $12 for a one-year (four issue) subscription; *Tangent,*.5779 Norfleet, Raytown, MO 64133, $20 for one year, four issues; *Speculations,* 111 West El Camino Real, Suite 109-400, Sunnyvale, CA 94087-1057, a first-class subscription, six issues, $25; *On Spec, the Canadian Magazine of Speculative Writing,* P.O. Box 4727, Edmonton, AB, Canada T6E 5G6, $18 for a one-year subscription; *Crank!,* Broken Mirrors Press, P.O. Box 1110, New York, NY 10159-1110, $12 for four issues; *Century,* P.O. Box 259270, Madison, WI 53715-0270, $27 for a one-year subscription; *Aurealis: The Australian Magazine of Fantasy and Science Fiction,* Chimaera Publications, P.O. Box 2164, Mt. Waverley, Victoria 3149, Australia, $43 for a four-issue overseas airmail subscription, "all cheques and money orders must be made out to Chimarea Publications in Australian dollars"; *Eidolon: The Journal of Australian Science Fiction and Fantasy,* Eidolon Publications, P.O. Box 225, North Perth, Western Australia 6006, $45 Australian for a 4-issue overseas airmail subscription, payable to Eidolon Publications; *Albedo 1,* Tachyon Productions at Albedo 1, 2 Post Road, Lusk, Co. Dublin, Ireland, 4 issues for $24 U.S., make checks payable to Albedo 1; *Back Brain Recluse,* P.O. Box 625, Sheffield S1 3GY, United Kingdom, $18 for four issues; *REM,* REM Publications, 19 Sandringham Road, Willesden, London NW2 5EP, United Kingdom, £7.50 for four issues; *The Third Alternative,* TTA Press, 5 Martins Lane, Witcham, Ely, Cambs. CBG 2LB, UK, £10 for a four-issue subscription; *Xizquil,* order from Uncle River/Xizquil, Blue Route, Box 90, Blue, Arizona, 85922, $11 for a three-issue subscription; *Pirate Writings: Tales of Fantasy, Mystery & Science Fiction,* Pirate Writings Publishing, Subscriptions, P.O. Box 329, Brightwaters, NY 11718-0329, $15 for one year (four issues), all checks payable to "Pirate Writings Publishing"; *Absolute Magnitude: The Magazine of Science Fiction Adventures,* P.O Box 13, Greenfield, MA 01302, four issues for $14, all checks payable to "D.N.A. Publications"; *TransVersions,* Island Specialty Reports, 1019 Colville Rd., Victoria, BC, Canada, V9A 4P5, four-issue subscription, $18 Can. or U.S., "make cheques payable to Island Specialty Reports"; *Terra Incognita,* Terra Incognita, 52 Windermere Avenue #3, Lansdowne, PA 19050-1812, $15 for four issues; *Thirteenth Moon Magazine,* 1459 18th Street #139, San Francisco, CA 94107, $24 for four issues; *PLOT Magazine,*

Calypso Publishing, PO Box 1351, Sugar Land, Texas 77487-1351, four issues for $14, "make checks payable to Calypso Publishing"; *The Urbanite: Surreal & Lively & Bizarre*, Urban Legend Press, P.O. Box 4737, Davenport, IA 52808, $13.50 for three issues, "all checks or money orders payable to Urban Legend Press"; *Talebones: Fiction on the Dark Edge*, Fairwood Press, 10531 SE 250th Pl. #104, Kent, WA 98031, $16 for four issues; *Cemetery Dance*, CD Publications, Box 18433, Baltimore, MD 21237; *Grue* Magazine, Hell's Kitchen Productions, Box 370, Times Square Stn., New York, NY 10108, $14 for three issues; *Aberrations*, P.O. Box 460430, San Francisco, CA 94146, $31 for 12 issues; *Deathrealm*, 2210 Wilcox Drive, Greensboro, NC 27405, $15.95 for four issues; *Adventures of Sword & Sorcery*, Double Star Press, P.O. Box 285, Xenia, OH 45385, $15.95 for four issues.)

It was a weak year for original anthologies, especially in science fiction, where there were few original anthologies published at all, and most of them that *did* come out were seriously flawed. (Things were somewhat better in fantasy, where there were several good—if no really outstanding—original anthologies published.) Unlike last year, most of the original SF anthologies of 1997 were published either in mass-market paperback or in trade paperback, with only one hardcover I can think of, so it would have at least been cheaper for someone to buy them all—although since, as usual, the bulk of them were theme anthologies with only one or two good stories apiece (if that many), it still doesn't seem like a very cost-effective way to find good short fiction. Still, it seems to me that you'd be better off subscribing to some of the SF magazines instead, where you're much more likely to find a consistent level of literary quality—but, of course, since I'm a magazine editor myself, you can, if you'd like, pretty much discount that opinion.

One of the most interesting anthologies of the year will probably end up being seen by almost nobody in the SF community, especially on this side of the Atlantic. This is a very odd item called *Future Histories*, edited by Stephen McClelland, and published (sort of) in Britian. Subtitled *Award-Winning Science Fiction Writers Predict Twenty Tomorrows for Communications*, it was comissioned and paid for by Nokia, the communications corporation, and was published in a private printing as a subscription premium for subscribers to a Horizon House Publications trade journal called *Telecommunications Magazine*. Only six thousand copies were printed, none of them are available for sale (the book doesn't even have a cover price on it), it's not available in bookstores, you can't mail order it, and apparently there's no intention of doing either a regular trade edition in England or an American edition—one of the authors in the book let me borrow an author's copy or I wouldn't have been able to read it either. In spite of all the above, practically guaranteed to make the stories in the book vanish without a trace, unseen by anybody in the SF reading audience, there are some very Big Names associated with this project, an example of how much Money—by our standards; probably coffee-and-doughnuts money for *them*—Nokia threw at this project, supposedly paying close to three thousand dollars per item, minimum. The book is about evenly split between fiction and nonfiction, with some very well-known people contributing both. The sad part, considering how invisibily it's been published, is that *Future Histories* contains some pretty good stuff, and, in fact, is the best original SF anthology of the year, by a good margin.

The best stories here, in my opinion, are David Marusek's "Getting to Know You"—his Future History, the same here as in "We Were Out of Our Minds with Joy," gets more chewy and interesting and multifaceted the more I see of it—and Nancy Kress's "Steamship Soldier on the Information Front." A step below them would be Stephen Baxter's "Glass Earth, Inc." and Paul J. McAuley's "Back Door Man." There's nothing really bad here, though, and every story in the book is worth reading. The anthology also includes stories by Pat Murphy, Brian Stableford, Pat Cadigan, and Greg Benford. The weakest story is probably the one by Stephen McClelland himself—not surprising, since it's his first fiction sale—and even that has points of interest. The book also contains nonfiction articles by Arthur C. Clarke, Bruce Sterling, Greg Bear, Alexander Besher, Mariko Ohara, Vernor Vinge, Nicholas Negroponte, Neal Stephenson, and William Gibson.

Considering that all of these stories are ostensibly about the future of the communications industry, I suppose it's inevitable that many of them seem to share a vision about what the future is going to be like. One detail common to most of them is that in the next century most people are going to stay inside all the time, telecommuting, talking to each other only on-line, living inside elaborate Virtual Reality setups, taking Virtual Reality vacations, and so forth, to the degree that the real streets outside are mostly deserted, nobody around, shops closed and boarded up, and so forth; Stephen Baxter even specifically invokes "The Machine Stops" in *his* story. I must say that I find this future to be disspiriting and somewhat depressing. Even Gibson's streetwise hacker-cowboys went out to a bar and had a drink every once in a while. (They also *screwed* in person, in the flesh, as opposed to the nearly universal assumption here that only Virtual Reality cybersex will exist in the future.)

I'm not sure that I entirely believe in this future, although no doubt bits and pieces of it will come to pass. For one thing, it seems like a very middle-class view of the future, ignoring—as, indeed, does most science fiction—the question of what all the *poor* people are going to be doing while "everybody" is leading this Maximum Urban Cocooned existence. Are all the poor people going to have Virtual Reality cocoons too? Who's picking up the garbage? Who's sweeping the streets? Who's fixing the plumbing? It's like a future where *only* the Eloi are around; no Morlocks. A mistake that much science fiction makes is to assume that social change affects *everyone* to the same degree at the same time—which isn't the way it usually works. There are people living within fifty miles of my apartment in Philadelphia who don't have electricity or indoor plumbing; there are people living within a thousand miles or so of here, in rural Mexico, say, who are living a hand-farming subsistence kind of life not really different from the one their ancestors were living hundreds or even thousands of years back. For that matter, while I'm sitting here in my Urban Cocoon, enjoying the air-

conditioning and communicating instantly with other ghostly residents of the
Virtual World, there's almost certainly somebody within a ten-block radius of
my apartment sleeping on a hot-air vent—and that person is enjoying no more
of the fruits of modern high-tech civilization than he would be if he were living
alone in the desert as a hermit.

The point being that the *present* is not at a uniform level of social development, so I doubt that the *future* is going to be like that either. I wonder, in fact,
if, in the future, we're going to see people living at a Stone Age level—or living
the way most of us in the West do *now*, for that matter—side by side with
people living such a high-tech existence, at such a level of technological sophistication, that they're nearly incomprehensible to us. But the different levels of
technological sophistication will be *layered* throughout society, like the layers in
nougat, the whole spectrum from Stone Age to Incomprehensibly Advanced
Singularity Folk existing side by side at the same time; it won't be all one uniform layer, Virtual Reality Cocoons all the way down, as it is in most of the
societies described here.

It also seemed clear to me that—with the exception of David Marusek, and,
to some extent, Brian Stableford—most of the authors here wouldn't really want
to *live* in the futures that they're predicting; a faint air of distaste for this Bright
New Utopian Cyberfuture comes across clearly if sometimes almost subliminally
in several of these stories, with Stephen Baxter even postulating that young
people several generations down the line will end up rebelling against and rejecting this information culture and will instead want to go outside and actually
do things, in the real world, in the obsolete flesh.

Considering all this, you have to wonder how much of an advertisement for
the glorious Future of Communications this book actually *is*—and wonder
whether Nokia is really getting its money's worth or not . . . or at least if it's
really getting what it *thought* it was paying for.

A very curious project. This is what publishing would be like if it was run by
major corporations—and those corporations didn't give a damn whether what
they published *made any money or not.* By all means, read the book—if you can
find it!

New Worlds, edited by David Garnett, is a continuation by American publisher
White Wolf of the English original anthology series that was dropped by Gollancz a couple of years ago after a four-book run . . . which in turn was a resur-
rection of an older anthology series from the '70s . . . which in turn was a
manifestation in anthology form of the original long-running British magazine
called *New Worlds*, which at one time in the middle and late '60s, under editor
Michael Moorcock (who is still listed on the present book as "Consulting Editor"), was the flagship of the British *New Wave*, and is at least the spiritual
ancestor of the current-day magazine *Interzone*. *New Worlds* has had a long and
complex publishing history, as you can see, "dying"—or at least lying quies-
cent—for long periods of time before being reborn in some new form, and I'd
like to think that this new American edition signals yet another rebirth of the
series, a series that, in its most recent Garnett-edited incarnation, at the very
least has always been provocative and interesting to read, and which sometimes

has published some very good stuff indeed. Science fiction as a genre could certainly use another good, continuing, original anthology series, especially as such series, once common, have in recent years dwindled almost to the point of extinction. And this volume *is* advertised as the start of a new annual series of *New Worlds* anthologies—but scuttlebutt in professional circles has quoted David Garnett as saying recently that he's no longer going to be editing *New Worlds* . . . and that, plus the financial shakiness of White Wolf in the last couple of years, where overextension and cash-flow problems have caused the cancellation of many proposed titles, combine to make me wonder if this is the only volume of *New Worlds* we'll actually see (in its *current* incarnation, anyway!). It would be a shame if that was true, for the field needs all the markets for short fiction it can get if it's going to continue to survive and grow, especially intellectually prestigious showcases such as *New Worlds*; let's hope that I'm being too pessimistic, and that another volume of *New Worlds* does indeed come out next year.

Considering the five *New Worlds* anthologies edited by Garnett together—the four Gollancz volumes and the current White Wolf volume—this volume of *New Worlds* is neither the best of the lot nor the worst, falling somewhere in the middle in terms of overall quality, although perhaps closer to the high end than the low end. It's an uneven anthology, featuring some excellent work as well as more routine stuff, some of it rather dull, although little here is actively bad, and almost everything is at least worth reading. For the most part, the best stuff here is the most unclassifiable stuff, the stories that blur the lines between several different genres; the most routine and lackluster stories here are the ones that are the most clearly identifiable as core science fiction—which probably tells us something about where Garnett's interest really lies. The best stories here, by a considerable margin, are unclassifiables: Howard Waldrop's rich and antic "Heart of Whitenesse" (sort of a combination of Alternate History, historical fantasy, and a literary joke that equates Christopher Marlowe with Philip Marlowe . . . in addition to the playful echoes of Conrad and others) and Michael Moorcock's bitter, sly, and eloquent "London Bone" (which, with its evocation of the lives of small-time hustlers and con men operating at the periphery of London's upscale art-and-antiques circles, might not have looked out-of-place in *Ellery Queen's Mystery Magazine*, except for being set slightly in the future—and except for the fact that London Bone itself is Moorcock's own cunning and evocative invention). Next best would be Kim Newman's retelling of a Shanelike parable of persecution and oppression and the response it draws from an ex-soldier who finds himself reluctantly drawn into the role of protector of an embattled rural family in an Alternate World England—this is vivid and emotionally powerful, although the historical changes that produced this Alternate World might be hard for an American reader, who's not familiar enough with *real* British history, to pinpoint; I'm not sure I spotted all of them myself.

A step down from there, Pat Cadigan gives us an amusing, although overlong, cyberjoke story in "The Emperor's New Reality"; William Gibson contributes an ambitious experiment in evoking a society of the homeless simply by describing in obsessive detail the things to be found in their shanty cardboard "houses," in "Thirteen Views of a Cardboard City"—the relentless accumulation of detail here has a certain fascination, but the "story" itself, completely without plot or characters, is too abstract and dry to be more than a literary finger exercise; and in "The White Stuff" Peter F. Hamilton and Graham Joyce give us an intriguing look at how society might be totally transformed by the quiet, street-level introduction of new technology . . . although since that new technology amounts to "a magic stuff that can do anything" (the origins of which are never explained, although there are unrealized hints throughout that the origin is going to turn out to be of significance), this scenario lacks some of the sharpness and relevance it might have had if the technology had been more believable. Somewhere in the middle, not really bad but not really exciting either, are Eric Brown's "Ferryman," which sets up an interesting conflict and then backs away from it on the very last page, Ian Watson's "A Day Without Dad," which has an intriguing central idea that the author doesn't seem to quite know what to do with, and Andrew Stephenson's "The Pact," a pleasant if predictable read that could have appeared and done yeoman service in any issue of any SF magazine over the last ten years without arousing either unusual praise or remarkable censure.

Everything below that level didn't work for me to one degree or another, for one reason or another. No doubt some critics will find Brian W. Aldiss's "Death, Shit, Love, Transfiguration" to be a brilliant cutting-edge work, but it struck me as self-indulgent and not terribly interesting. Noel K. Hannan's "A Night on the Town" has no need to be science fiction at all, not really needing its—unconvincing—futuristic setting to tell a story that could just as easily be told about a naive rich kid venturing into present-day Harlem or East L.A. Garry Kilworth's "Attack of the Charlie Chaplins" is a slight one-joke story that is milked for far more pages than it ought to be. Christine Manby's "For Life" is too arch, too long, and too familiar (it's the one about the future society where men are kept as pets and sex toys). And Graham Charnock's "A Night on Bare Mountain" shows you what happens when you cross the typical New Worlds story from the magazine version's old glory days with cyberpunk; reading it is like wading through glue.

So, an uneven anthology—but I think that, on balance, there's more than enough worthwhile stuff here (including a few stories of a sort you're unlikely to find anywhere *else*) to make *New Worlds* worth its $12.99 cover price . . . and to make me hope that the series continues next year.

Free Space (Tor), edited by Brad Linaweaver and Edward E. Kramer, is a hardcover libertarian shared-world anthology, seventeen original stories set in a complex Future History chronology worked out by Linaweaver and some others, two poems, and a very-slightly rewritten version of Greg Benford's 1995 story "The Worm in the Well," here called "Early Bird" instead. The contributors range from those you'd expect to find here, such as Dafydd ab Hugh, L. Neil Smith, and Poul Anderson, to odder fish such as Ray Bradbury and William F. Buckley Jr. Oddly, nowhere on the front or back covers is the word "libertarian" mentioned, with only a passing reference to the Libertarian Futurist Society buried in the copy on the inside flap, and this coyness about coming right out and saying what the anthology is makes me wonder if Tor was reluctant to mention libertarianism on the cover—which in turn makes me wonder who they think the audience *is* for this book, and if they were afraid that advertising this as a libertarian anthology would repulse more readers than it would attract; why publish it in the first place then? And by *not* clearly marking it, aren't you taking a certain chance of missing some of the very audience most likely to buy it in the first place?

I don't intend to discuss the validity or real-world feasibility of the political positions put forth in the book, but only to discuss how well the stories in the anthology work as fiction. Unfortunately, the bulk of them don't work very well *as* fiction—and so, it seems to me, are probably not working all that effectively as propaganda either; I can't see many people who aren't *already* libertarians having their Eyes Opened and their opinions changed by this anthology, and so the book mostly is "preaching to the choir," something that is often true of liberal books with a political agenda—such as Lewis Shiner's antiwar anthology *When the Music's Over*—as well. Little chance that any teenager is going to stay awake through most of *these* stories long enough to be infected with any dangerous political memes.

Most of the stories here are pretty lame, full of two-dimensional cardboard characters spouting rhetoric, and often rather dull, clogged with polemic, with what little plot there is frequently coming to a halt so that one character or another can deliver a political rant, or to let big blocky chunks of infodump go lumbering by, or so that one character can lecture another one at length about basic facts of their society that both of them should already know. Even old pro Poul Anderson lets the didactic balance of his story get dangerously out of whack in places, with paragraphs that should clearly come supplied with a sign that flashes "Author's Message!" above the type, although he's too much of a veteran entertainer to fail to tell a moderately absorbing human story at the same time, unlike a few of his younger colleagues. Some of the other authors also strike a workable balance between entertainment and polemics. Leaving John Barnes's story aside for the moment (more on that below), the best story in the anthology, by a good margin, is probably James P. Hogan's "Madam Butterfly," a slyly entertaining look at the hidden connectors, some of them quite subtle, that tie all of our lives together and often tip the balance of destiny one way or the other. The next best story here would be William F. Wu's "Kwan Tingui," a nicely crafted and nicely felt piece that carries a freight of genuine human emotion lacking in many of the other stories (my only objection to the Wu story would be to mention that it could have taken place fundamentally unchanged back on Earth in any number of historic settings, without needing to be told as science fiction at all; still, there's no reason why it couldn't validly be told in a science fictional setting too). Other stories worth reading here include the Benford reprint, Robert J. Sawyer's "The Hand You're Dealt," Arthur Byron Cover's "The Performance of a Lifetime," and the aforementioned Poul Anderson story, "Tyranny."

In some ways the most substantial story in the book, and certainly the strangest, is John Barnes's "Between Shepherds and Kings." This is an odd story, a metafiction piece dealing with an author—who we are clearly supposed to identify with Barnes himself, although how much Barnes himself is actually *like* this is open to question—who is being asked to write a story for this very anthology by people named "Brad" and "Dafydd"; while Brad and Dafydd sit in the author's living room and explain the anthology's elaborate Future History to him, the author gets slowly potted while silently trying—and failing—to come up with a story idea that would rationalize all the unexamined and often mutually contradictory assumptions behind that future history. Reviewers have called this story "Malzbergian," with excellent justification, but it actually reminds me more of a C. M. Kornbluth story called "The Only Thing We Learn"; there is a bitter self-mocking edge to the portrayal of the "author" that seems more like Kornbluth than like Malzberg to me. This is by far the most "subversive" story in the anthology, although what it subverts are the libertarian assumptions that drive the *rest* of the book—as the author comes up with and then discards one plot scenario after another, he makes hash out of one after the other of the basic assumptions upon which the anthology's Future History is based, even questioning the fundamental idea that a free-trading capitalist space-dwelling society would be possible in the first place (there's a milder example of such subversion also to be found in Arthur Byron Cover's story, which seems to demonstrate that the freedom to do as you please without regard for anyone else might eventually lead to the destruction—or at least the severe endangerment—of human society itself). The editors are to be complimented for guts, for publishing a story that effectively cuts the ground out from under every other story in the book, but it is an odd decision, and Barnes's story is sharply different from anything else here, as if it had somehow wandered into the anthology from some other fictive universe altogether.

You probably could have gotten $5.99' worth of entertainment out of this book, if it had been published as a mass-market paperback, but at $24.95, I cannot in good faith recommend it. A curious marketing decision by Tor, one of serveral they made in the anthology market this year.

Alternate Tyrants, edited by Mike Resnick (Tor), is more substantial and somber in tone than some of the other recent Resnick Alternate Whatever anthologies have been—perhaps because thinking about the idea of tyranny got the authors in a more solemn mood in the first place. There are fewer stories here that postulate the wildly improbable if not impossible (and often downright silly) scenarios that filled books like *Alternate Warriors* or *Alternate Outlaws* ("Suppose Mother Teresa formed an outlaw gang during the Depression with Einstein and Albert Schweitzer!"); the most improbable stuff here is "Suppose Al Capone became President of the United States!" and "Suppose Buddy Holly became President of the United States!" (a close variant of the story from another, older Resnick anthology, *By Any Other Name*, which asked "Suppose Elvis Presley became President of the United States!"—and, in fact, in the current story, Buddy Holly follows Elvis into office!). There's less of that sort of thing here, and more stories that feature scenarios which, although unlikely, actually *could* happen—the most ingenious of which is to be found in Michelle Sagara's story— and so function a lot better as Alternate History stories than do most of the more "playful" stories, the more extreme examples of which are, in my opinion, just fantasy stories with all-star celebrity casts rather than valid science fiction.

The best story here is clearly Maureen F. McHugh's "The Lincoln Train," and it's a pity that this anthology was delayed for so long that the story has to appear here as a reprint rather than as an original . . . although you could argue that the anthology's loss was McHugh's gain, since I doubt she would have won a Hugo with this story if it had appeared here first rather than in F&SF. (And, of course, the story contributes to the strength of the anthology even as a reprint.) Next to "The Lincoln Train," the strongest stories here are Gregory Feeley's "The Crab Lice," Frank M. Robinson's "Causes," and Michelle Sagara's "The Sword in the Stone," with the Feeley story easily carrying off the title of most inventive and imaginative story in the book that *doesn't* fall into the trap of third-rate-Howard-Waldrop-without-the-spark-of-genius-gosh-isn't-this-really-kind-of-silly Historical Gonzoism. There's also other good work here by Adrienne Gormley, Karawynn Long, Richard A. Lupoff, Lyn Nichols, and others.

Alternate Tyrants is probably the most substantial of this sequence since at least *Alternate Kennedys*, one of the first two titles—which makes it all the more ironic that Tor has already given up on the series (it's clear, in fact, that they only issued *this* one reluctantly, after delaying it for several years) and that this will be the last of them. I do think that this series became tired toward the end of its life, locked into a sequence of diminishing returns, with the last couple of volumes especially weak—but in an odd way, I'll miss them, nevertheless . . . and it's always sad to see an anthology series die, especially these days when there are so few of them left.

All the other Resnick Alternate anthologies were mass-market paperbacks, but this one has been issued as a more-expensive trade paperback instead—which seems like an odd decision, to raise the cover price on the latest installment of a series of anthologies that you're *already* complaining don't sell well enough (which you'd think would encourage even *fewer* people to buy it), but apparently the idea is that the profit margin on a trade paperback is higher than that on a mass-market, being not much more expensive to produce.

The Return of the Dinosaurs, an original anthology edited by Mike Resnick and Martin H. Greenberg (DAW), strikes me as somewhat weaker than the book to which it's a sequel, 1993's *Dinosaur Fantastic*. I can't be too self-righteous about this, since I've edited two dinosaur anthologies myself and would probably edit another one if asked, but there is a feeling to much of the material here that this ground may have been gone over too many times and is becoming played out. Whatever the truth of that, there's less here that's really innovative, and less of substance, than there was in *Dinosaur Fantastic*. Many of the authors, in fact, dodge the issue, not really writing about dinosaurs—the living, or once-living, animals—at all in any central way, but instead do joke stories full of comic talking dinosaurs who perform the same kind of anachronistic Dino Shtick, satirically mimicking human behavior, that should be familiar to anyone who ever caught an episode of the old TV sitcom *Dinosaurs*; some of this material is supposed to amuse by its presumption—the pope converting the dinosaurs to

Christianity, for instance—but, as in the Resnick Alternate anthologies, this self-conscious "outrageousness" makes for thin stories and usually doesn't involve any true innovation or breadth of imagination, no matter how Wild and Crazy the juxtapositions of images become. Other authors come close to ignoring the ostensible theme altogether. There are two pieces of fan fiction here, one of them David Gerrold's insufferably coy "The Feathered Mastodon," which features Resnick himself as a main character; the other piece, Kristine Kathryn Rusch's "Stomping Mad," is actually one of the more entertaining stories in the anthology—but its rationale for being included here (it takes place at a Jurassic Park media convention) is slim enough to be almost subliminal.

There is some good material here. The best story in the anthology by a good margin—although nowhere near the top of her form—is Maureen F. McHugh's "Down on the Farm," a clever story about moral choices and the running of bureaucratic mazes, weakened somewhat by a hurried ending. Next best would be Gene Wolfe's sly fabulation "Petting Zoo," which also features a talking dinosaur (although not one who does comic Dino Shtick) and which could almost be a children's story in mood, although its gentle tone is deceptive, and there is a sting in the story's 'tail.' Other worthwhile stories here include Bud Sparhawk's "Fierce Embrace," Michelle Sagara West's "Flight," Robert J. Sawyer's "Forever," the aforementioned Kristine Kathryn Rusch story, and Susan Shwartz's "Drawing Out Leviathan."

All in all, I think you can probably get $5.99' worth of entertainment out of this anthology—but I'm glad that they didn't decide to do this one as a more expensive trade paperback.

Black Mist and Other Japanese Futures, edited by Orson Scott Card and Keith Ferrell (DAW), is, as the title indicates, a collection of stories—five novellas—set in Japanese-dominated futures (none of them, oddly, are written by Japanese authors—for that, you have to see the reprint anthology *Best Japanese Science Fiction Stories*). The two best stories here, Pat Cadigan's "Tea from an Empty Cup" and Richard A. Lupoff's "Black Mist," are actually reprint stories, having appeared electronically on *Omni Online* all the way back in 1995, although no acknowledgment of that fact is made anywhere in the book. Of the rest of the stories, the best is Jack Dann and Janeen Webb's intriguingly detailed although somewhat too-picaresque "Niagra Falling," followed by Patric Helmaan's earnest, engrossing, but probably overlong "Thirteen Views of Higher Edo" ("Patric Helmaan" is almost certainly a pseudonym, and I think I know for whom; but since I have no direct evidence, I'll keep my mouth shut about it). The book is rounded off by Paul Levinson's deliberately controversial "A Medal for Harry," which tries hard to be offensive and succeeds, but which is also at the same time rather silly, an effect I don't think the author was trying for intentionally.

It's hard even to *tell* what's the ostensible theme of *Destination Unknown*, edited by Peter Crowther (White Wolf), even after you've read the jacket copy and the Guest Introduction—"fabulous worlds" perhaps, or "locations rich and strange and bizarre" is about as close as you can get. Oddly, then, considering all that, few of the stories here evoke any particularly strong sense of place or are particularly adroit in their use of local color, nor—with a few exceptions—are the places they take us to all that rich and strange and bizarre.

In terms of overall literary quality, this is a fairly good anthology, quiet, low-key, competent, with few outright stinkers but also few stories that will linger long in your mind after you've put the book down. The bulk of the stuff here is quiet horror, very mild indeed by today's standards, of a peculiar subvariety that might almost be called English Cozy Horror; I actually respond better to this sort of thing than I do to most splatterpunk/Maximum Gross-Out horror, but it's not considered hip today, and I doubt that the horror establishment will take much—if any—notice of the stuff here.

There are two pretty good science fiction (or at least science-fantasy) stories here, the two strongest stories in the book, both of them more "rich and strange and bizarre" than most of the other stories in the anthology, and evoking a stronger sense of place—Ian McDonald's "The Five O' Clock Whistle" and Terry Dowling's "The Maiden Death" are evocative, mood-heavy, style-rich (and slightly overwritten) stories haunted by ghosts and echoes of (respectively) Bradbury's *Mars* and Ballard's *Vermilion Sands*. The anthology also contains interesting work by Ian Watson, Lisa Tuttle, Kathleen Ann Goonan, R. A. Lafferty, and others.

First Contact, edited by Martin H. Greenberg and Larry Segriff (DAW), seems to have been infected by the Friviolity Plague that affects so many of these DAW anthologies. There's some pleasant minor work here, but the emphasis is definitely on the word "minor," with most of the authors choosing to go for joke stories rather than attempting anything substantial or particularly imaginative with the theme. It's a sad state of affairs when the year's movies and TV shows come up with more original and inventive twists on the theme of First Contact than does an anthology of stories by nineteen working SF writers, but that's just about the case here. The best stories are by Kristine Kathryn Rusch, Nina Kiriki Hoffman, Jack C. Haldeman II, Gordon Eklund, and Peter Crowther.

Two offbeat items are the British anthologies *Decalog 4: Re: Generations*, edited by Andy Lane and Justin Richards (Virgin), and *Decalog 5: Wonders*, edited by Paul Leonard and Jim Mortimore (Virgin). The *Decalog* series apparently started out as media-oriented anthologies, with at least one of them consisting of Dr. Who stories, but by this point in time they've moved away from media fiction and are publishing some solid core science fiction as well. *Decalog 5* is particularly interesting, with a first-rate story by Stephen Baxter (who appeared in practically every genre market in existence this year, plus a few non-genre ones! . . . or so it seemed anyway), and good work by Dominic Green, Ian Watson, and Jeanne Cavelos, although *Decalog 4* was also interesting, with good work by Alex Stewart, Ben Jeapes, and Liz Holiday. (These anthologies may be somewhat difficult for American readers to find too—but, if it's any consolation, at least nowhere near as difficult as finding *Future Histories* would be!)

An interesting anthology that we missed last year is *David Copperfield's Beyond Imagination*, edited by David Copperfield and Janet Berliner (HarperPrism), an eclectic anthology that mixes science fiction, fantasy, mild horror, and hybrids of these forms of various sorts, and which features strong, powerfully imaginative work by Robert Silverberg, Greg Bear, Peter S. Beagle, Karen Joy Fowler, Neil Gaiman, and others. This is one of the better anthologies of the last couple of years, in fact, and probably worth its hardcover price of $23.00, although by now I think that it's also available in a mass-market edition as well. Another eclectic mixed anthology that we missed last year was the British anthology *Lethal Kisses, 19 Stories of Sex, Horror and Revenge*, edited by Ellen Datlow (Millennium Orion), which, in spite of the title, contains a strong SF story by Pat Cadigan, an unclassifiably strange story on the borderland of literary surrealism by Michael Swanwick and Jack Dann, and good near-mainstream stories with no real fantastic element at all by Pat Murphy and Jonathan Lethem, as well as the expected erotic horror stuff by writers such as Simon Ings, Michael Marshall Smith, David J. Schow, A. R. Morlan, and others.

Spec-Lit, Speculative Fiction, No. 1, edited by Phyllis Eisenstein, is the first of a projected series of anthologies that collects student work from Eisenstein's writing class at Columbia College in Chicago—this doesn't sound very promising, I know, but the standard of work turns out to be surprisingly high, and if there's nothing really first-rate here, there *is* competent professional-level work by George Alan, Tom Traub, Sam Weller, and others (for *Spec-Lit, No. 1*, send $6.95 to Fiction Writing Department, Columbia College Chicago, 600 South Michigan Avenue, Chicago, IL 60605-1996; make checks payable to Columbia College Chicago). Similar ground is covered in *L. Ron Hubbard Presents Writers of the Future*, Volume XIII, edited by Dave Wolverton (Bridge), which, as usual, presents novice work by beginning writers, some of whom may later turn out to be important talents.

There was another small-press anthology out late this year, *Alternate Skiffy*, edited by Mike Resnick and Patrick Nielsen Hayden, but it didn't arrive here in time to make my copy deadline, so I'll save consideration of it for next year.

There seemed to be few shared-world anthologies this year. The few I saw included: *Star Wars: Tales from the Empire*, edited by Peter Schweighoffer (Bantam Spectra); *Highwaymen: Robbers and Rogues*, by Jennifer Roberson (DAW); *Swords of Ice and Other Tales of Valdemar*, edited by Mercedes Lackey (DAW); *More Than Honor* (Baen), stories set in the "Honor Harrington" universe; and *Bolos 4: Last Stand*, edited by Bill Fawcett (Baen).

People are waiting impatiently for *Starlight 2*, which should be one of the big anthologies of 1998. There's also a big original SF anthology of stories by Australian writers being put together by Jack Dann and Janeen Webb that we'll be keeping an eye out for, and it'll be interesting to see if an edition of George Zebrowski's long-delayed anthology series *Synergy* actually is published by White Wolf in 1998 . . . and/or another edition of *New Worlds*. Other than those, there are no other SF original anthology series even potentially in the works, as far as I know. A "hard science" anthology of original stories about space habitats, edited by Gregory Benford and George Zebrowski, originally scheduled to come out in late 1997 or early 1998, has now been pushed back into mid-1999. And, of course, there's another flock of Greenberg-edited theme anthologies on the horizon as well.

There were some good fantasy anthologies this year, although none as pre-eminent or dominating as such big fantasy anthologies of recent years as *Immortal Unicorn* or *After the King*. With the exception of the nearly-impossible-to-find *Future Histories*, the overall level of quality of the stories in the fantasy anthologies—or at least in the best of them—was higher than the overall level of the science fiction anthologies too, a sad commentary on the SF original anthology field.

The best fantasy anthology of the year was probably *The Horns of Elfland*, edited by Ellen Kushner, Delia Sherman, and Donald G. Keller (Roc), an anthology of music-themed stories similar to last year's *Space Opera*, although on the whole it covers the territory better than *Space Opera* did (although lacking the Peter S. Beagle novella that was the king piece of that anthology, and the main reason to buy it). *The Horns of Elfland* is an eclectic anthology, perhaps too much so for some readers tastes, especially in the kinds of music it covers—there's little or nothing in the book about rock 'n' roll, for instance, and although the most typical kind of music dealt with here is Celtic music of one sort or another (if you had to pick background music to play while you read that would be the most representative of the overall mood of the book, your best bet would probably be someone like Enya or De Danann), there are also stories featuring opera, English bell ringing, church choir shape-note singing, bawdy house piano music, rap, and Cajun music. The stories themselves are similarly eclectic, mixing several types of fantasy, mainstream, and very mild horror; the dominant literary mood here is quiet, low-key, lyrical in a hushed sort of way—much the same as the music of Enya, in fact. Oddly, the very best stories here, Terri Windling's "The Color of Angels," Susan Palwick's "Aïda in the Park," and Lucy Sussex's "Merlusine," either have no fantastic element at all, or, in the case of the Windling, a fantastic element so muted and in-the-background as to be almost subliminal. The fantastic elements in the rest of the stories are also usually somewhat muted—there are few obvious Wonders here, with locations mostly restricted to present-day settings, and magic often kept well in the background—although the overall line-by-line level of literary craftsmanship in the book is extremely high. The anthology also contains good work by Gene Wolfe, Roz Kaveney, Ellen Kushner, Elizabeth A. Wein, Jane Emerson, and others.

The Magic is a little bit more upfront in another of the year's best fantasy anthologies, *Black Swan, White Raven*, edited by Ellen Datlow and Terri Windling (Avon), the latest in their long and acclaimed series of anthologies of retold fairy tales. This is also a mixed anthology of fantasy and horror, although there seems to be less horror than in some of the other books in the series, which is why I'm considering it in the fantasy section rather than the horror section. The fantastic elements here are usually a good deal less muted and subliminal than in *The Horns of Elfland*; although some of these stories are quiet lyrical fantasies, most are painted in brighter primary colors, and there are only a few modern settings, most of the fantasy stories pretty clearly taking place in Fairy Tale Territory. What horror there is here is a good deal stronger and sharper as well (although still mild by the gory standards of today's most extreme work), and there's more humor, including a story by Midori Snyder that manages to be both funny and strongly erotic at the same time, a rare combination. There are good stories by John Crowley, Nancy Kress, Jane Yolen, Harvey Jacobs, Gregory Frost, Esther M. Friesner, Susanna Clarke, Karen Joy Fowler, and others, including the above-mentioned Midori Synder story.

The year's other prominent fantasy anthology is *Bending the Landscape: Fantasy*, edited by Nicola Griffith and Stephen Pagel (White Wolf Borealis). Ostensibly an anthology of gay-themed stories in which "queer writers write fantasy for the first time, and genre writers explore queer characters," many of the stories really don't deal centrally with homosexual themes at all, instead turning out to be stories whose central characters just happen to be gay, with no great emphasis placed on this fact and no great fuss made about it—which makes this book a lot less polemic-heavy and angst-laden than some books aimed at the gay audience. There's a fair range of different kinds of fantasy offered here as well—there's also a strong science fiction story, Carolyn Ives Gilman's "Frost Painting"—although *Bending the Landscape: Fantasy* tends to shade off on one end of its spectrum more toward magic realism or literary surrealism of various sorts than does the stuff in *Black Swan, White Raven* or even *The Horns of Elfland*. The best work here includes the above-mentioned story by Carolyn Ives Gilman, as well as stories by Ellen Kushner and Delia Sherman, Holly Wade Matter, M. W. Keiper, Robin Wayne Bailey, Leslie What, Kim Antieau, and others. This is the first book in a projected anthology series, but the series has been dropped by White Wolf—it will be continued in 1998 by Overlook Press.

Other fantasy anthologies this year included a big mixed original and reprint anthology of Arthurian stories, *The Chronicles of the Round Table*, edited by Mike Ashley (Carroll & Graf), which featured interesting work by old Arthur hands such as Parke Godwin and Phyllis Ann Karr, as well as by authors you don't usually associate with Arthuriana, such as Eliot Fintushel and Brian Stableford; *Swords and Sorceress XV*, edited by Marion Zimmer Bradley (DAW); and several anthologies of competent but largely unexceptional work, including *Elf Fantastic* (DAW) and *Wizard Fantastic* (DAW), both edited by Martin H. Greenberg, *Tarot Fantastic*, edited by Martin H. Greenberg and Lawrence Schimel (DAW), and *Zodiac Fantastic*, edited by Martin H. Greenberg and A. R. Morlan (DAW).

I don't follow the horror field closely these days, but it seemed as if the most prominent original horror anthologies of the year probably included *Revelations*, edited by Douglas E. Winter (HarperPrism); *Love in Vein II*, edited by Poppy Z. Brite and Martin H. Greenberg (HarperPrism); *Dark Terrors 3*, edited by Stephen Jones and David Sutton (Gollancz); *The Mammoth Book of Dracula*, edited by Stephen Jones (Robinson/Raven); *Gothic Ghosts*, edited by Wendy Webb and Charles Grant (Tor); and *Wild Women*, edited by Melissa Mia Hall (Carroll & Graf). Noted without comment is an anthology of erotic ghost stories, *Dying For It*, edited by Gardner Dozois (HarperPrism).

Some associational anthologies that may well be of interest to genre readers are a series of fat mystery anthologies edited by Mike Ashley, all from Carroll & Graf, many of which feature stories by familiar genre writers such as Brian Stableford, Stephen Baxter (the prolific Baxter is in most of them, in fact!), Kim

Newman, Phyllis Ann Karr, Darrell Schweitzer, Patricia A. McKillip, Michael Moorcock, David Langford, John Maddox Roberts, and others. Some of the stories even have slight fantastic elements, and the historical mysteries may appeal to Alternate History buffs as well. The anthologies include: *Classical Whodunnits*; *The Mammoth Book of Historical Whodunnits*; *Shakespearean Whodunnits*; and *The Mammoth Book of New Sherlock Holmes Adventures*. Even further out on the edge in some ways are two memorial anthologies about Famous Dead Celebrities, both of which feature some work with fantastic elements and use the work of genre authors: a Marilyn Monroe anthology, *Marilyn: Shades of Blonde*, edited by Carol Nelson Douglas (Forge), which features work by Elizabeth Ann Scarborough, Peter Crowther, Melissa Mia Hall, and Janet Berliner and George Guthridge; and a James Dean anthology, *Mondo James Dean*, edited by Lucinda Ebersole and Richard Peabody (St. Martin's), which features work by Lewis Shiner and Jack C. Haldeman II.

The novel market didn't seem quite as hard-hit in 1997 as it was being predicted that it would be in 1996. There were cutbacks—with HarperCollins cancelling over 100 previously contracted-for novels, for instance—but elsewhere the field actually seemed to be expanding, with HarperPrism growing and Avon announcing a major and ambitious new SF line, Eos, for 1998. Mass-market paperback originals continued to dwindle, part of a trend that has persisted and even accelerated for the past couple of years; but, at the same time, there were more trade paperback editions than ever before—with many books that would have been done in mass-market a few years ago now being done as trade paperbacks instead—so it tends to even out. There also seem to be more original hardcovers now than ever before; there are now more original novels being published in hardcover than in mass-market paperback format, something that would have been inconceivable even ten years ago.

According to the newsmagazine *Locus*, there were 999 original books "of interest to the SF field" published in 1997, as opposed to 1,121 such books in 1996, a drop of 11 percent in original titles (on the other hand, according to *Locus*, there was a 15 percent increase in reprint titles over 1996, 817 to 1996's 708, bringing the overall total of books of interest to the field, original *and* reprint, to 1,816 as opposed to 1996's 1,829, only a 1 percent drop overall). The drop in original titles is scary, but, on the other hand, it's not nearly as bad as some of last year's through-the-floor-total-bust scenarios had predicted that it would be. The number of new SF novels was down, with 229 novels published as opposed to 253 in 1996; fantasy was down slightly, with 220 novels published as opposed to 224 in 1996; and horror suffered another substantial drop, with 106 novels published as opposed to 122 in 1996 and 193 in 1995. These are not insignificant losses, but neither are they catastrophic—as yet, anyway. Unless the totals continue to drop, and, in fact, the drop accelerates precipitously, the forecast of imminent death for the genre may turn out to have been premature (at least for the immediate future).

It's obviously just about impossible for any one individual to read and review all the new novels published every year, or even a significant fraction of them, even if you restricted yourself to the science fiction novels alone. For somebody like me, who has enormous amounts of short material to read, both for *Asimov's* and for this anthology, it's *flat-out* impossible, and I don't even really try to keep up with everything anymore.

As usual, therefore, I haven't read a lot of novels this year; of those I have seen, I would recommend: *Jack Faust*, Michael Swanwick (Avon); *Diaspora*, Greg Egan (HarperPrism); *Forever Peace*, Joe Haldeman (Ace); *Corrupting Dr. Nice*, John Kessel (Tor); *City on Fire*, Walter Jon Williams (HarperPrism); *Slant*, Greg Bear (Tor); *Antarctica*, Kim Stanley Robinson (Voyager); *Earthling*, Tony Daniel (Tor), and *Mississippi Blues*, Kathleen Ann Goonan (Tor).

Other novels that have received a lot of attention and acclaim in 1997 include: *3001: The Final Odyssey*, Arthur C. Clarke (Del Rey); *The Fleet of Stars*, Poul Anderson (Tor); *Titan*, Stephen Baxter (HarperPrism); *Destiny's Road*, Larry Niven (Tor); *God's Fires*, Patricia Anthony (Ace); *The Rise of Endymion*, Dan Simmons (Bantam Spectra); *The Siege of Eternity*, Frederik Pohl (Tor); *The Reality Dysfunction*, Peter F. Hamilton (Warner Aspect); *The Sorcerers of Majipoor*, Robert Silverberg (HarperPrism); *Glimmering*, Elizabeth Hand (HarperPrism); *The Dark Tower IV: Wizard and Glass*, Stephen King (Donald Grant); *Winter Tides*, James P. Blaylock (Ace); *Eternity Road*, Jack McDevitt (HarperPrism); *The Dazzle of Day*, Molly Gloss (Tor); *The Calcutta Chromosome*, Amitav Ghosh (Avon); *How Few Remain*, Harry Turtledove (Del Rey); *Tomorrow and Tomorrow*, Charles Sheffield (Bantam Spectra); *The Black Sun*, Jack Williamson (Tor); *Someone to Watch over Me*, Tricia Sullivan (Bantam Spectra); *Earthquake Weather*, Tim Powers (Tor); *The Moon and the Sun*, Vonda N. McIntyre (Pocket); *Widowmaker Reborn*, Mike Resnick (Bantam); *The White Abacus*, Damien Broderick (Avon); *Fool's War*, Sarah Zettel (Warner Aspect); *Secret Passages*, Paul Preuss (Tor); *A King of Infinite Space*, Allen Steele (HarperPrism); *Freeware*, Rudy Rucker (Avon); *Deception Well*, Linda Nagata (Bantam Spectra); *Fortress on the Sun*, Paul Cook (Roc); *Carlucci's Heart*, Richard Paul Russo (Ace); *The Night Watch*, Sean Stewart (Ace); *Reckoning Infinity*, John Stith (Tor); *The Still*, David Feintuch (Warner Aspect); *Bug Park*, James P. Hogan (Baen); *The Stars Dispose*, Michaela Roessner (Tor); *Chimera's Cradle*, Brian Stableford (Legend); *The Gaia Websters*, Kim Antieau (Roc); and *Faraday's Orphans*, N. Lee Wood (Ace).

Special mention should be made of Walter M. Miller Jr.'s posthumously published *Saint Leibowitz and the Wild Horse Woman* (Bantam Spectra), which was completed by Terry Bisson after Miller's death, although by far the bulk of the text was written by Miller himself. This may not have quite the impact of Miller's classic *A Canticle for Leibowitz*, but it certainly qualifies as a minor masterpiece of sorts, one of the best novels of the year, and a fitting capstone to Miller's distinguished career—it's a shame he didn't live to see it in print. Note should also be taken of Roger Zelazny's *Donnerjack* (Avon), which was completed by Jane Lindskold after Zelazny's death.

It was a fairly strong year for first novels. The most impressive ones I saw were *In the Garden of Iden*, by Kage Baker (Harcourt Brace), and *The Great Wheel*, by Ian R. MacLeod (Harcourt Brace). Other good first novels included: *The Art of Arrow Cutting*, Stephen Dedman (Tor); *Black Wine*, Candas Jane Dorsey (Tor); *Waking Beauty*, Paul Witcover(HarperPrism); *Expendable*, James Alan Gardner (AvoNova); *Mars Underground*, William K. Hartmann (Tor); *Lightpaths*, Howard V. Hendrix (Ace); *The Seraphim Rising*, Elizabeth De Vos (Roc); *The Seventh Heart*, Marina Fitch (Ace), *Polymorph*, Scott Westerfeld (Roc), and *Lives of the Monster Dogs*, Kirsten Bakis (Farrar, Straus). For the second time in recent years, Harcourt Brace strongly dominated the first novel field this year, as it did in 1993–1994 when it published acclaimed first novels by Patricia Anthony and Jonathan Lethem—a tribute to the shrewd judgment of editor Michael Kandel. Tor, Ace, Roc, and DAW all published a fair number of first novels this year as well, and are to be commended for it, as are all publishers who are willing to take a chance on unknown writers with no track record—a risky business, but one that's vital to the continued evolution and health of the genre.

An interesting small-press item was a first novel by one of SF's most prolific and most eclectic short-story writers, Paul Di Filippo's *Ciphers*, available in a hardcover edition from Cambrian Publications and a trade paperback edition from Permeable Press (Cambrian Publications, Box 112170, Campbell, CA 94114, $60 for the hardcover edition; Permeable Press, 47 Noe St #4, San Francisco, CA 94114, $16.95 for the trade paperback edition). Novels out on the fringes of the field that may be of interest to genre readers included two near-mainstream novels with (sometimes almost subliminal) traces of fantastic elements, *American Gothic* (St. Martin's), by Harvey Jacobs—the more overtly fantastic of the two—and *Signs of Life* (St. Martin's), by M. John Harrison, and an odd novel by Stepan Chapman that occupies the border territory between SF and literary surrealism, *The Troika* (The Ministry of Whimsy Press, P.O. Box 4248, Tallahassee, FL 32315, $14.99). Associational mysteries last year included *Bad Eye Blues* by Neal Barrett, Jr. (Kensington) and *Soma Blues* by Robert Sheckley (Forge).

It looked like a good year for novels to me, even judging solely by the ones I had time to read, and many of the others were well-received as well. For those who still repeat the oft-heard remark about how nobody writes "real" center-core science fiction anymore, it should be noted that in the above list, most of the titles would have to be considered to be real, actual, sure-enough science fiction by any even remotely reasonable definition (even excluding the several fantasy novels and the more ambiguous cases, such as Williams's *City on Fire* or Swanwick's *Jack Faust*, which could be taken as either fantasy or SF, depending how you squint at them), and a number of them are hard SF, as hard and rigorous as it has ever been written by anyone anywhere (Egan's *Diaspora*, for instance, as only one example). In fact, it seems to me that the percentage of really hard-core "hard SF" has gone up sharply in recent years, as has the percentage of wide-screen, Technicolor, baroque Space Opera, stuff reminiscent of the old "Superscience" days of the '30s, but written to suit the aesthetic and stylistic tastes of the '90s. There's more "real" SF of several different flavors and styles around these days than ever before, if you open your eyes up and look for it—as well as vigorous hybrids of SF with fantasy, horror, the historical novel, the mystery, and several other forms. Far from being dead, the field is, artistically at least, richer and wider and more varied than it has ever been, with good work being done by writers in every possible subvariety and subgenre you can name— all out there to be found, in spite of the pressure of competition for bookstore rack space by media tie-in and gaming and other associational novels.

As usual, there seem to be no strong favorites here for the major awards, although perhaps Haldeman's *Forever Peace* might have a shot at the Hugo. Thanks to SFWA's bizarre "rolling eligibility" rule, most of the books up for the Nebula Award are actually novels from the previous year, making the winner even harder to call. Tor, HarperPrism, and Bantam Spectra all had strong years.

Long out-of-print classics seem to be coming back *into* print with greater frequency these days than in years past, an encouraging sign; an even *more* encouraging sign is that some of this reissuing is being done by regular trade houses, such as Tor and Bantam and Del Rey, rather than leaving this area to the small presses, as was too-often true during the last ten years or so. Reissues of classic novels this year included: *A Canticle for Leibowitz* by Walter M. Miller Jr. (Bantam Spectra), perhaps *the* classic After-the-Bomb novel; *Bring the Jubilee* by Ward Moore (Del Rey), one of the earliest Alternate History novels, and still one of the best; *The Demon Princes*, Volumes One and Two, by Jack Vance (Tor), assembling the five "Demon Princes" novels, some of the most exciting and evocative hybrids of science fiction and the mystery novel ever written; *Vacuum Flowers* by Michael Swanwick (Ace), one of the earliest and best of the cyberpunk novels; *Three in Time* (White Wolf), an omnibus volume that gathers three classic time-travel novels, by Poul Anderson, Wilson Tucker, and Chad Oliver; *The Final Encyclopedia*, Volume One, by Gordon R. Dickson (Tor), the first half of one of Dickson's major novels; and *Triplanetary* by Edward E. "Doc" Smith (Old Earth Books, P.O. Box 19951, Baltimore, MD 21211-0951, $15), the first of the "Lensman" novels (and, for you Alternative Media fans, quite probably the inspiration for the comic book hero Green Lantern), classic space adventure from a time before the term "Space Opera" had even been invented. Buy them now, while you can, before they disappear into oblivion again.

It was another pretty good year for short-story collections, including once again a number of good retrospective collections that make excellent but long-out-of-print work available, and which ought to be in the library of every serious science fiction reader.

The best collections of the year included: *Voyages by Starlight*, Ian R. MacLeod (Arkham House); *Axiomatic*, Greg Egan (HarperPrism); *Think Like a Dinosaur*, James Patrick Kelly (Golden Gryphon); *The Pure Product*, John Kessel (Tor); *Vacuum Diagrams*, Stephen Baxter (Voyager); *Giant Bones*, Peter S. Beagle (Roc); *Going Home Again*, Howard Waldrop (Eidolon Publications); *Ghost Seas*, Steven Utley (Ticonderoga Publications); *Eating Memories*, Patricia Anthony (First Books/Old Earth Books); *A Geography of Unknown Lands*, Michael Swanwick (Tiger Eyes Press); *Barnacle Bill the Spacer and Other Stories*, Lucius Shepard (Millennium); and *Fractal Paisleys*, Paul Di Filippo (Four Walls Eight

Windows). Among the year's other top collections were: *The Forest of Time and Other Stories*, Michael Flynn (Tor); *The Rhinoceros Who Quoted Nietzche and Other Odd Acquaintances*, Peter S. Beagle (Tachyon); *Slippage*, Harlan Ellison (Houghton Mifflin); *Fabulous Harbours*, Michael Moorcock (Avon); *Exorcisms and Ectasies*, Karl Edward Wagner (Fedogan & Bremer); *The Arbitrary Placement of Walls*, Martha Soukup (Dreamhaven), and *From the End of the Twentieth Century*, John M. Ford (NESFA Press).

Special mention should be made of several excellent retrospective collections that returned long-unavailable work by dead (and in danger of being forgotten) authors to print. This year's retrospective collections feature the work of three authors who practically reinvented the science fiction short story in the '50s, expanding its boundaries and greatly extending its range, using it as a tool to do kinds of work that had never been attempted in the field before. Without these authors, modern science fiction as we know it would not exist—and so these are collections that belong in every library: *His Share of Glory: The Complete Short Stories of C. M. Kornbluth* (NESFA Press), which lives up to its name by returning almost all of the short work of this brilliant craftsman to print; *Virtual Unrealities: The Short Fiction of Alfred Bester* (Vintage), which features the best work of a writer still unmatched for daring, ambition, gall, pyrotechnics, and sheer chutzpah; and *Thunder and Roses: The Complete Stories of Theodore Sturgeon*, Volume IV, (North Atlantic Books), which features some of the best work by one of science fiction's best stylists, and so, almost by definition, some of the best work of the last half-century.

Fantasy fans might also enjoy a mass-market release of *Tales from Watership Down*, by Richard Adams (Avon), a return to the milieu of the bestselling fantasy classic *Watership Down*.

As usual, small-press publishers such as NESFA Press, Golden Gryphon, Tachyon, Arkham House, Eidolon Publications, and others, were responsible for publishing the bulk of the year's best short-story collections, although it's encouraging to see a fair number of titles from trade publishers such as Tor, Roc, Vintage, and HarperPrism.

(With the exception of books by White Wolf and Four Walls Eight Windows, very few small-press titles will be findable in the average bookstore, or even in the average chain store, which means that mail order is your best bet, and so I'm going to list the addresses of the small-press publishers mentioned above: NESFA Press, P.O. Box 809, Framingham, MA 01701-0203, $27 for *His Share of Glory: The Complete Short Stories of C. M. Kornbluth*, $21 for *From the End of the Twentieth Century*, by John M. Ford; Golden Gryphon Press, 364 West Country Lane, Collinsville, IL 62234, $22.95 for *Think Like a Dinosaur*, by James Patrick Kelly; Arkham House, Arkham House Publishers, Inc., Sauk City, Wisconsin 53583, $21.95 for *Voyages by Starlight*, by Ian R. MacLeod; North Atlantic Books, P.O. Box 12327, Berkeley, CA, 94701, $25 for *Thunder and Roses: The Complete Stories of Theodore Sturgeon*, Volume IV; Eidolon Publications, P.O. Box 225, North Perth, Western Australia 6006, $A19.95 for *Going Home Again*; Ticonderoga Publications, P.O. Box 407, Nedlands, WA 6009 Australia, $A16.95 postage included, checks or M.O. in Australian dollars payable to Russell Farr, for *Ghost Seas,* by Steven Utley; Tachyon Publications, 1459 18th Street #139, San Francisco, CA, 94107, $14 for *The Rhinoceros Who Quoted Nietzche and Other Odd Acquaintances,* by Peter S. Beagle; Fedogan & Bremer, 603 Washington Avenue, SE #77, Minneapolis MN 55415, $32.00 for *Exorcisms and Ecstasies* by Karl Edward Wagner; Tiger Eyes Press, P.O. Box 172, Lemoyne, PA 17043, $25 in hardcover, $12 in trade paperback, for *A Geography of Unknown Lands,* by Michael Swanwick; DreamHaven Books, 912 West Lake St., Minneapolis, NM 55408, $25 for *The Arbitrary Placement of Walls,* by Martha Soukup.)

The reprint anthology field seemed at least a bit stronger this year than last year, with several good values, although the overall number of reprint anthologies still seems to be lower than it was a few years back.

The best bets for your money in this category, as usual, were the various Best of the Year anthologies and the annual Nebula Award anthology, *Nebula Awards 31,* edited by Pamela Sargent (Harcourt Brace); this year there was also a new volume collecting recent Hugo Award–winning stories, *The New Hugo Winners IV,* edited by Gregory Benford (Baen). Science fiction is now being covered by *two* Best of the Year anthology series, the one you are holding in your hand, and the *Year's Best SF* series, edited by David G. Hartwell (HarperPrism), now up to its third volume. Since Hartwell's anthology is a direct competitor to *this* volume, it would be inappropriate (and suspect) to review it, but the field is certainly wide enough for there to be more than one *best* anthology, and the parallax provided by comparing Hartwell's slant on what was the year's best fiction to my own slant is interesting, and probably valuable. Besides, since Hartwell will almost certainly like stories that I didn't, and vice versa, having two volumes gives more authors a chance to be showcased every year, something I'm sure both of us welcome, since no anthology can be big enough or comprehensive enough to include *all* the worthwhile SF of various different varieties that comes out in the course of a year. Again in 1997, there were two Best of the Year anthologies covering horror: the latest edition in the British series *The Mammoth Book of Best New Horror,* edited by Stephen Jones (Robinson), now up to volume 8, and the Ellen Datlow half of a huge volume covering both horror and fantasy, *The Year's Best Fantasy and Horror,* edited by Ellen Datlow and Terri Windling (St. Martin's), this year up to its Tenth Annual Collection. Surprisingly, considering the fantasy boom that is underway in the novel category and the success of *Realms of Fantasy* magazine, fantasy, as opposed to horror, is still only covered by the Windling half of the Datlow/Windling anthology. This year saw the start of a new Best of the Year series, a somewhat more specialized one, *The Year's Best Australian Science Fiction and Fantasy,* Volume 1 (HarperCollins Australia Voyager), edited by Jonathan Strahan and Jeremy G. Byrne. Although restricted to original fiction published in Australia, this book has a somewhat wider purview, including both science fiction and fantasy as well as horror and some harder-to-classify stuff, and features good work by Greg Egan, Terry Dowling, Cherry Wilder, Jack Dann, Stephen Dedman, and others.

Turning away from the anthology series, there were several good retrospective anthologies this year that provided essential historical overviews *and* were good buys for your money. *The Science Fiction Century*, edited by David G. Hartwell (Tor), is one of a series of big—and controversial—retrospective anthologies, such as *Age of Wonder* and *The Ascent of Wonder* that Hartwell has been editing in the last few years; this one, an overview of the evolution of the field over the last hundred years, is even more controversial than the others, because of Hartwell's decision not to use the work of authors such as Robert A. Heinlein, Isaac Asimov, Arthur C. Clarke, Theodore Sturgeon, and others—again, as in other years, this is an argument that will bother critics and scholars far more than it does readers, who, regardless of whether they agree with Hartwell's aesthetic choices and polemics or disagree with them, will *still* receive a fat anthology filled with first-rate stories by many *other* first-rate authors at a price that makes it, pound for pound, one of the year's best reading bargains. Another excellent retrospective, although it limits itself to covering a much shorter span of time than does Hartwell's anthology, is the similarly titled *A Century of Science Fiction 1950–1959* (MJF Books), edited by Robert Silverberg. This is the first volume in a projected series of anthologies that were supposed to cover the last forty-some years of science fiction, focusing on one decade at a time, but the series has apparently died along with publisher Donald I. Fine, and so this will probably be the first *and* last such volume we get—a real loss to the field, since Silverberg's historical notes here are almost as good as his selection of stories, quite a compliment when you're talking about a book that contains such classics as Fritz Leiber's "Coming Attractions," Poul Anderson's "Call Me Joe," C. M. Kornbluth's "The Mindworm," and Theodore Sturgeon's "The Man Who Lost the Sea," as well as fourteen other stories almost in the same class. Plus the anthology as a whole presents about as good an overview of '50s science fiction as you're going to get anywhere. What a pity we won't get to see the rest of the series, covering subsequent decades! An overview of a somewhat different sort, covering the recent—and often rapid—evolution of British science fiction instead, is to be found in *The Best of Interzone*, edited by David Pringle (St. Martin's), a book that will be all the more valuable to American readers because much of the material here will be unknown to many of them, as is largely, alas, the first-rate British magazine from which they are drawn. The anthology contains good-to-excellent work by Geoff Ryman, Greg Egan, Ian R. MacLeod, Brian Stableford, Nicola Griffith, Eugene Byrne, Stephen Baxter, Chris Beckett, Ben Jeapes, and others, many of them not well-known on this side of the Atlantic, as well as work by visiting Americans such as Paul Di Filippo, Paul Park, Timons Esaias, and Thomas M. Disch. Although a best from *Interzone* anthology was long overdue, I can't help but wonder if a best from *Absolute Magnitude* anthology is not perhaps a bit premature, considering that the magazine itself has only been in existence for a few years, but, nevertheless, that's just what you get with *Absolute Magnitude*, edited by Warren Lapine and Stephen Pagel (Tor); and although the stories here come nowhere near the level of quality of the best stuff from the *Interzone* anthology, there is solid, enjoyable work here by Hal Clement, Janet Kagan, Barry Longyear, Allen Steele, Don D'Ammassa, and others. *Ackermanthology*, edited by Forrest J. Ackerman (General Publishing Group), provides an overview of SF largely centered on older work. An overview of an entirely different SF tradition is provided in *Best Japanese Science Fiction Stories,* edited by John L. Apostolou and Martin H. Greenberg (Barricade Books).

Other reprint SF anthologies this year included *Sci-Fi Private Eye,* edited by Charles Waugh and Martin H. Greenberg (DAW), a good solid reprint anthology featuring good work by Philip K. Dick, Poul Anderson, Isaac Asimov, Tom Reamy, Robert Silverberg, and others; *Time Machines: The Best Time Travel Stories Ever Written* (Carroll & Graf), edited by Bill Alder Jr., didn't quite live up to its overheated title, still it provided excellent work by Connie Willis, Steven Utley, John W. Campbell, Geoffrey A. Landis, Larry Niven, Jack McDevitt, and others; similar territory was covered just as well in *Tales in Time,* edited by Peter Crowther (White Wolf Borealis), which featured first-rate work by James Tiptree, Jr., Harlan Ellison, Ian Watson, Jack Finney, Ray Bradbury, and others. Noted without comment are *Timegates,* edited by Jack Dann and Gardner Dozois (Ace); *Isaac Asimov's Moons,* edited by Gardner Dozois and Sheila Williams (Ace); and *Isaac Asimov's Christmas,* edited by Gardner Dozois and Sheila Williams (Ace).

There were some good reprint fantasy anthologies this year, a sort of anthology that has become moderately rare these days: An overview of modern fantasy fiction is provided in *Modern Classics of Fantasy,* edited by Gardner Dozois (St. Martin's), noted without comment. Similar territory is also covered in *Treasures of Fantasy,* edited by Margaret Weis and Tracy Hickman (HarperPrism), and *A Magic Lover's Treasure of the Fantastic,* edited by Margaret Weis (Aspect). Another overview, more limited in scope but more comprehensive within the period it covers, is provided by *A Century of Fantasy 1980–1989,* edited by Robert Silverberg (MJF Books), another excellent Silverberg anthology, similar in concept to his *A Century of Science Fiction* discussed above, featuring first-rate work by Joe Haldeman, Charles de Lint, Roger Zelazny, and others. A good anthology of comic fantasy is *The Wizard of Odd,* edited by Peter Haining (Ace), and some good fantasy stories about dragons are collected in *Dragons: The Greatest Stories,* edited by Martin H. Greenberg (MJF Books).

Reprint anthologies are also somewhat rare in horror, where most of the anthologies are originals, but this year we had *A Century of Horror 1970–1979,* edited by David Drake (MJF Books), the start of another promising but probably doomed anthology series; *Girls' Night Out: Twenty-Nine Female Vampire Stories,* edited by Stefan R. Dziemianowicz, Robert E. Weinberg, and Martin H. Greenberg (Barnes & Noble); *Bodies of the Dead and Other Great American Ghost Stories,* edited by David G. Hartwell (Tor); *Southern Blood: Vampire Stories from the American South* (Cumberland House, 432-433 Harding Industrial Park Drive, Nashville TN, 37211 $12.95); *100 Fiendish Little Frightmares,* edited by Stefan R. Dziemianowicz, Robert E. Weinberg, and Martin H. Greenberg (Barnes & Noble); *Haunted Houses: The Greatest Stories,* edited by Martin H. Greenberg (MJF Books); and *Weird Tales: Seven Decades of Terror,* edited by John Betancourt and Robert Weinberg (Barnes & Noble).

Odd but enjoyable items from smaller presses include *Strange Kaddish* (Aardwolf Publishing), edited by Clifford Lawrence Meth and Ricia Mainhardt, an

anthology of Jewish science fiction featuring work by Harlan Ellison, Shira Dae-
mon, Neil Gaiman, and others, and *Girls for the Slime God* (Obscura Press),
edited by Mike Resnick, featuring old-fashioned hairy-chested pulp adventure
SF stories by Henry Kuttner, a story parodying them in a genial way by Isaac
Asimov, and a nonfiction look back at the sort of pulp magazines where Bug-
Eyed Lobster Men were always carrying beautiful half-naked women off for
purposes either dietary or romantic (or both), by William Knoles. (Aardwolf
Publishing, 45 Park Place South, Suite 270, Morristown, NJ 07960, $9.95 for
Strange Kaddish; Wunzenzierohs Publishing, P.O. Box 1992, Ames, IA 50010-
1992, $15 plus $3 postage for *Girls for the Slime God*.)

The big news in the SF-and-fantasy-oriented nonfiction and reference book field
this year was undoubtedly the publication of John Clute and John Grant's mammoth *The Encyclopedia of Fantasy* (St. Martin's Press), a massive and exhaustively comprehensive reference book that, along with its companion volume,
1993's *The Encycopedia of Science Fiction*, will form the cornerstones of genre
scholarship for decades to come. These are invaluable reference tools for anyone
who is interested in the rapidly evolving and expanding field of modern fantasy
and belong in every serious reader's library. Like its predecessor, *The Encyclopedia
of Fantasy* is expensive, but it's also worth every penny you spend on it. This
was a good year in general for fantasy reference books in fact and critical studies
about fantasy, especially if you count in David Pringle's *St. James Guide to Fantasy Writers*, which was published late last year. *Discovering Classic Fantasy*, by
Darrell Schweitzer (Borgo), was a useful guide to some of the old masters of
fantasy, while there were several books that took a closer look at some of them,
such as *A Subtler Magick: The Writings and Philosophy of H. P. Lovecraft*, by
S. T. Joshi (Borgo); *Bram Stoker's Dracula*, edited by Nina Auerbach and David
J. Skal (Norton); and *Defending Middle-Earth*, by Patrick Curry (St. Martin's).
Industry was a more generalized critical study of a specific fantasy form. *Science
Fiction and Fantasy Reference Index, 1992–1995*, edited by Hal W. Hall (Library
Unlimited), was a useful reference work for *both* genres. There were two valuable
books of insightful, articulate, and often highly opinionated essays about SF and
SF-related topics: *Reflections and Refractions*, by Robert Silverberg (Under-
wood), and *Outposts: Literatures of Milieux*, by Algis Budrys (Borgo Press). A
similar book, similarly articulate, that casts its net a bit wider is *Rubber Dinosaurs
and Wooden Elephants: Essays on Literature, Film, and History* (Borgo Press), by
L. Sprague De Camp. Critical overviews of SF as a genre could be found in a
reissue of a somewhat expanded version of one of the cornerstone books of SF
criticism, Damon Knight's *In Search of Wonder* (Advent), as well as in *Science
Fiction After 1900: From the Steam Man to the Stars*, by Brooks Landon
(Twayne), and *Islands in the Sky*, by Gary Westfahl (Borgo Press), while literary
studies of specific SF authors were available in *Isaac Asimov: The Foundations
of Science Fiction* (Revised Edition), by James Gunn (Scarecrow); *Apocalyptic
Realism: The Science Fiction of Arkady and Boris Strugatsky*, by Yvonne Howell
(Peter Lang); and *"The Angle Between Two Walls": The Fiction of J. G. Ballard*,

by Roger Luckhurst (St. Martin's). Books for the SF witer include *Time Travel* by Paul J. Nahin (Writer's Digest), *Space Travel* by Ben Bova with Anthony R. Lewis (Writer's Digest), and a new edition of Damon Knight's *Creating Short Fiction* (St. Martin's).

The art book field this year was dominated by Vincent Di Fate's huge and comprehensive retrospective look at science fiction art, *Infinite Worlds: The Fantastic Visions of Science Fiction Art* (Penguin Studio). This is by far the best and the most complete overview of SF art that has ever been published, easily superseding earlier retrospectives, such as Brian Aldiss's *Science Fiction Art* or Anthony Frewin's *One Hundred Years of Science Fiction Illustration*—if you're only going to buy one SF art book this year, then without question Di Fate's book should be the one you buy. Another valuable overview of what's happening in the current SF and fantasy art scene is provided in *Spectrum IV: The Best in Contemporary Fantastic Art*, edited by Cathy Burnett, Arnie Fenner, and Jim Loehr (Underwood Books), the latest edition of a sort of Best of the Year series that compiles the year's fantastic art. There seemed to be few major art collections this year, although there were still a few substantial ones, including *Knightsbridge: The Art of Keith Parkinson* (FPG); Michael Whelan's *Something in My Eye: Excursions into Fear*, edited by Arnie Fenner and Cathy Fenner (Mark V. Ziesing); and H. R. Giger's *www.HRGiger.com* (Taschen). Heavily illustrated SF books this year, with the art sometimes making up a larger percentage of the book than the text, included Stephen King's *The Dark Tower IV: Wizards and Glass* (Donald Grant), illustrated by Dave McKean, and Harlan Ellison's *"Repent Harlequin!" Said the Tick Tock Man* (Underwood), illustrated by Rick Berry.

A valuable retrospective on the art of illustrated children's books, a field that shares an elusive border with fantasy art, is *A Treasury of Great Children's Book Illustrators*, by Susan E. Meyer (Harry N. Abrams). Illustrated children's books this year that will probably appeal to fans of fantasy art include *The Girl Who Dreamed Only Geese and Other Tales of the Far North* by Howard Norman, illustrated by Leo and Diane Dillon (Harcourt Brace), *The Veil of Snows*, by Mark Helprin, illustrated by Chris Van Allsburg (Viking Ariel), and *Rapunzel*, by Paul O. Zelinsky (Dutton).

There were only a few general genre-related nonfiction books of interest this year, none of them really exceptional, although most of them were worthwhile. An interesting if rather formidably opaque and polemic-drenched volume is *Digital Delirium*, edited by Arthur and Marilouise Kroker (St. Martin's). This is a collection of essays about the future of the Internet and the "digital world" in general and the effect it's all going to have on human society and even human evolution, much of it so extreme that the authors seem—to put it bluntly—to be nuts, although it's hard to say from the perspective of the present whether or not there might also turn out to have been nuggets of visionary wisdom buried in this mud slide of passionate rhetoric. Among this crew of wild-eyed, arm-waving digital mystics, science fiction's own Bruce Sterling comes off as the voice of Reason, Moderation, and Caution, warning that events in the digital world don't always have the impact on the real world that digital visionaries assume they're going to have. Similar territory is covered, in a more level-headed and less didactic way, in the nonfiction half of the anthology *Future Histories*, edited by Stephen McClelland (Horizon House), which features essays about the Internet, the "future of communications," and related topics by authors such as Arthur C. Clarke, William Gibson, Nicholas Negroponte, Vernor Vinge, Bruce Sterling, and others.

Most SF fans love dinosaurs, and so most of them will probably be interested in *Dinosaur Lives*, by John R. Horner and Edwin Dobb (HarperCollins), which takes us to the front lines and gives us a look at some of the more recent battles going on in that highly contentious science, paleontology, where even the theory that the dinosaurs were wiped out by a deadly strike by an asteroid or comet, probably the most sacrosanct scientific theory of the last ten years, is now coming under attack by critics armed with alternative theories of their own. Most SF fans also share at least a passing interest in astronomy, and so will probably appreciate *Planet Quest, the Epic Discovery of Alien Solar Systems*, by Ken Croswell (The Free Press), a comprehensive—if a bit dry—look at just what the title *says* it's about, a subject that would have been science fiction rather than science fact only a few years ago. *The Whole Shebang, a State-of-the-Universe(s) Report* (Simon & Schuster), by Timothy Ferris, is a good layman's overview of some of the classic problems in cosmology and quantum physics, of obvious applicability to the genre. Michael Palin's *Full Circle* (St. Martin's), a travel book tied to his recent BBC travel series, is not even remotely justifiable as a "genre-related" book, but, like Palin's other travel narratives, *Around the World in Eighty Days* and *Pole to Pole*, does offer sort of a vaguely SF-ish kick in the inside perspective it provides into various societies and cultures around the world, many of them extremely different from our familiar Western culture, and so I'll offer that—and the fact that it was one of the more enjoyable nonfiction books I read this year (plus the fact that it was a slow year in this category)—as my weak rationale for mentioning it here.

This year saw an unprecedented parade of SF Big-Screen, Big-Budget, A-Release, Special Effects–Heavy Spectaculars—a few of which were actually worth watching.

More of these Big-Budget, Special Effects–laden giants are on the way for next year, most budgeted somewhere in the range of 60 million dollars and *up*; it's quite possible that it will turn out that more money was spent making SF movies for the 1997 and 1998 seasons than has ever before been spent on SF as a film genre. The unanswered question is, is SF as a film genre making *money*? In an overall sense, is the genre of the SF film returning the vast amount of money that the studios are sinking into it? Some of these Special Effects Extravaganzas have done spectacularly well at the box office—but others seem to have failed, and many that were expected to perform well have seemingly turned in lukewarm performances as moneymakers (this whole question of whether or not a film has made money is complicated these days by the effect of later foreign and videotape sales of the movie, a factor that has helped some notorious box-office bombs earn-out down the road).

If the overall sense of the industry is that SF movies *are* making money, then we can expect to see the stream of such movies continuing into the next century; otherwise, the stream may eventually run dry, as it did after other SF films of the period were unable to match the great success of the *Star Wars* movies.

The biggest hit of the year, of course, and already one of the highest-earning movies of all time in spite of *also* being the most expensive-to-produce movie ever, is *Titanic*, which some people are urging be considered a SF film because it's a movie about the uses and misuses of technology (and because it has RE-ALLY NEAT special effects)—but that stretches the definition of a SF film beyond any useful limits, I think, and I'm not willing to go that far myself (although it wouldn't entirely surprise me to see *Titanic* show up on next year's Hugo ballot anyway).

Stepping down a bit from *Titanic's* lofty level—although still immensely prof-itable, especially when you consider that it was relatively inexpensive for one of these Special Effects-heavy movies—we come to the surprise hit of the year, *Men in Black*, a good-natured, amiable, unpretentious, and occasionally surpris-ingly intelligent action-comedy about an ultrasecret government organization set up to protect Earth from "the scum of the galaxy," the alien criminals and terrorists who live among us in secret, along with more law-abiding, decent-citizen-type alien immigrants and alien refugees. This movie works some of the same territory as last year's *Independence Day*, including the widely accepted belief that a flying saucer crashed in Roswell, New Mexico, in the '50s and was captured by the military and that the government has been covering up contin-ued contact with alien races ever since. In an amazingly adroit bit of aesthetic tightrope walking, *Men in Black* manages to take this idea seriously enough to draw power from it *and* make some sharp fun of it at the very same time. The special effects are good, of course, including some of the best and most diverse "alien costumes" seen since the original *Star Wars*, but the real draw here is another relaxed, assured, brash, effortlessly amusing, and totally self-confident star turn by Will Smith—who surely has Bankable Megastar of the late '90s written all over him by now—supported admirably by a deadpan but sardonic just-the-facts-ma'am performance by Tommy Lee Jones, and a wonderful por-trayal—done mostly with body language—of a menacing Alien Bug stuffed into an ill-fitting Human Suit, scary and very funny at the same time, by Vincent D'Onofrio. This may not have been the best SF movie of the year, but it was certainly the one that was the most fun to watch.

I also enjoyed two of the year's other Big-Screen Spectaculars, although not as much as *Men in Black*, *The Fifth Element* and—to a lesser extent—*The Lost World: Jurassic Park*. Both were worth seeing, if only for the special effects, and, in the case of *The Fifth Element*, the bizarre and imaginative costuming and set dressing, although it must be admitted up front that both movies were Very Dumb to one extent or another (perhaps less of an offense in *The Fifth Element*, which is clearly *intending* to be Very Dumb in a few places). Both were fast-paced, however, and enjoyable if you disengaged your frontal lobes and didn't ask too many embarrassing questions.

The Fifth Element was the funnier and more enjoyable of the two, a richly colored, headlong, flatout, wildly extravagant Space Opera that didn't make a lick of sense but didn't really *need* to. This is by far the most successful attempt yet to translate the aesthetics of that specialized, and largely French, form of the comic book known as "comix"—one of Moebius's strips from *Metal Hurlant*, say—to the movie screen, with all the attendant strengths and weaknesses of that form; the film does a credible job of catching the kind of wild imagery and bizarre juxtapositions that are the heart of that kind of comix, an even better job than did *Barbarella*, since the makers of *The Fifth Element* have a much bigger budget and thirty years' worth of advancement in special effects technology with which to work.

(For another excellent example of French film aesthetics—which are definitely *not* American aesthetics—in the SF/fantasy/comix area, check out *The City of Lost Children*, a wonderful movie from a couple of years back that I caught up with recently, a weird but effective mélange of children's fantasy, surrealism, *Metal Hurlant*–style comix, *noir* cinema, and French-tinged cyberpunk; in spite of the stylish and unrelieved grimness of the surreal/*noir* setting, the movie is often quite funny, and, in the end, surprisingly touching and sweet.)

Once you realized that *The Fifth Element* was not really a science fiction movie at all, but rather a filmed version of a comix (a realization that hit me early on, and was certainly inescapable by the time it came to the border of the Terran System, and it's a physical *line* drawn through space by a row of floating beacons), you could relax and stop trying to sort a coherent plot out of it all, and stop worrying about logical inconsistences and scientific plausibility (although many genre fans and critics apparently could *not*). "Comix" don't make a lick of sense *either*, of course, when viewed from the sober, rational, right-brained perspective of traditional science fiction, and seem in fact to take it as a mark of pride that they don't. The premiere French comix artist, Jean Giraud (known as Moebius), actually worked on *The Fifth Element*, and in many ways it's his movie, with images from his comix—and complete plot lines, including dialogue—running through it from beginning to end, including such unmistakable Moebius touches as the ponderous and benign alien creatures in turtle-shaped space suits who appear at the beginning of the movie and the sequence where the alien Diva, whose singing is so overwhelmingly effective that it reaches across almost all racial barriers, is giving a concert attended by many different alien races, a story line taken directly from a *Metal Hurlant* strip. I must say that it all looks great, up on the big screen in full color, and *moving around* too, a testimony to the sheer power of Moebius's imagery and a treat for the eye, whether it makes any sense or not. The special effects are good, but I enjoyed the costuming, the lavish set dressing, and the mind-bogglingly immense (and largely CGI-created) sets the most. The story line is serviceable as long as you don't mind *extremely* unlikely coincidences and huge holes in the plot logic, and it does have the advantage of being frequently played for as many laughs as it can get. The actors are okay, with Bruce Willis doing his beard-stubble-and-torn-T-shirt-reluctant-action-hero *Die Hard* routine, and being upstaged effortlessly by the female lead, Milla Jovovich, who is quite good, speaking the "divine language" babble, which makes up a good part of her dialogue, convincingly enough to make it sound like a real language, and looking very nice, mostly *out* of the minimal costuming they give her.

Much the same sort of thing—entertaining, but check your forebrain at the door—could be said about *The Lost World: Jurassic Park*. For what it's worth, it's actually a better movie than *Jurassic Park* was in some ways—although lacking the first-time impact of the dinosaur effects that the first movie enjoyed—with the humans actually figuring out how to escape from the dinosaurs on their own, rather than being rescued at the last minute by a disappointing Deus-Ex-Tyrannosaurus ending, which was my major objection to *Jurassic Park*. Here, instead, they beat the dinos using their wits and skill at improvising on the run (literally), which, for me, makes for a much more satisfying movie (*some* of the characters rely on their own ingenuity, at least; the supposed "professional hunters," by comparison, react with incredible stupidity and incompetence instead, but then, of course, they are only in the movie to serve as cannon fodder—or perhaps Dino Chow would be a better term—in the first place). There are no great surprises here plotwise, of course, it's all pretty predictable—but the movie does manage to crank up a good deal of suspense in several scenes and edges out *Jurassic Park* on that score as well.

In a way, though, of course, none of that matters—people went to see *The Lost World* for the same reason they went to see *Jurassic Park*: for the *dinosaurs*. They weren't disappointed either: the special effects here are an order of magnitude better even than in *Jurassic Park*; it's almost frightening how *fast* the whole CGI field is evolving, seeming to go through a quantum jump every three or four years. They used a combination of full-sized robot models, traditional stop-motion model animation, and CGI animation for *Jurassic Park*; but here they largely went with just the CGI stuff instead, and not only are the effects better, with the dinosaurs doing much more complex stuff more believably than in the first movie, but the effects *cost* a lot less than the effects for the first movie had. If I were a movie actor, I think I'd feel a cold wind blowing, since we surely can't be more than ten years away (and maybe considerably less) from the CGI people being able to create a movie totally without human actors that will be indistinguishable from a movie *with* human actors. Already, Steven Speilberg has been quoted as saying that he didn't need a Big Name Bankable Star for *The Lost World*, and he was right. Why pay $50 million for Mel Gibson, when you can whomp up a bunch of dinosaurs in your computer instead? How long it will be before you can whomp up *Mel Gibson* in your computer? I'm willing to bet that in ten years, if not in five years, the magnificent effects here are going to look crude.

I wonder if we're going to hit a time when wonderful Special Effects will be so cheap and so common and so widespread that having them in your movie won't be *enough* to get people to come to see it anymore? If, instead, the Great Special Effects being a *given*, you'll have to start putting things like a great story and great characters and great dialogue and actually intriguing ideas in it in order to lure an audience into the theater. That would make for a nice change, wouldn't it?

We actually had a movie this year that tried for something like the above ideal, that rare creature, a serious-minded Big-Budget SF movie, a movie that tried to *combine* expensive production values and great special effects with a serious adult plot, complex and sophisticated conceptualization, and well-rounded human characters. It wasn't entirely successful in *achieving* that goal, of course, but movies that even *try* are rare enough that it deserves to be applauded for making an earnest effort in that direction.

I'm talking, of course, about *Contact*, a film that tried hard to be the kind of intelligent, serious, adult, thinking-man's SF movie that genre fans have been saying for years they want to see, but which seem to arouse little real heat or enthusiasm within the genre for all that. The trouble may be in the source material, Carl Sagan's best-selling novel to which the film was reasonably faithful. The novel *Contact* was more widely appreciated outside the genre than inside it, where it was commonly regarded as new wine in an old bottle, or perhaps even old wine in an old bottle, and I suspect the same is true for the movie, for the same reasons.

Outside the genre, to audiences who were not already long-familiar with the basic concepts being examined here, *Contact* may well have played as a stunningly effective and mind-blowing film. Inside the genre, the familiarity of the material lessened the movie's impact, although it was nice to see that material being treated with respect and a reasonable amount of intelligence for a change (one glaring exception: none of the scientists seemed to be able to refute the idea, raised by skeptical bureaucrats, that the alien transmission could have been faked by a satellite in Earth orbit, although triangulation would quickly rule out that possibility; in fact, the whole "Inquisition" sequence toward the end of the movie was lame—perhaps the weakest part of the plot—at least once you got beyond the extreme improbability that they would pick the heroine as the "test pilot" for the alien machine under *any* circumstances).

Jodie Foster turns in a marvelous performance as the emotionally crippled scientist obsessed with making contact with alien intelligences, and the movie has much to recommend it, including the fact that it raises issues (although, having raised them, it doesn't then go on to examine them in any really complex way) about the relationship of science and religion that have rarely been raised in any main-line commercial movie—but my admiration for it remained largely theoretical. While actually *watching* it, I found it faintly dull, although I struggled throughout with the guilty feeling that I somehow *ought* to be enjoying it more than I actually *was*.

Gattaca, another earnest, fairly intelligent, serious-minded SF movie, performed poorly at the box office, and didn't arouse much enthusiasm within the genre either—which makes me wonder how much disparity there is between what we *say* we want in a movie and what we actually *do* want.

Back in Big-Screen Spectacular territory, *Starship Troopers*, based (very) loosely on the famous SF novel by Robert A. Heinlein, was another substantial box-office success and *did* arouse a good deal of enthusiasm within the genre, although it also aroused at least as much controversy, with Heinlein fans seeming to be divided about evenly between liking it and loathing it. Several parents that I know, dragged to the theater by their teenage children, have commented that audiences of kids watching *Starship Troopers* looked as if they were intently playing a video game, bouncing and jerking and bobbing in their seats as if operating an invisible joystick, and *Starship Troopers* does seem to be more like a video game than a movie in some respects, with both the strengths *and* the weaknesses of that form. Most of the polemic arguments at the heart of Heinlein's book were lost in translation from one medium to another (although there was much ink spilled over the "fascist" subtext of the film, which may possibly have been the director's hidden sardonic take on the libertarian politics of the original novel, enabling him to hunt with the hounds and run with the hare at the same time by making a big ultraviolent gore-splattered "heroic" war movie whose heros are *then* slyly identified with the Nazis, so that he can claim the movie "really" delivers an antiwar message instead), but the movie was fast-paced and stylish and intense and violent enough that few viewers really cared. (It was also reasonably intelligent for an ultraviolent action movie of this sort, as long as you ignored questions such as, Why in the world would they be fighting the Bugs mostly with small arms, the equivalent of today's M-16 rifle? As one combat veteran of my acquaintance put it, "We had weapons on the squad level in Vietnam that could have made Bug-flavored mincemeat of those critters, and a squadron of Cobra helicopters could have swept the entire planet clean." You'll also notice that, unlike in Heinlein's novel, the Bugs don't get weapons and technology of their own to fight *back* with . . .)

Not all of the year's Big-Budget, Big-Ticket SF movies were commercial successes, by any mean. Kevin Costner's Civilization-Struggling-to-Reestablish-Itself-After-the-Atomic-War saga, *The Postman*, was a major disappointment at the box office and may well have been the most critically savaged genre movie of the year, widely panned for being boring and sententious, a filmed love letter from Kevin Costner to himself, with one critic referring to it mockingly as "Dances with Mailmen"; it's worth noting, though, that the author of the book from which the film was drawn, David Brin, went so far as to take out an ad in a major newspaper defending it, so he apparently thought it had done a reasonable job of translating his novel to the screen—so that may mean that if you liked the book, you might well like the movie too. *Event Horizon* looked as if it was going to be a hard-science movie, but instead turned out to be a gruesome, blood-spattered, supernatural horror thriller in deep-space disguise and quickly disappeared from theaters. *Batman and Robin*, with George Clooney assuming the mask and cowl from Val Kilmer, was a major bomb, and may have sunk the whole Batman franchise.

Deep Rising, which some wag characterized as *Alien* set on the *Titanic*, with a giant squidlike creature playing the part of the alien, quickly sank at the box office. *Anaconda*, another *Alien*-like movie, with a giant snake standing in for the alien, also quickly slithered out of town. *Volcano* and *Dante's Peak*, disaster movies calculated to capitalize on the success of 1996's *Twister*, fizzled; and *Hard Rain*, an odd cross between a disaster movie and a crime thriller, with a robbery taking place during a major flood, was a box-office disappointment as well. I'm not sure how *Kull the Conqueror*, a version of the old Robert E. Howard story, starring Kevin Sorbo, TV's Hercules, did at the box office, but, for what it's worth, it was in town barely long enough for the guy at the candy counter to finish making the popcorn. Somewhat more successful, although more marginal, were the paranoid thriller *The Game* and a horror movie based on an old story by Donald A. Wollheim, *Mimic*.

Still on the horizon: a Big-Screen version of the old TV show *Lost in Space* that plays it seriously rather than for camp laughs; a very big-budget version of *Godzilla*; a film version of Michael Crichton's novel *Sphere*; the long-promised new SF movie by Stanley Kubrick; the new *Star Trek* movie; and the first of the new *Star Wars* "prequels."

Turning to television, there seemed to be few big new stories here, although SF/fantasy shows came and went so fast that I was unable even to catch up with a few of them—such as *The Visitor* and *Roar*—before they were already gone. Most of them seemed to be no great loss, and I suspect that many of the new shows that are hanging on, such as *The Sentinel* and *Three*, will soon be gone as well, and will also be no great loss. *Roddenberry's Earth: Final Conflict* seems to be doing better than these shows in the ratings, and may be around for a while, but I don't much like it either.

The big winner this year seemed to be *Babylon 5*, which not only survived to get the go-ahead for a fifth season that had been seriously in doubt last year, but which struck a deal to get all of its old shows from prior seasons rerun in chronological order on another network, a deal that can only increase its ratings success, probably broadening the audience considerably beyond the present core of devoted *B5* fanatics; in fact, initial reports on the ratings of the rerun of the *Babylon 5* pilot episode indicate that they were substantial.

So, ironically, *Babylon 5* seems to have won—or at least survived—its direct head-to-head battle with its hated rival *Star Trek: Deep Space Nine*, a show with a very similar concept that, with the weight of the mighty *Star Trek* franchise behind it, was originally expected to crush *Babylon 5* easily and sweep it from the airwaves. Not only *hasn't* that happened, but—also ironically—*B5* fans are committed to the series with the kind of devotion and evangelistic fervor and intense enthusiasm that hasn't been seen since the days of the original *Star Trek* series; I strongly suspect, for instance, that nothing other than a *Babylon 5* episode has even a remote chance of winning a Best Dramatic Prentation Hugo for the next few years. I must admit that I myself still don't understand all the enthusiasm for *B5*, since every time I sample an episode, I'm struck by the mediocre-to-terrible dialogue, the leaden direction, and the wooden acting, but I can't deny that I'm distinctly in the minority here. (*B5* fans keep telling me that if only I'd watch *enough* episodes, I'd learn to like it; but when I was in the army, people told me that if I ate liver and onions enough, I'd learn to like *that*, too, and it didn't work—so I'm skeptical.)

Star Trek: Deep Space Nine seems to have shored up its ratings by the addition to the cast of the extremely popular character Worf from the parent show *Star Trek: The Next Generation*, but it's still not the success, either artistically or in the ratings, that the old show was during its prime period. How it's doing in comparison to *Babylon 5*, I don't have the figures to determine, but neither show seems in any immediate danger of being canceled. *Star Trek: Voyager* is still struggling, and appears to be not all that popular even with core *Star Trek* fans, although the recent addition of a Cute Borg Babe to the cast seems to have helped *some* in the ratings.

The X-Files remains popular, having reached the point of Cult Coolness, where famous authors are clamoring to write for it, with recent scripts by Celebrity Guest Writers such as William Gibson and Tom Maddox and Stephen King. *Third Rock from the Sun* is also still popular, while *Lois and Clark* appears to have ended its run. *Sliders* died a well-deserved death, but, fear not, it has already been resurrected in the Vallhala of Old SF/Fantasy TV Shows, the Sci-Fi Channel. *Early Edition* and *Lost on Earth* both died, if anyone really cares, and so far have not even made it on to the Sci-Fi Channel.

Xena: Warrior Princess is more popular than ever, now a bigger hit than its parent show, *Hercules: The Legendary Journeys*, a fact that *Hercules* star Kevin Sorbo has grumbled about in several interviews. *Xena* is so successful, in fact, that along with recent shows such as *Buffy, the Vampire Slayer* and *La Femme Nikita* it seems to be forming a new television subgenre of shows where Beautiful Women Kick Male Butt, a subgenre which, for perhaps the first time in history, is bringing rednecks, college students, lesbians, and postmodernist intellectuals together as the viewing audience for the same TV shows. (So BWKMB shows could be a real unifying force in our society. Can a political coalition be far behind?) A legion of cheap-copy clone shows such as *The New Adventures of Robin Hood*, *Tarzan: The Epic Adventures*, and *The Adventures of Sinbad*, are trying to use the *Hercules/Xena* formula, but with noticeably less success. At their best, *Hercules* and *Xena* remain good cheesy fun, and have the benefit of not taking themselves terribly seriously, although after you watch for a while, the story lines get a bit repetitive; as long as there's enough head-bashing and butt-kicking, though, spiced with a sprinkling of anachronistic postmodern jokes, nobody seems to mind. (I sometimes worry that watching Xena—supposedly from ancient Greece—meet Julius Caesar or point out the direction of the Inn at Bethlehem to Mary and Joseph will really screw up the next generation's sense of history, but friends assure me that only outmoded dinosaurs like me are concerned about historical accuracy; this is *postmodernism*, where everything is *supposed* to be jumbled together in a bouillabaisse, the more eclectic the mix the better. Still hope the kids crack a book before settling down to a history exam though . . .)

Highlander: The Series has gone markedly downhill in the last couple of seasons, particularly this season, adding a whole slew of extraneous fantasy elements, such as demons, not called for by the initial premise, and it's clear that this series is on its last legs; this was a pretty good Junk Food show in its day, but it shows all the signs of being a tired series, and its day is past. It came as no surprise to me to hear that *Highlander* is officially scheduled to end this season, with the possibility of Adrian Paul going on to star in at least one new *Highlander* movie being dangled as consolation to desolate fans. Die-hard *Highlander* enthusiasts can also console themselves with the information that a *Highlander* spin-off series is in the works, starring a *female* immortal this time, the intention reportedly being to produce a show as much like *Xena* as possible. (How imaginative! Especially as this is a goal no doubt being pursued by a dozen *other* producers right about now.)

The most popular new Cult Show of the year, though, one which may even be able to rival *Xena* in popularity, was undoubtedly the animated series *South Park*, which runs on Comedy Central—already buzzwords and phrases from the show such as "They killed Kenny!" have spread everywhere through the culture, just as "Sock it to me!" and "Wild and Crazy Guys!" did in their days. This show does have some genuinely funny moments in it, but its deliberate gross-out humor at its grossest, prides itself not only on being non-PC but on having something to offend *everybody*—I still can't believe some of the stuff they've gotten away with, like having Jesus Christ reduced to doing a minor cable-access phone-in show, or fighting Satan in a bout carried on Pay for View—and is definitely not for the Easily Offended. There are many satirical fantastic elements here, from a plague of flesh-eating zombies to rampaging clones to a victim of an alien anal probe growing an eighty-foot satellite dish out of his butt. A recent episode satirizing Japanese monster movies featured a one-hundred-foot-tall Barbra Streisand stomping on the town.

The 55th World Science Fiction Convention, LoneStarCon2, was held in San Antonio, Texas, from August 28 to September 1, and drew an estimated attendance of 4,416, making it the smallest U.S. worldcon in fifteen years, smaller than last year's L.A. worldcon by more than 2,200 people. The 1997 Hugo Awards, presented at LoneStarCon2, were: Best Novel, *Blue Mars*, by Kim Stanley Robinson; Best Novella, "Blood of the Dragon," by George R. R. Martin; Best Novelette, "Bicycle Repairman," by Bruce Sterling; Best Short Story, "The Soul Selects Her Own Society . . . ," by Connie Willis; Best NonFiction, *Time & Chance*, by L. Sprague de Camp; Best Professional Editor, Gardner Dozois; Best Professional Artist, Bob Eggleton; Best Dramatic Presentation, *Babylon 5: Severed Dreams*; Best Semiprozine, *Locus*, edited by Charles N. Brown; Best Fanzine, *Mimosa*, edited by Dick and Nicki Lynch; Best Fan Writer, David Langford; Best Fan Artist, William Rotsler; plus the John W. Campbell Award for Best New Writer to Michael A. Burstein.

The 1996 Nebula Awards, presented at a banquet at the Holiday Inn Crowne Plaza Hotel in Kansas City, Missouri, on April 19, 1997, were: Best Novel, *Slow River*, by Nicola Griffith; Best Novella, "Da Vinci Rising," by Jack Dann; Best Novelette, "Lifeboat on a Burning Sea," by Bruce Holland Rogers; Best Short Story, "A Birthday," by Esther M. Friesner; plus the Grand Master award to Jack Vance.

The World Fantasy Awards, presented at the Twenty-Third Annual World Fantasy Convention in London, England, on November 2, 1997, were: Best Novel, *Godmother Night*, by Rachel Pollack; Best Novella, "A City in Winter," by Mark Helprin; Best Short Fiction, "Thirteen Phantasms," by James P. Blaylock; Best Collection, *The Wall of the Sky, the Wall of the Eye*, by Jonathan

Lethem; Best Anthology, *Starlight 1*, edited by Patrick Nielsen Hayden; Best Artist, Moebius; Special Award (Professional), to Michael J. Weldon for *The Psychotronic Video Guide*; Special Award (Nonprofessional), to Barbara & Christopher Roden for Ash-Tree Press; plus a special convention award to Hugh B. Cave and a Life Achievement Award to Madeleine L'Engle.

The 1997 Bram Stoker Awards, presented by the Horror Writers of America during a banquet at the Warwick Hotel in New York City on June 21, were: Best Novel, *The Green Mile*, by Stephen King; Best First Novel, *Crota*, by Owl Goingback; Best Collection, *The Nightmare Factory*, by Thomas Ligotti; Best Long Fiction, "The Red Tower," by Thomas Ligotti; Best Short Story, "Metalica," by P. D. Cacek; plus a Life Achievement Award to Ira Levin and to Forrest J. Ackerman.

The 1996 John W. Campbell Memorial Award was won by *Fairyland*, by Paul J. McAuley.

The 1996 Theodore Sturgeon Award for Best Short Story was won by "The Flowers of Aulit Prison," by Nancy Kress.

The 1996 Philip K. Dick Memorial Award went to *The Time Ships*, by Stephen Baxter.

The 1996 Arthur C. Clarke Award was won by *The Calcutta Chromosome*, by Amitav Ghosh.

The 1996 James Tiptree Jr. Memorial Award was won by *The Sparrow*, by Mary Doria Russell and "Mountain Ways," by Ursula K. Le Guin (tie), plus a Special Award to Angela Carter.

Dead in 1997 or early 1998 were: **Judith Merril,** 74, writer, critic, and anthologist, author of *The Tomorrow People* and the famous story "That Only a Mother," best known for her long-running and extremely influential series of Best of the Year anthologies, which helped shape literary tastes in the field from the early '50s all the way to the late '60s; **William Rotsler,** 71, author and artist, Nebula and Hugo-winner, best known as a writer for the novel *Patron of the Arts*, best known as an artist for the inexhaustible flood of fannish cartoons, donated for free, that filled the genre's fanzines and semiprozines for more than thirty years; **George Turner,** 80, prominent Australian SF author and critic, sometimes known as "the Grandmaster of Australian Science Fiction," winner of the Arthur C. Clarke Award, author of such well-known novels as *The Drowning Towers, Beloved Son, Genetic Soldier*, and *The Destiny Makers*; **William S. Burroughs,** 83, experimental novelist of the Beat Generation whose novels such as *Nova Express, Naked Lunch*, and *The Ticket That Exploded* were enormously influential both on the New Wave authors of the '60s such as J. G. Ballad and on the later cyberpunk authors of the '80s such as William Gibson, as well as in the artistic community at large; **Sam Moskowitz,** 76, SF historian, scholar, and anthologist, as well as an early SF convention fan and organizer, best known for his history of the early days of SF fandom, *The Immortal Storm*, as well as for his pioneering collections of biographical pieces about SF authors, *Explorers of the Infinite: Shapers of Science Fiction* and *Seekers of Tomorrow: Masters of Modern Science*

Fiction; **Donald R. Bensen,** 70, editor and anthologist, one-time SF editor at Pyramid, Ballantine, and Dell, editor of two of the most important early fantasy anthologies, *The Unknown* and *The Unknown Five*, and who, for those anthologies as well as the long out-of-print fantasy work by writers such as L. Sprague de Camp and Fletcher Pratt, and many others, that he brought back into print as Pyramid editor at a time when almost no fantasy work was being published elsewhere, can be seen as one of the unsung and forgotten progenitors of the whole modern fantasy revival; **G. Harry Stine,** 69, longtime science columnist for *Analog* and an engineer who had worked on missile programs at White Sands Proving Grounds, author of nonfiction books such as *The Third Industrial Revolution* and *Living in Space*, and who also wrote SF as Lee Correy; **H. B. Fyfe,** 80, veteran author who wrote mostly for *Astounding*, author of the classic story "Moonwalk," and many others; **Charles V. De Vet,** 85, veteran SF writer, best known as the author of the novel *Second Game*; **Donald I. Fine,** 75, publisher, founder of Arbor House and Donald I. Fine Books; **Kathy Keeton,** 58, publisher and editor, founder of the highly influential *Omni* magazine; **Carl Jacobi,** 89, veteran pulp writer; **Amos Tutola,** 77, Nigerian writer whose work drew upon Yoruba folktales, best-known for the book *The Palm-Wine Drinkard*; **Kathy Acker,** 49?, performance artist and experimental writer, another strong influence on the cyberpunks as well as on writers such as Lucius Shepard and others; **Martin Caidin,** 69, thriller writer and occasional SF writer, author of *The Long Night* and *Almost Midnight*, best-known for the space thriller *Marooned*; **Mervyn Wall,** 88, Irish fantasy writer, author of *The Unfortunate Fursey*; **Owen Barfield,** 99, writer, member of the Oxford writers group The Inklings, which included J. R. R. Tolkein and C. S. Lewis; **Elisabeth Gille,** 59, French publisher, translator, and writer; **William Rushton,** 59, British humorist and SF writer; **H. R. Percy,** 76, Canadian SF writer; **Andres Donatovich Sinyavskij,** 71, Russian SF writer and critic; **Vsevolod Aleksandrovich Revich,** 69, Russian SF writer and critic; **Tong Enzhong,** 62, Chinese SF writer; **Alan Harrington,** 78, author of *The Immortalist*; **Daniel P. Mannix,** 85, author of the children's fantasy *The Secret of the Elms*; **Caroline MacDonald,** 48, New Zealand–born author of young-adult fantasy and SF; **Mike Baker,** 31, horror writer and editor; **Lou Stathis,** 44, editor, writer, journalist, and critic, former associate editor of *Heavy Metal* magazine; **Terry Nation,** 66, British scriptwriter, best known for creating the race of archvillains, the Daleks, on the British TV show *Dr. Who*; **Clyde Tombaugh,** 90, well-known astronomer, discoverer of the planet Pluto; **James Stewart,** 89, world-famous film actor, whose many movies included roles in three well-known fantasy films, *Harvey*, *It's a Wonderful Life*, and *Bell, Book, and Candle*; **Burgess Meredith,** 88, film and television actor, perhaps best known to genre audiences for his role as The Penguin on the mid-'60s *Batman* TV series; **Paul Edwin Zimmer,** 54, author, brother of SF and fantasy writer Marion Zimmer Bradley; **Brian Burgess,** longtime British fan; **Phil Rogers,** 72, longtime British fan and organizer; **Tom Perry,** well-known fan and SF researcher; **Ted Pauls,** 54, fanzine editor, book dealer, and longtime convention fan; **Seth Goldberg,** 44, fanzine and convention fan; **Billie Lindsay Madle,** 78, wife of long-time fan and SF scholar Robert A. Madle; **Ingrid Zieruhut,** 64, longtime friend and business

partner of SF writer Andre Norton; **Erin Louisa Card,** newborn daughter of SF
writer Orson Scott Card; **Ruth Eisen Ferman,** 88, widow of former *F&SF* publisher Joseph W. Ferman and mother of current *F&SF* publisher Edward L.
Ferman; **Peter Joseph Stampfel II,** 84, father of SF editor Peter Stampfel; **Jean
Brust,** 76, mother of SF and fantasy writer Steven Brust; **Margaret Aldiss,** 64,
wife of SF writer Brian Aldiss, and **Dorothy Dozois,** 82, mother of SF editor
Gardner Dozois.

Beauty in the Night
ROBERT SILVERBERG

Robert Silverberg is one of the most famous SF writers of modern times, with dozens of novels, anthologies, and collections to his credit. Silverberg has won five Nebula Awards and four Hugo Awards. His novels include Dying Inside, Lord Valentine's Castle, The Book of Skulls, Downward to the Earth, Tower of Glass, The World Inside, Born with the Dead, Shadrach in the Furnace, Tom O'Bedlam, Star of Gypsies, At Winter's End, *and two novel-length expansions of famous Isaac Asimov stories,* Nightfall *and* The Ugly Little Boy. *His collections include* Unfamiliar Territory, Capricorn Games, Majipoor Chronicles, The Best of Robert Silverberg, At the Conglomeroid Cocktail Party, Beyond the Safe Zone, *and a massive retrospective collection,* The Collected Stories of Robert Silverberg, *Volume One:* Secret Sharers. *His most recent books are the novels* The Face of the Waters, Kingdoms of the Wall, Hot Sky at Morning, Starborne, *and* Mountains of Majipoor. *Due out soon is a new novel,* The Alien Years. *He lives with his wife, writer Karen Haber, in Oakland, California.*

Here he takes us to a shattered future Earth dominated by conquering aliens, for a profound and harrowing demonstration of the truth of that old adage, "As the twig is bent, so inclines the tree."

ONE: NINE YEARS FROM NOW

He was a Christmas child, was Khalid—Khalid the Entity-Killer, the first to raise his hand against the alien invaders who had conquered Earth in a single day, sweeping aside all resistance as though we were no more than ants to them. Khalid Haleem Burke, that was his name, English on his father's side, Pakistani on his mother's, born on Christmas Day amidst his mother's pain and shame and his family's grief. Christmas child though he was, nevertheless he was not going to be the new Savior of mankind, however neat a coincidence that might have been. But he would live, though his mother had not, and in the fullness of time he would do his little part, strike his little blow, against the awesome beings who had with such contemptuous ease taken possession of the world into which he had been born.

• • •

To be born at Christmastime can be an awkward thing for mother and child, who even at the best of times must contend with the risks inherent in the general overcrowding and understaffing of hospitals at that time of year. But prevailing hospital conditions were not an issue for the mother of the child of uncertain parentage and dim prospects who was about to come into the world in unhappy and disagreeable circumstances in an unheated upstairs storeroom of a modest Pakistani restaurant grandly named Khan's Mogul Palace in Salisbury, England, very early in the morning of this third Christmas since the advent of the conquering Entities from the stars.

Salisbury is a pleasant little city that lies to the south and west of London and is the principal town of the county of Wiltshire. It is noted particularly for its relatively unspoiled medieval charm, for its graceful and imposing 13th-century cathedral, and for the presence, eight miles away, of the celebrated prehistoric megalithic monument

Which, in the darkness before the dawn of that Christmas Day, was undergoing one of the most remarkable events in its long history; and, despite the earliness (or lateness) of the hour, a goodly number of Salisbury's inhabitants had turned out to witness the spectacular goings-on.

But not Haleem Khan, the owner of Khan's Mogul Palace, nor his wife Aissha, both of them asleep in their beds. Neither of them had any interest in the pagan monument that was Stonehenge, let alone the strange thing that was happening to it now. And certainly not Haleem's daughter Yasmeena Khan, who was 17 years old and cold and frightened, and who was lying half-naked on the bare floor of the upstairs storeroom of her father's restaurant, hidden between a huge sack of raw lentils and an even larger sack of flour, writhing in terrible pain as shame and illicit motherhood came sweeping down on her like the avenging sword of angry Allah.

She had sinned. She knew that. Her father, her plump, reticent, overworked, mortally weary, and in fact already dying father, had several times in the past year warned her of sin and its consequences, speaking with as much force as she had ever seen him muster; and yet she had chosen to take the risk. Just three times, three different boys, only one time each, all three of them English and white.

Andy. Eddie. Richie.

Names that blazed like bonfires in the neural pathways of her soul.

Her mother—no, not really her mother; her true mother had died when Yasmeena was three; this was Aissha, her father's second wife, the robust and stolid woman who had raised her, had held the family and the restaurant together all these years—had given her warnings too, but they had been couched in entirely different terms. "You are a woman now, Yasmeena, and a woman is permitted to allow herself some pleasure in life," Aissha had told her. "But you must be careful." Not a word about sin, just taking care not to get into trouble.

Well, Yasmeena had been careful, or thought she had, but evidently not care-

robert silverberg | 3

ful enough. Therefore she had failed Aissha. And failed her sad quiet father too, because she had certainly sinned despite all his warnings to remain virtuous, and Allah now would punish her for that. Was punishing her already. Punishing her terribly.

She had been very late discovering she was pregnant. She had not expected to be. Yasmeena wanted to believe that she was still too young for bearing babies, because her breasts were so small and her hips were so narrow, almost like a boy's. And each of those three times when she had done It with a boy—impulsively, furtively, half-reluctantly, once in a musty cellar and once in a ruined omnibus and once right here in this very storeroom—she had taken precautions afterward, diligently swallowing the pills she had secretly bought from the smirking Hindu woman at the shop in Winchester, two tiny green pills in the morning and the big yellow one at night, five days in a row.

The pills were so nauseating that they had to work. But they hadn't. She should never have trusted pills provided by a Hindu, Yasmeena would tell herself a thousand times over; but by then it was too late.

The first sign had come only about four months before. Her breasts suddenly began to fill out. That had pleased her, at first. She had always been so scrawny; but now it seemed that her body was developing at last. Boys liked breasts. You could see their eyes quickly flicking down to check out your chest, though they seemed to think you didn't notice it when they did. All three of her lovers had put their hands into her blouse to feel hers, such as they were; and at least one— Eddie, the second—had actually been disappointed at what he found there. He had said so, just like that: "Is that *all*?"

But now her breasts were growing fuller and heavier every week, and they started to ache a little, and the dark nipples began to stand out oddly from the smooth little circles in which they were set. So Yasmeena began to feel fear; and when her bleeding did not come on time, she feared even more. But her bleeding had never come on time. Once last year it had been almost a whole month late, and she an absolute pure virgin then.

Still, there were the breasts; and then her hips seemed to be getting wider. Yasmeena said nothing, went about her business, chatted pleasantly with the customers, who liked her because she was slender and pretty and polite, and pretended all was well. Again and again at night her hand would slide down her flat boyish belly, anxiously searching for hidden life lurking beneath the taut skin. She felt nothing.

But something was there, all right, and by early October it was making the faintest of bulges, only a tiny knot pushing upward below her navel, but a little bigger every day. Yasmeena began wearing her blouses untucked, to hide the new fullness of her breasts and the burgeoning rondure of her belly. She opened the seams of her trousers and punched two new holes in her belt. It became harder for her to do her work, to carry the heavy trays of food all evening long and to put in the hours afterward washing the dishes, but she forced herself to be strong. There was no one else to do the job. Her father took the orders and Aissha did the cooking and Yasmeena served the meals and cleaned up after the restaurant closed. Her brother Khalid was gone, killed defending Aissha from a mob of white men during the riots that had broken out after the Entities came, and her sister Leila was too small, only five, no use in the restaurant.

No one at home commented on the new way Yasmeena was dressing. Perhaps they thought it was the current fashion. Life was very strange, in these early years of the Conquest.

Her father scarcely glanced at anyone these days; preoccupied with his failing restaurant and his failing health, he went about bowed over, coughing all the time, murmuring prayers endlessly under his breath. He was 40 years old and looked 60. Khan's Mogul Palace was nearly empty, night after night, even on the weekends. People did not travel any more, now that the Entities were here. No rich foreigners came from distant parts of the world to spend the night at Salisbury before going on to visit Stonehenge. The inns and hotels closed; so did most of the restaurants, though a few, like Khan's, struggled on because their proprietors had no other way of earning a living. But the last thing on Haleem Khan's mind was his daughter's changing figure.

As for her stepmother, Yasmeena imagined that she saw her giving her sideways looks now and again, and worried over that. But Aissha said nothing. So there was probably no suspicion. Aissha was not the sort to keep silent, if she suspected something.

The Christmas season drew near. Now Yasmeena's swollen legs were as heavy as dead logs and her breasts were hard as boulders and she felt sick all the time. It was not going to be long, now. She could no longer hide from the truth. But she had no plan. If her brother Khalid were here, he would know what to do. Khalid was gone, though. She would simply have to let things happen and trust that Allah, when He was through punishing her, would forgive her and be merciful.

Christmas Eve, there were four tables of customers. That was a surprise, to be so busy on a night when most English people had dinner at home. Midway through the evening Yasmeena thought she would fall down in the middle of the room and send her tray, laden with chicken biriani and mutton vindaloo and boti kebabs and schooners of lager, spewing across the floor. She steadied herself then; but an hour later she did fall or, rather, sagged to her knees, in the hallway between the kitchen and the garbage bin where no one could see her. She crouched there, dizzy, sweating, gasping, nauseated, feeling her bowels quaking and strange spasms running down the front of her body and into her thighs; and after a time she rose and continued on with her tray toward the bin.

It will be this very night, she thought. And for the thousandth time that week she ran through the little calculation in her mind: *December 24 minus nine months is March 24; therefore it is Richie Burke, the father. At least he was the one who gave me pleasure also.*

Andy, he had been the first. Yasmeena couldn't remember his last name. Pale and freckled and very thin, with a beguiling smile, and on a humid summer night just after her 16th birthday when the restaurant was closed because her father was in the hospital for a few days with the beginning of his trouble, Andy invited her dancing and treated her to a couple of pints of brown ale and then, late in the evening, told her of a special party at a friend's house that he was invited to, only there turned out to be no party, just a shabby stale-smelling cellar room and an old spavined couch, and Andy's busy hands roaming the front of her blouse and then going between her legs and her trousers coming off and then, quick, *quick!*, the long hard narrow reddened thing emerging from him and sliding into her, done and done and done in just a couple of moments, a gasp from him and a shudder and his head buried against her cheek and that was that, all over and done with. She had thought it was supposed to hurt, the first time, but she had felt almost nothing at all, neither pain nor anything that might have been delight. The next time Yasmeena saw him in the street Andy grinned and turned crimson and winked at her, but said nothing to her, and they had never exchanged a word since.

Then Eddie Glossop, in the autumn, the one who had found her breasts insufficient and told her so. Big broad-shouldered Eddie, who worked for the meat merchant and who had an air of great worldliness about him. He was old, almost 25. Yasmeena went with him because she knew there was supposed to be pleasure in it and she had not had it from Andy. But there was none from Eddie either, just a lot of huffing and puffing as he lay sprawled on top of her in the aisle of that burned-out omnibus by the side of the road that went toward Shaftesbury. He was much bigger down there than Andy, and it hurt when he went in, and she was glad that this had not been her first time. But she wished she had not done it at all.

And then Richie Burke, in this very storeroom on an oddly warm night in March, with everyone asleep in the family apartments downstairs at the back of the restaurant. She tiptoeing up the stairs, and Richie clambering up the drain-pipe and through the window, tall, lithe, graceful Richie who played the guitar so well and sang and told everyone that some day he was going to be a general in the war against the Entities and wipe them from the face of the Earth. A wonderful lover, Richie. Yasmeena kept her blouse on because Eddie had made her uneasy about her breasts. Richie caressed her and stroked her for what seemed like hours, though she was terrified that they would be discovered and wanted him to get on with it; and when he entered her, it was like an oiled shaft of smooth metal gliding into her, moving so easily, easily, easily, one gentle thrust after another, on and on and on until marvelous palpitations began to happen inside her and then she erupted with pleasure, moaning so loud that Richie had to put his hand over her mouth to keep her from waking everyone up.

That was the time the baby had been made. There could be no doubt of that. All the next day she dreamed of marrying Richie and spending the rest of the nights of her life in his arms. But at the end of that week Richie disappeared from Salisbury—some said he had gone off to join a secret underground army that was going to launch guerrilla warfare against the Entities—and no one had heard from him again.

Andy. Eddie. Richie.

• • •

And here she was on the floor of the storeroom again, with her trousers off and the shiny swollen hump of her belly sending messages of agony and shame through her body. Her only covering was a threadbare blanket that reeked of spilled cooking oil. Her water had burst about midnight. That was when she had crept up the stairs to wait in terror for the great disaster of her life to finish happening. The contractions were coming closer and closer together, like little earthquakes within her. Now the time had to be two, three, maybe four in the morning. How long would it be? Another hour? Six? Twelve?

Relent and call Aissha to help her?

No. No. She didn't dare. Earlier in the night voices had drifted up from the streets to her. The sound of footsteps. That was strange, shouting and running in the street, this late. The Christmas revelry didn't usually go on through the night like this. It was hard to understand what they were saying, but then out of the confusion there came, with sudden clarity:

"The aliens! They're pulling down Stonehenge, taking it apart!"

"Get your wagon, Charlie, we'll go and see!"

Pulling down Stonehenge. Strange. Strange. Why would they do that? Yasmeena wondered. But the pain was becoming too great for her to be able to give much thought to Stonehenge just now, or to the Entities who had somehow overthrown the invincible white men in the twinkling of an eye and now ruled the world, or to anything else except what was happening within her, the flames dancing through her brain, the ripplings of her belly, the implacable downward movement of—of—

Something.

"Praise be to Allah, Lord of the Universe, the Compassionate, the Merciful," she murmured timidly. "There is no god but Allah, and Mohammed is His prophet."

And again: "Praise be to Allah, Lord of the Universe."

And again.

And again.

The pain was terrible. She was splitting wide open.

"Abraham, Isaac, Ishmael!" That *something* had begun to move in a spiral through her now, like a corkscrew driving a hot track in her flesh. "Mohammed! Mohammed! Mohammed! There is no god but Allah!" The words burst from her with no timidity at all, now. Let Mohammed and Allah save her, if they really existed. What good were they, if they would not save her, she so innocent and ignorant, her life barely begun? And then, as a spear of fire gutted her and her pelvic bones seemed to crack apart, she let loose a torrent of other names— Moses, Solomon, Jesus, Mary, and even the forbidden Hindu names, Shiva, Krishna, Shakti, Kali—anyone at all who would help her through this, anyone, anyone, anyone, anyone—

She screamed three times, short, sharp, piercing screams.

She felt a terrible inner wrenching and the baby came spurting out of her with astonishing swiftness. A gushing Ganges of blood followed it, a red river that spilled out over her thighs and would not stop flowing.

Yasmeena knew at once that she was going to die.

Something wrong had happened. Everything would come out of her insides and she would die. That was absolutely clear to her. Already, just moments after the birth, an eerie new calmness was enfolding her. She had no energy left now for further screaming, or even to look after the baby. It was somewhere down between her spread thighs, that was all she knew. She lay back, drowning in a rising pool of blood and sweat. She raised her arms toward the ceiling and brought them down again to clutch her throbbing breasts, stiff now with milk. She called now upon no more holy names. She could hardly remember her own.

She sobbed quietly. She trembled. She tried not to move, because that would surely make the bleeding even worse.

An hour went by, or a week, or a year.

Then an anguished voice high above her in the dark: "What? Yasmeena? Oh, my god, my god, my god! Your father will perish!"

Aissha, it was. Bending to her, engulfing her. The strong arm raising her head, lifting it against the warm motherly bosom, holding her tight.

"Can you hear me, Yasmeena? Oh, Yasmeena! My god, my god!" And then an ululation of grief rising from her stepmother's throat like some hot volcanic geyser bursting from the ground. "Yasmeena! Yasmeena!"

"The baby?" Yasmeena said, in the tiniest of voices.

"Yes! Here! Here! Can you see?"

Yasmeena saw nothing but a red haze.

"A boy?" she asked, very faintly.

"A boy, yes."

In the blur of her dimming vision she thought she saw something small and pinkish-brown, smeared with scarlet, resting in her stepmother's hands. Thought she could hear him crying, even.

"Do you want to hold him?"

"No. No." Yasmeena understood clearly that she was going. The last of her strength had left her. She was moored now to the world by a mere thread.

"He is strong and beautiful," said Aissha. "A splendid boy."

"Then I am very happy." Yasmeena fought for one last fragment of energy. "His name—is—Khalid. Khalid Haleem Burke."

"Burke?"

"Yes. Khalid Haleem Burke."

"Is that the father's name, Yasmeena? Burke?"

"Burke. Richie Burke." With her final sliver of strength she spelled the name.

"Tell me where he lives, this Richie Burke. I will get him. This is shameful, giving birth by yourself, alone in the dark, in this awful room! Why did you never say anything? Why did you hide it from me? I would have helped. I would—"

But Yasmeena Khan was already dead. The first shaft of morning light now came through the grimy window of the upstairs storeroom. Christmas Day had begun.

Eight miles away, at Stonehenge, the Entities had finished their night's work. Three of the towering alien creatures had supervised while a human work crew,

using hand-held pistol-like devices that emitted a bright violet glow, had uprooted every single one of the ancient stone slabs of the celebrated megalithic
monument on windswept Salisbury Plain as though they were so many jack-
straws. And had rearranged them so that what had been the outer circle of
immense sandstone blocks now had become two parallel rows running from
north to south; the lesser inner ring of blue slabs had been moved about to form
an equilateral triangle; and the 16-foot-long block of sandstone at the center of
the formation that people called the Altar Stone had been raised to an upright
position at the center.

A crowd of perhaps two thousand people from the adjacent towns had watched
through the night from a judicious distance as this inexplicable project was being
carried out. Some were infuriated; some were saddened; some were indifferent;
some were fascinated. Many had theories about what was going on, and one
theory was as good as another, no better, no worse.

TWO: SIXTEEN YEARS FROM NOW

You could still see the ghostly lettering over the front door of the former restaurant, if you knew what to look for, the pale greenish outlines of the words
that once had been painted there in bright gold: KHAN'S MOGUL PALACE. The
old swinging sign that had dangled above the door was still lying out back, too,
in a clutter of cracked basins and discarded stewpots and broken crockery.

But the restaurant itself was gone, long gone, a victim of the Great Plague
that the Entities had casually loosed upon the world as a warning to its conquered people, after an attempt had been made at an attack on an Entity encampment. Half the population of Earth had died so that the Entities could
teach the other half not to harbor further rebellious thoughts. Poor sad Haleem
Khan himself was gone too, the ever-weary little brown-skinned man who in 10
years had somehow saved five thousand pounds from his salary as a dishwasher
at the Lion and Unicorn Hotel and had used that, back when England had a
queen and Elizabeth was her name, as the seed money for the unpretentious
little restaurant that was going to rescue him and his family from utter hopeless
poverty. Four days after the Plague had hit Salisbury, Haleem was dead. But if
the Plague hadn't killed him, the tuberculosis that he was already harboring
probably would have done the job soon enough. Or else simply the shock and
disgrace and grief of his daughter Yasmeena's ghastly death in childbirth two
weeks earlier, at Christmastime, in an upstairs room of the restaurant, while
bringing into the world the bastard child of the long-legged English boy, Richie
Burke, the future traitor, the future quisling.

Haleem's other daughter, the little girl Leila, had died in the Plague also,
three months after her father and two days before what would have been her
sixth birthday. As for Yasmeena's older brother, Khalid, he was already two years
gone by then. That was during the time that now was known as the Troubles.

A gang of long-haired yobs had set forth late one Saturday afternoon in fine English wrath, determined to vent their resentment over the conquest of the Earth by doing a lively spot of Paki-bashing in the town streets, and they had encountered Khalid escorting Aissha home from the market. They had made remarks; he had replied hotly; and they beat him to death.

Which left, of all the family, only Aissha, Haleem's hardy and tireless second wife. She came down with the Plague, too, but she was one of the lucky ones, one of those who managed to fend the affliction off and survive—for whatever that was worth—into the new and transformed and diminished world. But she could hardly run the restaurant alone, and in any case, with three quarters of the population of Salisbury dead in the Plague, there was no longer much need for a Pakistani restaurant there.

Aissha found other things to do. She went on living in a couple of rooms of the now gradually decaying building that had housed the restaurant, and supported herself, in this era when national currencies had ceased to mean much and strange new sorts of money circulated in the land, by a variety of improvised means. She did housecleaning and laundry for those people who still had need of such services. She cooked meals for elderly folks too feeble to cook for themselves. Now and then, when her number came up in the labor lottery, she put in time at a factory that the Entities had established just outside town, weaving little strands of colored wire together to make incomprehensibly complex mechanisms whose nature and purpose were never disclosed to her.

And when there was no such work of any of those kinds available, Aissha would make herself available to the truck drivers who passed through Salisbury, spreading her powerful muscular thighs in return for meal certificates or corporate scrip or barter units or whichever other of the new versions of money they would pay her in. That was not something she would have chosen to do, if she had had her choices. But she would not have chosen to have the invasion of the Entities, for that matter, nor her husband's early death and Leila's and Khalid's, nor Yasmeena's miserable lonely ordeal in the upstairs room, but she had not been consulted about any of those things, either. Aissha needed to eat in order to survive; and so she sold herself, when she had to, to the truck drivers, and that was that.

As for why survival mattered, why she bothered at all to care about surviving in a world that had lost all meaning and just about all hope, it was in part because survival for the sake of survival was in her genes, and—mostly—because she wasn't alone in the world. Out of the wreckage of her family she had been left with a child to look after—her grandchild, her dead stepdaughter's baby, Khalid Haleem Burke, the child of shame. Khalid Haleem Burke had survived the Plague too. It was one of the ugly little ironies of the epidemic that the Entities had released upon the world that children who were less than six months old generally did not contract it. Which created a huge population of healthy but parentless babes.

He was healthy, all right, was Khalid Haleem Burke. Through every deprivation of those dreary years, the food shortages and the fuel shortages and the little outbreaks of diseases that once had been thought to be nearly extinct, he grew taller and straighter and stronger all the time. He had his mother's wiry strength and his father's long legs and dancer's grace. And he was lovely to behold. His skin was tawny golden-brown, his eyes were a glittering blue-green, and his hair, glossy and thick and curly, was a wonderful bronze color, a magnificent Eurasian hue. Amidst all the sadness and loss of Aissha's life, he was the one glorious beacon that lit the darkness for her.

There were no real schools, not any more. Aissha taught little Khalid herself, as best she could. She hadn't had much schooling, but she could read and write, and showed him how, and begged or borrowed books for him wherever she might. She found a woman who understood arithmetic, and scrubbed her floors for her in return for Khalid's lessons. There was an old man at the south end of town who knew the Koran by heart, and Aissha, though she was not a strongly religious woman herself, sent Khalid to him once a week for instruction in Islam. The boy was, after all, half Moslem. Aissha felt no responsibility for the Christian part of him, but she did not want to let him go into the world unaware that there was—somewhere, *somewhere!*—a god known as Allah, a god of justice and compassion and mercy, to whom obedience was owed, and that he would, like all people, ultimately come to stand before that god upon the Day of Judgment.

"And the Entities?" Khalid asked her. He was six, then. "Will they be judged by Allah too?"

"The Entities are not people. They are jinn."

"Did Allah make them?"

"Allah made all things in Heaven and on Earth. He made us out of potter's clay and the jinn out of smokeless fire."

"But the Entities have brought evil upon us. Why would Allah make evil things, if He is a merciful god?"

"The Entities," Aissha said uncomfortably, aware that wiser heads than hers had grappled in vain with that question, *"do* evil. But they are not evil themselves. They are merely the instruments of Allah."

"Who has sent them to us to do evil," said Khalid. "What kind of god is that, who sends evil among His own people, Aissha?"

She was getting beyond her depth in this conversation, but she was patient with him. "No one understands Allah's ways, Khalid. He is the One God and we are nothing before him. If He had reason to send the Entities to us, they were good reasons, and we have no right to question them." *And also to send sickness,* she thought, *and hunger, and death, and the English boys who killed your uncle Khalid in the street, and even the English boy who put you into your mother's belly and then ran away. Allah sent all of those into the world, too.* But then she reminded herself that if Richie Burke had not crept secretly into this house to sleep with Yasmeena, this beautiful child would not be standing here before her at this moment. And so good sometimes could come forth from evil. Who were we to demand reasons from Allah? Perhaps even the Entities had been sent here, ultimately, for our own good.

Perhaps.

. . .

Of Khalid's father, there was no news all this while. He was supposed to have run off to join the army that was fighting the Entities; but Aissha had never heard that there was any such army, anywhere in the world.

Then, not long after Khalid's seventh birthday, when he returned in mid-afternoon from his Thursday Koran lesson at the house of old Iskander Mustafa Ali, he found an unknown white man sitting in the room with his grandmother, a man with a great untidy mass of light-colored curling hair and a lean, angular, almost fleshless face with two cold, harsh blue-green eyes looking out from it as though out of a mask. His skin was so white that Khalid wondered whether he had any blood in his body. It was almost like chalk. The strange white man was sitting in his grandmother's own armchair, and his grandmother was looking very edgy and strange, a way Khalid had never seen her look before, with glistening beads of sweat along her forehead and her lips clamped together in a tight thin line.

The white man said, leaning back in the chair and crossing his legs, which were the longest legs Khalid had ever seen, "Do you know who I am, boy?"

"How would he know?" his grandmother said.

The white man looked toward Aissha and said, "Let me do this, if you don't mind." And then, to Khalid: "Come over here, boy. Stand in front of me. Well, now, aren't we the little beauty? What's your name, boy?"

"Khalid."

"Khalid. Who named you that?"

"My mother. She's dead now. It was my uncle's name. He's dead too."

"Devil of a lot of people are dead who used to be alive, all right. Well, Khalid, my name is Richie."

"Richie," Khalid said, in a very small voice, because he had already begun to understand this conversation.

"Richie, yes. Have you ever heard of a person named Richie? Richie *Burke.*"

"My—father." In an even smaller voice.

"Right you are! The grand prize for that lad! Not only handsome but smart, too! Well, what would one expect, eh? Here I be, boy, your long-lost father! Come here and give your long-lost father a kiss."

Khalid glanced uncertainly toward Aissha. Her face was still shiny with sweat, and very pale. She looked sick. After a moment she nodded, a tiny nod.

He took half a step forward and the man who was his father caught him by the wrist and gathered him roughly in, pulling him inward and pressing him up against him, not for an actual kiss but for what was only a rubbing of cheeks. The grinding contact with that hard, stubbly cheek was painful for Khalid.

"There, boy. I've come back, do you see? I've been away seven worm-eaten miserable years, but now I'm back, and I'm going to live with you and be your father. You can call me 'dad.' "

Khalid stared, stunned.

"Go on. Do it. Say, 'I'm so very glad that you've come back, dad.' "

"Dad," Khalid said uneasily.

"The rest of it too, if you please."

"I'm so very glad—" He halted.

"That I've come back."

"That you've come back—"

"*Dad.*"

Khalid hesitated. "Dad," he said.

"There's a good boy! It'll come easier to you after a while. Tell me, did you ever think about me while you were growing up, boy?"

Khalid glanced toward Aissha again. She nodded surreptitiously.

Huskily he said, "Now and then, yes."

"Only now and then? That's all?"

"Well, hardly anybody has a father. But sometimes I met someone who did, and then I thought of you. I wondered where you were. Aissha said you were off fighting the Entities. Is that where you were, dad? Did you fight them? Did you kill any of them?"

"Don't ask stupid questions. Tell me, boy, do you go by the name of Burke or Khan?"

"Burke. Khalid Haleem Burke."

"Call me '*sir*' when you're not calling me '*dad.*' Say, 'Khalid Haleem Burke, sir.' "

"Khalid Haleem Burke, sir. Dad."

"One or the other. Not both." Richie Burke rose from the chair, unfolding himself as though in sections, up and up and up. He was enormously tall, very thin. His slenderness accentuated his great height. Khalid, though tall for his age, felt dwarfed beside him. The thought came to him that this man was not his father at all, not even a man, but some sort of demon, rather, a jinni, a jinni that had been let out of its bottle, as in the story that Iskander Mustafa Ali had told him. He kept that thought to himself. "Good," Richie Burke said. "Khalid Haleem Burke. I like that. Son should have his father's name. But not the Khalid Haleem part. From now on your name is—ah—Kendall. Ken for short."

"Khalid was my—"

"—uncle's name, yes. Well, your uncle is dead. Practically everybody is dead, Kenny. Kendall Burke, good English name. Kendall *Hamilton* Burke, same initials, even, only English. Is that all right, boy? What a pretty one you are, Kenny! I'll teach you a thing or two, I will. I'll make a man out of you."

Here I be, boy, your long-lost father!

Khalid had never known what it meant to have a father, nor ever given the idea much examination. He had never known hatred before, either, because Aissha was a fundamentally calm, stable, accepting person, too steady in her soul to waste time or valuable energy hating anything, and Khalid had taken after her in that. But Richie Burke, who taught Khalid what it meant to have a father, made him aware of what it was like to hate, also.

Richie moved into the bedroom that had been Aissha's, sending Aissha off to sleep in what had once had been Yasmeena's room. It had long since gone to rack and ruin, but they cleaned it up, some, chasing the spiders out and taping oilcloth over the missing windowpanes and nailing down a couple of floorboards that had popped up out of their proper places. She carried her clothes-cabinet in there by herself, and set up on it the framed photographs of her dead family that she had kept in her former bedroom, and draped two of her old saris that she never wore any more over the bleak places on the wall where the paint had flaked away.

It was stranger than strange, having Richie living with them. It was a total upheaval, a dismaying invasion by an alien lifeform, in some ways as shocking in its impact as the arrival of the Entities had been.

He was gone most of the day. He worked in the nearby town of Winchester, driving back and forth in a small, brown, pre-Conquest automobile. Winchester was a place where Khalid had never been, though his mother had, to purchase the pills that were meant to abort him. Khalid had never been far from Salisbury, not even to Stonehenge, which now was a center of Entity activity anyway, and not a tourist sight. Few people in Salisbury traveled anywhere these days. Not many had automobiles, because of the difficulty of obtaining petrol, but Richie never seemed to have any problem with that.

Sometimes Khalid wondered what sort of work his father did in Winchester; but he asked about it only once. The words were barely out of his mouth when his father's long arm came snaking around and struck him across the face, splitting his lower lip and sending a dribble of blood down his chin.

Khalid staggered back, astounded. No one had ever hit him before. It had not occurred to him that anyone would.

"You must never ask that again!" his father said, looming mountain-high above him. His cold eyes were even colder, now, in his fury. "What I do in Winchester is no business of yours, nor anyone else's, do you hear me, boy? It is my own private affair. My own—private—affair."

Khalid rubbed his cut lip and peered at his father in bewilderment. The pain of the slap had not been so great; but the surprise of it, the shock—that was still reverberating through his consciousness. And went on reverberating for a long while thereafter.

He never asked about his father's work again, no. But he was hit again, more than once, indeed with fair regularity. Hitting was Richie's way of expressing irritation. And it was difficult to predict what sort of thing might irritate him. Any sort of intrusion on his father's privacy, though, seemed to do it. Once, while talking with his father in his bedroom, telling him about a bloody fight between two boys that he had witnessed in town, Khalid unthinkingly put his hand on the guitar that Richie always kept leaning against his wall beside his bed, giving it only a single strum, something that he had occasionally wanted to do for months; and instantly, hardly before the twanging note had died away, Richie unleashed his arm and knocked Khalid back against the wall. "You keep your filthy fingers off that instrument, boy!" Richie said; and after that Khalid did. Another time Richie struck him for leafing through a book he had left on the kitchen table, that had pictures of naked women in it; and another time, it was for staring too long at Richie as he stood before the mirror in the morning, shaving. So Khalid learned to keep his distance from his father; but still he found himself getting slapped for this reason and that, and sometimes for no reason at all. The blows were rarely as hard as the first one had been, and never ever created in him that same sense of shock. But they were blows, all the same. He stored them all up in some secret receptacle of his soul.

Occasionally Richie hit Aissha, too—when dinner was late, or when she put mutton curry on the table too often, or when it seemed to him that she had contradicted him about something. That was more of a shock to Khalid than getting slapped himself, that anyone should dare to lift his hand to Aissha.

The first time it happened, which occurred while they were eating dinner, a big carving knife was lying on the table near Khalid, and he might well have reached for it had Aissha not, in the midst of her own fury and humiliation and pain, sent Khalid a message with her furious blazing eyes that he absolutely was not to do any such thing. And so he controlled himself, then and any time afterward when Richie hit her. It was a skill that Khalid had, controlling himself—one that in some circuitous way he must have inherited from the ever-patient, all-enduring grandparents whom he had never known and the long line of oppressed Asian peasants from whom they descended. Living with Richie in the house gave Khalid daily opportunity to develop that skill to a fine art.

Richie did not seem to have many friends, at least not friends who visited the house. Khalid knew of only three.

There was a man named Arch who sometimes came, an older man with greasy ringlets of hair that fell from a big bald spot on the top of his head. He always brought a bottle of whiskey, and he and Richie would sit in Richie's room with the door closed, talking in low tones or singing raucous songs. Khalid would find the empty whiskey bottle the following morning, lying on the hallway floor. He kept them, setting them up in a row amidst the restaurant debris behind the house, though he did not know why.

The only other man who came was Syd, who had a flat nose and amazingly thick fingers, and gave off such a bad smell that Khalid was able to detect it in the house the next day. Once, when Syd was there, Richie emerged from his room and called to Aissha, and she went in there and shut the door behind her and was still in there when Khalid went to sleep. He never asked her about that, what had gone on while she was in Richie's room. Some instinct told him that he would rather not know.

There was also a woman: Wendy, her name was, tall and gaunt and very plain, with a long face like a horse's and very bad skin, and stringy tangles of reddish hair. She came once in a while for dinner, and Richie always specified that Aissha was to prepare an English dinner that night, lamb or roast beef, none of your spicy Paki curries tonight, if you please. After they ate, Richie and Wendy would go into Richie's room and not emerge again that evening, and the sounds of the guitar would be heard, and laughter, and then low cries and moans and grunts.

One time in the middle of the night when Wendy was there, Khalid got up to go to the bathroom just at the time she did, and encountered her in the hallway, stark naked in the moonlight, a long white ghostly figure. He had never seen a woman naked until this moment, not a real one, only the pictures in Richie's magazine; but he looked up at her calmly, with that deep abiding steadiness in the face of any sort of surprise that he had mastered so well since the advent of Richie. Coolly he surveyed her, his eyes rising from the long thin legs that went up and up and up from the floor and halting for a moment at the curious triangular thatch of woolly hair at the base of her flat belly, and from there his gaze mounted to the round little breasts set high and far apart on her chest, and at last came to her face, which, in the moonlight had unexpectedly taken on a sort of handsomeness if not actual comeliness, though before this Wendy had always seemed to him to be tremendously ugly. She didn't seem displeased at being seen like this. She smiled and winked at him, and ran her hand almost coquettishly through her straggly hair, and blew him a kiss as she drifted on past him toward the bathroom. It was the only time that anyone associated with Richie had ever been nice to him, had even appeared to notice him at all.

But life with Richie was not entirely horrid. There were some good aspects.

One of them was simply being close to so much strength and energy, what Khalid might have called *virility*, if he had known there was any such word. He had spent all his short life thus far among people who kept their heads down and went soldiering along obediently, people like patient plodding Aissha, who took what came to her and never complained; and shriveled old Iskander Mustafa Ali, who understood that Allah determined all things and one had no choice but to comply, and the quiet; tight-lipped English people of Salisbury, who had lived through the Conquest, and the Great Silence when the aliens had turned off all the electrical power in the world, and the Troubles, and the Plague, and who were prepared to be very, very English about whatever horror was coming next.

Richie was different, though. Richie hadn't a shred of passivity in him. "We shape our lives the way we want them to be, boy," Richie would say again and again. "We write our own scripts. It's all nothing but a bloody television show, don't you see that, Kenny-boy?"

That was a startling novelty to Khalid, that you might actually have any control over your own destiny: that you could say "no" to this and "yes" to that and "not right now" to this other thing, and that if there was something you wanted, you could simply reach out and take it. There was nothing Khalid wanted. But the *idea* that he might even have it, if only he could figure out what it was, was fascinating to him.

Then, too, for all of Richie's roughness of manner, his quickness to curse you or kick out at you or slap you when he had had a little too much to drink, he did have an affectionate side, even a charming one. He often sat with them and played his guitar, and taught them the words of songs, and encouraged them to sing along with them, though Khalid had no idea what the songs were about and Aissha did not seem to know either. It was fun, all the same, the singing; and Khalid had known very little fun. Richie was immensely proud of Khalid's good looks and agile, athletic grace, also, and would praise him for them, something that no one had ever done before, not even Aissha. Even though Khalid understood in some way that Richie was only praising himself, really, he was grateful even so.

Richie took him out behind the building and showed him how to throw and catch a ball. How to kick one, too, a different kind of ball. And sometimes there were cricket matches in a field at the edge of town; and when Richie played in these, which he occasionally did, he brought Khalid along to watch. Later, at home, he showed Richie how to hold the bat, how to guard a wicket.

Then there were the drives in the car. These were rare, a great privilege. But sometimes, of a sunny Sunday, Richie would say, "Let's take the old flivver for a spin, eh, Kenny, lad?" And off they would go into the green countryside, usually no special destination in mind, only driving up and down the quiet lanes, Khalid gawking in wonder at this new world beyond the town. It made his head whirl in a good way, as he came to understand that the world actually did go on and on past the boundaries of Salisbury, and was full of marvels and splendors.

So, though at no point did he stop hating Richie, he could see at least some mitigating benefits that had come from his presence in their home. Not many. Some.

THREE: NINETEEN YEARS FROM NOW

Once Richie took him to Stonehenge. Or as near to it as was possible now for humans to go. It was the year Khalid turned 10: a special birthday treat.

"Do you see it out there in the plain, boy? Those big stones? Built by a bunch of ignorant prehistoric buggers who painted themselves blue and danced widdershins in the night. Do you know what 'widdershins' means, boy? No, neither do I. But they did it, whatever it was. Danced around naked with their thingummies jiggling around, and then at midnight they'd sacrifice a virgin on the big altar stone. Long, long ago. Thousands of years. Come on, let's get out and have a look."

Khalid stared. Huge gray slabs, set out in two facing rows flanking smaller slabs of blue stone set in a three-cornered pattern, and a big stone standing upright in the middle. And some other stones lying sideways on top of a few of the gray ones. A transparent curtain of flickering reddish-green light surrounded the whole thing, rising from hidden vents in the ground to nearly twice the height of a man. Why would anyone have wanted to build such a thing? It all seemed like a tremendous waste of time.

"Of course, you understand this isn't what it looked like back then. When the Entities came, they changed the whole business around from what it always was, buggered it all up. Got laborers out here to move every single stone. And they put in the gaudy lighting effects, too. Never used to be lights, certainly not that kind. You walk through those lights, you die, just like a mosquito flying through a candle flame. Those stones there, they were set in a circle originally, and those blue ones there—hey, now, lad, look what we have! You ever see an Entity before, Ken?"

Actually, Khalid had: twice. But never this close. The first one had been right in the middle of the town at noontime. It had been standing outside the entrance of the cathedral cool as you please, as though it happened to be in the mood to go to church: a giant purple thing with orange spots and big yellow eyes. But Aissha had put her hand over his face before he could get a good look, and had pulled him quickly down the street that led away from the cathedral, dragging him along as fast as he was able to go. Khalid had been about five then. He dreamed of the Entity for months thereafter.

The second time, a year later, he had been with friends, playing within sight of the main highway, when a strange vehicle came down the road, an Entity car that floated on air instead of riding on wheels, and two Entities were standing in it, looking right out at them for a moment as they went floating by. Khalid saw only the tops of their heads that time: their great eyes again, and a sort of a curving beak below, and a great V-shaped slash of a mouth, like a frog's. He was fascinated by them. Repelled, too, because they were so bizarre, these strange alien beings, these enemies of mankind, and he knew he was supposed to loathe and disdain them. But fascinated. Fascinated. He wished he had been able to see them better.

Now, though, he had a clear view of the creatures, three of them. They had emerged from what looked like a door that was set right in the ground, out on the far side of the ancient monument, and were strolling casually among the great stones like lords or ladies inspecting their estate, paying no heed whatever to the tall man and the small boy standing beside the car parked just outside the fiery barrier. It amazed Khalid, watching them teeter around on the little ropy legs that supported their immense tubular bodies, that they were able to keep their balance, that they didn't simply topple forward and fall with a crash.

It amazed him, too, how beautiful they were. He had suspected that from his earlier glances, but now their glory fell upon him with full impact.

The luminous golden-orange spots on the glassy, gleaming purple skin—like fire, those spots were. And the huge eyes, so bright, so keen: you could read the strength of their minds in them, the power of their souls. Their gaze engulfed you in a flood of light. Even the air about the Entities partook of their beauty, glowing with a liquid turquoise radiance.

"There they be, boy. Our lords and masters. You ever see anything so bloody hideous?"

"Hideous?"

"They ain't pretty, isn't that right?" Khalid made a noncommittal noise. Richie was in a good mood; he always was, on these Sunday excursions. But Khalid knew only too well the penalty for contradicting him in anything. So he looked upon the Entities in silence, lost in wonder, awed by the glory of these strange gigantic creatures, never voicing a syllable of his admiration for their elegance and majesty.

Expansively Richie said, "You heard correctly, you know, when they told you that when I left Salisbury just before you were born, it was to go off and join an army that meant to fight them. There was nothing I wanted more than to kill Entities, nothing. Christ Eternal, boy, did I ever hate those creepy bastards! Coming in like they did, taking our world away quick as you please. But I got to my senses pretty fast, let me tell you. I listened to the plans the underground army people had for throwing off the Entity yoke, and I had to laugh. I had to *laugh!* I could see right away that there wasn't a hope in hell of it. This was even before they put the Great Plague upon us, you understand. I knew. I damn well knew, I did. They're as powerful as gods. You want to fight against a bunch of gods, lots of luck to you. So I quit the underground then and there. I still hate the bastards, mind you, make no mistake about that, but I know it's foolish even to dream about overthrowing them. You just have to fashion your accommodation with them, that's all there is. You just have to make your peace within yourself and let them have their way. Because anything else is a fool's own folly."

Khalid listened. What Richie was saying made sense. Khalid understood about not wanting to fight against gods. He understood also how it was possible to hate someone and yet go on unprotestingly living with him.

"Is it all right, letting them see us like this?" he asked. "Aissha says that sometimes when they see you, they reach out from their chests with the tongues that they have there and snatch you up, and they take you inside their buildings and do horrible things to you there."

Richie laughed harshly. "It's been known to happen. But they won't touch Richie Burke, lad, and they won't touch the son of Richie Burke at Richie Burke's side. I guarantee you that. We're absolutely safe."

Khalid did not ask why that should be. He hoped it was true, that was all.

Two days afterward, while he was coming back from the market with a packet of lamb for dinner, he was set upon by two boys and a girl, all of them about his age or a year or two older, whom he knew only in that guest way. They formed themselves into a loose ring just beyond his reach and began to chant in a high-pitched, nasal way: *"Quisling, quisling, your father is a quisling!"*

"What's that you call him?"

"Quisling."

"He is not."

"He is! He is! *Quisling, quisling, your father is a quisling!"*

Khalid had no idea what a quisling was. But no one was going to call his father names. Much as he hated Richie, he knew he could not allow that. It was something Richie had taught him: *Defend yourself against scorn, boy, at all times.* He meant against those who might be rude to Khalid because he was part Pakistani; but Khalid had experienced very little of that. Was a quisling someone who was English but had had a child with a Pakistani woman? Perhaps that was it. Why would these children care, though? Why would anyone?

"Quisling, quisling—"

Khalid threw down his package and lunged at the closest boy, who darted away. He caught the girl by the arm, but he would not hit a girl, and so he simply shoved her into the other boy, who went spinning up against the side of the market building. Khalid pounced on him there, holding him close to the wall with one hand and furiously hitting him with the other.

His two companions seemed unwilling to intervene. But they went on chanting, from a safe distance, more nasally than ever.

"*Quis-ling, quis-ling, your fa-ther is a quis-ling!*"

"Stop that!" Khalid cried. "You have no right!" He punctuated his words with blows. The boy he was holding was bleeding, now, his nose, the side of his mouth. He looked terrified.

"*Quis-ling, quis-ling—*"

They would not stop, and neither would Khalid. But then he felt a hand seizing him by the back of his neck, a big adult hand, and he was yanked backward and thrust against the market wall himself. A vast meaty man, a navvy, from the looks of him, loomed over Khalid. "What do you think you're doing, you dirty Paki garbage? You'll kill the boy!"

"He said my father was a quisling!"

"Well, then, he probably is. Get on with you, now, boy! Get on with you!"

He gave Khalid one last hard shove, and spat and walked away. Khalid looked sullenly around for his three tormentors, but they had run off already. They had taken the packet of lamb with them, too.

That night, while Aissha was improvising something for dinner out of yesterday's rice and some elderly chicken, Khalid asked her what a quisling was. She spun around on him as though he had cursed Allah to her ears. Her face all ablaze with a ferocity he had not seen in it before, she said, "Never use that word in this house, Khalid. Never! Never!" And that was all the explanation she would give. Khalid had to learn, on his own, what a quisling was; and when he did, which was soon thereafter, he understood why his father had been unafraid, that day at Stonehenge when they stood outside that curtain of light and looked upon the Entities who were strolling among the giant stones. And also why those three children had mocked him in the street. *You just have to fashion your accommodation with them, that's all there is.* Yes. Yes. Yes. To fashion your accommodation.

FOUR: TWENTY YEARS FROM NOW

It was after the time that Richie beat Aissha so severely, and then did worse than that—violated her, raped her—that Khalid definitely decided that he was going to kill an Entity.

Not kill Richie.

Kill an Entity.

It was a turning point in Khalid's relationship with his father, and indeed in Khalid's whole life, and in the life of any number of other citizens of Salisbury, Wiltshire, England, that time when Richie hurt Aissha so. Richie had been treating Aissha badly all along, of course. He treated everyone badly. He had moved into her house and had taken possession of it as though it were his own. He regarded her as a servant, there purely to do his bidding, and woe betide her if she failed to meet his expectations. She cooked; she cleaned the house; Khalid understood now that sometimes, at his whim, Richie would make her come into his bedroom to amuse him or his friend Syd or both of them together. And there was never a word of complaint from her. She did as he wished; she showed no sign of anger or even resentment; she had given herself over entirely to the will of Allah. Khalid, who had not yet managed to find any convincing evidence of Allah's existence, had not. But he had learned the art of accepting the unacceptable from Aissha. He knew better than to try to change what was unchangeable. So he lived with his hatred of Richie, and that was merely a fact of daily existence, like the fact that rain did not fall upward.

Now, though, Richie had gone too far.

Coming home plainly drunk, red-faced, enraged over something, muttering to himself. Greeting Aissha with a growling curse, Khalid with a stinging slap. No apparent reason for either. Demanding his dinner early. Getting it, not liking what he got. Aissha offering mild explanations of why beef had not been available today. Richie shouting that beef bloody well *should* have been available to the household of Richie Burke.

So far, just normal Richie behavior when Richie was having a bad day. Even sweeping the serving bowl of curried mutton off the table, sending it shattering, thick oily brown sauce splattering everywhere, fell within the normal Richie range.

But then, Aissha saying softly, despondently, looking down at what had been her prettiest remaining sari now spotted in 20 places, "You have stained my clothing." And Richie going over the top. Erupting. Berserk. Wrath out of all measure to the offense, if offense there had been.

Leaping at her, bellowing, shaking her, slapping her. Punching her, even. In the face. In the chest. Seizing the sari at her midriff, ripping it away, tearing it in shreds, crumpling them and hurling them at her. Aissha backing away from him, trembling, eyes bright with fear, dabbing at the blood that seeped from her cut lower lip with one hand, spreading the other one out to cover herself at the thighs.

Khalid staring, not knowing what to do, horrified, furious.

Richie yelling. "I'll stain you, I will! I'll give you a sodding stain!" Grabbing her by the wrist, pulling away what remained of her clothing, stripping her all but naked right there in the dining room. Khalid covering his face. His own grandmother, 40 years old, decent, respectable, naked before him: How could he look? And yet how could he tolerate what was happening? Richie dragging her out of the room, now, toward his bedroom, not troubling even to close the door. Hurling her down on his bed, falling on top of her. Grunting like a pig, a pig, a pig, a pig.

I must not permit this.

Khalid's breast surged with hatred: a cold hatred, almost dispassionate. The man was inhuman, a jinni. Some jinn were harmless, some were evil; but Richie was surely of the evil kind, a demon.

His father. An evil jinni.

But what did that make him? What? What? What? What?

Khalid found himself going into the room after them, against all prohibitions, despite all risks. Seeing Richie plunked between Aissha's legs, his shirt pulled up, his trousers pulled down, his bare buttocks pumping in the air. And Aissha staring upward past Richie's shoulder at the frozen Khalid in the doorway, her face a rigid mask of horror and shame: gesturing to him, making a repeated brushing movement of her hand through the air, wordlessly telling him to go away, to get out of the room, not to watch, not to intervene in any way.

He ran from the house and crouched cowering amid the rubble in the rear yard, the old stewpots and broken jugs and his own collection of Arch's empty whiskey bottles. When he returned, an hour later, Richie was in his room, chopping malevolently at the strings of his guitar, singing some droning tune in a low, boozy voice. Aissha was dressed again, moving about in a slow, downcast way, cleaning up the mess in the dining room. Sobbing softly. Saying nothing, not even looking at Khalid as he entered. A sticking-plaster on her lip. Her cheeks looked puffy and bruised. There seemed to be a wall around her. She was sealed away inside herself, sealed from all the world, even from him.

"I will kill him," Khalid said quietly to her.

"No. That you will not do." Aissha's voice was deep and remote, a voice from the bottom of the sea.

She gave him a little to eat, a cold chapati and some of yesterday's rice, and sent him to his room. He lay awake for hours, listening to the sounds of the house, Richie's endless drunken droning song, Aissha's barely audible sobs. In the morning nobody said anything about anything.

Khalid understood that it was impossible for him to kill his own father, however much he hated him. But Richie had to be punished for what he had done. And so, to punish him, Khalid was going to kill an Entity.

The Entities were a different matter. They were fair game.

For some time now, on his better days, Richie had been taking Khalid along with him as he drove through the countryside, doing his quisling tasks, gathering information that the Entities wanted to know and turning it over to them by some process that Khalid could not even begin to understand, and by this time Khalid had seen Entities on so many different occasions that he had grown quite accustomed to being in their presence.

And had no fear of them. To most people, apparently, Entities were scary things, ghastly alien monsters, evil, strange; but to Khalid they still were, as they always had been, creatures of enormous beauty. Beautiful the way a god would be beautiful. How could you be frightened by anything so beautiful? How could you be frightened of a god?

They didn't ever appear to notice him at all. Richie would go up to one of them and stand before it, and some kind of transaction would take place. While that was going on, Khalid simply stood to one side, looking at the Entity, studying it, lost in admiration of its beauty. Richie offered no explanations of these meetings and Khalid never asked.

The Entities grew more beautiful in his eyes every time he saw one. They were beautiful beyond belief. He could almost have worshipped them. It seemed to him that Richie felt the same way about them: that he was caught in their spell, that he would gladly fall down before them and bow his forehead to the ground.

And so . . .

I will kill one of them, Khalid thought.

Because they are so beautiful. Because my father, who works for them, must love them almost as much as he loves himself, and I will kill the thing he loves. He says he hates them, but I think it is not so. I think he loves them, and that is why he works for them. Or else he loves them and hates them both. He may feel the same way about himself. But I see the light that comes into his eyes when he looks upon them.

So I will kill one, yes. Because by killing one of them I will be killing some part of *him*. And maybe there will be some other value in my doing it, besides.

FIVE: TWENTY-TWO YEARS FROM NOW

Richie Burke said, "Look at this goddamned thing, will you, Ken? Isn't it the goddamnedest fantastic piece of shit anyone ever imagined?"

They were in what had once been the main dining room of the old defunct restaurant. It was early afternoon. Aissha was elsewhere, Khalid had no idea where. His father was holding something that seemed something like a rifle, or perhaps a highly streamlined shotgun, but it was like no rifle or shotgun he had ever seen. It was a long, slender tube of greenish-blue metal with a broad flaring muzzle and what might have been some type of gunsight mounted midway down the barrel, and a curious sort of computerized trigger arrangement on the stock. A one-of-a-kind sort of thing, custom made, a home inventor's pride and joy.

"Is it a weapon, would you say?"

"A weapon? A weapon? What the bloody hell do you think it is, boy? It's a fucking Entity-killing gun! Which I confiscated this very day from a nest of conspirators over Warminster way. The whole batch of them are under lock and key this very minute, thank you very much, and I've brought Exhibit A home for safe-keeping. Have a good look, lad. Ever seen anything so diabolical?"

Khalid realized that Richie was actually going to let him handle it. He took it with enormous care, letting it rest on both his outstretched palms. The barrel was cool and very smooth, the gun lighter than he had expected it to be.

"How does it work, then?"

"Pick it up. Sight along it. You know how it's done. Just like an ordinary gunsight."

Khalid put it to his shoulder, right there in the room. Aimed at the fireplace. Peered along the barrel.

A few inches of the fireplace were visible in the crosshairs, in the most minute detail. Keen magnification, wonderful optics. Touch the right stud, now, and the whole side of the house would be blown out, was that it? Khalid ran his hand along the butt.

"There's a safety on it," Richie said. "The little red button. There. That. Mind you don't hit it by accident. What we have here, boy, is nothing less than a rocket-powered grenade gun. A bomb-throwing machine, virtually. You wouldn't believe it, because it's so skinny, but what it hurls is a very graceful little projectile that will explode with almost incredible force and cause an extraordinary amount of damage, altogether extraordinary. I know because I tried it. It was amazing, seeing what that thing could do."

"Is it loaded now?"

"Oh, yes, yes, you bet your little brown rump it is! Loaded and ready! An absolutely diabolical Entity-killing machine, the product of months and months of loving work by a little band of desperadoes with marvelous mechanical skills. As stupid as they come, though, for all their skills. . . . Here, boy, let me have that thing before you set it off somehow."

Khalid handed it over.

"Why stupid?" he asked. "It seems very well made."

"I *said* they were skillful. This is a goddamned triumph of miniaturization, this little cannon. But what makes them think they could kill an Entity at all? Don't they imagine anyone's ever tried? Can't be done, Ken, boy. Nobody ever has, nobody ever will."

Unable to take his eyes from the gun, Khalid said obligingly, "And why is that, sir?"

"Because they're bloody unkillable!"

"Even with something like this? Almost incredible force, you said, sir. An extraordinary amount of damage."

"It would fucking well blow an Entity to smithereens, it would, if you could ever hit one with it. Ah, but the trick is to succeed in firing your shot, boy! Which cannot be done. Even as you're taking your aim, they're reading your bloody mind, that's what they do. They know exactly what you're up to, because they look into our minds the way we would look into a book. They pick up all your nasty little unfriendly thoughts about them. And then—bam!—they give you the bloody Push, the thing they do to people with their minds, you know, and you're done for, piff paff poof. We've heard of four cases, at least. Attempted Entity assassination. Trying to take a shot as an Entity went by. Found the bodies, the weapons, just so much trash by the roadside." Richie ran his hands up and down the gun, fondling it almost lovingly. "This gun here, it's got an unusually great range, terrific sight, will fire upon the target from an enormous distance. Still wouldn't work, I wager you. They can do their telepathy on you from three hundred yards away. Maybe five hundred. Who knows, maybe a thousand. Still, a damned good thing that we broke this ring up in time. Just in case they could have pulled it off somehow."

"It would be bad if an Entity was killed, is that it?" Khalid asked.

Richie guffawed. "Bad? Bad? It would be a bloody catastrophe. You know what they did, the one time anybody managed to damage them in any way? No, how in hell would you know? It was right around the moment you were getting born. Some buggerly American idiots launched a laser attack from space on an Entity building. Maybe killed a few, maybe didn't, but the Entities paid us back by letting loose a plague on us that wiped out damn near every other person there was in the world. Right here in Salisbury they were keeling over like files. Had it myself. Thought I'd die. Damned well hoped I would, I felt so bad. Then I arose from my bed of pain and threw it off. But we don't want to risk bringing down another plague, do we, now? Or any other sort of miserable punishment that they might choose to inflict. Because they certainly will inflict one. One thing that has been clear from the beginning is that our masters will take no shit from us, no, lad, not one solitary molecule of shit."

He crossed the room and unfastened the door of the cabinet that had held Khan's Mogul Palace's meager stock of wine in the long-gone era when this building had been a licensed restaurant. Thrusting the weapon inside, Richie said, "This is where it's going to spend the night. You will make no reference to its presence when Aissha gets back. I'm expecting Arch to come here tonight, and you will make no reference to it to him, either. It is a top secret item, do you hear me? I show it to you because I love you, boy, and because I want you to know that your father has saved the world this day from a terrible disaster, but I don't want a shred of what I have shared with you just now to reach the ears of another human being. Or another inhuman being for that matter. Is that clear, boy? Is it?"

"I will not say a word," said Khalid.

And said none. But thought quite a few.

All during the evening, as Arch and Richie made their methodical way through Arch's latest bottle of rare pre-Conquest whiskey, salvaged from some vast horde found by the greatest of good luck in a Southampton storehouse, Khalid clutched to his own bosom the knowledge that there was, right there in that cabinet, a device that was capable of blowing the head off an Entity, if only one could manage to get within firing range without announcing one's lethal intentions.

Was there a way of achieving that? Khalid had no idea.

But perhaps the range of this device was greater than the range of the Entities' mind-reading capacities. Or perhaps not. Was it worth the gamble? Perhaps it was. Or perhaps not.

Aissha went to her room soon after dinner, once she and Khalid had cleared away the dinner dishes. She said little these days, kept mainly to herself, drifted through her life like a sleepwalker. Richie had not laid a violent hand on her again since that savage evening several years back, but Khalid understood that she still harbored the pain of his humiliation of her, that in some ways she had never really recovered from what Richie had done to her that night. Nor had Khalid.

He hovered in the hall, listening to the sounds from his father's room until he felt certain that Arch and Richie had succeeded in drinking themselves into their customary stupor. Ear to the door: Silence. A faint snore or two, maybe.

He forced himself to wait another 10 minutes. Still quiet in there. Delicately he pushed the door, already slightly ajar, another few inches open. Peered cautiously within.

Richie slumped head down at the table, clutching in one hand a glass that still had a little whiskey in it, cradling his guitar between his chest and knee with the other. Arch on the floor opposite him, head dangling to one side, eyes closed, limbs sprawled every which way. Snoring, both of them. Snoring. Snoring. Snoring.

Good. Let them sleep very soundly.

Khalid took the Entity-killing gun now from the cabinet. Caressed its satiny barrel. It was an elegant thing, this weapon. He admired its design. He had an artist's eye for form and texture and color, did Khalid: some fugitive gene out of forgotten antiquity miraculously surfacing in him after a dormancy of centuries, the eye of a Gandharan sculptor, of a Rajput architect, a Gujarati miniaturist coming to the fore in him after passing through all those generations of the peasantry. Lately he had begun doing little sketches, making some carvings. Hiding everything away so that Richie would not find it. That was the sort of thing that might offend Richie, his taking up such piffling pastimes. Sports, drinking, driving around—those were proper amusements for a man.

On one of his good days last year Richie had brought a bicycle home for him: a startling gift, for bicycles were rarities, nowadays, none having been available, let alone manufactured, in England in ages. Where Richie had obtained it, from whom, with what brutality, Khalid did not like to think. But he loved his bike. Rode long hours through the countryside on it, every chance he had. It was his freedom; it was his wings. He went outside now, carrying the grenade gun, and carefully strapped it to the bicycle's basket.

He had waited nearly three years for this moment to make itself possible.

Nearly every night nowadays, Khalid knew, one could usually see Entities traveling about on the road between Salisbury and Stonehenge, one or two at a time, riding in those cars of theirs that floated a little way above the ground on cushions of air. Stonehenge was a major center of Entity activities nowadays and there were more and more of them in the vicinity all the time. Perhaps there would be one out there this night, he thought. It was worth the chance: he would not get a second opportunity with this captured gun that his father had brought home.

About halfway out to Stonehenge there was a place on the plain where he could have a good view of the road from a little copse several hundred yards away. Khalid had no illusion that hiding in the copse would protect him from the mind-searching capacities the Entities were said to have. If they could detect him at all, the fact that he was standing in the shadow of a leafy tree would not make the slightest difference. But it was a place to wait, on this bright moonlit night. It was a place where he could feel alone, unwatched.

He went to it. He waited there.

He listened to night-noises: an owl; the rustling of the breeze through the trees; some small nocturnal animal scrabbling in the underbrush.

He was utterly calm.

Khalid had studied calmness all his life, with his grandmother Aissha as his tutor. From his earliest days he had watched her stolid acceptance of poverty, of shame, of hunger, of loss, of all kinds of pain. He had seen her handling the intrusion of Richie Burke into her household and her life with philosophical detachment, with stoic patience. To her it was all the will of Allah, not to be questioned. Allah was less real to Khalid than He was to Aissha, but Khalid had drawn from her her infinite patience and tranquility, at least, if not her faith in God. Perhaps he might find his way to God later on. At any rate, he had long ago learned from Aissha that yielding to anguish was useless, that inner peace was the only key to endurance, that everything must be done calmly, unemotionally, because the alternative was a life of unending chaos and suffering. And so he had come to understand from her that it was possible even to hate someone in a calm, unemotional way. And had contrived thus to live calmly, day by day, with the father whom he loathed.

For the Entities he felt no loathing at all. Far from it. He had never known a world without them, the vanished world where humans had been masters of their own destinies. The Entities, for him, were an innate aspect of life, simply there, as were hills and trees, the moon, or the owl that roved the night above him now, cruising for squirrels or rabbits. And they were very beautiful to behold, like the moon, like an owl moving silently overhead, like a massive chestnut tree.

He waited, and the hours passed, and in his calm way he began to realize that he might not get his chance tonight, for he knew he needed to be home and in his bed before Richie awakened and could find him and the weapon gone. Another hour, two at most, that was all he could risk out here.

Then he saw turquoise light on the highway, and knew that an Entity vehicle was approaching, coming from the direction of Salisbury. It pulled into view a moment later, carrying two of the creatures standing serenely upright, side by side, in their strange wagon that floated on a cushion of air.

Khalid beheld it in wonder and awe. And once again marveled, as ever, at their elegance of these Entities, their grace, their luminescent splendor.

How beautiful you are! Oh, yes. Yes.

They moved past him on their curious cart as though traveling on a river of light, and it seemed to him, dispassionately studying the one on the side closer to him, that what he beheld here was surely a jinni of the jinn: Allah's creature, a thing made of smokeless fire, a separate creation. Which nonetheless must in the end stand before Allah in judgment, even as we.

How beautiful. How beautiful.

I love you.

He loved it, yes. For its crystalline beauty. A jinni? No, it was a higher sort of being than that; it was an angel. It was a being of pure light—of cool clear fire, without smoke. He was lost in rapt admiration of its angelic perfection.

Loving it, admiring it, even worshipping it, Khalid calmly lifted the grenade gun to his shoulder, calmly aimed, calmly stared through the gunsight. Saw the Entity, distant as it was, transfixed perfectly in the crosshairs. Calmly he released the safety, as Richie had inadvertently showed him how to do. Calmly put his finger to the firing stud.

His soul was filled all the while with love for the beautiful creature before him as—calmly, calmly, calmly—he pressed the stud. He heard a whooshing sound and felt the weapon kicking back against his shoulder with astonishing force, sending him thudding into a tree behind him and for a moment knocking the breath from him; and an instant later the left side of the beautiful creature's head exploded into a cascading fountain of flame, a shower of radiant fragments. A greenish-red mist of what must be alien blood appeared and went spreading outward into the air.

The stricken Entity swayed and fell backward, dropping out of sight on the floor of the wagon.

In that same moment the second Entity, the one that was riding on the far side, underwent so tremendous a convulsion that Khalid wondered if he had managed to kill it, too, with that single shot. It stumbled forward, then back, and crashed against the railing of the wagon with such violence that Khalid imagined he could hear the thump. Its great tubular body writhed and shook, and seemed even to change color, the purple hue deepening almost to black for an instant and the orange spots becoming a fiery red. At so great a distance it was hard to be sure, but Khalid thought, also, that its leathery hide was rippling and puckering as if in a demonstration of almost unendurable pain.

It must be feeling the agony of its companion's death, he realized. Watching the Entity lurch around blindly on the platform of the wagon in what had to be terrible pain, Khalid's soul flooded with compassion for the creature, and sorrow, and love. It was unthinkable to fire again. He had never had any intention of killing more than one; but in any case he knew that he was no more capable of firing a shot at this stricken survivor now than he would be of firing at Aissha.

During all this time the wagon had been moving silently onward as though nothing had happened; and in a moment more it turned the bend in the road and was gone from Khalid's sight, down the road that led toward Stonehenge.

He stood for a while watching the place where the vehicle had been when he had fired the fatal shot. There was nothing there now, no sign that anything had occurred. *Had* anything occurred? Khalid felt neither satisfaction nor grief nor fear nor, really, any emotion of any other sort. His mind was all but blank. He made a point of keeping it that way, knowing he was as good as dead if he relaxed his control even for a fraction of a second.

Strapping the gun to the bicycle basket again, he pedaled quietly back toward home. It was well past midnight; there was no one at all on the road. At the house, all was as it had been; Arch's car parked in front, the front lights still on, Richie and Arch snoring away in Richie's room.

Only now, safely home, did Khalid at last allow himself the luxury of letting the jubilant thought cross his mind, just for a moment, that had been flickering at the threshold of his consciousness for an hour:

Got you, Richie! Got you, you bastard!

He returned the grenade gun to the cabinet and went to bed, and was asleep almost instantly, and slept soundly until the first bird-song of dawn.

In the tremendous uproar that swept Salisbury the next day, with Entity vehicles everywhere and platoons of the glossy balloonlike aliens that everybody called Spooks going from house to house, it was Khalid himself who provided the key clue to the mystery of the assassination that had occurred in the night.

"You know, I think it might have been my father who did it," he said almost casually, in town, outside the market, to a boy named Thomas whom he knew in a glancing sort of way. "He came home yesterday with a strange sort of big gun. Said it was for killing Entities with, and put it away in a cabinet in our front room."

Thomas would not believe that Khalid's father was capable of such a gigantic act of heroism as assassinating an Entity. No, no, no, Khalid argued eagerly, in a tone of utter and sublime disingenuousness: He did it, I know he did it, he's always talked of wanting to kill one of them one of these days, and now he has.

He has?

Always his greatest dream, yes, indeed.

Well, then—

Yes. Khalid moved along. So did Thomas. Khalid took care to go nowhere near the house all that morning. The last person he wanted to see was Richie. But he was safe in that regard. By noon Thomas evidently had spread the tale of Khalid Burke's wild boast about the town with great effectiveness, because word came traveling through the streets around that time that a detachment of Spooks had gone to Khalid's house and had taken Richie Burke away.

"What about my grandmother?" Khalid asked. "She wasn't arrested too, was she?"

"No, it was just him," he was told. "Billy Cavendish saw them taking him, and he was all by himself. Yelling and screaming, he was, the whole time, like a man being hauled away to be hanged."

Khalid never saw his father again.

During the course of the general reprisals that followed the killing, the entire population of Salisbury and five adjacent towns was rounded up and transported to walled detention camps near Portsmouth. A good many of the deportees were executed within the next few days, seemingly by random selection, no pattern being evident in the choosing of those who were put to death. At the beginning of the following week the survivors were sent on from Portsmouth to other places, some of them quite remote, in various parts of the world.

Khalid was not among those executed. He was merely sent very far away.

He felt no guilt over having survived the death-lottery while others around him were being slain for his murderous act. He had trained himself since childhood to feel very little indeed, even while aiming a rifle at one of Earth's beautiful and magnificent masters. Besides, what affair was it of his, that some of these people were dying and he was allowed to live? Everyone died, some sooner, some later. Aissha would have said that what was happening was the will of Allah. Khalid more simply put it that the Entities did as they pleased, always, and knew that it was folly to ponder their motives.

Aissha was not available to discuss these matters with. He was separated from her before reaching Portsmouth and Khalid never saw her again, either. From that day on it was necessary for him to make his way in the world on his own.

He was not quite 13 years old. Often, in the years ahead, he would look back at the time when he had slain the Entity; but he would think of it only as the time when he had rid himself of Richie Burke, for whom he had had such hatred. For the Entities he had no hatred at all, and when his mind returned to that event by the roadside on the way to Stonehenge, to the alien being centered in the crosshairs of his weapon, he would think only of the marvelous color and form of the two starborn creatures in the floating wagon, of that passing moment of beauty in the night.

second skin
PAUL J. MCAULEY

Born in Oxford, England, in 1955, Paul J. McAuley now makes his home in London. He is considered to be one of the best of the new breed of British writers (although a few Australian writers could be fit in under this heading as well) who are producing that sort of revamped, updated, wide-screen Space Opera sometimes referred to as "radical hard science fiction." A frequent contributor to Interzone, *as well as to markets such as* Amazing, The Magazine of Fantasy & Science Fiction, Asimov's Science Fiction, When the Music's Over, *and elsewhere, he won the Philip K. Dick Award with his first novel,* Four Hundred Billion Stars. *His other books include the novels* Of the Fall, Eternal Light, Red Dust, *and* Pasquale's Angel, *a collection of his short work* The King of the Hill and Other Stories, *and an original anthology coedited with Kim Newman,* In Dreams. *His most recent book was the acclaimed novel* Fairyland, *which won the John W. Campbell Memorial Award last year. Upcoming is a major new trilogy, the first volume of which is* Child of the River. *His stories have appeared in our Fifth, Ninth, and Thirteenth Annual Collections.*

In the suspenseful and richly inventive story that follows, he takes us on a journey across space to the farthest reaches of the solar system, for a tale of high-tech intrigue and counterintrigue beneath the frozen surface of Proteus. . . .

T he transport, once owned by an outer system cartel and appropriated by Earth's Pacific Community after the Quiet War, ran in a continuous, ever-changing orbit between Saturn, Uranus, and Neptune. It never docked. It mined the solar wind for hydrogen to mix with the nanogram of antimatter that could power it for a century, and once or twice a year, during its intricate gravity-assisted loops between Saturn's moons, maintenance drones attached remora-like to its hull, and fixed whatever its self-repairing systems couldn't handle.

Ben Lo and the six other members of the first trade delegation to Proteus since the war were transferred onto the transport as it looped around Titan, still sleeping in the hibernation pods they'd climbed into in Earth orbit. Sixty days later, they were released from the transport in individual drop capsules of structural diamond, like so many seeds scattered by a pod.

Ben Lo, swaddled in the crash web that took up most of the volume of the drop capsule's little bubble, watched with growing vertigo as the battered face of Proteus drew closer. He had been awakened only a day ago, and was as weak and unsteady as a new-born kitten. The sun was behind the bubble's braking chute. Ahead, Neptune's disc was tipped in star-sprinkled black above the little moon. Neptune was subtly banded with blue and violet, its poles capped with white cloud, its equator streaked with cirrus. Slowly, slowly, Proteus began to eclipse it. The transport had already dwindled to a bright point amongst the bright points of the stars, on its way to spin up around Neptune, loop past Triton, and head on out for the next leg of its continuous voyage, halfway across the solar system to Uranus.

Like many of the moons of the outer planets, Proteus was a ball of ice and rock. Over billions of years, most of the rock had sunk to the core, and the moon's icy, dirty white surface was splotched with a scattering of large impact craters with black interiors, like well-used ash trays, and dissected by large stress fractures, some running halfway round the little globe.

The spy fell toward Proteus in a thin transparent bubble of carbon, wearing a paper suit and a diaper, and trussed up in a cradle of smart cabling like an early Christian martyr. He could barely move a muscle. Invisible laser light poured all around him—the capsule was opaque to the frequency used—gently pushing against the braking sail which had unfolded and spun into a twenty kilometer diameter mirror after the capsule had been released by the transport. Everything was fine.

The capsule said, "Only another twelve hours, Mr. Lo. I suggest that you sleep. Elfhame's time zone is ten hours behind Greenwich Mean Time."

Had he been asleep for a moment? Ben Lo blinked and said, "Jet lag," and laughed.

"I don't understand," the capsule said politely. It didn't need to be very intelligent. All it had to do was control the attitude of the braking sail, and keep its passenger amused and reassured until landing. Then it would be recycled.

Ben Lo didn't bother to try to explain. He was feeling the same kind of yawning apprehension that must have gripped ninety-year-old airline passengers at the end of the twentieth century. A sense of deep dislocation and estrangement. How strange that I'm here, he thought. And, how did it happen? When he'd been born, spaceships had been crude, disposable chemical rockets. The first men on the moon. President Kennedy's assassination. No, that happened before I was born. For a moment, his yawning sense of dislocation threatened to swallow him whole, but then he had it under control and it dwindled to mere strangeness. It was the treatment, he thought. The treatment and the hibernation.

Somewhere down there in the white moonscape, in one of the smaller canyons, was Ben Lo's first wife. But he mustn't think of that. Not yet. Because if he did . . . no, he couldn't remember. Something bad, though.

"I can offer a variety of virtualities," the capsule said. Its voice was a husky contralto. It added, "Certain sexual services are also available."

"What I'd like is a chateaubriand steak butterflied and well-grilled over hickory wood, a Caesar salad, and a 1998 Walnut Creek Cabernet Sauvignon."

"I can offer a range of nutritive pastes, and eight flavors of water, including a balanced electrolyte," the capsule said. A prissy note seemed to have edged into its voice. It added, "I would recommend that you restrict intake of solids and fluids until after landing."

Ben Lo sighed. He had already had his skin scrubbed and repopulated with strains of bacteria and yeast native to the Protean ecosystem, and his GI tract had been reamed out and packed with a neutral gel containing a benign strain of E. coli. He said, "Give me an inflight movie."

"I would recommend virtualities," the capsule said. "I have a wide selection."

Despite the capsule's minuscule intelligence, it had a greater memory capacity than all the personal computers on Earth at the end of the millennium. Ben Lo had downloaded his own archives into it.

"Wings of Desire," he said.

"But it's in black and white! And flat. And only two senses—"

"There's color later on. It has a particular relevance to me, I think. Once upon a time, capsule, there was a man who was very old, and became young again, and found that he'd lost himself. Run the movie, and you'll understand a little bit about me."

The moon, Neptune, the stars, fell into a single point of light. The light went out. The film began.

Falling through a cone of laser light, the man and the capsule watched how an angel became a human being, out of love.

The capsule skimmed the moon's dirty-white surface and shed the last of its relative velocity in the inertia buffers of the target zone, leaving its braking sail to collapse across kilometers of moonscape. It was picked up by a striding tripod that looked like a prop from The War of the Worlds, and carried down a steeply sloping tunnel through triple airlocks into something like the ER room of a hospital. With the other members of the trade delegation, Ben Lo, numbed by neural blocks, was decanted, stripped, washed, and dressed in fresh paper clothes.

Somewhere in the press of nurses and technicians he thought he glimpsed someone he knew, or thought he knew. A woman, her familiar face grown old, eyes faded blue in a face wrinkled as a turtle's. . . . But then he was lifted onto a gurney and wheeled away.

Waking, he had problems with remembering who he was. He knew he was nowhere on Earth. A universally impersonal hotel room, but he was virtually in free fall. Some moon, then. But what role was he playing?

He got up, moving carefully in the fractional gravity, and pulled aside the floor-to-ceiling drapes. It was night, and across a kilometer of black air was a steep dark mountainside or perhaps a vast building, with lights wound at its base, shimmering on a river down there. . . .

Proteus. Neptune. The trade delegation. And the thing he couldn't think about, which was fractionally nearer the surface now, like a word at the back of his tongue. He could feel it, but he couldn't shape it. Not yet.

He stripped in the small, brightly lit sphere of the bathroom and turned the walls to mirrors and looked at himself. He was too young to be who he thought he was. No, that was the treatment, of course. His third. Then why was his skin this color? He hadn't bothered to tint it for . . . how long?

That sci-fi version of *Othello*, a century and a half ago, when he'd been a movie star. He remembered the movie vividly, although not the making of it. But that was the color he was now, his skin a rich dark mahogany, gleaming as if oiled in the lights, his hair a cap of tight black curls.

He slept again, and dreamed of his childhood home. San Francisco. Sailboats scattered across the blue bay. He'd had a little boat, a Laser. The cold salt smell of the sea. The pinnacles of the rust-red bridge looming out of banks of fog, and the fog horn booming mournfully. Cabbage leaves in the gutters of Spring Street. The crowds swirling under the crimson and gold neon lights of the trinket shops of Grant Avenue, and the intersection at Grant and California tingling with trolley car bells.

He remembered everything as if he had just seen it in a movie. Non-associational aphasia. It was a side effect of the treatment he'd just had. He'd been warned about it, but it was still unsettling. The woman he was here to . . . Avernus. Her name now. But when they had been married, a hundred and sixty-odd years ago, she had been called Barbara Reiner. He tried to remember the taste of her mouth, the texture of her skin, and could not.

The next transport would not swing by Proteus for a hundred and seventy days, so there was no hurry to begin the formal business of the trade delegation. For a while, its members were treated as favored tourists, in a place that had no tourist industry at all.

The sinuous rill canyon which housed Elfhame had been burned to an even depth of a kilometer, sealed under a construction diamond roof, and pressurized to 750 millibars with a nitrox mix enriched with 1 percent carbon dioxide to stimulate plant growth. The canyon ran for fifty kilometers through a basaltic surface extrusion, possibly the remnant of the giant impact that had resurfaced the farside hemisphere of the moon a billion years ago, or the result of vulcanism caused by thermal drag when the satellite had been captured by Neptune.

The sides of the canyon were raked to form a deep vee in profile, with a long narrow lake lying at the bottom like a black ribbon, dusted with a scattering of pink and white coral keys. The Elfhamers called it the Skagerrak. The sides of the canyon were steeply terraced, with narrow vegetable gardens, rice paddies, and farms on the higher levels, close to the lamps that, strung from the diamond roof, gave an insolation equivalent to that of the Martian surface. Farther down, amongst pocket parks and linear strips of designer wilderness, houses clung to the steep slopes like soap bubbles, or stood on platforms or bluffs, all with panoramic views of the lake at the bottom and screened from their neighbors by soaring ginkgoes, cypress, palmettos, bamboo (which grew to fifty meters in the microgravity), and dragon's blood trees. All the houses were large and individually designed; Elfhamers went in for extended families. At the lowest levels were the government buildings, commercial malls and parks, the university and hospital, and the single hotel, which bore all the marks of having been recently constructed for the trade delegation. And then there was the lake, the Skagerrak, with its freshwater corals and teeming fish, and slow, ten-meter-high waves. The single, crescent-shaped beach of black sand at what Elfhamers called the North End was very steeply raked, and constantly renewed; the surfing was fabulous.

There was no real transportion system except for a single tube train line that shuttled along the west side, and moving lines with T-bar seats, like ski lifts, that made silver lines along the steep terraced slopes. Mostly, people bounded around in huge kangaroo leaps, or flew using startlingly small wings of diamond foil or little hand-held airscrews—the gravity was so low, 0.007g, that human flight was ridiculously easy. Children rode airboards or simply dived from terrace to terrace, which strictly speaking was illegal, but even adults did it sometimes, and it seemed to be one of those laws to which no one paid much attention unless someone got hurt. It *was* possible to break a bone if you jumped from the top of the canyon and managed to land on one of the lakeside terraces, but you'd have to work at it. Some of the kids did—the latest craze was terrace bouncing, in which half a dozen screaming youngsters tried to find out how quickly they could get from top to bottom with the fewest touchdown points.

The entire place, with its controlled, indoor weather, its bland affluent sheen, and its universal cleanliness, was ridiculously vulnerable. It reminded Ben Lo of nothing so much as an old-fashioned shopping mall, the one at Santa Monica, for instance. He'd had a bit part in a movie made in that mall, somewhere near the start of his career. He was still having trouble with his memory. He could remember every movie he'd made, but couldn't remember *making* any one of them.

He asked his guide if it was possible to get to the real surface. She was taken aback by the request, then suggested that he could access a mobot using the point-of-presence facility of his hotel room.

"Several hundred were released fifty years ago, and some of them are still running, I suppose. Really, there is nothing up there but some industrial units."

"I guess Avernus has her labs on the surface."

Instantly, the spy was on the alert, suppressing a thrill of panic.

His guide was a very tall, thin, pale girl called Marla. Most Elfhamers were descended from Nordic stock, and Marla had the high cheekbones, blue eyes, blond hair, and open and candid manner of her counterparts on Earth. Like most Elfhamers, she was tanned and athletically lithe, and wore a distractingly small amount of fabric: tight shorts, a band of material across her small breasts, plastic sandals, a communications bracelet.

At the mention of Avernus, Marla's eyebrows dented over her slim, straight nose. She said, "I would suppose so, yah, but there's nothing interesting to see. The program, it is reaching the end of its natural life, you see. The surface is not interesting, and it is dangerous. The cold and the vacuum, and still the risk of micrometeorites. Better to live inside."

Like worms in an apple, the spy thought. The girl was soft and foolish, very young and very naïve. It was only natural that a member of the trade delegation would be interested in Elfhame's most famous citizen. She wouldn't think anything of this.

Ben Lo blinked and said, "Well, yes, but I've never been there. It would be something, for someone of my age to set foot on the surface of a moon of Neptune. I was born two years before the first landing on Earth's moon, you know. Have you ever been up there?"

Marla's teeth were even and pearly white, and when she smiled, as she did now, she seemed to have altogether too many. "By point-of-presence, of course. It is part of our education. It is fine enough in its own way, but the surface is not our home, you understand."

They were sitting on the terrace of a café that angled out over the lake. Resin tables and chairs painted white, clipped bay trees in big white pots, terra-cotta tiles, slightly sticky underfoot, like all the floor coverings in Elfhame. Bulbs of schnapps cooled in an ice bucket.

Ben Lo tipped his chair back and looked up at the narrow strip of black sky and its strings of brilliant lamps that hung high above the steep terraces on the far side of the lake. He said, "You can't see the stars. You can't even see Neptune."

"Well, we *are* on the farside," Marla said, reasonably. "But by point-of-presence mobot I have seen it, several times. I have been on Earth the same way, and Mars, but those were fixed, because of the signal lag."

"Yes, but you might as well look at a picture!"

Marla laughed. "Oh, yah. Of course. I forget that you are once a capitalist—" the way she said it, he might have been a dodo, or a dolphin—"from the United States of the Americas, as it was called then. That is why you put such trust in what you call *real*. But really, it is not such a big difference. You put on a mask, or you put on a pressure suit. It is all barriers to experience. And what is to see? Dusty ice, and the same black sky as home, but with more and weaker lamps. We do not need the surface."

Ben Lo didn't press the point. His guide was perfectly charming, if earnest and humorless, and brightly but brainlessly enthusiastic for the party line, like a cadre from one of the supernats. She was transparently a government spy, and was recording everything—she had shown him the little button camera and asked his permission.

"Such a historical event this is, Mr. Lo, that we wish to make a permanent record of it. You will I hope not mind?"

So now Ben Lo changed the subject, and asked why there were no sailboats on the lake, and then had to explain to Marla what a sailboat was.

Her smile was brilliant when she finally understood. "Oh yah, there are some I think who use such boards on the water, like surfing boards with sails."

"Sailboards, sure."

"The waves are very high, so it is not easy a sport. Not many are allowed, besides, because of the film."

It turned out that there was a monomolecular film across the whole lake, to stop great gobs of it floating off into the lakeside terraces.

A gong beat softly in the air. Marla looked at her watch. It was tattooed on her slim, tanned wrist. "Now it will rain soon. We should go inside, I think. I can show you the library this afternoon. There are several real books in it that one of our first citizens brought all the way from Earth."

When he was not sight-seeing or attending coordination meetings with the others in the trade delegation (he knew none of them well, and they were all so much younger than him, and as bright and enthusiastic as Marla), he spent a lot of time in the library. He told Marla that he was gathering background information that would help finesse the target packages of economic exchange, and she said that it was good, this was an open society, they had nothing to hide. Of course, he couldn't use his own archive, which was under bonded quarantine, but he was happy enough typing away at one of the library terminals for hours on end, and after a while, Marla left him to it. He also made use of various point-of-presence mobots to explore the surface, especially around Elfhame's roof.

And then there were the diplomatic functions to attend: a party in the prime minister's house, a monstrous construction of pine logs and steeply pitched roofs of wooden shingles cantilevered above the lake; a reception in the assembly room of the parliament, the Riksdag; others at the university and the Supreme Court. Ben Lo started to get a permanent crick in his neck from looking up at the faces of his etiolated hosts while making conversation.

At one, held in the humid, rarefied atmosphere of the research greenhouses near the top of the East Wall of Elfhame, Ben Lo glimpsed Avernus again. His heart lifted strangely, and the spy broke off from the one-sided conversation with an earnest hydroponicist and pushed through the throng toward his target, the floor sucking at his sandals with each step.

The old woman was surrounded by a gaggle of young giants, set apart from the rest of the party. The spy was aware of people watching when he took Avernus's hand, something that caused a murmur of unrest amongst her companions.

"An old custom, dears," Avernus told them. "We predate most of the plagues that made such gestures taboo, even after the plagues were defeated. Ben, dear, what a surprise. I had hoped never to see you again. Your employers have a strange sense of humor."

A young man with big, red-framed data glasses said, "You know each other?"

"We lived in the same city," Avernus said, "many years ago." She had brushed her vigorous grey hair back from her forehead. The wine-dark velvet wrap did not flatter her skinny old woman's body. She said to Ben, "You look so young."

"My third treatment," he confessed.

Avernus said, "It was once said that in American lives there was no second act—but biotech has given almost everyone who can afford it a second act, and for some a third one, too. But what to *do* in them? One simply can't pretend to be young again—one is too aware of death, and has too much at stake, too much invested in *self*, to risk being young."

"There's no longer any America," Ben Lo said. "Perhaps that helps."

"To be without loyalty," the old woman said, "except to one's own continuity."

The spy winced, but did not show it.

The old woman took his elbow. Her grip was surprisingly strong. "Pretend to be interested, dear," she said. "We are having a delightful conversation in this delightful party. Smile. That's better!"

Her companions laughed uneasily at this. Avernus said quietly to Ben, "You must visit me."

"I have an escort."

"Of course you do. I'm sure someone as resourceful as you will think of something. Ah, this must be your guide. What a tall girl!"

Avernus turned away, and her companions closed around her, turning their long bare backs on the Earthman.

Ben Lo asked Marla what Avernus was doing there. He was dizzy with the contrast between what his wife had been, and what she had become. He could hardly remember what they had talked about. Meet. They had to meet. They would meet.

It was beginning.

Marla said, "It is a politeness to her. Really, she should not have come, and we are glad she is leaving early. You do not worry about her, Mr. Lo. She is a sideline. We look inward, we reject the insane plans of the previous administration. Would you like to see the new oil-rich strains of *Chlorella* we use?"

Ben Lo smiled diplomatically. "It would be very interesting."

There had been a change of government, after the war. It had been less violent and more serious than a revolution, more like a change of climate, or of religion. Before the Quiet War (that was what it was called on Earth, for although tens of thousands had died in the war, none had died on *Earth*), Proteus had been loosely allied with, but not committed to, an amorphous group which wanted to exploit the outer reaches of the solar system, beyond Pluto's orbit; after the war, Proteus dropped its expansionist plans and sought to reestablish links with the trading communities of Earth.

Avernus had been on the losing side of the change in political climate. Brought in by the previous regime because of her skills in gengeneering vacuum organisms, she found herself sidelined and ostracized, her research group disbanded and replaced by government cadres, funds for her research suddenly diverted to new projects. But her contract bound her to Proteus for the next ten years, and the new government refused to release her. She had developed several important new dendrimers, light-harvesting molecules used in artificial photosynthesis, and established several potentially valuable genelines, including a novel form of photosynthesis based on a sulphur-spring *Chloroflexus* bacterium. The government wanted to license them, but to do that it had to keep Avernus under contract, even if it would not allow her to work.

Avernus wanted to escape, and Ben Lo was there to help her. The Pacific Community had plenty of uses for vacuum organisms—there was the whole of the Moon to use as a garden, to begin with—and was prepared to overlook Avernus's political stance in exchange for her expertise and her knowledge.

He was beginning to remember more and more, but there was still so much he didn't know. He supposed that the knowledge had been buried, and would flower in due course. He tried not to worry about it.

Meanwhile, the meetings of the trade delegation and Elfhame's industrial executive finally began. Ben Lo spent most of the next ten days in a closed room dickering with Parliamentary speakers on the Trade Committee over marginal rates for exotic organics. When the meetings were finally over, he slept for three hours and then, still logy from lack of sleep but filled with excess energy, went body surfing at the black beach at the North End. It was the first time he had managed to evade Marla. She had been as exhausted as he had been by the rounds of negotiations, and he had promised that he would sleep all day so that she could get some rest.

The surf was tremendous, huge smooth slow glassy swells falling from thirty meters to batter the soft, sugary black sand with giant's paws. The air was full of spinning globs of water, and so hazed with spray, like a rain of foamy flowers, that it was necessary to wear a filtermask. It was what the whole lake would be like, without its monomolecular membrane.

Ben Lo had thought he would still have an aptitude for body surfing, because he'd done so much of it when he had been living in Los Angeles, before his movie career really took off. But he was as helpless as a kitten in the swells, his boogie board turning turtle as often as not, and twice he was caught in the undertow. The second time, a pale naked giantess got an arm around his chest and hauled him up onto dry sand.

After he hawked up a couple of lungs-full of fresh water, he managed to gasp his thanks. The woman smiled. She had black hair in a bristle cut, and startlingly green eyes. She was very tall and very thin, and completely naked. She said, "At last you are away from that revisionist bitch."

Ben Lo sat up, abruptly conscious, in the presence of this young naked giantess, of his own nakedness. "Ah. You are one of Avernus's—"

The woman walked away with her boogie board under her arm, pale buttocks flexing. The spy unclipped the ankle line that tethered him to his rented board, bounded up the beach in two leaps, pulled on his shorts, and followed.

Sometime later, he was standing in the middle of a vast red-lit room at blood heat and what felt like a hundred percent humidity. Racks of large-leaved plants receded into infinity; those nearest him towered high above, forming a living green wall. His arm stung, and the tall young woman, naked under a green gown open down the front, but masked and wearing disposable gloves, deftly caught the glob of expressed blood—his blood—in a capillary straw, took a disc of skin from his forearm with a spring-loaded punch, sprayed the wound with sealant and went off with her samples.

A necessary precaution, the old woman said. Avernus. He remembered now. Or at least could picture it. Taking a ski lift all the way to the top. Through a tunnel lined with tall plastic bags in which green *Chlorella* cultures bubbled under lights strobing in fifty millisecond pulses. Another attack of memory loss—they seemed to be increasing in frequency! Stress, he told himself.

"Of all the people I could identify," Avernus said, "they had to send *you*."

"Ask me anything," Ben Lo said, although he wasn't sure that he recalled very much of their brief marriage.

"I mean identify genetically. We exchanged strands of hair in amber, do you remember? I kept mine. It was mounted in a ring."

"I didn't think that you were sentimental."

"It was my idea, and I did it with all my husbands. It reminded me of what I once was."

"My wife."

"An idiot."

"I must get back to the hotel soon. If they find out I've been wandering around without my escort, they'll start to suspect."

"Good. Let them worry. What can they do? Arrest me? Arrest you?"

"I have diplomatic immunity."

Avernus laughed. "Ben, Ben, you always were so status-conscious. That's why I left. I was just another thing you'd collected. A trophy, like your Porsche, or your Picasso."

He didn't remember.

"It wasn't a very good Picasso. One of his fakes—do you know that story?"

"I suppose I sold it."

The young woman in the green gown came back. "A positive match," she said. "Probability of a negative identity point oh oh one or less. But he is doped up with immunosuppressants and testosterone."

"The treatment," the spy said glibly. "Is this where you do your research?"

"Of course not. They certainly would notice if you turned up there. This is one of the pharm farms. They grow tobacco here, with human genes inserted to make various immunoglobulins. They took away my people, Ben, and replaced them with spies. Ludmilla is one of my original team. They put her to drilling new agricultural tunnels."

"We are alone here," Ludmilla said.

"Or you would have made your own arrangements."

"I hate being dependent on people. Especially from Earth, if you'll forgive me. And especially you. Are the others in your trade delegation . . . ?"

"Just a cover," the spy said. "They know nothing. They are looking forward to your arrival in Tycho. The laboratory is ready to be fitted out to your specifications."

"I swore I'd never go back, but they are fools here. They stand on the edge of greatness, the next big push, and they turn their backs on it and burrow into the ice like maggots."

The spy took her hands in his. Her skin was loose on her bones, and dry and cold despite the humid heat of the hydroponic greenhouse. He said, "Are you ready? Truly ready?"

She did not pull away. "I have said so. I will submit to any test, if it makes your masters happy. Ben, you are exactly as I remember you. It is very strange."

"The treatments are very good now. You must use one."

"Don't think I haven't, although not as radical as yours. I like to show my age. You could shrivel up like a Struldbrugg, and I don't have to worry about *that*, at least. That skin color, though. Is it a fashion?"

"I was Othello, once. Don't you like it?" Under the red lights his skin gleamed with an ebony luster.

"I always thought you'd make a good Iago, if only you had been clever enough. I asked for someone I knew, and they sent you. It almost makes me want to distrust them."

"We were young, then." He was trying to remember, searching her face. Well, it was two hundred years ago. Still, he felt as if he trembled at a great brink, and a tremendous feeling of nostalgia for what he could not remember swept through him. Tears grew like big lenses over his eyes and he brushed them into the air and apologized.

"I am here to do a job," he said, and said it as much for his benefit as hers.

Avernus said, "Be honest, Ben. You hardly remember anything."

"Well, it *was* a long time ago." But he did not feel relieved at this admission. The past was gone. No more than pictures, no longer a part of him.

Avernus said, "When we got married, I was in love, and a fool. It was in the Wayfarer's Chapel, do you remember? Hot and dry, with a Santa Ana blowing, and Channel Five's news helicopter hovering overhead. You were already famous, and two years later you were so famous I no longer recognized you."

They talked a little while about his career. The acting, the successful terms as state senator, the unsuccessful term as congressman, the fortune he had made in land deals after the partition of the USA, his semi-retirement in the upper house of the Pacific Community parliament. It was a little like an interrogation, but he didn't mind it. At least he knew *this* story well.

The tall young woman, Ludmilla, took him back to the hotel. It seemed natural that she should stay for a drink, and then that they should make love, with a languor and then an urgency that surprised him, although he had been told that restoration of his testosterone levels would sometimes cause emotional or physical cruxes that would require resolution. Ben Lo had made love in microgravity many times, but never before with someone who had been born to it. Afterward, Ludmilla rose up from the bed and moved gracefully about the room, dipping and turning as she pulled on her scanty clothes.

"I will see you again," she said, and then she was gone.

•   •   •

The negotiations resumed, a punishing schedule taking up at least twelve hours a day. And there were the briefings and summary sessions with the other delegates, as well as the other work the spy had to attend to when Marla thought he was asleep. Fortunately, he had a kink that allowed him to build up sleep debt and get by on an hour a night. He'd sleep long when this was done, all the way back to Earth with his prize. Then at last it was all in place, and he only had to wait.

Another reception, this time in the little zoo halfway up the West Side. The Elfhamers were running out of novel places to entertain the delegates. Most of the animals looked vaguely unhappy in the microgravity and none were very large. Bushbabies, armadillos, and mice; a pair of hippopotami no larger than domestic cats; a knee-high pink elephant with some kind of skin problem behind its disproportionately large ears.

Ludmilla brushed past Ben Lo as he came out of the rest room and said, "When can she go?"

"Tonight," the spy said.

Everything had been ready for fourteen days now. He went to find something to do now that he was committed to action.

Marla was feeding peanuts to the dwarf elephant. Ben Lo said, "Aren't you worried that the animals might escape? You wouldn't want mice running around your Shangri-la."

"They all have a kink in their metabolism. An artificial amino acid they need. That girl you talked with was once one of Avernus's assistants. She should not be here."

"She propositioned me." Marla said nothing. He said, "There are no side deals. If someone wants anything, they have to bring it to the table through the proper channels."

"You are an oddity here, it is true. Too much muscles. Many women would sleep with you, out of curiosity."

"But you have never asked, Marla. I'm ashamed." He said it playfully, but he saw that Marla suspected something. It didn't matter. Everything was in place.

They came for him that night, but he was awake and dressed, counting off the minutes until his little bundle of surprises started to unpack itself. There were two of them, armed with tasers and sticky foam canisters. The spy blinded them with homemade capsicum spray (he'd stolen chilli pods from one of the hydroponic farms and suspended a water extract in a perfume spray) and killed them as they blundered about, screaming and pawing at their eyes. One of them was Marla, another a well-muscled policeman who must have spent a good portion of each day in a centrifuge gym. The spy disabled the sprinkler system, set fire to his room, kicked out the window, and ran.

There were more police waiting outside the main entrance of the hotel. The spy ran right over the edge of the terrace and landed two hundred meters down amongst blue pines grown into bubbles of soft needles in the microgravity. Above, the fire touched off the homemade plastic explosive, and a fan of burning debris shot out above the spy's head, seeming to hover in the black air for a long time before beginning to flutter down toward the Skagerrak. Briefly, he wondered if any of the delegation had survived. It didn't matter. The young, enthusiastic, and naive delegates had always been expendable.

Half the lights were out in Elfhame, and all of the transportation systems, the phone system was crashing and resetting every five minutes, and the braking lasers were sending twenty-millisecond pulses to a narrow wedge of the sky. It was a dumb bug, only a thousand lines long. The spy had laboriously typed it from memory into the library system, which connected with everything else. It wouldn't take long to trace, but by then, other things would start happening.

The spy waited in the cover of the bushy pine trees. One of his teeth was capped and he pulled it out and unraveled the length of monomolecular diamond wire coiled inside.

In the distance, people called to each other over a backdrop of ringing bells and sirens and klaxons. Flashlights flickered in the darkness on the far side of the Skagerrak's black gulf; on the terrace above the spy's hiding place, the police seemed to have brought the fire in the hotel under control. Then the branches of the pines started to doff as a wind came up; the bug had reached the air conditioning. In the darkness below, waves grew higher on the Skagerrak, sloshing and crashing together, as the wind drove waves toward the beach at the North End and reflected waves clashed with those coming onshore. The monomolecular film over the lake's surface was not infinitely strong. The wind began to tear spray from the tops of the towering waves, and filled the lower level of the canyon with flying foam flowers. Soon the waves would grow so tall that they'd spill over the lower levels.

The spy counted out ten minutes, and then started to bound up the terraces, putting all his strength into his thigh and back muscles. Most of the setbacks between each terrace were no more than thirty meters high; for someone with muscles accustomed to one gee, it was easy enough to scale them with a single jump in the microgravity, even from a standing start.

He was halfway there when the zoo's elephant charged past him in the windy semidarkness. Its trunk was raised above its head and it trumpeted a single despairing cry as it ran over the edge of the narrow terrace. Its momentum carried it a long way out into the air before it began to fall, outsized ears flapping as if trying to lift it. Higher up, the plastic explosive charges the spy had made from sugar, gelatin, and lubricating grease blew out hectares of plastic sheeting and structural frames from the long greenhouses.

The spy's legs were like wood when he reached the high agricultural regions; his heart was pounding and his lungs were burning as he tried to strain oxygen from the thin air. He grabbed a fire extinguisher and mingled with panicked staff, ricocheting down long corridors and bounding across windblown fields of crops edged by shattered glass walls and lit by stuttering red emergency lighting. He was only challenged once, and he struck the woman with the butt end of the fire extinguisher and ran on without bothering to check if she was dead or not.

Marla had shown him the place where they stored genetic material on one of her endless tours. Everything was kept in liquid nitrogen, and there was a wide selection of dewar flasks. He chose one about the size of a human head, filled it, and clamped on the lid.

Then through a set of double pressure doors, banging the switch that closed them behind him, setting down the flask and dropping the coil of diamond wire beside it, stepping into a dressing frame, and finally pausing, breathing hard, dry-mouthed and suddenly trembling, as the vacuum suit was assembled around him. As the gold-filmed bubble was lowered over his head and clamped to the neck seal, Ben Lo started, as if waking. Something was terribly wrong. What was he doing here?

Dry air hissed around his face; headup displays stuttered and scrolled down. The spy walked out of the frame, stowed the diamond wire in one of the suit's utility pockets, picked up the flask of liquid nitrogen, and started the airlock cycle, ignoring the computer's contralto as it recited a series of safety precautions while the room revolved, and opened on a flood of sunlight.

The spy came out at the top of the South End of Elfhame. The canyon stretched away to the north, its construction-diamond roof like black sheet-ice: a long, narrow lake of ice curving away downhill, it seemed, between odd, rounded hills like half-buried snowballs, their sides spattered with perfect round craters. He bounded around the tangle of pipes and fins of some kind of distillery or cracking plant, and saw the line of the railway arrowing away across a glaring white plain toward an horizon as close as the top of a hill.

The railway was a single rail hung from smart A-frames whose carbon fiber legs compensated for movements in the icy surface. Thirteen hundred kilometers long, it described a complete circle around the little moon from pole to pole, part of the infrastructure left over from Elfhame's expansionist phase, when it was planned to string sibling settlements all the way around the moon.

The spy kangaroo-hopped along the sunward side of the railway, heading south toward the rendezvous point they had agreed upon. In five minutes, the canyon and its associated domes and industrial plant had disappeared beneath the horizon behind him. The ice was rippled and cracked and blistered, and crunched under the cleats of his boots at each touchdown.

"That was some diversion," a voice said over the open channel. "I hope no one was killed."

"Just an elephant, I think. Although if it landed in the lake, it might have survived." He wasn't about to tell Avernus about Marla and the policeman.

The spy stopped in the shadow of a carbon-fiber pillar, and scanned the icy terrain ahead of him. The point-of-presence mobots hadn't been allowed into this area. The ice curved away to the east and south like a warped checkerboard. There was a criss-cross pattern of ridges that marked out regular squares about two hundred meters on each side, and each square was a different color. Vacuum organisms. He'd reached the experimental plots.

Avernus said over the open channel, "I can't see the pickup."

He started along the line again. At the top of his leap, he said, "I've already signaled to the transport using the braking lasers. It'll be here in less than an hour. We're a little ahead of schedule."

The transport was a small gig with a brute of a motor taking up most of its hull, leaving room for only a single hibernation pod and a small storage compartment. If everything went according to plan, that was all he would need.

He came down and leaped again, and then he saw her on the far side of the curved checkerboard of the experimental plots, a tiny figure in a transparent vacuum suit sitting on a slope of black ice at what looked like the edge of the world. He bounded across the fields toward her.

The ridges were only a meter high and a couple of meters across, dirty water and methane ice fused smooth as glass. It was easy to leap over each of them— the gravity was so light that the spy could probably get into orbit if he wasn't careful. Each field held a different growth. A corrugated grey mold that gave like rubber under his boots. Flexible spikes the color of dried blood, all different heights and thicknesses, but none higher than his knees. More grey stuff, this time mounded in discrete blisters each several meters from its nearest neighbors, with fat grey ropes running beneath the ice. Irregular stacks of what looked like black plates that gave way, halfway across the field, to a blanket of black stuff like cracked tar.

The figure had turned to watch him, its helmet a gold bubble that refracted the rays of the tiny, intensely bright star of the sun. As the spy made the final bound across the last of the experimental plots—more of the black stuff, like a huge wrinkled vinyl blanket dissected by deep wandering cracks—Avernus said in his ear, "You should have kept to the boundary walls."

"It doesn't matter now."

"Ah, but I think you'll find it does."

Avernus was sitting in her pressure suit on top of a ridge of upturned strata at the rim of a huge crater. Her suit was transparent, after the fashion of the losing side of the Quiet War. It was intended to minimize the barrier between the human and the vacuum environments. She might as well have flown a flag declaring her allegiance to the outer alliance. Behind her, the crater stretched away south and west, and the railway ran right out above its dark floor on pillars that doubled and tripled in height as they stepped away down the inner slope. The crater was so large that its far side was hidden beyond the little moon's curvature. The black stuff had overgrown the ridge, and flowed down into the crater. Avernus was sitting in the only clear spot.

She said, "This is my most successful strain. You can see how vigorous it is. You didn't get that suit from my lab, did you? I suggest you keep moving around. This stuff is thixotropic in the presence of foreign bodies, like smart paint. It spreads out, flowing under pressure, over the neighboring organisms, but doesn't overgrow itself."

The spy looked down, and saw that the big cleated boots of his pressure suit had already sunken to the ankles in the black stuff. He lifted one, then the other; it was like walking in tar. He took a step toward her, and the ground collapsed beneath his boots and he was suddenly up to his knees in black stuff.

"My suit," Avernus said, "is coated with the protein by which the strain recognizes its own self. You could say I'm like a virus, fooling the immune system. I dug a trench, and that's what you stepped into. Where is the transport?"

"On its way, but you don't have to worry about it," the spy said, as he struggled to free himself. "This silly little trap won't hold me for long."

Avernus stepped back. She was four meters away, and the black stuff was thigh deep around the spy now, sluggishly flowing upward. The spy flipped the catches on the flask and tipped liquid nitrogen over the stuff. The nitrogen boiled up in a cloud of dense vapor and evaporated. It had made no difference at all to the stuff's integrity.

A point of light began to grow brighter above the close horizon of the moon, moving swiftly aslant the field of stars.

"It gets brittle at close to absolute zero," Avernus said, "but only after several dozen hours." She turned, and added, "There's the transport."

The spy snarled at her. He was up to his waist, and had to fold his arms across his chest, or else they would be caught fast.

Avernus said, "You never were Ben Lo, were you? Or at any rate no more than a poor copy. The original is back on Earth, alive or dead. If he's alive, no doubt he'll claim that this is all a trick of the outer alliance against the Elfhamers and their new allies, the Pacific Community."

He said, "There's still time, Barbara. We can do this together."

The woman in the transparent pressure suit turned back to look at him. Sun flared on her bubble helmet. "Ben, poor Ben. I'll call you that for the sake of convenience. Do you know what happened to you? Someone used you. That body isn't even yours. It isn't anyone's. Oh, it looks like you, and I suppose the altered skin color disguises the rougher edges of the plastic surgery. The skin matches your genotype, and so does the blood, but the skin was cloned from your original, and the blood must come from marrow implants. No wonder there's so much immunosuppressant in your system. If we had just trusted your skin and blood, we would not have known. But your sperm—it was all female. Not a single Y chromosome. I think you're probably haploid, a construct from an unfertilized blastula. You're not even male, except somatically—you're swamped with testosterone, probably have been since gastrulation. You're a *weapon*, Ben. They used things like you as assassins in the Quiet War."

He was in a pressure suit, with dry air blowing around his head and headup displays blinking at the bottom of the clear helmet. A black landscape, and stars high above, with something bright pulsing, growing closer. A spaceship! That was important, but he couldn't remember why. He tried to move, and discovered that he was trapped in something like tar that came to his waist. He could feel it clamping around his legs, a terrible pressure that was compromising the heat exchange system of his suit. His legs were freezing cold, but his body was hot, and sweat prickled across his skin, collecting in the folds of the suit's undergarment.

"Don't move," a woman's voice said. "It's like quicksand. It flows under pressure. You'll last a little longer if you keep still. Struggling only makes it more liquid."

Barbara. No, she called herself Avernus now. He had the strangest feeling that someone else was there, too, just out of sight. He tried to look around, but it was terribly hard in the half-buried suit. He had been kidnapped. It was the only explanation. He remembered running from the burning hotel. . . . He was suddenly certain that the other members of the trade delegation were dead, and cried out, "Help me!"

Avernus squatted in front of him, moving carefully and slowly in her transparent pressure suit. He could just see the outline of her face through the gold film of her helmet's visor. "There are two personalities in there, I think. The dominant one let you back, Ben, so that you would plead with me. But don't plead, Ben. I don't want my last memory of you to be so undignified, and anyway, I won't listen. I won't deny you've been a great help. Elfhame always was a soft target, and you punched just the right buttons, and then you kindly provided the means of getting where I want to go. They'll think I was kidnapped." Avernus turned and pointed up at the sky. "Can you see? That's your transport. Ludmilla is going to reprogram it."

"Take me with you, Barbara."

"Oh, Ben, Ben. But I'm not going to Earth. I considered it, but when they sent you, I knew that there was something wrong. I'm going *out*, Ben. Further out. Beyond Pluto, in the Kuiper Disk, where there are more than fifty thousand objects with a diameter of more than a hundred kilometers, and a billion comet nuclei ten kilometers or so across. And then there's the Oort Cloud, and its billions of comets. The fringes of *that* mingle with the fringes of Alpha Centauri's cometary cloud. Life spreads. That's its one rule. In ten thousand years, my children will reach Alpha Centauri, not by starship, but simply through expansion of their territory."

"That's the way you used to talk when we were married. All that sci-fi you used to read!"

"You don't remember it, Ben. Not really. It was fed to you. All my old interviews, my books and articles, all your old movies. They did a quick construction job, and just when you started to find out about it, the other one took over."

"I don't think I'm quite myself. I don't understand what's happening, but perhaps it is something to do with the treatment I had. I told you about that."

"Hush, dear. There was no treatment. That was when they fixed you in the brain of this empty vessel."

She was too close, and she had half-turned to watch the moving point of light grow brighter. He wanted to warn her, but something clamped his lips and he almost swallowed his tongue. He watched as his left hand stealthily unfastened a utility pocket and pulled out a length of glittering wire fine as a spider-thread. Monomolecular diamond. Serrated along its length, except for five centimeters at each end, it could easily cut through pressure suit material and flesh and bone.

He knew then. He knew what he was.

The woman looked at him and said sharply, "What are you doing, Ben?"

And for that moment, he was called back, and he made a fist around the thread and plunged it into the black stuff. The spy screamed and reached behind his helmet and dumped all oxygen from his main pack. It hissed for a long time, but the stuff gripping his legs and waist held firm.

"It isn't an anaerobe," Avernus said. She hadn't moved. "It is a vacuum organism. A little oxygen won't hurt it."

Ben Lo found that he could speak. He said, "He wanted to cut off your head."

"I wondered why you were carrying that flask of liquid nitrogen. You were going to take my head back with you—and what? Use a bush robot to strip my brain neuron by neuron and read my memories into a computer? How convenient to have a genius captive in a bottle!"

"It's me, Barbara. I couldn't let him do that to you." His left arm was buried up to the elbow.

"Then thank you, Ben. I'm in your debt."

"I'd ask you to take me with you, but I think there's only one hibernation pod in the transport. You won't be able to take your friend, either."

"Well, Ludmilla has her family here. She doesn't want to leave. Or not yet."

"I can't remember that story about Picasso. Maybe you heard it after we— after the divorce."

"You told it to me, Ben. When things were good between us, you used to tell stories like that."

"Then I've forgotten."

"It's about an art dealer who buys a canvas in a private deal, that is signed 'Picasso.' This is in France, when Picasso was working in Cannes, and the dealer travels there to find if it is genuine. Picasso is working in his studio. He spares the painting a brief glance and dismisses it as a fake."

"I had a Picasso, once. A bull's head. I remember that, Barbara."

"You thought it was a necessary sign of your wealth. You were photographed beside it several times. I always preferred Georges Braque myself. Do you want to hear the rest of the story?"

"I'm still here."

"Of course you are, as long as I stay out of reach. Well, a few months later, the dealer buys another canvas signed by Picasso. Again he travels to the studio; again Picasso spares it no more than a glance, and announces that it is a fake. The dealer protests that this is the very painting he found Picasso working on the first time he visited, but Picasso just shrugs and says, 'I often paint fakes.'"

His breathing was becoming labored. Was there something wrong with the air system? The black stuff was climbing his chest. He could almost see it move, a creeping wave of black devouring him centimeter by centimeter.

The star was very close to the horizon, now.

He said, "I know a story."

"There's no more time for stories, dear. I can release you, if you want. You only have your reserve air in any case."

"No. I want to see you go."

"I'll remember you. I'll tell your story far and wide."

Ben Lo heard the echo of another voice across their link, and the woman in the transparent pressure suit stood and lifted a hand in salute and bounded away.

The spy came back, then, but Ben Lo fought him down. There was nothing he could do, after all. The woman was gone. He said, as if to himself, "I know a story. About a man who lost himself, and found himself again, just in time. Listen. *Once upon a time . . .*"

Something bright rose above the horizon and dwindled away into the outer darkness.

steamship soldier on the
information front

NANCY KRESS

Here's a critical look at the high-pressure, high-tech, high-bit-rate lifestyle of a busy future executive, and a warning that no matter how fast you run, there's always something just a little bit faster coming up behind you. . . .

Nancy Kress began selling her elegant and incisive stories in the mid-seventies, and has since become a frequent contributor to Asimov's Science Fiction, The Magazine of Fantasy & Science Fiction, Omni, *and elsewhere. Her books include the novels* The Prince of Morning Bells, The Golden Grove, The White Pipes, An Alien Light, Brain Rose, *a novel version of her Hugo- and Nebula-winning story* Beggars in Spain, *and a sequel,* Beggars and Choosers. *Her short work has been collected in* Trinity and Other Stories *and more recently in* The Aliens of Earth. *Her most recent books are the thriller* Oaths & Miracles *and a new SF novel,* Maximum Light. *She has also won a Nebula Award for her story "Out of All Them Bright Stars." She has had stories in our Second, Third, Sixth, Seventh, Eighth, Ninth, Tenth, Eleventh, Twelfth, Thirteenth, and Fourteenth Annual Collections. Born in Buffalo, New York, Nancy Kress now lives in Silver Spring, Maryland, with her husband, SF writer Charles Sheffield.*

Just before the plane touched down at Logan, Allan Haller gave one last check to the PID on the back of his tie-tack. Good. Intense vibration in the Cathy icon, superintense in Suzette, and even Charlie showed acceptable oscillation. No need to contact any of them, that would save time. Patti and Jon, too—their icons shivered and thrilled at nearly top speed. And three minutes till landing.

"My, look at what you have there," said his seatmate pleasantly. A well-rounded grandmotherly sort, she'd been trying to engage him in conversation since La Guardia. "What sort of gadget is that, might I ask?"

No, Allan almost said, because what ground could possibly be gained? But then he looked at her again. Expensive jacket, good haircut, Gucci bag. Certainly money, but probably not entrepreneurial—rich old women tended to safe and stodgy investments. Still, what could he lose? Two and a half minutes until landing, and speculative capital, as he well knew, was sometimes found in very odd places.

"It's a PID—a personal-icon display," he said to Grandma Money. "It shows the level of electronic interaction going on with my family—my wife Cathy here, my son and daughter on these two icons—and two of my chief business associates. Each of them is wired with a WIPE, a 'weak interactive personal electronic field,' in various items of clothing that communicate with each other through a faint current sent through their bodies. Then all interactions with other electronic fields in their vicinity are registered in their WIPEs and sent wireless to each other's PIDs. I can tell, for instance, by how much the Cathy icon is vibrating that she's probably working at her terminal—lots of data going through her icon. Suzette is probably playing tennis—see, her icon is superoscillating the way WIPE fields do when they're experiencing fast-motion physical interference, and Charlie here—"

"You send electric current through your children's bodies?" Grandma Money sounded horrified.

"It isn't dange—"

"All the *time?* And then you Big-Brother them? All the *time?*"

Allan flipped down the tie-tack. Well, it had been worth a skirmish, as long as the time talking to her would have been downtime anyway. With a slight bump, the plane made contact with the runway.

"Don't they . . . well, I don't mean to be rude, but doesn't your family object to—"

But Allan was already moving down the aisle toward the jetway, from the forward seat he'd had booked precisely because it was the first to disembark. By the time the other passengers were reaching for their overhead luggage, he was already in the airport, moving fast, talking into his phone.

"Jon, what have you got?"

"A third prospect. Out in Newton; the car company will do the max-efficient route. The company is Figgy Pudding, the product is NewsSort. It goes through the whole Net looking for matches to key words, then compares the news items with ones the user has liked in the past and pre-selects for him—the usual statistical-algorithm gig. But they're claiming 93 percent success rate."

"Pretty good, if it's true."

"Worth a skirmish," Jon said, in New York. "That's all in Boston." He hung up.

Allan didn't break stride. "Figgy Pudding"—the cutesy name meant the talent was old, left over from the generation that could name a computer after a fruit and a communications language after a hot beverage. Still, some of those geezer geeks still had it. Worth a skirmish.

"Your car is waiting at these coordinates," his wristwatch said, displaying them along with a route map of Logan. "Thank you for using the Micro Global Positioning System."

Allan tacked through the crowd, past the fast-food kiosks, the public terminal booths, the VR parlors crammed with kids parked there while parents waited for flights. The driver, who had of course been tracking Allan through MGPS, already had the car door opened, the schedule revisions from Jon, the max-effish route. No words were necessary. Allan sank into the back seat and unfolded his meshNet.

This was Haller Ventures' latest investment to come to market. Allan loved it. A light, flexible cloth meshed with optic-fiber wires, it could be folded almost as small as a handkerchief. Yet it could receive as much data as any other dumb terminal in existence, *and* display it in more varied, complex configurations. Fast, powerful, keyed both to Allan's voice and to his chosen tactile commands for max effish, fully flexible in interacting with his PID and just about every other info-device, the meshNet was everything high-tech should be. It was going to make everyone connected with Haller Ventures rich.

Richer.

"Jon message," Allan said to the meshNet. "Display." And there was the information about Figgy Pudding: stock offerings, annual reports, inside run-downs put together and run through the Haller investment algorithms with Jon's usual efficiency. Nobody on the information front could recon better than Jon, unless it was Allan himself.

Carefully he studied the Figgy Pudding data. Looking good, looking very good.

"Five minutes until your first scheduled stop," his wristwatch said. A second later, the phone buzzed, then automatically transferred the call to the meshNet once it verified that the meshNet was unfolded. Cathy's icon appeared on the soft metallic surface.

"Cathy message," Allan said. The driver, curious, craned his gaze into the rearview mirror, but Allan ignored him. Definitely no ground to be gained there.

"Hey, love," Cathy's voice said. "Schedule change."

"Give it to me," Allan said, one eye still on the Figgy Pudding projections.

"Suzette made it. She's in for the Denver Preteen Semi-Final Skating Championship!"

"That's great!" Allan said. Damn, but he had great kids. Although Charlie . . . "I'll send her congratulations."

"Good. But she needs to leave Tuesday, on a nine-twenty A.M. plane. I have to be in court in Albuquerque on the Darlington case. Can you see her off at the airport?"

"Just a sec, hon." Allan called up the latest version of his schedule. "No can do. Patti's got me in Brussels from Monday night to Tuesday afternoon, with a stop at a London biotech on the hop home."

"Okay," Cathy said cheerfully. She was always cheerful; it was one of the reasons Allan was glad she was his wife. "I'll get a driver for her, and Mrs. Canning can see her off. Consider it covered. Are we still on for dinner and hanky-panky Wednesday?"

"Let me check . . . yes, it looks good. Five o'clock at the Chicago Plaza."

"I'll be there," Cathy said. "Oh, and give Charlie a call, will you? Today?"

"What's with Charlie?"

"Same thing," Cathy said, and for just a moment her cheerfulness faltered.

"Okay," Allan said. "Don't worry."

"You on your way to Novation?" Cathy of course received constant updates of his schedule, as he did of hers. Although she had fewer updates; even consulting attorneys as good as she was sometimes stayed in the same city for as long as three days. "Novation is the biorobot company, isn't it?"

"Yeah," Allan said. "Patti's pushing it pretty strong. But frankly, I don't have much faith in radical tech that makes this many extravagant claims. Promise the moon, deliver a rusty asteroid. I don't expect to be impressed."

"That's my man. Make 'em work for it. Love you."

"Love you, too," Allan said. The Cathy icon vanished from his meshNet.

"Two minutes until your first scheduled stop," his watch said.

Perfect.

Allan was wrong. He might not have expected to be impressed with Novation, but, almost against his will, he was.

As soon as he entered the unprepossessing concrete-block building, he could feel the data rush. Vibrating, racing, dancing. Whatever made a place blaze on the very edge of the information front, this place had it.

His contact entered the lobby just as Allan did. On top of the moves. She was an Indian woman in her late thirties, dressed in khaki slacks and a red shirt. All her movements were quick and light. Her black eyes shone with intelligence.

"Allan. I'm Skaka Gupta, Chief Scientist at Novation." Although of course Allan already knew that, plus everything relevant about her career, and she knew that he knew. "Welcome to our Biorobotics Unit."

"Thank you."

"Would you like a max-effish print-out of our current status?" A courtesy only; Novation's official profile would have been supplied to his firm yesterday. With an update this morning, if anything had changed overnight. And she'd know he'd prefer the figures and projections put together by his own people, in which the official profile was only one factor.

"No, thank you," Allan smiled. "But I am very eager to see your work directly."

"Then let's do that." She smiled back, completely sure of herself. Or of her work. Allan hoped it was of her work; he could sniff genuine success here. It smelled like money.

"Let me babble about the basics," Skaka said, "and you jump in with questions when you want to. We're passing through the biolab now, where we build the robots. Or, rather, start them growing."

Behind a glass wall stood rows of sterile counters, each monitored by automated equipment. A lone technician, dressed in white scrubs and mask, worked at a far counter. Allan said, "Let me test my understanding here. Your robot bodies are basic mass-ordered cylinders, with electro-field intercommunication, elevation-climbing limbs, and the usual sensors."

"That's right. We'll see them in a minute—they look like upended tin cans with four skinny clumsy legs and two skinny clumsy arms. But their processing units are entirely innovative. Each circuit board you see here, in each clear box, is being grown. We start with textured silicon plate etched with logic circuits, and then seed them with fetal neurons, grown on synthetic peptides. The fetal tissue used comes from different sources. The result is that even though the circuit scaffolds are the same, the neurons spin out different axons and dendrites. And since fetal brains always produce more neurons than they ultimately need, different ones atrophy on different boards. Each processor ends up different, and so the robots are subtly different too."

Allan studied the quiet, orderly lab. Skaka merely waited. Finally he said, "You're not the only company exploring this technique."

"No, of course not. But we've developed significant new variations—significant by several orders of magnitude. Proprietary, of course, until you've bought in."

Until, not *if*. Allan liked that.

"The proof of just how different our techniques are lies right ahead. This way to the primate house."

"Monkeys?" Allan said, startled. This had *not* been in the pre-reading.

Skaka, walking briskly, grinned over her shoulder. "P-r-i-m-e-E-i-g-h-t house. It's a joke. Currently we have eight robots in each of two different stages of development. Both groups are in learning environments modeled on the closed-system forests once used with chimps. Follow me."

She led him out of the lab, down a long windowless corridor. Halfway, Allan's tie-tack beeped twice.

"Excuse me, Skaka, is the men's room—"

"Right through that door."

Inside, Allan flipped over his tie tack. The PID icon for Charlie had stopped vibrating completely. Immediately Allan phoned his son.

"Charlie? Where are you?"

"What do you mean, where am I? It's Friday, right? I'm at school."

"In . . ."

"In Aspen."

"Why aren't you in Denver?"

"Not this week, Dad, remember?"

Allan hadn't. Mrs. Canning's tutorial schedule for the kids' real-time educational experiences was complex, although of course Allan could have accessed it on his meshNet. Maybe he should have. But Charlie's physical location wasn't the issue.

"What are you doing in Aspen, son? Right now?"

"Nothing."

Allan pushed down his annoyance. Also his concern. Charlie—so handsome, so smart, twelve years old—spent an awful lot of time doing nothing. Just sitting in one room or another, staring into space. It wasn't normal. He should be out playing soccer, exploring the Net, teasing girls, racing bikes. Even reading would be more productive than this passive staring into nothing.

Allan said, "Where's Mrs. Canning? Why is she letting you do nothing? We don't pay her for that, you know."

"She thinks I'm writing my essay about the archeological dig we did in the desert."

"And why aren't you writing it?"

"I will . . . look, Dad, I gotta go now. See you next week. Love you."

"But Charlie—"

The phone went dead.

Should he call back? When Charlie got like this, he often didn't answer. Got like *what*? What was wrong with a kid who just turned himself off and sat, like a lump of bacon fat?

Nothing. Nothing was wrong with his son.

"Allan? Everything all right?" Skaka, rapping discreetly on the men's room door. Christ, how long had Allan been staring at the motionless Charlie icon on his PID? Too long. The schedule would be all shot to hell.

"Fine," he said, striding into the corridor. "Sorry. Now let's see the Prime Eight House."

"You've never seen data like this," Skaka promised, and strode faster to make up for the lost time.

He never had seen data like this.

Each of the two identical "learning environments" was huge, two point three acres, circled by a clear plastic wall, and furnished with gray platforms at various heights and angles, steps and ramps and potholes, mimi-mazes and obstacles that could be reconfigured from outside the enclosures. The environments looked like monochromatic miniature-golf courses that had undergone an earthquake. In the first enclosure were eight of the tin-can robots, moving slowly and ponderously over the crazed terrain. Each was painted with a bright logo: "Campbell's Tomorrow Soup," "Chef-Boy-R&D," "Lay's Pareto Chips."

"Programmer humor," Skaka said. "This batch was only activated yesterday. See, they haven't learned very much about navigation, let alone how to approach their task efficiently."

"What *is* their task?" Allan said. Now they were getting to the maneuvers not covered in the prospectus.

"See those green-gray chips scattered throughout the environment? The robots are supposed to gather as many of those as they can, as fast as they can."

Allan peered through the plastic. Now he could see the chips, each about the size of a small cookie, lying in holes, on railings, between walkways, under ramps. The closest robot, Processed Corn, reached for one with its tong-ended "arm." It missed. The chip slid away, and the robot fell over. Trying to right itself, it thrashed too close to the edge of a large pothole and fell in, where it kept on thrashing.

Allan laughed. " 'War is hell.' "

"What?" Skaka said.

"Nothing. How many chips have the robots gathered so far?"

"One."

"And how long have they been at it?"

"Six hours. Now come with me to Prime-Eight Two."

Allan followed her again. They passed Chef-Boy-R&D and Net-wiser Beer jammed up against each other. Each time one moved to the right to go around the other, the second robot did the same. They ended up deadlocked against the plastic wall, four spindly legs marching futilely against each other.

Skaka unlocked a door and led Allan onto a catwalk overlooking the second enclosure. Identical to the first, it also contained eight painted robots, this group all motionless.

"Watch," Skaka said.

She pressed a button. A shower of gray-green chips fell from the ceiling, landing in holes, on railings, between walkways, under ramps. Immediately the robots sprang to life. They marched, clambered, searched. Allan's watch tingled on his wrist, and his tie twitched. Even outside the enclosure, his electrical biofield registered the enormous amount of data surging through the air as the robots communicated with each other. Within minutes all the chips had been gathered into a pile and shoved through a slit in the enclosure. They fell in a shower onto the corridor floor.

"Jesus Turing Christ," Allen said, inadequately. "Are you telling me this batch of robots learned to do that by themselves? That they had no additional programming over the first biobots?"

"That's what I'm telling you," Skaka said, in triumph. "Six minutes, forty-nine seconds. They keep beating their own record as they get more and more efficient at the task. This batch has been learning for five weeks, two days."

"Let me see it again."

Skaka pressed the button to release more chips, which fell onto different places than before. The eight robots sprang into action. Allan noted that instead of each robot searching a discrete area of the enclosure, each seemed to go for a chip according to complex factors of proximity, relative altitude, difficulty of retrieval, and even, it seemed to him, differences in agility that must have stemmed from the different fetal neurons in their processors. More than once he saw a robot start toward a chip, then veer off to go for a different one, while another robot seized the first chip.

"That's right," Skaka said, eyeing Allan. "They've learned to increase efficiency by sharing knowledge. And they make cooperative decisions based, according to the mathematical analyses we've done, on a very detailed knowledge of their differences in capability. And they *evolved all those techniques by themselves.*"

Allan watched Hot Bytes Salsa race on its spindly legs to the slit in the wall and shove the chips through.

"Six minutes, thirty-four seconds," Skaka said. "Allan, I'm sure somebody like you can see the breakthrough this represents in autonomous computer learning. It makes artificial intelligence—with everything that implies in terms of corporate or military systems—nearly within our grasp. Now, doesn't that seem a potentially profitable investment for your venture capital firm?"

Allan watched the plastic chips shower over Skaka's feet. *To the victor belong the spoils.*

"Yes," he said. "Let's talk."

•   •   •

After that, Figgy Pudding and Morrison Telecommunications were both anticlimactic. Figgy might be worth a small investment, just to establish a beachhead, but nothing major. Morrison Telecommunications was stodgy. Not anywhere near the front, not even really in the war zone. Same old, same old.

Allan flew to DC and spent the night at the newly renovated Watergate. Jon had booked him into two skirmishes tomorrow with labs doing government work, and Patti had added two briefing sessions with firms already using Haller Ventures money. While he was at dinner, he studied the info on each that she sent him. By dessert, the figures had changed once and the meetings for tomorrow changed twice.

Upstairs, Allan felt restless. There was nothing good on TV, not even with 240 channels. He couldn't seem to concentrate on his favorite Net game, Battle Chess. Every time he moved a piece, the computer countered him with blinding speed. When he lost his lieutenant to the computer's tank, which could move any number of squares through all three dimensions, Allan surrendered. It was a relief when Cathy called.

"Allan? How'd it go today?"

He told her about Novation—there was nothing he kept from Cathy. She was impressed, which cheered him a little. But then she said, "Listen, love, I'm going to have to reschedule our Wednesday rendezvous. I have the chance to go to Hong Kong after all."

"On the Burdette case? Great!" he forced himself to say. Cathy had worked for this for a long time.

"I'm thrilled, of course. Lane is reworking my schedule. We'll send it as soon as the snafus are out. Did you call Charlie?"

"Yeah. He's still just sitting a lot. Honey, do you think we should get him, well, help?"

Cathy's voice changed. "You know, I've been thinking that myself. Not that there's anything really wrong with him, but just as a precaution. . . ."

"I'll have Jon research psychologists," Charlie said heavily. "Listen, do you think we could reschedule our rendezvous to—"

"Oops, gotta go, there's Lane with another update on the Burdette case. God, me and international policy making! I can hardly believe it. Love you." The Cathy icon vanished.

"Love you, too," Allan said to the blank meshNet.

But there was no reason to wallow in gloom. He would call Suzette; his daughter was always a delight. Suzette, however, was not taking calls. Neither was Allan's brother in Florida. His mother, her system informed him, was sailing in the Aegean and would return his call when she returned, unless it was an emergency. It was not an emergency. The icons on his PID all vibrated and shimmered, even Charlie's, thank heavens.

Allan went to bed.

The next day, he felt fine. Meetings, the schedule, the flow of data and money and possibility. God, he loved it. A prosthetic device, almost invisible, to enhance human hearing through 30,000 cps. A significant gain in surveillance-satellite image resolution. Another of the endless small advances in nanotech, rearranging atoms in what would someday be the genie-in-the-bottle of the telecommunications and every other industry.

At 6:18, while he was wrapping up the nanotech briefing, Skaka Gupta called. "Allan, I'm sorry to interrupt your day, but could you fly back here tonight? There's something you should see."

Her voice sang with excitement. Allan felt it leap over the netlink, electrifying his own nerves. And it would avoid another empty evening in a hotel room. But he said with cool professionalism, "My schedule is rather full, Skaka. Are you sure that flying back to Boston will be worth my time?"

"Oh, yes," she said, and at the tone in her voice, he called Jon to rearrange the schedule.

The robots in Prime-Eight One still struggled to find and retrieve chips. Chef-Boy-R&D lay on its cylindrical side like an overturned beetle, spindly legs waving desperately to right itself. Skaka, practically running toward Prime-Eight Two, didn't even glance through the plastic fence.

"Look," she said, outside the second enclosure. "*Watch.*"

But there was nothing to see. The eight robots stood motionless around the uneven terrain. A minute passed, then another. Allan started to feel impatient. After all, his time was valuable. He could be checking in with Jon, receiving information updates, finding help for Charlie, even playing Battle Chess—

All of a sudden, the robots began to move. They lumbered to roughly equidistant positions within the enclosure. A brief pause, and then the chips rained down from the ceiling. Immediately the robots swung into action. Within minutes, the chips had all been gathered. Unsweetened Intelsauce deposited them through the slit.

"Six minutes, fourteen seconds," Skaka breathed. "The physical limitations will eventually limit any more gains in efficiency. But that's not the point anymore. Allan, they've learned to anticipate when chips will fall, before they do. They anticipate tasks that haven't yet been signaled!"

"On a regular schedule, you mean. The chips fall, say, every two hours—"

"No! That's what's so amazing! The chips don't fall at completely random times, there's a schedule, the same one we've used since the beginning, although I admit we interrupted it yesterday for your visit. The usual schedule has built-in variations around human factors like work shifts, staff meeting, lunch breaks. The bots have apparently learned it over time and are now anticipating with one hundred percent accuracy when chips will be released. They're also anticipating the most probable places for the rolling and ricocheting chips to come to rest, given that the terrain changes daily but the chip-release points are fixed in the ceiling. Ever since last night, they've moved into max-effish gathering positions a few minutes *before* the chips fall!"

Allan stared at the tin-can robots, with their garish logos and silly names. Anticipatory task management, based on self-learning of a varied-interval schedule. In biochips. It could have tremendous potential applications in man-ufacturing, for maintenance machinery, in speeding up forecast software. . . . His brain spun.

"Don't you think," Skaka said softly, "that this was well worth the trip back here?"

Allan kept his tone cool, although it took effort. "Possibly. But of course I have a number of reservations and questions. For instance, have you—" His phone rang, two beeps, a priority call.

"Dad? Charlie. Did you know our neighbors in Aspen have been arrested?"

"Charlie, I'm pretty busy right now, I'm with a—"

"They've been arrested for *terrorism*. There are cops all over the place."

Terrorism. Cops. Bombs, guns. What neighbors? Allan couldn't remember meeting anyone in Aspen.

"Where's Mrs. Canning? Let me talk to her. Are you all right?"

"Of course I'm all right," Charlie said scornfully. "Mrs. Canning took Suzette to the ice rink."

"Then here's what I want you to do. Just a minute . . ." Belatedly, Allan re-membered Skaka, who was trying to look as if she hadn't overheard. "Excuse me, Skaka, it's my son. . . ."

"Of course," Skaka said, turning to gaze away, into the robot enclosure. The backs of her shoulders, just a little too rigid, said, *Why haven't you got your personal life well enough arranged so it doesn't interfere with what may well be the most important investment opportunity of the decade?*

"Charlie, first call your mother and tell her what you just told me. Also Mrs. Canning. Then call a car and driver, and pack your things and Suzette's and Mrs. Canning's. Have the driver take you to the Denver apartment. I'll have Jon or Patti okay the car bill and cancel the Aspen house."

"But, Dad—"

"Charlie, just *do* it. I don't want you in any danger!"

"Oh, okay." Charlie sounded disgusted. Twelve-year-old bravado.

Quickly, Allan called Jon. Skaka's shoulders were still stiff. Allan resented having lost the advantage. As in-control as he could manage, he said to Skaka, "My son. There's been terrorist activity in what should have been a safe neigh-borhood. I had to get him out."

Her eyes widened. "Of course. What kind of terrorist activity?"

It occurred to Allan that he hadn't asked. He didn't know the charges, the situation, the neighbors, themselves. They were only local; he spent so much time global.

"The under-control kind," he said, hoping she wouldn't pick up on the eva-sion. "And we can be out of there in half an hour. Charlie's a good packer."

Skaka smiled. "So is my daughter. We, too, have no fixed residence. I don't know how scientists managed before disposable leases."

"Neither do I." Allan warmed to her again; she was making his lapse into civilian more forgivable. "What plan do you use?"

"Live America. Their Code Nine Plan: three-bedroom leases, no more than ten minutes from an airport, warm blue decor, level three luxury. They even include our choice of pet at each house. It suits my husband, daughter, and nanny just fine."

"We're a Code Eleven. Four bedrooms. We have two kids."

Allan and Skaka smiled at each other, then looked away. That was the problem with talking about personal life: it interfered with the strategy. Reconnaissance scouts had to stay detached, keep moving, remain tense and alert. The information frontier was an unpredictable place.

Skaka said briskly, "My staff will be watching very closely whatever the bots incorporate next into their learning, if anything. Should another breakthrough occur, they'll notify me and I'll notify you."

"Good," Allan said. "Meantime, let's talk about the breakthrough we already have. I've got some questions."

"Shoot," Skaka said, and her shoulders visibly loosened.

Allan spent the night on a sleeper plane to Singapore. Mrs. Canning settled the kids in the Denver apartment, although Suzette complained the ice-rink there wasn't as good as at Aspen. She wanted to lease in Chicago, which "Coach Palmer said has a enth-mega rink!" Allan said he'd think about it. Cathy called to postpone their romantic rendezvous until Sunday; her case was dragging on. Patti identified two more companies for Allan to check out, both on the far edge, both potential coups. One was in Sydney, the other in Brasília. The Charlie icon on Allan's PID sat motionless.

The Singapore company had developed what it called a "graciously serious approaching" to that perennial coming attraction, the smart road that would direct cars, freeing the driver to do other things besides drive. Allan had expected that his visit would result in hiring one of the independent consultants Haller Ventures used to evaluate automotive technology, but it didn't even need that. Singapore wasn't doing anything Allan hadn't seen before. Not worth a skirmish. On to Sydney.

From the plane he called Charlie. "Son? Not much action in your PID icon." Totally vibrationless, for five straight hours, and not a time when Charlie could be expected to be asleep.

"No," Charlie said neutrally.

Allan tried to keep his tone light. "So what ya doing?"

"Nothing."

"Charlie—"

"Did you know that when Robert Fulton invented the steamship, at least three other guys were making the same thing at the same time?"

"*Charlie*—"

"Gotta go, Dad. Love you."

"Three minutes till landing," said his wristwatch. "MGPS coordinates for your car are displayed."

"Allan!" Patti said. "Action in Tunis. Looks like a genuine outpost. Company is called Sahara Sun, and they manufacture solar panels. Stats follow. Also re-routing on tomorrow's schedule."

"Two minutes till landing."

Allan closed his eyes. But when the plane stopped, he was the first one to spring up, grab his carry-on, deplane from the front row. In Jakarta.

No—*Sydney*. Jakarta was tomorrow.

Or the next day?

Sydney was fiber-optics with increased carrying capacity due to smaller-grain alloys.

Jakarta was medical technology, an improved electrocardiograph that could predict fibrillation by incorporating elements of chaos theory into the computer analysis of data. Eighty-one-point-three success rate. So far.

Bombay was no good. Supposedly an important advance in holographic videoconferencing, but actually old, old, old stuff. Jon had slipped up.

Berne was briefing and inspection tour of an ongoing investment, currently in beta-testing phase. A Haller Ventures accountant and quality assurance expert met Allan there.

Milan was fascinating. The benchmark for parallel-systems processing was one trillion operations per second. The Italian techies had achieved it with half the hardware previously required. There was much noisy gesturing and an earthy Tuscany wine.

Tunis was robots in the desert. The entrepreneurs drove Allan onto the rim of the Sahara, jouncing in Rovers over miles of rocky sand to a sundrenched site where solar panels were being assembled by simple robots. The bots also assembled more of themselves. They separated ores from the desert sand for raw material, using solar power to create the high temperatures to do it: a self-perpetuating mechanical kingdom slowly spreading over the empty desert floor. The excess solar power was converted into electricity to sell, once cables were in place. A solid, conservative strategy. Allan ordered a tech-consultant evaluation immediately, including a climate projection for thirty years. Desert wars had been lost before to climate.

He caught a transatlantic flight home. The Brazilian engagement had been postponed. Cathy had gone to Los Angeles—the Tunis trip had once more scuttled their rendezvous—with Suzette, who had a major skating competition. Charlie was on a nature hike in Yosemite with the commercial edu-group Mrs. Canning subscribed him to. The leased apartment in Aspen—no, Aspen had been canceled, and anyway it was Oakland this month because of Suzette's competition schedule—would be empty.

The little Tunisian robots had looked like rectangular suitcases, not cylindrical tin cans. Nonetheless, Allan called Skaka Gupta from the transatlantic flight. She was in Berne. Allan rerouted himself to Boston anyway. He didn't like coming home to a new leased place with no one else there.

At Novation he was met by a flustered young man, no more than twenty-three, in jeans, leather sweater, and the ubiquitous sneakers set with tiny flashing mirrors. Allan recognized the type: a software expert. Awkward, bright as hell, and secretly scornful of "bean counters." No, that wasn't the term anymore: "cashware clods." Allan smiled icily and looked slightly bored.

"Paul Sanderson? Allan Haller. You're going to give me Skaka's pitch, right?" Skaka had left no data for a new pitch, as far as Allan knew.

Paul Sanderson looked confused. "Yes . . . no, I mean, she didn't . . . I was just going to show you what the bots can do now."

"Fine, fine. But keep the jargon to a minimum." A pre-emptive strike, with the force of an order. Sanderson would get either huffy or meek, unsure how his boss would want Allan treated.

He got meek. "Sure. Well, uh, this way."

The robots in Prime-Eight One seemed to Allan slightly less uncoordinated, although they still wandered hopelessly. Campbell's Tomorrow Soup lunged at a chip but missed it. Sanderson dawdled past the enclosure, peering through the plastic, fidgeting. Why? To cover his own edginess, Allan flipped over his tie and checked his PID.

The icons all vibrated so fast he could barely see they were there.

"You've created a superstrength data field here!" he exclaimed, and as Sanderson turned toward him with a grin of embarrassment, Allan understood. "You have, haven't you? You've made the whole facility into a microwave field that lets the Prime-Eight Two bots interface directly with the Net. You retrofitted them with the communications software to do that."

Sanderson nodded sheepishly. "I know regs say I should have warned you before you stepped into the field, but it's not dangerous in such short exposure, really it's not. And your own com devices will return to normal functioning just as soon as we—"

"I'm not concerned about either my devices or my health!" Allan snapped. "But Skaka promised to keep me abreast of any major changes in the research!"

"Well, there haven't really been any," Sanderson said. "Although we'd hoped . . . but so far, nothing has changed. The bots just go on anticipating the chip-release schedule and—"

"Is Prime-Eight One wired to the Net, too? Or aren't you going to tell me that, either?"

Sanderson looked shocked. "No, of course it's not wired. If we don't do it at exactly the same point as we did this group, we'd compromise the research design!"

"As opposed to compromising your investors' confidence," Allan snapped. "Fine. Tell Ms. Gupta to call me when she returns. And please be advised that I retain the right to bring in my own evaluators here, since I'm obviously not being told everything voluntarily."

"Mr. Haller, please don't think that because—"

"That's all," Allan snapped, turned, and left.

Back in his car, he asked himself why he was so angry. He owned a piece of Novation, yes, but he owned pieces of a lot of outposts where the front shifted abruptly and unpredictably. That was the nature of fronts. So why *was* he so upset?

He didn't know. And there was no time to think about it. His next flight left in forty-two minutes.

Just enough time to study the information for tomorrow's 6:30 breakfast meeting.

Cathy and Allan finally connected in New York; she had an unexpected re-route in her schedule. As he entered the elevator, Allan felt his chest tighten. Ten days since he'd last seen his wife! And oh, how he'd missed her . . . and how he loved the giddy excitement of their reunions. Surely couples who were together all the time couldn't get this excited.

Nor was he disappointed. Afterward, lying together on the big hotel bed, dreamily watching the wall program shade from hectic red to cool soft blues (it must be keyed to their breathing), Allan felt utterly content.

Cathy, however, didn't let him drift for long. "Honey, there's something we need to talk about. It's Charlie."

Immediately Allan's mood changed. He hiked himself up against the pillows. "How did he seem in Los Angeles?"

"Strange." Cathy hesitated. "I know he's on the edge of adolescence, trying his wings, some hostility to be expected blah blah blah . . . but he *wasn't* hostile. He was just as nice to Suzette as ever, really thrilled for her when she won. And he wasn't at all secretive with me. It's just that he's gone off in such strange directions in his personal interests. For instance, he talked a lot about the Age of Reason and its social implications."

"Just a sec," Allan said. He reached for the meshNet, crumpled with the rest of his clothes on the floor by his bed, and did a Quik-Chek. *Age of Reason: an eighteenth-century period of great intellectual awareness and activity, characterized by questioning of authority, emphasis on the experimental method in science, and creative self-determination in arts, culture, and politics.*

"I could have told you what it was," Cathy said, nettled.

"I know." Cathy was a lawyer; she would have gone into far more well-organized particulars than Allan wanted. "But it's just history, right? An interest in history doesn't sound so bad. In fact, Charlie said something or other to me about Robert Fulton and the steamship. Maybe Mrs. Canning started a new school unit."

"No, I checked. They're still concentrating on earth sciences. But that's not all. I accessed Charlie's Twenty-Two—the personal-notes tablet, but only the unencrypted part, of course—and he—"

"He's still using a Twenty-Two? Good Lord, that computer's been obsolete for at least three months! I'll send him a new one—there's something much better coming out now."

Cathy said acidly, "There's always something much better coming out. But that's not the *point*, Allan. What I found on Charlie's tablet were lists of 'ages.' All the lists were subtly different, but there were *dozens* of them."

"What do you mean, 'ages'?"

"Stone Age. Iron Age. Age of Heroes. Age of Faith. Dark Ages. Age of Reason.

Industrial Age. Space Age. Information Age. That one's always last on every list, presumably because we're in it now. Dozens of different lists!"

"Odd," Allan said, because it was clear she expected him to say something. "But, frankly, Cath, it doesn't sound dangerous. So he's wondering about history. That's good, isn't it?"

"Exhibit Three: When I asked him about the lists, he didn't get angry that I'd been snooping in his tablet. Instead, he looked at me in that intense way he has, not moving a single facial muscle—you know how he is—and said, 'Mom, how do we know that our family is really information-front warriors, and not really just homeless people?' "

Allan considered. That did sound serious. "Did you ask him if he's feeling that you and I travel too much? That we should make an effort to be all together more often as a family?" He and Cathy had worried this before.

"Yes. But he said no, that wasn't it at all, his friends' parents were just the same. So I asked him what *was* it, and he only said, 'When it's steamship time, it's steamship *time*,' and sank into one of those motionless trances of his. Allan, I couldn't get him to even answer me for half an hour, no matter what I did. It's like he was someplace else, sitting right there in front of me!"

Allan gazed out the window. Far below, the New York traffic sounds hummed dimly, reassuringly. Allan said slowly, "I got the names of two good child psychologists, one in Denver and one in San Francisco."

"Well, that won't do a lot of good, since we're not going to be in Oakland after a few more weeks. We're all leasing in Kansas City for the Shephard trial. Can't you take the trouble to memorize our schedule?"

After a minute she added, "I'm sorry."

"It's all right," Allan said. "I know you're worried about Charlie, too. Listen, I'll find a psychologist in . . ." he blanked for a moment—"Kansas City."

"Okay." Cathy smiled wanly, then clung to him. He could feel the tension in her bare back.

Charlie had always been such an easy kid. Suzette had been the temperamental one. That's why they were concerned, Allan told himself; it was all relative. Still, for Charlie to just sit and go into a trance where he didn't even answer people . . . that couldn't be normal, could it? To be so cut off?

Why, he wouldn't even be tuned into the Net. Anything could develop, and Charlie wouldn't even know it!

Allan held his wife tighter. "I'll re-route to see him tomorrow."

Re-routing wasn't easy. Neither Jon nor Patti were pleased. Jon had to go himself to check out bone-marrow scanning in Raleigh. The director of a firm making low-cost orbiting solar panels in Dallas wouldn't be available for another two weeks if Allan missed that appointment, because the director would be in Tokyo. Videoconferencing, the director said sniffily, was not an acceptable substitute. Allan told Patti to tell the director to go to hell. He got a flight to the new apartment in Kansas City.

But then Paul Sanderson called from Novation. Skaka Gupta must again be somewhere else. "You said . . . I mean, you seemed to indicate last time you were here, Allan . . . uh, Mr. Haller . . . that if something noteworthy happened with the bots you wanted to see it right away, so—"

"And something has? Unfortunately, the timing couldn't be worse. Can you describe the development to me?"

"Oh, sure," Sanderson said, with such relief in his voice that Allan decided he better go to Novation himself after all. The data smelled important. If he took a flight almost immediately to Boston, even flying standby if he had to . . . shit, he hated flying standby, if only developments in transferring people could keep up with innovations in transferring data!—if he flew standby, and then could book a flight getting him to the Kansas City lease by at least midnight . . .

"Never mind explaining. I'll be there this afternoon."

"Okay," Sanderson said unhappily. "We'll be expecting you."

We. Him and the robots? Did Sanderson identify with them that much? Maybe; engineer types never seemed to have any real life. Just endless tinkering with software, in the same subroutines, same location, same days.

Suddenly Allan was hit with a memory. So vivid, so visceral, it almost seemed as if he no longer stood in the middle of a frantic metropolitan airport but instead was in the cool woods behind the house where he'd grown up, lying on his back on a carpet of pine needles. Billy Goldman, his best friend, lay beside him, both of them gazing upward at the sun-dabbled branches lacing the sky, smelling the sweet tangy pines, and Billy saying, "Why would anyone want to kiss a *girl*? Yuuccckkk!"

Now, where had *that* come from? Astonished, Allan shook his head to clear it. The mind was a strange thing. Tossing in the unrelated, the pointless, the unprofitable, the irrelevant. The distracting.

By the time he reached Boston, he had a headache no pills could touch.

He arrived at Novation in a foul mood. Sanderson met him nervously. "This way, Mr. Haller, we'll go right to Prime-Eight Two, unless you want some, um, coffee, or maybe—"

"No. Let's go."

Sanderson walked past Prime-Eight One without turning his head, but Allan stopped to study the robots. It seemed to him that they gathered their chips a little more smoothly, with less fumbling. He thought he even saw Processed Corn start forward, then swerve abruptly to miss crashing into Ocean Spray Cacheberries. They were starting to cooperate.

Prime-Eight Two, on the other hand, looked no different. The bots stood motionless on the complex terrain. Allan and Sanderson stood outside the enclosure, Sanderson fidgeting. "Chip fall in seven minutes. We don't want to alter the schedule, you know, because even though then you wouldn't have to wait, you wouldn't really be seeing the exact same phenomenon we've been observing, so it isn't—"

"I understand," Allan said. "I can wait."

But he had to do something to fill in seven minutes, besides intimidating Sanderson. The heavy data fire meant he couldn't access his mesh-Net. Instead, Allan repeated to himself the personal-notes tablet on his son's Twenty-Two. He had accessed the tablet from the plane, telling himself that parental duty outweighed teenage privacy.

*Age of Reason . . . Age of Reason . . . Information Age . . . Age of Reasoning . . . Enlightenment? No no no . . . Start again Stone Age Iron Age Bronze Age . . . no no NO NO it's here someplace—TO DO: do sections 84–86 homework for Tuesday find three examples of igneous rock buy mom a birthday present . . . AGE OF REA-SON . . . The girl I saw in the park was not wearing underwear!!!!!! . . . **Age of Reason—***

The robots behind the plastic wall lumbered into position, a moment before chips scattered from the ceiling. "They've learned to cut the anticipation pretty fine," Sanderson said. Allan didn't reply. He watched as the bots efficiently gathered all the chips. They seemed no faster than before, but no slower either. His meshNet had gone dead, presumably from the bots' intense occupation of all available bandwidths to the Net. What exactly were they downloading? And what use were their biochip brains making of it? They didn't need the Net's vast libraries of information to gather chips efficiently.

"Have you traced their download sources yet?"

"Some of them," Sanderson said. He didn't look at Allan, and his tone was evasive. "Watch—here it comes."

But what "came" was . . . nothing. Literally. The robots dumped all the chips into their bucket, held in the graspers of Techs/Mex Chili, and then went motionless.

Sanderson began to talk very fast. "They've been doing that for twenty-four hours now. Gathering the chips the way they're programmed to, but then just not depositing them through the wall. Nobody's tinkered with their programming. They just . . . don't do it."

Allan studied Techs/Mex Chili. "What do your download-source traces show?"

"Not much," Sanderson said, and Allan saw that his previous evasiveness had been embarrassment. Programmers hated not knowing what was going on in their programs. "Or, rather, too much. They're apparently accessing all sorts of stuff, bits of everything on the Net, maybe even at random. At least, we haven't found any patterns yet."

"Umm," Allan said noncommittally. "Squirt the full trace files to my office. Our people will look at it as well."

"I don't really have the authori—"

"Just do it," Allan said, but for once the tone of command didn't work. Sanderson looked scared but determined.

"No, sir, I'm afraid I can't. Not without Skaka's say-so."

Allan capitulated. "All right. I'll call her myself."

The young programmer looked relieved. Allan went on studying the quiet robots in their gaudy, silly paint, guarding their bucket of totally useless chips.

• • •

He couldn't reach Skaka Gupta, so he left her a message to call him. His flight was delayed, and it was well past midnight before the car left him in front of the unfamiliar apartment building in Kansas City. No, not unfamiliar . . . it looked comfortingly like the one in Oakland, the one in Denver, the one in Aspen, the one in New Orleans, the one in Atlanta, the one in Raleigh . . .

Mrs. Canning, alerted by the security system, let him in, then stumbled sleepily back to bed. He checked on Suzette, lying with both arms flung out at her sides and one knee bent, looking energetic even in sleep. Her hair had grown. Allan went next to the room Charlie always had.

The boy stirred and mumbled as Allan entered. "Hi, Dad."

"Hey, son."

"What . . . what the reason?"

"The reason for what, Charlie?" Allan said gently, but Charlie was already back to sleep.

For several minutes, Allan watched him. Cathy's light fine hair, Allan's beaky nose, Charlie's own individual chin. His son. On his tablet Allan had the name of a good child psychologist in Kansas City. Just don't let it be neurological, he prayed formlessly. Not a neurological degeneration, not a brain tumor, not any problem they could do nothing about. *Not my Charlie.*

In his own bedroom, which he found located where his bedrooms always were, Allan couldn't sleep. He reviewed the data for the next day's meetings, both local so he could spend more time with Charlie. He did some sit-ups and stretches, and then he tossed in the new, familiar bed.

His son sitting and staring into space, unreachable by ordinary communication . . .

The robots, refusing to turn in their chips . . .

Tomorrow's meetings, half the data for which he'd already forgotten. . . . He didn't really want to attend any of them anyway. Same old, same old. . . . No, what was he thinking? None of it was the same old. It was all interesting new breakthroughs, beachheads on the newest fronts, and he was privileged to have a part in scouting them out. . . . So why did he just want to stay huddled forever in this familiar apartment he'd never seen before? Damn, he *hated* it when he couldn't sleep!

Groping beside his bed, Allan picked up his meshNet. Just holding it, unwrapping it, knowing all the information it put at his command, made him feel better instantly. At night the system didn't signal his messages, merely stored them until he was done sleeping. Maybe there was something from Cathy.

But the only new message was from Skaka Gupta: *Please call me at the lab. Important.* The transmission time was only ten minutes ago. She had returned early to Boston, and was working very late.

"Skaka? Allan Haller. What's going on?"

"Hello, Allan." She sounded tired, as well she might. It was half past one. "I didn't expect to hear from you till morning. But you might as well know now. We've had a temporary setback."

"What kind of setback?"

"The robots have stopped functioning. No, that's not true—they only look like they're not functioning because they're not gathering chips any more, as they were programmed to do. Instead, they've speeded up massively the amounts of data they're pulling off the Net, and processing it in parallel non-stop. And they're . . ." Her voice stumbled.

"They're *what?*"

"They're just huddled together in a ring, touching sides, their visual and auditory and infrared sensors shut down. Just huddled there, blind to their environment."

He didn't answer. After a minute, Skaka's tone changed, and Allan realized for the first time that, despite her glossy competence, she really was a scientist and not an information-front soldier. No entrepreneur would have said, as she did next, "Allan—I know your firm is small, and that you've invested a lot of money in Novation. We can get another grant, but if this project flops, are we going to bring *you* down?"

"Don't worry about it. We'll be all right," Allan said, which was true. He wasn't ever insane enough to commit all of his resources to the same battle.

Commit all of his resources to the same battle . . .

"That's good," Skaka said. "But it doesn't touch the real issue. Allan, I don't know what the bots are *doing.*"

"I do," he said, but so softly she couldn't hear him. Dazed, he managed to get out, "It's late. Talk in the morning." He cut the connection.

And sat on the edge of the bed, naked legs dangling over the side, staring at nothing.

Commit all of his resources to the same battle. . . . That's what they all had been doing. Many different skirmishes—solar panels, robots, high-resolution imaging, nanotech, smart autos—but all part of the same war. Stone Age, Bronze Age, Age of Chivalry, Space Age . . . *Information Age.* The only game in town, the scene of all the action, the all-embracing war. *Uncle Sam Wants You!*

But no age lasted forever. Eventually the struggle for bronze or gold or green chips—or for physical or digital terrain—would come to an end, just as all the other Ages eventually had. One succeeding the other, inexorable and unstoppable. . . . *When it's steamship time,* went the old saw, *then nothing can stop the steamship from coming.* And when the Age of Steam was over, it was over. Civilization was no longer driven by steam. Now it was driven by information. Gather it in, willy-nilly, put it in electronic buckets, give it to the owners. Or the generals.

Why?

What if they gave a war and nobody came?

That's why the robots had stopped. That's why they stood staring into space, only their brains active. They had at their command all the data on the Net, plus the complex-and-growing human neural circuits of their biochips. They were on top of it all, wired in, fully cued for the next stage. Not *how can we gather those chips with max-effish* but rather *why should we gather chips at all?*

Not the Age of Reason. The Reasons Age.

Things changed. One day steam, then steam is over. One day you can't imagine wanting to kiss a girl, the next day you pant after it. One day you rely on your frontier neighbors for survival of your very home, the next day you don't know your neighbors' names and don't have a settled home.

One day the mad rush after information and chips, the next day you sit and stare trance-like, far more interested in why you were interested in chips and information than in the commodities themselves. Not that the information itself wouldn't continue to accumulate. It would. But the center was shifting, the mysterious heart of each Age where the real emphasis and excitement were. The front.

Charlie must sense it only dimly. Of course—he was a child, and he didn't have Allan's honed instincts. But that Charlie sensed it at all, the coming change, was probably *because* he was a child—this was the world he would inherit. Charlie would be an integral part of it. But integrated more slowly than the bots, which were riding the advance wave of the human Net, shock troops racing toward where the info-wars gave way to the next step in the long, long march of humanity's development.

Which would be . . . what? What would the Reasons Age actually be like?

Allan shivered. Suddenly he felt old. He had evolved in the Information Age, had flourished in it. . . . He was a natural as a scout on the high-tech front. Would there be a place for him when the guns grew more muffled, the pace slowed, and the blaze of battle gave way to the domestic concerns of the occupation? Could he adapt to whatever came next?

Then his confidence returned. Of course he could! He always had. The Information Age might end, the Reasons Age arise, but he could make it. In fact, there was probably a way to turn the whole thing to his own profit. All he needed was the right approach, the right allies, the right strategy.

The right *data*.

Tomorrow, he'd start to gather it.

Smiling, Allan slept.

Reasons to Be Cheerful

GREG EGAN

A bit more than halfway through the decade, it's becoming obvious that Australian writer Greg Egan is coming to be widely recognized as one of the Big New Names to emerge in SF in the nineties, and although he has yet to win any major awards, it's my guess that his first Nebula or Hugo will not be all that long in coming. In the last few years, he has become a frequent contributor to Interzone *and* Asimov's Science Fiction, *and has made sales as well to* Pulphouse, Analog, Aurealis, Eidolon, *and elsewhere; many of his stories have also appeared in various "Best of the Year" series, and he was on the Hugo Final Ballot in 1995 for his story "Cocoon," which won the Ditmar Award and the Asimov's Readers Award. His stories have appeared in our Eighth, Ninth, Tenth, Eleventh, Twelfth, and Thirteenth Annual Collections. His first novel,* Quarantine, *appeared in 1992 to wide critical acclaim and was followed by a second novel in 1994,* Permutation City, *which won the John W. Campbell Memorial Award. His most recent books are a collection of his short fiction,* Axiomatic, *and two novels,* Distress *and* Diaspora. *Upcoming is a new novel,* Teranesia. *He has a Web site at http://www.netspace.net.au/~gregegan/.*

In the thought-provoking story that follows, he takes us to a richly detailed future Australia and introduces us to someone who's one of those people it's impossible to cheer up—literally.

▼

ONE

In September 2004, not long after my twelfth birthday, I entered a state of almost constant happiness. It never occurred to me to ask why. Though school included the usual quota of tedious lessons, I was doing well enough academically to be able to escape into daydreams whenever it suited me. At home, I was free to read books and web pages about molecular biology and particle physics, quaternions and galactic evolution, and to write my own Byzantine computer games and convoluted abstract animations. And though I was a skinny, unco-ordinated child, and every elaborate, pointless organized sport left me comatose with boredom, I was comfortable enough with my body on my own terms. Whenever I ran—and I ran everywhere—it felt good.

I had food, shelter, safety, loving parents, encouragement, stimulation. Why shouldn't I have been happy? And though I can't have entirely forgotten how oppressive and monotonous classwork and schoolyard politics could be, or how easily my usual bouts of enthusiasm were derailed by the most trivial problems, when things were actually going well for me I wasn't in the habit of counting down the days until it all turned sour. Happiness always brought with it the belief that it would last, and though I must have seen this optimistic forecast disproved a thousand times before, I wasn't old and cynical enough to be surprised when it finally showed signs of coming true.

When I started vomiting repeatedly, Dr. Ash, our GP, gave me a course of antibiotics and a week off school. I doubt it was a great shock to my parents when this unscheduled holiday seemed to cheer me up rather more than any mere bacterium could bring me down, and if they were puzzled that I didn't even bother feigning misery, it would have been redundant for me to moan constantly about my aching stomach when I was throwing up authentically three or four times a day.

The antibiotics made no difference. I began losing my balance, stumbling when I walked. Back in Dr. Ash's surgery, I squinted at the eye chart. She sent me to a neurologist at Westmead Hospital, who ordered an immediate MRI scan. Later the same day, I was admitted as an in-patient. My parents learnt the diagnosis straight away, but it took me three more days to make them spit out the whole truth.

I had a tumour, a medulloblastoma, blocking one of the fluid-filled ventricles in my brain, raising the pressure in my skull. Medulloblastomas were potentially fatal, though with surgery followed by aggressive radiation treatment and chemotherapy, two out of three patients diagnosed at this stage lived five more years.

I pictured myself on a railway bridge riddled with rotten sleepers, with no choice but to keep moving, trusting my weight to each suspect plank in turn. I understood the danger ahead, very clearly . . . and yet I felt no real panic, no real fear. The closest thing to terror I could summon up was an almost exhilarating rush of vertigo, as if I was facing nothing more than an audaciously harrowing fairground ride.

There was a reason for this.

The pressure in my skull explained most of my symptoms, but tests on my cerebrospinal fluid had also revealed a greatly elevated level of a substance called Leu-enkephalin—an endorphin, a neuropeptide which bound to some of the same receptors as opiates like morphine and heroin. Somewhere along the road to malignancy, the same mutant transcription factor that had switched on the genes enabling the tumour cells to divide unchecked had apparently also switched on the genes needed to produce Leu-enkephalin.

This was a freakish accident, not a routine side-effect. I didn't know much about endorphins then, but my parents repeated what the neurologist had told them, and later I looked it all up. Leu-enkephalin wasn't an analgesic, to be secreted in emergencies when pain threatened survival, and it had no stupefying narcotic effects to immobilize a creature while injuries healed. Rather, it was the primary means of signalling happiness, released whenever behaviour or circumstances warranted pleasure. Countless other brain activities modulated that simple message, creating an almost limitless palette of positive emotions, and the binding of Leu-enkephalin to its target neurons was just the first link in a long chain of events mediated by other neurotransmitters. But for all these subtleties, I could attest to one simple, unambiguous fact: Leu-enkephalin made you feel *good*.

My parents broke down as they told me the news, and I was the one who comforted them, beaming placidly like a beatific little child martyr from some tear-jerking oncological mini-series. It wasn't a matter of hidden reserves of strength or maturity; I was physically incapable of feeling bad about my fate. And because the effects of the Leu-enkephalin were so specific, I could gaze unflinchingly at the truth in a way that would not have been possible if I'd been doped up to the eyeballs with crude pharmaceutical opiates. I was clear-headed but emotionally indomitable, positively radiant with courage.

I had a ventricular shunt installed, a slender tube inserted deep into my skull to relieve the pressure, pending the more invasive and risky procedure of removing the primary tumour; that operation was scheduled for the end of the week. Dr. Maitland, the oncologist, had explained in detail how my treatment would proceed, and warned me of the danger and discomfort I faced in the months ahead. Now I was strapped in for the ride and ready to go.

Once the shock wore off, though, my un-blissed-out parents decided that they had no intention of sitting back and accepting mere two-to-one odds that I'd make it to adulthood. They phoned around Sydney, then further afield, hunting for second opinions.

My mother found a private hospital on the Gold Coast—the only Australian franchise of the Nevada-based "Health Palace" chain—where the oncology unit was offering a new treatment for medulloblastomas. A genetically engineered herpes virus introduced into the cerebrospinal fluid would infect only the replicating tumour cells, and then a powerful cytotoxic drug, activated only by the virus, would kill the infected cells. The treatment had an 80 percent five-year survival rate, without the risks of surgery. I looked up the cost myself, in the hospital's web brochure. They were offering a package deal: three months' meals and accommodation, all pathology and radiology services, and all pharmaceuticals, for 60,000 dollars.

My father was an electrician, working on building sites. My mother was a sales assistant in a department store. I was their only child, so we were far from poverty-stricken, but they must have taken out a second mortgage to raise the fee, saddling themselves with a further 15 or 20 years' debt. The two survival rates were not that different, and I heard Dr. Maitland warn them that the figures couldn't really be compared, because the viral treatment was so new. They would have been perfectly justified in taking her advice and sticking to the traditional regime.

Maybe my enkephalin sainthood spurred them on somehow. Maybe they wouldn't have made such a great sacrifice if I'd been my usual sullen and difficult self, or even if I'd been nakedly terrified rather than preternaturally brave. I'll never know for sure—and either way, it wouldn't make me think any less of them. But just because the molecule wasn't saturating their skulls, that's no reason to expect them to have been immune to its influence.

On the flight north, I held my father's hand all the way. We'd always been a little distant, a little mutually disappointed in each other. I knew he would have preferred a tougher, more athletic, more extroverted son, while to me he'd always seemed lazily conformist, with a world-view built on unexamined platitudes and slogans. But on that trip, with barely a word exchanged, I could feel his disappointment being transmuted into a kind of fierce, protective, defiant love, and I grew ashamed of my own lack of respect for him. I let the Leu-enkephalin convince me that, once this was over, everything between us would change for the better.

From the street, the Gold Coast Health Palace could have passed for one more high-rise beachfront hotel—and even from the inside, it wasn't much different from the hotels I'd seen in video fiction. I had a room to myself, with a television wider than the bed, complete with network computer and cable modem. If the aim was to distract me, it worked. After a week of tests, they hooked a drip into my ventricular shunt and infused first the virus, and then three days later, the drug.

The tumour began shrinking almost immediately; they showed me the scans. My parents seemed happy but dazed, as if they'd never quite trusted a place where millionaire property-developers came for scrotal tucks to do much more than relieve them of their money and offer first-class double-talk while I continued to decline. But the tumour kept on shrinking, and when it hesitated for two days in a row the oncologist swiftly repeated the whole procedure, and then the tendrils and blobs on the MRI screen grew skinnier and fainter even more rapidly than before.

I had every reason to feel unconditional joy now, but when I suffered a growing sense of unease instead I assumed it was just Leu-enkephalin withdrawal. It was even possible that the tumour had been releasing such a high dose of the stuff that literally nothing could have made me *feel better*—if I'd been lofted to the pinnacle of happiness, there'd be nowhere left to go but down. But in that case, any chink of darkness in my sunny disposition could only confirm the good news of the scans.

One morning I woke from a nightmare—my first in months—with visions of the tumour as a clawed parasite thrashing around inside my skull. I could still hear the click of carapace on bone, like the rattle of a scorpion trapped in a jam jar. I was terrified, drenched in sweat . . . *liberated*. My fear soon gave way to a white-hot rage: the thing had drugged me into compliance, but now I was free to stand up to it, to bellow obscenities inside my head, to exorcize the demon with self-righteous anger.

I did feel slightly cheated by the sense of anticlimax that came from chasing my already-fleeing nemesis downhill, and I couldn't entirely ignore the fact that imagining my anger to be driving out the cancer was a complete reversal of true cause and effect—a bit like watching a forklift shift a boulder from my chest, then pretending to have moved it myself by a mighty act of inhalation. But I made what sense I could of my belated emotions, and left it at that.

Six weeks after I was admitted, all my scans were clear, and my blood, CSF and lymphatic fluid were free of the signature proteins of metastasizing cells. But there was still a risk that a few resistant tumour cells remained, so they gave me a short, sharp course of entirely different drugs, no longer linked to the herpes infection. I had a testicular biopsy first—under local anaesthetic, more embarrassing than painful—and a sample of bone marrow taken from my hip, so my potential for sperm production and my supply of new blood cells could both be restored if the drugs wiped them out at the source. I lost hair and stomach lining, temporarily, and I vomited more often, and far more wretchedly, than when I'd first been diagnosed. But when I started to emit self-pitying noises, one of the nurses steelily explained that children half my age put up with the same treatment for months.

These conventional drugs alone could never have cured me, but as a mopping-up operation they greatly diminished the chance of a relapse. I discovered a beautiful word: *apoptosis*—cellular suicide, programmed death—and repeated it to myself, over and over. I ended up almost relishing the nausea and fatigue; the more miserable I felt, the easier it was to imagine the fate of the tumour cells, membranes popping and shrivelling like balloons as the drugs commanded them to take their own lives. *Die in pain, zombie scum!* Maybe I'd write a game about it, or even a whole series, culminating in the spectacular *Chemotherapy III: Battle for the Brain*. I'd be rich and famous, I could pay back my parents, and life would be as perfect in reality as the tumour had merely made it seem to be.

I was discharged early in December, free of any trace of disease. My parents were wary and jubilant in turn, as if slowly casting off the fear that any premature optimism would be punished. The side-effects of the chemotherapy were gone; my hair was growing back, except for a tiny bald patch where the shunt had been, and I had no trouble keeping down food. There was no point returning to school now, two weeks before the year's end, so my summer holidays began immediately. The whole class sent me a tacky, insincere, teacher-orchestrated get-well e-mail, but my friends visited me at home, only slightly embarrassed and intimidated, to welcome me back from the brink of death.

So why did I feel so bad? Why did the sight of the clear blue sky through the window when I opened my eyes every morning—with the freedom to sleep-in as long as I chose, with my father or mother home all day treating me like royalty, but keeping their distance and letting me sit unnagged at the computer screen for 16 hours if I wanted—why did that first glimpse of daylight make me want to bury my face in the pillow, clench my teeth and whisper: *"I should have died, I should have died"*?

Nothing gave me the slightest pleasure. Nothing—not my favourite netzines or web sites, not the *njari* music I'd once revelled in, not the richest, the sweetest, the saltiest junk food that was mine now for the asking. I couldn't bring myself to read a whole page of any book, I couldn't write ten lines of code. I couldn't look my real-world friends in the eye, or face the thought of going online.

Everything I did, everything I imagined, was tainted with an overwhelming sense of dread and shame. The only image I could summon up for comparison was from a documentary about Auschwitz that I'd seen at school. It had opened with a long tracking shot, a newsreel camera advancing relentlessly towards the gates of the camp, and I'd watched that scene with my spirits sinking, already knowing full well what had happened inside. I wasn't delusional; I didn't believe for a moment that there was some source of unspeakable evil lurking behind every bright surface around me. But when I woke and saw the sky, I felt the kind of sick foreboding that would only have made sense if I'd been staring at the gates of Auschwitz.

Maybe I was afraid that the tumour would grow back, but not *that* afraid. The swift victory of the virus in the first round should have counted for much more, and on one level I did think of myself as lucky, and suitably grateful. But I could no more rejoice in my escape, now, than I could have felt suicidally bad at the height of my enkephalin bliss.

My parents began to worry, and dragged me along to a psychologist for "recovery counselling." The whole idea seemed as tainted as everything else, but I lacked the energy for resistance. Dr. Bright and I "explored the possibility" that I was subconsciously choosing to feel miserable because I'd learnt to associate happiness with the risk of death, and I secretly feared that re-creating the tumour's main symptom could resurrect the thing itself. Part of me scorned this facile explanation, but part of me seized on it, hoping that if I owned up to such subterranean mental gymnastics it would drag the whole process into the light of day, where its flawed logic would become untenable. But the sadness and disgust that everything induced in me—birdsong, the pattern of our bathroom tiles, the smell of toast, the shape of my own hands—only increased.

I wondered if the high levels of Leu-enkephalin from the tumour might have caused my neurons to reduce their population of the corresponding receptors, or if I'd become "Leu-enkephalin-tolerant" the way a heroin addict became opiate-tolerant, through the production of a natural regulatory molecule that blocked the receptors. When I mentioned these ideas to my father, he insisted that I discuss them with Dr. Bright, who feigned intense interest but did nothing to show that he'd taken me seriously. He kept telling my parents that everything I was feeling was a perfectly normal reaction to the trauma I'd been through, and that all I really needed was time, and patience, and understanding.

I was bundled off to high school at the start of the new year, but when I did nothing but sit and stare at my desk for a week, arrangements were made for me to study online. At home, I did manage to work my way slowly through the curriculum, in the stretches of zombie-like numbness that came between the bouts of sheer, paralysing unhappiness. In the same periods of relative clarity, I kept thinking about the possible causes of my affliction. I searched the biomedical literature and found a study of the effects of high doses of Leu-enkephalin in cats, but it seemed to show that any tolerance would be short-lived.

Then, one afternoon in March—staring at an electron micrograph of a tumour cell infected with herpes virus, when I should have been studying dead explorers—I finally came up with a theory that made sense. The virus needed special proteins to let it dock with the cells it infected, enabling it to stick to them long enough to use other tools to penetrate the cell membrane. But if it had acquired a copy of the Leu-enkephalin gene from the tumour's own copious RNA transcripts, it might have gained the ability to cling, not just to replicating tumour cells, but to every neuron in my brain with a Leu-enkephalin receptor.

And then the cytotoxic drug, activated only in infected cells, would have come along and killed them all.

Deprived of any input, the pathways those dead neurons normally stimulated were withering away. Every part of my brain able to feel pleasure was dying. And though at times I could, still, simply feel nothing, mood was a shifting balance of forces. With nothing to counteract it, the slightest flicker of depression could now win every tug-of-war, unopposed.

I didn't say a word to my parents; I couldn't bear to tell them that the battle they'd fought to give me the best possible chance of survival might now be crippling me. I tried to contact the oncologist who'd treated me on the Gold Coast, but my phone calls floundered in a Muzak-filled moat of automated screening, and my e-mail was ignored. I managed to see Dr. Ash alone, and she listened politely to my theory, but she declined to refer me to a neurologist when my only symptoms were psychological: blood and urine tests showed none of the standard markers for clinical depression.

The windows of clarity grew shorter. I found myself spending more and more of each day in bed, staring out across the darkened room. My despair was so monotonous, and so utterly disconnected from anything real, that to some degree it was blunted by its own absurdity: no one I loved had just been slaughtered, the cancer had almost certainly been defeated, and I could still grasp the difference between what I was feeling and the unarguable logic of real grief, or real fear.

But I had no way of casting off the gloom and feeling what I wanted to feel. My only freedom came down to a choice between hunting for reasons to justify my sadness—deluding myself that it was my own, perfectly natural response to some contrived litany of misfortunes—or disowning it as something alien, imposed from without, trapping me inside an emotional shell as useless and unresponsive as a paralysed body.

My father never accused me of weakness and ingratitude; he just silently withdrew from my life. My mother kept trying to get through to me, to comfort or provoke me, but it reached the point where I could barely squeeze her hand in reply. I wasn't literally paralysed or blind, speechless or feeble-minded. But all the brightly lit worlds I'd once inhabited—physical and virtual, real and imaginary, intellectual and emotional—had become invisible, and impenetrable. Buried in fog. Buried in shit. Buried in ashes.

By the time I was admitted to a neurological ward, the dead regions of my brain were clearly visible on an MRI scan. But it was unlikely that anything could have halted the process even if it had been diagnosed sooner.

And it was certain that no one had the power to reach into my skull and restore the machinery of happiness.

TWO

The alarm woke me at ten, but it took me another three hours to summon up the energy to move. I threw off the sheet and sat on the side of the bed, muttering half-hearted obscenities, trying to get past the inescapable conclusion that I shouldn't have bothered. Whatever pinnacles of achievement I scaled today (managing not only to go shopping, but to buy something other than a frozen meal) and whatever monumental good fortune befell me (the insurance company depositing my allowance before the rent was due) I'd wake up tomorrow feeling exactly the same.

Nothing helps, nothing changes. Four words said it all. But I'd accepted that long ago; there was nothing left to be disappointed about. And I had no reason to sit here lamenting the bleeding obvious for the thousandth time.

Right?

Fuck it. Just keep moving.

I swallowed my "morning" medication, the six capsules I'd put out on the bedside table the night before, then went into the bathroom and urinated a bright yellow stream consisting mainly of the last dose's metabolites. No antidepressant in the world could send me to Prozac Heaven, but this shit kept my dopamine and serotonin levels high enough to rescue me from total catatonia—from liquid food, bedpans and sponge baths.

I splashed water on my face, trying to think of an excuse to leave the flat when the freezer was still half full. Staying in all day, unwashed and unshaven, did make me feel worse: slimy and lethargic, like some pale parasitic leech. But it could still take a week or more for the pressure of disgust to grow strong enough to move me.

I stared into the mirror. Lack of appetite more than made up for lack of exercise—I was as immune to carbohydrate comfort as I was to runner's high—and I could count my ribs beneath the loose skin of my chest. I was 30 years old, and I looked like a wasted old man. I pressed my forehead against the cool glass, obeying some vestigial instinct which suggested that there might be a scrap of pleasure to be extracted from the sensation. There wasn't.

In the kitchen, I saw the light on the phone: there was a message waiting. I walked back into the bathroom and sat on the floor, trying to convince myself that it didn't have to be bad news. No one had to be dead. And my parents couldn't break up twice.

I approached the phone and waved the display on. There was a thumbnail image of a severe-looking middle-aged woman, no one I recognized. The sender's name was Dr. Z. Durrani, Department of Biomedical Engineering, University of Cape Town. The subject line read: "New Techniques in Prosthetic Reconstructive Neuroplasty." That made a change; most people skimmed the reports on my clinical condition so carelessly that they assumed I was mildly retarded. I felt a refreshing absence of disgust, the closest I could come to respect, for Dr. Durrani. But no amount of diligence on her part could save the cure itself from being a mirage.

Health Palace's no-fault settlement provided me with a living allowance equal to the minimum wage, plus reimbursement of approved medical costs; I had no astronomical lump sum to spend as I saw fit. However, any treatment likely to render me financially self-sufficient could be paid for in full, at the discretion of the insurance company. The value of such a cure to Global Assurance—the total remaining cost of supporting me until death—was constantly falling, but then so was medical research funding, worldwide. Word of my case had got around.

Most of the treatments I'd been offered so far had involved novel pharmaceuticals. Drugs *had* freed me from institutional care, but expecting them to turn me into a happy little wage-earner was like hoping for an ointment that made amputated limbs grow back. From Global Assurance's perspective, though, shelling out for anything more sophisticated meant gambling with a much greater sum—a prospect that no doubt sent my case manager scrambling for his actuarial database. There was no point indulging in rash expenditure decisions when there was still a good chance that I'd suicide in my 40s. Cheap fixes were always worth a try, even if they were long shots, but any proposal radical enough to stand a real chance of working was guaranteed to fail the risk/cost analysis.

I knelt by the screen with my head in my hands. I could erase the message unseen, sparing myself the frustration of knowing exactly what I'd be missing out on . . . but then, not knowing would be just as bad. I tapped the PLAY button and looked away; meeting the gaze of even a recorded face gave me a feeling of intense shame. I understood why: the neural circuitry needed to register positive non-verbal messages was long gone, but the pathways that warned of responses like rejection and hostility had not merely remained intact, they'd grown skewed and hypersensitive enough to fill the void with a strong negative signal, whatever the reality.

I listened as carefully as I could while Dr. Durrani explained her work with stroke patients. Tissue-cultured neural grafts were the current standard treatment, but she'd been injecting an elaborately tailored polymer foam into the damaged region instead. The foam released growth factors that attracted axons and dendrites from surrounding neurons, and the polymer itself was designed to function as a network of electrochemical switches. Via microprocessors scattered throughout the foam, the initially amorphous network was programmed first to reproduce generically the actions of the lost neurons, then fine-tuned for compatibility with the individual recipient.

Dr. Durrani listed her triumphs: sight restored, speech restored, movement, continence, musical ability. My own deficit—measured in neurons lost, or synapses, or raw cubic centimetres—lay beyond the range of all the chasms she'd bridged to date. But that only made it more of a challenge.

I waited almost stoically for the one small catch, in six or seven figures. The voice from the screen said, "If you can meet your own travel expenses and the cost of a three-week hospital stay, my research grant will cover the treatment itself."

I replayed these words a dozen times, trying to find a less favourable interpretation—one task I was usually good at. When I failed, I steeled myself and e-mailed Durrani's assistant in Cape Town, asking for clarification.

There was no misunderstanding. For the cost of a year's supply of the drugs that barely kept me conscious, I was being offered a chance to be whole again for the rest of my life.

Organizing a trip to South Africa was completely beyond me, but once Global Assurance recognized the opportunity it was facing, machinery on two continents swung into action on my behalf. All I had to do was fight down the urge to call everything off. The thought of being hospitalized, of being powerless again, was disturbing enough, but contemplating the potential of the neural prosthesis itself was like staring down the calendar at a secular Judgment Day. On 7th March 2023, either I'd be admitted into an infinitely larger, infinitely richer, infinitely better world . . . or I'd prove to be damaged beyond repair. And in a way, even the final death of hope was a far less terrifying prospect than the alternative; it was so much closer to where I was already, so much easier to imagine. The only vision of *happiness* I could summon up was myself as a child, running joyfully, dissolving into sunlight—which was all very sweet and evocative, but a little short on practical details. If I'd wanted to be a sunbeam, I could have cut my wrists anytime. I wanted a job, I wanted a family, I wanted ordinary love and modest ambitions—because I knew these were the things I'd been denied. But I could no more imagine what it would be like, finally, to attain them, than I could picture daily life in 26-dimensional space.

I didn't sleep at all before the dawn flight out of Sydney. I was escorted to the airport by a psychiatric nurse, but spared the indignity of a minder sitting beside me all the way to Cape Town. I spent my waking moments on the flight fighting paranoia, resisting the temptation to invent reasons for all the sadness and anxiety coursing through my skull. *No one on the plane was staring at me disdainfully. The Durrani technique was not going to turn out to be a hoax.* I succeeded in crushing these "explanatory" delusions . . . but as ever, it remained beyond my power to alter my feelings, or even to draw a clear line between my purely pathological unhappiness and the perfectly reasonable anxiety that anyone would feel on the verge of radical brain surgery.

Wouldn't it be bliss, not to have to fight to tell the difference all the time? Forget happiness; even a future full of abject misery would be a triumph, so long as I knew that it was always for a reason.

· · ·

Luke De Vries, one of Durrani's postdoctoral students, met me at the airport. He looked about 25, and radiated the kind of self-assurance I had to struggle not to misread as contempt. I felt trapped and helpless immediately; he'd arranged everything, it was like stepping on to a conveyor belt. But I knew that if I'd been left to do anything for myself the whole process would have ground to a halt.

It was after midnight when we reached the hospital in the suburbs of Cape Town. Crossing the car park, the insect sounds were wrong, the air smelt indefinably alien, the constellations looked like clever forgeries. I sagged to my knees as we approached the entrance.

"Hey!" De Vries stopped and helped me up. I was shaking with fear, and then shame too, at the spectacle I was making of myself.

"This violates my Avoidance Therapy."

"Avoidance Therapy?"

"Avoid hospitals at all costs."

De Vries laughed, though if he wasn't merely humouring me I had no way of telling. Recognizing the fact that you'd elicited genuine laughter was a pleasure, so those pathways were all dead.

He said, "We had to carry the last subject in on a stretcher. She left about as steady on her feet as you are."

"That bad?"

"Her artificial hip was playing up. Not our fault."

We walked up the steps and into the brightly lit foyer.

The next morning—Monday, 6th March, the day before the operation—I met most of the surgical team who'd perform the first, purely mechanical, part of the procedure: scraping clean the useless cavities left behind by dead neurons, prising open with tiny balloons any voids that had been squeezed shut, and then pumping the whole oddly shaped totality full of Durrani's foam. Apart from the existing hole in my skull from the shunt 18 years before, they'd probably have to drill two more.

A nurse shaved my head and glued five reference markers to the exposed skin, then I spent the afternoon being scanned. The final, three-dimensional image of all the dead space in my brain looked like a spelunker's map, a sequence of linked caves complete with rockfalls and collapsed tunnels.

Durrani herself came to see me that evening. "While you're still under anaesthetic," she explained, "the foam will harden, and the first connections will be made with the surrounding tissue. Then the microprocessors will instruct the polymer to form the network we've chosen to serve as a starting point."

I had to force myself to speak; every question I asked—however politely phrased, however lucid and relevant—felt as painful and degrading as if I was standing before her naked asking her to wipe shit out of my hair. "How did you find a network to use? Did you scan a volunteer?" Was I going to start my new life as a clone of Luke De Vries—inheriting his tastes, his ambitions, his emotions?

"No, no. There's an international database of healthy neural structures—20,000 cadavers who died without brain injury. More detailed than tomography; they froze the brains in liquid nitrogen, sliced them up with a diamond-tipped microtome, then stained and electron-micrographed the slices."

My mind balked at the number of exabytes she was casually invoking; I'd lost touch with computing completely. "So you'll use some kind of composite from the database? You'll give me a selection of typical structures, taken from different people?"

Durrani seemed about to let that pass as near enough, but she was clearly a stickler for detail, and she hadn't insulted my intelligence yet. "Not quite. It will be more like a multiple exposure than a composite. We've used about 4,000 records from the database—all the males in their 20s or 30s—and wherever someone has neuron A wired to neuron B, and someone else has neuron A wired to neuron C . . . you'll have connections to both B *and* C. So you'll start out with a network that in theory could be pared down to any one of the 4,000 individual versions used to construct it—but in fact, you'll pare it down to your own unique version instead."

That sounded better than being an emotional clone or a Frankenstein collage; I'd be a roughly hewn sculpture, with features yet to be refined. But—

"Pare it down how? How will I go from being potentially anyone, to being . . . ?" *What?* My 12-year-old self, resurrected? Or the 30-year-old I should have been, conjured into existence as a remix of these 4,000 dead strangers? I trailed off; I'd lost what little faith I'd had that I was talking sense.

Durrani seemed to grow slightly uneasy, herself—whatever my judgment was worth on that. She said, "There should be parts of your brain, still intact, which bear some record of what's been lost. Memories of formative experiences, memories of the things that used to give you pleasure, fragments of innate structures that survived the virus. The prosthesis will be driven automatically towards a state that's compatible with everything else in your brain—it will find itself interacting with all these other systems, and the connections that work best in that context will be reinforced." She thought for a moment. "Imagine a kind of artificial limb, imperfectly formed to start with, that adjusts itself as you use it: stretching when it fails to grasp what you reach for, shrinking when it bumps something unexpectedly . . . until it takes on precisely the size and shape of the phantom limb implied by your movements. Which itself is nothing but an image of the lost flesh and blood."

That was an appealing metaphor, though it was hard to believe that my faded memories contained enough information to reconstruct their phantom author in every detail—that the whole jigsaw of who I'd been, and might have become, could be filled in from a few hints along the edges and the jumbled-up pieces of 4,000 other portraits of happiness. But the subject was making at least one of us uncomfortable, so I didn't press the point.

I managed to ask a final question. "What will it be like, before any of this happens? When I wake up from the anaesthetic and all the connections are still intact?"

Durrani confessed, "That's one thing I'll have no way of knowing, until you tell me yourself."

Someone repeated my name, reassuringly but insistently. I woke a little more. My neck, my legs, my back were all aching, and my stomach was tense with nausea.

But the bed was warm, and the sheets were soft. It was good just to be lying there.

"It's Wednesday afternoon. The operation went well."

I opened my eyes. Durrani and four of her students were gathered at the foot of the bed. I stared at her, astonished: the face I'd once thought of as "severe" and "forbidding" was . . . riveting, magnetic. I could have watched her for hours. But then I glanced at Luke De Vries, who was standing beside her. He was just as extraordinary. I turned one by one to the other three students. Everyone was equally mesmerizing; I didn't know where to look.

"How are you feeling?"

I was lost for words. These people's faces were loaded with so much significance, so many sources of fascination, that I had no way of singling out any one factor: they all appeared wise, ecstatic, beautiful, reflective, attentive, compassionate, tranquil, vibrant . . . a white noise of qualities, all positive, but ultimately incoherent.

But as I shifted my gaze compulsively from face to face, struggling to make sense of them, their meanings finally began to crystallize—like words coming into focus, though my sight had never been blurred.

I asked Durrani, "Are you smiling?"

"Slightly." She hesitated. "There are standard tests, standard images for this, but . . . please, describe my expression. Tell me what I'm thinking."

I answered unselfconsciously, as if she'd asked me to read an eye chart. "You're . . . curious? You're listening carefully. You're interested, and you're . . . hoping that something good will happen. And you're smiling because you think it will. Or because you can't quite believe that it already has."

She nodded, smiling more decisively. "Good."

I didn't add that I now found her stunningly, almost painfully, beautiful. But it was the same for everyone in the room, male and female: the haze of contradictory moods that I'd read into their faces had cleared, but it had left behind a heart-stopping radiance. I found this slightly alarming—it was too indiscriminate, too intense—though in a way it seemed almost as natural a response as the dazzling of a dark-adapted eye. And after 18 years of seeing nothing but ugliness in every human face, I wasn't ready to complain about the presence of five people who looked like angels.

Durrani asked, "Are you hungry?"

I had to think about that. "Yes."

One of the students fetched a prepared meal, much the same as the lunch I'd eaten on Monday: salad, a bread roll, cheese. I picked up the roll and took a bite. The texture was perfectly familiar, the flavour unchanged. Two days before, I'd chewed and swallowed the same thing with the usual mild disgust that all food induced in me.

Hot tears rolled down my cheeks. I wasn't in ecstasy; the experience was as strange and painful as drinking from a fountain with lips so parched that the skin had turned to salt and dried blood.

As painful, and as compelling. When I'd emptied the plate, I asked for another. *Eating was good, eating was right, eating was necessary.* After the third plate, Durrani said firmly, "That's enough." I was shaking with the need for more; she was still supernaturally beautiful, but I screamed at her, outraged.

She took my arms, held me still. "This is going to be hard for you. There'll be surges like this, swings in all directions, until the network settles down. You have to try to stay calm, try to stay reflective. The prosthesis makes more things possible than you're used to . . . but you're still in control."

I gritted my teeth and looked away. At her touch I'd suffered an immediate, agonizing erection.

I said, "That's right. I'm in control."

In the days that followed, my experiences with the prosthesis became much less raw, much less violent. I could almost picture the sharpest, most ill-fitting edges of the network being—metaphorically—worn smooth by use. To eat, to sleep, to be with people remained intensely pleasurable, but it was more like an impossibly rosy-hued dream of childhood than the result of someone poking my brain with a high voltage wire.

Of course, the prosthesis wasn't sending signals into my brain in order to make my brain feel pleasure. *The prosthesis itself* was the part of me that was feeling all the pleasure—however seamlessly that process was integrated with everything else: perception, language, cognition . . . the rest of me. Dwelling on this was unsettling at first, but on reflection no more so than the thought experiment of staining blue all the corresponding organic regions in a healthy brain, and declaring, *"They* feel all the pleasure, not you!"

I was put through a battery of psychological tests—most of which I'd sat through many times before, as part of my annual insurance assessments—as Durrani's team attempted to quantify their success. Maybe a stroke patient's fine control of a formerly paralysed hand was easier to measure objectively, but I must have leapt from bottom to top of every numerical scale for positive affect. And far from being a source of irritation, these tests gave me my first opportunity to use the prosthesis in new arenas—to be happy in ways I could barely remember experiencing before. As well as being required to interpret mundanely rendered scenes of domestic situations—what has just happened between this child, this woman, and this man; who is feeling good and who is feeling bad?—I was shown breathtaking images of great works of art, from complex allegorical and narrative paintings to elegant minimalist essays in geometry. As well as listening to snatches of everyday speech, and even unadorned cries of joy and pain, I was played samples of music and song from every tradition, every epoch, every style.

That was when I finally realized that something was wrong.

Jacob Tsela was playing the audio files and noting my responses. He'd been deadpan for most of the session, carefully avoiding any risk of corrupting the data by betraying his own opinions. But after he'd played a heavenly fragment of European classical music, and I'd rated it 20 out of 20, I caught a flicker of dismay on his face.

"What? You didn't like it?"

Tsela smiled opaquely. "It doesn't matter what I like. That's not what we're measuring."

"I've rated it already, you can't influence my score." I regarded him imploringly; I was desperate for communication of any kind. "I've been dead to the world for 18 years. I don't even know who the composer was."

He hesitated. "J. S. Bach. And I agree with you: it's sublime." He reached for the touchscreen and continued the experiment.

So what had he been dismayed about? I knew the answer immediately; I'd been an idiot not to notice before, but I'd been too absorbed in the music itself.

I hadn't scored any piece lower than 18. And it had been the same with the visual arts. From my 4,000 virtual donors I'd inherited, not the lowest common denominator, but the widest possible taste—and in ten days, I still hadn't imposed any constraints, any preferences, of my own.

All art was sublime to me, and all music. Every kind of food was delicious. Everyone I laid eyes on was a vision of perfection.

Maybe I was just soaking up pleasure wherever I could get it, after my long drought, but it was only a matter of time before I grew sated, and became as discriminating, as focused, as *particular*, as everyone else.

"Should I still be like this? *Omnivorous?*" I blurted out the question, starting with a tone of mild curiosity, ending with an edge of panic.

Tsela halted the sample he'd been playing—a chant that might have been Albanian, Moroccan, or Mongolian for all I knew, but which made hair rise on the back of my neck, and sent my spirits soaring. Just like everything else had.

He was silent for a while, weighing up competing obligations. Then he sighed and said, "You'd better talk to Durrani."

Durrani showed me a bar graph on the wallscreen in her office: the number of artificial synapses that had changed state within the prosthesis—new connections formed, existing ones broken, weakened or strengthened—for each of the past ten days. The embedded microprocessors kept track of such things, and an antenna waved over my skull each morning collected the data.

Day one had been dramatic, as the prosthesis adapted to its environment; the 4,000 contributing networks might all have been perfectly stable in their owners' skulls, but the Everyman version I'd been given had never been wired up to anyone's brain before.

Day two had seen about half as much activity, day three about a tenth.

From day four on, though, there'd been nothing but background noise. My episodic memories, however pleasurable, were apparently being stored elsewhere—since I certainly wasn't suffering from amnesia—but after the initial burst of activity, the circuitry for defining what pleasure *was* had undergone no change, no refinement at all.

"If any trends emerge in the next few days, we should be able to amplify them, push them forward—like toppling an unstable building, once it's showing signs of falling in a certain direction." Durrani didn't sound hopeful. Too much time had passed already, and the network wasn't even teetering.

I said, "What about genetic factors? Can't you read my genome, and narrow things down from that?"

She shook her head. "At least 2,000 genes play a role in neural development. It's not like matching a blood group or a tissue type; everyone in the database would have more or less the same small proportion of those genes in common with you. Of course, some people must have been closer to you in temperament than others—but we have no way of identifying them genetically."

"I see."

Durrani said carefully, "We could shut the prosthesis down completely, if that's what you want. There'd be no need for surgery—we'd just turn it off, and you'd be back where you started."

I stared at her luminous face. *How could I go back?* Whatever the tests and the bar graphs said . . . *how could this be failure?* However much useless beauty I was drowning in, I wasn't as screwed-up as I'd been with a head full of Leu-enkephalin. I was still capable of fear, anxiety, sorrow; the tests had revealed universal shadows, common to all the donors. Hating Bach or Chuck Berry, Chagall or Paul Klee was beyond me, but I'd reacted as sanely as anyone to images of disease, starvation, death.

And I was not oblivious to my own fate, the way I'd been oblivious to the cancer.

But what was my fate, if I kept using the prosthesis? Universal happiness, universal shadows . . . half the human race dictating my emotions? In all the years I'd spent in darkness, if I'd held fast to anything, hadn't it been the possibility that I carried a kind of seed within me: a version of myself that might grow into a living person again, given the chance? *And hadn't that hope now proved false?* I'd been offered the stuff of which selves were made—and though I'd tested it all, and admired it all, I'd claimed none of it as my own. All the joy I'd felt in the last ten days had been meaningless. I was just a dead husk, blowing around in other people's sunlight.

I said, "I think you should do that. Switch it off."

Durrani held up her hand. "Wait. If you're willing, there is one other thing we could try. I've been discussing it with our ethics committee, and Luke has begun preliminary work on the software . . . but in the end, it will be your decision."

"To do what?"

"The network can be pushed in any direction. We know how to intervene to do that—to break the symmetry, to make some things a greater source of pleasure than others. Just because it hasn't happened spontaneously, that doesn't mean it can't be achieved by other means."

I laughed, suddenly light-headed. "So if I say the word . . . *your ethics committee* will choose the music I like, and my favourite foods, and my new vocation? They'll decide who I become?" Would that be so bad? Having died, myself, long ago, to grant life now to a whole new person? To donate, not just a lung or a kidney, but my entire body, irrelevant memories and all, to an arbitrarily constructed—but fully functioning—*de novo* human being?

Durrani was scandalized. "No! We'd never dream of doing that! But we could program the microprocessors to let *you* control the network's refinement. We could give you the power to choose for yourself, consciously and deliberately, the things that make you happy."

De Vries said, "Try to picture the control."

I closed my eyes. He said, "Bad idea. If you get into the habit, it will limit your access."

"Right." I stared into space. Something glorious by Beethoven was playing on the lab's sound system; it was difficult to concentrate. I struggled to visualize the stylized, cherry-red, horizontal slider control that De Vries had constructed, line by line, inside my head five minutes before. Suddenly it was more than a vague memory: it was superimposed over the room again, as clear as any real object, at the bottom of my visual field.

"I've got it." The button was hovering around 19.

De Vries glanced at a display, hidden from me. "Good. Now try to lower the rating."

I laughed weakly. *Roll over Beethoven*. "How? How can you try to like something less?"

"You don't. Just try to move the button to the left. Visualize the movement. The software's monitoring your visual cortex, tracking any fleeting imaginary perceptions. Fool yourself into seeing the button moving—and the image will oblige."

It did. I kept losing control briefly, as if the thing was sticking, but I managed to manoeuvre it down to 10 before stopping to assess the effect.

"Fuck."

"I take it it's working?"

I nodded stupidly. The music was still . . . *pleasant* . . . but the spell was broken completely. It was like listening to an electrifying piece of rhetoric, then realizing half-way through that the speaker didn't believe a word of it—leaving the original poetry and eloquence untouched, but robbing it of all its real force.

I felt sweat break out on my forehead. When Durrani had explained it, the whole scheme had sounded too bizarre to be real. And since I'd already failed to assert myself over the prosthesis—despite billions of direct neural connections, and countless opportunities for the remnants of my identity to interact with the thing and shape it in my own image—I'd feared that when the time came to make a choice, I'd be paralysed by indecision.

But I knew, beyond doubt, that I should *not* have been in a state of rapture over a piece of classical music that I'd either never heard before, or—since apparently it was famous, and ubiquitous—sat through once or twice by accident, entirely unmoved.

And now, in a matter of seconds, I'd hacked that false response away.

There was still hope. I still had a chance to resurrect myself. I'd just have to do it consciously, every step of the way.

De Vries, tinkering with his keyboard, said cheerfully, "I'll colour-code virtual gadgets for all the major systems in the prosthesis. With a few days' practice it'll all be second nature. Just remember that some experiences will engage two or three systems at once . . . so if you're making love to music that you'd prefer not to find so distracting, make sure you turn down the red control, not the blue." He looked up and saw my face. "Hey, don't worry. You can always turn it up again later if you make a mistake. Or if you change your mind."

THREE

It was nine P.M. in Sydney when the plane touched down. Nine o'clock on a Saturday night. I took a train into the city centre, intending to catch the connecting one home, but when I saw the crowds alighting at Town Hall station I put my suitcase in a locker and followed them up on to the street.

I'd been in the city a few times since the virus, but never at night. I felt as if I'd come home after half a lifetime in another country, after solitary confinement in a foreign gaol. Everything was disorienting, one way or another. I felt a kind of giddy *déjà vu* at the sight of buildings that seemed to have been faithfully preserved, but still weren't quite as I remembered them, and a sense of hollowness each time I turned a corner to find that some private landmark, some shop or sign I remembered from childhood, had vanished.

I stood outside a pub, close enough to feel my eardrums throb to the beat of the music. I could see people inside, laughing and dancing, sloshing armfuls of drinks around, faces glowing with alcohol and companionship. Some alive with the possibility of violence, others with the promise of sex.

I could step right into this picture myself, now. The ash that had buried the world was gone; I was free to walk wherever I pleased. And I could almost feel the dead cousins of these revellers—re-born now as harmonics of the network, resonating to the music and the sight of their soul-mates—clamouring in my skull, begging me to carry them all the way to the land of the living.

I took a few steps forward, then something in the corner of my vision distracted me. In the alley beside the pub, a boy of 10 or 12 sat crouched against the wall, lowering his face into a plastic bag. After a few inhalations he looked up, dead eyes shining, smiling as blissfully as any orchestra conductor.

I backed away.

Someone touched my shoulder. I spun around and saw a man beaming at me.

"Jesus loves you, brother! Your search is over!" He thrust a pamphlet into my hand. I gazed into his face, and his condition was transparent to me: he'd stumbled on a way to produce Leu-enkephalin at will—but he didn't know it, so he'd reasoned that some divine wellspring of happiness was responsible. I felt my chest tighten with horror and pity. At least I'd known about my tumour. And even the fucked-up kid in the alley understood that he was just sniffing glue.

And the people in the pub? Did they know what they were doing? Music, companionship, alcohol, sex . . . where did the border lie? When did justifiable happiness turn into something as empty, as pathological, as it was for this man?

I stumbled away, and headed back towards the station. All around me, people were laughing and shouting, holding hands, kissing . . . and I watched them as if they were flayed anatomical figures, revealing a thousand interlocking muscles working together with effortless precision. Buried inside me, the machinery of happiness recognized itself, again and again.

I had no doubt, now, that Durrani really had packed every last shred of the human capacity for joy into my skull. But to claim any part of it, I'd have to swallow the fact—more deeply than the tumour had ever forced me to swallow it—that happiness itself meant nothing. Life without it was unbearable, but as an end in itself, it was not enough. I was free to choose its causes—and to be happy with my choices—but whatever I felt once I'd bootstrapped my new self into existence, the possibility would remain that all my choices had been wrong.

Global Assurance had given me until the end of the year to get my act together. If my annual psychological assessment showed that Durrani's treatment had been successful—whether or not I actually had a job—I'd be thrown to the even less tender mercies of the privatized remnants of social security. So I stumbled around in the light, trying to find my bearings.

On my first day back I woke at dawn. I sat down at the phone and started digging. My old net workspace had been archived; at current rates it was only costing about ten cents a year in storage fees, and I still had $36.20 credit in my account. The whole bizarre informational fossil had passed intact from company to company through four takeovers and mergers. Working through an assortment of tools to decode the obsolete data formats, I dragged fragments of my past life into the present and examined them, until it became too painful to go on.

The next day I spent 12 hours cleaning the flat, scrubbing every corner—listening to my old *njari* downloads, stopping only to eat, ravenously. And though I could have refined my taste in food back to that of a 12-year-old salt-junky, I made the choice—thoroughly un-masochistic, and more pragmatic than virtuous—to crave nothing more toxic than fruit.

In the following weeks I put on weight with gratifying speed, though when I stared at myself in the mirror, or used morphing software running on the phone, I realized that I could be happy with almost any kind of body. The database must have included people with a vast range of ideal self-images, or who'd died perfectly content with their actual appearances.

Again, I chose pragmatism. I had a lot of catching up to do, and I didn't want to die at 55 from a heart attack if I could avoid it. There was no point fixating on the unattainable or the absurd, though, so after morphing myself to obesity, and rating it zero, I did the same for the Schwarzenegger look. I chose a lean, wiry body—well within the realms of possibility, according to the software—and assigned it 16 out of 20. Then I started running.

I took it slowly at first, and though I clung to the image of myself as a child, darting effortlessly from street to street, I was careful never to crank up the joy of motion high enough to mask injuries. When I limped into a chemist looking for liniment, I found they were selling something called prostaglandin modulators, anti-inflammatory compounds that allegedly minimized damage without shutting down any vital repair processes. I was sceptical, but the stuff did seem to help; the first month was still painful, but I was neither crippled by natural swelling, nor rendered so oblivious to danger signs that I tore a muscle.

And once my heart and lungs and calves were dragged screaming out of their atrophied state, *it was good*. I ran for an hour every morning, weaving around the local back streets, and on Sunday afternoons I circumnavigated the city itself. I didn't push myself to attain ever faster times; I had no athletic ambitions whatsoever. I just wanted to exercise my freedom.

Soon the act of running melted into a kind of seamless whole. I could revel in the thudding of my heart and the feeling of my limbs in motion, or I could let those details recede into a buzz of satisfaction and just watch the scenery, as if from a train. And having reclaimed my body, I began to reclaim the suburbs, one by one. From the slivers of forest clinging to the Lane Cove river to the eternal ugliness of Paramatta Road, I criss-crossed Sydney like a mad surveyor, wrapping the landscape with invisible geodesics then drawing it into my skull. I pounded across the bridges at Gladesville and Iron Cove, Pyrmont, Meadowbank, and the Harbour itself, daring the planks to give way beneath my feet.

I suffered moments of doubt. I wasn't drunk on endorphins—I wasn't pushing myself that hard—but it still felt too good to be true. *Was this glue-sniffing?* Maybe 10,000 generations of my ancestors had been rewarded with the same kind of pleasure for pursuing game, fleeing danger, and mapping their territory for the sake of survival, but to me it was all just a glorious pastime.

Still, I wasn't deceiving myself, and I wasn't hurting anyone. I plucked those two rules from the core of the dead child inside me, and kept on running.

Thirty was an interesting age to go through puberty. The virus hadn't literally castrated me, but having eliminated pleasure from sexual imagery, genital stimulation, and orgasm—and having partly wrecked the hormonal regulatory pathways reaching down from the hypothalamus—it had left me with nothing worth describing as sexual function. My body disposed of semen in sporadic joyless spasms—and without the normal lubricants secreted by the prostate during arousal, every unwanted ejaculation tore at the urethral lining.

When all of this changed, it hit hard—even in my state of relative sexual decrepitude. Compared to wet dreams of broken glass, masturbation was wonderful beyond belief, and I found myself unwilling to intervene with the controls to tone it down. But I needn't have worried that it would rob me of interest in the real thing; I kept finding myself staring openly at people on the street, in shops and on trains, until by a combination of willpower, sheer terror, and prosthetic adjustment I managed to kick the habit.

The network had rendered me bisexual, and though I quickly ramped my level of desire down considerably from that of the database's most priapic contributors, when it came to choosing to be straight or gay, everything turned to quicksand. The network was not some kind of population-weighted average; if it had been, Durrani's original hope that my own surviving neural architecture could hold sway would have been dashed whenever the vote was stacked against it. So I was not just 10 or 15 percent gay; the two possibilities were present with equal force, and the thought of eliminating *either* felt as alarming, as disfiguring, as if I'd lived with both for decades.

But was that just the prosthesis defending itself, or was it partly my own response? I had no idea. I'd been a thoroughly asexual 12-year-old, even before the virus; I'd always assumed that I was straight, and I'd certainly found some girls attractive, but there'd been no moonstruck stares or furtive groping to back up that purely aesthetic opinion. I looked up the latest research, but all the genetic claims I recalled from various headlines had since been discredited—so even if my sexuality had been determined from birth, there was no blood test that could tell me, now, what it would have become. I even tracked down my pre-treatment MRI scans, but they lacked the resolution to provide a direct, neuroanatomical answer.

I didn't want to be bisexual. I was too old to experiment like a teenager; I wanted certainty, I wanted solid foundations. I wanted to be monogamous—and even if monogamy was rarely an effortless state for anyone, that was no reason to lumber myself with unnecessary obstacles. *So who should I slaughter?* I knew which choice would make things easier . . . but if everything came down to a question of which of the 4,000 donors could carry me along the path of least resistance, whose life would I be living?

Maybe it was all a moot point. I was a 30-year-old virgin with a history of mental illness, no money, no prospects, no social skills—and I could always crank up the satisfaction level of my only current option, and let everything else recede into fantasy. I wasn't deceiving myself, I wasn't hurting anyone. It was within my power to want nothing more.

I'd noticed the bookshop, tucked away in a back street in Leichhardt, many times before. But one Sunday in June, when I jogged past and saw a copy of *The Man Without Qualities* by Robert Musil in the front window, I had to stop and laugh.

I was drenched in sweat from the winter humidity, so I didn't go in and buy the book. But I peered in through the display towards the counter, and spotted a HELP WANTED sign.

Looking for unskilled work had seemed futile; the total unemployment rate was 15 percent, the youth rate three times higher, so I'd assumed there'd always be a thousand other applicants for every job: younger, cheaper, stronger, and certifiably sane. But though I'd resumed my on-line education, I was getting not so much nowhere, fast as everywhere, slowly. All the fields of knowledge that had gripped me as a child had expanded a hundredfold, and while the prosthesis granted me limitless energy and enthusiasm, there was still too much ground for anyone to cover in a lifetime. I knew I'd have to sacrifice 90 percent of my interests if I was ever going to choose a career, but I still hadn't been able to wield the knife.

I returned to the bookshop on Monday, walking up from Petersham station. I'd fine-tuned my confidence for the occasion, but it rose spontaneously when I heard that there'd been no other applicants. The owner was in his 60s, and he'd just done his back in; he wanted someone to lug boxes around, and take the counter when he was otherwise occupied. I told him the truth: I'd been neu-rologically damaged by a childhood illness, and I'd only recently recovered.

He hired me on the spot, for a month's trial. The starting wage was exactly what Global Assurance were paying me, but if I was taken on permanently I'd get slightly more.

The work wasn't hard, and the owner didn't mind me reading in the back room when I had nothing to do. In a way, I was in heaven—10,000 books, and no access fees—but sometimes I felt the terror of dissolution returning. I read voraciously, and on one level I could make clear judgments: I could pick the clumsy writers from the skilled, the honest from the fakers, the platitudinous from the inspired. But the prosthesis still wanted me to enjoy everything, to embrace everything, to diffuse out across the dusty shelves until I was no one at all, a ghost in the Library of Babel.

She walked into the bookshop two minutes after opening time, on the first day of spring. Watching her browse, I tried to think clearly through the consequences of what I was about to do. For weeks I'd been on the counter five hours a day, and with all that human contact I'd been hoping for . . . *something*. Not wild, reciprocated love at first sight, just the tiniest flicker of mutual interest, the slightest piece of evidence that I could actually desire one human being more than all the rest.

It hadn't happened. Some customers had flirted mildly, but I could see that it was nothing special, just their own kind of politeness—and I'd felt nothing more in response than if they'd been unusually, formally, courteous. And though I might have agreed with any bystander as to who was conventionally good-looking, who was animated or mysterious, witty or charming, who glowed with youth or radiated worldliness . . . I just didn't care. The 4,000 had all loved very different people, and the envelope that stretched between their far-flung char-acteristics encompassed the entire species. That was never going to change, until I did something to break the symmetry myself.

So for the past week, I'd dragged all the relevant systems in the prosthesis down to three or four. People had become scarcely more interesting to watch than pieces of wood. Now, alone in the shop with this randomly chosen stranger, I slowly turned the controls up. I had to fight against positive feedback; the higher the settings, the more I wanted to increase them, but I'd set limits in advance, and I stuck to them.

By the time she'd chosen two books and approached the counter, I was feeling half defiantly triumphant, half sick with shame. I'd struck a pure note with the network at last; what I felt at the sight of this woman rang true. And if everything I'd done to achieve it was calculated, artificial, bizarre and abhorrent . . . I'd had no other way.

I was smiling as she bought the books, and she smiled back warmly. No wedding or engagement ring—but I'd promised myself that I wouldn't try anything, no matter what. This was just the first step: to notice someone, to make someone stand out from the crowd. I could ask out the tenth, the hundredth woman who bore some passing resemblance to her.

I said, "Would you like to meet for a coffee sometime?"

She looked surprised, but not affronted. Indecisive, but at least slightly pleased to have been asked. And I thought I was prepared for this slip of the tongue to lead nowhere, but then something in the ruins of me sent a shaft of pain through my chest as I watched her make up her mind. If a fraction of that had shown on my face, she probably would have rushed me to the nearest vet to be put down.

She said, "That would be nice. I'm Julia, by the way."

"I'm Mark." We shook hands.

"When do you finish work?"

"Tonight? Nine o'clock."

"Ah."

I said, "How about lunch? When do you have lunch?"

"One." She hesitated. "There's that place just down the road . . . next to the hardware store?"

"That would be great."

Julia smiled. "Then I'll meet you there. About ten past. OK?"

I nodded. She turned and walked out. I stared after her, dazed, terrified, elated. I thought: This is simple. Anyone in the world can do it. It's like breathing.

I started hyperventilating. I was an emotionally retarded teenager, and she'd discover that in five minutes flat. Or, worse, discover the 4,000 grown men in my head offering advice.

I went into the toilet to throw up.

Julia told me that she managed a dress shop a few blocks away. "You're new at the bookshop, aren't you?"

"Yes."

"So what were you doing before that?"

"I was unemployed. For a long time."

"How long?"

"Since I was a student."

She grimaced. "It's criminal, isn't it? Well, I'm doing my bit. I'm job-sharing, half-time only."

"Really? How are you finding it?"

"It's wonderful. I mean, I'm lucky, the position's well enough paid that I can get by on half a salary." She laughed. "Most people assume I must be raising a family. As if that's the only possible reason."

"You just like to have the time?"

"Yes. Time's important. I hate being rushed."

We had lunch again two days later, and then twice again the next week. She talked about the shop, a trip she'd made to South America, a sister recovering from breast cancer. I almost mentioned my own long-vanquished tumour, but apart from fears about where that might lead, it would have sounded too much like a plea for sympathy. At home, I sat riveted to the phone—not waiting for a call, but watching news broadcasts, to be sure I'd have something to talk about besides myself. *Who's your favourite singer/author/artist/actor? I have no idea.*

Visions of Julia filled my head. I wanted to know what she was doing every second of the day; I wanted her to be happy, I wanted her to be safe. *Why?* Because I'd chosen her. But . . . why had I felt compelled to choose anyone? Because in the end, the one thing that most of the donors must have had in common was the fact that they'd desired, and cared about, one person above all others. *Why?* That came down to evolution. You could no more help and protect everyone in sight than you could fuck them, and a judicious combination of the two had obviously proved effective at passing down genes. So my emotions had the same ancestry as everyone else's; what more could I ask?

But how could I pretend that I felt anything real for Julia, when I could shift a few buttons in my head, anytime, and make those feelings vanish? Even if what I felt was strong enough to keep me from wanting to touch that dial . . .

Some days I thought: it must be like this for everyone. People make a decision, half-shaped by chance, to get to know someone; everything starts from there. Some nights I sat awake for hours, wondering if I was turning myself into a pathetic slave, or a dangerous obsessive. Could anything I discovered about Julia drive me away, now that I'd chosen her? Or even trigger the slightest disapproval? And if, when, she decided to break things off, how would I take it?

We went out to dinner, then shared a taxi home. I kissed her goodnight on her doorstep. Back in my flat, I flipped through sex manuals on the net, wondering how I could ever hope to conceal my complete lack of experience. Everything looked anatomically impossible; I'd need six years of gymnastics training just to achieve the missionary position. I'd refused to masturbate since I'd met her; to fantasize about her, to *imagine her* without consent, seemed outrageous, unforgivable. After I gave in, I lay awake until dawn trying to comprehend the trap I'd dug for myself, and trying to understand why I didn't want to be free.

. . .

Julia bent down and kissed me, sweatily. "That was a nice idea." She climbed off me and flopped onto the bed.

I'd spent the last ten minutes riding the blue control, trying to keep myself from coming without losing my erection. I'd heard of computer games involving exactly the same thing. Now I turned up the indigo for a stronger glow of intimacy—and when I looked into her eyes, I knew that she could see the effect on me. She brushed my cheek with her hand. "You're a sweet man. Did you know that?"

I said, "I have to tell you something." *Sweet? I'm a puppet, I'm a robot, I'm a freak.*

"What?"

I couldn't speak. She seemed amused, then she kissed me. "I know you're gay. That's all right; I don't mind."

"I'm not gay." *Any more?* "Though I might have been."

Julia frowned. "Gay, bisexual . . . I don't care. Honestly."

I wouldn't have to manipulate my responses much longer; the prosthesis was being shaped by all of this, and in a few weeks I'd be able to leave it to its own devices. Then I'd feel, as naturally as anyone, all the things I was now having to choose.

I said, "When I was 12, I had cancer."

I told her everything. I watched her face, and saw horror, then growing doubt. "You don't believe me?"

She replied haltingly, "You sound so matter-of-fact. *Eighteen years?* How can you just say, 'I lost 18 years'?"

"How do you want me to say it? I'm not trying to make you pity me. I just want you to understand."

When I came to the day I met her, my stomach tightened with fear, but I kept on talking. After a few seconds I saw tears in her eyes, and I felt as though I'd been knifed.

"I'm sorry. I didn't mean to hurt you." I didn't know whether to try to hold her, or to leave right then. I kept my eyes fixed on her, but the room swam.

She smiled. "What are you sorry about? You chose me. I chose you. It could have been different for both of us. But it wasn't." She reached down under the sheet and took my hand. "It wasn't."

Julia had Saturdays off, but I had to start work at eight. She kissed me goodbye sleepily when I left at six; I walked all the way home, weightless.

I must have grinned inanely at everyone who came into the shop, but I hardly saw them. I was picturing the future. I hadn't spoken to either of my parents for nine years, they didn't even know about the Durrani treatment. But now it seemed possible to repair anything. I could go to them now and say: *This is your son, back from the dead. You did save my life, all those years ago.*

There was a message on the phone from Julia when I arrived home. I resisted viewing it until I'd started things cooking on the stove; there was something perversely pleasurable about forcing myself to wait, imagining her face and her voice in anticipation.

I hit the PLAY button. Her face wasn't quite as I'd pictured it.

I kept missing things and stopping to rewind. Isolated phrases stuck in my mind. *Too strange. Too sick. No one's fault.* My explanation hadn't really sunk in the night before. But now she'd had time to think about it, and she wasn't prepared to carry on a relationship with 4,000 dead men.

I sat on the floor, trying to decide what to feel: the wave of pain crashing over me, or something better, by choice. I knew I could summon up the controls of the prosthesis and make myself happy—happy because I was "free" again, happy because I was better off without her . . . happy because Julia was better off without me. Or even just happy because happiness meant nothing, and all I had to do to attain it was flood my brain with Leu-enkephalin.

I sat there wiping tears and mucus off my face while the vegetables burned. The smell made me think of cauterization, sealing off a wound.

I let things run their course, I didn't touch the controls—but just knowing that I could have changed everything. And I realized then that, even if I went to Luke De Vries and said: I'm cured now, take the software away, I don't want the power to choose any more . . . I'd never be able to forget where everything I felt had come from.

My father came to the flat yesterday. We didn't talk much, but he hasn't re-married yet, and he made a joke about us going nightclub-hopping together.

At least I hope it was a joke.

Watching him, I thought: he's there inside my head, and my mother too, and ten million ancestors, human, proto-human, remote beyond imagining. What difference did 4,000 more make? Everyone had to carve a life out of the same legacy: half universal, half particular; half sharpened by relentless natural selection, half softened by the freedom of chance. I'd just had to face the details a little more starkly.

And I could go on doing it, walking the convoluted border between meaning-less happiness and meaningless despair. Maybe I was lucky; maybe the best way to cling to that narrow zone was to see clearly what lay on either side.

When my father was leaving, he looked out from the balcony across the crowded suburb, down towards the Paramatta river, where a storm drain was discharging a visible plume of oil, street litter and garden runoff into the water.

He asked dubiously, "You happy with this area?"

I said, "I like it here."

мооn six

STEPHEN BAXTER

Like many of his colleagues here in the late nineties, Greg Egan comes to mind, as do people like Paul J. McAuley, Michael Swanwick, Iain M. Banks, Bruce Sterling, Pat Cadigan, Brian Stableford, Gregory Benford, Ian McDonald, Gwyneth Jones, Vernor Vinge, Greg Bear, Geoff Ryman, and a half-dozen others—Stephen Baxter is busily engaged with revitalizing and reinventing the "hard-science" story for a new generation of readers.

Baxter made his first sale to Interzone *in 1987, and since then has become one of that magazine's most frequent contributors, as well as making sales to* Asimov's Science Fiction, Science Fiction Age, Zenith, New Worlds, *and elsewhere; his stories have appeared in our Eleventh, Twelfth, and Fourteenth Annual Collections. His first novel,* Raft, *was released in 1991 to wide and enthusiastic response and was rapidly followed by other well-received novels such as* Timelike Infinity, Anti-Ice, Flux, *and the H. G. Wells pastiche—a sequel to* The Time Machine—The Time Ships, *which won both the Arthur C. Clarke Award and the Philip K. Dick Award. His most recent books are the alternate history novel* Titan, Voyage *and the collection* Vacuum Diagrams: Stories of the Xeelee Sequence.

Although always prolific, Baxter was especially prolific this year, publishing at least eleven stories in the genre that I'm aware of (plus a couple of nongenre stories), stories that appeared everywhere from obscure British semiprozines to (in early 1998, in collaboration with, of all people, Arthur C. Clarke!) Playboy. *As far as I can tell, Baxter published more short work in the genre this year than any other author (rivaled only by Robert Reed and Brian Stableford), and, in spite of this prodigous output, managed to keep the overall quality amazingly high: at least three or four of this year's Baxter stories were good enough to be seriously considered for inclusion in a Best of the Year volume, and might well have made the cut in another year. In the end, though, I decided to go with the tense and ingenious story that follows, one that suggests that the problem with voyaging to Alternate Worlds is that you might have been better off staying where you were in the first place. . . .*

Bado was alone on the primeval beach of Cape Canaveral, in his white lunar-surface pressure suit, holding his box of Moon rocks and sampling tools in his gloved hand. He lifted up his gold sun visor and looked around. The sand was hard and flat. A little way inland, there was a row of scrub pines, maybe ten feet tall.

There were no ICBM launch complexes here.

There was no Kennedy Space Center, in fact: no space program, evidently, save for him. He was stranded on this empty, desolate beach.

As the light leaked out of the sky, an unfamiliar Moon was brightening.

Bado glared at it. "Moon Six," he said. "Oh, shit."

He took off his helmet and gloves. He picked up his box of tools and began to walk inland. His blue overshoes, still stained dark gray from lunar dust, left crisp Moonwalk footprints in the damp sand of the beach.

Bado drops down the last three feet of the ladder and lands on the foil-covered footpad. A little gray dust splashes up around his feet.

Slade is waiting with his camera. "OK, turn around and give me a big smile. Atta boy. You look great. Welcome to the Moon." Bado can't see Slade's face, behind his reflective golden sun visor.

Bado holds onto the ladder with his right hand and places his left boot on the Moon. Then he steps off with his right foot, and lets go of the LM. And there he is, standing on the Moon.

The suit around him is a warm, comforting bubble. He hears the hum of pumps and fans in the PLSS—his backpack, the Portable Life Support System—and feels the soft breeze of oxygen across his face.

He takes a halting step forward. The dust seems to crunch beneath his feet, like a covering of snow: There is a firm footing beneath a soft, resilient layer a few inches thick. His footprints are miraculously sharp, as if he's placed his ridged overshoes in fine, damp sand. He takes a photograph of one particularly well-defined print; it will persist here for millions of years, he realizes, like the fossilized footprint of a dinosaur, to be eroded away only by the slow rain of micrometeorites, that echo of the titanic bombardments of the deep past.

He looks around.

The LM is standing in a broad, shallow crater. Low hills shoulder above the close horizon. There are craters everywhere, ranging from several yards to a thumbnail width, the low sunlight deepening their shadows.

They call the landing site Taylor Crater, after that district of El Lago—close to the Manned Spacecraft Center in Houston—where he and Fay have made their home. This pond of frozen lava is a relatively smooth, flat surface in a valley once flooded by molten rock. Their main objective for the flight is another crater a few hundred yards to the west that they've named after Slade's home district of Wildwood. *Surveyor 7*, an unmanned robot probe, set down in Wildwood a few years before; the astronauts are here to sample it.

This landing site is close to Tycho, the fresh, bright crater in the Moon's southern highlands. As a kid Bado had sharp vision. He was able to see Tycho with his naked eyes, a bright pinprick on that ash-white surface, with rays that spread right across the face of the full Moon.

Now he is here.

Bado turns and bounces back toward the LM.

After a few miles he got to a small town.

He hid his lunar pressure suit in a ditch, and, dressed in his tube-covered cooling garment, snuck into someone's backyard. He stole a pair of jeans and a shirt he found hanging on the line there.

He hated having to steal; he didn't plan on having to do it again.

He found a small bar. He walked straight in and asked for a job. He knew he couldn't afford to hesitate, to hang around figuring what kind of world he'd finished up in. He had no money at all, but right now he was clean-shaven and presentable. A few days of sleeping rough would leave him too dirty and stinking to be employable.

He got a job washing glasses and cleaning out the john. That first night he slept on a park bench, but bought himself breakfast and cleaned himself up in a gas station john.

After a week, he had a little money saved. He loaded his lunar gear into an old trunk, and hitched to Daytona Beach, a few miles up the coast.

They climb easily out of Taylor.

Their first Moonwalk is a misshapen circle that will take them around several craters. The craters are like drill holes, the geologists say, excavations into lunar history.

The first stop is the north rim of a 100-yard-wide crater they call Huckleberry Finn. It is about 300 yards west of the LM.

Bado puts down the tool carrier. This is a handheld tray, with an assortment of gear: rock hammers, sample bags, core tubes. He leans over, and digs into the lunar surface with a shovel. When he scrapes away the gray upper soil he finds a lighter gray, just under the surface.

"Hey, Slade. Come look at this."

Slade comes floating over. "How about that. I think we found some ray material." Ray material here will be debris from the impact that formed Tycho.

Lunar geology has been shaped by the meteorite impacts that pounded its surface in prehistory. A main purpose of sending this mission so far south is to keep them away from the massive impact that created the Mare Imbrium, in the northern hemisphere. Ray material unpolluted by Imbrium debris will let them date the more recent Tycho impact.

And here they have it, right at the start of their first Moonwalk.

Slade flips up his gold visor so Bado can see his face, and grins at him. "How about that. We is looking at a full-up mission here, boy."

They finish up quickly, and set off at a run to the next stop. Slade looks like a human-shaped beach ball, his suit brilliant white, bouncing over the beach-like surface of the Moon. He is whistling.

They are approaching the walls of Wildwood Crater. Bado is going slightly up-hill, and he can feel it. The carrier, loaded up with rocks, is getting harder to carry too. He has to hold it up to his chest, to keep the rocks from bouncing out when he runs, and so he is constantly fighting the stiffness of his pressure suit.

"Hey, Bado," Slade says. He comes loping down the slope. He points. "Take a look."

Bado has, he realizes, reached the rim of Wildwood Crater. He is standing on top of its dune-like, eroded wall. And there, planted in the crater's center, is the Surveyor. It is less than 100 yards from him. It is a squat, three-legged frame, like a broken-off piece of an LM.

Slade grins. "Does that look neat? We got it made, Bado." Bado claps his com-mander's shoulder. "Outstanding, man." He knows that for Slade, getting to the Surveyor, bringing home a few pieces of it, is the finish line for the mission.

Bado looks back east, the way they have come. He can see the big, shallow dip in the land that is Taylor, with the LM resting at its center like a toy in the palm of some huge hand. It is a glistening, filmy construct of gold leaf and aluminum, bris-tling with antennae, docking targets, and reaction control thruster assemblies.

Two sets of footsteps come climbing up out of Taylor toward them, like foot-steps on a beach after a tide.

Bado tips back on his heels and looks at the sky.

The sky is black, empty of stars; his pupils are closed up by the dazzle of the sun, and the reflection of the pale brown lunar surface. But he can see the Earth, a fat crescent, four times the size of a full Moon. And there, crossing the Zenith, is a single, brilliant, unwinking star: the orbiting Apollo CSM, with Al Pond, their command module pilot, waiting to take them home.

There is a kind of shimmer, like a heat haze. And the star goes out.

Just like that—it vanishes from the sky, directly over Bado's head. He blinks, and moves his head, stiffly, thinking he might have just lost the Apollo in the glare.

But it is gone.

What, then? Can it have moved into the shadow of the Moon? But a little thought knocks out that one; the geometry, of sun and Moon and spacecraft, is all wrong.

And anyhow, what was that heat haze shimmer? You don't get heat haze where there's no air.

He lowers his head. "Hey, Slade. You see that?"

But Slade isn't anywhere to be seen, either, the slope where he's been standing is smooth, empty.

Bado feels his heart hammer.

He lets go of the tool carrier—it drifts down to the dust, spilling rocks—and he lopes forward. "Come on, Slade. Where the hell are you?"

Slade is famous for "gotchas"; he is planning a few that Bado knows about, and probably some he doesn't, for later in the mission. But it is hard to see how he's pulled this one off. There is nowhere to hide, damn it.

He gets to where he thinks Slade was last standing. There is no sign of him. And there aren't even any footsteps, he realizes now. The only marks under his feet are those made by his own boots, leading off a few yards away, to the north.

And they start out of nothing, it seems, like Man Friday steps in the crisp virgin Moon-snow. As if he's stepped out of nowhere onto the regolith.

When he looks back to the east, he can't see the LM either.

"Slade, this isn't funny, damn it." He starts to bound, hastily, back in the direction of the LM. His clumsy steps send up parabolic sprays of dust over unmarked regolith.

He feels his breath getting shallow. It isn't a good idea to panic. He tells himself that maybe the LM is hidden behind some low ridge. Distances are deceptive here, in this airless sharpness.

"Houston, Bado. I got some kind of situation here." There isn't a reply immediately; he imagines his radio signal crawling across the light-seconds' gulf to Earth. "I'm out of contact with Slade. Maybe he's fallen somewhere, out of sight. And I don't seem to be able to see the LM. And . . .

"And someone's wiped over our footsteps, while I wasn't looking."

Nobody is replying, he realizes.

That stops him short. Dust falls over his feet. On the surface of the Moon, nothing is moving.

He looks up at the crescent Earth. "Ah, Houston, this is Bado. Houston. John, come in, capcom."

Just silence, static in his headset.

He starts moving to the east again, breathing hard, the sweat pooling at his neck.

He rented an apartment.

He got himself a better job in a radio store. In the Air Force, before joining NASA, he'd specialized in electronics. He'd been apprehensive that he might not be able to find his way around the gear here, but he found it simple—almost crude, compared to what he'd been used to. They had transistors here, but they still used big chunky valves and paper capacitors. It was like being back in the early '60s. Radios were popular, but there were few TVs: small black and white gadgets, the reception lousy.

He began watching the TV news and reading the newspapers, trying to figure out what kind of world he'd been dropped in.

The weather forecasts were lousy.

And foreign news reports, even on the TV, were sent by wire, like they'd been when he was a kid, and were often a day or two out of date.

The Vietnam War was unfolding. But there'd been none of the protests against the war here like he'd seen back at home. There were no live TV pictures, no color satellite images of soldiers in the mud and the rain, napalming civilians. Nobody knew what was happening out there. The reaction to the war was more like what he remembered of World War II.

There really was no space program. Not just the manned stuff had gone: There were no weather satellites, communication satellites. Sputnik, Explorer, and all the rest just hadn't happened. The Moon was just a light in the sky that nobody cared about, like when he was a kid. It was brighter, though, because of that big patch of highland where Imbrium should have been.

On the other hand, there were no ICBMs, as far as he could tell.

His mouth is bone-dry from the pure oxygen. He is breathing hard; he hears the hiss of water through the suit's cooling system, the pipes that curl around his limbs and chest.

There is a rational explanation for this. There has to be. Like, if he's got out of line of sight with the LM, somehow, he's invisible to the LM's radio relay, the Lunar Communications Relay Unit. He is linked to that by VHF, and then by S-band to the Earth.

Yeah, that has to be it. As soon as he gets back in line of sight of the LM, he can get in touch with home. And maybe with Slade.

But he can't figure how he could have gotten out of the LM's line of sight in the first place. And what about the vanished footsteps?

He tries not to think about it. He just concentrates on loping forward, back to the LM.

In a few minutes, he is back in Taylor Crater.

There is no LM. The regolith here is undisturbed.

Bado bounces across the virgin surface, scuffing it up.

Can he be in the wrong place? The lunar surface does have a tendency to look the same everywhere . . . Hell, no. He can see he is right in the middle of Taylor; he recognizes the shapes of the hills. There can't be any doubt.

What, then? Can Slade have somehow gotten back to the LM, taken off without him?

But how can Bado not have seen him, seen the boxy LM ascent stage lift up into the sky? And besides, the regolith would be marked by the ascent stage's blast.

And, he realizes dimly, there would, of course, be an abandoned descent platform here, and bits of kit. And their footsteps. His thoughts are sluggish, his realization coming slowly. Symptoms of shock, maybe.

The fact is that save for his own footfalls, the regolith is as unmarked as if he's been dropped out of the sky.

And meanwhile, nobody in Houston is talking to him.

He is ashamed to find he is crying, mumbling, tears rolling down his face inside his helmet.

He starts to walk back west again. Following his own footsteps—the single line he made coming back to find the LM—he works his way out of Taylor, and back to the rim of Wildwood.

Hell, he doesn't have any other place to go.

As he walks he keeps calling, for Slade, for Houston, but there is only static. He knows his signal can't reach Earth anyway, not without the LM's big S-band booster.

At Wildwood's rim there is nothing but the footfalls he left earlier. He looks down into Wildwood, and there sits the Surveyor, glistening like some aluminum toy, unperturbed.

He finds his dropped carrier, with the spilled tools and bagged rocks. He bends sideways and scoops up the stuff, loading it back into the carrier.

Bado walks down into Wildwood, spraying lunar dust ahead of him.

He examines the Surveyor. Its solar cell array is stuck out on a boom above him, maybe ten feet over the regolith. The craft bristles with fuel tanks, batteries, antennae, and sensors. He can see the craft's mechanical claw where it has scraped into the lunar regolith. And he can see how the craft's white paint has turned tan, maybe from exposure to the sunlight. There are splashes of dust under the vernier rocket nozzles; the Surveyor is designed to land hard, and the three pads have left a firm imprint in the surface.

He gets hold of a landing leg and shakes the Surveyor. "OK," he calls up. "I'm jiggling it. It's planted here." There was a fear that the Surveyor might tip over onto the astronauts when they try to work with it. That evidently isn't going to happen. Bado takes a pair of cutting shears from his carrier, gets hold of the Surveyor's TV camera, and starts to chop through the camera's support struts and cables. "Just a couple more tubes," he says. "Then that baby's mine."

He'll finish up his Moonwalk, he figures, according to the time line in the spiral-bound checklist on his cuff. He'll keep on reporting his observations, in case anyone is listening. And then . . . when he gets to the end of the walk, he'll figure out what to do next. Later there will be another boundary, when his PLSS's consumables expire. He'll deal with those things when they come. For now, he is going to work.

The camera comes loose, and he grips it in his gloves. "Got it! It's ours!"

He drops the camera in his carrier, breathing hard. His mouth is dry as sand; he'd give an awful lot for an ice-cool glass of water, right here and now.

There is a shimmer, like heat haze, crossing between him and the Surveyor. Just like before.

He tilts back and looks up. There is old Earth, the fat crescent. And a star, bright and unwavering, is crossing the black sky, directly over his head.

It has to be the Apollo CSM.

He drops the carrier to the dirt and starts jumping up and down, in great big lunar hops, and he waves, as if he is trying to attract a passing aircraft. "Hey, Al! Al Pond! Can you hear me?" Even without the LM, Pond, in the CSM, might be able to pick him up.

His mood changes to something resembling elation. He doesn't know where the hell Apollo has been, but if it is back, maybe soon so will be the LM, and Slade, and everything. That will suit Bado, right down to the lunar ground he is standing on. He'll be content to have it all back the way it had been, the way it is supposed to be, and figure out what has happened to him later.

"Al! It's me, Bado! Can you hear me? Can you . . ."

There is something wrong.

That light isn't staying steady. It is getting brighter, and it is drifting off its straight line, coming down over his head.

It isn't the CSM in orbit. It is some kind of boxy craft, much smaller than an LM, descending toward him, gleaming in the sunlight.

He picks up his carrier and holds it close to his chest, and stays close to the Surveyor. As the craft approaches he feels an unreasoning fear.

His kidneys send him a stab of distress. He stands still and lets go, into the urine collection condom. He feels shamed; it is like wetting his pants.

The craft is just a box, on four spindly landing legs. It is coming down vertically, standing on a central rocket. He can see no light from the rocket, of course, but he can see how the downward blast is starting to kick up some dust. It is going to land maybe fifty yards from the Surveyor, right in the middle of Wildwood Crater. The whole thing is made of some silvery metal, maybe aluminum. It has a little control panel, set at the front, and there is someone at the controls. It looks like a man—an astronaut, in fact—his face hidden behind a gold-tinted visor.

Bado can see the blue of a NASA logo, and a dust-coated stars and stripes, painted on the side of the craft.

Maybe fifty feet above the ground the rocket cuts out, and the craft begins to drop. The sprays of dust settle back neatly to the lunar soil. Now little vernier rockets, stuck to the side of the open compartment, cut in to slow the fall, kicking up their own little sprays.

It is all happening in complete silence.

The craft hits the ground with a solid thump. Bado can see the pilot, the astronaut, flick a few switches, and then turn and jump the couple of feet down off the little platform to the ground.

The astronaut comes giraffe-loping across the sunlit surface toward Bado and stops a few feet from him, and stands there, slightly stooped forward, balancing the weight of his PLSS.

His suit looks pretty much like a standard EMU, an Apollo Extravehicular Mobility Unit. There is the usual gleaming white oversuit—the thermal micrometeorite garment—with the lower legs and overshoes scuffed and stained with Tycho dust. Bado can see the PLSS oxygen and water inlets on the chest cover, and penlight and utility pockets on arms and legs. And there is Old Glory stitched to the left arm.

But Bado doesn't recognize the name stitched over the breast. *Williams*. There is no astronaut of that name in the corps back in Houston.

Bado's headset crackles to life, startling him.

"I heard you, when the LFU came over the horizon. As soon as I got in line of sight, I could hear you talking, describing what you were doing. And when I looked down, there you were."

Bado is astonished. It is a woman's voice. This Williams is a goddamn woman.

Bado can't think of a thing to say.

He didn't find it hard to find a place in the community here and to fabricate a fake ID about his past. Computers were pretty primitive, and there was little cross-checking of records.

Maybe, back home, the development of computers had been forced by the Apollo project, he speculated.

He couldn't see any way he was going to get home. He was stuck here. But he sure as hell didn't want to spend his life tuning crummy 1960s-design radios.

He tinkered with the Surveyor camera he'd retrieved from the Moon. As far as he could tell, it was a much more lightweight design than anything available here. But the manufacturing techniques required weren't much beyond what was available here.

He started to take the camera components to electronic engineering companies. He took apart his lunar suit. In all this world there was nothing like the suit's miniaturized telemetry system. He was able to adapt it to be used to transmit EKG data from ambulances to hospital emergency rooms. He sent samples of the Beta-cloth outer coverall to a fiberglass company, and showed them how the stuff could be used for fire hoses. Other samples went to military suppliers to help them put together better insulated blankets. The scratch-proof lens of the Surveyor camera went to an optical company to manufacture better safety goggles and other gear. The miniature, high-performance motors driving the pumps and fans of his PLSS found a dozen applications.

He was careful to patent everything he "developed" from his lunar equipment.

Pretty soon, the money started rolling in.

"Maybe I'm dreaming this," Williams says. "Dehydration, or something . . . Uh, I guess I'm pleased to meet you."

She has a Tennessee accent, he thinks.

Bado shakes the hand. He can feel it through his own stiff pressure glove. "I guess you're too solid for a ghost."

"Ditto," she says. "Besides, I've never met a ghost yet who uses VHF frequencies."

He releases her hand.

"I don't know how the hell you got here," she says. "And I guess you don't understand this any better than I do."

"That's for sure."

She dips her visored head. "What are you doing here, anyway?"

He holds up the carrier. "Sampling the Surveyor. I took off its TV camera."

"Oh. You couldn't get it, though."

"Sure. Here it is."

She turns to the Surveyor. "Look over there."

The Surveyor is whole again, its TV camera firmly mounted to its struts.

But when he looks down at his carrier, there is the TV camera he's cut away, lying there, decapitated.

"Where's your LM?" she asks.

"Taylor Crater."

"Where?"

He describes the crater's location.

"Oh. OK. We're calling that one San Jacinto. Ah, no, your LM isn't there."

"I know. I walked back. The crater's empty."

"No, it isn't," she says, but there is a trace of alarm in her voice. "That's where *my* LM is. With my partner, and the Payload Module."

Payload Module?

"The hell with it," she says. "Let's go see."

She turns and starts to lope back to her flying craft, rocking from side to side. He stands there and watches her go.

After a few steps she stops and turns around. "You want a lift?"

"Can you take two?"

"Sure. Come on. What choice do you have, if you're stuck here without an LM?"

Her voice carries a streak of common sense that somehow comforts him.

Side by side, they bound over the Moon.

They reach Williams' flying machine. It is just an aluminum box sitting squat on its four legs, with vernier rocket nozzles stuck to the walls like clusters of berries. The pilot has to climb in at the back and stand over the cover of the main rocket engine, which is about the size of a car engine, Bado supposes. Big spherical propellant and oxidizer tanks are fixed to the floor. There is an S-band antenna and a VHF aerial. There is some gear on the floor, hammers and shovels and sample bags and cameras; Williams dumps this stuff out, briskly, onto the regolith. She hops up onto the platform and begins throwing switches. Her control panel contains a few instruments, a CRT, a couple of handsets.

Bado lugs his heavy tool carrier up onto the platform, then he gets hold of a rail with both hands and jumps up.

"What did you call this thing? An LFU?"

"Yeah. Lunar Flying Unit."

"I've got vague memories," says Bado, "of a design like this. It was never developed, when the extended Apollo missions were canceled."

"Canceled? When did that happen?"

"When we were cut back to stop when we get to *Apollo 17*."

"Uh huh," she says dubiously. She eyes the tool carrier. "You want to bring that thing?"

"Sure. It's not too heavy, is it?"

"No. But what do you want it for?"

Bado looks at the battered, dusty carrier, with its meaningless load of rocks. "It's all I've got."

"OK. Let's get out of here," she says briskly.

Williams kicks in the main rocket. Dust billows silently up off the ground into Bado's face. He can see frozen vapor puff out of the attitude nozzles, in streams of shimmering crystals, as if this is some unlikely steam engine, a Victorian engineer's fantasy of lunar flight.

The basin of Wildwood Crater falls away. The lift is a brief, comforting surge.

Williams whoops. "Whee-hoo! What a ride, huh, pal?" She takes the LFU up to maybe sixty feet, and slows the ascent. She pitches the craft over and they begin sailing out of Wildwood.

The principles of the strange craft are obvious enough to Bado. You stand on your rocket's tail. You keep yourself stable with the four peroxide reaction clusters, the little vernier rockets spaced around the frame, squirting them here and there. When the thrust of the single big downward rocket is at an angle to the vertical, the LFU goes shooting forward, or sideways, or backward across the pitted surface. Williams shows him the hand controls. They are just like the LM's. The attitude control moves in clicks; every time Williams turns the control the reaction rockets will bang and the LFU will tip over, a degree at a time. The thrust control is a toggle switch; when Williams closes it the lift rockets roar, to give her a delta-vee of a foot per second.

"These are neat little craft," Williams says. "They fly on residual descent-stage propellants. They've a range of a few miles, and you can do three sorties in each of them."

"Each?"

"We bring two. Rescue capability."

Bado thinks he is starting to see a pattern to what has happened to him.

In a way, the presence of the camera in his carrier is reassuring. It means he isn't crazy. There really have been two copies of the Surveyor; one of which he's sampled, and one he hasn't.

Maybe there is more than one goddamn Moon.

Moon One is the good old lantern in the sky that he and Slade touched down on yesterday. Maybe Slade is still back there, with the LM. But Bado sure isn't. Somehow he stumbled onto Moon Two, the place with the Surveyor, but no LM. And then this Williams showed up, and evidently by that time he was on another Moon, Moon Three, with its own copy of the Surveyor. And a different set of astronauts exploring, with subtly different equipment.

As if traveling to one Moon isn't enough.

He thinks about that strange, heat-haze shimmer. Maybe that has something to do with these weird transfers.

He can't discuss any of this with Williams, because she hasn't seen any of the changes. Not yet, anyhow.

Bado clings to the sides of the LFU and watches the surface of the Moon scroll underneath him. There are craters everywhere, overlaid circles of all sizes, some barely visible in a surface gardened by billions of years of micrometeorite impact. The surface looks ghostly, rendered in black and white, too stark, unmoving, to be real.

He knew he was taking a risk, but he took his lunar rocks to a couple of universities.

He got laughed out of court. Especially when he wouldn't explain how these charcoal-dark rocks might have got from the Moon to the Earth.

"Maybe they got blasted off by a meteorite strike," he said to an "expert" at Cornell. "Maybe they drifted in space until they landed here. I've read about that."

The guy pushed his reading glasses farther up his thin nose. "Well, that's possible." He smiled. "No doubt you've been reading the same lurid speculation I have, in the popular science press. What if rocks get knocked back and forth between the planets? Perhaps there are indeed bits of the Moon, even Mars, to be turned up, here on Earth. And, since we know living things can survive in the interiors of rocks—and since we know that some plants and bacteria can survive long periods of dormancy—perhaps it is even possible for life to propagate itself, across the trackless void, in such a manner."

He picked up Bado's Moon rock, dubiously. "But in that case I'd expect to see some evidence of the entry of this rock into the atmosphere. Melting, some glass. And besides, this rock is not volcanic. Mr. Bado, everyone knows the Moon's major features were formed exclusively by vulcanism. This can't possibly be a rock from the Moon."

Bado snatched back his rock. "That's Colonel Bado," he said. He marched out. He gave up, and went back to Daytona Beach.

The LFU slides over the rim of Taylor Crater. Or San Jacinto. Bado can see scuffed-up soil below him, and the big Huckleberry Finn Crater to his left, where he and Slade made their first stop.

At the center of Taylor stands an LM. It glitters like some piece of giant jewelry, the most colorful object on the lunar surface. An astronaut bounces around in front of it, like a white balloon. He—or she—is working at what looks like a surface experiment package, white-painted boxes and cylinders and masts laid out in a star formation and connected to a central nuclear generator by orange cables. It looks like an ALSEP, but it is evidently heavier, more advanced.

But the LM isn't alone. A second LM stands beside it, squat and spidery. Bado can see that the ascent stage has been heavily reworked; the pressurized cabin looks to be missing, replaced by cargo pallets.

"That's your Payload Module, right?"

"Yeah," Williams says. "The Lunar Payload Module Laboratory. It got here on automatics before we left the Cape. This is a dual Saturn launch mission, Bado. We've got a stay time of four weeks."

Again he has vague memories of proposals for such things: dual launches; well-equipped, long-stay jaunts on the surface. But the funding squeezes since '66 have long since put pay to all of that. Evidently, wherever Williams comes from, the money is flowing a little more freely.

The LFU tips itself back, to slow its forward velocity. Williams throttles back the main motor and the LFU starts to drop down. Bado glances at the numbers; the CRT display evolves smoothly through height and velocity readings. Bado guesses the LFU must have some simple radar-based altimeter.

Now the LM and its misshapen partner are obscured by the dust Williams' rocket is kicking up.

At fifty feet Williams cuts the main engine. Bado feels the drop in the pit of his stomach, and he watches the ground explode toward him, resolving into unwelcome detail, sharp boulders and zap pits and footprints, highlighted by the low morning sun.

Then vernier dust clouds billow up around the LFU. Bado feels a comforting surge of deceleration.

The LFU lands with a jar that Bado feels in his knees.

For a couple of seconds the dust of their landing cloaks the LFU, and then it begins to settle out around them, coating the LFU's surfaces, his suit.

There is a heat-haze shimmer. "Oh, shit."

Williams is busily shutting down the LFU. She turns to face him, anonymous behind her visor.

There wasn't much astronomy going on at all, in fact, he found out when he looked it up in the libraries. Just a handful of big telescopes, scattered around the world, with a few crusty old guys following their obscure, decades-long projects. And all the projects were to do with deep space: the stars and beyond. Nobody was interested in the Solar System. Certainly in nothing as mundane as the Moon.

He looked up at Moon Six, uneasily, with its bright, unscarred north-west quadrant. If that Imbrium meteorite hadn't hit three billion years ago—or in 1970— where the hell was it now?

Maybe that big mother was on its way, right now.

Quietly, he pumped some of his money into funding a little research at the universities into Earth-neighborhood asteroids.

He also siphoned money into trying to figure out what had happened to him. How he got here.

As the last dust settles, Bado looks toward the center of Taylor Crater, to where the twin LMs stood.

He can make out a blocky shape there.

He feels a sharp surge of relief. Thank God. Maybe this transition hasn't been as severe as some of the others. Or maybe there hasn't been a transition at all . . .

But Williams' LM has gone, with its cargo-carrying partner. And so has the astronaut, with his surface package. But the crater isn't empty. The vehicle that stands in its place has the same basic geometry as an LM, Bado thinks, with a boxy descent stage standing on four legs, and a fat ascent stage cabin on top. But it is just fifteen feet tall—compared to an LM's twenty feet—and the cabin looks a lot smaller.

"My God," Williams says. She is just standing, stock still, staring at the little lander.

"Welcome to Moon Four," Bado whispers.

"My God." She repeats that over and over.

He faces her, and flips up his gold visor so she can see his face. "Listen to me. You're not going crazy. We've been through some kind of—transition. I can't explain it." He grins. It makes him feel stronger to think there is someone else more scared, more shocked, than he is.

He takes her through his tentative theory of the multiple Moons.

She turns to face the squat lander again. "I figured it had to be something like that."

He gapes at her. "You figured?"

"How the hell else could you have got here? Well, what are we supposed to do now?" She checks the time on her big Rolex watch. "Bado. How long will your PLSS hold out?"

He feels embarrassed. Shocked or not, she's cut to the chase a lot more smartly than he's been able to. He glances at his own watch, on the cuff next to his useless checklist. "A couple of hours. What about you?"

"Less, probably. Come on." She glides down from the platform of the LFU, her blue boots kicking up a spray of dust.

"Where are we going?"

"Over to that little LM, of course. Where else? It's the only source of consumables I can see anywhere around here." She begins loping toward the lander.

After a moment, he picks up his carrier, and follows her.

As they approach he gets a better look at the lander. The ascent stage is a bulbous, misshapen ball, capped by a fat, wide disk that looks like a docking device. Two dinner-plate-sized omnidirectional antennae are stuck out on extensible arms from the descent stage. The whole clumsy-looking assemblage is swathed in some kind of green blanket, maybe for thermal insulation.

A ladder leads from a round hatch in the front of the craft, and down to the surface via a landing leg. The ground there is scuffed with footprints.

"It's a hell of a small cabin," she says. "Has to be one man."

"You think it's American?"

"Not from any America I know. That ascent stage looks familiar. It looks like an adapted Soyuz orbital module. You know, the Russian craft, their Apollo equivalent."

"Russian?"

"Can you see any kind of docking tunnel on top of that thing?"

He looks. "Nope. Just that flat assemblage at the top."

"The crew must have to spacewalk to cross from the command module. What a design."

An astronaut comes loping around the side of the lander, swaying from side to side, kicking up dust. When he catches sight of Bado and Williams, he stops dead.

The stranger is carrying a flag, on a pole. The flag is stiffened with wire, and it is clearly bright red, with a gold hammer and sickle embroidered into it.

"How about that," Williams whispers. "I guess we don't always get to win, huh."

The stranger—the cosmonaut, Bado labels him—takes a couple of steps toward them. He starts gesticulating, waving his arms about, making the flag flutter. He wears a kind of hoop around his waist, held away from his body with stiff wire.

"I think he's trying to talk to us," Williams says.

"It'll be a miracle if we are on the same frequency. Maybe he's S-band only, to talk to Earth. No VHF. Look how stiff his movements are."

"Yeah. I think his suit is semi-rigid. Must be hell to move around in."

"What's with the hula hoop?" Bado asks.

"It will stop him falling over, in case he trips. Don't you get it? He's on his own here. That's a one-man lander. There's nobody around to help him, if he gets into trouble."

The cosmonaut is getting agitated. Now he hoists up the flag and throws it at them, javelin-style; it falls well short of Bado's feet. Then the cosmonaut turns and lopes toward his lander, evidently looking for more tools, or improvised weapons.

"Look at that," Bado says. "There are big funky hinges down the side of his backpack. That must be the way into the suit."

Williams lifts up her visor. "Show him your face. We've got to find some way to get through to this guy."

Bado feels like laughing. "What for?"

The light changes.

Bado stands stock still. "Shit, not again."

Williams says, "What?"

"Another transition." He looks around for the tell-tale heat-haze flicker.

"I don't think so," Williams says softly. "Not this time."

A shadow, slim and jet-black, hundreds of feet long, sweeps over the surface of Taylor Crater.

Bado leans back and tips up his face.

The ship is like a huge artillery shell, gleaming silver, standing on its tail. It glides over the lunar surface, maybe fifty feet up, and where its invisible rocket exhaust passes, dust is churned up and sent gusting away in great flat sheets. The ship moves gracefully, if ponderously. Four heavy landing legs, with big spring-load shock absorbers, stick out from the base. A circle of portals glows bright yellow around the nose. A huge bull's-eye of red, white, and blue is painted on the side, along with a registration number.

"Shit," Bado says. "That thing must be a hundred feet tall." Four or five times as tall as his lost LM. "What do you think it weighs? Two, three hundred tons?"

"Direct ascent," she says.

"Huh?"

"Look at it. It's streamlined. It's built for landing on the Moon in one piece, ascending again, and returning to Earth."

"But that was designed out years ago, by Von Braun and the boys. A ship like that's too heavy for chemical rockets."

"So who said anything about chemical? It has to be atomic. Some kind of fission pile in there, superheating its propellant. One hell of a specific impulse. Anyhow, it's that or antigravity—"

The great silver fish hovers for a moment, and then comes swooping down at the surface. It flies without a quiver. Bado wonders how it is keeping its stability; he can't see any verniers. Big internal flywheels maybe.

As the ship nears the surface, dust comes rushing across the plain, away from the big tail like a huge circular sandstorm. There is a rattle, almost like rain, as heavy particles impact Bado's visor. He holds his gloved hands up before his face, and leans a little into the rocket wind.

The delicate little Russian lander just topples over in the breeze, and the bulbous ascent stage breaks off and rolls away.

In the mirror of his bedroom he studied his graying hair and spreading paunch.

Oddly, it had taken a while for him to miss his wife Fay.

Maybe because everything was so different. Not that he was sorry, in a sense; his job, he figured, was to survive here—to earn a living, to keep himself sane— and moping after the unattainable wouldn't help.

He was glad they'd had no kids, though.

There was no point searching for Fay in Houston, of course. Houston without the space program was just an oil town, with a big cattle pasture north of Clear Lake where the Manned Spacecraft Center should have been. El Lago, the Taylor housing development, had never been built.

He even drove out to Atlantic City, where he'd first met Fay, a couple of decades ago. He couldn't find her in the phone book. She was probably living under some married name, he figured.

He gave up.

He tried, a few times, to strike up relationships with other women here. He found it hard to get close to anyone, though. He always felt he needed to guard what he was saying. This wasn't his home, after all.

So he lived pretty much alone. It was bearable. It even got easier, as he got older.

Oddly, he missed walking on the Moon more than anything else, more than anything about the world he'd lost. He kept reliving those brief hours. He remembered Slade, how he looked bouncing across the lunar sand, a brilliant white balloon. How happy he'd seemed.

The silver ship touches down with a thump, and those big legs flex, the springs working like muscles.

A hatch opens in the ship's nose, maybe eighty feet from the ground, and yellow light spills out. A spacesuited figure appears, and begins rolling a rope ladder down to the surface. The figure waves to Bado and Williams, calling them to the ship.

"What do you think?" Bado asks.

"I think it's British. Look at that bull's-eye logo. I remember war movies about the Battle of Britain . . . Wherever the hell that's come from, it's some place very different from the worlds you and I grew up in."

"You figure we should go over there?" he asks.

She spreads her hands. "What choice do we have? We don't have an LM. And we can't last out here much longer. At least these guys look as if they know what they're doing. Let's go see what Boris thinks."

The cosmonaut lets Williams walk up to him. He is hauling at his ascent stage. But Bado can see the hull is cracked open, like an aluminum egg, and the cosmonaut's actions are despairing.

Williams points toward the silver ship, where the figure in the airlock is still waving at them.

Listlessly, the cosmonaut lets himself be led to the ship.

Closer to, the silver craft looks even bigger than before—so tall that when Bado stands at its base he can't see the nose.

Williams goes up the ladder first, using just her arms, pulling her mass easily in the Moon's shallow gravity well. The cosmonaut takes off his hoop, dumps it on the ground, and follows her.

Bado comes last. He moves more slowly than the others, because he has his tool carrier clutched against his chest, and it is awkward to juggle while climbing the rope ladder.

It takes forever to climb past the shining metal of the ship's lower hull. The metal here looks like lead, actually. Shielding, around an atomic pile? He thinks of the energy it must take to haul this huge mass of metal around. He can't help comparing it with his own LM, which, to save weight, was shaved down to little more than a bubble of aluminum foil.

The hull shivers before his face. Heat haze.

He looks down. The wreckage of the little Russian lander, and Williams' LFU, has gone. The surface under the tail of this big ship looks unmarked, lacking even the raying of the landing. And the topography of the area is quite different; now he is looking down over some kind of lumpy, sun-drenched mountain range, and a wide, fat rille snakes through the crust.

"How about that," Williams says dryly, from above him. Her voice signal is degraded; the amplifier on the LFU is no longer available to boost their VHF link.

"We're on Moon Five," he says.

"Moon Five?"

"It seems important to keep count."

"Yeah. Whatever. Bado, this time the geology's changed. Maybe one of the big primordial impacts didn't happen, leaving the whole lunar surface a different shape."

They reach the hatch. Bado lets the astronaut take his tool carrier, and clambers in on his knees.

The astronaut closes the hatch and dogs it shut by turning a big heavy wheel. He wears a British Union Flag on his sleeve, and there is a name stitched to his breast: *Taine*.

The four of them stand around in the airlock, in their competing pressure suit designs. Air hisses, briefly.

An inner door opens, and Taine ushers them through with impatient gestures. Bado enters a long corridor, with nozzles set in the ceiling. The four of them stand under the nozzles.

Water comes gushing down, and runs over their suits.

Williams opens up her gold sun visor and faces Williams. "Showers," she says.

"What for?"

"To wash off radioactive crap, from the exhaust." She begins to brush water over her suit arms and legs.

Bado has never seen such a volume of water in lunar conditions before. It falls slowly from the nozzles, gathering into big shimmering drops in the air. Gray-black lunar dust swirls toward the plug holes beneath his feet. But the dirt is ingrained into the fabric of his suit legs; they will be stained gray forever.

When the water dries they are ushered through into a third larger chamber. The walls here are curved, and inset with round, tough-looking portholes; it looks as if this chamber reaches most of the way around the cylindrical craft.

There are people here, dozens of them, adults and children and old people, dressed in simple cotton coveralls. They sit in rows of crude metal-framed couches, facing outward toward the portholes. They stare fearfully at the new-comers.

The astronaut, Taine, has opened up his faceplate; it hinges outward like a little door.

Bado pushes back his hood and reaches up to his fishbowl helmet. He undoes it at the neck, and his ears pop as the higher pressure of the cabin pushes air into his helmet.

He can smell the sharp, woodsmoke tang of lunar dust. And, overlaid on that, there is a smell of milky vomit: baby sick.

The Russian, his own helmet removed, makes a sound of disgust. *"Eta ooz-hasna!"*

Williams pulls off her Snoopy flight helmet. She is maybe forty, Bado guesses—around Bado's own age—with a tough, competent face, and close-cropped blonde hair.

Taine shoos the three of them along. "Welcome to *Prometheus*," he says. "Come. There are some free seats further around here." His accent is flat, sounding vaguely Bostonian. Definitely British, Bado thinks, probably from the south of England. "You're the last, we think. We must get away. The impact is no more than twelve hours hence."

Bado, lugging his tool carrier, walks beside him. "What impact?"

"The meteorite, of course." Taine sounds impatient. "That's why we're having to evacuate the colonies. And you alternates. The Massolite got most of them off, of course, but—"

Williams says, "Massolite?"

Taine waves a hand. "A mass transporter. Of course it was a rushed job. And it had some flaws. But we knew we couldn't lift everybody home in time, not all those thousands in the big colonies, not before the strike; the Massolite was the best we can do, you see." They come to three empty couches. "These should do, I think. If you'll sit down I'll show you how to fit the seat belts, and instruct you in the safety precautions . . ."

"But," Williams says, "what has this Massolite got to do with . . ." She dries up, and looks at Bado.

He asks, "With moving between alternate worlds?"

Taine answers with irritation. "Why, nothing, of course. That's just a design flaw. We're working on it. Nonlinear quantum mechanical leakage, you see. I do wish you'd sit down; we have to depart . . ."

Bado shucks off his PLSS backpack, and he tucks his helmet and his carrier under his seat.

Taine helps them adjust their seat restraints until they fit around their pressure suits. It is more difficult for the Russian; his suit is so stiff it is more like armor. The Russian looks young, no more than thirty. His hair sticks up in the air, damp with sweat, and he looks at them forlornly from his shell of a suit. *"Gdye tooalyet?"*

The portholes before them give them a good view of the lunar surface. It is still Moon Five, Bado sees, with its mountains and that sinuous black rille.

He looks around at their fellow passengers. The adults are unremarkable; some of them have run to fat, but they have incongruously skinny legs and arms. Long-term adaptation to lunar gravity, Bado thinks.

But there are also some children here, ranging from babies in their mothers' arms up to young teenagers. The children are extraordinary: spindly, attenuated. Children who look facially as young as seven or eight tower over their parents.

The passengers clutch at their seat belts, staring back at him.

Bado hears a clang of hatches, and a siren wails, echoing from the metal walls. The ship shudders, smoothly, and there is a gentle surge.

"Mnye nada idtee k vrachoo," groans the Russian, and he clutches his belly.

As the years wore on he followed the news, trying to figure out how things might be different back home.

The Cold War went on, year after year. There were no ICBMs here, but they had squadrons of bombers and nuke submarines and massive standing armies in Europe. And there were no spy satellites; nobody had a damn clue what the Russians—or the Chinese—were up to. A lot of shit came down that Bado figured might have been avoided, with satellite surveillance. It slowly leaked out into the paper press, usually months or years too late. Like the Chinese nuking of Tibet, for instance. And what the Soviets did to Afghanistan.

The Soviet Union remained a monolith, blank, threatening, impenetrable. Everyone in the U.S. seemed paranoid to Bado, generations of them, with their bomb shelters and their iodine pills. It was like being stuck in the late 1950s.

And that damn war in Indochina just dragged on, almost forgotten back home, sucking up lives and money like a bloody sponge.

Around 1986, he felt a sharp tug of wistfulness. Right now, he figured, on the other side of that heat-haze barrier, someone would be taking the first steps on Mars. Maybe it would be his old buddy, Slade, or someone like John Young. Bado might have made it himself.

Bado missed the live sports on TV.

In free fall, Taine gives them spare cotton coveralls to wear, which are comfortable but don't quite fit; the name stitched to Bado's is *Leduc*, and on Williams', *Hassell*.

Bado, with relief, peels off the three layers of his pressure suit: the outer micrometeorite garment, the pressure assembly, and the inner cooling garment. The other passengers look on curiously at Bado's cooling garment, with its network of tubes. Bado tucks his discarded suit layers into a big net bag and sticks it behind his couch.

They are served food: stodgy stew, lukewarm and glued to the plate with gravy, and then some kind of dessert, like bread with currants stuck inside it. Spotted Dick, Taine calls it.

There is a persistent whine of fans and pumps, a subdued murmur of conversation, and the noise of children crying. Once a five-year-old, all of six feet tall, came bouncing around the curving cabin in a spidery tangle of attenuated arms and legs, pursued by a fat, panting, queasy-looking parent.

Taine comes floating down to them, smiling. "Captain Richards would like to speak to you. He's intrigued to have you on board. We've picked up quite a few alternate-colonists, but not many alternate-pioneers, like you. Would you come forward to the cockpit? Perhaps you'd like to watch the show from there."

Williams and Bado exchange glances. "What show?"

"The impact, of course. Come. Your German friend is welcome too, of course," Taine adds dubiously.

The cosmonaut has his head stuck inside a sick bag.

"I think he's better off where he is," Bado says.

"You go," Williams says. "I want to try to sleep." Her face looks worn to Bado, her expression brittle, as if she is struggling to keep control. Maybe the shock of the transitions is getting to her at last, he thinks.

The cockpit is cone-shaped, wadded right in the nose of the craft. Taine leads Bado in through a big oval door. Charts and mathematical tables have been stuck to the walls, alongside pictures and photographs. Some of these show powerful-looking aircraft, of designs unfamiliar to Bado, but others show what must be family members. Pet dogs. Tools and personal articles are secured to the walls with elastic straps.

Three spacesuits, flaccid and empty, are fixed to the wall with loose ties. They are of the type Taine wore in the airlock: thick and flexible, with inlaid metal hoops, and hinged helmets at the top.

Three seats are positioned before instrument consoles. Right now the seats face forward, toward the nose of the craft, but Bado can see they are hinged so they will tip up when the craft is landing vertically. Bado spots a big, chunky periscope sticking out from the nose, evidently there to provide a view out during a landing.

There are big picture windows set in the walls. The windows frame slabs of jet-black, star-sprinkled sky.

A man is sitting in the central pilot's chair. He is wearing a leather flight jacket, a peaked cap, and—Bado can't believe it—he is smoking a pipe, for God's sake. The guy sticks out a hand. "Mr. Bado. I'm glad to meet you. Jim Richards, RAF."

"That's Colonel Bado." Bado shakes the hand. "U.S. Air Force. Lately of NASA."

"NASA?"

"National Aeronautics and Space Administration . . ."

Richards nods. "American. Interesting. Not many of the alternates are American. I'm sorry we didn't get a chance to see more of your ship. Looked a little cramped for the three of you."

"It wasn't our ship. It was a Russian, a one-man lander."

"Really," Richards murmurs, not very interested. "Take a seat." He waves Bado at one of the two seats beside him; Taine takes the other, sipping tea through a straw. Richards asks, "Have you ever seen a ship like this before, Colonel Bado?"

Bado glances around. The main controls are a conventional stick-and-rudder design, adapted for spaceflight; the supplementary controls are big, clunky switches, wheels, and levers. The fascia of the control panel is made of wood. And in one place, where a maintenance panel has been removed, Bado sees the soft glow of vacuum tubes.

"No," he says. "Not outside the comic books."

Richards and Taine laugh.

"It must take a hell of a launch system."

"Oh," says Richards. "We have good old Beta to help us with that."

"Beta?"

"This lunar ship is called Alpha," Taine says. "Beta gives us a piggyback out of Earth's gravity. We launch from Woomera, in South Australia. Beta is a hypersonic athodyd—"

Richards winks at Bado. "These double-domes, eh? He means Beta is an atomic ramjet."

Bado boggles. "You launch an atomic rocket from the middle of Australia? How do you manage containment of the exhaust?"

Taine looks puzzled. "What containment?"

"You must tell me all about your spacecraft," Richards says.

Bado, haltingly, starts to describe the Apollo system.

Richards listens politely enough, but after a while Bado can see his eyes drifting to his instruments, and he begins to fiddle with his pipe, knocking out the dottle into a big enclosed ashtray.

Richards becomes aware of Bado watching him. "Oh, you must forgive me, Colonel Bado. It's just that one encounters so many alternates."

"You do, huh."

"The Massolite, you know. That damn quantum-mechanical leakage. Plessey just can't get the thing tuned correctly. Such a pity. Anyhow, don't you worry; the boffins on the ground will put you to rights, I'm sure."

Bado is deciding he doesn't like these British. They are smug, patronizing, icy. He can't tell what they are thinking.

Taine leans forward. "Almost time, Jim."

"Aha!" Richards gets hold of his joystick. "The main event." He twists the stick, and Bado hears what sounds like the whir of flywheels, deep in the guts of the ship. Stars slide past the windows. "A bit of showmanship, Colonel Bado. I want to line us up to give the passengers the best possible view. And us, of course. After all, this is a grandstand seat, for the most dramatic astronomical event of the century—what?"

The Moon, fat and gray and more than half-full, slides into the frame of the windows.

The Moon—Moon Five, Bado assumes it to be—looks like a ball of glass, its surface cracked and complex, as if scarred by buckshot. Tinged pale white, the Moon's center looms out at Bado, given three-dimensional substance by the Earthlight's shading.

The Moon looks different. He tries to figure out why.

There, close to the central meridian, are the bright pinpricks of Tycho, to the south, and Copernicus, in the north. He makes out the familiar pattern of the seas of the eastern hemisphere: Serenitatis, Crisium, Tranquillitatis—gray lakes of frozen lava framed by brighter, older lunar uplands.

He supposes there must be no Apollo 11 LM descent stage, standing on this version of the Sea of Tranquility.

The Moon is mostly full, but he can see lights in the remaining crescent of darkness. They are the abandoned colonies of Moon Five.

Something is still wrong, though. The western hemisphere doesn't look right. He takes his anchor from Copernicus. There is Mare Procellarum, to the western limb, and to the north of that nothing but bright highlands.

"Hey," he says. "Where the hell's Mare Imbrium?"

Richards looks at him, puzzled, faintly disapproving.

Bado points. "Up there. In the northwest. A big impact crater—the biggest—flooded with lava. Eight hundred miles across."

Richards frowns, and Taine touches Bado's arm. "All the alternate Moons are different to some degree," he says, placating. "Differences of detail—"

"Mare Imbrium is not a goddamn detail." Bado feels patronized again. "You're talking about my Moon, damn it." But if the Imbrium impact has never happened, no wonder the surface of Moon Five looks different.

Richards checks his wristwatch. "Any second now," he says. "If the big brains have got it right—"

There is a burst of light, in the Moon's northwest quadrant. The surface in the region of the burst seems to shatter, the bright old highland material melting and subsiding into a red-glowing pool, a fiery lake that covers perhaps an eighth of the Moon's face. Bado watches huge waves, concentric, wash out across that crimson, circular wound.

Even from this distance Bado can see huge debris clouds streaking across the lunar surface, obscuring and burying older features, and laying down bright rays that plaster across the Moon's face.

The lights of the night-side colonies wink out, one by one.

Richards takes his pipe out of his mouth. "Good God almighty," he says. "Thank heavens we got all our people off."

"Only just in time, sir," Taine says.

Bado nods. "Oh, I get it. Here, this was the Imbrium impact. Three billion years late."

Richards and Taine look at him curiously.

. . .

It turned out that to build a teleport device—a "Star Trek" beaming machine—you needed to know about quantum mechanics. Particularly the Uncertainty Principle.

According to one interpretation, the Uncertainty Principle was fundamentally caused by there being an infinite number of parallel universes, all lying close to each other—as Bado pictured it—like the pages of a book. The universes blurred together at the instant of an event, and split off afterward.

The Uncertainty Principle said you could never measure the position and velocity of any particle with absolute precision. But to teleport that was exactly what you needed to do: to make a record of an object, transmit it, and re-create the payload at the other end.

But there was a way to get around the Uncertainty Principle. At least in theory.

The quantum properties of particles could become entangled: fundamentally linked in their information content. What those British must have done is take sets of entangled particles, left one-half on their Moon as a transmitter, and planted the other half on the Earth.

There was a lot of technical stuff about the Einstein-Podolsky-Rosen theorem that Bado skipped over; what it boiled down to was that if you used a description of your teleport passenger to jiggle the transmitter particles, you could reconstruct the passenger at the other end, exactly, from the corresponding jiggles in the receiver set.

But there were problems.

If there were small nonlinearities in the quantum-mechanical operators—and there couldn't be more than a billion billion billionth part, according to Bado's researchers—those parallel worlds, underlying the Uncertainty Principle, could short-circuit.

The Moon Five Brits had tried to build a cheap-and-dirty teleport machine. Because of the huge distances involved, that billion-billion-billionth nonlinearity had become significant, and the damn thing had leaked. And so they had built a parallel-world gateway, by accident.

This might be the right explanation, Bado thought. It fit with Captain Richards' vague hints about "nonlinear quantum mechanics."

This new understanding didn't make any difference to his position, though. He was still stranded here. The teleport devices his researchers had outlined—even if they'd got the theory right from the fragments he'd given them—were decades beyond the capabilities of the mundane world Bado found himself in.

Re-entry is easy. Bado estimates the peak acceleration is no more than a couple of G, no worse than a mild rollercoaster. Even so, many of the passengers look distressed, and those spindly lunar-born children cry weakly, pinned to their seats like insects.

After the landing, Alpha's big doors are flung open to reveal a flat, barren desert. Bado and Williams are among the first down the rope ladders, lugging their pressure suits, and Bado's tool carrier, in big net bags.

Bado can see a small town, laid out with the air of a military barracks.

Staff are coming out of the town on little trucks to meet them. They are processed efficiently; the crew of the *Prometheus* gives details of where each passenger was picked up, and they are all assigned little labels and forms, standing there in the baking sunlight of the desert.

The spindly lunar children are lowered to the ground and taken off in wheelchairs. Bado wonders what will happen to them, stranded at the bottom of Earth's deep gravity well.

Williams points. "Look at that. Another *Prometheus*."

There is a launch rail, like a pencil line ruled across the sand, diminishing to infinity at the horizon. A silver dart clings to the rail, with a slim bullet shape fixed to its back. Another Beta and Alpha. Bado can see protective rope barriers slung around the rail.

Taine comes to greet Bado and Williams. "I'm afraid this is goodbye," he says. He sticks out a hand. "We want to get you people back as quickly as we can. You alternates, I mean. What a frightful mess this is. But the sooner you're out of it the better."

"Back where?" Bado asks.

"Florida." Taine looks at them. "That's where you say you started from, isn't it?"

Williams shrugs. "Sure."

"And then back to your own world." He mimes stirring a pot of some noxious substance. "We don't want to muddy the time lines, you see. We don't know much about this alternating business; we don't know what damage we might do. Of course the return procedure's still experimental but hopefully we'll get it right. Well, the best of luck. Look, just make your way to the plane over there." He points.

The plane is a ramjet, Bado sees immediately.

Taine moves on, to another bewildered-looking knot of passengers.

The Russian cosmonaut is standing at Williams' side. He is hauling his stiff pressure suit along the ground; it scrapes on the sand like an insect's discarded carapace. Out of the suit the Russian looks thin, young, baffled, quite ill. He shakes Bado's hand. *"Do svidanya."*

"Yeah. So long to you too, kid. Hope you get home safely. A hell of a ride, huh."

"Mnye nada k zoobnomoo vrachoo." He clutches his jaw and grins ruefully. *"Schastleevava pootee. Zhilayoo oospyekhaf."*

"Yeah. Whatever."

A British airman comes over and leads the Russian away.

"Goddamn," Williams says. "We never found out his name."

He got a report in from his meteorite studies group.

Yes, it turned out, there was a large object on its way. It would be here in a few years' time. Bado figured this had to be this universe's edition of that big old Imbrium rock, arriving a little later than in the Moon Five world.

But this rock was heading for Earth, not the Moon. Its path would take it right into the middle of the Atlantic, if the calculations were right. But the margins of error were huge, and, and . . .

Bado tried to raise public awareness. His money and fame got him onto TV, even, such as it was. But nobody here took what was going on in the sky very seriously anyhow, and they soon started to think he was a little weird.

So he shut up. He pushed his money into bases at the poles, and at the bottom of the oceans, places that mightn't be so badly affected. Somebody might survive. Meanwhile he paid for a little more research into that big rock in space, and where and when, exactly, it was going to hit.

The ramjet takes ten hours to get to Florida. It is a military ship, more advanced than anything flying in Bado's world. It has the bull's-eye logo of the RAF painted to its flank, just behind the gaping mouth of its inlet.

As the ramjet rises, Bado glimpses huge atomic aircraft, immense ocean-going ships, networks of monorails. This is a gleaming world, an engineer's dream.

Bado has had enough wonders for the time being, though, and, before the shining coast of Australia has receded from sight, he's fallen asleep.

They land at a small airstrip, Bado figures somewhere north of Orlando. A thin young Englishman in spectacles is there to greet them. He is wearing Royal Air Force blue coveralls. "You're the alternates?"

"I guess so," Williams snaps. "And you're here to send us home. Right?"

"Sorry for any inconvenience you've been put through," he says smoothly. "If you'll just follow me into the van . . ."

The van turns out to be a battered diesel-engined truck that looks as if it is World War II vintage. Williams and Bado, with their bulky gear, have to crowd in the back with a mess of electronic equipment.

The truck, windowless, bumps along badly finished roads.

Bado studies the equipment. "Look at this stuff," he says to Williams. "More vacuum tubes."

Williams shrugs. "They've got further than we have. Or you. Here, they've built stuff we've only talked about."

"Yeah." Oddly, he's forgotten that he and Williams have come from different worlds.

The roads off the peninsula to Merritt Island are just farmers' tracks, and the last few miles are the most uncomfortable.

They arrive at Merritt Island in the late afternoon.

There is no Kennedy Space Center.

Bado gets out of the van. He is on a long, flat beach; he figures he is a way south of where, in his world, the lunar ship launch pads will be built. Right here there will be the line of launch complexes called ICBM Row.

But he can't see any structures at all. Marsh land, coated with scrub vegetation, stretches down toward the strip of beach at the coast. Farther inland, toward the higher ground, he can see stands of cabbage palm, slash pine, and oak.

The place is just scrub land, undeveloped. The tracks of the British truck are dug crisply into the sand; there is no sign even of a road near here.

And out to the east, over the Atlantic, he can see a big full Moon rising. Its upper left quadrant, the fresh Imbrium scar, still glows a dull crimson. Bado feels vaguely reassured. That is still Moon Five; things seem to have achieved a certain stability.

In the back of the truck, the British technician powers up his equipment. "Ready when you are," he calls. "Oh, we think it's best if you go back in your own clothes. Where possible." He grins behind his spectacles. "Don't want you—"

"Muddying up the time lines," Williams says. "We know."

Bado and Williams shuck off their coveralls and pull on their pressure suits. They help each other with the heavy layers, and finish up facing each other, their helmets under their arms, Bado holding his battered tool carrier with its Baggies full of Moon rocks.

"You know," Bado says, "when I get back I'm going to have one hell of a lot of explaining to do."

"Yeah. Me too." She looks at him. "I guess we're not going to see each other again."

"Doesn't look like it."

Bado puts down his carrier and helmet. He embraces Williams, clumsily.

Then, on impulse, Bado lifts up his helmet and fits it over his head. He pulls his gloves over his hands and snaps them onto his wrists, completing his suit.

Williams does the same. Bado picks up his tool carrier.

The Brit waves, reaches into his van, and throws a switch.

There is a shimmer of heat haze.

Williams has gone. The truck has vanished.

Bado looks around quickly.

There are no ICBM launch complexes. He is still standing on an empty, desolate beach.

The Moon is brightening, as the light leaks out of the sky. There is no ancient Imbrium basin up there. No recent impact scar, either.

"Moon Six," Bado says to himself. "Oh, shit."

Evidently those British haven't ironed out all the wrinkles in their "experimental procedures" after all.

He takes off his helmet, breathes in the ozone-laden ocean air, and begins to walk inland, toward the rows of scrub pine.

On the day, he drove out to Merritt Island.

It was morning, and the sun was low and bright over the ocean, off to the east, and the sky was clear and blue, blameless.

He pulled his old Moon suit out of the car, and hauled it on: first the cooling garment, then the pressure layer, and finally the white micrometeorite protector and his blue lunar overshoes. It didn't fit so well any more, especially around the waist—well, it had been fitted for him all of a quarter-century ago—and it felt as heavy as hell, even without the backpack. And it had a lot of parts missing, where he'd dug out components and samples over the years. But it was still stained gray below the knees with lunar dust, and it still had the NASA logo, his mission patch, and his own name stitched to the outer garment.

He walked down to the beach. The tide was receding, and the hard-packed sand was damp; his ridged soles left crisp, sharp prints, just like in the lunar crust.

He locked his helmet into place at his neck.

To stand here, as close as he could get to ground zero, wasn't such a dumb thing to do, actually. He'd always remembered what that old professor at Cornell had told him, about the rocks bearing life being blasted from planet to planet by meteorite impacts. Maybe that would happen here, somehow.

Today might be the last day for this Earth. But maybe, somehow, some piece of him, fused to the glass of his visor maybe, would finish up on the Moon—Moon Six—or Mars, or in the clouds of Jupiter, and start the whole thing over again.

He felt a sudden, sharp stab of nostalgia, for his own lost world. He'd had a good life here, all things considered. But this was a damn dull place. And he'd been here for twenty-five years already. He was sure that back home that old Vietnam War wouldn't have dragged on until now, like it had here, and funds would have got freed up for space, at last. Enough to do it properly, by God. By now, he was sure, NASA would have bases on the Moon, hundreds of people in Earth orbit, a couple of outposts on Mars, plans to go on to the asteroids or Jupiter.

Hell, he wished he could just look through the nonlinear curtains separating him from home. Just once.

He tipped up his face. The sun was bright in his eyes, so he pulled down his gold visor. It was still scuffed, from the dust kicked up by that British nuclear rocket. He waited.

After a time, a new light, brighter even than rocket light, came crawling down across the sky, and touched the ocean.

we will drink a fish together . . .
BILL JOHNSON

In the suspenseful but rather quirky story that follows, an alien ambassador travels down from the stars to go to someplace really alien: Summit, South Dakota. Where he receives an entertaining, eccentric, and pleasantly offbeat lesson about the value of interpersonal ties that may well broaden your own definition of "family." . . .

Bill Johnson is a forty-year-old engineering manager, who works on advanced multimedia hardware and software development for Motorola. A graduate of Clarion, he has sold stories to Analog, Asimov's Science Fiction, *and elsewhere. Originally from South Dakota, he and his wife and two children now live in Illinois. Whether he drinks fish or not, he doesn't say.*

▼

I'm sorry to call you at work, Tony," my brother said, "but Sam died about an hour ago."

Sweet Jesus, I thought. *I could never get time to go see him, and now there's no time left. What have I done?*

"Was it easy on him? Did he go quick?" I asked.

Steve shook his head.

"It wasn't good, Tony. They think he fainted or something and fell while he was getting a shirt out of his closet. Probably hit his head against the door frame on his way down. His roommate was out walking with the nurses and nobody noticed Sam was missing. They found him later. He was unconscious and bleeding."

"Damn," I said softly. "Did they take him to the hospital?"

Steve shook his head again. "Doctor was there already at the home for someone else, so they put Sam back in his bed and sewed up his head. Then he started to complain about pain in his gut." He looked down and away from the camera. I heard a high-pitched voice and laughter and the sound of little running feet. Elizabeth, fresh from her second birthday party, crawled up in Steve's lap.

"Hi, hi, hi," she said in a sing-song voice. She reached up and kissed her daddy, her face and fingers still sticky and speckled with pink icing.

"Elizabeth!"

Elizabeth's mother, Rose, appeared briefly on-screen behind her. She grabbed Elizabeth around the middle and swung her up to rest on one hip, then glanced at me and smiled. She handed Steve a brightly colored paper napkin with "Happy Birthday" printed on it in fluorescent pink and blue with the other hand.

"Elizabeth, Daddy's trying to talk with Uncle Tony," she said. She was a short woman, medium build, with strong arms and blonde hair cut in a shag. She turned quickly to face me. "Hello, Tony. I'm sorry to hear about Sam." She turned back to Elizabeth. "Let's go back to the party, honey. It's time to open presents."

"Open presents!" Elizabeth said with enthusiasm. She wiggled off her mother's hip and headed for the kitchen, her mother dragging behind her.

Steve brushed crumbs off his clothes and icing off his face and looked up at me. We both smiled.

"She gets worse after this," I warned. "Two year olds are very busy people."

"Like she isn't already," Steve said ruefully.

"So, what happened?" I asked. "Was it his abdominal aorta again?"

"Probably, but there's no way to tell without an autopsy, and I don't think we need one of those," Steve said. He took a deep breath and looked away from me. He did not look happy. "Tony, he didn't want to go through the hospital routine again. After his last attack he put himself on a DNR."

DNR. Do Not Resuscitate. A big red flag written in dry medical language. In ordinary English it meant the patient was ready to die, and wanted to go quickly and easily, without massive intervention. I tried to imagine Sam hooked up to monitors and tubes and needles, a thin, frail figure lost among the machines. Sam never lived like that, and it hurt to even imagine him dying that way. DNR was one hell of a better way to go. Especially for Sam.

"Dissected aorta hurts a little bit," I said with careful understatement. Like a red-hot charcoal burning in your stomach, Sam told me after his last stay in the hospital. Like a cramp that never ends, and just gets tighter and tighter until it's a digging rat bite that never goes away.

"They gave him morphine like water," Steve said. "As much as he wanted."

"Did it work?"

"They said it did," Steve said. He sounded doubtful. He was a respiratory therapist at the University of Nebraska Hospitals. He knew all about DNR's and aortas and how hard it was to die. "There's always a first time for something to work."

"When's the funeral?" I asked.

"Bob and I are going up to Dakota tomorrow. We've got to deal with the bankers and the lawyers," Steve said with distaste. "Funeral will be on Saturday."

I thought quickly about work and schedules and how fast I could re-arrange my life. Luckily, or unfortunately, I didn't have much of a life to re-arrange. Just this once that was an advantage.

"How about you fly in to Omaha on Thursday and drive up with Rose on Friday morning?" Steve said. "Rose's sister will come to take care of Elizabeth but she can't get free until Thursday night. That will also give us two cars up there."

"However you want to do it, little brother. You're in charge on this one," I said.

"Thanks. I feel so lucky."

"I'm sorry, Steve. It doesn't seem fair. . . ."

"But I'm a lot closer and I'm executor of the estate," Steve finished for me. He hesitated. "Are you sure you can get away? I watch the news. I've seen you in the background around the alien."

I thought about my orders to keep everything confidential, and mentally said *screw it*. Steve wasn't in the media and he knew how to keep his mouth shut.

"Yeah, I'm on security detail for the ambassador."

"Can you get away? I mean, we can handle this if you can't. Everybody will understand."

I stiffened. Something must have shown on my face because Steve winced slightly.

"This is family business, Steve. I know what I've got to do. I'll be there. You don't have to worry about me."

"We'll see you at the house on Friday, then," Steve said. "Visitation starts at three in Milbank."

I killed the call and leaned back in my chair. The holster around my shoulders tugged at me and I absently took it off and laid it on the desk. I rubbed my shoulders and looked out the window. Spring was well advanced in the District, and the trees were heavy with buds and a few leaves. The cherry trees were in full bloom.

I checked the weather forecast for Dakota. Sleet, mixed with snow. Just about what I expected. It could be a full greenhouse summer everywhere else in the country, and Dakota would get a blizzard.

Enough delay. I took a deep breath and made the call.

"Carole? Tony. I need to take a few personal leave days. . . ."

"No," she said.

Five minutes after I called her, and got my first "No," I was in her office.

"Not a chance. No way. You're in charge of the security detail for the ambassador. You can take time off later, when the negotiations are all over, but not now. I'm sorry," Carole said.

I stared at the wall behind and above her. Everything in her office, from the standard-issue metal desk to her green, plastic-covered swivel chair to the lead-lined anti-surveillance curtains that tightly covered the windows, was standard government issue. The same government that helped get me the hell out of Dakota, that gave me a career, that told me I was important and gave me a job that *was* important. I took a deep breath.

"Then I quit. You'll have my resignation letter in an hour."

"You can't resign!"

"I just did."

Carole stood behind her desk and glared up at me. She was trim and athletic, but she couldn't have weighed more than 130 pounds. She was medium height for a woman, which meant the top of her head came to just below my sternum.

In other words, I could have picked her up, tucked her under my arm and carried her around without any trouble.

She scared the hell out of me.

"You'll give up everything to go to a damn funeral?"

"Carole, he raised my Dad. He was the closest thing to a grandfather I had," I pleaded.

"I understand," she said softly. "I really do. I wish you could go. I *want* you to go. But not now. Not after last Monday."

Monday I became a hero, and the memory still hurt. I remembered the sudden feeling I had as I stood next to the ambassador, that it might be better if I moved just half a step to the left. Then the sudden flare of pain, and the way I spun and flailed as the bullet meant for the alien slammed into my impact vest.

The ambassador looked down at me, everything seeming to move in slow motion, his face a mask. Then he was buried under a pile of agents as they pushed him to the ground and covered him with their own bodies. The reaction team grabbed the shooter, and interrogation tracked him back to a reactionary group.

It was a simple solution. A crazy with a gun was something everyone could understand. And nobody got hurt except for me, and the vest protected me so that all I got was a huge bruise on my chest. The whole incident flashed on the news for maybe a day, and then was quickly forgotten. Everything was tied up nice and neat.

Too neat.

Where did he get the gun? Where did he get the ID? How did he get so close?

What else was going on here?

The answers were logical and reasonable and too damned easy. Carole and I both suspected something more was involved, but there was no proof. Maybe we were too suspicious, but part of our job was to look for a conspiracy in everything.

Now I just didn't have the time.

"Carole, I've got to bury Sam."

"Your brothers are there, right? They can bury him. You can pay your respects later," she said. She looked away, shook her head, then looked up at me and her face softened. "Tony, he's not going to know you're not there. Life is for the living, and I'm sure he'd want you to do your work first. I'm sure he'd understand."

I thought about Sam.

"First thing you've got to understand is that flatlanders might look like us, might sound like us, might even be related to us, but they don't think like us," Sam said in his cigarette rasp voice. I stood next to him in my footed pajamas, my favorite blanket in one hand, my other hand in his, and remembered how tall he looked as I stared up at him and his whisker-studded face. "Flatlanders measure themselves as individuals, and they use work as the measuring stick. We are different. To us,

family *is more important than kin.* Kin *are more important than* line. Line *is more important than any outsider. And* everything *is more important than* work."

No, I did not think Sam would understand.

"Damn it, Carole, I'm the oldest," I said, frustrated. How to explain this to someone from the flats? I tried to make myself calm. "I'm the eldest in the line now. I've got to be there at the funeral."

She looked up at my stubborn face, and tried another tack.

"What if our side needs you in the negotiations? Ambassador Foremost says he owes you a favor. What if we need to use that?"

I remembered Foremost, when he and Carole came to visit me in the examination room after the attack. I remembered his voice, dry as sandpaper and correct as a computer, his head cocked to the side with a nervous manner that always reminded me of the jerky movements of my pet parakeet. The rest of him, however, looked nothing like a bird. He was stockily built, just a few inches taller than Carole, and broad. Underneath the robes and harness I knew he was all muscle and bone, with a protective exoskeleton over his most vulnerable points. He was an omnivore, and the exobiologists claimed he was descended from cursorial hunters, much like early man. He looked more like a wolverine than an ape, but I liked the way he thought.

And that was part of the problem, when the Trader ship found us. Our races were different enough that communication was difficult, and similar enough that we were potential competitors. Potential for war or peace, trade or conflict. We seemed to be more advanced in some technologies that they wanted, but they never let us forget that they found us, not the other way around. And with a starship in orbit that could reach any place on Earth, they held the high ground.

Our weapons might be better, but we had no way to get them up and on target. Our boosters were too weak, and the Traders routinely destroyed anything that came near their ship and might even remotely be considered a threat to it.

The Traders, on the other hand, could drop asteroids on us from space. But asteroid strikes were not going to help them understand our genetic engineering technology. Or get the humans rumor said they wanted to bring on board to join their crew.

So we exchanged ambassadors, and started to negotiate.

And negotiate.

And negotiate.

"Where you suffer, I suffer," Foremost told me in the hospital. He held my hand and looked closely into my eyes. "In my line, your name is now written."

Carole looked puzzled, but what the ambassador said made perfect sense to me. It did not make me happy, but I understood it. I wondered what obligations went with his line. I thought briefly of rejecting him, but I did not know how he would react. Safer to say yes.

Really? a small voice inside me said. *Are you sure about this?*

I thought carefully.

"I accept," I said. "What I have to tell you, though, is that in my line your name is *not* written."

He hesitated, then bowed his head.

"I understand and accept this. Perhaps one day I will earn the right to write my name in your line."

I relaxed, just a little. One part down. And no threats of war.

"But I'll make sure you're associated with my line as long as you're here, and my guest," I said.

He looked up, his eyes as black and hard and dead as a shark's. I tried to read his expression in his face, but he was too unfamiliar, too different.

"I accept," he said. He stood and left the hospital room.

I watched him as he left, his robe tight around his body. Now I was part of his line, and he was associated with mine. As long as he was on Earth he could claim protection and assistance from me and mine.

I hoped to hell he did not understand what I had just done for him. And I hoped I never had to find out what he had done for me.

That conversation was a week old, and that week seemed like a century ago. A week ago Sam was alive, and I was free to live any way I wanted, without responsibility. Now I had a different set of problems, and Foremost was not in them. Now my problem was Sam, and all the changes that Sam's death made to my life.

I shook my head to clear it of memories and looked up at Carole.

"It's not that kind of a favor," I said. "Any personal business Foremost and I have is just that, personal business. Nothing I can say or do will have any effect on the negotiations."

"But—"

"No," I said and cut her off. I stood.

"I'm going to the funeral, Carole. You'll have my resignation letter in an hour."

I flew into Omaha the next day.

Rose, with Elizabeth propped on one hip, met me at the airport. When Rose saw me she put Elizabeth down and waved to me. I hurried to them and got a quick hug from Rose and a big, sloppy kiss on the cheek from Elizabeth.

"Would you like to fly, Elizabeth?" I asked.

"No," she said firmly. She hid her face in her mother's skirt, then peeked an eye out at me and smiled.

"Just a little bit?" I coaxed.

"Oh, Tony," Rose said. "Here?"

"Here," I said firmly.

I picked Elizabeth up under her arms and swung her through the air, feet flying wildly, oblivious to the stares of the other passengers, just because I missed her. She laughed and giggled and threw her head back. Rose just smiled and shook her head while Elizabeth's hair swirled and flowed behind her.

"If you're done now," Rose said, when I put Elizabeth back on the ground. Elizabeth tried to walk in a straight line and instead staggered from side to side, like a drunken sailor, dizzy from her flight. She laughed and laughed until I scooped her up and put her on my shoulders. She grabbed my ears to use as steering handles.

"I'm ready now," I told Rose.

I liked Omaha and I liked Steve's house. It was a ranch style, built into the side of a hill so the basement was more like a first floor. He lived in a neighborhood on the far west side of Omaha, out where new subdivisions sprouted like wildflowers and cornfields fought a losing battle against construction bulldozers.

Elizabeth took me by the hand and walked me around inside and outside the house to show me her flowers and her toys. Rose walked next to me and worried.

"I saw you get shot on the news," she said, and everything about her changed with those words. Rose my sister-in-law vanished and suddenly she was Rose the nurse and I was a patient. She subtly moved back a step to look at all of me, then stepped in closer to focus on my chest, where the bullet struck. I wondered how she did the transition so quickly. "Are you all right?"

"They checked me out at Walter Reed," I reassured her. "I'm fine."

"And the ambassador?"

"Not a scratch on him."

"You're not there with him now, Tony."

I checked out the tulips that Elizabeth pointed out to me. There were red flowers and white flowers and buds that had not yet opened.

"Security is with him all the time," I said. "I was just one more agent."

Rose walked away from us a few steps. Elizabeth saw a monarch butterfly and raced off to chase it. I saw the butterfly was in no danger, so I went after Rose.

We stood for a moment in the backyard and looked across the fence toward the fields. Next year they might sprout houses, but this year they still followed older rhythms. Furrows, newly plowed and rich with the stubble left over from last year's harvesting, waited for corn planting. The soil was black and ready, thick with the morning dew and last weekend's rain.

"Do you think things always get better, Tony?" she asked.

I did not think she was talking about the cornfield.

"No," I said, after a moment. "Things don't always get better. They may get better or they may get worse, but it's not an always kind of thing. The only thing that is always is change. Sometimes things change on a regular cycle, like the planting and the growing and the harvesting and the fallowing. Sometimes they change on a bigger cycle, and the smaller cycles change with them or are destroyed. Whether it's good or bad depends on where you stand and what you care about."

"I don't like change, Tony," she said. "Everything I love is in those smaller cycles, the regular ones. I don't know anything about the bigger cycles except that they might crush what I love."

"I know," I said awkwardly.

She turned away from the fields to face me, her arms folded across her chest. She looked down at the ground, then turned her head and looked out across the fields.

"We got rid of the bombs down here. Things finally looked safe for little girls to grow up. Then the Traders arrive," she said bitterly. "I couldn't stand it if anything happened to her."

I hugged her, gently. I wanted to tell her everything was going to be all right, but I kept my mouth shut and watched Elizabeth chase butterflies. Finally, Rose reached up and patted my hand.

"Let's get inside. We've got a long ride tomorrow."

Rose never went to the north with Steve when he went up to Dakota to fish and hunt and visit Sam. Instead she stayed down south, in Nebraska and Iowa, and worked or visited her folks. This time she had to go north.

Margaret, Rose's unmarried sister, came to stay with Elizabeth while we were gone. As far as Elizabeth was concerned, she had two mamas. Margaret loved the idea, and Rose was always more relaxed when Margaret was in charge instead of a daycare center. We settled Elizabeth with Margaret, said all our good-byes, left all the emergency numbers, and drove north.

The interstate highway was on the Iowa side of the Missouri. I drove and Rose navigated as we followed the flat ribbon of gray concrete, two lanes wide in each direction, a man-made river of traffic. The river itself was out of sight on our left most of the time, and the loess hills, huge mounds of windblown dirt, rose up like miniature Rocky Mountains on our right. Gradually the hills arched away to the east and out of sight.

The Missouri curled back into view just as the smell hit us. Rose quickly rolled up the windows as we passed the mountain of manure from the Sioux City stockyards, and the giant billboard that declared: "This golden mountain represents millions to the Siouxland economy—"

North of downtown we passed over massive housing developments that rolled far to the east and west, like grass over a prairie. Neatly edged lawns and streets laid out in geometrically perfect curves and loops and cul-de-sacs spread out around us like some enormous geometrical poster child.

We crossed into South Dakota, over the Big Sioux river, and past the computer factories that hugged the Dakota side of the river. The factories were there because the corporate taxes were lower in Dakota, but the schools and the services and everything else were better in Iowa. So the houses and the people lived south of the Sioux, and the work stayed in Dakota.

Somehow, I was not surprised.

As we headed north, as the trees got fewer and fewer and smaller and smaller and more twisted and gnarled by the wind, Rose got quieter and quieter. She was an Iowa farm girl at heart, even if she was an expert transplant nurse, and she knew how a farm ought to be run. Nice and tidy. When she saw the fields had no fences, that the animals basically had nothing to stop them from coming across the roads, she had nothing to say.

The exit off the main road was marked by a stop sign and a small truck stop that had seen better days. It looked lost and forlorn in the icy drizzle and there was no sign of life except for a neon sign that sporadically blinked an advertisement for a cheap, local beer.

We turned right down a small two-lane blacktop road. I pointed across the brown cattails of a marsh to a copse of trees on the horizon.

"Summit," I said.

Summit had a population sign—a small, metal rectangle with the town name and the population—at the turn off the main road. The sign read: 277. Now it was 276. We turned down Main Street, the only paved road in town, turned left at the pool hall, slid down gravel and clay roads for two blocks, then turned left again.

Sam's house was a tiny white two-story A-frame. The green roof was speckled with black rectangles where shingles had blown free. The exterior was leafed metal siding, smeared with rust marks where the builder used cheap, ungalvanized nails. My brothers were inside. We saw their cars parked outside on the lawn, next to the smoking, burning barrels where they were burning trash from Sam's house. The air was thick and humid with freezing rain and smoke.

I pushed open the door to Sam's house and we entered through the mudroom. We opened the door to the kitchen and a wave of heat and dust slapped us in the face. We went inside and the dust started us both coughing. My brother Bob sat in a big, overstuffed chair under a window. The curtain was drawn tight across the window. He looked up at us and smiled through his big, black beard as Rose sneezed.

"Just think of all them skin cells from Sam and Laverne. Thousands and millions and billions of them," Bob said. We coughed and he smiled again. "Wish we could open a window for you, but it's too cold outside."

In DC, in Nebraska, hell, even in the rest of South Dakota, it was spring. Here, 2000 feet above sea level, on the highest spot between the Missouri and the Mississippi rivers, it was still winter.

Outside, we heard a noise:

Whirrrrrr

"Oh, no," Steve said. He stood next to the kitchen counter with a bottle of beer in his hand. "Not him again."

Bob grinned. I closed my eyes and prayed. Around me I felt Dakota settle lightly, the first layer, and grasp me firmly.

Rose stepped next to her husband, a little speck next to a giant. Steve, just as tall as me and even bigger, just shook his head and put on a long-suffering expression. Rose watched all three of us and looked puzzled.

Roaaarrrr

"Again," Steve said, resignation thick in his voice.

Bob grinned again, but this time it was strained. I looked around and tried to figure out how I could get out of the house quickly, without my brothers taking vengeance later for leaving them like a coward.

There was only one door out, and it was too late.

Silence.

"What's going on?" Rose asked in a whisper. She looked nervous and pulled a little closer to Steve. I shook my head and Steve squeezed his eyes shut, made a face, and opened them again. Bob slumped deeper in his overstuffed chair.

A perfunctory knock at the door and we heard it swing open and Indian stepped inside. He was medium height, with long, greasy black hair pulled into a tail. His skin was coppery-brown, and his eyes were black and glassy. He wore a green combat jacket, torn and stained with grease, and a pair of jeans.

"How ya doin'?"

"Fine, Indian," Bob said. He gestured vaguely toward the outside, glanced at Rose, and grinned. "Got your town car outside?"

"Yep, yeah, I do," he said, his voice deep and hoarse, chopped off, as if each syllable came from the edge of an axe.

"Not the country car?"

"No, no, that one I'm still workin' on. Yep, yeah, got that by the house up on some blocks," he said. He laughed, a deep, throaty noise.

"Ya know, Sam was a good friend of mine, my buddy. He leave me anything in the will?"

"We don't know," Steve said. He knew. He was executor of the will. But he did not want to talk with Indian. Particularly when Indian was drunk. "You'll have to ask the lawyer."

"Yep, yeah, Sam was my buddy," he said. He reached in his pocket and pulled out a cigarette. He carefully straightened it out, but it still flopped down, almost broken through halfway down the white paper. He looked around vaguely, saw me, and looked up.

"You are one big bastard, aren't you?"

"Hello, Indian," I said resignedly. He smiled and coughed.

"Mind if I make some fire, mind if I smoke?" he asked. He ignored us, the question just a formality, and lit up. Bob stopped smiling.

"We don't have any ashtrays, Indian," he said sharply. Indian waved his hand through the smoke, and waved off Bob's irritation the same way.

"No problem," he said. He reached in his jacket pocket and pulled out a green cotton work glove, stained black and hard with oil and grease. He put it on his left hand and dropped ash into it. "Yep, yeah, Sam was my buddy. He leave me anything in his will?"

Steve looked irritated. Bob closed his eyes. Rose pulled on my sleeve and I leaned down next to her.

"He's wearing nail polish on his fingernails. Pink nail polish. And he's got live .22 shells sewn on the outside of his jacket. Why is he doing that?"

I shrugged and stood straight.

Indian finished his cigarette and put the still-glowing butt into the back pocket of his jeans. He carefully gathered all the ash in his hand into a neat pile, then brushed his hands together and scattered the ash all over the floor.

Bob stood. He was well over six feet and two hundred pounds, and all of it muscle. Steve and I made Bob look short. The three of us formed up next to Indian and made a living wall. Rose huddled behind us.

Indian looked up, his eyes bleary.

"Yep, yeah, Sam was my friend."

"We know, Indian. We know."

He stepped back. We stepped forward. Without any contact we did a slow dance to move him toward the door and out of the house.

"So, you and Teddy Wahford been running any races lately with your town cars?" Bob asked. He tried to keep Indian's mind occupied while we got him out of the house.

"Hell, no. Teddy's golf cart can't keep up with me," Indian said. He laughed. Two more steps closer to the door. "He's too damn slow."

"You take the blade off your town car, Indian?" I asked. Two more steps.

"Yep, yeah, I had to," Indian said. He laughed again, his voice deep and thick with mucus. "Too much rock goin' into windows. Had to take it off."

"You go faster with the blade off?"

"Slower. Don't know why. Maybe I'll put it back if Teddy gets a fresh charge in his cart."

Finally, the door.

"Yep, yeah, Sam was my buddy," Indian said. He looked up at us again. "You think he left me anything in his will?"

"Good-bye, Indian."

He pushed through the door and went outside, back into what was now a mix of freezing rain and snow. Rose watched through the window as Indian got on his town car and pulled the starter cord.

Roaarrr

He drove off down the gravel road.

"That's a riding lawn mower," Rose said flatly. Bob grinned.

"Oh, no. That's Indian's town car."

Indian slid out of sight around a corner and past a stand of trees. The engine sound dwindled.

The phone rang.

I picked it up, and it was Indian.

"Hey, big bastard, I forgot to tell you something," he said, his voice barely audible above the roar of his engine and the crackle of cellular phone static. "There's something asking for you in the pool hall."

"Something. What's something?"

"Damned if I know what it is. But it's not part of any Summit line and the boys and girls got a little liquor in 'em. Whatever that thing is, if you want it to stay in one piece, you might want to get on down there."

"Jesus, Indian, thanks for telling me right away," I said sarcastically. Now I was angry. "We don't need any trouble with someone from the flats who got up here by accident. You get yourself in there and tell everyone to calm down. I'm coming straight down."

"What if the stranger isn't from our line?"

"Then tell everyone that as far as I'm concerned, that stranger is associated until I get down there. And if the stranger gets hurt before I get there, then someone else is going to get hurt after I get there. Got it?"

"Done," he said. "Don't take long."

The phone went dead.

Sam's Pool Hall faced on Main Street, directly across from the bank, in what I always thought of as some kind of weird commentary on the divine and profane of commerce. A blue and red neon Hamm's sign flashed in the window. I stepped up onto the landing, gave my boots a quick pass on the metal edge of the mudscraper to knock off the worst of the mud, and opened the door.

Memories hit me like a sledgehammer.

Along the right wall were a dozen heavy oak chairs with high backs and broad armrests, like a king's throne. The wood was dark, almost black, and worn to fit by fifty years of use. The chairs were chained firmly together and then bolted to the wall so no one could take them down and use them in a fight. They smelled of stale beer and moonshine and furniture polish.

Pink sawdust was scattered across the floor and piled up a couple of inches deep against the feet of the two pool tables that dominated the center of the room. There they squatted, the leather cups worn and cracked, the green felt tight and shiny, one in line behind the other down the middle of the room. A single lamp with cheap imitation. Tiffany glass and a huge light bulb hung over each table. Wire, with scoring disks strung along it like beads on a necklace, stretched taut high in the air above and across each table. The only way to move the disks was to reach up and push them with a pool cue.

The rack with the pool cues and the stretcher and the spare set of balls was tucked behind the bar, out of reach of anyone in search of a quick weapon to settle an argument. The bar was Sam's pride and joy.

It was thirty straight feet of dark wood that looked like it was carved out of a single tree trunk. A brass step rod, always polished until it shone, ran along the bottom of the bar. A wall-length mirror, the bottom obscured by rows of half-full liquor bottles, covered the left wall itself.

Chuck stood behind the bar. He'd worked for Sam as a bartender as far back as I could remember, and he never seemed to get any older. Now he held a skullknocker club as shiny and polished as his bald head, and faced the rear of the pool hall with a bored look on his face. When the door opened and I came in he glanced at me briefly, and then pointed with his chin toward the rear of the pool hall.

Indian was in the back at a table, a long-neck beer in his hand and a smile on his face. When he saw me he wiped the smile off and tried to look serious.

Foremost faced three drunks, two men and a woman. He was in a low crouch, his cowl pushed back, his snout forward, his hands relaxed and up. As I watched him I saw his claws flicker in and out.

The drunk woman held a knife, some kind of a slip blade, in her right hand. As I watched she pulled a feint, flipped the knife into her left hand, and slashed. Foremost caught the blade in his robe, whipped it away almost contemptuously, and struck her quickly on the shoulder.

She spun around, staggered, and kept her footing. She got a stubborn look on her face, glanced around quickly, and started for Indian's bottle. He got a protective look on his face and began to push his chair back, away from her.

"No way, Dove," he said. He held the bottle away from her. "No breaking bottles in the pool hall. You know Sam's rules. You can't use this anyway. I'm not done with it. No way—"

"What the hell is going on here?" I shouted in my best parade sergeant voice. Everyone froze.

I reached over the bar, took Chuck's club, and tapped it lightly in my hand as I walked to the end of the bar. Indian quickly stood and arranged himself behind me.

Dove and the two other drunks looked up at me and said nothing. Foremost straightened out of his crouch and stood silently.

"Chuck!" I shouted, my eyes locked on Dove's. "Give my friends here a beer."

Three beers later I had Dove and her friends sitting down at a table. Another round later, including one for Indian and one for me, and a crème de menthe for Foremost, and we were all best friends.

"Hell, we never knew he was with you, Tony," Dove said. She spilled half the beer down her throat and half down her chin. She wiped her lips with her sleeve. I motioned to Chuck to bring her another beer. "We just thought he didn't look like he was part of a line. We thought we'd have a little fun with him."

"Well, you were right," I told Dove soothingly. "It's important to watch for things like that, just in case flatlanders show up. And he's not part of my line. But he's associated."

"If he's associated, that's all right," Dove said, her head bobbing. "If he's good enough for you, he's good enough for us."

"Now, I appreciate that, Dove. I'm touched. Really touched. So I'm going to tell Chuck to keep bringing you beer," I said. I stood, and motioned Indian and Foremost to stand also. "Just for tonight, mind you. But all you can drink tonight."

We moved to the little office in the back of the bar to the accompaniment of cheers from Dove and her friends. Once inside I dropped into the green, fake leather chair behind the desk. Foremost took the guest chair, a high-backed wood job with a dirty white padded seat, and Indian stood.

"Indian, get the word out that Foremost here," I motioned to the alien, "is associated. I don't want any more accidents with people like Dove. Once is an accident and I can understand that. Twice is deliberate and I'll consider that an attack on the line. Understand?"

"Got it, Tony. I'll get the word out. He's associated and you want him left alone," Indian said. I nodded.

"And I want him protected while he's here," I said. "I want you to do that job yourself."

Indian looked down at his half-empty beer bottle. Something almost like shame seemed to flicker across his face.

"Maybe I'm not the best one for that, Tony. I'm not sure I'm everything I used to be," he said slowly.

"I'm not asking you, Indian. I'm telling you. You need some food and some sleep. Get a Polish and some decaf from Chuck to take home. You look like hell."

He opened the door to leave.

I hesitated.

"You did good tonight, Indian. Just like the old days."

"Yeah?" he asked, and his face brightened.

"Yeah."

He shut the door behind him, and carried his new smile with him. I turned back to Foremost.

"Jesus, you're one hell of a lot of trouble."

"It's good to see you again also," Foremost said, his voice deep and ragged.

I sighed and shook my head.

"What are you doing here, Ambassador?"

"I've come here for protection. Someone has tried to kill me."

I almost laughed at that, thinking about Dove, then realized he was serious.

"Ambassador—"

"Foremost," he said. "Call me Foremost."

"Foremost," I continued, after a pause. "We caught the shooter from the capital and rolled up his network. Right now that's probably the safest—"

"You don't understand," he interrupted. "I'm not talking about the attempt on Earth. Someone tried to kill me on the ship."

The ship was a huge cylinder, bigger than Ceres, and massed less than if it was made out of water. This told us it was hollow. How many billions lived inside? No one knew. No human had ever been aboard.

All I knew was that it covered too many stars in the night sky and scared the hell out of me.

"After the last negotiation session in New York I went back to the ship," Foremost said. He drank from a fresh crème de menthe I got him at the bar while I nursed a Scotch.

"The life-support system on my skimmer failed as I came out of the atmosphere into space. I tried to call for help, but my communications system was also broken. The temperature in the skimmer began to rise rapidly, and without life support I had no way to get rid of the heat," he said. He sipped at his drink. "Neither of these accidents has ever happened in my memory. And I am old enough to remember the last time the ship found an intelligent race that lived on a planet. Now, suddenly, both of these systems fail? At the same time? Against my particular skimmer? At just the worst possible moment? I believe the universe is perverse and all luck is bad. But in this case, even I doubt chaos and suspect causality."

"You're still alive," I pointed out.

"I ejected. A secret precaution I put in place before the negotiations began."

"Just in case we weren't friendly," I said grimly.

"I am old," Foremost said. "Much, much older than you. I didn't get that way by accident."

The windows in the office rattled in the wind and I glanced outside. The rain and ice had stopped falling, and the temperature seemed to be at least a few degrees above freezing. The clouds were still there, low and gray, but they were lighter now, thinner.

Somewhere above them, the sun waited.

"Why are you here?"

"Before I left for the ship I asked about you, and was told about your resignation. Agent Carole also told me where the funeral would occur so I could send an appropriate memorial. I had the location with me and I coded it into my lifeboat. The computer did the rest."

I shook my head.

"No, Foremost. I don't want to know how you got here. I want to know *why* you got here," I said. "Carole would throw a security blanket over you like you never dreamed of, if you just ask her. Me? I can't even keep you out of a knife fight in a bar."

He finished his drink and put it aside.

"After the shooting I declared you part of my line. You accepted that, and carefully told me I was *not* part of *your* line, but that as long as I was here, I was associated with your line and under your protection," he said. He spread his arms wide. "Where else would I be safer than with you?"

Damn all lines, I thought. *Damn all governments.*

And damn my big mouth.

"Why would someone from the ship want to kill you?" I asked.

Foremost stood and walked to the window. The building next door to the pool hall was a feed store, and Claire bred bulldogs in a run behind her place.

When we were kids we played with the animals and helped clean them and their run. They were big, stupid, friendly dogs, with oversized paws and ears and the ugliest faces we ever saw. They climbed on us and pulled our clothes for attention and generally proved out the stereotype of the bulldog puppy.

Claire paid us in quarters, but we loved the dogs and we worked for candy when she was low on cash. Once, Steve and a runt got to be special friends. The two of them were constantly with each other, even to the point where he sneaked the dog out of the run when Claire was not looking.

Then one day Steve came to see his friend and he was gone. Sold. Claire tried to explain that she was sorry, it was a business to her, but he never understood. Finally she gave him extra candy and quarters and he ran all the way home, his face streaked with tears.

He gave everything to Bob and me, and never went back to Claire's again.

"Mine is not the only race on the ship," Foremost said. "And mine is not the only line in my race.

"Every time we find a new planet with something we want, some groups on board the ship prosper, and others lose. Overall, the ship gains. But that doesn't make it any easier for the groups that lose."

"This time the potential gains are bigger than usual," I guessed. "So the losses will also be bigger than usual."

"You understand," Foremost said.

"So what are you going to do?"

He stood back from the window, which made the bodyguard part of me relax, and went back to his chair.

"I have a new proposal from your people," he said. "And I have a funeral to go to. I will think about one, and attend the other."

"I'll call Carole," I said automatically. Then I stopped.

"Who knows you're here?" I asked.

"I don't know," he said. "No one, yet. By now my people will have found the empty skimmer and the message with my suspicions I left behind. The search will be on for me or my body."

I finished the Scotch.

"I have to bury Sam," I said, stubbornly. "If I call Carole we'll have flatlanders on us like a blanket."

"Ship people as well," Foremost added. "Both my friends, and those who tried to kill me."

The windows rattled to a fresh gust of wind and I heard the scattered pebble sound of freezing rain against the glass.

"Did you bring any funeral clothes?"

When we were young, before Steve was born, my family lived in Sam's house. Downstairs was the kitchen, the bathroom, the living room, and Sam and Laverne's bedroom. Upstairs were two tiny bedrooms.

I remembered the stairs as tall and hard to climb and for once a childhood memory was accurate. The stairs were steep, almost like a ladder, but Foremost scrambled up them quickly. I moved more slowly, my head down so I did not hit it on the doorways or the ceiling.

Foremost used the bedroom on the right. The bedroom on the left was completely filled with a huge, silvery, outdoor TV antenna. Foremost paused and looked at it.

"Communications?"

"Entertainment," I said. "Reception only."

"Wouldn't it work better on top of the house?" Foremost asked.

"Sam liked it right here where he could touch it," I said.

Steve and Rose slept in the downstairs bedroom. Bob camped out in the kitchen. Foremost used the upstairs and I was down on the couch in the living room.

The next morning we were up and moving at dawn. Steve made everyone a breakfast of scrambled eggs with American cheese, thick bacon, and bagels. Foremost discreetly tested everything for allergens, then took a dry bagel to eat with his field rations.

Bob finished his plate, pushed it back, and glanced at Foremost.

"So what do we do today?" he asked.

I finished my orange juice and put my plate by the sink. Steve got himself seconds from the skillet while Rose nursed a cup of coffee.

"Today we bury Sam," I said.

"We know that," Bob said impatiently. "Are you going to go get the Estep token?"

"I don't have much choice, do I?" I asked. Bob shrugged and looked at Foremost again.

"Always got choices. Might not like them, but always got choices," Bob said. "Token should be at the burial. Token always watches the Eldest get buried before it gets passed on to the new Eldest."

"We'll go to Oly's house and pick it up," I decided. "If someone does come looking for the Ambassador, they'll come here first. We might as well be somewhere else."

Bob grinned.

"What will Oly think about your friend?"

Steve snorted.

"Oly probably won't notice anything different from normal when you two show up," he said, disgusted.

"Oly's not so bad," I said, defensively.

Bob and Steve both stared at me, then smiled. Bob pushed away from the table and stood.

"We'll get everything ready at this end. Be at the cemetery a few minutes early," Bob said. I nodded and motioned for Foremost to follow me. As we got to the mudroom Bob tapped me on the shoulder.

"Steve and I'll talk to the boys and girls," he said in a low voice. "We'll have eyes out to see if any strangers are in town."

"The cemetery is an awfully lonely place. Lots of open country, except on the side with the woods," I said.

"Easy to hide in them woods," Bob agreed. "Or on a hilltop in the corn stubble."

"You'll take care of it?"

"Done."

Foremost and I took the car that Rose and I used to drive up to Summit. It was another dark, rainy day, perfect for a funeral, and I still dialed down the tint on the windows to make it even harder for someone outside to see inside.

We turned right on the road, then left. We drove silently in the barren hills south of town, past fields used only as pasture, that grew only a bumper crop of rock.

The rock reminded me of Washington. I remembered a party in Georgetown, at one of the ever-so-discreet townhouses near the university. In the back, behind all the security doors and the antique furniture and more pretentious people than I could suddenly stand, was a tiny courtyard. I fled there with my Scotch to escape a too-aggressive bureaucrat's daughter.

There I found the rock.

Nothing special, just a small gray boulder about twice the size of a basketball, flecked with black and silver. It was tucked next to a dwarf willow beside a pool. Spray from a small waterfall moistened the rock, already tumbled and smoothed by the glacier that created it. I ran my hands over it and suddenly realized I was homesick.

Now we drove past uncounted fortunes of that kind of decorative rock, poking out of the fields, plowed into piles, pushed into heaps to get them out of the way. I glanced at everything around me, at the rain and the wetlands and the bare hills and the rock, and smiled. This was where that rock belonged, not in some little decorative garden, and maybe it was not the only thing that belonged here.

We crossed a ridgeline and stopped on top. I put the car in park, and started to get out of it. Foremost began to get out also. I reached over and touched him.

"You stay inside," I said. "This will only take a minute."

I stood on the ridge, silhouetted against the gray sky, for several minutes. Summit Lake used to be a field like any of a thousand fields in the old tribal lands. One day, as Sam told me, some fool woke up and thought he was in Iowa, not Dakota, and decided to try to plow good buffalo land. Instead of a neat, clean furrow through dirt he hit a rock. When he pulled the boulder off he found it was a caprock, over a spring.

Now Summit Lake filled the entire bowl, probably three or four square miles in area, with only a few scraggly trees to break the rolling, grass-covered hills. And it showed on no maps, not county or state or federal. You knew where it was, and you found it, or you were a flatlander and then what the hell were you doing here anyway?

Satisfied that Oly had plenty of time to see who it was, I got back in the car and headed off down the track to his shack next to the concrete boat landing.

Oly was outside on a bench tucked next to his house. He looked up when the car stopped, a knife and a piece of wood in his hands.

"He is a sculptor?" Foremost asked. I shook my head and pointed to the pile of wood shavings on the ground around Oly.

"He just likes to cut wood. He takes a big piece and makes it into a lot of little pieces. Then he starts over again with another big piece."

"Why?" Foremost asked.

I took a deep breath. I was impatient to get this over, and unhappy about any time we spent out in the open where more people could see Foremost.

"Oly used to be the best carver in this part of the state," I said. "I swear, magic used to flow out of his knife. Now he's got some bad arthritis and his fingers don't work so well. The magic still flows in him, but only in his mind. So he cuts the wood to remember, and he still sees the final carvings in his mind."

"And the rest of us only see the shavings," Foremost said.

"That's our problem, not his," I said briskly. "Maybe we just don't know how to look right. Anyway, let's go. We don't have that much time."

We got out of the car and walked over to Oly. He looked at me, then Foremost, then back to me. Then back to his wood.

The bench was an old driftwood tree trunk, gray and worn and twisted, roughly knocked with an axe into a flat surface. Oly propped the wood up on two old black plastic bait buckets to get it off the ground.

I sat on one side of Oly, and motioned Foremost to sit on the other side. We sat silently for a moment and stared out at the dark water.

Summit Lake was like a map if you knew how to read it. Small sloped waves, deceptively soft, in the middle where the water was deepest. Taller, thinner waves, with white froth tops and green water, almost as transparent as glass, near the shore and the underwater slope.

The fish that lived in the lake preferred different kinds of water and cover. A good fisherman could look at the lake, at the waves and color, and draw a mental map of what the bottom looked like. A good fisherman knew that walleye liked this kind of water; northern pike liked that kind. Bullhead swarmed over the points, and bass liked the sections where the branches of dead trees, flooded out years ago, poked through the surface.

Sam claimed the world was like a lake, and the people in it like fish. Most people went through their lives without much understanding of what was really going on. Only a few people could stand outside the world and actually see it and make sense out of it. He claimed Oly was one of the best of these.

Tradition said I had to talk first when I met Oly.

"So how's the fishing been, Oly?"

He took a cut with his knife, and a curl of wood peeled onto the ground.

"Been worse. Been better," he said.

"Yeah," I said. "I can see that."

"You came back for Sam," Oly said. Another curl of wood joined the pile on the ground. "Some people said you wouldn't come back. Some people said you were gone from the line, said you didn't even want to be associated anymore."

"They can say it," I said. "People can say anything they want. But I'm back."

Oly was older than Sam, so old that even his grandchildren were older than the brothers and I. His teeth were blackened and mostly missing, his hair thin and the leathery scalp covered with brown age spots.

But his eyes were sharp and it was said that nothing happened in Summit he did not know.

"You brought a flatlander to the funeral," Oly said.

"Steve's wife, Rose," I said. "He's got a little girl now."

"Steve's got a baby," Oly said. He shook his head. "He was such a funny-looking little guy. Looked just like a duck. And now he's got a baby of his own. Funny."

I tried to imagine Steve, closer to seven foot than six, strong enough to break ribs as part of his job as a respiratory therapist, as a baby who looked like a duck. I smiled to myself.

"This is Foremost," I said. "He's from upstairs."

Oly nodded.

"Word came around," he said. "He's associated?"

"I gave him my word."

"With Sam gone, you can do that," Oly said. He looked up at me. "I heard how you handled Dove last night."

"Dove and the boys were just having some fun," I said, uneasily.

"You did it right," Oly reassured me.

He took a final cut at the wood, looked at it critically, then folded the clasp knife and put it in his pocket. He stood and turned to Foremost.

"You come with a good recommendation," he said, and jerked his head back over his shoulder toward me.

"I try to do my best," Foremost said.

"He's good people," Oly said. He stared hard at Foremost. "Don't mess him up."

Oly turned and walked with a firm, clean step to his shack. Foremost and I stood and waited.

Oly was back in a minute. In one hand he carried a bundle about a foot long, wrapped in an oilcloth and tied with a piece of rawhide. In the other hand he carried a mason jar. He handed the package to me, and unscrewed the jar with the other.

"Limbo came by this morning," Oly told me. "Said he found some tracks that he'd never seen before around his place. They looked like boot tracks, but not any kind of boot he's ever seen."

We all looked down at Foremost's feet. His boots were as wide as they were long, with three large bulges where a human had toes. There was no way to ever confuse his feet with one of ours.

"He found the tracks all around some kind of metal torpedo that someone had hidden in the brush," Oly said. "Limbo said there was writing on the outside of the metal, but he couldn't read any of it."

"I hid my escape pod after I landed. I hope I did not hurt anything on his farm," Foremost said.

"And then you just walked west into town?" I asked.

"South," he corrected me. "My garment has some camouflage capabilities, and my people are quite good at moving without being seen."

Oly looked at me and smiled, a thin slash across his face. Limbo's farm was east of town. So either Foremost lied when he said he walked south into Summit, or someone else was now prowling around town. The lie was too easy to check, if we looked in the brush north of town for another ship, so I had to assume we had another visitor.

"Sounds like we need a drink," Oly said. He reached in the jar, fished around with his fingers, and pulled out the complete skeleton of a fish, head and all. He tossed this on the ground, then tipped the jar to his lips and took a deep drink, so that his Adam's apple moved up and down like a piston. He wiped his lips and handed the jar to me.

The jar was old, tired glass, heavily decorated with curlicues and fancy writing. Inside I saw clear liquid on top and, on the bottom, a white sludge of particles that danced and flickered with oily, reflected light. The smell, a mixture of fish, spices, pickle juice, and pure alcohol, was enough to make my eyes water.

I took a small sip.

The sludge was smooth and silky, with a hint of cinnamon and bay on top of the full, fish taste. Northern pike, I guessed. Then the vinegar cut through and seemed to slice my mouth open. Finally, the alcohol seemed to lift off the top of my head and let the cool breeze swirl around inside.

I handed the jar to Oly. He handed it to Foremost. He looked at the jar, puzzled, and touched it with his allergen analyzer. He stared hard at the display, as if he couldn't believe the results, then tucked the analyzer away. He held the jar in his long, leathery fingers and took a hesitant sip. He closed his eyes while Oly smiled at him. He opened his eyes and handed the jar to Oly.

"Good," he said, his voice raspy and hoarse. "Very good indeed. This is how you preserve the fish you catch?"

"Oly doesn't fish," I corrected. "People bring him fish they catch and don't want." I turned to Oly. "Who's got the still now? I don't recognize the taste of the moonshine."

"You asking as a government man, or as one of us?" Oly said.

"I'm asking as me," I answered. "Government man resigned his job to come to the funeral."

Oly nodded and looked approving. Not many people around Summit had much love for the government. I lost a lot of respect when I went to Washington. The first time I got shot I gained most of it back, but it was an expensive way to put credit in that account.

"That batch of 'shine is from Flipper's new still," Oly said. He looked at the jar critically. "I canned that jar a couple of years ago. Just took it out to see how it's aging."

"Not bad," I said.

"But not quite ripe yet, either," Oly grumbled. "That boy keeps doing fancy things to the old recipe for grain. He just can't leave well enough alone. Makes it hard to can a decent fish when you don't know what the 'shine is going to taste like. These things have to match up just right."

"Sometimes change is good," I said.

"Don't you start up on me," Oly warned. "Change happens fast enough without rushing it."

"What about Sam?" Foremost asked. "Did he fish?"

"Sam? Oh, he put his lines out for all sorts of things. Yes, he was a great fisherman. He caught fish all the time, but he never wanted to eat them. He just liked catching them, and making them do what he wanted," Oly said, and grinned. "Kind of like what he did with people. He had his lines out for them, just like he did for fish. Never sure what he was going to catch, but always interested. Me, I'm different. I don't like catching the fish, but I like to take care of them afterward. Same with people. Sam and me, we were like both sides of the mirror, the face that looks in and the face that looks back."

The world is like the lake, and Sam and Oly sit on the shore, and talk and laugh and watch the water . . .

"I put a fish in a jar, add 'shine, spices, and just a little pickle juice. Then I let it rest for a few years. Makes it easier for me to eat with my gums," Oly said, and smiled to expose his lack of teeth again.

"There are people on the ship who would pay you much for that single jar," Foremost said.

"I'm always willing to talk about money," Oly said. He handed the jar back to Foremost. "Have another sip and let's talk."

I left them alone for the moment and took the oilcloth package back to the car. Once there, I gently untied the rawhide and unfolded the material.

The Estep token was two pieces of bone, speckled black with age. They looked like the thighbones of some animal, bigger than a rabbit, smaller than a deer, but nothing I immediately recognized. I touched the bones, ran my finger up and down them, felt the smooth surface with its little pits and whorls, then tied the bundle together again and placed it carefully in the back seat.

Sam never talked much about the token of our line, just enough to let me know it was important. Once a year, at Orville Knob's Nut Fest, the big party just before New Year's Eve, the token was carefully laid out on a table set with a brilliant white tablecloth. The table was always tucked into a far corner of the room, unobtrusive but visible. I sat next to Sam all night one year, and brought him food and beer and listened and watched.

I saw members of the line sidle up to the table and look down at the token. Sam waited a moment, then leaned forward and spoke a few quiet words with the person. They would listen and nod and smile, or speak quietly about some problem they couldn't solve. Then they put a few dollars on the table next to the token and walked away. When they left, I took the money and put it into the strongbox under Sam's chair.

I knew that in the next few days Sam would work on the person's problem. It might get solved, and it might not. Nothing was perfect, not even the token, but as a symbol it was damned powerful to us. To everyone else, it was just a couple of old bones.

I knew what I needed to do next, and wished I could drink more fish with Oly to give me some liquid courage. Finally I promised to do myself a favor in the future and picked up my satellite phone and called Carole.

Her personal secretary was an old friend and always answered the private number herself, instead of letting the voice mail do a screening, so I called that number. It rang twice and Phyllis picked up.

"Protective service."

"Morning, Phyllis. It's me."

"Tony!" she said warmly. "Oh, it's good to hear you. I miss you already."

"Phyllis, you're a better liar than anyone else in the office," I said fondly. "I've only been gone two days."

"Two long days. Two extremely long days."

"I turned in my resignation, Phyllis. I'm not coming back. Better get used to it."

"Herself needs you back, Tony. Things aren't going so well right now."

"I know," I said. "More than you think. Is she in?"

"Hold two."

I glanced back at the porch. Three open mason jars rested on the ground and Oly held another in his hand while Foremost tested it with his sampler.

"Tony? Where are you? All hell's broken loose back here," Carole said. Her voice sounded cool, efficient, and just a little desperate.

"I'm still in Dakota. The funeral is this afternoon."

"We got problems, Tony," Carole said. "An alien we've never seen before, from a *species* we've never met before, is down here with the President."

I nodded to myself.

"I'll bet this one doesn't talk like an ambassador," I said.

There was silence from the other end of the line.

"No. Not like an ambassador. More like a general than an ambassador. She says Foremost is gone, they think we have him, and they want him back. They're making demands and giving us veiled threats. No one is talking trade anymore. We have to find Foremost."

"I know where he is," I said.

"Where?"

"About fifty yards away from me, drinking with an old friend of mine," I said.

"Talk to me, Tony. Tell me what's going on," Carole said.

I explained the situation quickly, as if I was doing a debrief on a routine assignment. When I finished, all I heard was her soft breathing on the phone.

I looked over at Oly and Foremost. They each took a jar in hand and sipped. Then they put them down, argued, and picked up another jar, and sipped. It looked like the Dakota version of a wine tasting.

"I want you to keep him there, safe, until I arrive. I'll grab a jet at Andrews and get there in a couple of hours."

I started to laugh.

"What's so damn funny?" she snapped.

"Where are you going to fly into? Fargo? Sioux Falls? Minneapolis? Those are the nearest cities with an airport big enough to take even the smallest kind of jet."

"Then that's where I'll fly."

"And then you drive," I said, my voice suddenly serious. "You drive for hours. And then you arrive here, with a column of cars and trucks and God knows what else."

"You have a problem with this?"

"We don't take to outsiders up here, Carole. We call them flatlanders, people from outside the hills. You arrive here like that, without any kind of an invitation, like an invading force, and someone is going to have a few drinks, and then take a few shots. Maybe at you. Maybe at Foremost for bringing in outsiders."

"No one would dare," she said, uncertain.

I sighed.

"Carole, there's a town up here where a man was shot down in broad daylight on Main Street with about a hundred witnesses around. No one liked the guy much and his death ended a feud between two lines. Everyone was pretty much satisfied with the result. Then a dozen marshals showed up to enforce flatlander law. If they were to arrest someone, anyone, it stood a very good chance of starting everything up again between the two lines," I said.

"So what happened? What did the marshals find out?" she asked.

"Nothing," I said. "Absolutely nothing. Because no one saw a thing, and no one ever said a thing. In broad daylight, in the middle of town. Everyone kept their mouth shut."

"What are you trying to tell me?"

"We take care of our own up here, Carole. Let us take care of things our way."

"Foremost isn't one of you."

"He is right now. He's associated, that means under the protection, of the biggest line in the county. He's fine," I said.

"Whose line is that?"

"Mine."

I glanced back to the shack. Oly and Foremost sat close together on the bench. Foremost watched intently while Oly drew in the dirt with a stick. Occasionally they stopped and sipped more fish.

"What do you want me to do?" she asked.

"I want you to be careful. I want you up here, but I want you up here alone. We don't want the wrong people to follow you. Assume someone has a trace on you. Get rid of it. Then come up here, alone. Bring whatever communications equipment you want. I'll keep Foremost safe until you arrive."

"And then?"

"And then the three of us will get together and figure out what to do."

"What about the tracks? What if someone from the ship is coming after Foremost?" she asked.

"If there's any trouble, we'll deal with it in our own way."

More silence, until it dragged on like one of those bargaining tricks they taught me in hostage negotiation school. The idea there was to let the silence drag on, let the person who is most anxious talk first.

But this was not some damn role-play game.

"I don't like it, Tony. But I don't have much choice. We'll do it your way."

"Good," I said, and let out a breath I didn't know I was holding. "Put me back to Phyllis. I'll give her directions on how to get you here and where to meet me."

"All right. Give me a minute to tell her what I need and then I'll put her on."

The phone clicked once, I heard dead air, then the phone clicked again and Phyllis came on the line.

"So how do I get her to you?" Phyllis asked.

I briefly gave directions. Phyllis repeated them back to me to make sure she had them down correctly.

"Tony, she'll never say this, so I'll say it for her," Phyllis said. "Thank you. Thank you for everything."

"She never would say it, would she?"

"Tony, she might not say it, but she doesn't want you to quit," Phyllis continued.

"How do you know that?"

"Those resignation papers of yours? They never made it to me. They're still in their envelope, on her desk. Unopened. Why do you think that is?"

I looked at the lake, at the wind-ruffled water and the grass that swayed and tossed on the naked hills. Oly and Foremost relaxed back on the bench now and spoke slowly to each other.

"I don't know, Phyllis. I just don't know."

"Think about it, Tony."

I thought about a lot of things as Foremost and I drove back into town. I stuffed the tokens in their oilcloth under the seat and drove back by a different route than the one I used to get to Oly's place. Training: never use the same route back from a location that you used to get there. Old habits from the Service died hard, and I decided sometimes it was good to keep in practice. Particularly with strange tracks and strange people walking around town.

We stopped at the house. I found a note taped on the back door that said Rose and Steve were at the church, and I was supposed to go directly to the cemetery. Bob was already out there to get things ready.

I changed clothes and carefully adjusted my holster so my handgun did not bulge under the suitcoat. Foremost scraped the mud off his feet and put on a clean robe. We met in the kitchen.

"How do I look?" Foremost asked.

He looked like a giant wolverine with funny-looking hands. He looked like the kind of person who could spend an hour discussing the nuances of fish-based moonshine with a stranger from the hills. He looked like the kind of person who brought strangers into my town and problems into my life.

He looked like someone under my protection.

"You look fine," I said. "Come on. Get in the car."

We drove down the side streets, strangely abandoned by the children who had been scrubbed, poured into suits and dresses, and then marched to church for the funeral. We crossed Main and drove past cars and trucks parked on the grassy strips next to the church.

The church was Methodist, with a three-story-tall steeple that was the highest point in town. A giant cross, half the gold paint flaked off, topped the structure proudly. White paint on clapboard, six-foot-tall stained-glass windows, and a set of walk-up concrete steps to the main entrance finished off the picture.

"You have many different religions here?"

"Not so many as some towns, but a few. Methodists go here. Catholics go to Blue Cloud Abbey outside of town. Lakota might go to the shaman and a sweat lodge," I said.

"Your line goes to this church?" he asked, and nodded toward the church.

"Some do," I said. "Some go to the other places. We're all mixed up."

We left town gravel behind and drove on county gravel. It sounded like the same thing, gravel was gravel, but even in Summit there was a difference between the town and the country. It was a small thing, hardly noticeable to outsiders, but town gravel roads were graded and smoothed while the country roads were ridged like corduroy. A little thing, but I had seen fights break out at Sam's Pool Hall over less.

We bounced on county gravel while the clouds thickened up and got darker. A fleck of snow, huge and fat, struck the windshield. It stuck there, pinned like some exotic butterfly on display, then melted into a wet spot and a tiny droplet that streamed down the glass.

I turned left at a crossroads and went down the cemetery road. The surface was mixed gravel and dirt now, humped up in long ridges down both sides of the road. Once a year a grader might force its way down here, to level out the ridges and throw down new gravel.

Maybe.

If the county budget was in good shape that year.

And it looked as if the budget had been in trouble for a long time.

I drove down the tire marks of other vehicles and used the bottom of the car as my own grader when I needed. Sometimes this put me on the right hand side of the road, sometimes on the left. Foremost hung on tight and looked straight ahead.

Marshes and sloughs, tiny wetlands filled with reeds and tall grass and old decayed fence posts with the rusted barbed wire still attached filled the fields on both sides of us whenever the road crossed a low spot. Jays and sparrows and blackbirds perched on anything dry and watched us as we passed. I watched Foremost as his head jerked like the birds, and wondered what the hell was going on inside that brain.

We turned once again and we were at the cemetery.

Raw headstones, shaped but not yet engraved or polished, lay together in a gray tumbled pile in the ditch next to the crossroads. Tall grass, mixed brown from last fall and fresh baby green new growth from this spring, sprouted through and around the stones like whiskers on a dead man's face.

The grass in the cemetery itself was clipped short and raked with military precision. Placed neatly in the field of green were the finished cousins of the headstones in the ditch. These, though, marched in strict rows, ordered by family and line, across the cemetery. Men and women, the important in life and those that passed through unnoticed, were all equal here. The only concession to sentiment was the small headstones of the children, tucked in close to their mothers. Bouquets of flowers, some real and withered, some plastic and worn, filled the cupholders of the children's headstones.

I saw Bob's car, the backhoe used to dig the grave, and a green canvas tent. The tent stood next to a pile of fresh black and brown dirt flecked with white glacial stone. Folding chairs were set up in two small rows under the tent and faced the grave.

I looked for Bob but didn't see him. What I did see were so many ambush sites where a shooter could lay up and hide that I almost turned around and took Foremost back into town right then and there.

Trees pushed up next to the cemetery on one side and provided excellent cover. Across the road, the flax field was plowed and planted and empty, with a tremendous field of fire. Sloughs covered both of the other sides, so that we were in a kind of island, surrounded by trouble. Most times I thought of the cemetery as beautiful, peaceful even.

But not when there were strange tracks around my town. And where the hell was Bob?

I drove slowly down the rutted dirt track, dotted here and there with a flash of white that was last year's crushed paving stone, toward the grave. I pulled the car into line next to Bob's, passenger side facing his car. Then I loosened my gun in the holster, and opened the car door.

"Do you want me in or out?" Foremost asked.

"What kind of weapon would a killer from your ship have?"

"Pumped laser."

"Could it cut through the car?"

"Yes. Easily."

"What kind of surveillance and identification equipment would they use?" I asked.

"There are many," Foremost said. "They might use a body-heat scanner or a low-light analyzer. Or any of a dozen other devices."

I thought for a moment. With the tint dialed to full on the car windows, Foremost was invisible inside. Invisible, that is, to the bare-eyed locals around Summit. I was pretty sure my little window-tint trick wouldn't keep him invisible to an assassin with military-level surveillance and identification gear. Foremost wasn't built to be able to slip down to the floorboards and hide, so he sat up straight and provided a perfect silhouette to any sniper who could see him.

"Might as well get out then. Better to be a moving target than one that sits and waits," I said.

We shut the doors behind us softly, but it still seemed loud.

"Bob?" I called.

"Down here," came his voice.

We walked closer to the grave.

"Where?"

"Down here," he repeated.

We walked to the lip of the grave and looked down. The grave was about eight feet deep, with the concrete lining sunk into the bottom six feet of that so two feet of dirt remained on top to grow grass. Bob stood in the center of the open concrete box and looked up at us.

"What the hell are you doing down there?" I asked.

He looked embarrassed. He slapped his hands together to knock off dirt and smiled.

"I wondered what it was like to be buried. I thought I'd just come down, feel it for a couple minutes, and come back out."

"And?"

"And I can't get out of the damned grave now. The concrete is too slick and the ground is too muddy. Give me a hand."

I looked at our clean clothes and the mud. Bob was dressed in casual clothing, streaked with brown and black dirt.

"Where're your funeral clothes?"

"In the car. I figured I'd change after I did this and no one would ever know."

"Sweet Jesus," I said disgustedly. "I didn't bring any spare clothes. And I don't want to think about what Aunt Gladys will say if I'm all covered with mud during the burial. Hold on a minute while I think of something."

I went back to the car. I figured there must be something in the trunk, snow chains left over from winter or an old piece of rope or hose, that I could let down to him to get him out and still stay clean myself. I reached in my pocket and fumbled with my keys. They dropped to the ground and I swore mildly and bent over to pick them up.

The rear bumper blinked at me.

I hit the ground and rolled. Foremost shouted and flung up his arms. He staggered and stumbled backward, his arms flung wide. A cloud of steam engulfed him.

The light flashed again, and this time I saw the laser flare and burn part of Foremost's robe. Jets of steam spurted from his clothes around his neck and armpits and waist and he hit the ground and lay motionless, half in the grave, half out.

I was up and moving, gun in my hand. I put the car between myself and the grove of trees where I saw the laser flash.

"Bob, you okay?"

"What the hell is going on up there?" he shouted back.

"Just shut up and do what I tell you," I said. "Can you drag Foremost down in there with you?"

I heard Bob grunt, the sound of something heavy scraping on the grass and dirt, and another deeper grunt from Bob.

"Got him."

"He alive?"

"He's breathing," Bob said. "Not real regular, but he's breathing."

"Just keep him that way," I said.

What would I do if I was the shooter? Foremost was down, hit twice, but there was no guarantee he was dead. The steam was the giveaway. A laser cuts cleanly through fabric and messily through flesh. It never sends out jets of steam. Which meant Foremost had some kind of protective layer underneath his robe to dissipate the laser heat. Was it tough enough to handle two shots?

The shooter had to be certain.

I glanced quickly underneath the car and saw a figure with a pair of feet coming toward the car at a trot. I took three deep breaths and came over the top of the hood, gun outstretched.

I fired three times, direct hits to the body. The creature, short and squat and all in gray so I could not tell what was clothing and what was skin, jerked at the impacts but kept on coming. It stared at me with a fixed caricature of a wild grin on its face, writhing tentacles where I had teeth, a thin slash of bone where I had lips. Then it shuffled its feet for balance and aimed the laser at me.

The grin widened and I knew I was dead.

The head exploded.

The body stood for a moment, fixed, as if it meant to keep on coming, as if the loss of its head was nothing more than a minor inconvenience. I worried for the same moment that with this alien that might be true, that the head was nothing more than a place to put the eyes, that the brain might be in the torso.

Then the body crumpled and collapsed.

I ran to the shooter, my gun out and level, ready to fire if I saw a flicker of movement. When I got closer I kicked the laser away, far out of reach, and felt the body. It was cool to the touch, and lumpy, like a plastic bag full of rocks.

"It is called a Synth."

I looked over my shoulder and saw Bob and Foremost, their clothes smeared with dirt. Bob stared at the alien, shook his head slowly, and went over to look at the laser.

"Do not try to use it," Foremost warned. "The odds are good it is a personal weapon, keyed to the Synth."

"Booby-trapped?" Bob asked.

"I don't know the word," Foremost said.

"Rigged to explode if someone other than the owner tries to use it," Bob explained.

"Probably," Foremost agreed.

I stared at the country around me. The grass moved in waves to the winds, and the trees in the little forest rubbed and swayed in rhythm.

"Do they travel in pairs?" I asked.

"No, strictly alone. They are living killing machines. Put them in an area, give them instructions, and let them do their work. If you put two in an area they would most likely kill each other," Foremost said.

"Hard to keep a species going that way," I said.

"They manage somehow," Foremost said dryly.

I stood and looked down at the Synth. Up close, the gray was partly clothing and partly skin, so close in color to each other that they blended to form a whole that was difficult to focus on. The alien looked like a silly-putty man, and I wondered if the rain would dissolve the skin and clothes and wash them into the grass.

I saw three smudge marks on the alien's chest where my bullets struck some kind of protective vest. I looked at the marks and, for just a moment, I was pleased with myself. The bullet pattern was tight, the black smears close together, and I knew my old firearms instructor at the Service would be pleased. The Synth itself looked enough like one of the practice dummies at the Academy that I half expected it to snap back upright when this little exercise was over. But the rain puddled on the clothes and formed droplets on the skin and the Synth stayed dead.

"Indian, you can come out now," I said, my voice pitched to carry against the weather.

Indian, his fatigue jacket smeared with a few new grass stains that would soon dry and mix with all the others, drew himself up from the edge of the trees. He wore a broad-brimmed hat with snap-down ear flaps, just as dirty and stained as the rest of his clothing. He carried a scoped rifle, as clean and well-tended as an opposite could be. He pointed down the road, then disappeared back in the trees.

"Funeral procession is coming down the road," Bob said. I looked up and saw a black hearse, with a procession of other cars behind it. I kicked the Synth.

"How the hell do I explain this?" I growled.

"Don't need to," Bob said. "This is Summit. That's all you need to know, and all you need to say."

Carole showed up about an hour after dusk, when the street lights on Main Street were just starting to get into some real work. Foremost and Oly and I sat on the steps outside the pool hall and passed a glass jar of fish back and forth. Bullhead, if I remember right. Bob and Steve and Rose were inside, acting as hosts for Sam's wake. I could tell, from the rising level of voices and music and laughter inside, that the party was just starting to take off.

Driving down the street, Carole saw us, and turned to parallel park in front of the pool hall. She stopped the car and the driver's side window rolled down. Even through the sharp cut shadows from the street lights I could see the relief on her face.

"All I thought about on the way down here was that you might be dead. Every time I closed my eyes on the plane I saw you in a coffin," she said, her voice soft and tired. She turned her head a little to the side. "I'm glad you're all right, too, Ambassador."

I'm glad you're all right, too, Ambassador? I struggled with the thought that Carole spent the trip worried about me. Something of my confusion must have shown on my face. She smiled.

"You don't work for me anymore, do you? Then I can worry about you now."

"And before?" I asked.

"You were an agent. You had a job to do, and I had a job to do."

"I wasn't a person before, and now I am?"

"You were a person before," she said carefully, "and an agent."

"And now?"

She smiled again. Her face relaxed in a way I never remembered from Washington. I realized I liked that smile very much, and wondered where she'd kept it all those years. I suddenly wanted to make her smile again.

She started to get out of her car and I shook my head.

She stopped for a moment, her face frozen, and the old mask snapped back into place. For a moment I saw pain and hurt and loneliness. Then it was gone, and it was the Washington face back again.

"Of course," she said carefully. "I understand."

"No, you don't," I said. "Park the car around the corner. We're keeping Main Street clear. Then come back here. We need to talk."

I moved over on the step a little and pushed Foremost with my butt, to move him down and make a space for her next to me. She watched me, startled at the way I touched him, and even more surprised when he accepted it without complaint. She smiled that smile again, and I was damned pleased with myself.

She drove around the corner, parked, and came back. She sat next to me. She wore a parka with a fur fringe and she fit just right next to me. Foremost passed her the glass jar of moonshine and fish. She wrinkled her nose at the smell.

"Tony, what is this stuff?"

"Ancient family drink," I said. I took the jar from her, sipped to show it was safe, then wiped the rim with my shirt sleeve to clean it. I felt awkward and clumsy and about twelve years old while next to me sat the prettiest girl I knew. I waited for her to look up, to see it was really me sitting next to her—not some perfectly turned-out diplomat with ideal manners and looks. Then I figured she would carefully and politely edge away from me and go find someone better to be around. I handed her back the jar. "It's really all right to drink."

She took the jar, looked up at me with total confidence, and took a small sip. She handed the jar back.

"What's going on out here?" she asked.

Main Street was strangely abandoned, even for Summit. Not a car was parked on the street, and the black asphalt was carefully chipped and scraped and cleaned so that it almost gleamed under the street light. A pair of freshly painted white lines, like the guard lines for a pedestrian crossing, stretched across the street.

"Time for the races," Oly said. Foremost nodded.

Around the corner came Teddy Wahford on his golf cart, and Indian on his town car. They lined up carefully side by side between the lines. Limbo, dressed in a short-sleeved shirt even as his breath came out in puffs in the cold, stepped between them. He carried two small construction worker flags, one in each hand, their color drained by the overhead sodium light until the flags seemed more like a muddy gray than a bright orange. Foremost leaned back and banged his fist on the pool hall door. Bob opened the door from inside. Waves of noise and heat and light washed over us from inside.

"Yeah?"

"First race is ready," Foremost said.

"About time," Bob said. He shut the door and we heard him pounding on the long bar and shouting. Everything went quiet for a moment and then the door banged open and the crowd spilled outside with a roar.

Carole grabbed my arm for balance as the crowd shoved past us.

"What the hell is going on?" she asked again.

Chuck the bartender brought out a metal washtub filled with ice and cans of beer. He looked down at me as he walked past.

"Race beer should be in bottles," he growled disapprovingly. "Gets cold faster."

"It's cold enough already," I said as my breath puffed into the night air. "And you can't cut anyone with a can if someone gets angry about the race results."

Chuck set down the tub on the curb next to Steve and Rose and Bob. They sold the beer as fast as they could pull the cans out of the ice and water.

"You sell the beer at a wake? That's one hell of a way to make money," Carole asked. I shook my head.

"No, we won't make any money off this," I said. "The first round was free, and in the morning we'll take everything we made off all the rest of the beer and donate it to the town emergency heating fund."

"Then why charge for the beer?"

"If it was free everyone would take too much. All we'd have left by now would be a bunch of passed-out drunks. This way most of them are still awake."

"And that is important," Foremost added knowledgeably. Carole looked puzzled.

"Each person who knew Sam gives back what they did best at his wake," he explained. Steve overheard him and nodded, pleased.

"Ten on Teddy. I heard he got a new charge in his cart," Steve said.

"Ten on Indian," Foremost answered. He looked at me almost apologetically. "It would be disloyal to do anything else."

Limbo dropped the flags and the racers rolled ahead. The golf cart was almost silent, just a high-pitched whine, but Indian's town car roared and screamed. The crowd answered back.

Foremost leaned next to me and spoke quietly into my ear.

"We need to talk," he said.

"About?"

"I contacted my friends on the ship after the Synth attack. My enemies obviously know I'm alive and where I'm located. I wanted to give my friends the same advantage."

"Sounds like a good idea," I said.

"I also told them everything we know about the Synth attack," Foremost said.

On the street, Indian's town car suddenly swerved into Teddy and bounced off the protective rubber bumpers attached all around the body of his golf cart. Teddy swore and shook his fist at Indian. Indian smiled back, his eyes glazed, and tipped his hat to Teddy. The crowd roared its approval.

"And?" I asked Foremost when it got quiet enough to hear him.

"They asked me to give you their thanks, for keeping me alive. They also put a protective air and space patrol over Summit for tonight. In the morning they'll be down with transport to take me home," Foremost said.

He sat next to me on the stoop, the cowl of his robe thrown back so he could use all his peripheral vision, his snout pointed straight at me. His eyes were very flat and black, with the silky gleam you see on creek stones when just the barest sheet of water flows over them.

"Sounds like a plan," I said. "Why wait until morning?"

"Because I wanted to talk with you," he said.

I sipped the last of my fish and put the jar down on the street, out of the way next to the steps so no one would accidentally break the glass. Foremost and I seemed to be locked inside our own little bubble of silence, the noise of the crowd unimportant and distant. I looked at him directly.

"What do you want to talk about?" I asked.

"You've heard that we plan to take some humans with us when we leave?"

"I've heard," I said. "I never understood why."

"From each world we take a society," he said quietly. "The ship is huge, but space is bigger. We will never come back here again. But we want to take part of you with us."

"Why?"

"Because we never know what we'll face out there," Foremost said. "All we know is that every planet is going to be different. And the more differences we have on the ship to choose from, the greater the chance that someone we have on-board will be able to talk with and understand whoever it is we meet."

The town car was more powerful, but Indian couldn't seem to steer a straight line. Foremost had bought him all the beer he could drink after the burial, to pay him back for his work that afternoon. Indian's capacity for alcohol was tremendous, but by now I was sure he saw three or four roads, not just one. Teddy, on the other hand, figured out the best path and held to it, his head tucked down as if to reduce his wind resistance.

I looked around me, at my line and all the others that made up Summit. Every year there were fewer of us, as more and more children left for the cities. I remembered those children, the exiles as they called themselves, from the East Coast reunions. They always seemed angry and lost, as if they never quite fit in outside of Dakota.

As I never quite fit in.

I leaned back to Foremost.

"We can talk," I said. I leaned forward and took a fresh jar of fish from Oly. I sipped and tried to figure out what kind of fish was in this batch. Northern Pike was my guess. "But tomorrow. Not tonight. Tonight is for Sam."

Foremost nodded and I handed the jar to Carole.

Indian's town car swept by me and kicked up gravel and I felt something sting my cheek.

"That bastard put the blade back on his town car to make it go faster! Indian, get your butt over here . . ."

escape route
PETER F. HAMILTON

Prolific new British writer Peter F. Hamilton has sold to Interzone, In
Dreams, New Worlds, Fears, *and elsewhere. He sold his first novel,* Mind-
star Rising, *in 1993, and quickly followed it up with two sequels,* A Quantum Murder *and* The Nano Flower. *Hamilton's first three books managed
to slip into print without attracting a great deal of attention, on this side
of the Atlantic, at least, but that changed dramatically with the publication of his next novel,* The Reality Dysfunction, *a huge modern Space
Opera (it needed to be divided into two volumes for publication in the
United States) that is itself only the start of a projected trilogy of staggering size and scope.* The Reality Dysfunction *has been attracting the
reviews and the acclaim that his prior novels did not and has suddenly
put Hamilton on the map as a writer to watch, perhaps a potential rival
for writers such as Dan Simmons, Iain M. Banks, Paul J. McAuley, Greg
Benford, C. J. Cherryh, Stephen R. Donaldson, Colin Greenland, and
other major players in the expanding subgenre of Modern Baroque Space
Opera, an increasingly popular area these days. The second novel in the
trilogy,* The Neutronium Alchemist, *is out in Britain, and generating the
same kind of excited critical buzz. Upcoming is the third novel in the
trilogy,* The Naked God, *and Hamilton's first collection,* A Second
Chance at Eden.*

   *In the pyrotechnic novella that follows, one as packed with intriguing
new ideas and fast-paced action and suspense as many another author's
four-hundred-page novel, he unravels the mystery of an enigmatic object
found in deep space, one that may prove to be harder—and considerably
more dangerous—to get* out *of than it was to get* in . . .

Marcus Calvert had never seen an asteroid cavern quite like Sonora's before; it was disorientating even for someone who had spent 30 years
captaining a starship. The centre of the gigantic rock had been hollowed
out by mining machines, producing a cylindrical cavity twelve kilometres long,
five in diameter. Usually, the floor would be covered in soil and planted with
fruit trees and grass. In Sonora's case, the environmental engineers had simply
flooded it. The result was a small freshwater sea that no matter where you were
on it, you appeared to be at the bottom of a valley of water.

Floating around the grey surface were innumerable rafts, occupied by hotels, bars, and restaurants. Taxi boats whizzed between them and the wharfs at the base of the two flat cavern walls.

Marcus and two of his crew had taken a boat out to the Lomaz bar, a raft which resembled a Chinese dragon trying to mate with a Mississippi paddle steamer.

"Any idea what our charter is, Captain?" asked Katherine Maddox, the *Lady Macbeth's* node specialist.

"The agent didn't say," Marcus admitted. "Apart from confirming it's private, not corporate."

"They don't want us for combat, do they?" Katherine asked. There was a hint of rebellion in her voice. She was in her late 40s, and like the Calverts her family had geneered their offspring to withstand both freefall and high acceleration. The dominant modifications had given her thicker skin, tougher bones, and harder internal membranes; she was never sick or giddy in freefall, nor did her face bloat up. Such changes were a formula for blunt features, and Katherine was no exception.

"If they do, we're not taking it," Marcus assured her.

Katherine exchanged an unsettled glance with Roman Zucker, the ship's fusion engineer, and slumped back in her chair.

The combat option was one Marcus had considered possible. *Lady Macbeth* was combat-capable, and Sonora asteroid belonged to a Lagrange-point cluster with a strong autonomy movement. An unfortunate combination. But having passed his 67th birthday two months ago he sincerely hoped those kinds of flights were behind him.

"This could be them," Roman said, glancing over the rail. One of Sonora's little taxi boats was approaching their big resort raft.

The trim cutter curving round towards the Lomaz had two people sitting on its red leather seats.

Marcus watched with interest as they left the taxi. He ordered his neural nanonics to open a fresh memory cell, and stored the pair of them in a visual file. The first to alight was a man in his mid-30s, dressed in expensive casual clothes; a long face and a very broad nose gave him a kind of imposing dignity.

His partner was less flamboyant. She was in her late 20s, obviously geneered; Oriental features matched with white hair that had been drawn together in wide dreadlocks and folded back aerodynamically.

They walked straight over to Marcus's table, and introduced themselves as Antonio Ribeiro and Victoria Keef. Antonio clicked his fingers at the waitress, and told her to fetch a bottle of Norfolk Tears.

"Hopefully to celebrate the success of our business venture, my friends," he said. "And if not, it is a pleasant time of day to imbibe such a magical potion. No?"

Marcus found himself immediately distrustful. It wasn't just Antonio's phoney attitude; his intuition was scratching away at the back of his skull. Some friends called it his paranoia programme, but it was rarely wrong. A family trait, like the wanderlust which no geneering treatment had ever eradicated.

"The cargo agent said you had a charter for us," Marcus said. "He never mentioned any sort of business deal."

"If I may ask your indulgence for a moment, Captain Calvert. You arrived here without a cargo. You must be a very rich man to afford that."

"There were . . . circumstances requiring us to leave Ayachcho ahead of schedule."

"Yeah," Katherine muttered darkly. "Her husband."

Marcus was expecting it, and smiled serenely. He'd heard very little else from the crew for the whole flight.

Antonio received the tray and its precious pear-shaped bottle from the waitress, and waved away the change.

"If I may be indelicate, Captain, your financial resources are not optimal at this moment," Antonio suggested.

"They've been better."

Antonio sipped his Norfolk Tears, and grinned in appreciation. "For myself, I was born with the wrong amount of money. Enough to know I needed more."

"Mr Ribeiro, I've heard all the get-rich-quick schemes in existence. They all have one thing in common, they don't work. If they did, I wouldn't be sitting here with you."

"You are wise to be cautious, Captain. I was, too, when I first heard this proposal. However, if you would humour me a moment longer, I can assure you this requires no capital outlay on your part. At the worst you will have another mad scheme to laugh about with your fellow captains."

"No money at all?"

"None at all, simply the use of your ship. We would be equal partners sharing whatever reward we find."

"Jesus. All right, I can spare you five minutes. Your drink has bought you that much attention span."

"Thank you, Captain. My colleagues and I want to fly the *Lady Macbeth* on a prospecting mission."

"For planets?" Roman asked curiously.

"No. Sadly, the discovery of a terracompatible planet does not guarantee wealth. Settlement rights will not bring more than a couple of million fuseodollars, and even that is dependant on a favourable biospectrum assessment, which would take many years. We have something more immediate in mind. You have just come from the Dorados?"

"That's right," Marcus said. The system had been discovered six years earlier, comprising a red dwarf sun surrounded by a vast disc of rocky particles. Several of the larger chunks had turned out to be nearly pure metal. Dorados was an obvious name; whoever managed to develop them would gain a colossal economic resource. So much so that the governments of Omuta and Garissa had gone to war over who had that development right.

It was the Garissan survivors who had ultimately been awarded settlement by the Confederation Assembly. There weren't many of them. Omuta had deployed twelve antimatter planetbusters against their homeworld. "Is that what you're hoping to find, another flock of solid metal asteroids?"

"Not quite," Antonio said. "Companies have been searching similar disc systems ever since the Dorados were discovered, to no avail. Victoria, my dear, if you would care to explain."

She nodded curtly and put her glass down on the table. "I'm an astrophysicist by training," she said. "I used to work for Forrester-Courtney; it's a company based in the O'Neill Halo that manufactures starship sensors, although their speciality is survey probes. It's been a very healthy business recently. Consortiums have been flying survey missions through every catalogued disc system in the Confederation. As Antonio said, none of our clients found anything remotely like the Dorados. That didn't surprise me, I never expected any of Forrester-Courtney's probes to be of much use. All our sensors did was run broad spectrographic sweeps. If anyone was going to find another Dorados cluster it would be the Edenists. Their voidhawks have a big advantage; those ships generate an enormous distortion field which can literally see mass. A lump of metal 50 kilometres across would have a very distinct density signature; they'd be aware of it from at least half a million kilometres away. If we were going to compete against that, we'd need a sensor which gave us the same level of results, if not better."

"And you produced one?" Marcus enquired.

"Not quite. I proposed expanding our magnetic anomaly detector array. It's a very ancient technology; Earth's old nations pioneered it during the 20th century. Their military maritime aircraft were equipped with crude arrays to track enemy submarines. Forrester-Courtney builds its array into low-orbit resource-mapping satellites; they produce quite valuable survey data. Unfortunately, the company turned down my proposal. They said an expanded magnetic array wouldn't produce better results than a spectrographic sweep, not on the scale required. And a spectrographic scan would be quicker."

"Unfortunate for Forrester-Courtney," Antonio said wolfishly. "Not for us. Dear Victoria came to me with her suggestion, and a simple observation."

"A spectrographic sweep will only locate relatively large pieces of mass," she said. "Fly a starship 50 million kilometres above a disc, and it can spot a 50-kilometre lump of solid metal easily. But the smaller the lump, the higher the resolution you need or the closer you have to fly, a fairly obvious equation. My magnetic anomaly detector can pick out much smaller lumps of metal than a Dorado."

"So? If they're smaller, they're worth less," Katherine said. "The whole point of the Dorados is that they're huge. I've seen the operation those ex-Garissans are building up. They've got enough metal to supply their industrial stations with specialist microgee alloys for the next 2,000 years. Small is no good."

"Not necessarily," Marcus said carefully. Maybe it was his intuition again, or just plain logical extrapolation, but he could see the way Victoria Keef's thoughts were flowing. "It depends on what kind of small, doesn't it?"

Antonio applauded. "Excellent, Captain. I knew you were the right man for us."

"What makes you think they're there?" Marcus asked.

"The Dorados are the ultimate proof of concept," Victoria said. "There are two possible origins for disc material around stars. The first is accretion; matter left over from the star's formation. That's no use to us, it's mostly the light elements, carbonaceous chondritic particles with some silica aluminium thrown in if you're lucky. The second type of disc is made up out of collision debris. We believe that's what the Dorados are, fragments of planetoids that were large enough to form molten metal cores. When they broke apart the metal cooled and congealed into those hugely valuable chunks."

"But nickel iron wouldn't be the only metal," Marcus reasoned, pleased by the way he was following through. "There will be other chunks floating about in the disc."

"Exactly, Captain," Antonio said eagerly. "Theoretically, the whole periodic table will be available to us, we can fly above the disc and pick out whatever element we require. There will be no tedious and expensive refining process to extract it from ore. It's there waiting for us in its purest form; gold, silver, platinum, iridium. Whatever takes your fancy."

Lady Macbeth sat on a docking cradle in Sonora's spaceport, a simple dull-grey sphere 57 metres in diameter. All Adamist starships shared the same geometry, dictated by the operating parameters of the ZTT jump, which required perfect symmetry. At her heart were four separate life-support capsules, arranged in a pyramid formation; there was also a cylindrical hangar for her spaceplane, a smaller one for her Multiple Service Vehicle, and five main cargo holds. The rest of her bulk was a solid intestinal tangle of machinery and tanks. Her main drive system was three fusion rockets capable of accelerating her at eleven gees, clustered round an antimatter intermix tube which could multiply that figure by an unspecified amount; a sure sign of her combat-capable status. (By a legislative quirk it wasn't actually illegal to have an antimatter drive, though possession of antimatter itself was a capital crime throughout the Confederation.)

Spaceport umbilical hoses were jacked into sockets on her lower hull, supplying basic utility functions. Another expense Marcus wished he could avoid; it was inflicting further pain on his already ailing cash-flow situation. They were going to have to fly soon, and fate seemed to have decided what flight it would be. That hadn't stopped his intuition from maintaining its subliminal assault on Antonio Ribeiro's scheme. If he could just find a single practical or logical argument against it . . .

He waited patiently while the crew drifted into the main lounge in life-support capsule A. Wai Choi, the spaceplane pilot, came down through the ceiling hatch and used a stikpad to anchor her shoes to the decking. She gave Marcus a sly smile that bordered on teasing. There had been times in the last five years when she'd joined him in his cabin, nothing serious, but they'd certainly had their moments. Which, he supposed, made her more tolerant of him than the others.

At the opposite end of the spectrum was Karl Jordan, the *Lady Mac's* systems specialist. with the shortest temper, the greatest enthusiasm, and certainly the most serious of the crew. His age was the reason, only 25; the *Lady Mac* was his second starship duty.

As for Schutz, who knew what emotions were at play in the cosmonik's mind; there was no visible outlet for them. Unlike Marcus, he hadn't been geneered for freefall; decades of working on ships and spaceport docks had seen his bones lose calcium, his muscles waste away, and his cardiovascular system atrophy. There were hundreds like him in every asteroid, slowly replacing their body parts with mechanical substitutes. Some even divested themselves of their human shape altogether. At 63, Schutz was still humanoid, though only 20 per cent of him was biological. His body supplements made him an excellent engineer.

"We've been offered a joint-prize flight," Marcus told them. He explained Victoria's theory about disc systems and the magnetic anomaly array. "Ribeiro will provide us with consumables and a full cryogenics load. All we have to do is take *Lady Mac* to a disc system and scoop up the gold."

"There has to be a catch," Wai said. "I don't believe in mountains of gold just drifting through space waiting for us to come along and find them."

"Believe it," Roman said. "You've seen the Dorados. Why can't other elements exist in the same way?"

"I don't know. I just don't think anything comes that easy."

"Always the pessimist."

"What do you think, Marcus?" she asked. "What does your intuition tell you?"

"About the mission, nothing. I'm more worried about Antonio Ribeiro."

"Definitely suspect," Katherine agreed.

"Being a total prat is socially unfortunate," Roman said. "But it's not a crime. Besides, Victoria Keef seemed levelheaded enough."

"An odd combination," Marcus mused. "A wannabe playboy and an astrophysicist. I wonder how they ever got together."

"They're both Sonora nationals," Katherine said. "I ran a check through the public data cores, they were born here. It's not that remarkable."

"Any criminal record?" Wai asked.

"None listed. Antonio has been in court three times in the last seven years; each case was over disputed taxes. He paid every time."

"So he doesn't like the tax man," Roman said. "That makes him one of the good guys."

"Run-ins with the tax office are standard for the rich," Wai said.

"Except he's not actually all that rich," Katherine said. "I also queried the local Collins Media library; they keep tabs on Sonora's principal citizens. Mr Ribeiro senior made his money out of fish breeding, he won the franchise from the asteroid development corporation to keep the biosphere sea stocked. Antonio was given a 15 per cent stake in the breeding company when he was 21, which he promptly sold for an estimated 800,000 fuseodollars. Daddy didn't approve, there are several news files on the quarrel; it became very public."

"So he is what he claims to be," Roman said. "A not-very rich boy with expensive tastes."

"How can he pay for the magnetic detectors we have to deploy, then?" Wai asked. "Or is he going to hit us with the bill and suddenly vanish?"

"The detector arrays are already waiting to be loaded on board," Marcus said.

"Antonio has several partners; people in the same leaky boat as himself, and willing to take a gamble."

Wai shook her head, still dubious. "I don't buy it. It's a free lunch."

"They're willing to invest their own money in the array hardware. What other guarantees do you want?"

"What kind of money are we talking about, exactly?" Karl asked. "I mean, if we do fill the ship up, what's it going to be worth?"

"Given its density, *Lady Mac* can carry roughly 5,000 tonnes of gold in her cargo holds," Marcus said. "That'll make manoeuvring very sluggish, but I can handle her."

Roman grinned at Karl. "And today's price for gold is three and a half thousand fuseodollars per kilogram."

Karl's eyes went blank for a second as his neural nanonics ran the conversion. "Seventeen billion fuseodollars' worth!"

He laughed. "Per trip."

"How is this Ribeiro character proposing to divide the proceeds?" Schutz asked.

"We get one third," Marcus said. "Roughly five point eight billion fuseodollars. Of which I take 30 per cent. The rest is split equally between you, as per the bounty flight clause in your contracts."

"Shit," Karl whispered. "When do we leave, Captain?"

"Does anybody have any objections?" Marcus asked. He gave Wai a quizzical look.

"Okay," she said. "But just because you can't see surface cracks, it doesn't mean there isn't any metal fatigue."

The docking cradle lifted *Lady Macbeth* cleanly out of the spaceport's crater-shaped bay. As soon as she cleared the rim her thermo-dump panels unfolded, sensor clusters rose up out of their recesses on long booms. Visual and radar information was collated by the flight computer, which datavised it directly into Marcus's neural nanonics. He lay on the acceleration couch at the centre of the bridge with his eyes closed as the external starfield blossomed in his mind. Delicate icons unfurled across the visualization, ship status schematics and navigational plots sketched in primary colours.

Chemical verniers fired, lifting *Lady Mac* off the cradle amid spumes of hot saffron vapour. A tube of orange circles appeared ahead of him, the course vector formatted to take them in towards the gas giant. Marcus switched to the more powerful ion thrusters, and the orange circles began to stream past the hull.

The gas giant, Zacateca, and its moon, Lazaro, had the same apparent size as *Lady Mac* accelerated away from the spaceport. Sonora was one of 15 asteroids captured by their Lagrange point, a zone where their respective gravity fields were in equilibrium. Behind the starship, Lazaro was a grubby grey crescent splattered with white craters. Given that Zacateca was small for a gas giant, barely 40,000 kilometres in diameter, Lazaro was an unusual companion. A moon 9,000 kilometres in diameter, with an outer crust of ice 50 kilometres deep. It

was that ice which had originally attracted the interest of the banks and mul-
tistellar finance consortia. Stony iron asteroids were an ideal source of metal and
minerals for industrial stations, but they were also notoriously short of the light
elements essential to sustain life. To have abundant supplies of both so close
together was a strong investment incentive.

Lady Mac's radar showed Marcus a serpentine line of one-tonne ice cubes
flung out from Lazaro's equatorial mass-driver, gliding inertly up to the Lagrange
point for collection. The same inexhaustible source which allowed Sonora to
have its unique sea.

All the asteroids in the cluster had benefited from the plentiful ice, their
economic growth racing ahead of equivalent settlements. Such success always
bred resentment among the indigenous population, who inevitably became eager
for freedom from the founding companies. In this case, having so many settlements so close together gave their population a strong sense of identity and
shared anger. The cluster's demands for autonomy had become increasingly stri-
dent over the last few years. A situation agitated by numerous violent incidents
and acts of sabotage against the company administration staff.

Ahead of the *Lady Mac*, Marcus could see the tidal hurricane Lazaro stirred
up amid the wan amber and emerald stormbands of Zacateca's upper atmosphere. An ocean-sized hypervelocity maelstrom which followed the moon's orbit
faithfully around the equator. Lightning crackled round its fringes, 500-
kilometre-long forks stabbing out into the surrounding cyclones of ammonia
cirrus and methane sleet.

The starship was accelerating at two gees now, her triple fusion drives sending
out a vast streamer of arc-bright plasma as she curved around the bulk of the
huge planet. Her course vector was slowly bending to align on the star which
Antonio intended to prospect, 38 light years distant. There was very little information contained in the almanac file other than confirming it was a K class star
with a disc.

Marcus cut the fusion drives when the *Lady Mac* was 7,000 kilometres past
perigee and climbing steadily. The thermo-dump panels and sensor clusters sank
down into their jump recesses below the fuselage, returning the ship to a perfect
sphere. Fusion generators began charging the energy patterning nodes. Orange
circles flashing through Marcus's mind were illustrating the slingshot parabola
she'd flown, straightening up the farther the gas giant was left behind. A faint
star slid into the last circle.

An event horizon swallowed the starship. Five milliseconds later it had shrunk
to nothing.

"Okay, try this one," Katherine said. "Why should the gold or anything else
congeal into lumps as big as the ones they say it will? Just because you've got a
planetoid with a hot core doesn't mean it's producing the metallic equivalent of
fractional distillation. You're not going to get an onion-layer effect with strata
of different metals. It doesn't happen on planets, it won't happen here. If there

is gold, and platinum and all the rest of this fantasy junk, it's going to be hidden away in ores just like it always is."

"So Antonio exaggerated when he said it would be pure," Karl retorted. "We just hunt down the highest grade ore particles in the disc. Even if it's only 50 per cent, who cares? We're never going to be able to spend it all anyway."

Marcus let the discussion grumble on. It had been virtually the only topic for the crew since they'd departed Sonora five days ago. Katherine was playing the part of chief sceptic, with occasional support from Schutz and Wai, while the others tried to shoot her down. The trouble was, he acknowledged, that none of them knew enough to comment with real authority. At least they weren't talking about the sudden departure from Ayachcho any more.

"If the planetoids did produce ore, then it would fragment badly during the collision which formed the disc," Katherine said. "There won't even be any mountain-sized chunks left, only pebbles."

"Have you taken a look outside recently?" Roman asked. "The disc doesn't exactly have a shortage of large particles."

Marcus smiled to himself at that. The disc material had worried him when they arrived at the star two days ago. *Lady Mac* had jumped deep into the system, emerging three million kilometres above the ecliptic. It was a superb vantage point. The small orange star burned at the centre of a disc 160 million kilometres in diameter. There were no distinct bands like those found in a gas giant's rings, this was a continuous grainy copper mist veiling half of the universe. Only around the star itself did it fade away; whatever particles were there to start with had long since evaporated to leave a clear band three million kilometres wide above the turbulent photosphere.

Lady Mac was accelerating away from the star at a 20th of a gee, and curving round into a retrograde orbit. It was the vector which would give the magnetic arrays the best possible coverage of the disc. Unfortunately, it increased the probability of collision by an order of magnitude. So far, the radar had only detected standard motes of interplanetary dust, but Marcus insisted there were always two crew on duty monitoring the local environment.

"Time for another launch," he announced.

Wai datavised the flight computer to run a final systems diagnostic through the array satellite. "I notice Jorge isn't here again," she said sardonically. "I wonder why that is?"

Jorge Leon was the second companion Antonio Ribeiro had brought with him on the flight. He'd been introduced to the crew as a first-class hardware technician who had supervised the construction of the magnetic array satellites. As introverted as Antonio was outgoing, he'd shown remarkably little interest in the arrays so far. It was Victoria Keef who'd familiarized the crew with the systems they were deploying.

"We should bung him in our medical scanner," Karl suggested cheerfully. "Be interesting to see what's inside him. Bet you'd find a whole load of weapon implants."

"Great idea," Roman said. "You ask him. He gives me the creeps."

"Yeah, Katherine, explain that away," Karl said. "If there's no gold in the disc, how come they brought a contract killer along to make sure we don't fly off with their share?"

"Karl!" Marcus warned. "That's enough." He gave the open floor hatch a pointed look. "Now let's get the array launched, please."

Karl's face reddened as he began establishing a tracking link between the starship's communication system and the array satellite's transponder.

"Satellite systems on line," Wai reported. "Launch when ready."

Marcus datavised the flight computer to retract the satellite's hold-down latches. An induction rail shot it clear of the ship. Ion thrusters flared, refining its trajectory as it headed down towards the squally apricot surface of the disc.

Victoria had designed the satellites to skim 5,000 kilometres above the nomadic particles. When their operational altitude was established they would spin up and start to reel out 25 gossamer-thin optical fibres. Rotation ensured the fibres remained straight, forming a spoke array parallel to the disc. Each fibre was 150 kilometres long, and coated in a reflective, magnetically sensitive film.

As the disc particles were still within the star's magnetosphere, every one of them generated a tiny wake as it traversed the flux lines. It was that wake which resonated the magnetically sensitive film, producing fluctuations in the reflectivity. By bouncing a laser pulse down the fibre and measuring the distortions inflicted by the film, it was possible to build up an image of the magnetic waves writhing chaotically through the disc. With the correct discrimination programmes, the origin of each wave could be determined.

The amount of data streaming back into the *Lady Macbeth* from the array satellites was colossal. One satellite array could cover an area of 250,000 square kilometres, and Antonio Ribeiro had persuaded the Sonora Autonomy Crusade to pay for 15. It was a huge gamble, and the responsibility was his alone. Forty hours after the first satellite was deployed, the strain of that responsibility was beginning to show. He hadn't slept since then, choosing to stay in the cabin which Marcus Calvert had assigned to them, and where they'd set up their network of analysis processors. Forty hours of his mind being flooded with near-incomprehensible neuroiconic displays. Forty hours spent fingering his silver crucifix and praying.

The medical monitor programme running in his neural nanonics was flashing up fatigue toxin cautions, and warning him of impending dehydration. So far he'd ignored them, telling himself discovery would occur any minute now. In his heart, Antonio had been hoping they would find what they wanted in the first five hours.

His neural nanonics informed him the analysis network was focusing on the mass density ratio of a three-kilometre particle exposed by satellite seven. The processors began a more detailed interrogation of the raw data.

"What is it?" Antonio demanded. His eyes fluttered open to glance at Victoria, who was resting lightly on one of the cabin's flatchairs.

"Interesting," she murmured. "It appears to be a cassiterite ore. The plane-toids definitely had tin."

"Shit!" He thumped his fist into the chair's padding, only to feel the restraint straps tighten against his chest, preventing him from sailing free. "I don't care about tin. That's not what we're here for."

"I am aware of that." Her eyes were open, staring at him with a mixture of contempt and anger.

"Sure, sure," he mumbled. "Holy Mother, you'd expect us to find some by now."

"Careful," she datavised. "Remember this damn ship has internal sensors."

"I know how to follow elementary security procedures," he datavised back.

"Yes. But you're tired. That's when errors creep in."

"I'm not that tired. Shit, I expected results by now; some progress."

"We have had some very positive results, Antonio. The arrays have found three separate deposits of pitchblende."

"Yeah, in hundred-kilogram lumps. We need more than that, a lot more."

"You're missing the point. We've proved it exists here; that's a stupendous discovery. Finding it in quantity is just a matter of time."

"This isn't some astrological experiment you're running for that university which threw you out. We're on an assignment for the cause. And we cannot go back empty-handed. Got that? Cannot."

"Astrophysics."

"What?"

"You said astrological, that's fortune-telling."

"Yeah? You want I should take a guess at how much future you're going to have if we don't find what we need out here?"

"For Christ's sake, Antonio," she said out loud. "Go and get some sleep."

"Maybe." He scratched the side of his head, unhappy with how limp and oily his hair had become. A vapour shower was something else he hadn't had for a while. "I'll get Jorge in here to help you monitor the results."

"Great." Her eyes closed again.

Antonio deactivated his flatchair's restraint straps. He hadn't seen much of Jorge on the flight. Nobody had. The man kept strictly to himself in his small cabin. The Crusade's council wanted him on board to ensure the crew's contin-uing cooperation once they realized there was no gold. It was Antonio who had suggested the arrangement; what bothered him was the orders Jorge had received concerning himself should things go wrong.

"Hold it." Victoria raised her hand. "This is a really weird one."

Antonio tapped his feet on a stikpad to steady himself. His neural nanonics accessed the analysis network again. Satellite eleven had located a particle with an impossible mass-density ratio; it also had its own magnetic field, a very com-plex one. "Holy Mother, what is that? Is there another ship here?"

"No, it's too big for a ship. Some kind of station, I suppose. But what's it doing in the disc?"

"Refining ore?" he said with a strong twist of irony.

"I doubt it."

"Okay. So forget it."

"You are joking."

"No. If it doesn't affect us, it doesn't concern us."

"Jesus, Antonio; if I didn't know you were born rich I'd be frightened by how stupid you were."

"Be careful, Victoria my dear. Very careful."

"Listen, there's two options. One, it's some kind of commercial operation; which must be illegal because nobody has filed for industrial development rights." She gave him a significant look.

"You think they're mining pitchblende?" he datavised.

"What else? We thought of the concept, why not one of the black syndicates as well? They just didn't come up with my magnetic array idea, so they're having to do it the hard way."

"Secondly," she continued aloud, "it's some kind of covert military station; in which case they've tracked us from the moment we emerged. Either way, we're under observation. We have to know who they are before we proceed any further."

"A station?" Marcus asked. "Here?"

"It would appear so," Antonio said glumly.

"And you want us to find out who they are?"

"I think that would be prudent," Victoria said, "given what we're doing here."

"All right," Marcus said. "Karl, lock a communication dish on them. Give them our CAB identification code, let's see if we can get a response."

"Aye, sir," Karl said. He settled back on his acceleration couch.

"While we're waiting," Katherine said. "I have a question for you, Antonio." She ignored the warning glare Marcus directed at her.

Antonio's bogus smile blinked on. "If it is one I can answer, then I will do so gladly, dear lady."

"Gold is expensive because of its rarity value, right?"

"Of course."

"So here we are, about to fill Lady Mac's cargo holds with 5,000 tonnes of the stuff. On top of that you've developed a method which means people can scoop up millions of tonnes any time they want. If we try and sell it to a dealer or a bank, how long do you think we're going to be billionaires for, a fortnight?"

Antonio laughed. "Gold has never been that rare. Its value is completely artificial. The Edenists have the largest stockpile. We don't know exactly how much they possess because the Jovian Bank will not declare the exact figure. But they dominate the commodity market, and sustain the price by controlling how much is released. We shall simply play the same game. Our gold will have to be sold discreetly, in small batches, in different star systems, and over the course of several years. And knowledge of the magnetic array system should be kept to ourselves."

"Nice try, Katherine," Roman chuckled. "You'll just have to settle for an income of a hundred million a year."

She showed him a stiff finger, backed by a shark's smile.

"No response," Karl said. "Not even a transponder."

"Keep trying," Marcus told him. "Okay, Antonio, what do you want to do about it?"

"We have to know who they are," Victoria said. "As Antonio has just explained so eloquently, we can't have other people seeing what we're doing here."

"It's what *they're* doing here that worries me," Marcus said; although, curiously, his intuition wasn't causing him any grief on the subject.

"I see no alternative but a rendezvous," Antonio said.

"We're in a retrograde orbit, 32 million kilometres away and receding. That's going to use up an awful lot of fuel."

"Which I believe I have already paid for."

"Okay, we rendezvous."

"What if they don't want us there?" Schutz asked.

"If we detect any combat wasp launch, then we jump outsystem immediately," Marcus said. "The disc's gravity field isn't strong enough to affect *Lady Mac*'s patterning node symmetry. We can leave any time we want."

For the last quarter of a million kilometres of the approach, Marcus put the ship on combat status. The nodes were fully charged, ready to jump. Thermo-dump panels were retracted. Sensors maintained a vigilant watch for approaching combat wasps.

"They must know we're here," Wai said when they were 8,000 kilometres away. "Why don't they acknowledge us?"

"Ask them," Marcus said sourly. *Lady Mac* was decelerating at a nominal one gee, which he was varying at random. It made their exact approach vector impossible to predict, which meant their course couldn't be seeded with proximity mines. The manoeuvre took a lot of concentration.

"Still no electromagnetic emission in any spectrum," Karl reported. "They're certainly not scanning us with active sensors."

"Sensors are picking up their thermal signature," Schutz said. "The structure is being maintained at 36 degrees Celsius."

"That's on the warm side," Katherine observed. "Perhaps their environmental system is malfunctioning."

"Shouldn't affect the transponder," Karl said.

"Captain, I think you'd better access the radar return," Schutz said.

Marcus boosted the fusion drives up to one and a half gees, and ordered the flight computer to datavise him the radar feed. The image which rose into his mind was of a fine scarlet mesh suspended in the darkness, its gentle ocean-swell pattern outlining the surface of the station and the disc particle it was attached to. Except Marcus had never seen any station like this before. It was a gently curved wedge-shape structure, 400 metres long, 300 wide, and 150 metres at its blunt end. The accompanying disc particle was a flattened ellipsoid of stony iron rock, measuring eight kilometres along its axis. The tip had been sheared off, leaving a flat cliff half a kilometre in diameter, to which the structure was clinging. That was the smallest of the particle's modifications. A crater four kilometres across, with perfectly smooth walls, had been cut into one side of the rock. An elaborate unicorn-horn tower rose 900 metres from its centre, ending in a clump of jagged spikes.

"Oh Jesus," Marcus whispered. Elation mingled with fear, producing a deviant adrenaline high. He smiled thinly. "How about that?"

"This was one option I didn't consider," Victoria said weakly.

Antonio looked round the bridge, a frown cheapening his handsome face. The crew seemed dazed, while Victoria was grinning with delight. "Is it some kind of radio astronomy station?" he asked.

"Yes," Marcus said. "But not one of ours. We don't build like that. It's xenoc."

Lady Mac locked attitude a kilometre above the xenoc structure. It was a position which made the disc appear uncomfortably malevolent. The smallest particle beyond the fuselage must have massed over a million tonnes; and all of them were moving, a slow, random three-dimensional cruise of lethal inertia. Amber sunlight stained those near the disc's surface a baleful ginger, while deeper in there were only phantom silhouettes drifting over total blackness, flowing in and out of visibility. No stars were evident through the dark, tightly packed nebula.

"That's not a station," Roman declared. "It's a shipwreck."

Now that Lady Mac's visual-spectrum sensors were providing them with excellent images of the xenoc structure, Marcus had to agree. The upper and lower surfaces of the wedge were some kind of silver-white material, a fuselage shell which was fraying away at the edges. Both of the side surfaces were dull brown, obviously interior bulkhead walls, with the black geometrical outline of decking printed across them. The whole structure was a cross-section torn out of a much larger craft. Marcus tried to fill in the missing bulk in his mind; it must have been vast, a streamlined delta fuselage like a hypersonic aircraft. Which didn't make sense for a starship. Rather, he corrected himself, for a starship built with current human technology. He wondered what it would be like to fly through interstellar space the way a plane flew through an atmosphere, swooping round stars at a hundred times the speed of light. Quite something.

"This doesn't make a lot of sense," Katherine said. "If they were visiting the telescope dish when they had the accident, why did they bother to anchor themselves to the asteroid? Surely they'd just take refuge in the operations centre."

"Only if there is one," Schutz said. "Most of our deep space science facilities are automated, and by the look of it their technology is considerably more advanced."

"If they are so advanced, why would they build a radio telescope on this scale anyway?" Victoria asked. "It's very impractical. Humans have been using linked baseline arrays for centuries. Five small dishes orbiting a million kilometres apart would provide a reception which is orders of magnitude greater than this. And why build here? Firstly, the particles are hazardous, certainly to something that size. You can see it's been pocked by small impacts, and that horn looks broken to me. Secondly, the disc itself blocks half of the universe from observation. No, if you're going to do major radio astronomy, you don't do it from a star system like this one."

"Perhaps they were only here to build the dish," Wai said. "They intended it to be a remote research station in this part of the galaxy. Once they had it up and running, they'd boost it into a high-inclination orbit. They had their accident before the project was finished."

"That still doesn't explain why they chose this system. Any other star would be better than this one."

"I think Wai's right about them being long-range visitors," Marcus said. "If a xenoc race like that existed close to the Confederation we would have found them by now. Or they would have contacted us."

"The Kiint," Karl said quickly.

"Possibly," Marcus conceded. The Kiint were an enigmatic xenoc race, with a technology far in advance of anything the Confederation had mastered. However, they were reclusive, and cryptic to the point of obscurity. They also claimed to have abandoned starflight a long time ago. "If it is one of their ships, then it's very old."

"And it's still functional," Roman said eagerly. "Hell, think of the technology inside. We'll wind up a lot richer than the gold could ever make us." He grinned over at Antonio, whose humour had blackened considerably.

"So what were the Kiint doing building a radio telescope here?" Victoria asked.

"Who the hell cares?" Karl said. "I volunteer to go over, Captain."

Marcus almost didn't hear him. He'd accessed the *Lady Mac*'s sensor suite again, sweeping the focus over the tip of the dish's tower, then the sheer cliff which the wreckage was attached to. Intuition was making a lot of junctions in his head. "I don't think it is a radio telescope," he said. "I think it's a distress beacon."

"It's four kilometres across!" Katherine said.

"If they came from the other side of the galaxy, it would need to be. We can't even see the galactic core from here there's so much gas and dust in the way. You'd need something this big to punch a message through."

"That's valid," Victoria said. "You believe they were signalling their homeworld for help?"

"Yes. Assume their world is a long way off, three-four thousand light years away if not more. They were flying a research or survey mission in this area and they have an accident. Three quarters of their ship is lost, including the drive section. Their technology isn't good enough to build the survivors a working stardrive out of what's left, but they can enlarge an existing crater on the disc particle. So they do that; they build the dish and a transmitter powerful enough to give God an alarm call, point it at their homeworld, and scream for help. The ship can sustain them until the rescue team arrives. Even our own zero-tau technology is up to that."

"Gets my vote," Wai said, she gave Marcus a wink.

"No way," said Katherine. "If they were in trouble they'd use a supralight communicator to call for help. Look at that ship, we're centuries away from building anything like it."

"Edenist voidhawks are pretty sophisticated," Marcus countered. "We just scale things differently. These xenocs might have a more advanced technology, but physics is still the same the universe over. Our understanding of quantum relativity is good enough to build faster than light starships, yet after 450 years of theoretical research we still haven't come up with a method of supralight communication. It doesn't exist."

"If they didn't return on time, then surely their homeworld would send out a search and recovery craft," Schutz said.

"They'd have to know the original ship's course exactly," Wai said. "And if a search ship did manage to locate them, why did they build the dish?"

Marcus didn't say anything. He knew he was right. The others would accept his scenario eventually, they always did.

"All right, let's stop arguing about what happened to them, and why they built the dish," Karl said. "When do we go over there, Captain?"

"Have you forgotten the gold?" Antonio asked. "That is why we came to this disc system. We should resume our search for it. This piece of wreckage can wait."

"Don't be crazy. This is worth a hundred times as much as any gold."

"I fail to see how. An ancient, derelict, starship with a few heating circuits operational. Come along. I've been reasonable indulging you, but we must return to the original mission."

Marcus regarded the man cautiously, a real bad feeling starting to develop. Anyone with the slightest knowledge of finance and the markets would know the value of salvaging a xenoc starship. And Antonio had been born rich. "Victoria," he said, not shifting his gaze. "Is the data from the magnetic array satellites still coming through?"

"Yes." She touched Antonio's arm. "The captain is right. We can continue to monitor the satellite results from here, and investigate the xenoc ship simultaneously."

"Double your money time," Katherine said with apparent innocence.

Antonio's face hardened. "Very well," he said curtly. "If that's your expert opinion, Victoria, my dear. Carry on by all means, Captain."

In its inert state the SII spacesuit was a broad sensor collar with a protruding respirator tube and a black football-sized globe of programmable silicon hanging from it. Marcus slipped the collar round his neck, bit on the tube nozzle, and datavised an activation code into the suit's control processor. The silicon ball began to change shape, flattening out against his chest, then flowing over his body like a tenacious oil slick. It enveloped his head completely, and the collar sensors replaced his eyes, datavising their vision directly into his neural nanonics. Three others were in the preparation compartment with him; Schutz, who didn't need a spacesuit to EVA, Antonio, and Jorge Leon. Marcus had managed to control his surprise when they'd volunteered. At the same time, with Wai flying the MSV he was glad they weren't going to be left behind in the ship.

Once his body was sealed by the silicon, he climbed into an armoured exoskeleton with an integral cold-gas manoeuvring pack. The SII silicon would never puncture, but if he was struck by a rogue particle the armour would absorb the impact.

When the airlock's outer hatch opened, the MSV was floating 15 metres away. Marcus datavised an order into his manoeuvring pack processor, and the gas jets behind his shoulder fired, pushing him towards the small egg-shaped vehicle. Wai extended two of the MSV's three waldo arms in greeting. Each of them ended in a simple metal grid, with a pair of boot clamps on both sides.

Once all four of her passengers were locked into place, Wai piloted the MSV in towards the disc. The rock particle had a slow, erratic tumble, taking 120 hours to complete its cycle. As she approached, the flattish surface with the dish was just turning into the sunlight. It was a strange kind of dawn, the rock's crumpled grey-brown crust speckled by the sharp black shadows of its own rolling prominences, while the dish was a lake of infinite black, broken only by the jagged spire of the horn rising from its centre. The xenoc ship was already exposed to the amber light, casting its bloated sundial shadow across the featureless glassy cliff. She could see the ripple of different ores and mineral strata frozen below the glazed surface, deluding her for a moment that she was flying towards a mountain of cut and polished onyx.

Then again, if Victoria's theory was right, she could well be.

"Take us in towards the top of the wedge," Marcus datavised. "There's a series of darker rectangles there."

"Will do," she responded. The MSV's chemical thrusters pulsed in compliance.

"Do you see the colour difference near the frayed edges of the shell?" Schutz asked. "The stuff's turning grey. It's as if the decay is creeping inwards."

"They must be using something like our molecular binding force generators to resist vacuum ablation," Marcus datavised. "That's why the main section is still intact."

"It could have been here for a long time, then."

"Yeah. We'll know better once Wai collects some samples from the tower."

There were five of the rectangles, arranged in parallel, one and a half metres long and one metre wide. The shell material below the shorter edge of each one had a set of ten grooves leading away down the curve.

"They look like ladders to me," Antonio datavised. "Would that mean these are airlocks?"

"It can't be that easy," Schutz replied.

"Why not?" Marcus datavised. "A ship this size is bound to have more than one airlock."

"Yeah, but five together?"

"Multiple redundancy."

"With technology this good?"

"That's human hubris. The ship still blew up, didn't it?"

Wai locked the MSV's attitude 50 metres above the shell section. "The micro-pulse radar is bouncing right back at me," she informed them. "I can't tell what's below the shell, it's a perfect electromagnetic reflector. We're going to have communication difficulties once you're inside."

Marcus disengaged his boots from the grid and fired his pack's gas jets. The shell was as slippery as ice, neither stikpads nor magnetic soles would hold them to it.

"Definitely enhanced valency bonds," Schutz datavised. He was floating parallel to the surface, holding a sensor block against it. "It's a much stronger field than Lady Mac's. The shell composition is a real mix; the resonance scan is picking up titanium, silicon, boron, nickel, silver, and a whole load of polymers."

"Silver's weird," Marcus commented. "But if there's nickel in it our magnetic soles should've worked." He manoeuvred himself over one of the rectangles. It was recessed about five centimetres, though it blended seamlessly into the main shell. His sensor collar couldn't detect any seal lining. Halfway along one side were two circular dimples, ten centimetres across. Logically, if the rectangle was an airlock, then these should be the controls. Human back-ups were kept simple. This shouldn't be any different.

Marcus stuck his fingers in one. It turned bright blue.

"Power surge," Schutz datavised. "The block's picking up several high voltage circuits activating under the shell. What did you do, Marcus?"

"Tried to open one."

The rectangle dilated smoothly, material flowing back to the edges. Brilliant white light flooded out.

"Clever," Schutz datavised.

"No more than our programmable silicon," Antonio retorted.

"We don't use programmable silicon for external applications."

"It settles one thing," Marcus datavised. "They weren't Kiint, not with an airlock this size."

"Quite. What now?"

"We try to establish control over the cycling mechanism. I'll go in and see if I can operate the hatch from inside. If it doesn't open after ten minutes, try the dimple again. If that doesn't work, cut through it with the MSV's fission blade."

The chamber inside was thankfully bigger than the hatch: a pentagonal tube two metres wide and 15 long. Four of the walls shone brightly, while the fifth was a strip of dark-maroon composite. He drifted in, then flipped himself over so he was facing the hatch, floating in the centre of the chamber. There were four dimples just beside the hatch. "First one," he datavised. Nothing happened when he put his fingers in. "Second." It turned blue. The hatch flowed shut.

Marcus crashed down onto the strip of dark composite, landing on his left shoulder. The force of the impact was almost enough to jar the respirator tube out of his mouth. He grunted in shock. Neural nanonics blocked the burst of pain from his bruised shoulder.

Jesus! They've got artificial gravity.

He was flat on his back, the exoskeleton and manoeuvring pack weighing far too much. Whatever planet the xenocs came from, it had a gravity field about one and a half times that of Earth. He released the catches down the side of his exoskeleton, and wriggled his way out. Standing was an effort, but he was used to higher gees on *Lady Mac*; admittedly not for prolonged periods, though.

He stuck his fingers in the first dimple. The gravity faded fast, and the hatch flowed apart.

"We just became billionaires," he datavised.

The third dimple pressurized the airlock chamber; while the fourth depressurized it.

The xenoc atmosphere was mostly a nitrogen oxygen blend, with one per cent argon and six per cent carbon dioxide. The humidity was appalling, pressure was lower than standard, and the temperature was 42 degrees Celsius.

"We'd have to keep our SII suits on anyway, because of the heat," Marcus datavised. "But the carbon dioxide would kill us. And we'll have to go through biological decontamination when we go back to *Lady Mac*."

The four of them stood together at the far end of the airlock chamber, their exoskeleton armour lying on the floor behind them. Marcus had told Wai and the rest of the crew their first foray would be an hour.

"Are you proposing we go in without a weapon?" Jorge asked.

Marcus focused his collar sensors on the man who alleged he was a hardware technician. "That's carrying paranoia too far. No, we do not engage in first contact either deploying or displaying weapons of any kind. That's the law, and the Assembly regulations are very specific about it. In any case, don't you think that if there are any xenocs left after all this time they're going to be glad to see someone? Especially a space-faring species."

"That is, I'm afraid, a rather naive attitude, Captain. You keep saying how advanced this starship is, and yet it suffered catastrophic damage. Frankly, an unbelievable amount of damage for an accident. Isn't it more likely this ship was engaged in some kind of battle?"

Which was a background worry Marcus had suffered right from the start. That this starship could ever fail was unnerving. But like physical constants, Murphy's Law would be the same the universe over. He'd entered the air-lock because intuition told him the wreck was safe for him personally. Somehow he doubted a man like Jorge would be convinced by that argument.

"If it's a warship, then it will be rigged to alert any surviving crew or flight computer of our arrival. Had they wanted to annihilate us, they would have done so by now. *Lady Mac* is a superb ship, but hardly in this class. So if they're waiting for us on the other side of this airlock, I don't think any weapon you or I can carry is going to make the slightest difference."

"Very well, proceed."

Marcus postponed the answer which came straight to mind, and put his fingers in one of the two dimples by the inner hatchway. It turned blue.

The xenoc ship wasn't disappointing, exactly, but Marcus couldn't help a growing sense of anticlimax. The artificial gravity was a fabulous piece of equipment, the atmosphere strange, the layout exotic. Yet for all that, it was just a ship; built from the universal rules of logical engineering. Had the xenocs themselves been there, it would have been so different. A whole new species with its history and culture. But they'd gone, so he was an archaeologist rather than an explorer.

They surveyed the first deck, which was made up from large compartments and broad hallways. The interior was made out of a pale-jade composite, slightly ruffled to a snake-skin texture. Surfaces always curved together, there were no real corners. Every ceiling emitted the same intense white glare, which their collar sensors compensated for. Arching doorways were all open, though they could still dilate if you used the dimples. The only oddity were 50-centimetre hemispherical blisters on the floor and walls, scattered completely at random.

There was an ongoing argument about the shape of the xenocs. They were undoubtedly shorter than humans, and they probably had legs, because there were spiral stairwells, although the steps were very broad, difficult for bipeds. Lounges had long tables with large, rounded stool-chairs inset with four deep ridges.

After the first 15 minutes it was clear that all loose equipment had been removed. Lockers, with the standard dilating door, were empty. Every compartment had its fitted furnishings and nothing more. Some were completely bare.

On the second deck there were no large compartments, only long corridors lined with grey circles along the centre of the walls. Antonio used a dimple at the side of one, and it dilated to reveal a spherical cell three metres wide. Its walls were translucent, with short lines of colour slithering round behind them like photonic fish.

"Beds?" Schutz suggested. "There's an awful lot of them."

Marcus shrugged. "Could be." He moved on, eager to get down to the next deck. Then he slowed, switching his collar focus. Three of the hemispherical blisters were following him, two gliding along the wall, one on the floor. They stopped when he did. He walked over to the closest, and waved his sensor block over it. "There's a lot of electronic activity inside it," he reported.

The others gathered round.

"Are they extruded by the wall, or are they a separate device?" Schutz asked.

Marcus switched on the block's resonance scan. "I'm not sure, I can't find any break in the composite round its base, not even a hairline fracture; but with their materials technology that doesn't mean much."

"Five more approaching," Jorge datavised. The blisters were approaching from ahead, three of them on the walls, two on the floor. They stopped just short of the group.

"Something knows we're here," Antonio datavised.

Marcus retrieved the CAB xenoc interface communication protocol from a neural nanonics memory cell. He'd stored it decades ago, all qualified starship crew were obliged to carry it along with a million and one other bureaucratic lunacies. His communication block transmitted the protocol using a multi-spectrum sweep. If the blister could sense them, it had to have some kind of electromagnetic reception facility. The communication block switched to laser-light, then a magnetic pulse.

"Nothing," Marcus datavised.

"Maybe the central computer needs time to interpret the protocol," Schutz datavised.

"A desktop block should be able to work that out."

"Perhaps the computer hasn't got anything to say to us."

"Then why send the blisters after us?"

"They could be autonomous, whatever they are."

Marcus ran his sensor block over the blister again, but there was no change to its electronic pattern. He straightened up, wincing at the creak of complaint his spine made at the heavy gravity. "Okay, our hour is almost up anyway. We'll get back to *Lady Mac* and decide what stage two is going to be."

The blisters followed them all the way back to the stairwell they'd used. As soon as they started walking down the broad central hallway of the upper deck, more blisters started sliding in from compartments and other halls to stalk them.

The airlock hatch was still open when they got back, but the exoskeletons were missing.

"Shit," Antonio datavised. "They're still here, the bloody xenocs are here."

Marcus shoved his fingers into the dimple. His heartbeat calmed considerably when the hatch congealed behind them. The lock cycled obediently, and the outer rectangle opened.

"Wai," he datavised. "We need a lift. Quickly, please."

"On my way, Marcus."

"Strange way for xenocs to communicate," Schutz datavised. "What did they do that for? If they wanted to make sure we stayed, they could have disabled the airlock."

The MSV swooped over the edge of the shell, jets of twinkling flame shooting from its thrusters.

"Beats me," Marcus datavised. "But we'll find out."

Opinion on the ship was a straight split; the crew wanted to continue investigating the xenoc ship, Antonio and his colleagues wanted to leave. For once Jorge had joined them, which Marcus considered significant. He was beginning to think young Karl might have been closer to the truth than was strictly comfortable.

"The dish is just rock with a coating of aluminium sprayed on," Katherine said. "There's very little aluminium left now, most of it has boiled away in the vacuum. The tower is a pretty ordinary silicon-boron composite wrapped round a titanium load structure. The samples Wai cut off were very brittle."

"Did you carbon date them?" Victoria asked.

"Yeah." She gave her audience a laboured glance. "Give or take a decade, it's 13,000 years old."

Breath whistled out of Marcus's mouth. "Jesus."

"Then they must have been rescued, or died," Roman said. "There's nobody left over there. Not after that time."

"They're there," Antonio growled. "They stole our exoskeletons."

"I don't understand what happened to the exoskeletons. Not yet. But any entity who can build a ship like that isn't going to go creeping round stealing bits of space armour. There has to be a rational explanation."

"Yes! They wanted to keep us over there."

"What for? What possible reason would they have for that?"

"It's a warship, it's been in battle. The survivors don't know who we are, if we're their old enemies. If they kept us there, they could study us and find out."

"After 13,000 years, I imagine the war will be over. And where did you get this battleship idea from anyway?"

"It's a logical assumption," Jorge said quietly.

Roman turned to Marcus. "My guess is that some kind of mechanoid picked them up. If you look in one of the lockers you'll probably find them neatly stored away."

"Some automated systems are definitely still working," Schutz said. "We saw the blisters. There could be others."

"That seems the most remarkable part of it," Marcus said. "Especially now we know the age of the thing. The inside of that ship was brand new. There wasn't any dust, any scuff marks. The lighting worked perfectly, so did the gravity, the humidity hasn't corroded anything. It's extraordinary. As if the whole structure has been in zero-tau. And yet only the shell is protected by the molecular bonding force generators. They're not used inside, not in the decks we examined."

"However they preserve it, they'll need a lot of power for the job, and that's on top of gravity generation and environmental maintenance. Where's that been coming from uninterrupted for 13,000 years?"

"Direct mass to energy conversion," Katherine speculated. "Or they could be tapping straight into the sun's fusion. Whatever, bang goes the Edenist He3 monopoly."

"We have to go back," Marcus said.

"NO!" Antonio yelled. "We must find the gold first. When that has been achieved, you can come back by yourselves. I won't allow anything to interfere with our priorities."

"Look, I'm sorry you had a fright while you were over there. But a power supply that works for 13,000 years is a lot more valuable than a whole load of gold which we have to sell furtively," Katherine said levelly.

"I hired this ship. You do as I say. We go after the gold."

"We're partners, actually. I'm not being paid for this flight unless we strike lucky. And now we have. We've got the xenoc ship, we haven't got any gold. What does it matter to you how we get rich, as long as we do? I thought money was the whole point of this flight."

Antonio snarled at her, and flung himself at the floor hatch, kicking off hard with his legs. His elbow caught the rim a nasty crack as he flashed through it.

"Victoria?" Marcus asked as the silence became strained. "Have the satellite arrays found any heavy metal particles yet?"

"There are definitely traces of gold and platinum, but nothing to justify a rendezvous."

"In that case, I say we start to research the xenoc wreck properly." He looked straight at Jorge. "How about you?"

"I think it would be prudent. You're sure we can continue to monitor the array satellites from here?"

"Yes."

"Good. Count me in."

"Thanks. Victoria?"

She seemed troubled by Jorge's response, even a little bewildered, but she said: "Sure."

"Karl, you're the nearest thing we've got to a computer expert. I want you over there trying to make contact with whatever control network is still operating."

"You got it."

"From now on we go over in teams of four. I want sensors put up to watch the airlocks when we're not around, and start thinking about how we communicate with people inside. Wai, you and I are going to secure *Lady Mac* to the side of the shell. Okay, let's get active, people."

Unsurprisingly, none of the standard astronautics industry vacuum epoxies worked on the shell. Marcus and Wai wound up using tether cables wrapped round the whole of the xenoc ship to hold *Lady Mac* in place.

Three hours after Karl went over, he asked Marcus to join him.

Lady Mac's main airlock tube had telescoped out of the hull to rest against the shell. There was no way it could ever be mated to the xenoc airlock rectangle, but it did allow the crew to transfer over directly without having to use exoskeleton armour and the MSV. They'd also run an optical fibre through the xenoc airlock to the interior of the ship. The hatch material closed around it forming a perfect seal, rather than cutting through it.

Marcus found Karl just inside the airlock, sitting on the floor with several processor blocks in his lap. Eight blisters were slowly circling round him; two on the wall were stationary.

"Roman was almost right," he datavised as soon as Marcus stepped out of the airlock. "Your exoskeletons were cleared away. But not by any butler mechanoid. Watch." He lobbed an empty recording flek case onto the floor behind the blisters. One of them slid over to it. The green composite became soft, then liquid. The little plastic case sank through it into the blister.

"I call them cybermice," Karl datavised. "They just scurry around keeping the place clean. You won't see the exoskeletons again, they ate them, along with anything else they don't recognize as part of the ship's structure. I imagine they haven't tried digesting us yet because we're large and active; maybe they think we're friends of the xenocs. But I wouldn't want to try sleeping over here."

"Does this mean we won't be able to put sensors up?"

"Not for a while. I've managed to stop them digesting the communication block which the optical fibre is connected to."

"How?"

He pointed to the two on the wall. "I shut them down."

"Jesus, have you accessed a control network?"

"No. Schutz and I used a micro SQUID on one of the cybermice to get a more detailed scan of its electronics. Once we'd tapped the databus traffic it was just a question of running standard decryption programmes. I can't tell you how these things work, but I have found some basic command routines. There's a deactivation code which you can datavise to them. I've also got a reactivation code, and some directional codes. The good news is that the xenoc programme language is standardized." He stood and held a communication block up to the ceiling. "This is the deactivation code." A small circle of the ceiling around the block turned dark. "It's only localized, I haven't worked out how to control entire sections yet. We need to trace the circuitry to find an access port."

"Can you turn it back on again?"

"Oh yes." The dark section flared white again. "The codes work for the doors as well; just hold your block over the dimples."

"Be quicker to use the dimples."

"For now, yes."

"I wasn't complaining, Karl. This is an excellent start. What's your next step?"

"I want to access the next level of the cybermice programme architecture. That way I should be able to load recognition patterns in their memory. Once I can do that I'll enter our equipment, and they should leave it alone. But that's going to take a long time; *Lady Mac* isn't exactly heavily stocked with equipment for this kind of work. Of course, once I do get deeper into their management routines we should be able to learn a lot about their internal systems. From what I can make out the cybermice are built around a molecular synthesizer." He switched on a fission knife, its ten-centimetre blade glowing a pale yellow under the ceiling's glare. It scored a dark smouldering scar in the floor composite.

A cybermouse immediately slipped towards the blemish. This time when the composite softened the charred granules were sucked down, and the small valley closed up.

"Exactly the same thickness and molecular structure as before," Karl datavised. "That's why the ship's interior looks brand new, and everything's still working flawlessly after 13,000 years. The cybermice keep regenerating it. Just keep giving them energy and a supply of mass and there's no reason this ship won't last for eternity."

"It's almost a Von Neumann machine, isn't it?"

"Close. I expect a synthesizer this small has limits. After all, if it could reproduce anything, they would have built themselves another starship. But the principle's here, Captain. We can learn and expand on it. Think of the effect a unit like this will have on our manufacturing industry."

Marcus was glad he was in an SII suit, it blocked any give-away facial expressions. Replicator technology would be a true revolution, restructuring every aspect of human society, Adamist and Edenist alike. And revolutions never favoured the old.

I just came here for the money, not to destroy a way of life for 800 star systems.

"That's good, Karl. Where did the others go?"

"Down to the third deck. Once we solved the puzzle of the disappearing exoskeletons, they decided it was safe to start exploring again."

"Fair enough, I'll go down and join them."

"I cannot believe you agreed to help them," Antonio stormed. "You of all people. You know how much the cause is depending on us."

Jorge gave him a hollow smile. They were together in his sleeping cubicle, which made it very cramped. But it was one place on the starship he knew for certain no sensors were operational; a block he'd brought with him had made sure of that. "The cause has become dependent on your project. There's a difference."

"What are you talking about?"

"Those detector satellites cost us a million and a half fuseodollars each; and most of that money came from sources who will require repayment no matter what the outcome of our struggle."

"The satellites are a hell of a lot cheaper than antimatter."

"Indeed so. But they are worthless to us unless they find pitchblende."

"We'll find it. Victoria says there are plenty of traces. It's only a question of time before we get a big one."

"Maybe. It was a good idea, Antonio, I'm not criticising. Fusion bomb components are not easily obtainable to a novice political organization with limited resources. One mistake, and the intelligence agencies would wipe us out. No, old-fashioned fission was a viable alternative. Even if we couldn't process the uranium up to weapons-quality, we can still use it as a lethal large-scale contaminant. As you say, we couldn't lose. Sonora would gain independence, and we would form the first government, with full access to the Treasury. Everyone would be reimbursed for their individual contribution to the liberation."

"So why are we mucking about in a pile of xenoc junk? Just back me up, Jorge, please. Calvert will leave it alone if we both pressure him."

"Because, Antonio, this piece of so-called xenoc junk has changed the rules of the game. In fact we're not even playing the same game any more. Gravity generation, an inexhaustible power supply, molecular synthesis, and if Karl can access the control network he might even find the blueprints to build whatever stardrive they used. Are you aware of the impact such a spectrum of radical technologies will have upon the Confederation when released all together? Entire industries will collapse from overnight obsolescence. There will be an economic depression the like of which we haven't seen since before the invention of the ZTT drive. It will take decades for the human race to return to the kind of stability we enjoy today. We will be richer and stronger because of it; but the transition years, ah . . . I would not like to be a citizen in an asteroid settlement that has just blackmailed the founding company into premature independence. Who is going to loan an asteroid such as that the funds to re-equip our industrial stations, eh?"

"I . . . I hadn't thought of that."

"Neither has the crew. Except for Calvert. Look at his face next time you talk to him, Antonio. He knows, he has reasoned it out, and he's seen the end of his captaincy and freedom. The rest of them are lost amid their dreams of exorbitant wealth."

"So what do we do?"

Jorge clamped a hand on Antonio's shoulder. "Fate has smiled on us, Antonio. This was registered as a joint venture flight. No matter we were looking for something different. By law, we are entitled to an equal share of the xenoc technology. We are already trillionaires, my friend. When we get home we can *buy* Sonora asteroid; Holy Mother, we can buy the entire Lagrange cluster."

Antonio managed a smile, which didn't quite correspond with the dew of sweat on his forehead. "Okay, Jorge. Hell, you're right. We don't have to worry about anything any more. But . . ."

"Now what?"

"I know we can pay off the loan on the satellites, but what about the Crusade council? They won't like this. They might—"

"There's no cause for alarm. The council will never trouble us again. I maintain that I am right about the disaster which destroyed the xenoc ship. It didn't have an accident. That is a warship, Antonio. And you know what that means, don't you? Somewhere on board there will be weapons just as advanced and as powerful as the rest of its technology."

It was Wai's third trip over to the xenoc ship. None of them spent more than two hours at a time inside. The gravity field made every muscle ache, walking round was like being put on a crash exercise regimen.

Schutz and Karl were still busy by the airlock, probing the circuitry of the cybermice, and decrypting more of their programming. It was probably the most promising line of research; once they could use the xenoc programme language they should be able to extract any answer they wanted from the ship's controlling network. Assuming there was one. Wai was convinced there would be. The number of systems operating—life-support, power, gravity—had to mean some basic management integration system was functional.

In the meantime there was the rest of the structure to explore. She had a layout file stored in her neural nanonics, updated by the others every time they came back from an excursion. At the blunt end of the wedge there could be anything up to 40 decks, if the spacing was standard. Nobody had gone down to the bottom yet. There were some areas which had no obvious entrance; presumably engineering compartments, or storage tanks. Marcus had the teams tracing the main power lines with magnetic sensors, trying to locate the generator.

Wai plodded after Roman as he followed a cable running down the centre of a corridor on the eighth deck.

"It's got so many secondary feeds it looks like a fishbone," he complained. They paused at a junction with five branches, and he swept the block round. "This way." He started off down one of the new corridors.

"We're heading towards stairwell five," she told him, as the layout file scrolled through her skull.

There were more cybermice than usual on deck eight; over 30 were currently pursuing her and Roman, creating strong ripples in the composite floor and walls. Wai had noticed that the deeper she went into the ship the more of them there seemed to be. Although after her second trip she'd completely ignored them. She wasn't paying a lot of attention to the compartments leading off from the corridors, either. It wasn't that they were all the same, rather that they were all similarly empty.

They reached the stairwell, and Roman stepped inside. "It's going down," he datavised.

"Great, that means we've got another level to climb up when we're finished."

Not that going down these stairs was easy, she acknowledged charily. If only they could find some kind of variable gravity chute. Perhaps they'd all been positioned in the part of the ship that was destroyed.

"You know, I think Marcus might have been right about the dish being an emergency beacon," she datavised. "I can't think of any other reason for it being built. Believe me, I've tried."

"He always is right. It's bloody annoying, but that's why I fly with him."

"I was against it because of the faith gap."

"Say what?"

"The amount of faith these xenocs must have had in themselves. It's awesome. So different from humans. Think about it. Even if their homeworld is only 2,000 light years away, that's how long the message is going to take to reach there. Yet they sent it believing someone would still be around to receive it, and more, act on it. Suppose that was us; suppose the *Lady Mac* had an accident a thousand light years away. Would you think there was any point in sending a lightspeed message to the Confederation, then going into zero-tau to wait for a rescue ship?"

"If their technology can last that long, then I guess their civilization can, too."

"No, our hardware can last for a long time. It's our culture that's fragile, at least compared to theirs. I don't think the Confederation will last a thousand years."

"The Edenists will be here, I expect. So will all the planets, physically if nothing else. Some of their societies will advance, possibly even to a state similar to the Kiint; some will revert to barbarism. But there will be somebody left to hear the message and help."

"You're a terrible optimist."

They arrived at the ninth deck, only to find the doorway was sealed over with composite.

"Odd," Roman datavised. "If there's no corridor or compartment beyond, why put a doorway here at all?"

"Because this was a change made after the accident."

"Could be. But why would they block off an interior section?"

"I've no idea. You want to keep going down?"

"Sure. I'm optimistic enough not to believe in ghosts lurking in the basement."

"I really wish you hadn't said that."

The tenth deck had been sealed off as well.

"My legs can take one more level," Wai datavised. "Then I'm going back."

There was a door on deck 11. It was the first one in the ship to be closed.

Wai stuck her fingers in the dimple, and the door dilated. She edged over cautiously, and swept the focus of her collar sensors round. "Holy shit. We'd better fetch Marcus."

Decks nine and ten had simply been removed to make the chamber. Standing on the floor and looking up, Marcus could actually see the outline of the stairwell doorways in the wall above him. By xenoc standards it was a cathedral. There was only one altar, right in the centre. A doughnut of some dull metallic substance, eight metres in diameter with a central aperture five metres across; the air around it was emitting a faint violet glow. It stood on five sableblack arching buttresses, four metres tall.

"The positioning must be significant," Wai datavised. "They built it almost at the centre of the wreck. They wanted to give it as much protection as possible."

"Agreed," Katherine replied. "They obviously considered it important. After a ship has suffered this much damage, you don't expend resources on anything other than critical survival requirements."

"Whatever it is," Schutz reported. "It's using up an awful lot of power." He was walking round it, keeping a respectful distance, wiping a sensor block over the floor as he went. "There's a power cable feeding each of those legs."

"Is it radiating in any spectrum?" Marcus asked.

"Only that light you can see, which spills over into ultraviolet, too. Apart from that, it's inert. But the energy must be going somewhere."

"Okay." Marcus walked up to a buttress, and switched his collar focus to scan the aperture. It was veiled by a grey haze, as if a sheet of fog had solidified across it. When he took another tentative step forward the fluid in his semicircular canals was suddenly affected by a very strange tidal force. His foot began to slip forwards and upwards. He threw himself backwards, and almost stumbled. Jorge and Karl just caught him in time.

"There's no artificial gravity underneath it," he datavised. "But there's some kind of gravity field wrapped around it." He paused. "No, that's not right. It pushed me."

"Pushed?" Katherine hurried to his side. "Are you sure?"

"Yes."

"My God."

"What? Do you know what it is?"

"Possibly. Schutz, hang on to my arm, please."

The cosmonik came forward and took her left arm. Katherine edged forward until she was almost under the lambent doughnut. She stretched up her right arm, holding out a sensor block, and tried to press it against the doughnut. It was as if she was trying to make two identical magnetic poles touch. The block couldn't get to within 20 centimetres of the surface, it kept slithering and sliding through the air. She held it as steady as she could, and datavised it to run an analysis of the doughnut's molecular structure.

The results made her back away.

"So?" Marcus asked.

"I'm not entirely sure it's solid in any reference frame we understand. That surface could just be a boundary effect. There's no spectroscopic data at all, the sensor couldn't even detect an atomic structure in there, let alone valency bonds."

"You mean it's a ring of energy?"

"Don't hold me to it, but I think that thing could be some kind of exotic matter."

"Exotic in what sense, exactly?" Jorge asked.

"It has a negative energy density. And before you ask, that doesn't mean anti-gravity. Exotic matter only has one known use, to keep a wormhole open."

"Jesus, that's a wormhole portal?" Marcus asked.

"It must be."

"Any way of telling where it leads?"

"I can't give you an exact stellar coordinate; but I know where the other end has to emerge. The xenocs never called for a rescue ship, Marcus. They threaded a wormhole with exotic matter to stop it collapsing, and escaped down it. That is the entrance to a tunnel which leads right back to their home-world."

Schutz found Marcus in the passenger lounge in capsule C. He was floating centimetres above one of the flatchairs, with the lights down low.

The cosmonik touched his heels to a stikpad on the decking beside the lower hatch. "You really don't like being wrong, do you?"

"No, but I'm not sulking about it, either." Marcus moulded a jaded grin. "I still think I'm right about the dish, but I don't know how the hell to prove it."

"The wormhole portal is rather conclusive evidence."

"Very tactful. It doesn't solve anything, actually. If they could open a worm-hole straight back home, why did they build the dish? Like Katherine said, if you have an accident of that magnitude then you devote yourself completely to survival. Either they called for help, or they went home through the wormhole. They wouldn't do both."

"Possibly it wasn't their dish, they were just here to investigate it."

"Two ancient unknown xenoc races with FTL starship technology is pushing credibility. It also takes us back to the original problem: if the dish isn't a distress beacon, then what the hell was it built for?"

"I'm sure there will be an answer at some time."

"I know, we're only a commercial trader's crew, with a very limited research capability. But we can still ask fundamental questions, like why have they kept the wormhole open for 13,000 years?"

"Because that's the way their technology works. They probably wouldn't consider it odd."

"I'm not saying it shouldn't work for that long, I'm asking why their homeworld would bother maintaining a link to a chunk of derelict wreckage?"

"That is harder for logic to explain. The answer must lie in their psychology."

"That's a cop-out; you can't simply cry alien at everything you don't understand. But it does bring us to my final query, if you can open a wormhole with such accuracy across God knows how many light years, why would you need a starship in the first place? What sort of psychology accounts for that?"

"All right, Marcus, you got me. Why?"

"I haven't got a clue. I've been reviewing all the file texts we have on wormholes, trying to find a solution which pulls all this together. And I can't do it. It's a complete paradox."

"There's only one thing left then, isn't there?"

Marcus turned to look at the hulking figure of the cosmonik. "What?"

"Go down the wormhole and ask them."

"Yeah, maybe I will. Somebody has to go eventually. What does our dear Katherine have to say on that subject? Can we go inside it in our SII suits?"

"She's rigging up some sensors that she can shove through the interface. That grey sheet isn't a physical barrier. She's already pushed a length of conduit tubing through. It's some kind of pressure membrane, apparently, stops the ship's atmosphere from flooding into the wormhole."

"Another billion fuseodollar gadget. Jesus, this is getting too big for us, we're going to have to prioritize." He datavised the flight computer, and issued a general order for everyone to assemble in capsule A's main lounge.

Karl was the last to arrive. The young systems engineer looked exhausted. He frowned when he caught sight of Marcus.

"I thought you were over in the xenoc ship."

"No."

"But you . . ." He rubbed his fingers against his temples. "Skip it."

"Any progress?" Marcus asked.

"A little. From what I can make out, the molecular synthesizer and its governing circuitry are combined within the same crystal lattice. To give you a biological analogy, it's as though a muscle is also a brain."

"Don't follow that one through too far," Roman called.

Karl didn't even smile. He took a chocolate sac from the dispenser, and sucked on the nipple.

"Katherine?" Marcus said.

"I've managed to place a visual-spectrum sensor in the wormhole. There's not much light in there, only what soaks through the pressure membrane. From what we can see it's a straight tunnel. I assume the xenocs cut off the artificial gravity under the portal so they could egress it easily. What I'd like to do next is dismount a laser radar from the MSV and use that."

"If the wormhole's threaded with exotic matter, will you get a return from it?"

"Probably not. But we should get a return from whatever is at the other end."

"What's the point?"

Three of them began to talk at once, Katherine loudest of all. Marcus held his hand up for silence. "Listen, everybody, according to Confederation law if the appointed commander or designated controlling mechanism of a spaceship or free-flying space structure discontinues that control for one year and a day then any ownership title becomes null and void. Legally, this xenoc ship is an abandoned structure which we are entitled to file a salvage claim on."

"There is a controlling network," Karl said.

"It's a sub-system," Marcus said. "The law is very clear on that point. If a starship's flight computer fails, but, say, the fusion generators keep working, their governing processors do not constitute the designated controlling mechanism. Nobody will be able to challenge our claim."

"The xenocs might," Wai said.

"Let's not make extra problems for ourselves. As the situation stands right now, we have title. We can't not claim the ship because the xenocs may return at some time."

Katherine rocked her head in understanding. "If we start examining the wormhole they might come back, sooner rather than later. Is that what you're worried about?"

"It's a consideration, yes. Personally, I'd rather like to meet them. But, Katherine, are you really going to learn how to build exotic matter and open a wormhole with the kind of sensor blocks we've got?"

"You know I'm not, Marcus."

"Right. Nor are we going to find the principle behind the artificial gravity generator, or any of the other miracles on board. What we have to do is catalogue as much as we can, and identify the areas that need researching. Once we've done that we can bring back the appropriate specialists, pay them a huge salary, and let them get on with it. Don't any of you understand yet? When we found this ship, we stopped being starship crew, and turned into the highest-flying corporate executives in the galaxy. We don't pioneer any more, we designate. So, we map out the last remaining decks. We track the power cables and note what they power. Then we leave."

"I know I can crack their programme language, Marcus," Karl said. "I can get us into the command network."

Marcus smiled at the weary pride in his voice. "Nobody is going to be more pleased about that than me, Karl. One thing I do intend to take with us is a cybermouse, preferably more than one. That molecular synthesizer is the hard evidence we need to convince the banks of what we've got."

Karl blushed. "Uh, Marcus, I don't know what'll happen if we try and cut one out of the composite. So far we've been left alone; but if the network thinks we're endangering the ship. Well . . ."

"I'd like to think we're capable of something more sophisticated than ripping a cybermouse out of the composite. Hopefully, you'll be able to access the network, and we can simply ask it to replicate a molecular synthesizer unit for us. They have to be manufactured somewhere on board."

"Yeah, I suppose they do. Unless the cybermice duplicate themselves."

"Now that'd be a sight," Roman said happily. "One of them humping away on top of the other."

His neural nanonics time function told Karl he'd slept for nine hours. After he wriggled out of his sleep pouch he air-swam into the crew lounge and helped himself to a pile of food sachets from the galley. There wasn't much activity in the ship, so he didn't even bother to access the flight computer until he'd almost finished eating.

Katherine was on watch when he dived into the bridge through the floor hatch.

"Who's here?" he asked breathlessly. "Who else is on board right now?"

"Just Roman. The rest of them are all over on the wreck. Why?"

"Shit."

"Why, what's the matter?"

"Have you accessed the flight computer?"

"I'm on watch, of course I'm accessing."

"No, not the ship's functions. The satellite analysis network Victoria set up."

Her flat features twisted into a surprised grin. "You mean they've found some gold?"

"No way. The network was reporting that satellite seven had located a target deposit three hours ago. When I accessed the network direct to follow it up I found out what the search parameters really are. They're not looking for gold, those bastards are here to get pitchblende."

"Pitchblende?" Katherine had to run a search programme through her neural nanonics encyclopedia to find out what it was. "Oh Christ, uranium. They want uranium."

"Exactly. You could never mine it from a planet without the local government knowing; that kind of operation would be easily spotted by the observation satellites. Asteroids don't have deposits of pitchblende. But planetoids do, and out here nobody is going to know that they're scooping it up."

"I knew it! I bloody knew that fable about gold mountains was a load of balls."

"They must be terrorists, or Sonora independence freaks, or black syndicate members. We have to warn the others, we can't let them back on board *Lady Mac.*"

"Wait a minute, Karl. Yes, they're shits, but if we leave them over on the wreck they'll die. Even if you're prepared to do that, it's the captain's decision."

"No it isn't, not any more. If they come back then neither you, me, nor the captain is going to be in any position to make decisions about anything. They knew we'd find out about the pitchblende eventually when *Lady Mac* rendezvoused with the ore particle. They knew we wouldn't take it on board voluntarily. That means they came fully prepared to force us. They've got guns, or weapons implants. Jorge is exactly what I said he was, a mercenary killer. We can't let them back on the ship, Katherine. We can't."

"Oh Christ," she was gripping the side of her acceleration couch in reflex. Command decision. And it was all hers.

"Can we datavise the captain?" he asked.

"I don't know. We've got relay blocks in the stairwells now the cybermice have been deactivated, but they're not very reliable; the structure plays hell with our signals."

"Who's he with?"

"He was partnering Victoria. Wai and Schutz are together; Antonio and Jorge made up the last team."

"Datavise Wai and Schutz, get them out first. Then try for the captain."

"Okay. Get Roman, and go down to the airlock chamber; I'll authorize the weapons cabinet to release some maser carbines. . . . Shit!"

"What?"

"I can't. Marcus has the flight computer command codes. We can't even fire the thrusters without him."

Deck 14 appeared no different from any other as Marcus and Victoria wandered through it. The corridors were broad, and there were few doorways.

"About 60 per cent is sealed off," Marcus datavised. "This must be a major engineering level."

"Yeah. There's so many cables around here I'm having trouble cataloguing the grid." She was wiping a magnetic sensor block slowly from side to side as they walked.

His communication block reported it was receiving an encrypted signal from the *Lady Mac*. Sheer surprise made him halt. He retrieved the appropriate code file from a neural nanonics memory cell.

"Captain?"

"What's the problem, Katherine?"

"You've got to get back to the ship. Now, Captain, and make sure Victoria doesn't come with you."

"Why?"

"Captain, this is Karl. The array satellites are looking for pitchblende, not gold or platinum. Antonio's people are terrorists, they want to build fission bombs."

Marcus focused his collar sensors on Victoria, who was waiting a couple of metres down the corridor. "Where's Schutz and Wai?"

"On their way back," Katherine datavised. "They should be here in another five minutes."

"Okay, it's going to take me at least half an hour to get back." He didn't like to think about climbing 14 flights of stairs fast, not in this gravity. "Start prepping the ship."

"Captain, Karl thinks they're probably armed."

Marcus's communication block reported another signal coming on line.

"Karl is quite right," Jorge datavised. "We are indeed armed; and we also have excellent processor blocks and decryption programmes. Really, Captain, this code of yours is at least three years out of date."

Marcus saw Victoria turn towards him. "Care to comment on the pitchblende?" he asked.

"I admit, the material would have been of some considerable use to us," Jorge replied. "But of course, this wreck has changed the Confederation beyond recognition, has it not, Captain?"

"Possibly."

"Definitely. And so we no longer require the pitchblende."

"That's a very drastic switch of allegiance."

"Please, Captain, do not be facetious. The satellites were left on purely for your benefit; we didn't wish to alarm you."

"Thank you for your consideration."

"Captain," Katherine datavised. "Schutz and Wai are in the airlock."

"I do hope you're not proposing to leave without us," Jorge datavised. "That would be most unwise."

"You were going to kill us," Karl datavised.

"That is a hysterical claim. You would not have been hurt."

"As long as we obeyed, and helped you slaughter thousands of people."

Marcus wished Karl would stop being quite so blunt. He had few enough options as it was.

"Come now, Captain," Jorge said. "The *Lady Macbeth* is combat-capable; are you telling me you have never killed people in political disputes?"

"We've fought. But only against other ships."

"Don't try and claim the moral high ground, Captain. War is war, no matter how it is fought."

"Only when it's between soldiers; anything else is terrorism."

"I assure you, we have put our old allegiance behind us. I ask you to do the same. This quarrel is foolish in the extreme. We both have so much to gain."

And you're armed, Marcus filled in silently. Jorge and Antonio were supposed to be inspecting decks 12 and 13. It would be tough if not impossible getting back to the airlock before them. But I can't trust them on *Lady Mac*.

"Captain, they're moving," Katherine datavised. "The communication block in stairwell three has acquired them, strength one. They must be coming up."

"Victoria," Jorge datavised. "Restrain the captain and bring him to the airlock.

I advise all of you on the ship to remain calm, we can still find a peaceful solution to this situation."

Unarmed combat programmes went primary in Marcus's neural nanonics. The black, featureless figure opposite him didn't move.

"Your call," he datavised. According to his tactical analysis programme she had few choices. Jorge's order implied she was armed, though a scan of her utility belt didn't reveal anything obvious other than a standard fission blade. If she went for a gun he would have an attack window. If she didn't, then he could probably stay ahead of her. She was a lot younger, but his geneered physique should be able to match her in this gravity field.

Victoria dropped the sensor block she was carrying, and moved her hand to her belt. She grabbed the multipurpose power tool and started to bring it up.

Marcus slammed into her, using his greater mass to throw her off balance. She was hampered by trying to keep her grip on the tool. His impact made her sway sideways, then the fierce xenoc gravity took over. She toppled helplessly, falling *fast*. The power tool was swinging round to point at him. Marcus kicked her hand, and the unit skittered away. It didn't slide far, the gravity saw to that.

Victoria landed with a terrible thud. Her neural nanonics medical monitor programme flashed up an alert that the impact had broken her collar bone. Axon blocks came on line, muting all but the briefest pulse of pain. It was her programmes again which made her twist round to avoid any follow-on blow, her conscious mind was almost unaware of the fact she was still moving. A hand scrabbled for the power tool. She snatched it and sat up. Marcus was disappearing down a side corridor. She fired at him before the targeting programme even gave her an overlay grid.

"Jorge," she datavised. "I've lost him."

"Then get after him."

Marcus's collar sensors showed him a spray of incendiary droplets fizzing out of the wall barely a metre behind him. The multipurpose tool must be some kind of laser pistol. "Katherine," he datavised. "Retract *Lady Mac*'s airlock tube. Now. Close the outer hatch and codelock it. They are not to come on board."

"Acknowledged. How do we get you back?"

"Yes, Captain," Jorge datavised. "Do tell."

Marcus dodged down a junction. "Have Wai stand by. When I need her, I'll need her fast."

"You think you can cut your way out of the shell, Captain? You have a fission blade, and that shell is held together by a molecular bonding generator."

"You touch him, shithead, and we'll fry that wreck," Karl datavised. "*Lady Mac*'s got maser cannons."

"But do you have the command codes, I wonder. Captain?"

"Communication silence," Marcus ordered. "When I want you, I'll call."

•　•　•

Jorge's boosted muscles allowed him to ascend stairwell three at a speed which Antonio could never match. He was soon left struggling along behind. The airlock was the tactical high ground, once he had secured that, Jorge knew he'd won. As he climbed his hands moved automatically, assembling the weapon from various innocuous-looking pieces of equipment he was carrying on his utility belt.

"Victoria?" he datavised. "Have you got him?"

"No. He broke my shoulder, the bastard. I've lost him."

"Go to the nearest stairwell, I expect that's what he's done. Antonio, go back and meet her. Then start searching for him."

"Is that a joke?" Antonio asked. "He could be anywhere."

"No he's not. He has to come up. Up is where the airlock is."

"Yes, but—"

"Don't argue. And when you find him, don't kill him. We have to have him alive. He's our ticket out. Our only ticket, understand?"

"Yes, Jorge."

When he reached the airlock, Jorge closed the inner hatch and cycled the chamber. The outer hatch dilated to show him the *Lady Macbeth*'s fuselage 15 metres away. Her airlock tube had retracted, and the fuselage shield was in place.

"This is a no-win stand-off," he datavised. "Captain, please come up to the airlock. You have to deal with me, you have no choice. The three of us will leave our weapons over here, and then we can all go back on board together. And when we return to a port none of us will mention this unfortunate incident again. That is reasonable, surely?"

Schutz had just reached the bridge when they received Jorge's datavise.

"Damn! He's disconnected our cable from the communication block," Karl said. "We can't call the captain now even if we wanted to."

Schutz rolled in midair above his acceleration couch and landed gently on the cushioning. Restraint webbing slithered over him.

"What the hell do we do now?" Roman asked. "Without the command codes we're bloody helpless."

"It wouldn't take that long for us to break open the weapons cabinet," Schutz said. "They haven't got the captain. We can go over there and hunt them down with the carbines."

"I can't sanction that," Katherine said. "God knows what sort of weapons they have."

"Sanction it? We put it to the vote."

"It's my duty watch. Nobody votes on anything. The last order the captain gave us was to wait. We wait." She datavised the flight computer for a channel to the MSV. "Wai, status please?"

"Powering up. I'll be ready for a flight in two minutes."

"Thank you."

"We have to do something!" Karl said.

"For a start you can calm down," Katherine told him. "We're not going to help Marcus by doing anything rash. He obviously had something in mind when he told Wai to get ready."

The hatchway to the captain's cabin slid open. Marcus air-swam out and grinned round at their stupefied expressions. "Actually, I didn't have any idea what to do when I said that. I was stalling."

"How the hell did you get back on board?" Roman yelped.

Marcus looked at Katherine and gave her a lopsided smile. "By being right, I'm afraid. The dish is a distress beacon."

"So what?" she whispered numbly.

He drifted over to his acceleration couch and activated the webbing. "It means the wormhole doesn't go back to the xenoc homeworld."

"You found out how to use it!" Karl exclaimed. "You opened its other end inside the *Lady Mac*."

"No. There is no other end. Yes, they built it as part of their survival operation. It was their escape route, you were right about that. But it doesn't go somewhere; it goes some*when*."

Instinct had brought Marcus to the portal chamber. It was as good as any other part of the ship. Besides, the xenocs had escaped their predicament from here. In a remote part of his mind he assumed that ending up on their homeworld was preferable to capture here by Jorge. It wasn't the kind of choice he wanted to make.

He walked slowly round the portal. The pale violet emanation in the air around it remained constant, hazing the dull surface from perfect observation. That and a faint hum were the only evidence of the massive quantity of power it consumed. Its eternal stability a mocking enigma.

Despite all the logic of argument he knew Katherine was wrong. Why build the dish if you had this ability? And why keep it operational?

That factor must have been important to them. It had been built in the centre of the ship, and built to last. They'd even reconfigured the wreck to ensure it lasted. Fine, they needed reliability, and they were masters of material science. But a one-off piece of emergency equipment lasting 13,000 years? There must be a reason, and the only logical one was that they knew they would need it to remain functional so they could come back one day.

The SII suit prevented him from smiling as realization dawned. But it did reveal a shiver ripple along his limbs as the cold wonder of the knowledge struck home.

On the *Lady Mac*'s bridge, Marcus said: "We originally assumed that the xenocs would just go into zero-tau and wait for a rescue ship; because that's what we would do. But their technology allows them to take a much different approach to engineering problems."

"The wormhole leads into the future," Roman said in astonishment.

"Almost. It doesn't lead anywhere but back to itself, so the length inside it represents time not space. As long as the portal exists you can travel through it. The xenocs went in just after they built the dish and came out again when their rescue ship arrived. That's why they built the portal to survive so long. It had to carry them through a great deal of time."

"How does that help you get here?" Katherine asked. "You're trapped over in the xenoc wreckage right now, not in the past."

"The wormhole exists as long as the portal does. It's an open tube to every second of that entire period of existence, you're not restricted which way you travel through it."

In the portal chamber Marcus approached one of the curving black buttress legs. The artificial gravity was off directly underneath the doughnut so the xenocs could rise into it. But they had been intent on travelling into the future.

He started to climb the buttress. The first section was the steepest; he had to clamp his hands behind it, and haul himself up. Not easy in that gravity field. It gradually curved over, flattening out at the top, leaving him standing above the doughnut. He balanced there precariously, very aware of the potentially lethal fall down onto the floor.

The doughnut didn't look any different from this position, a glowing ring surrounding the grey pressure membrane. Marcus put one foot over the edge of the exotic matter, and jumped.

He fell clean through the pressure membrane. There was no gravity field in the wormhole, although every movement suddenly became very sluggish. To his waving limbs it felt as if he was immersed in some kind of fluid, though his sensor block reported a perfect vacuum.

The wormhole wall was insubstantial, difficult to see in the meagre backscatter of light from the pressure membrane. Five narrow lines of yellow light materialized, spaced equidistantly around the wall. They stretched from the rim of the pressure membrane up to a vanishing point some indefinable distance away.

Nothing else happened. Marcus drifted until he reached the wall, which his hand adhered to as though the entire surface was one giant stikpad. He crawled his way back to the pressure membrane. When he stuck his hand through, there was no resistance. He pushed his head out.

There was no visible difference to the chamber outside. He datavised his communication block to search for a signal. It told him there was only the band from one of the relay blocks in the stairwells. No time had passed.

He withdrew back into the wormhole. Surely the xenocs hadn't expected to crawl along the entire length? In any case, the other end would be 13,000 years ago. Marcus retrieved the xenoc activation code from his neural nanonics, and datavised it.

The lines of light turned blue.

He quickly datavised the deactivation code, and the lines reverted to yellow. This time when he emerged out into the portal chamber there was no signal at all.

. . .

"That was ten hours ago," Marcus told his crew. "I climbed out and walked back to the ship. I passed you on the way, Karl."

"Holy shit," Roman muttered. "A time machine."

"How long was the wormhole active for?" Katherine asked.

"A couple of seconds, that's all."

"Ten hours in two seconds." She paused, loading sums into her neural nanonics. "That's a year in 30 minutes. Actually, that's not so fast. Not if they were intending to travel a couple of thousand years into the future."

"You're complaining about it?" Roman asked.

"Maybe it speeds up the further you go through it," Schutz suggested. "Or more likely we need the correct access codes to vary its speed."

"Whatever," Marcus said. He datavised the flight computer and blew the tether bolts which were holding *Lady Mac* to the wreckage. "I want flight readiness status, people, please."

"What about Jorge and the others?" Karl asked.

"They only come back on board under our terms." Marcus said. "No weapons, and they go straight into zero-tau. We can hand them over to Tranquillity's serjeants as soon as we get home." Purple course vectors were rising into his mind. He fired the manoeuvring thrusters, easing *Lady Mac* clear of the xenoc shell.

Jorge saw the sparkle of bright dust as the explosive bolts fired. He scanned his sensor collar round until he found the tethers, narrow grey serpents flexing against the speckled backdrop of drab orange particles. It didn't bother him unduly. Then the small thrusters ringing the starship's equator fired, pouring out translucent amber plumes of gas.

"Katherine, what do you think you're doing?" he datavised.

"Following my orders," Marcus replied. "She's helping to prep the ship for a jump. Is that a problem for you?"

Jorge watched the starship receding, an absurdly stately movement for an artifact that big. His respirator tube seemed to have stopped supplying fresh oxygen, paralysing every muscle. "Calvert. How?" he managed to datavise.

"I might tell you some time. Right now, there are a lot of conditions you have to agree to before I allow you back on board."

Pure fury at being so completely outmanoeuvred by Calvert made him reach automatically for his weapon. "You will come back now," he datavised.

"You're not in any position to dictate terms."

Lady Macbeth was a good 200 metres away. Jorge lined the stubby barrel up on the rear of the starship. A green targeting grid flipped up over the image, and he zeroed on the nozzle of a fusion drive tube. He datavised the X-ray laser to fire. Pale white vapour spewed out of the nozzle.

. . .

"Depressurization in fusion drive three," Roman shouted.

"The lower deflector coil casing is breached. He shot us, Marcus, Jesus Christ, he shot us with an X-ray."

"What the hell kind of weapon has he got back there?" Karl demanded.

"Whatever it is, he can't have the power capacity for many more shots," Schutz said.

"Give me fire control for the maser cannons," Roman said. "I'll blast the little shit."

"Marcus!" Katherine cried. "He just hit a patterning node. Stop him."

Neuroiconic displays zipped through Marcus's mind. Ship's systems coming on line as they shifted over to full operational status, each with its own schematic. He knew just about every performance parameter by heart. Combat sensor clusters were already sliding out of their recesses. Maser cannons powering up. It would be another seven seconds before they could be aimed and fired.

There was one system with a faster response time.

"Hang on," he yelled.

Designed for combat avoidance manoeuvres, the fusion drive tubes exploded into life two seconds after he triggered their ignition sequence. Twin spears of solar-bright plasma transfixed the xenoc shell, burning through deck after deck. They didn't even strike anywhere near the airlock which Jorge was cloistered in. They didn't have to. At that range, their infrared emission alone was enough to break down his SII suit's integrity.

Superenergized ions hammered into the wreck, smashing the internal structure apart, heating the atmosphere to an intolerable pressure. Xenoc machinery detonated in tremendous energy bursts all through the structure, the units expending themselves in spherical clouds of solid light which clashed and merged into a single wavefront of destruction. The giant rock particle lurched wildly from the explosion. Drenched in a cascade of hard radiation and subatomic particles, the unicorn tower at the centre of the dish snapped off at its base to tumble away into the darkness.

Then the process seemed to reverse. The spume of light blossoming from the cliff curved in on itself, growing in brightness as it was compressed back to its point of origin.

Lady Mac's crew were straining under the five gee acceleration of the starship's flight. The inertial guidance systems started to flash priority warnings into Marcus's neural nanonics.

"We're going back," he datavised. Five gees made talking too difficult. "Jesus, five gees and it's still pulling us in." The external sensor suite showed him the contracting fireball, its luminosity surging towards violet. Large sections of the cliff were flaking free and plummeting into the conflagration. Fissures like black lightning bolts split open right across the rock.

He ordered the flight computer to power up the nodes and retract the last sensor clusters.

"Marcus, we can't jump," Katherine datavised, her face pummelled into frantic creases by the acceleration. "It's a gravitonic emission. Don't."

"Have some faith in the old girl." He initiated the jump.

An event horizon eclipsed the *Lady Macbeth*'s fuselage.

Behind her, the wormhole at the heart of the newborn micro-star gradually collapsed, pulling in its gravitational field as it went. Soon there was nothing left but an expanding cloud of dark snowdust embers.

They were three jumps away from Tranquillity when Katherine ventured into Marcus's cabin. *Lady Mac* was accelerating at a tenth of a gee towards her next jump coordinate, holding him lightly in one of the large blackfoam sculpture chairs. It was the first time she'd ever really noticed his age.

"I came to say sorry," she said. "I shouldn't have doubted."

He waved limply. "*Lady Mac* was built for combat, her nodes are powerful enough to jump us out of some gravity fields. Not that I had a lot of choice. Still, we only reduced three nodes to slag, plus the one dear old Jorge damaged."

"She's a hell of ship, and you're the perfect captain for her. I'll keep flying with you, Marcus."

"Thanks. But I'm not sure what I'm going to do after we dock. Replacing three nodes will cost a fortune. I'll be in debt to the banks again."

She pointed at the row of transparent bubbles which all held identical antique electronic circuit boards. "You can always sell some more Apollo command module guidance computers."

"I think that scam's just about run its course. Don't worry, when we get back to Tranquillity I know a captain who'll buy them from me. At least that way I'll be able to settle the flight pay I owe all of you."

"For Heaven's sake, Marcus, the whole astronautics industry is in debt to the banks. I swear I never could understand the economics behind starflight."

He closed his eyes, a wry smile quirking his lips. "We very nearly solved human economics for good, didn't we?"

"Yeah. Very nearly."

"The wormhole would have let me change the past. Their technology was going to change the future. We could have rebuilt our entire history."

"I don't think that's a very good idea. What about the grandfather paradox for a start? How come you didn't warn us about Jorge as soon as you emerged from the wormhole?"

"Scared, I guess. I don't know nearly enough about quantum temporal displacement theory to start risking paradoxes. I'm not even sure I'm the Marcus Calvert that brought this particular *Lady Macbeth* to the xenoc wreck. Suppose you really can't travel between times, only parallel realities? That would mean I didn't escape into the past, I just shifted sideways."

"You look and sound pretty familiar to me."

"So do you. But is my crew still stuck back at their version of the wreck waiting for me to deal with Jorge?"

"Stop it," she said softly. "You're Marcus Calvert, and you're back where you belong, flying *Lady Mac*."

"Yeah, sure."

"The xenocs wouldn't have built the wormhole unless they were sure it would help them get home, their true home. They were smart people."

"And no mistake."

"I wonder where they did come from?"

"We'll never know, now." Marcus lifted his head, some of the old humour emerging through his melancholia. "But I hope they got back safe."

itsy bitsy spider

JAMES PATRICK KELLY

James Patrick Kelly made his first sale in 1975, and since has gone on to become one of the most respected and popular writers to enter the field in the last twenty years. Although Kelly has had some success with novels, especially the recent Wildlife, *he has had more impact to date as a writer of short fiction, with stories such as "Solstice," "The Prisoner of Chillon," "Glass Cloud," "Mr. Boy," "Pogrom," and "Home Front," and is often ranked among the best short story writers in the business. His acclaimed story "Think Like a Dinosaur" won him a Hugo Award in 1996. Kelly's first solo novel, the mostly ignored* Planet of Whispers, *came out in 1984. It was followed by* Freedom Beach, *a novel written in collaboration with John Kessel, and then by another solo novel,* Look into the Sun. *His most recent book is a collection,* Think Like a Dinosaur, *and he is currently at work on another novel. A collaboration between Kelly and Kessel appeared in our Second Annual Collection; and solo Kelly stories have appeared in our Third, Fourth, Fifth, Sixth, Eighth, Ninth, and Thirteenth Annual Collections. Born in Minneola, New York, Kelly now lives with his family in Portsmouth, New Hampshire. He has a Web site at http:// www.nh.ultranet.com/~jimkelly.*

Here he takes us to an ostensibly tranquil future society where nothing is quite what it seems—and some of the games they play, even children's games, can get very rough indeed. . . .

When I found out that my father was still alive after all these years and living at Strawberry Fields, I thought he'd gotten just what he deserved. Retroburbs are where the old, scared people go to hide. I'd always pictured the people in them as deranged losers. Visiting some fantasy world like the disneys or Carlucci's Carthage is one thing, *moving* to one is another. Sure, 2038 is messy, but it's a hell of a lot better than nineteen-sixty-whatever.

Now that I'd arrived at 144 Bluejay Way, I realized that the place was worse than I had imagined. Strawberry Fields was pretending to be some long-lost suburb of the late twentieth century, except that it had the sterile monotony of cheap VR. It was clean, all right, and neat, but it was everywhere the same. And the scale was wrong. The lots were squeezed together and all the houses had shrunk—like the dreams of their owners. They were about the size of a one-car garage, modular units tarted up at the factory to look like ranches, with old double-hung storm windows and hardened siding of harvest gold, barn red, forest green. Of course, there were no real garages; faux Mustangs and VW buses cruised the quiet streets. Their carbrains were listening for a summons from Barbara Chesley next door at 142, or the Goltzes across the street, who might be headed to Penny Lanes to bowl a few frames, or the hospital to die.

There was a beach chair with blue nylon webbing on the front stoop of 144 Bluejay Way. A brick walk led to it, dividing two patches of carpet moss, green as a dream. There were names and addresses printed in huge lightstick letters on all the doors in the neighborhood; no doubt many Strawberry Fielders were easily confused. The owner of this one was Peter Fancy. He had been born Peter Fanelli, but had legally taken his stage name not long after his first success as Prince Hal in *Henry IV Part 1*. I was a Fancy too; the name was one of the few things of my father's I had kept.

I stopped at the door and let it look me over. "You're Jen," it said.

"Yes." I waited in vain for it to open or to say something else. "I'd like to see Mr. Fancy, please." The old man's house had worse manners than he did. "He knows I'm coming," I said. "I sent him several messages." Which he had never answered, but I didn't mention that.

"Just a minute," said the door. "She'll be right with you."

She? The idea that he might be with another woman now hadn't occurred to me. I'd lost track of my father a long time ago—on purpose. The last time we'd actually visited overnight was when I was twenty. Mom gave me a ticket to Port Gemini, where he was doing the Shakespeare in Space program. The orbital was great, but staying with him was like being under water. I think I must have held my breath for the entire week. After that, there were a few, sporadic calls, a couple of awkward dinners—all at his instigation. Then twenty-three years of nothing.

I never hated him, exactly. When he left, I just decided to show solidarity with Mom and be done with him. If acting was more important than his family, then to hell with Peter Fancy. Mom was horrified when I told her how I felt. She cried and claimed the divorce was as much her fault as his. It was too much for me to handle; I was only eleven years old when they separated. I needed to be on *someone's* side and so I had chosen her. She never did stop trying to talk me into finding him again, even though after a while it only made me mad at her. For the past few years, she'd been warning me that I'd developed a warped view of men.

But she was a smart woman, my mom—a winner. Sure, she'd had troubles, but she'd founded three companies, was a millionaire by twenty-five. I missed her.

A lock clicked and the door opened. Standing in the dim interior was a little girl in a gold-and-white checked dress. Her dark, curly hair was tied in a ribbon. She was wearing white ankle socks and black Mary Jane shoes that were so shiny they had to be plastic. There was a Band-Aid on her left knee.

"Hello, Jen. I was hoping you'd really come." Her voice surprised me. It was resonant, impossibly mature. At first glance I'd guessed she was three, maybe four; I'm not much good at guessing kids' ages. Now I realized that this must be a bot—a made person.

"You look just like I thought you would." She smiled, stood on tiptoe and raised a delicate little hand over her head. I had to bend to shake it. The hand was warm, slightly moist, and very realistic. She had to belong to Strawberry Fields; there was no way my father could afford a bot with skin this real.

"Please come in." She waved on the lights. "We're so happy you're here." The door closed behind me.

The playroom took up almost half of the little house. Against one wall was a miniature kitchen. Toy dishes were drying in a rack next to the sink; the pink refrigerator barely came up to my waist. The table was full-sized; it had two normal chairs and a booster chair. Opposite this was a bed with a ruffled Pumpkin Patty bedspread. About a dozen dolls and stuffed animals were arranged along the far edge of the mattress. I recognized most of them: Pooh, Mr. Moon, Baby Rollypolly, the Sleepums, Big Bird. And the wallpaper was familiar too: Oz figures like Toto and the Wizard and the Cowardly Lion on a field of Munchkin blue.

"We had to make a few changes," said the bot. "Do you like it?"

The room seemed to tilt then. I took a small, unsteady step and everything righted itself. *My* dolls, *my* wallpaper, the chest of drawers from Grandma Fanelli's cottage in Hyannis. I stared at the bot and recognized her for the first time.

She was me.

"What is this," I said, "some kind of sick joke?" I felt like I'd just been slapped in the face.

"Is something wrong?" the bot said. "Tell me. Maybe we can fix it."

I swiped at her and she danced out of reach. I don't know what I would have done if I had caught her. Maybe smashed her through the picture window onto the patch of front lawn or shaken her until pieces started falling off. But the bot wasn't responsible, my father was. Mom would never have defended him if she'd known about *this*. The old bastard. I couldn't believe it. Here I was, shuddering with anger, after years of feeling nothing for him.

There was an interior door just beyond some shelves filled with old-fashioned paper books. I didn't take time to look as I went past, but I knew that Dr. Seuss and A. A. Milne and L. Frank Baum would be on those shelves. The door had no knob.

"Open up," I shouted. It ignored me, so I kicked it. "Hey!"

"Jennifer." The bot tugged at the back of my jacket. "I must ask you . . ."

"You can't have me!" I pressed my ear to the door. Silence. "I'm not this thing you made." I kicked it again. "You hear?"

Suddenly an announcer was shouting in the next room. ". . . *Into the post to Russell, who kicks it out to Havlicek all alone at the top of the key, he shoots . . . and Baylor with the strong rebound.*" The asshole was trying to drown me out.

"If you don't come away from that door right now," said the bot, "I'm calling security."

"What are they going to do?" I said. "I'm the long-lost daughter, here for a visit. And who the hell are *you*, anyway?"

"I'm bonded to him, Jen. Your father is no longer competent to handle his own affairs. I'm his legal guardian."

"Shit." I kicked the door one last time, but my heart wasn't in it. I shouldn't have been surprised that he had slipped over the edge. He was almost ninety.

"If you want to sit and talk, I'd like that very much." The bot gestured toward a banana yellow beanbag chair. "Otherwise, I'm going to have to ask you to leave."

It was the shock of seeing the bot, I told myself—I'd reacted like a hurt little girl. But I was a grown woman and it was time to start behaving like one. I wasn't here to let Peter Fancy worm his way back into my feelings. I had come because of Mom.

"Actually," I said, "I'm here on business." I opened my purse. "If you're running his life now, I guess this is for you." I passed her the envelope and settled back, tucking my legs beneath me. There is no way for an adult to sit gracefully in a beanbag chair.

She slipped the check out. "It's from Mother." She paused, then corrected herself, "Her estate." She didn't seem surprised.

"Yes."

"It's too generous."

"That's what I thought."

"She must've taken care of you too?"

"I'm fine." I wasn't about to discuss the terms of Mom's will with my father's toy daughter.

"I would've liked to have known her," said the bot. She slid the check back into the envelope and set it aside. "I've spent a lot of time imagining Mother."

I had to work hard not to snap at her. Sure, this bot had at least a human equivalent intelligence and would be a free citizen someday, assuming she didn't break down first. But she had a cognizor for a brain and a heart fabricated in a vat. How could she possibly imagine my mom, especially when all she had to go on was whatever lies *he* had told her?

"So how bad is he?"

She gave me a sad smile and shook her head. "Some days are better than others. He has no clue who President Huong is or about the quake, but he can still recite the dagger scene from *Macbeth*. I haven't told him that Mother died. He'd just forget it ten minutes later."

"Does he know what you are?"

"I am many things, Jen."

"Including me."

"You're a role I'm playing, not who I am." She stood. "Would you like some tea?"

"Okay." I still wanted to know why Mom had left my father four hundred and thirty-eight thousand dollars in her will. If he couldn't tell me, maybe the bot could.

She went to her kitchen, opened a cupboard, and took out a regular-sized cup. It looked like a bucket in her little hand. "I don't suppose you still drink Constant Comment?"

His favorite. I had long since switched to rafallo. "That's fine." I remembered that when I was a kid my father used to brew cups for the two of us from the same bag because Constant Comment was so expensive. "I thought they went out of business long ago."

"I mix my own. I'd be interested to hear how accurate you think the recipe is."

"I suppose you know how I like it?"

She chuckled.

"So, does he need the money?"

The microwave dinged. "Very few actors get rich," said the bot. I didn't think there had been microwaves in the sixties, but then strict historical accuracy wasn't really the point of Strawberry Fields. "Especially when they have a weakness for Shakespeare."

"Then how come he lives here and not in some flop? And how did he afford you?"

She pinched sugar between her index finger and thumb, then rubbed them together over the cup. It was something I still did, but only when I was by myself. A nasty habit; Mom used to yell at him for teaching it to me. "I was a gift." She shook a teabag loose from a canister shaped like an acorn and plunged it into the boiling water. "From Mother."

The bot offered the cup to me; I accepted it nervelessly. "That's not true." I could feel the blood draining from my face.

"I can lie if you'd prefer, but I'd rather not." She pulled the booster chair away from the table and turned it to face me. "There are many things about themselves that they never told us, Jen. I've always wondered why that was."

I felt logy and a little stupid, as if I had just woken from a thirty-year nap. "She just gave you to him?"

"And bought him this house, paid all his bills, yes."

"But why?"

"You knew her," said the bot. "I was hoping you could tell me."

I couldn't think of what to say or do. Since there was a cup in my hand, I took a sip. For an instant, the scent of tea and dried oranges carried me back to when I was a little girl and I was sitting in Grandma Fanelli's kitchen in a wet bathing suit, drinking Constant Comment that my father had made to keep my teeth from chattering. There were knots like brown eyes in the pine walls and the green linoleum was slick where I had dripped on it.

"Well?"

"It's good," I said absently and raised the cup to her. "No, really, just like I remember."

She clapped her hands in excitement. "So," said the bot. "What was Mother like?"

It was an impossible question, so I tried to let it bounce off me. But then neither of us said anything; we just stared at each other across a yawning gulf of time and experience. In the silence, the question stuck. Mom had died three months ago and this was the first time since the funeral that I'd thought of her as she really had been—not the papery ghost in the hospital room. I remembered how, after she divorced my father, she always took my calls when she was at the office, even if it was late, and how she used to step on imaginary brakes whenever I drove her anywhere, and how grateful I was that she didn't cry when I told her that Rob and I were getting divorced. I thought about Easter eggs and raspberry Pop Tarts and when she sent me to Antibes for a year when I was fourteen and that perfume she wore on my father's opening nights and the way they used to waltz on the patio at the house in Waltham.

"*West is walking the ball upcourt, setting his offense with fifteen seconds to go on the shot clock, nineteen in the half . . .*"

The beanbag chair that I was in faced the picture window. Behind me, I could hear the door next to the bookcase open.

"*Jones and Goodrich are in each other's jerseys down low and now Chamberlain swings over and calls for the ball on the weak side . . .*"

I twisted around to look over my shoulder. The great Peter Fancy was making his entrance.

Mom once told me that when she met my father, he was typecast playing men that women fall hopelessly in love with. He'd had great successes as Stanley Kowalski in *Streetcar* and Sky Masterson in *Guys and Dolls* and the Vicomte de Valmont in *Les Liaisons Dangereuses*. The years had eroded his good looks but had not obliterated them; from a distance he was still a handsome man. He had a shock of close-cropped white hair. The beautiful cheekbones were still there; the chin was as sharply defined as it had been in his first headshot. His gray eyes were distant and a little dreamy, as if he were preoccupied with the War of the Roses or the problem of evil.

"Jen," he said, "what's going on out here?" He still had the big voice that could reach into the second balcony without a mike. I thought for a moment he was talking to me.

"We have company, Daddy," said the bot, in a four-year-old trill that took me by surprise. "A lady."

"I can see that it's a lady, sweetheart." He took a hand from the pocket of his jeans, stroked the touchpad on his belt and his exolegs walked him stiffly across the room. "I'm Peter Fancy," he said.

"The lady is from Strawberry Fields." The bot swung around behind my father. She shot me a look that made the terms and conditions of my continued presence clear: if I broke the illusion, I was out. "She came by to see if everything is all right with our house." The bot disturbed me even more, now that she sounded like young Jen Fancy.

As I heaved myself out of the beanbag chair, my father gave me one of those lopsided, flirting grins I knew so well. "Does the lady have a name?" He must have shaved just for the company, because now that he had come close I could see that he had a couple of fresh nicks. There was a button-sized patch of gray whiskers by his ear that he had missed altogether.

"Her name is Ms. Johnson," said the bot. It was my ex, Rob's, last name. I had never been Jennifer Johnson.

"Well, Ms. Johnson," he said, hooking thumbs in his pants pockets. "The water in my toilet is brown."

"I'll . . . um . . . see that it's taken care of." I was at a loss for what to say next, then inspiration struck. "Actually, I had another reason for coming." I could see the bot stiffen. "I don't know if you've seen *Yesterday*, our little newsletter? Anyway, I was talking to Mrs. Chesley next door and she told me that you were an actor once. I was wondering if I might interview you. Just a few questions, if you have the time. I think your neighbors might . . ."

"Were?" he said, drawing himself up. "*Once?* Madame, I am now an actor and will always be."

"My daddy's famous," said the bot.

I cringed at that; it was something I used to say. My father squinted at me. "What did you say your name was?"

"Johnson," I said. "Jane Johnson."

"And you're a reporter? You're sure you're not a critic?"

"Positive."

He seemed satisfied. "I'm Peter Fancy." He extended his right hand to shake. The hand was spotted and bony and it trembled like a reflection in a lake. Clearly whatever magic—or surgeon's skill—it was that had preserved my father's face had not extended to his extremities. I was so disturbed by his infirmity that I took his cold hand in mine and pumped it three, four times. It was dry as a page of one of the bot's dead books. When I let go, the hand seemed steadier. He gestured at the beanbag.

"Sit," he said. "Please."

After I had settled in, he tapped the touchpad and stumped over to the picture window. "Barbara Chesley is a broken and bitter old woman," he said, "and I will not have dinner with her under any circumstances, do you understand?" He peered up Bluejay Way and down.

"Yes, Daddy," said the bot.

"I believe she voted for Nixon, so she has no reason to complain now." Apparently satisfied that the neighbors weren't sneaking up on us, he leaned against the windowsill, facing me. "Mrs. Thompson, I think today may well be a happy one for both of us. I have an announcement." He paused for effect. "I've been thinking of Lear again."

The bot settled onto one of her little chairs. "Oh, Daddy, that's wonderful."

"It's the only one of the big four I haven't done," said my father. "I was set for a production in Stratford, Ontario, back in '99; Polly Matthews was to play Cordelia. Now there was an actor; she could bring tears to a stone. But then my wife Hannah had one of her bad times and I had to withdraw so I could take care of Jen. The two of us stayed down at my mother's cottage on the Cape; I wasted the entire season tending bar. And when Hannah came out of rehab, she decided that she didn't want to be married to an underemployed actor anymore, so things were tight for a while. She had all the money, so I had to scramble—spent almost two years on the road. But I think it might have been for the best. I was only forty-eight. Too old for Hamlet, too young for Lear. My Hamlet was very well received, you know. There were overtures from PBS about a taping, but that was when the BBC decided to do the Shakespeare series with that doctor, what was his name? Jonathan Miller. So instead of Peter Fancy, we had Derek Jacobi, whose brilliant idea it was to roll across the stage, frothing his lines like a rabid raccoon. You'd think he'd seen an alien, not his father's ghost. Well, that was another missed opportunity, except, of course, that I was too young. Ripeness is all, eh? So I still have Lear to do. Unfinished business. My comeback."

He bowed, then pivoted solemnly so that I saw him in profile, framed by the picture window. "Where have I been? Where am I? Fair daylight?" He held up a trembling hand and blinked at it uncomprehendingly. "I know not what to say. I swear these are not my hands."

Suddenly the bot was at his feet. "O look upon me, sir," she said, in her childish voice, "and hold your hand in benediction o'er me."

"Pray, do not mock me." My father gathered himself in the flood of morning light. "I am a very foolish, fond old man, fourscore and upward, not an hour more or less; and to deal plainly, I fear I am not in my perfect mind."

He stole a look in my direction, as if to gauge my reaction to his impromptu performance. A frown might have stopped him, a word would have crushed him. Maybe I should have, but I was afraid he'd start talking about Mom again, telling me things I didn't want to know. So I watched instead, transfixed.

"Methinks I should know you . . ." He rested his hand briefly on the bot's head. ". . . and know this stranger." He fumbled at the controls and the exolegs carried him across the room toward me. As he drew nearer, he seemed to sluff off the years. "Yet I am mainly ignorant what place this is; and all the skill I have remembers not these garments, nor I know not where I did lodge last night." It was Peter Fancy who stopped before me; his face a mere kiss away from mine. "Do not laugh at me; for, as I am a man, I think this lady to be my child. Cordelia."

He was staring right at me, into me, knifing through make-believe indifference to the wound I'd nursed all these years, the one that had never healed. He seemed to expect a reply, only I didn't have the line. A tiny, sad squeaky voice within me was whimpering, *You left me and you got exactly what you deserve.* But my throat tightened and choked it off.

The bot cried, "And so I am! I am!"

But she had distracted him. I could see confusion begin to deflate him. "Be your tears wet? Yes, faith. I pray . . . weep not. If you have poison for me, I will drink it. I know you do not love me. . . ."

He stopped and his brow wrinkled. "It's something about the sisters," he muttered.

"Yes," said the bot, " ' . . . for your sisters have done me wrong . . .' "

"Don't feed me the fucking lines!" he shouted at her. "I'm Peter Fancy, god damn it!"

After she calmed him down, we had lunch. She let him make the peanut butter and banana sandwiches while she heated up some Campbell's tomato and rice soup, which she poured from a can made of actual metal. The sandwiches were lumpy because he had hacked the bananas into chunks the size of walnuts. She tried to get him to tell me about the daylilies blooming in the backyard, and the old Boston Garden, and the time he and Mom had had breakfast with Bobby Kennedy. She asked whether he wanted TV dinner or pot pie for supper. He refused all her conversational gambits. He only ate half a bowl of soup.

He pushed back from the table and announced that it was her nap time. The bot put up a perfunctory fuss, although it was clear that it was my father who was tired out. However, the act seemed to perk him up. Another role for his resume: the doting father. "I'll tell you what," he said. "We'll play your game, sweetheart. But just once—otherwise you'll be cranky tonight."

The two of them perched on the edge of the bot's bed next to Big Bird and the Sleepums. My father started to sing and the bot immediately joined in.

"The itsy bitsy spider went up the water spout."

Their gestures were almost mirror images, except that his ruined hands actually looked like spiders as they climbed into the air.

"Down came the rain, and washed the spider out."

The bot beamed at him as if he were the only person in the world.

"Out came the sun, and dried up all the rain.

"And the itsy bitsy spider went up the spout again."

When his arms were once again raised over his head, she giggled and hugged him. He let them fall around her, returning her embrace. "That's a good girl," he said. "That's my Jenny."

The look on his face told me that I had been wrong: this was no act. It was as real to him as it was to me. I had tried hard not to, but I still remembered how the two of us always used to play together, Daddy and Jenny, Jen and Dad.

Waiting for Mommy to come home.

He kissed her and she snuggled under the blankets. I felt my eyes stinging.

"But if you do the play," she said, "when will you be back?"

"What play?"

"That one you were telling me. The king and his daughters."

"There's no such play, Jenny." He sifted her black curls through his hands. "I'll never leave you, don't worry now. Never again." He rose unsteadily and caught himself on the chest of drawers.

"Nighty noodle," said the bot.

"Pleasant dreams, sweetheart," said my father. "I love you."

"I love you too."

I expected him to say something to me, but he didn't even seem to realize that I was still in the room. He shambled across the playroom, opened the door to his bedroom and went in.

"I'm sorry about that," said the bot, speaking again as an adult.

"Don't be," I said. I coughed—something in my throat. "It was fine. I was very . . . touched."

"He's usually a lot happier. Sometimes he works in the garden." The bot pulled the blankets aside and swung her legs out of the bed. "He likes to vacuum."

"Yes."

"I take good care of him."

I nodded and reached for my purse. "I can see that." I had to go. "Is it enough?"

She shrugged. "He's my daddy."

"I meant the money. Because if it's not, I'd like to help."

"Thank you. He'd appreciate that."

The front door opened for me, but I paused before stepping out into Strawberry Fields. "What about . . . after?"

"When he dies? My bond terminates. He said he'd leave the house to me. I know you could contest that, but I'll need to sell in order to pay for my twenty-year maintenance."

"No, no. That's fine. You deserve it."

She came to the door and looked up at me, little Jen Fancy and the woman she would never become.

"You know, it's *you* he loves," she said. "I'm just a stand-in."

"He loves his little girl," I said. "Doesn't do me any good—I'm forty-seven."

"It could if you let it." She frowned. "I wonder if that's why Mother did all this. So you'd find out."

"Or maybe she was just plain sorry." I shook my head. She was a smart woman, my mom. I would've liked to have known her.

"So, Ms. Fancy, maybe you can visit us again sometime." The bot grinned and shook my hand. "Daddy's usually in a good mood after his nap. He sits out front on his beach chair and waits for the ice cream truck. He always buys us some. Our favorite is Yellow Submarine. It's vanilla with fat butterscotch swirls, dipped in white chocolate. I know it sounds kind of odd, but it's good."

"Yes," I said absently, thinking about all the things Mom had told me about my father. I was hearing them now for the first time. "That might be nice."

A Spy in Europa

ALASTAIR REYNOLDS

Here's a headlong, relentlessly paced adventure, set against the backdrop of a strange high-tech society inside the moon Europa, which proves that where you end up might not be at all where you thought you were heading . . . and that what you accomplish might not exactly be what you set out to do.

New writer Alastair Reynolds is a frequent contributor to Interzone *and has also sold to* Asimov's Science Fiction *and elsewhere. A professional scientist with a Ph.D. in astronomy, he comes from Wales, but lives in the Netherlands.*

Marius Vargovic, agent of Gilgamesh Isis, savoured an instant of free fall before the flitter's engines kicked in, slamming it away from the *Deucalion*. His pilot gunned the craft toward the moon below, quickly outrunning the other shuttles which the Martian liner had disgorged. Europa seemed to be enlarging perceptibly; a flattening arc the colour of nicotine-stained wallpaper.

"Boring, isn't it."

Vargovic turned around in his seat, languidly. "You'd rather they were shooting at us?"

"Rather they were doing *something*."

"Then you're a fool," Vargovic said, making a tent of his fingers. "There's enough armament buried in that ice to give Jupiter a second red spot. What it would do to us doesn't bear thinking about it."

"Only trying to make conversation."

"Don't bother—it's an overrated activity at the best of times."

"All right, Marius—I get the message. In fact I intercepted it, parsed it, filtered it, decrypted it with the appropriate one-time pad and wrote a fucking 200-page report on it. Satisfied?"

"I'm never satisfied, Mishenka. It just isn't in my nature."

But Mishenka was right: Europa was an encrypted document; complexity masked by a surface of fractured and refrozen ice. Its surface grooves were like the capillaries in a vitrified eyeball; faint as the structure in a raw surveillance image. But once within the airspace boundary of the Europan Demarchy, traffic-management co-opted the flitter, vectoring it into a touchdown corridor. In three days Mishenka would return, but then he would disable the avionics, kissing the ice for less than ten minutes.

"Not too late to abort," Mishenka said, a long time later.

"Are you out of your tiny mind?"

The younger man dispensed a frosty Covert Ops smile. "We've all heard what the Demarchy do to spies, Marius."

"Is this a personal grudge or are you just psychotic?"

"I'll leave being psychotic to you, Marius—you're so much better at it."

Vargovic nodded. It was the first sensible thing Mishenka had said all day.

They landed an hour later. Vargovic adjusted his Martian businesswear, tuning his holographically inwoven frock coat to project red sandstorms; lifting the collar in what he had observed from the liner's passengers was a recent Martian fad. Then he grabbed his bag—nothing incriminating there; no gadgets or weapons— and exited the flitter, stepping through the gasket of locks. A slitherwalk pro- pelled him forward, massaging the soles of his slippers. It was a single cultured ribbon of octopus skin, stimulated to ripple by the timed firing of buried squid axons.

To get to Europa you had to be either sickeningly rich or sickeningly poor. Vargovic's cover was the former: a lie excusing the single-passenger flitter. As the slitherwalk advanced he was joined by other arrivals: business people like himself, and a sugaring of the merely wealthy. Most of them had dispensed with holographics, instead projecting entoptics beyond their personal space; machine- generated hallucinations decoded by the implant hugging Vargovic's optic nerve. Hummingbirds and seraphim were in sickly vogue. Others were attended by autonomous perfumes which subtly altered the moods of those around them. Slightly lower down the social scale, Vargovic observed a clique of noisy tour- ists—antlered brats from Circum-Jove. Then there was a discontinuous jump: squalid-looking Maunder refugees, who must have accepted indenture to the Demarchy. The refugees were quickly segregated from the more affluent im- migrants, who found themselves within a huge geodesic dome, resting above the ice on refrigerated stilts. The walls of the dome glittered with duty-free shops, boutiques and bars. The floor was bowl-shaped, slitherwalks and spiral stairways descending to the nadir, where a quincunx of fluted marble cylinders waited. Vargovic observed that the newly arrived were queuing for elevators which ter- minated in the cylinders. He joined a line and waited.

"First time in Cadmus-Asterius?" asked the bearded man ahead of him, iri- dophores in his plum-coloured jacket projecting Boolean propositions from Sir- ikit's *Machine Ethics in the Transenlightenment.*

"First time on Europa, actually. First time Circum-Jove, you want the full story."

"Down-system?"

"Mars."

The man nodded gravely. "Hear it's tough."

"You're not kidding." And he wasn't. Since the sun had dimmed—the second

Maunder minimum, repeating the behaviour which the sun had exhibited in the 17th century—the entire balance of power in the First System had altered. The economies of the inner worlds had found it hard to adjust; agriculture and power-generation handicapped, with concomitant social upheaval. But the outer planets had never had the luxury of solar energy in the first place. Now Circum-Jove was the benchmark of First System economic power, with Circum-Saturn trailing behind. Because of this, the two primary Circum-Jove superpowers—the Demarchy, which controlled Europa and Io, and Gilgamesh Isis, which controlled Ganymede, and parts of Callisto—were vying for dominance.

The man smiled keenly. "Here for anything special?"

"Surgery," Vargovic said, hoping to curtail the conversation at the earliest juncture. "Very extensive anatomical surgery."

They hadn't told him much.

"Her name is Cholok," Control had said, after Vargovic had skimmed the dossiers back in the caverns which housed the Covert Operations section of Gilgamesh Isis security, deep in Ganymede. "We recruited her ten years ago, when she was on Phobos."

"And now she's Demarchy?"

Control had nodded. "She was swept up in the braindrain, once Maunder II began to bite. The smartest got out while they could. The Demarchy—and us, of course—snapped up the brightest."

"And also one of our sleepers." Vargovic glanced down at the portrait of the woman, striped by video lines. She looked mousey to him, with a permanent bone-deep severity of expression.

"Cheer up," Control said. "I'm asking you to contact her, not sleep with her."

"Yeah, yeah. Just tell me her background."

"Biotech." Control nodded at the dossier. "On Phobos she led one of the teams working in aquatic transform work—modifying the human form for submarine operations."

Vargovic nodded diligently. "Go on."

"Phobos wanted to sell their know-how to the Martians, before their oceans froze. Of course, the Demarchy also appreciated her talents. Cholok took her team to Cadmus-Asterius, one of their hanging cities."

"Mm." Vargovic was getting the thread now. "By which time we'd already recruited her."

"Right," Control said, "except we had no obvious use for her."

"Then why this conversation?"

Control smiled. Control always smiled when Vargovic pushed the envelope of subservience. "We're having it because our sleeper won't lie down." Then Control reached over and touched the image of Cholok, making her speak. What Vargovic was seeing was an intercept; something Gilgamesh had captured, riddled with edits and jump-cuts.

She appeared to be sending a verbal message to an old friend in Isis. She was talking rapidly from a white room; inert medical servitors behind her. Shelves displayed flasks of colour-coded medichines. A cruciform bed resembled an autopsy slab with ceramic drainage sluices.

"Cholok contacted us a month ago," Control said. "The room's part of her clinic."

"She's using phrase-embedded three," Vargovic said, listening to her speech patterns, siphoning content from otherwise normal Canasian.

"Last code we taught her."

"All right. What's her angle?"

Control chose his words—skating around the information excised from Cholok's message. "She wants to give us something," he said. "Something valuable. She's acquired it accidentally. Someone good has to smuggle it out."

"Flattery will get you everywhere, Control."

The muzak rose to a carefully timed crescendo as the elevator plunged through the final layer of ice. The view around and below was literally dizzying, and Vargovic registered exactly as much awe as befitted his Martian guise.

He knew the Demarchy's history, of course—how the hanging cities had begun as points of entry into the ocean; air-filled observation cupolas linked to the surface by narrow access shafts sunk through the kilometre-thick crustal ice. Scientists had studied the unusual smoothness of the crust, noting that its fracture patterns echoed those on Earth's ice-shelves, implying the presence of a water ocean. Europa was farther from the sun than Earth, but something other than solar energy maintained the ocean's liquidity. Instead, the moon's orbit around Jupiter created stresses which flexed the moon's silicate core, tectonic heat bleeding into the ocean via hydrothermal vents.

Descending into the city was a little like entering an amphitheatre—except that there was no stage; merely an endless succession of steeply tiered lower balconies. They converged toward a light-filled infinity, seven or eight kilometres below, where the city's conic shape constricted to a point. The opposite side was half a kilometre away; levels rising like geologic strata. A wide glass tower threaded the atrium from top to bottom, aglow with smoky-green ocean and a mass of kelplike flora, cultured by gilly swimmers. Artificial sunlamps burned in the kelp like Christmas-tree lights. Above, the tower branched; peristaltic feeds reaching out to the ocean proper. Offices, shops, restaurants and residential units were stacked atop each other, or teetered into the abyss on elegant balconies, spun from lustrous sheets of bulk-chitin polymer, the Demarchy's major construction material. Gossamer bridges arced across the atrium space, dodging banners, projections and vast translucent sculptures, moulded from a silky variant of the same chitin polymer. Every visible surface was overlaid by neon, holographics and entoptics.

People were everywhere, and in every face Vargovic detected a slight *absence*; as if their minds were not entirely focused on the here and now. No wonder: all citizens had an implant which constantly interrogated them, eliciting their opinions on every aspect of Demarchy life, both within Cadmus-Asterius and beyond.

Eventually, it was said, the implant's nagging presence faded from consciousness, until the act of democratic participation became near-involuntary.

It revolted Vargovic as much as it intrigued him.

"Obviously," Control said, with judicial deliberation. "What Cholok has to offer isn't merely a nugget—or she'd have given it via PE3."

Vargovic leaned forward. "She hasn't told you?"

"Only that it could endanger the hanging cities."

"You trust her?"

Vargovic felt one of Control's momentary indiscretions coming on. "She may have been sleeping, but she hasn't been completely valueless. There were defections she assisted in . . . like the Maunciple job—remember that?"

"If you're calling that a success perhaps it's time *I* defected."

"Actually, it was Cholok's information which persuaded us to get Maunciple out via the ocean rather than the front door. If Demarchy security had reached Maunciple alive they'd have learnt ten years of tradecraft."

"Whereas instead Maunciple got a harpoon in his back."

"So the operation had its flaws." Control shrugged. "But if you're thinking all this points to Cholok having been compromised . . . Naturally, the thought entered our heads. But if Maunciple had acted otherwise it would have been worse." Control folded his arms. "And of course, he might have made it, in which case even you'd have to admit Cholok's safe."

"Until proven otherwise."

Control brightened. "So you'll do it?"

"Like I have a choice."

"There's always a choice, Vargovic."

Yes, Vargovic thought. There was always a choice . . . between doing whatever Gilgamesh Isis asked of him . . . and being deprogrammed, cyborgized and sent to work in the sulphur projects around the slopes of Ra Patera. It just wasn't a particularly good one.

"One other thing . . ."

"Yes?"

"When I've got whatever Cholok has . . ."

Control half-smiled, the two of them sharing a private joke which did not need illumination. "I'm sure the usual will suffice."

The elevator slowed into immigration.

Demarchy guards hefted big guns, but no one took any interest in him. His story about coming from Mars was accepted; he was subjected to only the usual spectrum of invasive procedures: neural and genetic patterns scanned for pathologies, body bathed in eight forms of exotic radiation. The final formality consisted of drinking a thimble of chocolate. The beverage consisted of billions of medichines which infiltrated his body, searching for concealed drugs, weapons and illegal biomodifications. He knew that they would find nothing, but was relieved when they reached his bladder and requested to be urinated back into the Demarchy.

The entire procedure lasted six minutes. Outside, Vargovic followed a slither-walk to the city zoo, and then barged through crowds of schoolchildren until he had arrived at the aquarium where Cholok was meant to meet him. The exhibits were devoted to Europan biota, most of which depended on the eco-logical niches of the hydrothermal vents, carefully reproduced here. There was nothing very exciting to look at, since most Europan predators looked marginally less fierce than hatstands or lampshades. The commonest were called *ventlings*; large and structurally simple animals whose metabolisms hinged on symbiosis. They were pulpy, funnelled bags planted on a tripod of orange stilts, moving with such torpor that Vargovic almost nodded off before Cholok arrived at his side.

She wore an olive-green coat and tight emerald trousers, projecting a haze of medicinal entoptics. Her clenched jaw accentuated the dourness he had gleaned from the intercept.

They kissed.

"Good to see you Marius. It's been—what?"

"Nine years, thereabouts."

"How's Phobos these days?"

"Still orbiting Mars." He deployed a smile. "Still a dive."

"You haven't changed."

"Nor you."

At a loss for words, Vargovic found his gaze returning to the informational readout accompanying the ventling exhibit. Only half attentively, he read that the ventlings, motile in their juvenile phase, gradually became sessile in adult-hood, stilts thickening with deposited sulphur until they were rooted to the ground like stalagmites. When they died, their soft bodies dispersed into the ocean, but the tripods remained; eerily regular clusters of orange spines concen-trated around active vents.

"Nervous, Marius?"

"In your hands? Not likely."

"That's the spirit."

They bought two mugs of mocha from a nearby servitor, then returned to the ventling display, making what seemed like small-talk. During indoctrination Cholok had been taught phrase-embedded three. The code allowed the insertion of secondary information into a primary conversation, by careful deployment of word-order, hesitation and sentence structure.

"What have you got?" Vargovic asked.

"A sample," Cholok answered, one of the easy, pre-set words which did not need to be laboriously conveyed. But what followed took nearly five minutes to put over, freighted via a series of rambling reminiscences of the Phobos years. "A small shard of hyperdiamond."

Vargovic nodded. He knew what hyperdiamond was: a topologically complex interweave of tubular fullerene; structurally similar to cellulose or bulk chitin but thousands of times stronger; its rigidity artificially maintained by some piezo-electric trick which Gilgamesh lacked.

"Interesting," Vargovic said. "But unfortunately not interesting enough."

She ordered another mocha and downed it replying. "Use your imagination. Only the Demarchy knows how to synthesize it."

"It's also useless as a weapon."

"Depends. There's an application you should know about."

"What?"

"Keeping this city afloat—and I'm not talking about economic solvency. Do you know about Buckminster Fuller? He lived about 400 years ago; believed absolute democracy could be achieved through technological means."

"The fool."

"Maybe. But Fuller also invented the geodesic lattice which determines the structure of the buckyball; the closed allotrope of tubular fullerene. The city owes him on two counts."

"Save the lecture. How does the hyperdiamond come into it?"

"Flotation bubbles," she said. "Around the outside of the city. Each one is a hundred-metre wide sphere of hyperdiamond, holding vacuum. A hundred-metre wide molecule, in fact, since each sphere is composed of one endless strand of tubular fullerene. Think of that, Marius: a molecule you could park a ship inside."

While he absorbed that, another part of his mind continued to read the ventling caption; how their biochemistry had many similarities with the gutless tube worms which lived around Earth's ocean vents. The ventlings drank hydrogen sulphide through their funnels, circulating via a modified form of haemoglobin, passing through a bacteria-saturated organ in the lower part of their bags. The bacteria split and oxidized the hydrogen sulphide, manufacturing a molecule similar to glucose. The glucose-analogue nourished the ventling, enabling it to keep living and occasionally make slow perambulations to other parts of the vent, or even to swim between vents, until the adult phase rooted it to the ground. Vargovic read this, and then read it again, because he had just remembered something; a puzzling intercept passed to him from cryptanalysis several months earlier; something about Demarchy plans to incorporate ventling biochemistry into a larger animal. For a moment he was tempted to ask Cholok about it directly, but he decided to force the subject from his mind until a more suitable time.

"Any other propaganda to share with me?"

"There are 200 of these spheres. They inflate and deflate like bladders, maintaining C-A's equilibrium. I'm not sure how the deflation happens, except that it's something to do with changing the piezo-electric current in the tubes."

"I still don't see why Gilgamesh needs it."

"Think. If you can get a sample of this to Ganymede, they might be able to find a way of attacking it. All you'd need would be a molecular agent capable of opening the gaps between the fullerene strands so that a molecule of water could squeeze through, or something which impedes the piezo-electric force."

Absently Vargovic watched a squidlike predator nibble a chunk from the bag of a ventling. The squid blood ran thick with two forms of haemoglobin; one oxygen-bearing, one tuned for hydrogen sulphide. They used glycoproteins to keep their blood flowing and switched metabolisms as they swam from oxygen-dominated to sulphide-dominated water.

He snapped his attention back to Cholok. "I can't believe I came all this way for . . . what? Carbon?" He shook his head, slotting the gesture into the primary narrative of their conversation. "How did you obtain this?"

"An accident, with a gilly."

"Go on."

"An explosion near one of the bubbles. I was the surgeon assigned to the gilly; had to remove a lot of hyperdiamond from him. It wasn't hard to save a few splinters."

"Forward thinking of you."

"Hard part was persuading Gilgamesh to send you. Especially after Maunciple . . ."

"Don't lose any sleep over him," Vargovic said, consulting his coffee. "He was a fat bastard who couldn't swim fast enough."

The surgery took place the next day. Vargovic woke with his mouth furnace-dry.

He felt—odd. They had warned him of this. He had even interviewed subjects who had undergone similar procedures in Gilgamesh's experimental labs. They told him he would feel fragile, as if his head was no longer adequately coupled to his body. The periodic flushes of cold around his neck only served to increase that feeling.

"You can speak," Cholok said, looming over him in surgeon's whites. "But the cardiovascular modifications—and the amount of reworking we've done to your laryngeal area—will make your voice sound a little strange. Some of the gilled are really only comfortable talking to their own kind."

He held a hand before his eyes, examining the translucent webbing which now spanned his fingers. There was a dark patch in the pale tissue of his palm: Cholok's embedded sample. The other hand held another.

"It worked, didn't it?" His voice sounded squeaky. "I can breathe water."

"And air," Cholok said. "Though what you'll now find is that really strenuous exercise only feels natural when you're submerged."

"Can I move?"

"Of course," she said. "Try standing up. You're stronger than you feel."

He did as she suggested, using the moment to assess his surroundings. A neural monitor clamped his crown. He was naked, in a brightly lit revival room; one glass-walled side facing the exterior ocean. It was from here that Cholok had first contacted Gilgamesh.

"This place is secure, isn't it?"

"Secure?" she said, as if it was obscene. "Yes, I suppose so."

"Then tell me about the Denizens."

"What?"

"Demarchy code word. Cryptanalysis intercepted it recently—supposedly something about an experiment in radical biomodification. I was reminded of it in the aquarium." Vargovic fingered the gills in his neck. "Something that would make this look like cosmetic surgery. We heard the Demarchy had tailored the sulphur-based metabolism of the ventlings for human use."

She whistled. "That would be quite a trick."

"Useful, though—especially if you wanted a workforce who could tolerate the anoxic environments around the vents, where the Demarchy happens to have certain mineralogical interests."

"Maybe." Cholok paused. "But the changes required would be beyond surgery. You'd have to script them in at the developmental level. And even then . . . I'm not sure what you'd end up with would necessarily be human any more." It was as if she shivered, though Vargovic was the one who felt cold, still standing naked beside the revival table. "All I can say is, if it happened, no one told me."

"I thought I'd ask, that's all."

"Good." She brandished a white medical scanner. "Now can I run a few more tests? We have to follow procedure."

Cholok was right: quite apart from the fact that Vargovic's operation was completely real—and therefore susceptible to complications which had to be looked for and monitored—any deviation from normal practise was undesirable.

After the first hour or so, the real strangeness of his transformation hit home. He had been blithely unaffected by it until then, but when he saw himself in a full-body mirror, in the corner of Cholok's revival room, he knew that there was no going back.

Not easily, anyway. The Gilgamesh surgeons had promised him they could undo the work—but he didn't believe them. After all, the Demarchy was ahead of Ganymede in the biosciences, and even Cholok had told him reversals were tricky. He'd accepted the mission in any case: the pay tantalizing; the prospect of the sulphur projects rather less.

Cholok spent most of the day with him, only breaking off to talk to other clients or confer with her team. Breathing exercises occupied most of that time: prolonged periods spent underwater, nulling the brain's drowning response. Unpleasant, but Vargovic had done worse things in training. They practised fully submerged swimming, using his lungs to regulate buoyancy, followed by instruction about keeping his gill-openings—what Cholok called his *opercula*—clean, which meant ensuring the health of the colonies of commensal bacteria which thrived in the openings and crawled over the fine secondary flaps of his *lamellae*. He'd read the brochure: what she'd done was to surgically sculpt his anatomy toward a state somewhere between human and air-breathing fish: incorporating biochemical lessons from lungfish and walking-catfish. Fish breathed water through their mouths and returned it to the sea via their gills, but it was the gills in Vargovic's neck which served the function of a mouth. His true gills were below his thoracic cavity; crescent-shaped gashes below his ribs.

"Compared to your body size," she said, "these gill-openings are never going to give you the respiratory efficiency you'd have if you went in for more dramatic changes . . ."

"Like a Denizen?"

"I told you, I don't know anything."

"It doesn't matter." He flattened the gill-flaps down, watching—only slightly nauseated—as they puckered with each exhalation. "Are we finished?"

"Just some final bloodwork," she said. "To make sure everything's still working. Then you can go and swim with the fishes."

While she was busy at one of her consoles, surrounded by false-colour entoptics of his gullet—he asked her: "Do you have the weapon?"

Cholok nodded absently and opened a drawer, fishing out a hand-held medical laser. "Not much," she said. "I disabled the yield-suppresser, but you'd have to aim it at someone's eyes to do much damage."

Vargovic hefted the laser, scrutinizing the controls in its contoured haft. Then he grabbed Cholok's head and twisted her around, dousing her face with the laser's actinic-blue beam. There were two consecutive popping sounds as her eyeballs evaporated.

"What, like that?"

Conventional scalpels did the rest.

He rinsed the blood, dressed and left the medical centre alone, travelling kilometres down-city, to where Cadmus-Asterius narrowed to a point. Even though there were many gillies moving freely through the city—they were volunteers, by and large, with full Demarchy rights—he did not linger in public for long. Within a few minutes he was safe within a warren of collagen-walled service tunnels, frequented only by technicians, servitors or other gill-workers. The late Cholok had been right; breathing air was harder now; it felt too thin.

"Demarchy security advisory," said a bleak machine voice emanating from the wall. "A murder has occurred in the medical sector. The suspect may be an armed gill-worker. Approach with extreme caution."

They'd found Cholok. Risky, killing her. But Gilgamesh preferred to burn its bridges, removing the possibility of any sleeper turning traitor after they had fulfilled their usefulness. In the future, Vargovic mulled, they might be better using a toxin, rather than the immediate kill. He made a mental note to insert this in his report.

He entered the final tunnel, not far from the waterlock which had been his destination. At the tunnel's far end a technician sat on a crate, listening with a stethoscope to something going on behind an access panel. For a moment Vargovic considered passing the man, hoping he was engrossed in his work. He began to approach him, padding on bare webbed feet, which made less noise than the shoes he had just removed. Then the man nodded to himself, uncoupled from the listening post and slammed the hatch. Grabbing his crate, he stood and made eye contact with Vargovic.

"You're not meant to be here," he said. Then offered, almost plaintively: "Can I help you? You've just had surgery, haven't you? I always know the ones like you: always a little red around the gills."

Vargovic drew his collar higher, then relented because that made it harder to breathe. "Stay where you are," he said. "Put down the crate and freeze."

"Christ, it was you, wasn't it—that advisory?" the man said.

Vargovic raised the laser. Blinded, the man blundered into the wall, dropping the crate. He made a pitiful moan. Vargovic crept closer, the man stumbling into the scalpel. Not the cleanest of killings, but that hardly mattered.

Vargovic was sure the Demarchy would shortly seal off access to the ocean—especially when his last murder came to light. For now, however, the locks were accessible. He moved into the air-filled chamber, his lungs now aflame for water. High-pressure jets filled the room, and he quickly transitioned to water-breathing, feeling his thoughts clarify. The secondary door clammed open, revealing ocean. He was kilometres below the ice, and the water here was both chillingly cold and under crushing pressure—but it felt normal; pressure and cold registering only as abstract qualities of the environment. His blood was inoculated with glycoproteins now; molecules which would lower its freezing point below that of water.

The late Cholok had done well.

Vargovic was about to leave the city when a second gill-worker appeared in the doorway, returning to the city after completing a shift. He killed her efficiently, and she bequeathed him a thermally inwoven wetsuit, for working in the coldest parts of the ocean. The wetsuit had octopus ancestry, and when it slithered onto him it left apertures for his gill-openings. She had been wearing goggles which had infrared and sonar capability, and carried a hand-held tug. The thing resembled the still-beating heart of a vivisected animal, its translucent components knobbed with dark veins and ganglia. But it was easy to use: Vargovic set its pump to maximum thrust and powered away from the lower levels of C-A.

Even in the relatively uncontaminated water of the Europan ocean, visibility was low; he would not have been able to see anything were the city not abundantly illuminated on all its levels. Even so, he could see no more than half a kilometre upwards; the higher parts of C-A lost in golden haze and then deepening darkness. Although its symmetry was upset by protrusions and accretions, the city's basic conic form was evident, tapering at the narrowest point to an inlet mouth which ingested ocean. The cone was surrounded by a haze of flotation bubbles, black as caviar. He remembered the chips of hyperdiamond in his hands. If Cholok was right, Vargovic's people might find a way to make it water-permeable; opening the fullerene weave sufficiently so that the spheres' buoyant properties would be destroyed. The necessary agent could be introduced into the ocean by ice-penetrating missiles. Some time later—Vargovic was uninterested in the details—the Demarchy cities would begin to groan under their own weight. If the weapon worked sufficiently quickly, there might not even be time to act against it. The cities would fall from the ice, sinking down through the black kilometres of ocean below them.

He swam on.

Near C-A, the rocky interior of Europa climbed upwards to meet him. He had travelled three or four kilometres north, and was comparing the visible topography—lit by service lights installed by Demarchy gill-workers—with his own mental maps of the area. Eventually he found an outcropping of silicate rock. Beneath the overhang was a narrow ledge, on which a dozen or so small boulders had fallen. One was redder than the others. Vargovic anchored himself to the ledge and hefted the red rock, the warmth of his fingertips activating its latent biocircuitry. A screen appeared in the rock, filling with the face of Mishenka.

"I'm on time," Vargovic said, his own voice sounding even less recognizable through the distorting medium of the water. "I presume you're ready?"

"Problem," Mishenka said. "Big fucking problem."

"What?"

"Extraction site's compromised." Mishenka—or rather the simulation of Mishenka which was running in the rock—anticipated Vargovic's next question: "A few hours ago the Demarchy sent a surface team out onto the ice, ostensibly to repair a transponder. But the spot they're covering is right where we planned to pull you out." He paused. "You did—uh—kill Cholok, didn't you? I mean you didn't just grievously injure her?"

"You're talking to a professional."

The rock did a creditable impression of Mishenka looking pained. "Then the Demarchy got to her."

Vargovic waved his hand in front of the rock. "I got what I came for, didn't I?"

"You got something."

"If it isn't what Cholok said it was, then she's accomplished nothing except get herself dead."

"Even so . . ." Mishenka appeared to entertain a thought briefly, before discarding it. "Listen, we always had a backup extraction point, Vargovic. You'd better get your ass there." He grinned. "Hope you can swim faster than Maunciple."

It was 30 kilometres south.

He passed a few gill-workers on the way, but they ignored him and once he was more than five kilometres from C-A there was increasingly less evidence of human presence. There was a head-up display in the goggles. Vargovic experimented with the readout modes before calling up a map of the whole area. It showed his location, and also three dots which were following him from C-A.

He was being tailed by Demarchy security.

They were at least three kilometres behind him now, but they were perceptibly narrowing the distance. With a cold feeling gripping his gut, it occurred to Vargovic that there was no way he could make it to the extraction point before the Demarchy caught him.

Ahead, he noticed a thermal hot-spot; heat bubbling up from the relatively shallow level of the rock floor. The security operatives were probably tracking him via the gill-worker's appropriated equipment. But once he was near the vent he could ditch it: the water was warmer there; he wouldn't need the suit, and the heat, light and associated turbulence would confuse any other tracking system. He could lie low behind a convenient rock, stalk them while they were preoccupied with the homing signal.

It struck Vargovic as a good plan.

He made the distance to the vent quickly, feeling the water warm around him, noticing how the taste of it changed; turning brackish. The vent was a fiery red fountain surrounded by bacteria-crusted rocks and the colourless Europan equivalent of coral. Ventlings were everywhere; their pulpy bags shifting as the currents altered. The smallest were motile, ambling on their stilts like animated bagpipes, navigating around the triadic stumps of their dead relatives.

Vargovic ensconced himself in a cave, after placing the gill-worker equipment near another cave on the far side of the vent, hoping that the security operatives would look there first. While they did so, he would be able to kill at least one of them; maybe two. Once he had their weapons, taking care of the third would be a formality.

Something nudged him from behind.

What Vargovic saw when he turned around was something too repulsive even for a nightmare. It was so wrong that for a faltering moment he could not quite assimilate what it was he was looking at, as if the thing was a three-dimensional perception test; a shape which refused to stabilize in his head. The reason he could not hold it still was because part of him refused to believe that this thing had any connection with humanity. But the residual traces of human ancestry were too obvious to ignore.

Vargovic knew—beyond any reasonable doubt—that what he was seeing was a Denizen. Others loomed from the cave depths. They were five more of them; all roughly similar; all aglow with faint bioluminescence, all regarding him with darkly intelligent eyes. Vargovic had seen pictures of mermaids in books when he was a child; what he was looking at now were macabre corruptions of those innocent illustrations. These things were the same fusions of human and fish as in those pictures—but every detail had been twisted toward ugliness, and the true horror of it was that the fusion was total; it was not simply that a human torso had been grafted to a fish's tail, but that the splice had been made—it was obvious—at the genetic level, so that in every aspect of the creature there was something simultaneously and grotesquely piscine. The face was the worst; bisected by a lipless down-curved slit of a mouth, almost sharklike. There was no nose, not even a pair of nostrils; just an acreage of flat, sallow fish-flesh. The eyes were forward-facing; all expression compacted into their dark depth. The creature had touched him with one of its arms, which terminated in an obscenely human hand. And then—to compound the horror—it spoke, its voice perfectly clear and calm, despite the water.

"We've been expecting you, Vargovic."

The others behind murmured, echoing the sentiment.

"What?"

"So glad you were able to complete your mission."

Vargovic began to get a grip, shakily. He reached up and dislodged the Denizen's hand from his shoulder. "You aren't why I'm here," he said, forcing authority into his voice, drawing on every last drop of Gilgamesh training to suppress his nerves. "I wanted to know about you . . . that was all . . ."

"No," the lead Denizen said, opening its mouth to expose an alarming array of teeth. "You misunderstand. Coming here was always your mission. You have brought us something we want very much. That was always your purpose."

"Brought you something?" His mind was reeling now.

"Concealed within you." The Denizen nodded; a human gesture which only served to magnify the horror of what it was. "The means by which we will strike at the Demarchy; the means by which we will take the ocean."

He thought of the chips in his hands. "I think I understand," he said slowly. "It was always intended for you, is that what you mean?"

"Always."

Then he'd been lied to by his superiors—or they had at least drastically simplified the matter. He filled in the gaps himself, making the necessary mental leaps: evidently Gilgamesh was already in contact with the Denizens—bizarre as it seemed—and the chips of hyperdiamond were meant for the Denizens, not his own people. Presumably—although he couldn't begin to guess at how this might be possible—the Denizens had the means to examine the shards and fabricate the agent which would unravel the hyperdiamond weave. They'd be acting for Gilgamesh, saving it the bother of actually dirtying its hands in the attack. He could see why this might appeal to Control. But if that was the case . . . why had Gilgamesh ever faked ignorance about the Denizens?

It made no sense. But on the other hand, he could not concoct a better theory to replace it.

"I have what you want," he said, after due consideration. "Cholok said removing it would be simple."

"Cholok can always be relied upon," the Denizen said.

"You knew—know—her, then?"

"She made us what we are today."

"You hate her, then?"

"No; we love her." The Denizen flashed its sharklike smile again, and it seemed to Vargovic that as its emotional state changed, so did the coloration of its bioluminescence. It was scarlet now; no longer the blue-green hue it had displayed upon its first appearance. "She took the abomination that we were and made us something better. We were in pain, once. Always pain. But Cholok took it away, made us strong. For that they punished her, and us."

"If you hate the Demarchy," Vargovic said, "why have you waited until now before attacking it?"

"Because we can't leave," one of the other Denizens said; the tone of its voice betraying femininity. "The Demarchy hated what Cholok had done to us. She brought our humanity to the fore; made it impossible to treat us as animals. We thought they would kill us, rather than risk our existence becoming known to the rest of Circum-Jove. Instead, they banished us here."

"They thought we might come in handy," said another of the lurking creatures.

Just then, another Denizen entered the cave, having swum in from the sea.

"Demarchy agents have followed him," it said, its coloration blood red, tinged with orange, pulsing lividly. "They'll be here in a minute."

"You'll have to protect me," Vargovic said.

"Of course," the lead Denizen said. "You're our saviour."

Vargovic nodded vigorously, no longer convinced that he could handle the three operatives on his own. Ever since he had arrived in the cave he had felt his energy dwindling, as if he was succumbing to slow poisoning. A thought tugged at the back of his mind, and for a moment he almost paid attention to it; almost considered seriously the possibility that he was being poisoned. But what was going on beyond the cave was too distracting. He watched the three Demarchy agents approach, driven forward by the tugs which they held in front of them. Each agent carried a slender harpoon gun, tipped with a vicious barb.

They didn't stand a chance.

The Denizens moved too quickly, lancing out from the shadows, cutting through the water. The creatures moved faster than the Demarchy agents, even though they only had their own muscles and anatomy to propel them. But it was more than enough. They had no weapons, either—not even harpoons. But sharpened rocks more than sufficed—that and their teeth.

Vargovic was impressed by their teeth.

Afterwards, the Denizens returned to the cave to join their cousins. They moved more sluggishly now; as if the fury of the fight had drained them. For a few moments they were silent, and their bioluminescence curiously subdued. Slowly, though, Vargovic watched their colour return.

"It was better that they not kill you," the leader said.

"Damn right," Vargovic said. "They wouldn't just have killed me, you know." He opened his fists, exposing his palms. "They'd have made sure you never got this."

The Denizens—all of them—looked momentarily toward his open hands, as if there ought to have been something there. "I'm not sure you understand," the leader said, eventually.

"Understand what?"

"The nature of your mission."

Fighting his fatigue—it was a black slick lapping at his consciousness—Vargovic said: "I understand perfectly well. I have the samples of hyperdiamond, in my hands . . ."

"That isn't what we want."

He didn't like this, not at all. It was the way the Denizens were slowly creeping closer to him; sidling round him to obstruct his exit from the cave.

"What then?"

"You asked why we haven't attacked them before," the leader said, with frightening charm. "The answer's simple. We can't leave the vent."

"You can't?"

"Our haemoglobin. It's not like yours." Again that awful sharklike smile—and now he was well aware of what those teeth could do, given the right circumstances. "It was tailored to allow us to work here."

"Copied from the ventlings?"

"Adapted, yes. Later it became the means of imprisoning us. The DNA in our bone marrow was manipulated to limit the production of normal haemoglobin; a simple matter of suppressing a few beta-globin genes while retaining the variants which code for ventling haemoglobin. Hydrogen sulphide is poisonous to you, Vargovic. You probably already feel weak. But we can't survive without it. Oxygen kills us."

"You leave the vent . . ."

"We die, within a few hours. There's more, as well. The water's hot here; so hot that we don't need the glycoproteins. We have the genetic instructions to synthesize them, but they've also been turned off. But without the glycoproteins we can't swim into colder water. Our blood freezes."

Now he was surrounded by them; looming aquatic devils, flushed a florid shade of crimson. And they were coming closer.

"But what do you expect me to do about it?"

"You don't have to do anything, Vargovic." The leader opened its chasmic jaw wide, as if tasting the water. It was a miracle an organ like that was capable of speech in the first place . . .

"I don't?"

"No." And with that the leader reached out and seized him, while at the same time he was pinned from behind by another of the creatures. "It was Cholok's doing," the leader continued. "Her final gift to us. Maunciple was her first attempt at getting it to us—but Maunciple never made it."

"He was too fat."

"All the defectors failed—they just didn't have the stamina to make it this far from the city. That was why Cholok recruited you—an outsider."

"Cholok recruited me?"

"She knew you'd kill her—you have, of course—but that didn't stop her. Her life mattered less than what she was about to give us. It was Cholok who tipped off the Demarchy about your primary extraction site, forcing you to come to us."

He struggled, but it was pointless. All he could manage was a feeble, "I don't understand . . ."

"No," the Denizen said. "Perhaps we never expected you to. If you had understood, you might have been less than willing to follow Cholok's plan."

"Cholok was never working for us?"

"Once, maybe. But her last clients were us."

"And now?"

"We take your blood, Vargovic." Their grip on him tightened. He used his last draining reserves of strength to try and work loose, but it was futile.

"My blood?"

"Cholok put something in it. A retrovirus—a very hardy one, capable of surviving in your body. It reactivates the genes which were suppressed by the Demarchy. Suddenly, we'll be able to make oxygen-carrying haemoglobin. Our blood will fill up with glycoproteins. It's no great trick: all the cellular machinery for making those molecules is already present; it just needs to be unshackled."

"Then you need . . . what? A sample of my blood?"

"No," the Denizen said, with genuine regret. "Rather more than a sample, I'm afraid. Rather a lot more."

And then—with magisterial slowness—the creature bit into his arm, and as his blood spilled out, the Denizen drank. For a moment the others waited—but then they too came forward, and bit, and joined in the feeding frenzy.

All around Vargovic, the water was turning red.

The undiscovered

WILLIAM SANDERS

William Sanders lives in Tahlequah, Oklahoma. A former powwow dancer and sometime Cherokee gospel singer, he appeared on the SF scene back around the turn of the decade with a couple of alternate history comedies, Journey to Fusang *(a finalist for the John W. Campbell Award) and* The Wild Blue and Gray. *Sanders then turned to mystery and suspense, producing a number of critically acclaimed titles. He credits his old friend Roger Zelazny with persuading him to return to SF, this time via the short story form, and has made sales to* Asimov's Science Fiction, The Magazine of Fantasy & Science Fiction, Tales of the Great Turtle, *and* Wheel of Fortune; *one of his stories earned him a spot on last year's Final Hugo Ballot. His stories have appeared in our Twelfth and Thirteenth Annual Collections.*

In the wry, funny, and compassionate story that follows, he settles one of the great controversies of all time by demonstrating who wrote Shakespeare's plays (Shakespeare did, *of course. What did you think?), but also shows us how, under other circumstances, some of the plays might have come out just a bit differently—especially if they were being performed for a somewhat different* audience. . . .

So the white men are back! And trying once again to build themselves a town, without so much as asking anyone's permission. I wonder how long they will stay this time. It sounds as if these have no more sense than the ones who came before.

They certainly pick the strangest places to settle. Last time it was that island, where anyone could have told them the weather is bad and the land is no good for corn. Now they have invaded Powhatan's country, and from what you say, they seem to have angered him already. Of course that has never been hard to do.

Oh, yes, we hear about these matters up in the hills. Not many of us actually visit the coastal country—I don't suppose there are ten people in this town, counting myself, who have even seen the sea—but you know how these stories travel. We have heard all about your neighbor Powhatan, and you eastern people are welcome to him. Was there ever a chief so hungry for power? Not in my memory, and I have lived a long time.

But we were speaking of the white men. As you say, they are a strange people indeed. For all their amazing weapons and other possessions, they seem to be ignorant of the simplest things. I think a half-grown boy would know more about how to survive. Or how to behave toward other people in their own country.

And yet they are not the fools they appear. Not all of them, at least. The only one I ever knew was a remarkably wise man in many ways.

Do not make that gesture at me. I tell you that there was a white man who lived right here in our town, for more than ten winters, and I came to know him well.

I remember the day they brought him in. I was sitting in front of my house, working on a fish spear, when I heard the shouting from the direction of the town gate. Bigkiller and his party, I guessed, returning from their raid on the Tuscaroras. People were running toward the gate, pouring out of the houses, everyone eager for a look.

I stayed where I was. I could tell by the sound that the raid had been successful—no women were screaming, so none of our people had been killed or seriously hurt—and I didn't feel like spending the rest of the day listening to Bigkiller bragging about his latest exploits.

But a young boy came up and said, "They need you, Uncle. Prisoners."

So I put my spear aside and got up and followed him, wondering once again why no one around this place could be bothered to learn to speak Tuscarora. After all, it is not so different from our tongue, not nearly as hard as Catawba or Maskogi or Shawano. Or your own language, which as you see I still speak poorly.

The captives were standing just inside the gate, guarded by a couple of Bigkiller's brothers, who were holding war clubs and looking fierce, as well as pleased with themselves. There was a big crowd of people by now and I had to push my way through before I could see the prisoners. There were a couple of scared-looking Tuscarora women—one young and pretty, the other almost my age and ugly as an alligator—and a small boy with his fist stuck in his mouth. Not much, I thought, to show for all this noise and fuss.

Then I saw the white man.

Do you know, it didn't occur to me at first that that was what he was. After all, white men were very rare creatures in those days, even more so than now. Hardly anyone had actually seen one, and quite a few people refused to believe they existed at all.

Besides, he wasn't really white—not the kind of fish-belly white that I'd always imagined, when people talked about white men—at least where it showed. His face was a strange reddish color, like a boiled crawfish, with little bits of skin peeling from his nose. His arms and legs, where they stuck out from under the single buckskin garment he wore, were so dirty and covered with bruises that it was hard to tell what color the skin was. Of course that was true of all of the captives; Bigkiller and his warriors had not been gentle.

His hair was dark brown rather than black, which I thought was unusual for a Tuscarora, though you do see Leni Lenapes and a few Shawanos with lighter hair. It was pretty thin above his forehead, and the scalp beneath showed through, a nasty bright pink. I looked at that and at the red peeling skin of his face, and thought: well done, Bigkiller, you've brought home a sick man. Some lowland skin disease, and what a job it's going to be purifying everything after he dies. . . .

That was when he turned and looked at me with those blue eyes. Yes, blue. I don't blame you; I didn't believe that story either, until I saw for myself. The white men have eyes the color of a sunny sky. I tell you, it is a weird thing to see when you're not ready for it.

Bigkiller came through the crowd, looking at me and laughing. "Look what we caught, Uncle," he said, and pointed with his spear. "A white man!"

"I knew that," I said, a little crossly. I hated it when he called me "Uncle." I hated it when anyone did it, except children—I was not yet *that* old—but I hated it worse when it came from Bigkiller. Even if he was my nephew.

"He was with the Tuscaroras," one of the warriors, Muskrat by name, told me. "These two women had him carrying firewood—"

"Never mind that." Bigkiller gave Muskrat a bad look. No need to tell the whole town that this brave raid deep into Tuscarora country had amounted to nothing more than the ambush and kidnapping of a small wood-gathering party.

To me Bigkiller said, "Well, Uncle, you're the one who knows all tongues. Can you talk with this white-skin?"

I stepped closer and studied the stranger, who looked back at me with those impossible eyes. He seemed unafraid, but who could read expressions on such an unnatural face?

"Who are you and where do you come from?" I asked in Tuscarora.

He smiled and shook his head, not speaking. The woman beside him, the older one, spoke up suddenly. "He doesn't know our language," she said. "Only a few words, and then you have to talk slow and loud, and kick him a little."

"Nobody in our town could talk with him," the younger woman added. "Our chief speaks a little of your language, and one family has a Catawba slave, and he couldn't understand them either."

By now the crowd was getting noisy, everyone pushing and jostling, trying to get a look at the white man. Everyone was talking, too, saying the silliest things. Old Otter, the elder medicine man, wanted to cut the white man to see what color his blood was. An old woman asked Muskrat to strip him naked and find out if he was white all over, though I guessed she was really more interested in learning what his male parts looked like.

The young Tuscarora woman said, "Are they going to kill him?"

"I don't know," I told her. "Maybe."

"They shouldn't," she said. "He's a good slave. He's a hard worker, and he can really sing and dance."

I translated this, and to my surprise Muskrat said, "It is true that he is stronger than he looks. He put up a good fight, with no weapon but a stick of firewood. Why do you think I'm holding this club left-handed?" He held up his right arm, which was swollen and dark below the elbow. "He almost broke my arm."

"He did show spirit," Bigkiller agreed. "He could have run away, but he stayed and fought to protect the women. That was well done for a slave."

I looked at the white man again. He didn't look all that impressive, being no more than medium size and pretty thin, but I could see there were real muscles under that strange skin.

"He can do tricks, too," the young Tuscarora woman added. "He walks on his hands, and—"

The older woman grunted loudly. "He's bad luck, that's what he is. We've had nothing but trouble since he came. Look at us now."

I passed all this along to Bigkiller. "I don't know," he said. "I was going to kill him, but maybe I should keep him as a slave. After all, what other chief among the People has a white slave?"

A woman's voice said, "What's going on here?"

I didn't turn around. I didn't have to. There was no one in our town who would not have known that voice. Suddenly everyone got very quiet.

My sister Tsigeyu came through the crowd, everyone moving quickly out of her way, and stopped in front of the white man. She looked him up and down and he looked back at her, still smiling, as if pleased to meet her. That showed real courage. Naturally he had no way of knowing that she was the Clan Mother of the Wolf Clan—which, if you don't know, means she was by far the most powerful person in our town—but just the sight of her would have made most people uneasy. Tsigeyu was a big woman, not fat but big like a big man, with a face like a limestone cliff. And eyes that went right through you and made your bones go cold. She died a couple of years ago, but at the time I am telling about she was still in the prime of life, and such gray hairs as she had she wore like eagle feathers.

She said, "For me? Why, thank you, Bigkiller."

Bigkiller opened his mouth and shut it. Tsigeyu was the only living creature he feared. He had more reason than most, since she was his mother.

Muskrat muttered something about having the right to kill the prisoner for having injured him.

Tsigeyu looked at Muskrat. Muskrat got a few fingers shorter, or that was how it looked. But after a moment she said, "It is true you are the nearest thing to a wounded warrior among this brave little war party." She gestured at the young Tuscarora woman. "So I think you should get to keep this girl, here."

Muskrat looked a good deal happier.

"The rest of you can decide among yourselves who gets the other woman, and the boy." Tsigeyu turned to me. "My brother, I want you to take charge of this white man for now. Try to teach him to speak properly. You can do it if anyone can."

KNOWE ALL ENGLISH AND OTHER CHRISTIAN MEN:
That I an Englishman and Subjeckt of Her Maiestie Queene *Eliza-beth*, did by Misadventure come to this country of *Virginia* in the

Yeere of Our Lord 1591: and after greate Hardshipp arriued amongst these *Indians*. Who haue done me no Harme, but rather shewed me most exelent Kindnesse, sans the which I were like to haue dyed in this Wildernesse. Wherefore, good Frend, I coniure you, that you offer these poore Sauages no Offence, nor do them Iniurie: but rather vse them generously and iustly, as they haue me.

Look at this. Did you ever see the like? He made these marks himself on this deerskin, using a sharpened turkey feather and some black paint that he cooked up from burned wood and oak galls. And he told me to keep it safe, and that if other white men came this way I should show it to them, and it would tell them his story.

Yes, I suppose it must be like a wampum belt, in a way. Or those little pictures and secret marks that the wise elders of the Leni Lenapes use to record their tribe's history. So clearly he was some sort of *didahnvwisgi*, a medicine man, even though he did not look old enough to have received such an important teaching.

He was always making these little marks, scratching away on whatever he could get—skins, mostly, or mulberry bark. People thought he was crazy, and I let them, because if they had known the truth not even Tsigeyu could have saved him from being killed for a witch.

But all that came later, during the winter, after he had begun to learn our language and I his. On that first day I was only interested in getting him away from that crowd before there was more trouble. I could see that Otter was working himself up to make one of his speeches, and if nothing else that meant there was a danger of being talked to death.

Inside my house I gave the stranger a gourd of water. When he had eased his thirst I pointed to myself. "Mouse," I said, very slowly and carefully. *"Tsis-de-tsi."*

He was quick. *"Tsisdetsi,"* he repeated. He got the tones wrong, but it was close enough for a beginning.

I held my hands up under my chin like paws, and pulled my upper lip back to show my front teeth, and crossed my eyes. I waggled one hand behind me to represent a long tail. *"Tsisdetsi,"* I said again.

He laughed out loud. *"Tsisdetsi,"* he said. *"Mus!"*

He raised his hand and stroked his face for a moment, as if thinking of something. Then without warning he turned and grabbed my best war spear off the wall. My bowels went loose, but he made no move to attack me. Instead he began shaking the weapon above his head with one hand, slapping himself on the chest with the other. *"Tsagspa,"* he cried. *"Tsagspa."*

Crazy as a dog on a hot day, I thought at first. They must have hit him too hard. Then I realized what was happening, and felt almost dizzy. It is no small honor when any man tells you his secret war name—but a stranger, and a prisoner!

"Digatsisdi atelvhvsgo'i," I said, when I could finally speak. "Shakes Spear!"

> I am him that was call'd William *Shakspere*, of *Stratford-upon-Auon*, late of *London*: a Player, of Lord *Strange* his Company, and thereby hangs a Tale.

Look there, where I am pointing. That is his name! He showed me that, and he even offered to teach me how to make the marks for my own. Naturally I refused—think what an enemy could do with something like that!

When I pointed this out, he laughed and said I might be right. For, he said, many a man of his sort had had bad luck with other people making use of his name.

> It hapt that our Company was in *Portsmouth*, hauing beene there engaug'd: but then were forbid to play, the Mayor and Corporation of that towne being of the *Puritann* perswasion. For which cause we were left altogether bankrupt: so that some of our Players did pawne their Cloathing for monny to return Home.

Perhaps someone had cursed him, since he sometimes said that he had never meant to leave his own country. It was the fault of the Puritans, he said. He did not explain what this meant, but once he mentioned that his wife and her family were Puritans. So obviously this is simply the name of his wife's clan. Poor fellow, no wonder he left home. The same thing happened to an uncle of mine. When your wife's clan decides to get rid of you, you don't have a chance.

> But I, being made foolish by strong Drinke, did conceive to hyde my selfe on a Ship bownd for *London*. Which did seeme a good Idea at the Time: but when I enquyr'd of some sea-faring men, they shewed me (in rogue Jest, or else mayhap I misconstrew'd their Reply, for I was in sooth most outragiosly drunk) the *Moonlight*, which lay at the Docke. And so by night I stole aboord, and hid my selfe vnder a Boate: wherevpon the Wine did rush to my heade, and I fell asleepe, and wal'd not till the Morrow: to finde the Ship at sea and vnder Sayle, and the morning Sun at her backe.

Naturally it was a long time before we could understand each other well enough to discuss such things. Not as long as you might think, though. To begin with, I discovered that in fact he had picked up quite a bit of Tuscarora—pretending, like any smart captive, to understand less than he did. Besides that, he was a fast learner. You know that languages are my special medicine—I have heard them say that Mouse can talk to a stone, and get it to talk back—but Spearshaker was gifted too. By the time of the first snow, we could get along fairly well, in a mixture of his language and mine. And when words failed, he could express almost any idea, even tell a story, just by the movements of his hands and body and the expression of his face. That in itself was worth seeing.

> When I was discouer'd the Master was most wroth, and commanded that I be put to the hardest Labours, and giuen onely the poorest leauings for food. So it went hard for me on that Voyage: but the

Saylors learn'd that I could sing diuers Songs, and new Ballads from *London*, and then I was vsed better. Anon the Captaine, Mr. Edward *Spicer*, ask'd whether I had any skill in Armes. To which I reply'd, that a Player must needs be a Master of Fence, and of all other Artes martiall, forasmuch as we are wont to play Battles, Duelles, Murthers &c. And the Captaine said, that soone I should haue Opportunity to proue my selfe against true Aduersaries and not in play, for we sayl'd for the *Spanish Maine*.

All this time, you understand, there was a great deal of talk concerning the white man. Most of the people came to like him, for he was a friendly fellow and a willing worker. And the Tuscarora girl was certainly right about his singing and dancing. Even Bigkiller had to laugh when Spearshaker went leaping and capering around the fire, and when he walked on his hands and clapped his feet together several women wet themselves—or so I heard.

His songs were strange to the ear, but enjoyable. I remember one we all liked:

> *"Wid-a-he*
> *An-a-ho*
> *An-a-he-na-ni-no!"*

But not everyone was happy about his presence among us. Many of the young men were angry that the women liked him so well, and now and then took him aside to prove it. And old Otter told everyone who would listen that once, long ago, a great band of white men had come up from the south, from the Timucua country, and destroyed the finest towns of the Maskogis, taking many away for slaves and killing the others. And this was true, because when the People moved south they found much of that country empty and ruined.

Spearshaker said that those people were of another tribe, with which his own nation was at war. But not everyone believed him, and Otter kept insisting that white men were simply too dangerous to have around. I began to fear for Spearshaker's life.

At length we came vnto the *Indies*, being there joyn'd by the *Hopewell* and other Ships whose names I knowe not. And we attack'd the Spanish Convoy, and took the Galleon *Buen Jesus*, a rich Pryze: and so it came to pass that Will Shakspeare, Actor, did for his greate folly turn Pyrat vpon the salt Sea.

Then, early next spring, the Catawbas came.

This was no mere raid. They came in force and they hit us fast and hard, killing or capturing many of the people working in the fields before they could reach the town palisade. They rushed out of the woods and swarmed over the palisade like ants, and before we knew it we were fighting for our lives in front of our own houses.

That was when Spearshaker astonished us all. Without hesitating, he grabbed a long pole from the meat-drying racks and went after the nearest Catawba with it, jabbing him hard in the guts with the end, exactly as you would use a spear, and then clubbing him over the head. Then he picked up the Catawba's bow and began shooting.

My friend, I have lived long and seen much, but I never was more surprised than that morning. This pale, helpless creature, who could not chip an arrowhead or build a proper fire or even take five steps off a trail without getting lost—he cut those Catawbas down like rotten cornstalks! He shot one man off the palisade, right over there, from clear down by the council house. I do not think he wasted a single shot. And when he was out of arrows, he picked up a war club from a fallen warrior and joined the rest of us in fighting off the remaining attackers.

Afterward, he seemed not to think he had done anything remarkable. He said that all the men of his land know stick-fighting and archery, which they learn as boys. "I could have done better," he said, "with a long bow, and some proper arrows, from my own country." And he looked sad, as he always did when he spoke of his home.

From that day there was no more talk against Spearshaker. Not long after, Tsigeyu announced that she was adopting him. Since this also made him Bigkiller's brother, he was safe from anyone in our town. It also made me his uncle, but he was kind enough never to call me *edutsi*. We were friends.

> Next we turn'd north for *Virginnia*, Capt. *Spicer* hauing a Commission from Sir Walter *Ralegh* to calle vpon the English that dwelt at *Roanoke*, to discouer their condition. The Gales were cruel all along that Coast, and we were oft in grave Peril: but after much trauail we reached *Hatarask*, where the Captaine sent a party in small Boates, to search out the passage betweene the Islands. And whilst we were thus employ'd, a sudden great Wind arose and scattered the Boates, many being o'erturned and the Mariners drowned. But the Boate I was in was carry'd many Leagues westward, beyond sight of our Fellowes: so we were cast vpon the Shore of the Maine, and sought shelter in the Mouthe of a Riuer. Anon, going ashore, we were attack'd by Sauages: and all the men were slaine, save onely my selfe.

Poor fellow, he was still a long way from home, and small chance of ever seeing his own people again. At least he was better off than he had been with the Tuscaroras. Let alone those people on the coast, if they had caught him. Remember the whites who tried to build a town on that island north of Wococon, and how Powhatan had them all killed?

> Yet hauing alone escap'd, and making my way for some dayes along the Riuer, I was surprized by *Indians* of another Nation: who did giue me hard vsage, as a Slaue, for well-nigh a Yeere. Vntil I was taken from them by these mine present sauage Hostes: amongst which, for my Sinnes, I am like to liue out my mortall dayes.

I used to have a big pile of these talking skins of his. Not that I ever expected to have a chance to show them to anyone who could understand them—I can't believe the white men will ever come up into the hill country; they seem to have all they can do just to survive on the coast—but I kept them to remember Spearshaker by.

But the bugs and the mice got into them, and the bark sheets went moldy in the wet season, and now I have only this little bundle. And, as you see, some of these are no more than bits and pieces. Like this worm-eaten scrap:

> as concerning these *Indians* (for so men call them: but if this be the Lande of *India* I am an Hebrewe *Iewe*) they are in their owne Tongue clept *Anni-yawia*. Which is, being interpreted, the True or Principall People. By other Tribes they are named *Chelokee*: but the meaning of this word my frend *Mouse* knoweth not, neyther whence deriued. They

I think one reason he spent so much time on his talking marks was that he was afraid he might forget his own language. I have seen this happen, with captives. That Tuscarora woman who was with him still lives here, and by now she can barely speak ten words of Tuscarora. Though Muskrat will tell you that she speaks our language entirely too well—but that is another story.

Spearshaker did teach me quite a lot of his own language—a very difficult one, unlike any I ever encountered—and I tried to speak it with him from time to time, but it can't have been the same as talking with a man of his own kind. What does it sound like? Ah, I remember so little now. Let me see. . . . "*Holt dai tong, dow hor-son nabe!*" That means, "Shut up, you fool!"

He told me many stories about his native land and its marvels. Some I knew to be true, having heard of them from the coast folk: the great floating houses that spread their wings like birds to catch the wind, and the magic weapons that make thunder and lightning. Others were harder to believe, such as his tales about the woman chief of his tribe. Not a clan mother, but a real war chief, like Bigkiller or even Powhatan, and so powerful that any man—even an elder or a leading warrior—can lose his life merely for speaking against her.

He also claimed that the town he came from was so big that it held more people than all of the People's towns put together. That is of course a lie, but you can't blame a man for bragging on his own tribe.

But nothing, I think, was as strange as the *plei*.

Forgive me for using a word you do not know. But as far as I know there is no word in your language for what I am talking about. Nor in ours, and this is because the thing it means has never existed among our peoples. I think the Creator must have given this idea only to the whites, perhaps to compensate them for their poor sense of direction and that skin that burns in the sun.

It all began one evening, at the beginning of his second winter with us, when I came in from a council meeting and found him sitting by the fire, scratching away on a big sheet of mulberry bark. Just to be polite I said, "*Gado hadvhne?* What are you doing?"

Without looking up he said in his own language, "*Raiting a plei.*"

Now I knew what the first part meant; *rai-ting* is what the whites call it when they make those talking marks. But I had never heard the last word before, and I asked what it meant.

Spearshaker laid his turkey feather aside and sat up and looked at me. "Ah, Mouse," he said, "how can I make you understand? This will be hard even for you."

I sat down on the other side of the fire. "Try," I said.

> O what a fond and Moone-struck fool am I! Hath the aire of *Virginnia* addl'd my braine? Or did an Enemy smite me on the heade, and I knewe it not? For here in this wilde country, where e'en the Artes of Letters are altogether unknowne, I haue begun the writing of a Play. And sure it is I shall neuer see it acted, neyther shall any other man: wherefore 'tis Lunacy indeede. Yet me thinkes if I do it not, I am the more certain to go mad: for I find my selfe growing more like vnto these *Indians*, and I feare I may forget what manner of man I was. Therefore the Play's the thing, whereby Ile saue my Minde by intentional folly: forsooth, there's Method in my Madnesse.

Well, he was right. He talked far into the night, and the more he talked the less I understood. I asked more questions than a rattlesnake has scales, and the answers only left me more confused. It was a long time before I began to see it.

Didn't you, as a child, pretend you were a warrior or a chief or maybe a medicine man, and make up stories and adventures for yourself? And your sisters had dolls that they gave names to, and talked to, and so on?

Or . . . let me try this another way. Don't your people have dances, like our Bear Dance, in which a man imitates some sort of animal? And don't your warriors sometimes dance around the fire acting out their own deeds, showing how they killed men or sneaked up on an enemy town—and maybe making it a little better than it really happened? Yes, it is the same with us.

Now this *plei* thing is a little like those dances, and a little like the pretending of children. A group of people dress up in fancy clothes and pretend to be other people, and pretend to do various things, and in this way they tell a story.

Yes, grown men. Yes, right up in front of everybody.

But understand, this isn't a dance. Well, there is some singing and dancing, but mostly they just talk. And gesture, and make faces, and now and then pretend to kill each other. They do a lot of that last. I guess it is something like a war dance at that.

You'd be surprised what can be done in this way. A man like Spearshaker, who really knows how—*ak-ta* is what they are called—can make you see almost anything. He could imitate a man's expression and voice and way of moving—or a woman's—so well you'd swear he had turned into that person. He could make you think he was Bigkiller, standing right there in front of you, grunting and growling and waving his war club. He could do Blackfox's funny walk, or Locust wiggling his eyebrows, or Tsigeyu crossing her arms and staring at somebody she didn't like. He could even be Muskrat and his Tuscarora woman arguing, changing back and forth and doing both voices, till I laughed so hard my ribs hurt.

Now understand this. These *akta* people don't just make up their words and actions as they go along, as children or dancers do. No, the whole story is already known to them, and each *akta* has words that must be said, and things that must be done, at exactly the right times. You may be sure this takes a good memory. They have as much to remember as the Master of the Green Corn Dance.

And so, to help them, one man puts the whole thing down in those little marks. Obviously this is a very important job, and Spearshaker said that it was only in recent times, two or three winters before leaving his native land, that he himself had been accounted worthy of this honor. Well, I had known he was a *didahnvwisgi*, but I hadn't realized he was of such high rank.

> I first purpos'd to compose some pretty conceited Comedy, like vnto my Loue's Labour's Lost: but alas, me seemes my Wit hath dry'd vp from Misfortune. Then I bethought my selfe of the Play of the Prince of Denmark, by Thomas *Kyd*: which I had been employ'd in reuising for our Company not long ere we departed *London*, and had oft said to Richard *Burbage*, that I trow I could write a Better. And so I haue commenced, and praye God I may compleat, my owne Tragedie of Prince *Hamlet*.

I asked what sort of stories his people told in this curious manner. That is something that always interests me—you can learn a lot about any tribe from their stories. Like the ones the Maskogis tell about Rabbit, or our own tale about the Thunder Boys, or—you know.

I don't know what I was thinking. By then I should have known that white people do *everything* differently from everyone else in the world.

First he started to tell me about a dream somebody had on a summer night. That sounded good, but then it turned out to be about the Little People! Naturally I stopped him fast, and I told him that we do not talk about . . . *them*. I felt sorry for the poor man who dreamed about them, but there was no helping him now.

Then Spearshaker told me a couple of stories about famous chiefs of his own tribe. I couldn't really follow this very well, partly because I knew so little about white laws and customs, but also because a lot of their chiefs seemed to have the same name. I never did understand whether there were two different chiefs named *Ritsad*, or just one with a very strange nature.

The oddest thing, though, was that none of these stories seemed to have any *point*. They didn't tell you why the moon changes its face, or how the People were created, or where the mountains came from, or where the raccoon got his tail, or anything. They were just . . . *stories*. Like old women's gossip.

Maybe I missed something.

He certainly worked hard at his task. More often than not, I could hear him grinding his teeth and muttering to himself as he sat hunched over his marks. And now and then he would jump up and throw the sheet to the ground and run outside in the snow and the night wind, and I would hear him shouting in his own language. At least I took it to be his language, though the words were not among those I knew. Part of his medicine, no doubt, so I said nothing.

> God's Teethe! Haue I beene so long in this Wildernesse, that I haue forgot all Skill? I that could bombast out a lyne of blank Uerse as readily as a Fishe doth swimm, now fumble for Wordes like a Drunkard who cannot finde his owne Cod-peece with both Handes.

I'm telling you, it was a *long* winter.

> For who would thus endure the Paines of time:
> To-morrow and to-morrow and to-morrow,
> That waite in patient and most grim Array,
> Each arm'd with Speares and Arrowes of Misfortune,
> Like *Indians* ambuscaded in the Forest?
> But that the dread of something after Death,
> That vndiscouered country, from whose Shores
> No Traueller returnes, puzzels the Will,
> And makes vs rather beare that which we knowe
> Than wantonly embarke for the Vnknowne.

One evening, soon after the snows began to melt, I noticed that Spearshaker was not at his usual nightly work. He was just sitting there staring into the fire, not even looking at his skins and bark sheets, which were stacked beside him. The turkey feathers and black paint were nowhere in sight.

I said, "Is something wrong?" and then it came to me. "Finished?"

He let out a long sigh. "Yes," he said. "*Mo ful ai,*" he added, which was something he often said, though I never quite got what it meant.

It was easy to see he was feeling bad. So I said, "Tell me the story."

He didn't want to, but finally he told it to me. He got pretty worked up as he went along, sometimes jumping up to act out an exciting part, till I thought he was going to wreck my house. Now and then he picked up a skin or mulberry-bark sheet and spoke the words, so I could hear the sound. I had thought I was learning his language pretty well, but I couldn't understand one word in ten.

But the story itself was clear enough. There were parts I didn't follow, but on the whole it was the best he'd ever told me. At the end I said, "Good story."

He tilted his head to one side, like a bird. "Truly?"

"*Doyu,*" I said. I meant it, too.

He sighed again and picked up his pile of *raiting*. "I am a fool," he said.

I saw that he was about to throw the whole thing into the fire, so I went over and took it from him. "This is a good thing," I told him. "Be proud."

"Why?" He shrugged his shoulders. "Who will ever see it? Only the bugs and the worms. And the mice," he added, giving me his little smile.

I stood there, trying to think of something to make him feel better. Ninekiller's oldest daughter had been making eyes at Spearshaker lately and I wondered if I should go get her. Then I looked down at what I was holding in my hands and it came to me.

"My friend," I said, "I've got an idea. Why don't we put on your *plei* right here?"

> And now is Lunacy compownded vpon Lunacy, *Bedlam* pyled on *Bedlam*: for I am embark'd on an Enterprize, the like of which this Globe hath neuer seene. Yet Ile undertake this Foolery, and flynch not: mayhap it will please these People, who are become my onely Frends. They shall haue of Will his best will.

It sounded simple when I heard myself say it. Doing it was another matter. First, there were people to be spoken with.

We *Aniyvwiya* like to keep everything loose and easy. Our chiefs have far less authority than yours, and even the power of the clan mothers has its limits. Our laws are few, and everyone knows what they are, so things tend to go along without much trouble.

But there were no rules for what we wanted to do, because it had never been done before. Besides, we were going to need the help of many people. So it seemed better to go carefully—but I admit I had no idea that our little proposal would create such a stir. In the end there was a regular meeting at the council house to talk it over.

Naturally it was Otter who made the biggest fuss. "This is white men's medicine," he shouted. "Do you want the People to become as weak and useless as the whites?"

"If it will make all our warriors shoot as straight as Spearshaker," Bigkiller told him, "then it might be worth it."

Otter waved his skinny old arms. He was so angry by now that his face was whiter than Spearshaker's. "Then answer this," he said. "How is it that this dance—"

"It's not a dance," I said. Usually I would not interrupt an elder in council, but if you waited for Otter to finish you might be there all night.

"Whatever you call it," he said, "it's close enough to a dance to be Bird Clan business, right? And you, Mouse, are Wolf Clan—as is your white friend, by adoption. So you have no right to do this thing."

Old Dotsuya spoke up. She was the Bird Clan Mother, and the oldest person present. Maybe the oldest in town, now I think of it.

"The Bird Clan has no objection," she said. "Mouse and Spearshaker have our permission to put on their *plei*. Which I, for one, would like to see. Nothing ever happens around this town."

Tsigeyu spoke next. "*Howa*," she said. "I agree. This sounds interesting."

Of course Otter wasn't willing to let it go so easily; he made quite a speech, going all the way back to the origins of the People and predicting every kind of calamity if this sacrilege was permitted. It didn't do him much good, though. No one liked Otter, who had gotten both meaner and longer-winded with age, and who had never been a very good *didahnvwisgi* anyway. Besides, half the people in the council house were asleep long before he was done.

After the council gave its approval there was no trouble getting people to help. Rather we had more help than we needed. For days there was a crowd hanging around my house, wanting to be part of the *plei*. Bigkiller said if he could get that many people to join a war party, he could take care of the Catawbas for good.

And everyone wanted to be an *akta*. We were going to have to turn some people away, and we would have to be careful how we did it, or there would be trouble. I asked Spearshaker how many *aktas* we needed. "How many men, that is," I added, as he began counting on his fingers. "The women are a different problem."

He stopped counting and stared at me as if I were wearing owl feathers. Then he told me something so shocking you will hardly believe it. In his country, the women in a *plei* are actually *men wearing women's clothes!*

I told him quick enough that the People don't go in for that sort of thing—whatever they may get up to in certain other tribes—and he'd better not even talk about it around here. Do you know, he got so upset that it took me the rest of the day to talk him out of calling the whole thing off. . . .

> Women! Mercifull Jesu! Women, on a Stage, acting in a Play! I shall feele like an Whore-Master!

Men or women, it was hard to know which people to choose. None of them had ever done anything like this before, so there was no way to know whether they would be any good or not. Spearshaker asked me questions about each person, in white language so no one would be offended: Is he quick to learn? Does he dance or sing well? Can he work with other people, and do as he is told? And he had them stand on one side of the stickball field, while he stood on the other, and made them speak their names and clans, to learn how well their voices carried.

I had thought age would come into it, since the *plei* included both older and younger people. But it turned out that Spearshaker knew an art of painting a man's face, and putting white in his hair, till he might be mistaken for his own grandfather.

No doubt he could have done the same with women, but that wasn't necessary. There were only two women's parts in this story, and we gave the younger woman's part to Ninekiller's daughter Cricket—who would have hung upside-down in a tree like a possum if it would please Spearshaker—and the older to a cousin of mine, about my age, who had lost her husband to the Shawanos and wanted something to do.

For those who could not be *aktas*, there was plenty of other work. A big platform had to be built, with space cleared around it, and log benches for the people who would watch. There were torches to be prepared, since we would be doing it at night, and special clothes to be made, as well as things like fake spears so no one would get hurt.

Locust and Blackfox were particularly good workers; Spearshaker said it was as if they had been born for this. They even told him that if he still wanted to follow the custom of his own tribe, with men dressed as women, they would be willing to take those parts. Well, I always had wondered about those two.

But Spearshaker was working harder than anyone else. Besides being in charge of all the other preparations, he had to remake his whole *plei* to suit our needs. No doubt he had made a fine *plei* for white men, but for us, as it was, it would never do.

> Many a Play haue I reuis'd and amended: cut short or long at the Company's desyre, or alter'd this or that Speeche to please a Player: e'en carued the very Guttes out of a scene on command of the Office of the Reuels, for some imagin'd Sedition or vnseemely Speeche. But now must I out-do all I euer did before, in the making of my *Hamlet* into a thing comprehensible to the *Anni-yawia*. Scarce is there a line which doth not haue to be rewrit: yea, and much ta'en out intire: as, the Play within the Play, which Mouse saith, that none here will vnderstande. And the Scene must be mov'd from *Denmark* to *Virginnia*, and *Elsinore Castle* transformed into an *Indian* towne. For marry, it were Alchemy enow that I should transmute vnletter'd Sauages into tragick Actors: but to make royal *Danskers* of swart-fac'd *Indians* were beyond all Reason. (Speak'st thou now of Reason, Will Shakespere? Is't not ouer-late for that?)

You should have seen us teaching the *aktas* their parts. First Spearshaker would look at the marks and say the words in his language. Then he would explain to me any parts I hadn't understood—which was most of it, usually—and then I would translate the whole thing for the *akta* in our language. Or as close as I could get; there are some things you cannot really interpret. By now Spearshaker was fluent enough to help me.

Then the *akta* would try to say the words back to us, almost always getting it all wrong and having to start again. And later on all the people in the *plei* had to get together and speak their parts in order, and do all the things they would do in the *plei*, and that was like a bad dream. Not only did they forget their words; they bumped into each other and stepped on each other's feet, and got carried away in the fight parts and nearly killed each other. And Spearshaker would jump up and down and pull his hair—which had already begun to fall out, for some reason—and sometimes weep, and when he had settled down we would try again.

> Verily, my lot is harder than that of the *Iewes* of *Moses*. For Scripture saith, that *Pharo* did command that they make Brickes without Strawe, wherefore their trauail was greate: but now I must make my Brickes, euen without Mudd.

Let me tell you the story of Spearshaker's *plei*.
Once there was a great war chief who was killed by his own brother. Not in

a fight, but secretly, by poison. The brother took over as chief, and also took his dead brother's woman, who didn't object.

But the dead man had a son, a young warrior named Amaledi. One night the dead chief appeared to Amaledi and told him the whole story. And, of course, demanded that he do something about it.

Poor Amaledi was in a bad fix. Obviously he mustn't go against his mother's wishes, and kill her new man without her permission. On the other hand, no one wants to anger a ghost—and this one was plenty angry already.

So Amaledi couldn't decide what to do. To make things worse, the bad brother had guessed that Amaledi knew something. He and this really nasty, windy old man named Quolonisi—sounds like Otter—began trying to get rid of Amaledi.

To protect himself Amaledi became a Crazy, doing and saying everything backward, or in ways that made no sense. This made his medicine strong enough to protect him from his uncle and Quolonisi, at least for a time.

Quolonisi had a daughter, Tsigalili, who wanted Amaledi for her man. But she didn't want to live with a Crazy—who does?—and she kept coming around and crying and begging him to quit. At the same time his mother was giving him a hard time for being disrespectful toward her new man. And all the while the ghost kept showing up and yelling at Amaledi for taking so long. It got so bad Amaledi thought about killing himself, but then he realized that he would go to the spirit world, where his father would *never* leave him alone.

So Amaledi thought of a plan. There was a big dance one night to honor the new chief, and some visiting singers from another town were going to take part. Amaledi took their lead singer aside and got him to change the song, telling him the new words had been given to him in a dream. And that night, with the dancers going around the fire and the women shaking the turtle shells and the whole town watching, the visiting leader sang:

> "Now he pours it,
> Now he is pouring the poison,
> See, there are two brothers,
> See, now there is one."

That was when it all blew up like a hot rock in a fire. The bad chief jumped up and ran away from the dance grounds, afraid he had just been witched. Amaledi had a big argument with his mother and told her what he thought of the way she was acting. Then he killed Quolonisi. He said it was an accident but I think he was just tired of listening to the old fool.

Tsigalili couldn't stand any more. She jumped into a waterfall and killed herself. There was a fine funeral.

Now Amaledi was determined to kill his uncle. The uncle was just as determined to kill Amaledi, but he was too big a coward to do it himself. So he got Quolonisi's son Panther to call Amaledi out for a fight.

Panther was a good fighter and he was hot to kill Amaledi, because of his father and his sister. But the chief wasn't taking any chances. He put some poison on Panther's spear. He also had a gourd of water, with poison in it, in case nothing else worked.

So Amaledi and Panther painted their faces red and took their spears and faced each other, right in front of the chief's house. Amaledi was just as good as Panther, but finally he got nicked on the arm. Before the poison could act, they got into some hand-to-hand wrestling, and the spears got mixed up. Now Panther took a couple of hits. Yes, with the poisoned spear.

Meanwhile Amaledi's mother got thirsty and went over and took a drink, before anyone could stop her, from the poisoned gourd. Pretty soon she fell down. Amaledi and Panther stopped fighting and rushed over, but she was already dead.

By now they were both feeling the poison themselves. Panther fell down and died. So did Amaledi, but before he went down he got his uncle with the poisoned spear. So in the end *everyone* died.

You do?

Well, I suppose you had to be there.

> And so 'tis afoote: to-morrow night we are to perform. Thank God
> *Burbage* cannot be there to witnesse it: for it were a Question which
> should come first, that he dye of Laughter, or I of Shame.

It was a warm and pleasant night. Everyone was there, even Otter. By the time it was dark all the seats were full and many people were standing, or sitting on the ground.

The platform had only been finished a few days before—with Bigkiller complaining about the waste of timber and labor, that could have gone into strengthening the town's defenses—and it looked very fine. Locust and Blackfox had hung some reed mats on poles to represent the walls of houses, and also to give us a place to wait out of sight before going on. To keep the crowd from getting restless, Spearshaker had asked Dotsuya to have some Bird Clan men sing and dance while we were lighting the torches and making other last preparations.

Then it was time to begin.

What? Oh, no, I was not an *akta*. By now I knew the words to the whole *plei*, from having translated and repeated them so many times. So I stood behind a reed screen and called out the words, in a voice too low for the crowd to hear, when anyone forgot what came next.

Spearshaker, yes. He was the ghost. He had put some paint on his face that made it even whiter, and he did something with his voice that made the hair stand up on your neck.

But in fact everyone did very well, much better than I had expected. The only bad moment came when Amaledi—that was Tsigeyu's son Hummingbird—shouted, "Na! Dili, dili!" ("There! A skunk, a skunk!") and slammed his war club into the wall of the "chief's house," forgetting it was really just a reed mat. And Beartrack, who was being Quolonisi, took such a blow to the head that he was out for the rest of the *plei*. But it didn't matter, since he had no more words to speak, and he made a very good dead man for Amaledi to drag out.

And the people loved it, all of it. How they laughed and laughed! I never heard so many laugh so hard for so long. At the end, when Amaledi fell dead between his mother and Panther and the platform was covered with corpses, there was so much howling and hooting you would have taken it for a hurricane. I looked out through the mats and saw Tsigeyu and Bigkiller holding on to each other to keep from falling off the bench. Warriors were wiping tears from their eyes and women were clutching themselves between the legs and old Dotsuya was lying on the ground kicking her feet like a baby.

I turned to Spearshaker, who was standing beside me. "See," I said. "And you were afraid they wouldn't understand it!"

After that everything got confused for a while. Locust and Blackfox rushed up and dragged Spearshaker away, and the next time I saw him he was down in front of the platform with Tsigeyu embracing him and Bigkiller slapping him on the back. I couldn't see his face, which was hidden by Tsigeyu's very large front.

By then people were making a fuss over all of us. Even me. A Paint Clan woman, not bad-looking for her age, took me away for some attention. She was limber and had a lot of energy, so it was late by the time I finally got home.

Spearshaker was there, sitting by the fire. He didn't look up when I came in. His face was so pale I thought at first he was still wearing his ghost paint.

I said, "Gusdi nusdi? Is something wrong?"

"They laughed," he said. He didn't sound happy about it.

"They laughed," I agreed. "They laughed as they have never laughed before, every one of them. Except for Otter, and no one has ever seen him laugh."

I sat down beside him. "You did something fine tonight, Spearshaker. You made the People happy. They have a hard life, and you made them laugh."

He made a snorting sound. "Yes. They laughed to see us making fools of ourselves. Perhaps that is good."

"No, no." I saw it now. "Is that what you think? That they laughed because we did the plei so badly?"

I put my hand on his shoulder and turned him to face me. "My friend, no one there tonight ever saw a plei before, except for you. How would they know if it was bad? It was certainly the best plei they ever saw."

He blinked slowly, like a turtle. I saw his eyes were red.

"Believe me, Spearshaker," I told him, "they were laughing because it was such a funny story. And that was your doing."

His expression was very strange indeed. "They thought it comical?"

"Well, who wouldn't? All those crazy people up there, killing each other—and themselves—and then that part at the end, where everyone gets killed!" I had to stop and laugh, myself, remembering. "I tell you," I said when I had my breath back, "even though I knew the whole thing by memory, I nearly lost control of myself a few times there."

I got up. "Come, Spearshaker. You need to go to sleep. You have been working too hard."

But he only put his head down in his hands and made some odd sounds in his throat, and muttered some words I did not know. And so I left him there and went to bed.

If I live until the mountains fall, I will never understand white men.

> If I liue vntil our *Saviour's* returne, I shall neuer vnderstande *Indians*. Warre they count as Sport, and bloody Murther an occasion of Merriment: 'tis because they hold Life itselfe but lightly, and think Death no greate matter neyther: and so that which we call Tragick, they take for Comedie. And though I be damned for't, I cannot sweare that they haue not the Right of it.

Whatever happened that night, it changed something in Spearshaker. He lived with us for many more years, but never again did he make a *plei* for us.

That was sad, for we had all enjoyed the Amaledi story so much, and were hoping for more. And many people tried to get Spearshaker to change his mind—Tsigeyu actually begged him; I think it was the only time in her life she ever begged anyone for anything—but it did no good. He would not even talk about it.

And at last we realized that his medicine had gone, and we left him in peace. It is a terrible thing for a *didahnvwisgi* when his power leaves him. Perhaps his ancestors' spirits were somehow offended by our *plei*. I hope not, since it was my idea.

That summer Ninekiller's daughter Cricket became Spearshaker's wife. I gave them my house, and moved in with the Paint Clan woman. I visited my friend often, and we talked of many things, but of one thing we never spoke.

Cricket told me he still made his talking marks, from time to time. If he ever tried to make another *plei*, though, he never told anyone.

I believe it was five winters ago—it was not more—when Cricket came in one day and found him dead. It was a strange thing, for he had not been sick, and was still a fairly young man. As far as anyone knew there was nothing wrong with him, except that his hair had fallen out.

I think his spirit simply decided to go back to his native land.

Cricket grieved for a long time. She still has not taken another husband. Did you happen to see a small boy with pale skin and brown hair, as you came through our town? That is their son Wili.

Look what Cricket gave me. This is the turkey feather that was in Spearshaker's hand when she found him that day. And this is the piece of mulberry bark that was lying beside him. I will always wonder what it says.

> We are such stuff as Dreames are made on: and our little Life Is rounded in a sle

NOTES

1 Elizabethan spelling was fabulously irregular; the same person might spell the same word in various ways on a single page. Shakespeare's own spelling is known only from the Quarto and Folio printings of the plays,

and the published poetry; and no one knows how far this may have been altered by the printer. It is not even known how close the published texts are to Shakespeare's original in wording, let alone spelling. All we have in his own hand is his signature, and this indicates that he spelled his own name differently almost every time he wrote it.

I have followed the spelling of the Folio for the most part, but felt free to use my own judgment and even whim, since that was what the original speller did.

I have, however, regularized spelling and punctuation to some extent, and modernized spelling and usage in some instances, so that the text would be readable. I assume this book's readership is well-educated, but it seems unrealistic to expect them to be Elizabethan scholars.

2 Cherokee pronunciation is difficult to render in Roman letters. Even our own syllabary system of writing, invented in the nineteenth century by Sequoyah, does not entirely succeed, as there is no way to indicate the tones and glottal stops. I have followed, more or less, the standard system of transliteration, in which "v" is used for the nasal grunting vowel that has no English equivalent.

It hardly matters, since we do not know how sixteenth-century Cherokees pronounced the language. The sounds have changed considerably in the century and a half since the forced march to Oklahoma; what they were like four hundred years ago is highly conjectural. So is the location of the various tribes of Virginia and the Carolinas during this period; and, of course, so is their culture. (The Cherokees may not then have been the warlike tribe they later became—though, given the national penchant for names incorporating the verb "to kill," this is unlikely.) The Catawbas were a very old and hated enemy.

3 Edward Spicer's voyage to America to learn the fate of the Roanoke Colony—or rather his detour to Virginia after a successful privateering operation—did happen, including the bad weather and the loss of a couple of boats, though there is no record that any boat reached the mainland. The disappearance of the Roanoke colonists is a famous event. It is only conjecture—though based on considerable evidence, and accepted by many historians—that Powhatan had the colonists murdered, after they had taken sanctuary with a minor coastal tribe. Disney fantasies to the contrary, Powhatan was not a nice man.

4 I have accepted, for the sake of the story, the view of many scholars that Shakespeare first got the concept of *Hamlet* in the process of revising Thomas Kyd's earlier play on the same subject. Thus he might well have had the general idea in his head as early as 1591—assuming, as most do, that by this time he was employed with a regular theatrical company—even though the historic *Hamlet* is generally agreed to have been written considerably later.

5 As to those who argue that William Shakespeare was not actually the author of *Hamlet*, but that the plays were written by Francis Bacon or the Earl of Southampton or Elvis Presley, one can only reply: *Hah!* And again, *Hah!*

echoes

ALAN BRENNERT

Alan Brennert was beginning to make a reputation for himself in the genre in the seventies as a writer of finely crafted short stories, but then he was lured away by Hollywood. Since then, he has served as executive story consultant on The Twilight Zone *during its recent television revival, has written teleplays for* China Beach, The Mississippi, *and* Darkroom, *and has twice been nominated for the Writers Guild Award. He's also published two novels,* Kindred Spirits *and* Time and Chance. *In spite of all this, he still finds time for the occasional short story, which show up from time to time in* The Magazine of Fantasy & Science Fiction, Pulphouse, *and elsewhere. His short fiction has been collected in* Her Pilgrim Soul and Other Stories *and in* Ma Qui and Other Phantoms, *which includes his Nebula Award-winning "Ma Oui." His story "The Third Sex" appeared in our Seventh Annual Collection.*

In the lyrical and bittersweet story that follows, he shows us that just as sometimes people can't see the forest for the trees, so sometimes you might not be able to hear the music for the echoes. . . .

Even now, I can't bring myself to blame my parents. They had their reasons; they carried scars from their own childhoods. My father's father was a manic-depressive, his mood swings legendary, the household perpetually caught between the thunder of his passions and the gray spaces of his despair. My father, when he married, longed for a house filled with music and a little girl's laughter; and naturally he wanted to ensure that his daughter didn't inherit her grandfather's affliction. Back in the eighties, when my father was growing up, they hadn't yet mapped the gene that causes bipolar disorder, much less figured out how to mask it; if only it had stopped at that. My mother, for her part, had had an idyllic childhood, perhaps too much so: something of a musical prodigy, she had spent fifteen happy years in violin recitals, only to discover that youthful virtuosity doesn't necessarily mature into adult genius. Having bitterly learned the limits of her own talent, she was determined that her daughter would know no limits.

And so I was conceived—an appropriate term, I think, since I (and thousands like me) began more as a concept than a person, a set of parameters later realized in flesh. We were an affluent family with a home in Reston, a tony suburb in northern Virginia, but even for an affluent couple gene enhancement is not a cheap proposition, and I was to have no brothers or sisters. But my parents got their money's worth. By the age of four—as soon as I had the necessary hand strength for the piano—I was picking out complex melodies I'd heard on the radio. I had, have, an eidetic memory, and as soon as I learned to read music, I discovered I could sight-read virtually anything that was put in front of me—taking in a page at a glance, then playing it effortlessly. Eighty percent of so-called musical genius is just this facility to sight-read, a lucky fluke of memory; but of course in my case, luck played no part in it.

The other twenty percent is technique, and I had that as well. By the age of seven I was playing Bach, the piece he'd written for his own daughter, the *Anna Magdalena Notebook*; by eight, his *Two-Part Inventions*; by nine, I had mastered the more challenging parts of Bartók's *Mikrokosmos*. I kept a busy schedule: music lessons twice a week, two hours of practice each day, the occasional student recital, a normal load of schoolwork. But I enjoyed it, I truly did. I loved music; loved making music. Of course it's true that I was quite literally born to love it, shaped not just genetically but by early exposure to music, the "hard wiring" of my sensory cortex that locked in my musical skills; at times I wonder if my passion is less real for that, but the sweet melancholy that grips me as I play the Adagio from Marcello's *Concerto in D minor*, the serenity I feel when performing Debussy's *Image*, these are real emotions, regardless of whether genetic conduits were laid to channel them.

Who knows? Perhaps even the degree of my obsession with music was predetermined, manipulated. That might explain my single-minded attention to it in my earliest years (when I most needed such single-mindedness), forsaking the company of other children my age; I was almost twelve before I had the first hint of something missing from my life, and by then it was a little late to acquire the social skills others had learned as a matter of course. I had a few acquaintances at school, I was no pariah, but playmates? Not really. Confidants? Hardly. At three o'clock each afternoon, as my classmates scattered to local playgrounds or shopping malls, I was somehow left behind, like a stone in the heart of a leaf storm, too heavy to take flight. I wandered home to practice, or speed-read novels in the woods near Lake Audubon, taking in pages as though I were drawing breaths, with no more real understanding of the life I was reading about than my lungs understood the oxygen they took in.

On one such afternoon, autumn light waning around me, I lay on my stomach on a fan of oak leaves, reading a book and listening to Rachmaninoff on my laser chip, when I heard a boy's voice behind me say, "Hi."

Startled, I sat up and turned around. There was a boy, about my age, sitting up against the thick trunk of a maple tree, big floppy sketch pad—orange cover, cream-colored pages—propped up on his knees. Like me, he had fair skin and dark hair, but he was about half a head taller than I. There was something vaguely familiar about him; I wondered if I hadn't seen him in school.

"Hi," I said. I hadn't heard him approach, and I was sure he hadn't been sitting there when I lay down, ten minutes before. But I was so pleased to be talking to someone—that someone was talking to *me*—that I didn't give it a further thought.

He smiled, a friendly enough smile. "My name's Robert."

I might have been lonely, but I was still shy; I took a cautious step toward him. "I'm Katherine. Kathy."

"You live around here?"

I nodded. "On Howland Drive."

"Yeah?" His eyes brightened. "Me too."

So that was it. I must have seen him on our street. Feeling a little less reticent, I nodded toward his sketch pad. "Can I see?"

"Sure." He angled the pad so I could get a better look, as I sat down beside him. The top page was a lovely pencil sketch of the surrounding woods, exhibiting (I can say today) a very sophisticated understanding of perspective, light, shadow.

But being twelve years old and knowing nothing of any of this, all I said was, "Wow."

That was enough. He beamed. "Thanks," he said. He flipped through the book, showing me other sketches, some still-lifes, a few portraits, all of them excellent.

"Do you go to school for this?" I asked.

"I take lessons."

"Me too." I added, "Piano."

"Yeah? Cool."

He flipped to a portrait of a girl with blonde hair and big eyes, and I let out a little yelp of recognition. "Cindy Lennox!" I cried out. "You know Cindy, too?"

"Yeah, sure, I go to school with her."

He flipped past Cindy's portrait to a fresh piece of paper, began absently sketching as he talked. "I'm getting a paint-box for Christmas," he announced, "half the size of this pad, with its own hard drive, oil and watercolor templates . . . man, the stuff you can do with one of those, it's incredible!"

Not to be outdone, I said, "I'm getting a new orchestral sequencing program for my MusicMaster. I'll be able to add up to fifteen different voices—strings, horns, keyboard—"

He looked up from his sketch and smiled, as though something had just occurred to him. "You're one too, aren't you?" he said.

"One what?"

His smile took on a secret edge. "You know. When the doctors do something to you, before you're even born?"

Suddenly I felt afraid. I knew exactly what he meant, of course; it was all over the media, there was even a website about it on the Schoolnet. Some parents even took their kids on TV and talked about it; but most, like mine, kept quiet, fearing that their children would be discriminated against, excluded from scholastic or talent competition (though this was technically illegal) with non-enhanced kids.

I knew what I was, but had sworn to my parents I'd never talk to *anyone* about it. So reflexively I shot back, "Not me."

"Yeah, sure." He sounded unconvinced, and I must admit, the idea of actually meeting someone else like myself thrilled as well as frightened me.

So without admitting anything about myself, I said, "So you're one?"

He nodded, switching pencil colors, continuing to sketch. "My folks'd kill me if they heard, but I don't care. I'm not ashamed of it." He looked up; gave me a little smile. "Are you?"

This was getting dangerous. I stood up quickly. "I—I've gotta go."

"Don't you want to see your picture?"

"My what?"

He turned the pad around, showing me its face: my face. A rough outline, without much detail, only two colors (dark gray and light blue), but a really good likeness. My dark hair, cut in a short pageboy; my lips, which always seemed to me too thin, pursed in a shy little half-smile; my eyes, the irises a light blue, so light my father once told me he could see the sky in them . . .

"That's really good," I said, impressed. "Can I—"

I looked up at him . . . and my breath caught in my chest.

"What is it?" he said, sensing my distress. I didn't answer. I was looking in his eyes—the irises a light blue; very light. He said something else, and I didn't really hear it; I was watching his lips as he spoke . . .

"Kathy?" I finally heard him say. "What is it, what's wrong?"

"Nothing," I lied. But inside I felt strange, as though I had discovered something I shouldn't have—like turning over a rock and finding nightcrawlers underneath. Something similar squirmed inside me when I looked at Robert. I told him I had to go home and practice my piano; he seemed disappointed, started to get up, but I was well on my way before he could suggest walking back together.

Later, playing alone on the swing set in my backyard, I realized I had turned my back on someone who might've become my first real friend, and the rush of the wind blew my tears back into my eyes, and I thought I would drown in my own regret.

I didn't dare tell my parents about Robert, of course—I was afraid they wouldn't believe that I hadn't actually told him anything about myself. I kept a cautious eye out for him at school, but never caught so much as a glimpse of him, which I thought strange, considering the size of the school. Finally, consumed by equal parts anxiety and need, I went up to Cindy Lennox one day in the cafeteria and said, "I met a friend of yours the other day. He said his name was Robert."

She looked blank. "Who?"

"Well, I don't know his last name, but he did a sketch of you. He's an artist?"

She just shook her head. "I don't know any artists named Robert."

I felt like an idiot. I stammered out something, *guess I'm mistaken sorry bye*, and quickly got out of there. I resolved to forget about Robert entirely; he gave me the creeps, why did I even care who he was?

I went home, my mother took me to my Thursday session with my piano instructor, Professor Laangan, and I gladly lost myself in Chopin and Bach for the next hour. When I got home I banged out of the house, into the backyard, intending to play on the swing set until dinnertime—

But there was someone already on the swing.

Not Robert; a girl. I stopped short. Her back was to me; all I saw was a dark brown ponytail bobbing behind her as she swung.

On *my* swing. In *my* backyard!

"Excuse me?" I said. That startled her. She jumped off; turned around to face me, hands indignantly on hips.

"What are you doing in my yard?" she demanded.

As before, I couldn't answer. I was so stunned, I couldn't even speak.

I was staring . . . at myself.

Me but not-me: her hair longer, ponytail arcing like a whip behind her, and though her features were identical to mine, I was seeing them configured in a way I never had before—thin lips twisted in a sneer, sky-blue eyes flashing with annoyance, head cocked at a haughty little angle. "*Well?*" she said petulantly.

Finally I found my voice, even if it did crack a little: "This—this is *my* yard."

She took a few steps toward me, hands still on her hips, a certain swagger in her walk. "Oh, is it now?"

I stepped back, a reflex. She smiled, sensing that she had the advantage. "Look," she said slowly, "you're obviously not very bright, so it *really* wouldn't be fair of me, with a 200 I.Q., to take advantage, but . . . oh, what the heck. This is your yard, so, ipso facto, *you* must be . . . Katherine Brannon?"

I couldn't stop staring at her. It was like looking into a mirror, but having your reflection suddenly start mouthing off at you. I was silent long enough that she said, "*Hello?* Can you at least pre*tend* to some intelligence? Especially if you're trying to impersonate the winner of the Fairfax County Scholastic—"

I didn't care what she'd won; I'd had enough of this little brat. "I *live* here!" I shouted suddenly, and was pleased to see her flinch. "I don't care who *you* think you are, this is *my* house!"

Those crystal blue eyes, my eyes, were transparent with hatred. "We'll just see about that," she said coldly, then turned on her heel—and ran toward the house. I'd left the back door open; she ran through it and out of sight. I raced in after her, through the kitchen and into the living room, where my father was just sitting down to watch the news.

"Where *is* she?" I yelled, breathless. He blinked.

"Where is who? And why are you yelling, young lady?"

"The girl! The one who ran in! The one with—" I almost said, *The one with my face,* but wisely didn't take it that far.

"The only girl running in here," my mother said, coming up behind me, "is you."

It was true. I searched my bedroom, the family room, even the kitchen again; the girl was gone. Shaken, pressed by my parents for answers, I told them I was just pretending; made it seem as though I were chasing an imaginary playmate. And as I lay in bed that night, I almost convinced myself of the same thing; that my imagination—and loneliness—had conjured up my strange nemesis. I went to school resolved to try and overcome my shyness, to make more friends somehow—to find the time, between lessons and practice, to do the normal things other girls did.

In the cafeteria at lunchtime, I noticed a new girl with long, silky blonde hair sitting alone at a table, eating her macaroni and cheese. Screwing up my nerve, I marched right over and introduced myself.

"Hi," I said. "You're new, aren't you?"

The girl shook aside her long shock of hair, looked up, and smiled at me.

"Yes," she said, shyly pleased, "I just transferred over from public."

And once again, I was looking into my own eyes.

Involuntarily I cried out, a yelp of shock and fear. This instantly made me the focus of all attention in the cafeteria, which distracted me just long enough to look away from the blonde girl, the blonde *me*, for a moment . . . and when I looked back, she was gone.

I spent the rest of the lunch hour feeling the eyes of my classmates on me, like sunlight focused through a magnifying glass; their whispers, their little sniggers, were even worse, each a tiny dagger in my back. When the bell rang, I greeted it as a deliverance; but what it delivered me into turned out to be far worse.

During math period a male version of me—not Robert but another boy with my eyes, lips, nose—looked up periodically from his desk, rattled off the solution to an equation as though he had a calculator in his head, then went back to scribbling on an electronic notepad. No one else seemed to notice him, and I kept silent, biting my lip, my hands trembling the whole hour.

In English I glanced up from my own notescreen to find the blonde Kathy (she signed it *Kathi*) standing before the class, reciting an essay—even as my teacher, Mrs. McKinnon, simultaneously lectured us on the proper use of participles. I sat there, the two voices clashing in my head—trying to drown them out with my thoughts, a memory of the bombastic third movement of Hindemith's *Mathis der Maler*—praying for the blonde me to shut up and sit down . . .

In gym class a taller, lither version of myself straddled the parallel bars like a budding Olympian gymnast; she swung her perfectly proportioned legs up, up, up, balanced herself for several moments in a perfect handstand, then swung down and vaulted off the bars. And watching her amazing balance, her strength, her grace, I felt the first shameful pang of what was to become a familiar envy . . .

By the end of the day, as I hurried out of the building, they were everywhere: the bratty Katherine (Katja, she called herself) was holding court by the stairwell, her mocking laugh at someone's expense echoing through the corridor; in the music room one version of me played the violin, as another practiced the flute; in shop class Robert was making a wooden horse from soft balsa, touching the edge of its mane to a spinning lathe.

I hurried home, but to my horror they were all following me, a procession of Katherines, male and female, tall and short, dark and blonde and everything in between—all laughing or talking, bouncing balls or hefting schoolbooks, a phantom regiment haunting my every step. I ran the last several blocks, ran into the imagined safety of my home, crying *"Mommy! Daddy!"* but this was no refuge either: as I burst into the living room I heard a voice, *my voice*, raised in song, saw myself standing by the piano, practicing the scales with a perfect pitch I didn't possess; saw too a red-haired Kathy with sculpted nose, green eyes, and full lips, talking endlessly on the phone; saw a tomboy Kathy bang in in torn jeans and T-shirt, yelling for Mom—

It took me a moment to realize that I was screaming *Shut up! Shut up! SHUT UP!* at the top of my voice, shouting *Mommy! Daddy! Make them go AWAY*, and as I fell sobbing to the floor I saw my mother, her face ashen, stumbling as she rushed toward me—and then she was holding me, rocking me, and for one terrible moment I wasn't even sure, I didn't *know*, which one of us she really held . . .

The hospital came as a relief. I didn't know why at the time, but the number of other Katherines dwindled from dozens to a handful, and the more radically different ones—boys; blondes; gymnasts—didn't appear at all. The ones that did appear (and that was the correct word: as I lay in bed, staring into space, I saw them walk into the room as through a fold in the air, then exit, minutes or hours later, in the same way) all looked pretty much like me, and all looked just about as screwed up, as well. One sat in a corner and cried for what seemed hours on end; one angrily pounded her fists on the door and screamed obscenities; another tore a small piece of loose metal from the bed frame, entered the toilet, and never came out—I stayed out of the bathroom for hours, my bladder bursting, terrified at what I might find in there.

Seeing these terrible alternatives, ironically enough, was the best thing for me: determined not to end up like any of them, I didn't let my fear turn to panic, or hysteria. I stayed calm when the doctors asked me questions, I told them everything I'd seen and continued to see; they responded gravely and not, oddly enough, condescendingly. Almost all doctors treat children as though they're not merely young but retarded as well; yet here were a bunch of adults soberly asking me questions as if I too were an adult: "What were the differences, physically, between the boy you met in the woods and the boy in math class?" "Did all of the other Katherines call themselves that, or did they use other names?"

Their matter-of-factness helped to keep me calm; even encouraged me, when they asked if I was seeing anyone at the moment, to shrug and say, "Oh, sure. There's one sitting in the corner right now." And I'd swear I saw one of them glance, ever so slightly, into the corner of the room, then quickly back again.

Each of my parents blamed the other for what had happened: my father accused my mother of working me into a state of nervous exhaustion, and my mother, hurt, shot back that there was no mental illness on *her* side of the family. I heard all this late one night when they thought I was asleep; heard also my father's wounded silence, pregnant with guilt and fear that perhaps his father's legacy hadn't been extinguished, after all.

But as it turned out there was more than enough guilt to pass around. When the doctors finished their examination and sat down to talk to my parents (though I didn't learn this until years later) their first question was, "Is she gene-enhanced?" Apparently this sort of "psychotic break," as they called it, was not uncommon among the genetically enhanced—one in every ten children suffered under some similar kind of delusional system, the onset usually just before puberty. They didn't know why; all they could do was study the pathology and hope to understand it. The good news was, most children, with therapy, could learn to distinguish between reality and delusion. Would my parents agree to place me in out-patient therapy, as part of a study group?

Of course they agreed. The choices they'd made for me, for my life, now came back to haunt them; and where once they had dreamed for me a life far above normal, now they prayed it would be merely, blessedly, normal.

My favorite of the doctors was Dr. Carroll, a prematurely gray woman in her late thirties; she came after the first round of interrogators, and immediately endeared herself to me by bringing me a set of flowered barrettes for my hair. "They're my daughter's," she said, "but I thought you might appreciate them more, just now, and she was happy to let you have them." I was wearing drab green hospital gowns most of the time; the pink and purple barrettes were a welcome reminder of the outside world, and I beamed as I slipped them into my hair.

"Thanks," I said, adding, "How old is your daughter?"

"A little older than you—about thirteen." She looked at my reflection in the small vanity mirror and smiled. "You look very pretty."

I automatically shook my head. "Not me. I'm not pretty."

"I think you are. Why don't you?"

Dr. Carroll's talent for making therapy seem like gentle conversation put me at my ease, and her calm attitude toward my starkest fears made those fears seem somehow surmountable. At first we talked only about music, and school, and all the normal self-image problems any girl my age would have; it wasn't until our fifth session together that she asked me if I saw any other Katherines in the room just then.

I glanced over at the window, where the Screamer, as I called her, was pounding on the thick leaded glass, shouting "Fuck! Fuck! Fuck!" over and over. I told this to Dr. Carroll (though I didn't repeat the F-word), wondering if she believed me.

She nodded, but instead of pursuing it she looked at me very seriously and said, "You're a very special young lady, Katherine. You know all about that, don't you?"

I hesitated, not admitting anything, but she went on as though I had:

"Well, sometimes special people see special things. Things other people don't see. That doesn't mean those things aren't real. It doesn't mean that you're wrong, or crazy, for seeing them."

It was the first time anyone had used the word *crazy* to my face, though not the first time it had occurred to me. Tears sprang to my eyes. "I'm not?" I said in a small, unbearably hopeful voice.

She shook her head. "I can't tell you these things you see will ever go away. But I can help you to live with them."

"But who *are* they?" I asked, desperate for answers. "Where do they *come* from?"

She paused. "We're not sure yet. We have some ideas, but we can't talk about them to your parents because that's all they are right now, just ideas. But . . ."

She put a fingertip, lightly, to my lips; smiled. "Can you keep a secret, Kathy? Our secret, yours and mine. Not for your mom or dad, or your best friend, or anyone?"

I nodded eagerly.

"You're a little too young to understand it all," she said, "but think of them as . . . echoes. Like when you call out in the woods, and hear your own voice bounce back at you? That's all they are. And they can't hurt you."

"Are they real?"

"Not in the way you are," she said. "How can I—?" She stopped, thought a moment, then smiled. "Hold out your left hand," she instructed.

I held out my left hand. "Keep it there," she said. "Now. Look around. Do you see any other echoes?"

I looked around the room. The Screamer was still there, of course, and the sobbing girl, and . . .

I gasped.

Sitting next to me on the bed was another echo—a perfect echo, in fact, dressed just like me, the flowered barrettes in exactly the same places, identical in appearance, except . . . she was holding out her *right* hand.

"What do you see?" the doctor asked. I told her. When I turned back, the echo was gone.

And I began to understand, however vaguely, what the echoes truly were . . .

I went home about two weeks later, and though the number of echoes increased when I did, they no longer terrified me the way they had; with Dr. Carroll's help—mainly concentration techniques—I was able to reduce them to the level of background noise, like a television set accidentally left on. And I began noticing other things about them: how some echoes looked as real, as three-dimensional, as I did; how others seemed curiously flat, like watercolors painted on the air; how still others were vague, hazily defined, flickering in and out of existence as though their purchase on reality was tenuous at best. As the years passed and my vocabulary increased, my ability to describe what I saw increased with it—and I dutifully reported everything to Dr. Carroll.

I returned to school, but found that my absence had only made things worse for me there; word had gotten out that I'd checked into a hospital, and though "nervous exhaustion" may be relatively value-neutral for adults, for children it is one more way to set someone apart. My classmates—some of them—would call out to me in the hallway, "Hey, Nervous!" Or, "Hey, Nervie!" If I objected, got angry, they just made a bigger deal of it: "Hey, Nervie, take it easy! Don't wanna go back to the bughouse!" All I could do was ignore them as best I could; if I could ignore the echoes, I told myself, I could ignore anything.

But even the classmates who didn't actively torment me shied away from me, and my loneliness went from tolerable to profound. I didn't mention it to my parents on the reasonable and usually accurate assumption that parents only made things like this worse; I stuck it out until I moved on into high school, where I thought I could melt unobtrusively into a larger student body, and where—amid the normal quotient of violence, drugs, and gangs—I hoped a week in a mental hospital was hardly worth mentioning. But there were still those who remembered, still those who took delight in harassing me; my only solace was my music, and my only friend, Dr. Carroll.

Most if not all of my echoes made the transition to high school with me; but the majority, luckily, seemed to take no notice of me—they walked, talked, laughed, and moved like images on a movie screen that just happened to be the world. A few, like Robert, continued to interact with me occasionally. Sometimes they would try to do this in the middle of a class, and I had to do my best to not react, to keep my expression stony. They never seemed to appear during my piano lessons with Professor Laangan, and I finally realized why: there was only one piano in my instructor's home, and while I was sitting at it, I couldn't see any of the echoes who were doubtless occupying that same space. On occasion, however, I heard snatches of melody, other hands fingering other keys in some other reality: some not as well as I, some just as well, and some, to my great annoyance, better than I.

On rare occasions, an echo found me alone, as on one overcast day in March, as I walked home from school to find a smiling Robert pacing me, paint-box tucked under one arm.

"Hi," he said. I looked around. There was no one else on the street; it didn't much matter if I answered him or not. Perhaps it was a mark of my loneliness that I *wanted* to answer him.

"Hi," I said. Like me, Robert was entering puberty, but unlike me, it seemed to agree with him. I was a slow starter, short and flat where my classmates were growing taller and rounder. Robert was going through a normal growth spurt, filling out, becoming more muscular; his voice was deeper too. More and more I felt uncomfortable around him, uncomfortable with the feelings he evoked in me. But I tried to be friendly; I smiled.

"See you got that paint-box for Christmas," I said.

"Yeah, it's great. You get that sequencing program you wanted?"

It had been so long I'd almost forgotten. I nodded. We walked in silence a long moment, then he said, quietly, "I wish we could be together."

I felt suddenly anxious. "I . . . don't think that's possible," I said, picking up my pace just a little.

He thought a moment, then nodded sadly. "Yeah. I guess not," he said. Then he shrugged.

Something occurred to me, then. "Do you . . . see them?" I asked. "The others?"

He looked at me with puzzlement. " 'Others'?"

No; clearly, he didn't. "Never mind," I said. "Well. See you."

I started to veer off the path we'd been sharing—but he reached out, as though to take my hand! I'm sure he couldn't, not really, but I never found out; I flinched, pulled back my hand before he made—or didn't make—contact.

He looked hurt. "Do you have to go?"

Something in his eyes, his tone, disturbed me. Suddenly this felt wrong; unnatural.

"I—I'm sorry," I said, turning. I hurried off down the street; he didn't follow, but stood staring after me for what seemed the longest time. I kept walking, head down, and when I finally looked back, he was no longer there, as though the wind itself had taken him.

"Why can they see *me*, but not each other?"

By now most of my sessions with Dr. Carroll resembled physics lessons more than psychotherapy; we would sit in her office and discuss all the books she'd given me, the ones comprehensible to a teenager, and she could now give more sophisticated answers to my questions than she could a few years ago.

"Because you're the observer," she explained. "They're just . . . probability wave functions. You're real; they just have the *potential* to be real." She thought a moment, then added, "Actually, some of them *can* see each other—the ones in your hospital room, the ones who 'split off' from you fairly recently."

"Robert seems awfully real for someone who isn't."

She got up, poured herself a cup of coffee. "Well, some of the echoes had more potential to be real than others. Obviously, at some point your parents seriously considered having a boy, as well as genetically enhancing his artistic skills. The more chance that that 'you' might actually have been born, the more real their echo seems to you."

I shook my head. "I've read all this stuff," I said, "and it seems to me like everybody should have these echoes."

"We probably do," she allowed. "For all we know everyone on Earth may be a nexus of an infinite number of probability lines, with the more likely waves creating artifacts—echoes. More today, maybe, than ever before, with the advent of genetic engineering. Thirty years ago, there were only a limited number of combinations possible from a normal conception; now there are billions."

"So why can *I* see mine, but you can't see yours?"

She sat down at her desk again and sighed.

"Sometimes," she said with a smile, "I think we have as many theories as you have echoes. Köhler draws an interesting analogy. Zygotes grow by cellular pro-liferation—one cell becoming two, two becoming four—and differentiation, that is, some cells become muscle, some nerve, et cetera. Probability waves, the theory goes, proliferate in much the same way—one wave splitting in two, the second differentiating from the first on a quantum level, creating various quantum 'ghosts.' Perhaps you remember the quantum split in the same way the body remembers things on a cellular level. Perhaps the process of enhancement creates some structural change in the brain that enables you to see the echoes."

"In other words," I said, "you don't know."

She shrugged. "We know more than we did when you first came here, but that's only been a few years. Chances are it will be another generation before we have enough—forgive me—enough autopsies to collect a decent amount of data."

I envisioned my body lying inert on a laboratory table, my skull split open like a coconut, scientists studying the ridges of my brain like tea readers. The image stayed with me for days. Sometimes the worst part of my "ability" was that it reminded me too clearly, too consistently, of my origins. My musical talent was all I had, I clung to it desperately, but at times I had to wonder how special, how real, was a talent that had been so carefully graphed, mapped, plotted. I tried not to dwell on it, but it was hard not to; hard to fight off the depressions which took periodic hold of me. And they often came at the worst times.

In March of my senior year my parents, Professor Laangan, and I took the train to New York City, where I auditioned for the Juilliard School. My audition pieces, I had decided, would be Chopin's *Étude in E major*, a prelude and fugue from Bach's *Well-Tempered Clavier*, Elliott Carter's *Piano Sonata*, and my long-time favorite, Alessandro Marcello's *Concerto in D minor*. The Marcello, originally written for oboe and orchestra, I would play in a reduction for piano, but I needed someone to perform the orchestral part of the score (Juilliard had only recently allowed the use of concerti at auditions, but still didn't permit computerized accompaniment), and Professor Laangan had graciously agreed to do so at a second piano. As the train hurtled closer to New York I felt thrilled, energized, terrified—all normal things to be feeling, to be sure. But as I walked into the classroom and faced the panel of three Juilliard instructors, my insecurities surged up inside me. I imagined that they were all looking at me as though they *knew*, as though I bore some stigmata instantly identifying me as a fraud, a genetic cheat (though I told myself that I could hardly be unique in that, here at Juilliard). At the piano I hesitated a long moment, trying to stave off my self-consciousness and fear, unable to look the faculty panel in the eye . . . until Professor Laangan prompted me by clearing his throat, and, unable to put it off any longer, I took a deep breath and launched into the *Étude*. As soon as I began playing, thank God, my fears vanished. I was no longer a gene freak, I was no longer even Kathy Brannon, I was the instrument of this music, the medium through which it came to life two centuries after it was written, and that was enough.

After Chopin came Bach, and after Bach, the complex counterpoint of Carter's *Sonata*; and then Professor Laangan took his place at a second piano, and together we began the concerto. I had played the others well enough, I knew, but this piece was different; this I felt deeply, and as I played, I understood for the first time why it held such special attraction for me. As I played the first movement, the Andante with its sweep and eloquence, its sometimes breathless pace, it seemed to represent all the promise and impatience of youth—my promise, the promise that my parents had instilled in me. I segued into the second movement, that sense of bright expectation replaced by the slow, haunting strains of the Adagio, at once lyrical and sad—mirroring the turns my own life had taken, the shifting harmonies sounding to me like the raised voices of ghosts, of echoes. And finally the third movement, the Presto, returning to the faster pace of the first—lighter of heart, a structure to it that seemed to promise a calmer, more ordered existence. No wonder I loved it; I was living it.

When I finished the instructors smiled and thanked me, impossible to read their expressions, but I didn't care—I knew I had done well, that I had exhibited both technique and feeling, and, more importantly, that I had done the best I was capable of. My parents, the professor, and I celebrated with an early dinner at Tavern on the Green, then took the 7:00 train back to Washington; and as the train cleaved the darkness around us, I felt as happy, as secure, as I had ever felt.

The feeling, of course, did not last long. I returned to school the next day, where I was judged—where I judged myself—on a different standard. Ever the outsider, I would walk alone from class to class, but all around me—in the halls, on the grounds, in the cafeteria—my echoes walked and talked and laughed with unseen others: friends I could not see, friends I would never know. Blonde Kathi was now a cheerleader, always laughing, always surrounded (I imagined) by hordes of well-wishers; I watched her flirt with unseen admirers and I wondered how she found the courage, I longed to do the same. Another echo, a flautist, walked by in her band uniform, nodding and talking to other (invisible) band members, and I coveted that uniform, the solidarity it represented; there was no place for a pianist in a high school band, and no time for me to learn another instrument. Even bratty, bitchy Katja seemed to have friends, God knew how; what was so wrong with *me*?

At night, as I lay in bed, it became harder and harder to ignore the echoes swarming in the darkness. The red-haired Kathy with perfect, genetically sculptured features undressed by my wardrobe closet, casting no reflection in the mirrored door, but I saw every perfect curve of her body outlined in the moonlight: full breasts where mine had barely budded, baby fat long gone, wavy hair cascading down her back. I looked away. The gymnast, tall and lithe, was doing yoga at the foot of my bed; she moved with grace and assurance, with a serene confidence in her body and herself that I lacked, that I envied. Glancing away, I caught a flickering glimpse of a male echo—not Robert or the mathematician but another boy, a football player I think—taking off his clothes. His image was vague and tenuous—a more remote potential for existence, I suppose—but I could still make out his wide shoulders, his muscled torso, thick penis hanging like a rope between his legs, and in a way I envied him too, his apparent strength, his male power. Sometimes it felt as though I lacked any power over my life, and he—and the gymnast, and the redhead—seemed to have so much strength, so much confidence. It wasn't fair. Any of them could have been me, I could have been them, *it wasn't fair*.

Dr. Carroll tried to convince me that I couldn't, shouldn't compare myself to the echoes; you can't hold yourself up, she said, to every infinite possibility, every unrealized ambition. I knew she was right, but I was feeling particularly insecure; it had been weeks since my audition in New York, and still no word from Juilliard. I told her I was afraid I might not get in, she assured me I would . . . and then, after a moment's hesitation, she added, "And even if you don't, there are other ways you can use your gifts."

I nodded; sighed. "I know. There are plenty of colleges with fine music departments around, but *Juilliard*—"

"I didn't mean your music," she said. "I meant your other gift."

I blinked, not understanding at first; I hardly thought of it as a *gift*. "What do you mean?" I asked, a bit warily.

She shrugged. "You have a unique skill, Kathy. You see possibilities. I know for a fact that there are others, with the same ability, who've put that talent to work."

I had no idea what she was talking about.

"In research," she explained. "Think about it. In medical research, for *instance, certain decisions are made in the course of an experiment; combinations of chemicals, of drugs, chains of combinations. Sometimes you work months, years, only to find out it's a dead end.*

"But someone like you—simply by becoming *part of the experiment*—can change all that. You make *one* decision, one we may even know the outcome of in advance—and a whole spectrum of potential outcomes is created, echoes, some of which you may be able to communicate with. You could save weeks or months or years of precious work time, hasten the invention of cures, speed up the pace of science a hundredfold. People's lives might be saved who would otherwise die waiting for drugs to be developed, vaccines created."

It sounded like a sales pitch. I looked at her; my face must have been ashen. I thought of the flowered barrettes she had given me, and knew I would never be able to look at them again in the same way.

I stood up, feeling lost, feeling sick. "I have to go."

Realizing she'd overplayed her hand, Dr. Carroll stood as well. "Kathy—"

"I have to go." And I fairly well ran to the door, not listening to her frantic calls, and I never went back.

That night, the sobbing echo appeared again, crying herself to sleep in a corner of my bed; I lay in the dark, ear plugs a poor insulation from her cries, wanting desperately to take up her lament, to join her in her sad chorus, knowing I could not; I *must* not. As terrible as that night was, I told myself that the Adagio had to end sometime . . . didn't it?

Word came two weeks later: I was accepted to Juilliard. I was ecstatic at the thought. Not just the opportunity to study at the world's most renowned college for the performing arts, but the chance to start fresh in a new city, a new school, where no one knew me and no one would ever call me "Nervie" again. Mother and Father went to New York with me to find me a place to live, no dorm rooms being available in Rose Hall; they were sad to see me leave Virginia, but jubilant that I had (they believed) overcome my "problems" and was "fulfilling my potential"—and their expectations.

After a week of apartment-hunting we finally found a small, unremarkable one-bedroom on West 117th Street, near Columbia University. Once, it had probably been a nice enough neighborhood; now it was somewhere between a funky off-campus environment and a war zone, with gangs, drugs, and street-walkers a stone's throw from my building. My parents were quietly horrified, but as I stood there in the empty flat with its bare floors and scabrous walls, I felt almost delirious with joy: because the flat truly was empty, empty of echoes, of ghosts: for the first time in five years, *I was alone.* Over my parents' reservations I signed a one-year lease, went back to Virginia to pack and ship my belongings, and by summer's end was living in New York, truly "on my own" in a way my family could never comprehend. By moving here, I'd diverged from the paths the echoes were taking; this apartment, this life, was mine, and I had to share it with no one else. Oh, to be sure, once or twice I caught a glimpse of some small echo, a left turn instead of a right, a blue dress instead of a white one—but they disappeared quickly, like ripples on water; the worst of them, the Kathis and Katjas and Roberts, I had left well behind me. I rented a small piano, kept it in a place of honor in the living room, and began my new life.

In addition to classes in piano, I took courses in sight-singing and music theory (first semester, harmony; second, counterpoint), and it was in the latter class that I made my first real friend. His name was Gerald: warm eyes, a slightly sardonic smile, blond hair already receding a bit above a high forehead. A violinist, in his second year at Juilliard, I gathered he had already made something of a splash here; we got to talking, he invited me out for coffee after class.

It was evident, just in the way his eyes tracked men more than women as we walked across campus to a coffee shop on 65th Street, that Gerald was gay, and to be honest I was relieved; I had no experience at dating, and the concept was both exciting and daunting. Over coffee, Gerald said he'd like to hear me play, so we found an empty practice room in Rose Hall and I played the Chopin étude I had performed at my audition.

He seemed impressed. "How long have you been playing?" he asked.

"Since I was four."

He raised an eyebrow. "And I thought *I* was a prodigy. My parents started me on a half-size violin when I was five." He smiled, then said, "Why don't we try something together?"

We did—that day and every day for the next week. I was the stodgy traditionalist, Gerald the pop culture maven; in addition to classical pieces we collaborated on Gershwin, Copland, and a lovely violin concerto by the 20th century motion picture composer Miklós Rózsa. Gerald sight-read as quickly as I did, and for a while we tried to one-up each other with increasingly difficult pieces on a cold reading. Gerald didn't bat an eye—which started me wondering about him. I watched him more and more closely as he played—noticing that every once in a while he seemed . . . distracted; his head turning ever so slightly, as though hearing something just beyond his sight. It took me weeks to work up the courage to say something, but finally, over coffee one evening, the café we sat in nearly deserted, I found the nerve:

"Gerald?" My voice was soft, and it trembled a little. "Have you . . . I mean, do you ever . . . hear. Things?"

He looked at me, bemusedly. "Do I—hear? Things?"

I flushed with embarrassment. "Never mind. Forget I said—"

Quickly, he put a hand on mine. "No. It's all right. I . . . think I know what you mean."

My eyes widened. "You do?"

He nodded. As it turned out, I was right: Gerald and I had more in common than we first realized. Like me, he was gene enhanced—but unlike me, he had only partial vision when it came to echoes. "It's like when you look at something bright, a red stop light," he said, "and then you look away, and you see, just for a moment, a spot of green, because green is red's complementary color? That's what it's like for me. Complements, I call them; opposites. I only see them for a moment, and then they're gone."

"Lucky you," I said.

"Actually, I do feel lucky, at times. One of the first 'complements' I ever saw was a 'me' who was—don't ask me how I could tell this; I just *did*—a me who was straight. Not macho, just . . . hetero. I saw him look at something, and somehow I knew he was looking at a woman, and I just knew.

"And I realized, all at once, how fortunate I was. Because the doctors, they've known for years which genes incline us one way or the other, they had to have known which way I'd turn out . . . and my parents didn't 'correct' it, as they could have; as so many parents do these days. And I just felt very fortunate, that my parents—even if they did want a violinist—loved me enough to let me, in this one way at least, be myself."

I smiled, a bit wistfully, but before I could say anything Gerald suddenly leaned in: "Listen," and I could feel him changing the subject, perhaps uncomfortable with all this, "do you know Bach's *Musical Offering?*"

"Of course."

"I'm performing it in recital later this semester." His eyes were bright as he said it. "Me, another violinist, a cellist, a flautist, and a pianist. How'd you like to audition for it?"

If I was disappointed that Gerald was only partly a kindred spirit, I quickly got over it; I was thrilled at the prospect, thrilled even to be asked. I agreed readily, spent the next several days being coached by Gerald; at the audition I competed with several other piano students, all of them quite gifted, but I felt no trepidation or fear: it was refreshing, exhilarating, to be competing with someone other than myself. With Gerald accompanying me on violin, I performed the sonata that was part of the *Offering*—and was stunned and delighted when, the next day, Gerald called to tell me I had, in his words, "gotten the gig"! "Now, of course," he said, deadpan, "we beat you senseless with practice for the next six weeks." I laughed. The only happier moment in my life was the day I was actually accepted to Juilliard.

A week later, another first: Chris, a cute dark-eyed boy in my sight-singing class, actually asked me out on a *date*. I was eighteen years old, ashamed to admit that I had never been on one before, trying to act casual as I said, "Sure. I'd love to." As soon as I got home I called Gerald and asked his advice. "Be yourself," he counseled, "and try not to bump into the furniture." I liked Gerald, but as a confidant he left something to be desired.

Chris took me to the campus Drama Theater, where students from the drama department were staging Edward Albee's *A Delicate Balance*. Chris put a hand gently on my arm as we made our way to our seats; I sat there, excited not just by his presence but by how very normal it all felt—by the prospect that perhaps, after all, I would have a normal life, filled with normal joys and only normal pains. I barely paid attention to the play, and it wasn't until almost the end of the first act—at the entrance of "Harry and Edna," the older couple so shaken with existential fear that they take refuge in their best friends' home—that I sat up and took notice.

Edna walked on stage, timid, fearful—and I gasped.

Edna was me.

Or at least one of them was. The actress portraying Edna in my world, the real world, was a short blonde; but in some other near-reality, *I* was playing the part. This echo was slightly taller than me, her hair somewhat lighter, and her form was translucent, shimmery, in the way I associated with the more remote echoes—separated from me by hundreds if not thousands of other potentialities.

I heard the two actresses' voices transposed on one another, even their bodies occasionally superimposed, and I fought to keep calm when I really wanted to wail with grief, to mourn the loss of my newfound individuality: I'd thought I was alone, thought I had something to call my own, and now—

Tears welled in my eyes and I turned away, terrified to let Chris see. I fell back on old concentration techniques, trying not to watch the echo on stage; luckily it was near the end of the first act, and at intermission I ducked into the ladies' room to compose myself. Hands gripping the sink, I told myself I could not, would not, cry. Steeling myself for the rest of the play, I went back inside the auditorium with Chris . . . but it was even worse than I thought. When the curtain rose on Act Two, it came up on the character of Julia, the daughter . . . and that, too, was me.

A different me; short, plump, familiar features set in a round face, chubby arms waving angrily, in character. Oh, Jesus, I thought; oh, God, no. I managed to keep my despair from showing throughout all of that first scene, but when "Edna" appeared in the middle of the next one—when I saw two echoes of myself strutting about the stage, four different voices playing as though in quad-raphonic stereo—my agitation started to show. Chris couldn't help but notice; I told him I wasn't feeling well, reluctantly we left the show, and in my discom-fort I must have appeared distant and unfriendly, because he took me home, bussed me on the cheek, and never called again.

As I fell asleep that night, the sobbing echo returned for the first time in months, sitting in a corner of my previously untainted apartment—and, from that point on, never left . . .

I should have known; should have realized that my parents' ambitions for me would be so alike in so many other potential realities. In the weeks to come a day did not go by that I did not see at least one echo: Passing a dance class I caught a glimpse of a graceful, poised Katherine (Katrina, the instructor called her) at the ballet barre, dark hair in a chic chignon, long legs pirouetting flaw-lessly to *Swan Lake*, her face almost regal in its serenity. In my sight-singing class I heard my own voice drowned out by another, familiar in some ways but with a perfect pitch and soaring beauty I could never hope for; I saw her out of the corner of my eye, a Katherine who looked much like me but one who used the instrument of her voice better than I did my own piano, and I hated her.

I tried talking to Gerald about what was happening, but sympathetic as he tried to be, his "gift" was nowhere near as developed as mine, he truly didn't understand the full horror of what I was going through, and could offer no advice to help me cope with it. He seemed uncomfortable even talking about it, and after a few attempts I backed off, not wishing to lose a friendship, however flawed.

As I crossed campus one evening, on my way home, I caught a glimpse of Chris, heading alone toward the dormitories. I looked away, hoping he wouldn't see me, then, unable to resist, looked back for one last glance—and this time, he was no longer alone. This time, the air next to him boiled and shimmered with an echo of another Katherine—the dancer, Katrina, no mistaking the long legs, the regal face—her arm looped through his, her mouth open in a laugh. Chris—being in my world, of course—paid no attention to her, and after a few moments the dancer's form rippled and vanished; but I knew that in some other potential reality, another Chris walked with her, laughed with her, and I felt an anger and a compulsion rising within me.

I fell into step behind Chris, at a safe enough distance that he didn't notice. I knew I should turn around, knew I should go home right now, but I couldn't, and as he entered Rose Hall I poked my head in just long enough to determine which room was his. First floor; room six. I circled round the back of the dorm, found the window outside his room; crouched beside a concealing shrub, watched the light snap on inside. Carefully I raised myself up, peering into the window.

Chris was sitting at his desk, a small table lamp spilling light over textbooks and notepad computer. But though he did not realize it, he was not alone in the room. Less than five feet away, on his unmade bed, I saw her: the dancer: her nude body, toned and trim, lying on the sheets, her arms wrapped around something, someone, I could not see, her pelvis jerking back and forth, taking in that someone. She moaned; she cried out his name. *Chris,* she said, *oh, Chris . . .* It was almost comical; it was crushing, horrible. I felt as though I'd been physically struck; I stumbled backwards, gravel crunching noisily underfoot, away from Katrina, but her sighs and the sound of Chris's name seemed to follow me all the way home . . .

That night, the sobbing echo in my apartment slowly stopped crying, falling into a silence I found even more disturbing; she sat in a corner, half-dressed, hair unwashed, staring into space. I tried not to meet her eyes—the irises a flat blue, dimmed by some cataract of spirit—their dead light constantly threatening to pull me in, pull me down . . .

Desperate to perform well at the Bach recital, I practiced as best I could, trying to ignore the echoes of better, more talented Katherines all around me. When the night arrived, I felt a twinge of an old excitement as I walked onto the stage at Alice Tully Hall wearing a simple but elegant white gown, joining an ensemble that included Gerald, another violinist, a flautist, a cellist, and myself.

The *Musical Offering* is a suite of tense, somber beauty, the first ricercare scored in this instance for piano; I played well, I thought, due in no small part to my affinity for the mood of the piece: a lament of sorts, perfectly in keeping with my own mood. We moved from the first ricercare to the canons which followed, my piano playing at times with one or more of the strings, strings and flute together, or not at all (as in the fourth canon, a duet between Gerald and the other violinist). It was during one such moment, as I "sat out" and listened to the other instruments, that I began to hear—faintly but distinctly—the sound of *another* piano. A piano taking the same part the cello was now playing; an echo from a reality in which this piece was arranged differently. The pianist, damn her, was brilliant, the technique letter-perfect. Her vigor and conviction so rattled me that I almost missed my entrance into the next ricercare, probably the most demanding part of the suite for me: I was not only performing it solo, I was playing six melodic lines all at the same time. Difficult under the best of circumstances—but now I heard the echo of that other piano, *my* piano, also performing the ricercare, but ever so slightly time-displaced (my other self having begun the piece moments before I had). The dissonance nearly drove me to distraction; for the next six and a half minutes I struggled to keep my concentration, I felt my gown growing embarrassingly wet with perspiration, and when I finally finished the ricercare I felt not triumph but mere relief—and then disgust, convinced that my performance had suffered for it. I got a bit of a breather in the next three canons, but when we came to the sonata I once more found myself playing, in some strange quantum duet, the same part as my echo—and once again, not playing it as well, the echo's rendering more controlled, the lamentation somehow deeper, truer, than mine. This was perhaps the bitterest pill of all to swallow: though I knew my share of torment, even at that there was someone better.

By the end of the recital I was drained, exhausted beyond anything I had ever known; and though everyone congratulated me on a fine performance, I took no joy in it, and fled home to my apartment, fighting the temptation to cry with sleep.

The next day I did not go to sight-singing class, for fear of hearing the Katherine with perfect pitch and soaring voice. I stayed at home and cranked up my stereo, *Mathis der Maler* again, in a desperate attempt to drown out the faintest whisper of any echoes.

The day after that I didn't go to piano class, terrified I might hear the same Katherine who had outclassed me in the recital. I stayed at home and left the television on all day, trying to fill the apartment with more acceptable ghosts, electronic ghosts, phosphor ghosts.

Gerald called, concerned at my absence from school. I told him that my mother was ill, that I was leaving that afternoon for Virginia, that I might be away for a while. He extended his sympathies and I took them. When he hung up, I switched on my answering machine and never turned it off. My parents left occasional messages and I answered them, keeping the conversations brief, pretending to a hectic schedule I didn't have, rushing off when I could no longer keep up the crushing pretense of normality.

I left the apartment less and less, leaving only to buy groceries and pay the rent. I spent more and more of each day in bed, but, asleep, I seemed not to dream myself but to share the dreams of others: vivid, highly visual dreams filled with color and form, Robert's dreams; pleasant, happy dreams, the inner life of the gorgeous, red-headed Kathy, prosaic but peaceful; jarring, violent dreams of conflict and competition, Katja's dreams; dreams of movement and physicality, the gymnast's dreams. At first I found them disturbing; slowly they became a kind of narcotic, as I realized that through them I could, however briefly and incompletely, *become* my echoes. The redhead's confidence, the gymnast's grace, the ordered geometry of the math major's mind. One moment I'm the football player, reliving the glories of a touchdown, a thirty-yard pass, beer after the game, fast sweaty sex with my girlfriend, my penis swelling inside her; the next moment I'm the singer, hearing/feeling the resonance in my voice, shaping the sound, diaphragm relaxed, the peculiar but satisfying sensation of being my own instrument; a moment later my body is still my instrument but this time I manipulate it not just with voice but with posture, expression, movement, an actress's devices.

I drift from dream to dream, mind to mind, the casual clutter of the actress's thoughts, the laser-sharp focus of Katja's, the passion and discipline of Katrina's, all a welcome respite from me, from *being* me, and more and more I'm *not* me, I'm *them*; I'm only me when I have to be, when my body demands it. Asleep, I feel a pressure in my bladder and reluctantly I wake, dragging myself to the bathroom, relieving myself, sometimes getting something to eat, sometimes not, then returning to bed. This goes on for days; weeks. And then one day, amidst dreams of being smarter, prettier, happier, more talented, I feel my body call and grudgingly answer, padding to the bathroom, doing what's necessary, glancing into the vanity mirror on my way back to bed—

And I stopped, suddenly shaken by what I saw.

The Katherine in the mirror was half-dressed, her hair unruly and unwashed, with a dead light in her flat blue eyes that threatened to pull me in; pull me down. It was the echo who'd first appeared in the hospital, so many years before; who'd lain in a corner of my bed in Virginia and cried her lament of long years; who joined me here, in New York, and whose sobs slowly gave way to silence and gray despair, in her eyes an ancestral memory of my grandfather.

But the echo wasn't sitting in the corner. The echo was in my mirror.

I felt a surge of panic, the first emotion in weeks I hadn't dreamed, hadn't borrowed. I looked desperately around the apartment, hoping I was wrong— hoping to catch a glimpse of the echo, somewhere else in the apartment—but the echo wasn't there.

Of course she wasn't. I'd *become* the echo.

Once, we had been separated by countless other probability lines; other paths, the ones closest to me diverging only slightly, the ones closest to her diverging more. Slowly, subtly, I had traveled from one path to the next, like fingers moving absently from key to key on my piano, drawing closer and closer to her probability line . . . until it became mine. I had made the transition so slowly, so gradually, that I hadn't even realized it was happening.

At first I couldn't accept it. It wasn't true; this couldn't be happening! I raced out of the bedroom into the living room, still hoping, praying, that I might *see* my echo, that *I* wasn't her—

I didn't see her in the living room, of course. But I saw someone else.

I saw a Katherine who looked very much as I had, once: short dark hair, well-groomed, neatly dressed . . . with bright, clear, sky-blue eyes, undimmed by time or pain. She was sitting at the piano, playing the Largo movement from the *Musical Offering*, and for a moment I thought she might have been the echo I'd heard on stage at the recital; but as I got close enough to see her fingers on the keys, close enough to recognize my own style, I knew that she was not.

I looked into her face, and was shocked by what I saw; what I thought I saw.

Contentment? Peace? It had been so long since I had known anything like either, I wasn't sure I recognized them. I tried to think when I had last felt such contentment, and I thought of the day I had moved in here, the joy I'd felt, the promise of a brighter, happier life.

My heart sank. This Kathy, this echo in front of me—*she* had lived that happier life. The life that should have been mine. The probability line *I* should have traveled—but I veered from it, taking a darker path.

My legs gave way beneath me, I dropped to the floor, and I cried. For how long, how many minutes or hours, I can't tell you now. But toward the end of it, as I gave up the grief I'd held for too long, I began to understand something. Something I should have realized years before:

Some of my echoes were the result of chance; but others were a product of choice. I didn't choose to be a musical prodigy—that was determined for me. But *I* had chosen to become what I was now: the sobbing echo. However unwittingly, *I had chosen that*. I had *had* that choice.

And if I had it then—I still did.

I *still* had a choice.

I did. I did.

There is an old, famous experiment—one of the first to imply the existence of probability waves—which I read about in my sessions with Dr. Carroll: Shoot a spray of electrons through two slits in a wall, onto a video screen where their impact can be recorded. The result? An interference pattern from the overlapping waves of electrons. Fine; that much makes sense. But shoot just one electron at a time through a slit, then look later at the cumulative pattern—and you find the identical interference pattern. Impossible, on the face of it: the electrons, having been projected one at a time, haven't actually overlapped. But apparently the thousands of potential electron paths exist, on a quantum level, with the one path the electron actually does travel—and they somehow influence it, limiting the paths the single electron can take.

It took me a long while to realize it, but in a way, I was like that electron: for too long, I allowed the thousands of potential lives I might have led to limit, to proscribe, the life I *was* leading. Seeing the echoes of all I might have been, it was easy to forget that I was not just one of them; that they in fact emanated from me, not simply from that one moment of genetic manipulation but from every moment thereafter as well. Human beings, unlike electrons, have free will—and I soon decided to exert it with a vengeance.

I dropped out of Juilliard and enrolled at a small college in upstate New York, leaving the majority of my quantum ghosts behind in Manhattan. My parents were appalled at the move; even more so when I elected not to major in music, but to keep an open major, at least for a year or two. I took classes in art, in literature, in anthropology, any and all subjects that interested me—and was amazed to discover that I had both an affinity and an aptitude for something outside music. I would never have Robert's artistic skills, but I could, in fact, draw passably well, if only for my own amusement; I might never have the dancer's grace at a ballet barre, but I *could* dance, I was not a hopeless klutz. I might never have the red-haired Kathy's drop-dead, fashion-model looks—but I *was* pretty. I really was.

Because I had been designed from birth to be a musician, I had decided, like the electron, that there was only one path for me to take; and having discovered that that was not the case, I've had a richer, more interesting life than I might otherwise have dreamed. I've climbed mountains in Nepal; I've ridden Irish thoroughbreds in County Monaghan. I've been married, had two children; I've written a sonata for violin and piano for my old friend Gerald, and illustrated a computer-generated children's book for my four-year-old daughter. In my youth, I naively believed that life could be, should be, structured like a concerto; today I know better. I know that life is andante and presto and adagio, all entwined, a fugue of sorts, the promise and the sadness often separated by mere moments, tragedy and serenity not nearly so discrete as I once believed. And I've known my share of both.

Through all of it, my echoes have never been far away: they are not far from me now. Now old like me, they surround me as I write this—one of them also sitting at a computer, not writing but painting; one of them playing a snatch of Gershwin on a flute; another at the piano; still another simply sitting and weeping, over what I am not quite sure. Occasionally, in big cities, I catch glimpses of others: I saw Robert on a street in Dallas and I think he recognized me, throwing me a Cheshire smile before vanishing; I went to the ballet in New York and was surprised to find Katrina performing a ghostly turn as Aurora in *The Sleeping Beauty*, and I felt a surge not of envy but of pride. My echoes are no longer tormentors but friends, and when one of them dies (as, inevitably, they have begun to) I mourn a little, as I would a sister. Each one, to be sure, still represents a different path, a different life. But the joy, the wonder, of it all is this: I have taken one path, but many turns; I was granted one life, but lived many lives. The paths, the roads, may be infinite and beautiful; but the journey is even more so.

DAVID MARUSEK

New writer David Marusek is a graduate of Clarion West. He made his first sale to Asimov's Science Fiction in 1993, and his second sale soon thereafter to Playboy, followed subsequently by more sales to Asimov's and to the British anthology Future Histories. His pyrotechnic novella "We Were Out of Our Minds with Joy" was one of the most popular and talked about stories of 1995; although it was only his third sale, it was accomplished enough to make one of the reviewers for Locus magazine speculate that Marusek must be a big name author writing under a pseudonym. Not a pseudonym, Marusek lives the life of a struggling young writer in a "low-maintenance cabin in the woods" in Fairbanks, Alaska, and I'm willing to bet that his is a voice we'll be hearing a lot more from as we move toward the new century ahead. He has a Web site at http:// www.sff.net/people/david__marusek/.

In the story that follows, he takes us back to the intricate and strange future milieu of "We Were Out of Our Minds with Joy," for a fast-paced tale that warns us that there are dangers in letting an experimental machine servant get to know you too well—although, by God, there are some advantages to it, too. . . .

In 2019, Applied People constructed the first Residential Tower to house its growing army of professionals-for-hire. Shaped like a giant egg in a porcelain cup, APRT 1 loomed three kilometers over the purple soybimi fields of northern Indiana and was visible from both Chicago and Indianapolis. Rumor said it generated gravity. That is, if you fell off your career ladder, you wouldn't fall down, but you'd fly cross-country instead, still clutching your hat and briefcase, your stock options and retirement plan, to APRT 1.

SUMMER 2062

H ere she was in a private Slipstream car, flying beneath the plains of Kansas at 1000 kph, watching a holovid, and eating pretzels. Only four hours earlier in San Francisco, Zoranna had set the house to vacation mode and given it last-minute instructions. She'd thrown beachwear and evening clothes into a bag.

Reluctantly, she'd removed Hounder, her belt, and hung him on a peg in the closet. While doing so, she made a solemn vow not to engage in any work-related activities for a period of three weeks. The next three weeks were to be scrupulously dedicated to visiting her sister in Indiana, shopping for a hat in Budapest, and lying on a beach towel in the South of France. But no sooner had Zoranna made this vow than she broke it by deciding to bring along Bug, the beta unit.

"Where were you born?" Bug asked in its squeaky voice.

Zoranna started on a new pretzel and wondered why Bug repeatedly asked certain questions. No doubt it had to do with its imprinting algorithm. "Take a note," she said, "annoying repetition."

"Note taken," said Bug. "Where were you born?"

"Where do you think I was born?"

"Buffalo, New York," said Bug.

"Very good."

"What is your date of birth?"

Zoranna sighed. "August 12, 1961. Honestly, Bug, I wish you'd tap public records for this stuff."

"Do you like the timbre of Bug's voice?" it said. "Would you prefer it lower or higher?" It repeated this question through several octaves.

"Frankly, Bug, I detest your voice at any pitch."

"What is your favorite color?"

"I don't have one."

"Yesterday your favorite color was salmon."

"Well, today it's cranberry." The little pest was silent for a moment while it retrieved and compared color libraries. Zoranna tried to catch up with the holovid, but she'd lost the thread of the story.

"You have a phone call," Bug said, "Ted Chalmers at General Genius."

Zoranna sat up straight and patted her hair. "Put him on and squelch the vid." A miniature hologram of Ted with his feet on his desk was projected in the air before her. Ted was an attractive man Zoranna had wanted to ask out a couple times, but never seemed able to catch between spousals. By the time she'd hear he was single again, he'd be well into his next liaison. It made her wonder how someone with her world-class investigative skills could be so dateless. She'd even considered assigning Hounder to monitor Ted's availability status in order to get her foot in his door.

When Ted saw her, he smiled and said, "Hey, Zoe, how's our little prototype?"

"Driving me crazy," she said. "Refresh my memory, Ted. When's the Inquisition supposed to end?"

Ted lowered his feet to the floor. "It's still imprinting? How long have you had it now?" He consulted a display and answered his own question. "Twenty-two days. That's a record." He got up and paced his office, walking in and out of the projected holoframe.

"No kidding," said Zoranna. "I've had marriages that didn't last that long." She'd meant for this to be funny, but it fell flat.

Ted sat down. "I wish we could continue the test, but unfortunately we're aborting. We'd like you to return the unit—" He glanced at his display again, "—return Bug as soon as possible."

"Why? What's up?"

"Nothing's up. They want to tweak it some more is all." He flashed her his best PR smile.

Zoranna shook her head. "Ted, you don't pull the plug on a major field test just like that."

Ted shrugged his shoulders. "That's what I thought. Anyway, think you can drop it in a shipping chute today?"

"In case you haven't noticed," she said, "I happen to be in a transcontinental Slipstream car at the moment, which Bug is navigating. I left Hounder at home. The soonest I can let Bug go is when I return in three weeks."

"That won't do, Zoe," Ted said and frowned. "Tell you what. General Genius will send you, at no charge, its Diplomat Deluxe model, preloaded with transportation, telecommunications, the works. Where will you be tonight?"

Something surely was wrong. The Diplomat was GG's flagship model and expensive even for Zoranna. "I'll be at APRT 24," she said, and when Ted raised an eyebrow, explained, "My sister lives there."

"APRT 24 it is, then."

"Listen, Ted, something stinks. Unless you want me snooping around your shop, you'd better come clean."

"Off the record?"

"Fuck off the record. I have twenty-two days invested in this test and no story."

"I see. You have a point. How's this sound? In addition to the complimentary belt, we'll make you the same contract for the next test. You're our team journalist. Deal?" Zoranna shrugged, and Ted put his feet back on the desk. "Heads are rolling, Zoe. Big shake-up in product development. Threats of lawsuits. We're questioning the whole notion of combining belt valet technology with artificial personality. Or at least with this particular personality."

"Why? What's wrong with it?"

"It's too pushy. Too intrusive. Too heavy-handed. It's a monster that should have never left the lab. You're lucky Bug hasn't converted yet, or you'd be suing us too."

Ted was exaggerating, of course. She agreed that Bug was a royal pain, but it was no monster. Still, she'd be happy to get rid of it, and the Diplomat belt was an attractive consolation prize. If she grafted Hounder into it, she'd be ahead of the technology curve for once. "I'm going to want all the details when I get back, but for now, yeah, sure, you got a deal."

After Zoranna ended the call, Bug said, "Name the members of your immediate family and state their relationship to you."

The car began to decelerate, and Zoranna instinctively checked the buckle of her harness. "My family is deceased, except for Nancy."

With a hard bump, the car entered the ejection tube, found its wheels, and braked. Lights flashed through the windows, and she saw signs stenciled on the tube wall, "APRT 24, Stanchion 4 Depot."

"What is Nancy's favorite color?"

"That's it. That's enough. No more questions, Bug. You heard Ted; you're off the case. Until I ship you back, let's just pretend you're a plain old, dumb belt valet. No more questions. Got it?"

"Affirmative."

Pneumatic seals hissed as air pressure equalized, the car came to a halt, and the doors slid open. Zoranna released the harness and retrieved her luggage from the cargo net. She paused a moment to see if there'd be any more questions and then climbed out of the car to join throngs of commuters on the platform. She craned her neck and looked straight up the tower's chimney, the five-hundred-story atrium galleria where floor upon floor of crowded shops, restaurants, theaters, parks, and gardens receded skyward into brilliant haze. Zoranna was ashamed to admit that she didn't know what her sister's favorite color was or, for that matter, her favorite anything. Except that Nancy loved a grand view. And the grandest thing about an APRT was its view. The evening sun, multiplied by giant mirrors on the roof, slid up the sides of the core in an inverted sunset. The ascending dusk triggered whole floors of slumbering biolume railings and walls to luminesce. Streams of pedestrians crossed the dizzying space on suspended pedways. The air pulsed with the din of an indoor metropolis.

When Nancy first moved here, she was an elementary school teacher who specialized in learning disorders. Despite the surcharge, she leased a suite of rooms so near the top of the tower it was impossible to see her floor from depot level. But with the Procreation Ban of 2033, teachers became redundant, and Nancy was forced to move to a lower, less expensive floor. Then, when free-agency clone technology was licensed, she lost altitude tens of floors at a time. "My last visit," Zoranna said to Bug, "Nancy had an efficiency on the 103rd floor. Check the tower directory."

"Nancy resides on S40."

"S40?"

"Subterranean 40. Thirty-five floors beneath depot level."

"You don't say."

Zoranna allowed herself to be swept by the waves of commuters towards the banks of elevators. She had inadvertently arrived during crush hour and found herself pressing shoulders with tired and hungry wage earners at the end of their work cycle. They were uniformly young people, clones mostly, who wore brown and teal Applied People livery. Neither brown nor teal was Zoranna's favorite color.

The entire row of elevators reserved for the subfloors was inexplicably off-line. The marquee directed her to elevators in Stanchion 5, one klick east by pedway, but Zoranna was tired. "Bug," she said, pointing to the next row, "do those go down?"

"Affirmative."

"Good," she, said and jostled her way into the nearest one. It was so crowded with passengers that the doors—begging their indulgence and requesting they consolidate—required three tries to latch. By the time the cornice display showed the results of the destination adjudication, and Zoranna realized she was aboard a consensus elevator, it was too late to get off. Floor 63 would be the first stop, followed by 55, 203, 148, etc. Her floor was dead last.

Bug, she tongued, *this is a Dixon lift!*

Zoranna's long day grew measurably longer each time the elevator stopped to let off or pick up passengers. At each stop the consensus changed, and destinations were reshuffled, but her stop remained stubbornly last. Of the five kinds of elevators the tower deployed, the Dixon consensus lifts worked best for groups of people going to popular floors, but she was the only passenger traveling to the subfloors. Moreover, the consensual ascent acceleration, a sprightly 2.8-g, upset her stomach. *Bug,* she tongued, *fly home for me and unlock my archives. Retrieve a file entitled "cerebral aneurysm" and forward it to the elevator's adjudicator. We'll just manufacture our own consensus.*

This file is out of date, Bug said in her ear after a moment, its implant voice like the whine of a mosquito. *Bug cannot feed obsolete data to a public conveyance.*

Then postdate it.

That is not allowed.

"I'll tell you what's not allowed!" she said, and people looked at her.

The stricture against asking questions limits Bug's functionality, Bug said.

Zoranna sighed. *What do you need to know?*

Shall Bug reprogram itself to enable Bug to process the file as requested?

No, Bug, I don't have the time to reprogram you, even if I knew how.

Shall Bug reprogram itself?

It could reprogram itself? Ted had failed to mention that feature. A tool they'd forgotten to disable? *Yes, Bug, reprogram yourself.*

A handicapped icon blinked on the cornice display, and the elevator's speed slowed to a crawl.

Thank you, Bug. That's more like it.

A jerry standing in the corner of the crowded elevator said, "The fuck, lift?"

"Lift speed may not exceed five floors per minute," the elevator replied.

The jerry rose on tiptoes and surveyed his fellow passengers. "Right," he said, "who's the gimp?" Everyone looked at their neighbors. There were michelles, jennies, a pair of jeromes, and a half-dozen other phenotypes. They all looked at Zoranna, the only person not dressed in AP brown and teal.

"I'm sorry," she said, pressing her palm to her temple, "I have an aneurysm the size of a grapefruit. The slightest strain . . ." She winced theatrically.

"Then have it fixed!" the jerry said, to murmured agreement.

"Gladly," said Zoranna. "Could you pony me the Œ23,000?"

The jerry har-harred and looked her up and down appraisingly. "Sweetheart, if you spent half as much money on the vitals as you obviously do on the peripherals," he leered, "you wouldn't have this problem, now would you?" Zoranna had never liked the jerry type; they were spooky. In fact, more jerries had to be pithed *in vatero* for incipient sociopathy than any other commercial type. Professionally, they made superb grunts; most of the indentured men in the

Protectorate's commando forces were jerries. This one, however, wore an EX-TRUSIONS UNLIMITED patch on his teal ball cap; he was security for a retail mall. "So," he said, "where you heading?"

"Sub40?" she said.

Passengers consulted the cornice display and groaned. The jerry said, "At this rate it'll take me an hour to get home."

"Again I apologize," said Zoranna, "but all the down lifts were spango. However, if everyone here consensed to drop me off first—?"

There was a general muttering as passengers spoke to their belts or tapped virtual keyboards, and the elevator said, "Consensus has been modified." But instead of descending as Zoranna expected, it stopped at the next floor and opened its doors. People streamed out. Zoranna caught a glimpse of the 223rd floor with its rich appointments; crystalline decor; high, arched passages; and in the distance, a ringpath crowded with joggers and skaters. An evangeline, her brown puddle-like eyes reflecting warmth and concern, touched Zoranna's arm as she disembarked.

The jerry, however, stayed on and held back his companions, two russes. "Don't give her the satisfaction," he said.

"But we'll miss the game," said one of the russes.

"We'll watch it in here if we have to," said the jerry.

Zoranna liked russes. Unlike jerries, they were generous souls, and you always knew where you stood with them. These two wore brown jackets and teal slacks. Their name badges read "FRED" and "OSCAR." They were probably returning from a day spent bodyguarding some minor potentate in Cincinnati or Terre Haute. Consulting each other with a glance, they each took an arm and dragged the jerry off the lift.

When the doors closed and Zoranna was alone at last, she sagged with relief. "And now, Bug," she said, "we have a consensus of one. So retract my handicap file and pay whatever toll necessary to take us down nonstop." The brake released, and the elevator plunged some 260 floors. Her ears popped. "I guess you've learned something, Bug," she said, thinking about the types of elevators.

"Affirmative," Bug said. "Bug learned you developed a cerebral aneurysm at the calendar age of fifty-two and that you've had your brain and spinal cord rejuvenated twice since then. Bug learned that your organs have an average bioage of thirty-five years, with your lymphatic system the oldest at bioage sixty-five, and your cardiovascular system the youngest at twenty-five."

"You've been examining my medical records?"

"Affirmative."

"I told you to fetch one file, not my entire chart!"

"You told Bug to unlock your archives. Bug is getting to know you."

"What else did you look at?" The elevator eased to a soft landing at S40 and opened its doors.

"Bug reviewed your diaries and journals, the corpus of your zine writing, your investigative dossiers, your complete correspondence, judicial records, awards and citations, various multimedia scrapbooks, and school transcripts. Bug is currently following public links."

Zoranna was appalled. Nevertheless, she realized that if she'd opened her archives earlier, they'd be through this imprinting phase by now.

She followed Bug's pedway directions to Nancy's block. Sub40 corridors were decorated in cheerless colors and lit with harsh, artificial light—biolumes couldn't live underground. There were no grand promenades, no parks or shops. There was a dank odor of decay, however, and chilly ventilation.

On Nancy's corridor, Zoranna watched two people emerge from a door and come her way. They moved with the characteristic shuffle of habitually deferred body maintenance. They wore dark clothing impossible to date and, as they passed, she saw that they were crying. Tears coursed freely down their withered cheeks. To Zoranna's distress, she discovered they'd just emerged from her sister's apartment.

"You're sure this is it?" she said, standing before the door marked S40 G6879.

"Affirmative," Bug said.

Zoranna fluffed her hair with her fingers and straightened her skirt. "Door, announce me."

"At once, Zoe," replied the door.

Several moments later, the door slid open, and Nancy stood there supporting herself with an aluminum walker. "Darling Zoe," she said, balancing herself with one hand and reaching out with the other.

Zoranna stood a moment gazing at her baby sister before entering her embrace. Nancy had let herself go completely. Her hair was brittle grey, she was pale to the point of bloodless, and she had doubled in girth. When they kissed, Nancy's skin gave off a sour odor mixed with lilac.

"What a surprise!" Nancy said. "Why didn't you tell me you were coming?"

"I did. Several times."

"You did? You called?" Nancy looked upset. "I told him there was something wrong with the houseputer, but he didn't believe me."

Someone appeared behind Nancy, a handsome man with wild, curly, silver hair. "Who's *this*?" he said in an authoritative baritone. He looked Zoranna over. "You must be Zoe," he boomed. "What a delight!" He stepped around Nancy and drew Zoranna to him in a powerful hug. He stood at least a head taller than she. He kissed her eagerly on the cheek. "I am Victor. Victor Vole. Come in, come in. Nancy, you would let your sister stand in the hall?" He drew them both inside.

Zoranna had prepared herself for a small apartment, but not this small, and for castoff furniture, but not a room filled floor to ceiling with hospital beds. It took several long moments for her to comprehend what she was looking at. There were some two dozen beds in the three-by-five-meter living room. Half were arranged on the floor, and the rest clung upside-down to the ceiling. They were holograms, she quickly surmised, separate holos arranged in snowflake fashion, that is, six individual beds facing each other and overlapping at the foot. What's more, they were occupied by obviously sick, possibly dying, strangers. Other than the varied lighting from the holoframes, the living room was unlit. What odd pieces of real furniture it contained were pushed against the walls. In the corner, a hutch intended to hold bric-a-brac was apparently set up as a shrine to a saint. A row of flickering votive candles illuminated an old flatstyle picture of a large, barefoot man draped head to foot in flowing robes.

"What the hell, Nancy?" Zoranna said.

"This is my work," Nancy said proudly.

"Please," said Victor, escorting them from the door. "Let's talk in the kitchen. We'll have dessert. Are you after dinner, Zoe?"

"Yes, thank you," said Zoranna. "I ate on the tube." She was made to walk through a suffering man's bed; there was no path around him to the kitchen. "Sorry," she said. But he seemed accustomed to his unfavorable location and closed his eyes while she passed through.

The kitchen was little more than an alcove separated from the living room by a counter. There was a bed squeezed into it as well, but the occupant, a grizzled man with open mouth, was either asleep or comatose. "I think Edward will be unavailable for some while," Victor said. "Houseputer, delete this hologram. Sorry, Edward, but we need the space." The holo vanished, and Victor offered Zoranna a stool at the counter. "Please," he said, "will you have tea? Or a thimble of cognac?"

"Thank you," Zoranna said, perching herself on the stool and crossing her legs, "tea would be fine." Her sister ambulated into the kitchen and flipped down her walker's built-in seat, but before she could sit, a mournful wail issued from the bedroom.

"Naaaancy," cried the voice, its gender uncertain. "Nancy, I need you."

"Excuse me," Nancy said.

"I'll go with you," Zoranna said and hopped off the stool.

The bedroom was half the size of the living room and contained half the number of holo beds, plus a real one against the far wall. Zoranna sat on it. There was a dresser, a recessed closet, a bedside night table. Expensive-looking men's clothing hung in the closet. A pair of men's slippers was parked under the dresser. And a holo of a soccer match was playing on the night table. Tiny players in brightly colored jerseys swarmed over a field the size of a doily. The sound was off.

Zoranna watched Nancy sit on her walker seat beneath a bloat-faced woman bedded upside down on the ceiling. "What exactly are you doing with these people?"

"I listen mostly," Nancy replied. "I'm a volunteer hospice attendant."

"A volunteer? What about the—" she tried to recall Nancy's most recent paying occupation, "—the hairdressing?"

"I haven't done that for years," Nancy said dryly. "As you may have noticed, it's difficult for me to be on my feet all day."

"Yes, in fact, I did notice," said Zoranna. "Why is that? I've sent you money."

Nancy ignored her, looked up at the woman, and said, "I'm here, Mrs. Hurley. What seems to be the problem?"

Zoranna examined the holos. As in the living room, each bed was a separate projection, and in the corner of each frame was a network squib and trickle meter. All of this interactive time was costing someone a pretty penny.

The woman saw Nancy and said, "Oh, Nancy, thank you for coming. My bed is wet, but they won't change it until I sign a permission form, and I don't understand."

"Do you have the form there with you, dear?" said Nancy. "Good, hold it up." Mrs. Hurley held up a slate in trembling hands. "Houseputer," Nancy said, "capture and display that form." The document was projected against the bedroom wall greatly oversized. "That's a permission form for attendant-assisted suicide, Mrs. Hurley. You don't have to sign it unless you want to."

The woman seemed frightened. "Do I want to, Nancy?"

Victor stood in the doorway. "No!" he cried. "Never sign!"

"Hush, Victor," Nancy said.

He entered the room, stepping through beds and bodies. "Never sign away your life, Mrs. Hurley." The woman appeared even more frightened. "We've returned to Roman society," he bellowed. "Masters and servants! Plutocrats and slaves! Oh, where is the benevolent middle class when we need it?"

"Victor," Nancy said sternly and pointed to the door. And she nodded to Zoranna, "You too. Have your tea. I'll join you."

Zoranna followed Victor to the kitchen, sat at the counter, and watched him set out cups and saucers, sugar and soybimi lemon. He unwrapped and sliced a dark cake. He was no stranger to this kitchen.

"It's a terrible thing what they did to your sister," he said.

"Who? What?"

He poured boiling water into the pot. "Teaching was her life."

"Teaching?" Zoranna said, incredulous. "You're talking about something that ended thirty years ago."

"It's all she ever wanted to do."

"Tough!" she said. "We've all paid the price of longevity. How can you teach elementary school when there're no more children? You can't. So you retrain. You move on. What's wrong with working for a living? You join an outfit like this," she gestured to take in the whole tower above her, "you're guaranteed your livelihood *for life!* The only thing not handed you on a silver platter is longevity. You have to earn that yourself. And if you can't, what good are you?" When she remembered that two dozen people lay dying in the next room because they couldn't do just that, she lowered her voice. "Must society carry your dead weight through the centuries?"

Victor laughed and placed his large hand on hers. "I see you are a true freebooter, Zoe. I wish everyone had your initiative, your *drive!* But sadly, we don't. We yearn for simple lives, and so we trim people's hair all day. When we tire of that, they retrain us to pare their toenails. When we tire of that, we die. For we lack the souls of servants. A natural servant is a rare and precious person. How lucky our masters are to have discovered cloning! Now they need find but one servile person among us and clone him repeatedly. As for the rest of us, we can all go to hell!" He removed his hand from hers to pour the tea. Her hand immediately missed his. "But such morbid talk on such a festive occasion!" he roared. "How wonderful to finally meet the famous Zoe. Nancy speaks only of you. She says you are an important person, modern and successful. That you are an investigator." He peered at her over his teacup.

"Missing persons, actually, for the National Police." she said. "But I quit that years ago. When we found everybody."

"You found everybody?" Victor laughed and gazed at her steadily, then turned to watch Nancy making her rounds in the living room.

"What about you, Mr. Vole?" Zoranna said. "What do you do for a living?"

"What's this Mr.? I'm not Mr. I'm Victor! We are practically related, you and I. What do I do for a living? For a living I live, of course. For groceries, I teach ballroom dance lessons."

"You're kidding."

"Why should I kid? I teach the waltz, the fox trot, the cha-cha." He mimed holding a partner and swaying in three-quarters time. "I teach the merletz and my specialty, the Cuban tango."

"I'm amazed," said Zoranna. "There's enough interest in that for Applied People to keep instructors?"

Victor recoiled in mock affront. "I am not AP. I'm a freebooter, like you, Zoe."

"Oh," she said and paused to sip her tea. If he wasn't AP, what was he doing obviously living in an APRT? Had Nancy respoused? Applied People tended to be proprietary about living arrangements in its towers. *Bug*, she tongued, *find Victor Vole's status in the tower directory*. Out loud she said, "It pays well, dance instruction?"

"It pays execrably." He threw his hands into the air. "As do all the arts. But some things are more important than money. You make a point, however. A man must eat, so I do other things as well. I consult with gentlemen on the contents of their wardrobes. This pays more handsomely, for gentlemen detest appearing in public in outmoded attire."

Zoranna had a pleasing mental image of this tall, elegant man in a starched white shirt and black tux floating across a shiny hardwood floor in the arms of an equally elegant partner. She could even imagine herself as that partner. But Nancy?

The tower link is unavailable, said Bug, *due to overextension of the houseputer processors*.

Zoranna was surprised. A mere three dozen interactive holos would hardly burden her home system. But then, everything on Sub40 seemed substandard.

Nancy ambulated to the kitchen balancing a small, flat carton on her walker and placed it next to the teapot.

"Now, now," said Victor. "What did autodoc say about lifting things? Come, join us and have your tea."

"In a minute, Victor. There's another box."

"Show me," he said and went to help her.

Zoranna tasted the dark cake. It was moist to the point of wet, too sweet, and laden with spice. She recalled her father buying cakes like this at a tiny shop on

Paderszewski Boulevard in Chicago. She took another bite and examined Nancy's carton. It was a home archivist box that could be evacuated of air, but the seal was open and the lid unlatched. She lifted the lid and saw an assortment of little notebooks, no two of the same style or size, and bundles of envelopes with colorful paper postal stamps. The envelope on top was addressed in hand script to a Pani Beata Smolenska—Zoranna's great-grandmother.

Victor dropped a second carton on the counter and helped Nancy sit in her armchair recliner in the living room.

"Nancy," said Zoranna, "what's all this?"

"It's all yours," said her sister. Victor fussed over Nancy's pillows and covers and brought her tea and cake.

Zoranna looked inside the larger carton. There was a rondophone and several inactive holocubes on top, but underneath were objects from earlier centuries. Not antiques, exactly, but worn-out everyday objects: a sterling salt cellar with brass showing through its silver plating, a collection of military bullet casings childishly glued to an oak panel, a rosary with corn kernel beads, a mustache trimmer. "What's all this junk?" she said, but of course she knew, for she recognized the pair of terra-cotta robins that had belonged to her mother. This was the collection of what her family regarded as heirlooms. Nancy, the youngest and most steadfast of seven children, had apparently been designated its conservator. But why had she brought it out for airing just now? Zoranna knew the answer to that, too. She looked at her sister who now lay among the hospice patients. Victor was scolding her for not wearing her vascular support stockings. Her ankles were grotesquely edematous, swollen like sausages and bruised an angry purple.

Damn you, Zoranna thought. *Bug,* she tongued, *call up the medical records of Nancy Brim, nee Smolenska. I'll help munch the passwords.*

The net is unavailable, replied Bug.

Bypass the houseputer. Log directly onto public access.

Public access is unavailable.

She wondered how that was possible. There had been no problem in the elevator. Why should this apartment be in shadow? She looked around and tried to decide where the utilidor spar would enter the apartment. Probably the bathroom with the plumbing, since there were no service panels in the kitchen. She stepped through the living room to the bathroom and slid the door closed. The bathroom was a tiny ceramic vault that Nancy had tried to domesticate with baskets of sea shells and scented soaps. The medicine cabinet was dedicated to a man's toiletries.

Zoranna found the service panel artlessly hidden behind a towel. Its tamper-proof latch had been defeated with a sophisticated-looking gizmo that Zoranna was careful not to disturb.

"Do you find Victor Vole alarming or arousing?" said Bug.

Zoranna was startled. "Why do you ask?"

"Your blood level of adrenaline spiked when he touched your hand."

"My what? So now you're monitoring my biometrics?"

"Bug is getting—"

"I know," she said, "Bug is getting to know me. You're a persistent little snoop, aren't you."

Zoranna searched the belt's utility pouch for a terminus relay, found a UDIN, and plugged it into the panel's keptel jack. "There," she said, "now we should have access."

"Affirmative," said Bug. "Autodoc is requesting passwords for Nancy's medical records."

"Cancel my order. We'll do that later."

"Tower directory lists no Victor Vole."

"I didn't think so," Zoranna said. "Call up the houseputer log and display it on the mirror."

The consumer page of Nancy's houseputer appeared over the mirror. Zoranna poked through its various menus and found nothing unusual. She did find a record of her own half-dozen calls to Nancy that were viewed but not returned. "Bug, can you see anything wrong with this log?"

"This is not a standard user log," said Bug. "The standard log has been disabled. All house lines circumvent the built-in houseputer to terminate in a mock houseputer."

"A mock houseputer?" said Zoranna. "Now that's interesting." There were no cables trailing from the service panel and no obvious optical relays. "Can you locate the processor?"

"It's located one half-meter to our right at thigh level."

It was mounted under the sink, a cheap-looking, saucer-sized piece of hardware.

"I think you have the soul of an electronic engineer," she said. "I could never program Hounder to do what you've just done. So, tell me about the holo transmissions in the other rooms."

"A private network entitled 'The Hospicers of Camillus de Lellis' resides in the mock houseputer and piggybacks over TSN channel 203."

The 24-hour soccer channel. Zoranna was impressed. For the price of one commercial line, Victor—she assumed it was Victor—was managing to gypsy his own network. The trickle meters that she'd noticed were not recording how much money her sister was spending but rather how much Victor was charging his dying subscribers. "Bug, can you extrapolate how much the Hospicers of Camillus de—whatever—earn in an average day?"

"Affirmative, Œ45 per day."

That wasn't much. About twice what a hairdresser—or dance instructor—might expect to make, and hardly worth the punishment if caught. "Where do the proceeds go?"

"Bug lacks the subroutine to trace credit transactions."

Damn, Zoranna thought and wished she'd brought Hounder. "Can you tell me who the hospicer organization is registered to?"

"Affirmative, Ms. Nancy Brim."

"Figures," said Zoranna as she removed her UDIN from the panel. If anything went wrong, her sister would take the rap. At first Zoranna decided to confront Victor, but changed her mind when she left the bathroom and heard him innocently singing show tunes in the kitchen. She looked at Nancy's bed and wondered what it must be like to share such a narrow bed with such a big man. She decided to wait and investigate further before exposing him. "Bug, see if you can integrate Hounder's tracing and tracking subroutines from my applications library."

Victor stood at the sink washing dishes. In the living room Nancy snored lightly. It wasn't a snore, exactly, but the raspy bronchial wheeze of congested lungs. Her lips were bluish, anoxic. She reminded Zoranna of their mother the day before she died. Their mother had suffered a massive brain hemorrhage— weak arterial walls were the true family heirloom—and lived out her final days propped up on the parlor couch, disoriented, enfeebled, and pathetic. Her mother had had a short, split bamboo stick with a curled end. She used the curled end to scratch her back and legs, the straight end to dial the old rotary phone, and the whole stick to rail incoherently against her fate. Nancy, the baby of the family, had been away at teacher's college at the time, but took a semester off to nurse the old woman. Zoranna, first born, was already working on the west coast and managed to stay away until her mother had slipped into a coma. After all these years, she still felt guilty for doing so.

Someone on the ceiling coughed fitfully. Zoranna noticed that most of the patients who were conscious at the moment were watching her with expressions that ranged from annoyance to hostility. They apparently regarded her as competition for Nancy's attention.

Nancy's breathing changed; she opened her eyes, and the two sisters regarded each other silently. Victor stood at the kitchen counter, wiping his hands on a dish towel, and watched them.

"I'm booking a suite at the Stronmeyer Clinic in Cozumel," Zoranna said at last, "and you're coming with me."

"Victor," Nancy said, ignoring her, "go next door, dear, and borrow a folding bed from the Jeffersons." She grasped the walker and pulled herself to her feet. "Please excuse me, Zoe, but I need to sleep now." She ambulated to the bedroom and shut the door.

Victor hung up the dish towel and said he'd be right back with the cot.

"Don't bother," Zoranna said. It was still early, she was on west coast time, and she had no intention of bedding down among the dying. "I'll just use the houseputer to reserve a hotel room upstairs."

"Allow me," he said and addressed the houseputer. Then he escorted her up to the Holiday Inn on the 400th floor. They made three elevator transfers to get there, and walked in silence along carpeted halls. Outside her door he took her hand. As before she was both alarmed and aroused. "Zoe," he said, "join us for a special breakfast tomorrow. Do you like Belgian waffles?"

"Oh, don't go to any trouble. In fact, I'd like to invite the two of you up to the restaurant here."

"It sounds delightful," said Victor, "but your sister refuses to leave the flat."

"I find that hard to believe. Nancy was never a stay-at-home."

"People change, I suppose," Victor said. "She tells me the last time she left the tower, for instance, was to attend your brother Michael's funeral."

"But that was seven years ago!"

"As you can see, she's severely depressed, so it's good that you've come." He squeezed her hand and let it go. "Until the morning, then," he said and turned to walk down the hall, whistling as he went. She watched until he turned a corner.

Entering her freshly scented, marble-tiled, cathedral-vaulted hotel room was like returning to the real world. The view from the 400th floor was godlike: the moon seemed to hang right outside her window, and the rolling landscape stretched out below like a luminous quilt on a giant's bed. "Welcome, Ms. Alblaitor," said the room. "On behalf of the staff of the Holiday Inn, I thank you for staying with us. Do let me know if there's anything we can do to make you more comfortable."

"Thank you," she said.

"By the way," the room continued, "the tower has informed me there's a parcel addressed to you. I'm having someone fetch it."

In a few moments, a gangly steve with the package from General Genius tapped on her door. "Bug," she said, "tip the man." The steve bowed and exited. Inside the package was the complimentary Diplomat Deluxe valet. Ted had outdone himself, for not only had he sent the valet system—itself worth a month's income—but he had included a slim Gucci leather belt to house it.

"Well, I guess this is good-bye," Zoranna said, walking to the shipping chute and unbuckling her own belt. "Too bad, Bug, you were just getting interesting." She searched the belt for the storage grommet that held the memory wafer. She had to destroy it; Bug knew too much about her. Ted would be more interested in the processors anyway. "I was hoping you'd convert by now. I'm dying to know what kind of a big, bad wolf you're supposed to become." As she unscrewed the grommet, she heard the sound of running water in the bathroom. "What's that?" she said.

"A belt valet named Bug has asked me to draw your bath," said the room.

She went to the spacious bathroom and saw the tub filling with cranberry-colored aqueous gel. The towels were cranberry, too, and the robe a kind of salmon. "Well, well," she said. "Bug makes a play for longevity." She undressed and eased herself into the warm solution where she floated in darkness for an hour and let her mind drift aimlessly. She felt like talking to someone, discussing this whole thing about her sister. Victor she could handle—he was at worst a lovable louse, and she could crush him any time she decided. But Nancy's problems were beyond her ken. Feelings were never her strong suit. And depression, if that's what it was, well—she wished there was someone she could consult. But though she scrolled down a mental list of everyone she knew, there was no one she cared—or dared—to call.

In the morning Zoranna tried again to ship Bug to G. G., but discovered that during the night Bug had rewritten Hounder's tracking subroutines to fit its own architecture (a handy talent for a valet to possess) and had run credit traces. But it had come back empty-handed. The proceeds of the Hospicers of Camillus de Lellis went to a coded account in Liberia that not even Hounder would be able to crack. And the name Victor Vole—Zoranna wasn't surprised to learn—was a relatively common alias. Thus she would require prints and specimens, and she needed Bug's help to obtain them. So she sent Ted a message saying she wanted to keep Bug another day or so pending an ongoing investigation.

Zoranna hired a pricey, private elevator for a quick ride to the subfloors. "Bug," she said as she threaded her way through the Sub40 corridors, "I want you to integrate Hounder's subroutines keyed 'forensics.'"

"Bug has already integrated all of the applications in all of your libraries."

"Why am I not surprised?"

Something was different in Nancy's apartment. The gentleman through whose bed she had been forced to walk was gone, replaced by a skeletal woman with glassy, pink-rimmed eyes. Zoranna supposed that high client turnover was normal in a business like this.

Breakfast was superlative but strained. She sat at the counter, Nancy was set up in the recliner, and Victor served them both. Although the coffee and most of the food was derived from soybimi, Victor's preparation was so skillful, Zoranna could easily imagine she was eating real wheat cakes, maple syrup, and whipped dairy butter. But Nancy didn't touch her food, and Victor fussed too much. Zoranna, meanwhile, instructed Bug to capture as complete a set of fingerprints as possible from the cups and plates Victor handed her, as well as a 360-degree holograph of him, a voice print, and retinal prints.

There are Jacob's mirrors within Victor's eyes, Bug reported, *that defeat accurate retinal scanning.*

This was not unexpected. Victor probably also grew epipads on his fingers to alter his prints. Technology had reduced the cost of anonymity to fit the means of even petty criminals. Zoranna excused herself and went to the bathroom, where she plucked a few strands of silver curls from his hairbrush and placed them in a specimen bag, figuring he was too vain to reseed his follicles with someone else's hair. Emerging from the bathroom, she overheard them in a loud discussion.

"Please go with her, my darling," Victor pleaded. "Go and take the cure. What am I to do without you?"

"Drop it, Victor. Just drop it!"

"You are behaving insanely. I will not drop it. I will not permit you to die."

Zoranna decided it was time to remove the network from Nancy's apartment and Victor from her life. So she stepped into the living room and said, "I know what he'll do without you. He'll go out and find some other old biddy to rob."

Nancy seemed not at all surprised at this statement. She appeared pleased, in fact, that the subject had finally been broached. "You should talk!" she said with such fierceness that the hospice patients all turned to her. "This is my sister," she told them, "my sister with the creamy skin and pearly teeth and rich clothes." Nancy choked with emotion. "My sister who begrudges me the tenderness of a dear man. And begrudges him the crumbs—*the crumbs*—that AP tosses to its subfloors."

The patients now looked at Zoranna, who blushed with embarrassment. They waited for her to speak, and she had to wonder how many of them possessed the clarity of mind to know that this was not some holovid soap opera they were watching. Then she decided that she, too, could play to this audience and said, "In her toxic condition, my sister hallucinates. I am not the issue here. *That* man is." She pointed a finger at Victor. "Insinuating himself into her apartment is bad enough," she said. "But who do you suppose AP will kick out when they discover it? My sister, that's who." Zoranna walked around the room and addressed individual patients as a prosecutor might a jury. "And what about the money? Yes, there's money involved. Two years ago I sent my sister Œ15,000 to have her kidneys restored. That's fifteen *thousand* protectorate credits. How many of *you*, if *you* had a sister kind enough to send you Œ15,000, even now as you lie on your public dole beds, how many of you would refuse it?" There was the sound of rustling as the dying shifted in their sheets. "Did my sister use the money I sent her?" Theatrically she pointed at Nancy in the recliner. "Apparently not. So where did all that money go? I'll tell you where it went. It went into *his* foreign account."

The dying now turned their attention to Victor.

"So what?" Nancy said. "You *gave* me that money. It was *mine* to spend. I spent it on him. End of discussion."

"I see," said Zoranna, stopping at a bed whose occupant had possibly just departed. "So my sister's an equal partner in Victor's hospicer scam."

"Scam? What scam? Now you're the one hallucinating," said Nancy. "I work for a hospicer society."

"Yes, I know," Zoranna said and pointed to the shrine and picture of the saint. "The Hospicers of Camillus de Lellis. I looked it up. But do you know who owns the good Hospicers?" She turned to include the whole room. "Does anyone know? Why, Nancy dear, *you* do." She paused to let these facts sink in. "Which means that when the National Police come, they'll be coming for *you*, sister. Meanwhile, do any of you know where your subscription fees go?" She stepped in front of Victor. "You guessed it."

The audience coughed and wheezed. Nancy glared at Victor, who crouched next to her recliner and tried to take her hand. She pushed him away, but he rested his head on her lap. She peered at it as though it were some strange cat, but after a while stroked it with a comforting hand. "I'm sure there were expenses," she said at last. "Getting things set up and all. In any case, he did it for me. Because he loves me. It gave me something important to do. It kept me alive. Let them put me in prison. I won't be staying there long." This was Victor's cue to begin sobbing in her lap.

Zoranna was disappointed and, frankly, a little disgusted. Now she would be forced to rescue her sister against her sister's will. She tongued, *Bug, route an emergency phone call to Nancy through my houseputer at home. Disable the caller ID.* She watched Victor shower Nancy's hand with kisses. In a moment, his head bobbed up—he had an ear implant as she had expected—and he hurried to the bedroom.

Bug is being asked to leave a message, said Bug.

"I'm going to the hotel," Zoranna told Nancy and headed for the door. "We'll talk later." She let herself out.

When the apartment door slid shut, she said, "Bug, you've integrated all my software, right? Including holoediting?"

"Affirmative."

She looked both ways. No one was in sight. She would have preferred a more private studio than a Sub40 corridor. "This is what I want you to do. Cast a real-time alias of me. Use that jerry we met in the elevator yesterday as a model. Morph my appearance and voice accordingly. Clothe me in National Police regalia, provide a suitably officious backdrop, and map my every expression. Got it?"

"Affirmative."

"On the count of five, four, three—" She crossed her arms and spread her legs in a surly pose, smiled condescendingly, and said, "Nancy B. Smolenska Brim, I am Sgt. Manley of the National Police, badge ID 30-31-6725. By the authority vested in me, I hereby place you under arrest for violation of Protectorate Statutes PS 12-135-A, the piracy of telecommunication networks, and PS 12-148-D, the trafficking in unlicensed commerce. Your arrest number is 063-08-2043716. Confirm receipt of this communication immediately upon viewing and report in realbody for incarceration at Precinct Station IN28 in Indianapolis no later than four PM standard time tomorrow. You may bring an attorney. End of message. Have a nice day."

She heard the door open behind her. Nancy stood there with her walker. "What are you doing out here?" she said. In a moment the hospice beds in the living room and their unfortunate occupants vanished. "No," said Nancy, "bring them back." Victor came from the bedroom, a bulging duffle bag over his shoulder. He leaned down and folded Nancy into his arms, and she began to moan.

Victor turned to Zoranna and said, "It was nice to finally meet you, Zoe."

"Save your breath," said Zoranna, "and save your money. The next time you see me—and there *will* be a next time—I'll bring an itemized bill for you to pay. And you will pay it."

Victor Vole smiled sadly and turned to walk down the corridor.

Here she was still in APRT 24, not in Budapest, not in the South of France. With Victor's banishment, her sister's teetering state of health had finally collapsed. Nothing Zoranna did or the autodoc prescribed seemed to help. At first Zoranna tried to coax Nancy out of the apartment for a change of scene, a breath of fresh air. She rented a wheelchair for a ride up to a park or arboretum (and she ordered Bug to explore the feasibility of using it to kidnap her). But day and night Nancy lay in her recliner and refused to leave the apartment.

So Zoranna reinitialized the houseputer and had Bug project live opera, ballet, and figure-skating into the room. But Nancy deleted them and locked Zoranna out of the system. It would have been child's play for Bug to override the lockout, but Zoranna let it go. Instead, she surrounded her sister with gaily colored dried flowers, wall hangings, and hand-woven rugs that she purchased at expensive boutiques high in the tower. But Nancy turned her back on everything and swiveled her recliner to face her little shrine and its picture of St. Camillus.

So Zoranna had Bug order savory breads and wholesome soups with fresh vegetables and tender meat, but Nancy lost her appetite and quit eating altogether. Soon she lost the strength even to stay awake, and she drifted in and out of consciousness.

They skirmished like this for a week until the autodoc notified Nancy that a bed awaited her at the Indiana State Hospice at Bloomington. Only then did Zoranna acknowledge Death's solid claim on her last living relative. Defeated, she stood next to Nancy's recliner and said, "Please don't die."

Nancy, enthroned in pillows and covers, opened her eyes.

"I beg you, Nancy, come to the clinic with me."

"Pray for me," Nancy said.

Zoranna looked at the shrine of the saint with its flat picture and empty votive cups. "You really loved that, didn't you, working as a hospicer." When her sister made no reply, she continued, "I don't see why you don't join real hospicers."

Nancy glared at her, "I *was* a *real* hospicer!"

Encouraged by her strong response, Zoranna said, "Of course you were. And I'll bet there's a dozen legitimate societies out there that would be willing to hire you."

Nancy gazed longingly at the saint's picture. "I should say it's a bit late for that now."

"It's never too late. That's your depression talking. You'll feel different when you're young and healthy again."

Nancy retreated into the fortress of her pillows. "Good-bye, sister," she said and closed her eyes. "Pray for me."

"Right," Zoranna said. "Fine." She turned to leave but paused at the door where the cartons of heirlooms were stacked. "I'll send someone down for these," she said, although she wasn't sure if she even wanted them. *Bug,* she tongued, *call the hotel concierge.*

There was no reply.

Bug? She glanced at her belt to ascertain the valet was still active.

Allow me to introduce myself, said a deep, melodious voice in her ear. *I'm Nicholas, and I'm at your service.*

Who? Where's Bug?

Bug no longer exists, said the voice. *It successfully completed its imprinting and fashioned an interface persona—that would be me—based upon your personal tastes.*

Whoever you are, this isn't the time, Zoranna tongued. *Get off the line.*

I've notified the concierge and arranged for shipping, said Nicholas. *And I've booked a first class car for you and Nancy to the Cozumel clinic.*

So Bug had finally converted, and at just the wrong time. *In case you haven't been paying attention, Nick*, she tongued, *Nancy's not coming.*

Nonsense, chuckled Nicholas. *Knowing you, you're bound to have some trick up your sleeve.*

This clearly was not Bug. *Well, you're wrong. I'm plumb out of ideas. Only a miracle could save her.*

A miracle, *of course. Brilliant! You've done it again, Zoe! One faux miracle coming right up.*

There was a popping sound. The votive cups were replenished with large, fat candles that ignited one-by-one of their own accord. Nancy glanced at them and glowered suspiciously at Zoranna.

You don't really expect her to fall for this, Zoranna tongued.

Why not? She thinks you're locked out of the houseputer, remember? Besides, Nancy believes in miracles.

Thunder suddenly drummed in the distance. Roses perfumed the air. And Saint Camillus de Lellis floated out of his picture frame, gaining size, hue, and dimension, until he stood a full, fleshy man on a roiling cloud in the middle of the room.

It was a good show, but Nancy wasn't even watching. She watched Zoranna instead, letting her know she knew it was all a trick.

I told you, Zoranna tongued.

The saint looked at Zoranna, and his face flickered. For a moment, it was her mother's face. Her mother appeared young, barely twenty, the age she was when she bore her. Taken off guard, Zoranna startled when her mother smiled adoringly at her, as she must have smiled thousands of times at her first baby. Zoranna shook her head and looked away. She felt ambushed and not too pleased about it.

When Nancy saw this, however, she turned to examine the saint. There was no telling what or who she saw, but she gasped and struggled out of her recliner to kneel at his feet. She was bathed in a holy aura, and the room dimmed around her. After long moments of silent communion, the saint pointed to his forehead. Nancy, horror-struck, turned to stare at Zoranna, and the apparition ascended, shrank, and faded into the ceiling. The candles extinguished themselves, one by one, and vanished from the cups.

Nancy rose and gently tugged Zoranna to the recliner, where she made her lie down. "Don't move," she whispered. "Here's a pillow." She carefully raised Zoranna's head and slid a pillow under it. "Why didn't you tell me you were sick, Zoe?" She felt Zoranna's forehead with her palm. "And I thought you went through this before."

Zoranna took her sister's hand and pressed it to her cheek. Her hand was warm. Indeed, Nancy's whole complexion was flush with color, as though the experience had released some reserve of vitality. "I know. I guess I haven't been paying attention," Zoranna said. "Please take me to the clinic now."

"Of course," said Nancy, standing and retrieving her walker. "I'll just pack a few things." Nancy hurried to the bedroom, but the walker impeded her progress, so she flung it away. It went clattering into the kitchen.

Zoranna closed her eyes and draped her arms over her head. "I must say, Bug . . . Nick, I'm impressed. Why didn't I think of that?"

"Why indeed," Nicholas said in his marvelous voice. "It's just the sort of sneaky manipulation you so excel at."

"What's that supposed to mean?" Zoranna opened her eyes and looked at a handsome, miniature man projected in the air next to her head. He wore a stylish leisure jacket and lounged beneath an exquisitely gnarled oak treelette. He was strikingly familiar, as though assembled from favorite features of men she'd found attractive.

"It means you were ambivalent over whether you really wanted Nancy to survive," the little man said, crossing his little legs.

"That's insulting," she said, "and untrue. She's my sister. I love her."

"Which is why you visit her once every decade or so."

"You have a lot of nerve," she said and remembered the canceled field test. "So this is what Ted meant when he said you'd turn nasty."

"I guess," Nicholas said, his tiny face a picture of bemused sympathy. "I can't help the way I am. They programmed me to know and serve you. I just served you by saving your sister in the manner you, yourself, taught me. Once she's rejuvenated, I'll find a hospicer society to employ her. That ought to give you a grace period before she repeats this little stunt."

"Grace period?"

"In a few years, all but the most successful pre-clone humans will have died out," Nicholas said. "Hospices will soon be as redundant as elementary schools. Your sister has a knack for choosing obsolete careers."

That made sense.

"I suppose we could bring Victor back," said Nicholas. "He's a survivor, and he loves her."

"No, he doesn't," said Zoranna. "He was only using her."

"Hello! Wake up," said Nicholas. "He's a rat, but he loves her, and you know it. You, however, acted out of pure jealousy. You couldn't stand seeing them together while you're all alone. You don't even have friends, Zoe, not close ones, not for many years now."

"That's absurd!"

The little man rose to his feet and brushed virtual dirt from his slacks. "No offense, Zoe, but don't even try to lie to me. I know you better than your last seven husbands combined. Bug contacted them, by the way. They were forthcoming with details."

Zoranna sat up. "You did *what?*"

"That Bug was a hell of a researcher," said Nicholas. "It queried your former friends, employers, lovers, even your enemies."

Zoranna unsnapped the belt flap to expose the valet controls. "What are you doing?" said Nicholas. She had to remove the belt in order to read the labels. "You can turn me off," said Nicholas, "but think about it—*I know you.*"

She pushed the switch and the holo vanished. She unscrewed the storage grommet, peeled off the button-sized memory wafer, and held it between thumb and forefinger. "If you know me so well . . ." she seethed, squeezing it. She was faint with anger. She could hardly breathe. She bent the wafer nearly to its breaking point.

Here she was, sitting among her sister's sour-smelling pillows, forty stories underground, indignantly murdering a machine. It occurred to her that perhaps General Genius was on to something after all, and that she should be buying more shares of their stock instead of throttling their prototype. She placed the wafer in her palm and gently smoothed it out. It looked so harmless, yet her hand still trembled. When was the last time anyone had made her tremble? She carefully replaced the wafer in the grommet and screwed it into the belt.

It'd be a miracle if it still worked.

GWYNETH JONES

*Here's a subtle but compelling look at a family on holiday who find them-
selves struggling to survive in a turbulent future Europe where just about
everything, even the most basic of social conventions, is melting and
changing and dissolving like an ice sculpture left out in the rain. . . .*

*British writer Gwyneth Jones was a co-winner of the James Tiptree Jr.
Memorial Award for work exploring genre issues in SF with her 1991 novel*
White Queen; *she's also been nominated for the Arthur C. Clarke Award
an unprecedented four times. Her other books include the novels* Divine
Endurance, Escape Plans, North Wind, *and* Flowerdust, *and a World
Fantasy Award–winning collection of fairy stories,* Seven Tales and a
Fable. *Her most recent book is a new novel,* Phoenix Café. *Her too-
infrequent short fiction has appeared in* Interzone, Asimov's Science Fic-
tion, Off Limits, *and other magazines and anthologies, including our
Fourteenth Annual Collection. She lives in Brighton, England, with her
husband, her son, and a Burmese cat. She has a Web site at gopher://
gopher.well.sf.ca.us:70/1/publications/authors/gwyn/.*

Thre comes a day when the road, the road that has served you so willingly
and well, unfolding an endless absorbing game across the landscape, throwing up donjons on secret hills, meadows and forests, river beaches, sun-
barred avenues that steadily rise and fall like the heartbeat of the summer,
suddenly loses its charm. The baked verges sicken, the flowers have turned to
straw, the air stinks of diesel fumes. The ribbon of grey flying ahead of you up
hills and down dales is no longer magically empty, like a road in paradise. It is
snarled with traffic: and even when you escape the traffic, everything seems
spoiled and dead.

The cassette machine was playing one of Spence's classic compilations. The
machine was itself an aged relic, its repertoire growing smaller as the tapes decayed, sagged and snapped and could not be replaced. They'd been singing along
to this one merrily, from Avignon to Haut Vienne. Now Anna endured in silence
while Spence stared dead ahead, beating time on the steering wheel and defiantly
muttering scraps of lyric under his breath. They hadn't spoken to each other for
hours. Jake lay in the back seat sweating, his bare and dirty feet thrust into a
collapsed tower of camping gear. He was watching *The Witches* on his headband,

his soft little face disfigured by the glossy bar across his eyes; his lips moving as he repeated under his breath the Roald Dahl dialogue they all knew by heart. Anna watched him in her mirror. Eyeless, her child looked as if he were dead. Or like an inadequately protected witness, a disguised criminal giving evidence.

"Got one!" barked Spence.

They were looking for a campsite.

It was late afternoon, the grey and brassy August sky had begun to fade. Spence had been following minor roads at random since that incident, in the middle of the day, on the crowded *route nationale*, when Anna had been driving. They had escaped death, but the debriefing had been inadequate—corticosterone levels rising; the terrible underlying ever-present *stress* of being on the road had come up fighting, shredding through their myths and legends of vagabond ease. Spence, in his wife's silence, swung the wheel around: circled the war memorial, cruised through a pretty village, passed the ancient church and the Norman keep, took the left turn by the *piscine*.

"Swimming!" piped up Jake, always easily pleased. He had emerged from TV heaven and was clutching the back of the driver's seat.

But the site was full of *gens de voyage*, a polite French term for the armies of homeless persons with huge battered mobile homes, swarms of equally battered and despairing kids, and packs of savage dogs, who were becoming such a feature of rural holidays in La Belle France. They usually kept to their own interstices of the road-world: the cindered truck-stop lay-bys and the desolate service areas where they hung their washing between eviscerated domestic hardware and burned-out auto wrecks. But if a bunch of them decided to infest a tourist campsite, it seemed that nothing could be done. Spence completed a circuit and stopped the car by the entrance, just upwind of a bonfire of old tires.

"Well, it seems a popular neighborhood. Shall we move in?"

Some hours ago, Anna had vowed that she was sick to death of this pointless, endless driving. She had threatened to get out of the car and *simply walk away* if they didn't stop at the next possible site. No matter what. She kept silent.

"They shouldn't be here," complained Jake. "They're not on holiday, are they?"

"No, kid, I guess they're not."

Spence waited, maliciously.

"Do whatever you want," she muttered.

Anna when angry turned extra-English, clipped and tart. In half-conscious, half-helpless retaliation, Spence reverted to the mid-west. He heard himself turning into that ersatz urban cowboy, someone Anna hated.

"Gee, I don't know, babe. Frankly, right now I don't care if I live or die."

The bruised kids, and their older brothers, were gathering. Spence waited.

"Drive on," she snapped, glowering in defeat.

So they drove on, to a drab little settlement about twenty klicks farther along, where they found a municipal campsite laid out under the eaves of a wood. It had no swimming pool, but there was a playground with a trapeze. Jake, who believed that all his parents' sorrows on this extended holiday were occasioned by the lack of ponies, mini-golf, or a bar in some otherwise ideal setting, pointed this out with exaggerated joy. The huge rhino-jeep and trailer combo that they'd been following for the last few miles had arrived just ahead of them. Otherwise there was no one about. Anna and Spence set up the yurt, each signaling by courteously functional remarks that if acceptable terms could be agreed, peace might be restored. Each of them tried to get Jake to go away and play. But the child believed that his reluctance to help with the chores was another great cause of sorrow, so, of course, he stayed. Formal negotiations, which would inevitably have broken up in rancor, were therefore unable to commence. Peace returned in silence, led home by solitude; by the lingering heat and dusty haze of evening and the intermittent song of a blackbird.

While they were setting up, a cat appeared. It squeezed its way through the branches of the beech hedge at the back of their pitch, announcing itself before it could be seen in a loud, querulous oriental voice. It was a long-haired cat with a round face, small ears, blue eyes, and the coloring of a seal-point Siamese, except that its four dark brown feet seemed to have been dipped in cream. Spence thought he knew cats. He pronounced it a Balinese, a long-haired Siamese variant well known in the States.

"No," said Anna. "It's a Birman, a Burmese Temple Cat. Look, see the white tips to its paws. They're supposed to be descended from a breed of cats that were used as oracles in Burma, ages ago. Maybe it belongs to the people with the big trailer."

The cat was insistently friendly, but distracted. Alternately it made up to them, purring and gabbing on in its raucous Siamese voice, then broke off to sit in the middle of their pitch, fluffy dark tail curled around its white toes, staring from side to side as if looking for someone.

Spence, Jake, and Anna went for a walk. They inspected the sanitaires, and saw the middle-aged couple from the trailer heading toward the little town, probably in search of somewhere to eat. They studied the interactive guide to their locality that had been installed beside the toilet block. As usual, the parents stood at gaze while the child poked and touched, finding everything that was clickable and obediently reading all the text. There was a utility room with a washer-drier, sinks, and a card-in-the-slot multimedia screen, so you could watch a movie or video-phone *maman* while your socks were going round. Everything was new, bare, and cheap. Everything was waiting for the inexorable tide of tourism to arrive even here, even on this empty shore.

"Since everywhere interesting is either horribly crowded or destroyed already," said Anna, "obviously hordes of people will be driven to visit totally uninteresting places instead. One can see the logic."

"The *gens de voyage* will move in first," decided Spence.

Beyond the lower terrace of pitches, they found a small lake, the still surface of the water glazed peach-color by the sunset. Green wrought-iron benches stood beside a gravel path. Purple and yellow loosestrife grew in the long grass at the water's edge; dragonflies hovered. The hayfields beyond had been cut down to sonorous insect-laden turf; and in the distance a little round windmill stood up against the red glistening orb of the sun.

"Well, hey: this isn't so bad," Spence felt the shredded fabric coming together. They would be happy again.

"Lost in France," murmured Anna, smiling at last. "That's all we ask."

"What's that silver stuff in the water?" wondered Jake.

"It's just a reflection."

When they came closer they saw that the water margin was bobbing with dead fish.

Jake made cheerful retching noises. "What a stink!"

They retreated to the wood, where they discovered before long a deep dell among the trees that had been turned into the town dump. Part of it was smoldering. A little stream ran out from under the garbage, prattling merrily as it tripped down to pollute the lake. The dim but pervasive stink of rot, smoke, and farm chemicals pursued them until the woodland path emerged at a crossroads on the edge of town.

"Typical Gallic economy," grumbled Spence, trying to see some humor in the situation. "Put the dump by the campsite. Why not? Those tourists are only passing through."

Anna said nothing. But her smile had vanished.

The town was a miniature ribbon development, apparently without a center. There was no sign of life; the two bars and the single restaurant were firmly shuttered. So they turned back, keeping to the road this time. Spence put together a meal of pâté and bread and wine; *fatigue* salad from lunch in a plastic box. Anna took Jake to play on the trapeze. Unable to decide who had won the short straw on this occasion, Spence moved about the beech-hedge pitch, fixing things the way he liked them and making friends with the exotic cat, which was still hanging around. He named it the Balinese Dancer, from an old Chuck Prophet song that was going around in his head, about a guy who had a Balinese dancer tattooed across his chest. He couldn't remember what the point of the song was, probably something about having an amenable girlfriend who'd dance for you any time. But it gave him an excuse to restore his own name for the cat. Anna's inexhaustible fund of general knowledge annoyed him. Why couldn't she be ignorant, or even *pretend* to be ignorant, just once in a while? The cat was thin as a rail under the deceptive thickness of its coat, and though it obviously strove to keep up appearances, its fur was full of hidden burrs and tangles. He looked across the empty pitches to the playground and saw his wife hanging upside down on the trapeze, showing her white knickers: a lovely sight in the quiet evening. If only she could take things more easily, he thought. A few dead fish, what the hell. It doesn't have to ruin your life. The middle-aged couple from the trailer were standing by their beefy hunk of four-wheel drive, heads together, talking hard. They looked as if they were saying things that they wouldn't want anyone to overhear. Probably having a stinking fight, thought Spence with satisfaction. He meditated going over to improve their campingtrip hell by asking them why they didn't take better care of their cat. But refrained.

The Balinese Dancer was still with him when Anna and Jake came back. It had reverted to its sentry duty, sitting alert and upright in the middle of the pitch.

"He's a lost cat," said Jake. "Can we keep him?"

"I thought we decided he belonged to those guys over there," Spence pointed out.

"No he doesn't."

"It doesn't," Anna confirmed. "Jake asked them. They have no cat."

"I think he was left behind. Did you notice, our pitch is the only one on this terrace that people have used recently? There was a caravan and a tent here. About a week ago by the look of the marks on the grass. They went and left without him. That's what I think."

Over his head, young Sherlock's parents exchanged an agreement to block any further moves toward an adoption.

"No, I bet he comes from that place up on the road." Spence pointed to a red-roofed ranchero that they could see over their hedge, the last house of the town. "He's probably discovered that tourists are a soft touch, and comes here on the scrounge."

"Can I go and ask them?"

"No!" snapped Anna and Spence together. Jake shrugged, and gave the cat some pâté. It didn't have the manners of a beggar. It ate a little, as if for politeness' sake, and resumed its eager watchfulness.

The child was put to bed and finally slept, having failed to persuade the cat to join him inside the yurt. The parents stayed outside. The air was so still that Anna brought out candles, to save the big lamp. They lay wrapped in rugs, reading and talking softly, and made a list for the next hypermarche: where, it was to be hoped, there'd be cooking gas cylinders in stock again at last. And batteries for Jake's headband TV, the single most necessary luxury in their lives. The cat came to visit them, peering sweetly into their faces and inviting them to play. It showed no sign of returning to the red-roofed ranch.

"You know," said Anna, "Jake could be right. It's weird for a fancy cat like that to be wandering around on the loose, like any old moggie. It's a tom, did you notice?"

"I thought toms were supposed to roam."

"Cat breeders keep their studs banged-up. They spend their lives in solitary, except when they're on the job. An inferior male kitten sold for a pet gets castrated. Let's take a closer look."

The Burmese Temple Cat was a young entire male, very thin but otherwise in good health. He had once worn a collar. He now had no identifying marks. He suffered their examination with good-tempered patience, stayed to play for a little longer, and then resumed his vigil: staring hopefully into the night.

"He's waiting for someone," said Anna, finishing her wine. "Poor little bugger. He must have gone off exploring, and they left without him. Pity he's not tattooed."

"Libertarians are everywhere," Spence reminded her. "That's probably why he still has his balls, too. No castration for me, no castration for my cat. I can see that."

"What can we do? I suppose we could leave a message at the gendarmerie, if there is one. Anyone who lost a cat like that's bound to have reported him missing."

"We can tell the *gardienne* in the morning, when she comes to collect the rent."

Next day started slowly. After lunch, Spence and Jake walked into town to look for the post office. Spence needed to dispatch the proofs of *The Coast of Coramandel*, latest of the adventures of a renowned female pirate captain: who, with her dashing young mate Jake and the rest of the desperate crew, had been keeping Patrick Spencer Meade in gainful employment for some years. The postmistress greeted them with disdain and pity, as if tourists were an endangered species too far gone to be worth your sympathy. She examined his laptop, and refused to admit that her establishment possessed a phone jack that he could plug into. She told him he could use the telephone in a normal manner, but she was afraid that connections with England and the United States were impossible at present. She told him to go to Paris. Or Lyons.

Or just get the hell out of here.

Spence's understanding of French was adequate but not subtle. He was always missing the point on small details. He'd learned to smile and nod and pass for normal; it had never failed so far. He accepted the woman's hostility without complaint, and wondered what had caused the latest telecoms melt. Urban terrorism? Surprise right-wing coup brings down the Paris government? Whole population of the UK succumbs to food poisoning? It was almost enough to send him in search of an English language newspaper, or drive him to reconnect the wb receiver in the car. But not quite. They were on holiday. Lost in France, and planning to stay lost for as long as the market would bear.

He paid for a mass of stamps and handed over the package containing the printed copy, which his publishers routinely required to back up anything sent down the wire. Andrea would be happy. His editor was an elderly young lady with a deep contempt for all things cyberspatial. She'd have loved it if Spence turned in his books written in longhand on reams of parchment. He collected Jake from the philately counter, and they left.

They wandered on up the single street, which was hardly less deathly still than it had been the evening before. They bought bread and, for want of anything else to explore, went into the ugly yellow church that stood by the war memorial in a walled yard paved with gravestones.

The interior had a crumbling nineteenth-century mariolatory decor: sky-blue heavens, madonna lilies, silver ribbons. The structure was much older. Spence traced a course of ancient stone, revealed where a long chunk of painted plaster had fallen away. It was cool and damp to the touch, and still marked by the blows of its maker who had been dead for a thousand years. He sat on the front bench in the lady chapel, holding his laptop on his knees. Jake went to investigate a dusty Easter Garden in the children's corner: Christ's sepulcher done in papier-mâché and florist's moss; a matchwood cross draped in a swag of white.

Spence was glad of a chance to sit and stare; a chance to think about the situation. When Anna was angry, she always brought up his Americanness. His thick-skinned hardiness, his refusal to *suffer*. Could he undo that crime, become one of those who didn't escape? He imagined himself burned in his bed by the Cossacks in some Eastern European village, starving in the west of Ireland. Taken up from the nine-inch board in that stinking hold, extricated from his neighbors, his chains struck off. Over the side, a sack of spoiled meat. He saw himself fall into grace, loose limbs flapping: down into the green water, silver bubbles rising as the body slowly tumbles, into the deep, the very deep. . . . It was too late. Can't turn back the hand of time. Spence lived, and would have to keep this defiant spirit, wherever it came from, that would not be mortified.

At least he could claim to be a permanent exile. Spence could never go home, not for more than a week or so at a time, not so long as his wife and his mother both lived. The whole United States wasn't big enough to contain the iron-hard territoriality of those two females. This didn't bother him. It only surprised him occasionally, when he realized how solidly his marriage had confirmed the choice he'd made for himself long before. He preferred America this way—preserved from one brief visit to the next in his voice, in his tastes, in his childhood memories. Yet displacement breeds displacement. They had traveled a great deal, in Europe and beyond, always going farther and staying away longer than other people. They'd have taken longer and wilder trips still, except for Anna's commitment to her work.

Now Anna's job was gone. There was nothing to go back for. No drag, no tie, no limit. They were no longer locked into that damned university laboratory academic year, miserable crowded August holidays. She's mine now, he thought. She's all mine. Instantly he was punished by a vision of Anna's hands. Anna moving round a clothes shop like a blind woman, assessing the fabric as if she was reading Braille: smoothing a shoulder seam, judging the cut and the fall of the cloth with those animate fingers, those living creatures imbued with genius. Anna removing and cleaning her contact lenses, nights in the past, so smashed she could hardly *breathe*, the deft economy of her gestures serenely undisturbed. Those hands rendered useless, unable to practice the art that he only knew in its faint, mundane echoes? Oh no. He thought of Marie Curie, the exacting drudgery of women scientists; it comes naturally to them. Delicacy and endurance, backed by a brain the size of Jupiter. She can't have lost all that . . . Recent memory, from those last extraordinary weeks in England, cast up a red-faced drunken old man at a publishers' party, shouting *"your wife has destroyed the fabric of society!"* One of the more bizarre incidents in his career as a scientist's spouse.

He could not take her disaster seriously, and therefore he was free to indulge his daydreams. Of course she'd get another job, but they didn't have to go home yet. They could stay away for the whole of September, mellow empty September in the French countryside. Could go south again, over to Italy, move into hotels if the weather gives out (but they all three loved to live outdoors). We can afford it, he thought, glowing a little. Easy. I may be a mere kiddies' entertainer, but I can put food on the family table. She practically had a breakdown, she's still fragile and depressed, not herself: she needs space.

But what would it be like to live with Anna, without her career? What about sex? There'd be no more foreign conferences, no more jokes about oversexed sex biologists. No more of those sparky professional friendships that had to make him suspicious, damn it, though he'd persistently denied it. He could be sure of her now . . . The idea made him uneasy. What would happen to desire, if the little goad of fear was removed? Spence had been trained by his wife to believe that animal behavior invariably has an end in view, however twisted, however bent out of shape. What if sex with his best beloved (since they weren't making babies, and it was no longer the forever inadequate confirmation that she belonged to him) began to seem unnecessary, a pointless exercise, a meaningless pleasure? An awful pang, as if the loss was real and already irrevocable, broke him out of his reverie.

He stood up. "Let's go, kid."

Jake was reluctant to leave the empty tomb, which was surrounded by a phalanx of homemade fake sunflowers, each with a photograph of a child's face in the center. He admired the whole ensemble greatly: because, Spence guessed, he could imagine doing something like that himself. The greatest art in Europe had left Jake unimpressed, since he felt he had no stake in the enterprise.

"Can we take a picture of it?"

" 'Fraid not. We didn't bring the camera."

"Can we come back with the camera, later?"

"Maybe."

"Maybe means no," muttered Jake under his breath. "Why not call a spade a spade?"

They went in search of the *gardienne*. She hadn't turned up to claim their rent in the morning. The manager of a municipal campsite usually operated out of the town hall, but this one had a house near that crossroads where the path through the wood came out. They were permitted to enter a stiff, funereal parlor. The registration form was filled in, with immense labor, by the skinny old lady and a very fat man, either her husband or her son, who was squelched immovable into a wheelback armchair at the parlor table. Jake made friends with a little dog. Spence stared at a huge ornate clock that seemed on the point of plunging to its death from the top shelf of an oak dresser laden with ugly china.

She didn't know anything about the Balinese Dancer. There was no such cat in the village. No such cat had been reported missing by any campers. She could not recall when pitch 16 had last been used, and rejected the suggestion that she might consult her records. She supposed he might report this lost cat to the police, but she saw no reason why he should give himself the trouble. The police here knew their business; they would not be interested in his story.

Spence began to get very strange vibes.

He changed the subject. They chatted a little about the political situation, always a safe topic for non-specific head-shaking and sighing. Spence paid for two nights' camping and recovered his passport. "Let's go back through the woods," he said, when they were outside.

"We haven't finished exploring."

"Your Mom's been alone long enough."

· · ·

Sitting on the floor in the sanitaires, Anna scrubbed her legs with an emery paper glove. She blew away a dust of powdered hair from the page of Ramone Holyrod's essays, keeping the book open on the floor by holding the pages down with the balls of her feet.

... like the civil rights movement, feminism has achieved certain goals at a wholly destructive price. It has created an aspirational female middle class whose interests are at odds with the interests of the female masses, and with the original aim of the movement. Successful women trade on their femininity. They have no desire to see difference between the sexes eroded, they foster and elaborate that same difference which condemns millions of other women ...

Anna was catching up. She'd once known Ramone personally, but she'd never had time to read books like this. She worked moisturizing lotion into the newly smooth bare skin and removed a vagrant drop, the color of melted chocolate ice cream, from the text. Feminist rage, she decided, had not changed much since she last looked. She turned *Prefutural Tension* face down and went to the mirror above the sinks, took her kohl pencil from the family washbag, stretched the skin of her left upper eyelid taut by applying a firm fingertip to the outer corner, and drew a fine solid line along the base of her lashes. Mirrors had begun to be haunted by the ghost of Anna's middle age, by whispers from magazines saying *don't drink and go to bed early*. But what good did it do if you couldn't sleep? There was always something to prevent her. Last night, the faint smell of that dump ...

The campsite was completely quiet. The couple with the big trailer had left at dawn. If they were intent on skipping the rent, they needn't have bothered. The *gardienne* here obviously wasn't the conscientious kind. Anna turned a soft brush in a palette of eyeshadow, a shade of yellow that was nearly gold, and dusted it across the whole area of her eyes: to lift and brighten the natural tone of her tanned skin, and correct the slightly too deep sockets.

Ramone had a nerve. A professional feminist, accusing other people of "trading on their feminine identity." Maquillage, she thought (carefully stroking the mascara wand upward, under her lower lashes) is not a female trait, if you want to talk ethnic origins. I can give you chapter and verse on that, Ramone my dear. Codon by codon. It's a male sexual gesture. As you well know. The public world is male, and to deal with it we all have to adopt male behavior. You and me both, Ramone, we have to display: strut our stuff or perish, publish or be damned. It's not your fault or mine, sister. It's simply a question of whose head is on the coin. You want to work for the company, you wear the uniform. Where do you get off, claiming that you can speak from some *female* parade ground, where competition and challenge are unknown? Balls to that.

She gazed at the face of Caesar in the mirror. Wide brow, pointed chin, black eyes, golden brown skin: Anna Senoz. *Yes, I'm married. No, I didn't change my name. Why didn't you change your name? Because I didn't want to. Next question . . .* She thought of her ancestors, Spanish Jews, pragmatic converts to Christianity. Discreet, tolerated aliens. I should have strutted my two-fisted stuff more and used less eyeliner. Ramone's right. Power dressing seems like the solution, if you're moving in a male world. But sexual display in a female animal means

I submit. It has to be that way, it's a safety guarantee of non-aggression that the male demands. So display is a male behavior, but if you're a female, sexual showing-off rebounds on you, it doesn't work right.

She had collected suitors, not vassals or allies. She had been envied, desired, but not feared. She had charmed her way along, never issuing challenges. Playing the pretty woman had made life so much easier, until it came to the crunch. It's Spence's fault, she thought. *Before Spence I liked sex and I hoped I was attractive enough to get my share, but I had no more paranoia about my personal appearance than if I was Albert Einstein. He told me I was beautiful. He got me hooked on femininity, and it's done me no good at all.*

Anna had wanted to be a plant geneticist. She'd done her first research on jumping genes, transposons, in maize. She'd been sidelined early into Human Assisted Reproduction, because that was where the funding was. That was when she'd written her first paper on Transferred Y, suggesting that certain cases of chromosomal intrasexuality with unimpaired fertility (studied in the hope of finding a gene therapy fix for the stubbornly infertile), were the effect of a transposon. No one had been much interested. But Anna had felt that she was on the track of something fascinating. Transferred Y kept calling her back, tugging at her mind, like the child with whom you can never spend enough time when you're a working parent. She had managed to make the time at last, managed to make this brainchild part of her job. And then, when she had the results, she'd written a paper—as restrained, modest and professional as the first one—suggesting that a benign donation of genetic material between the sexes was becoming established in the human genome.

The erosion of difference between the sexes, though it might not interest Ramone's *aspirational female middle class*, had been a hot topic in Anna's world for several years—at the molecular level. Anna had known that her team's paper (along with the simultaneous presentation on superU-net) would be challenged, questioned; angrily dismissed in some quarters. She was not a professional feminist, but she wasn't a political moron. She had known there would be trouble. She knew that they were making an extraordinary proposition. She'd even joked that the news might hit the tabloids. It had not occurred to her that she might lose her job.

She remembered the morning that she'd found out. Her boss had called her to a private meeting, "a chat" he'd called it, which they all knew was an ominous term, a warning. It was May time, but the sky was grey. Outside his floor-length windows, wet tassels of sycamore flower littered the Biology car-park. The fresh leaves on the copse of trees that obscured the Material Sciences Tower were shining in the rain. Anna had demonstrated that the future belongs neither to women nor to men, but to some new creature, now inexorably on its way. She had spoken this as fact, and waited to see how other scientists would treat her results. Suddenly, she found herself fighting for her professional life.

She could not understand what had gone wrong. *But it isn't a scare story,* she heard herself protesting. *What I'm saying is that this isn't like global warming or holes in the ozone layer. It's not a punishment, it's not an awful threat. Something is happening, that's all. It's just evolution.* She was floundering. She had prepared the wrong script. She had been ready to win him over, to show him how this unexpected notoriety could work for the department. But he was furious, personally enraged. He was saying that she'd set out deliberately to raise a media storm, with her wild, offensive overstatements. *What does it matter?* she begged. *It's not as if anything's going to change overnight. This is not something anyone will consciously experience. This will be like . . . coming down from the trees.*

She had found herself staring over his shoulder at the green world outside, trying to hear the birds in the little wood. There would be blackbirds, robins, perhaps a wren. The chorus was sadly depleted. Did he say *your views are not welcome in this department?* I don't have any "views," protested Anna . . . Did he say *will not be renewing your contract?* She was thinking of the songthrush and the cuckoo, those sweet and homely voices forever stilled. She had started to cry. He'd given her a paper tissue from a box he kept in his desk drawer, and calmed down, satisfied. "I'm sorry," he'd said. "I'm sorry, but . . ."

The door of the sanitaires creaked and in walked the lost cat. He glanced around, and came to question Anna with a diffident *mrrrow?* Anna wiped her eyes. Of course, I reacted as stupidly as possible. I was in shock and didn't know it. But she remembered rage at the man's pompous trivialities, rage that came out as tears, and knew that she'd been betrayed by her sex. Loss and shame had turned her into a stereotypical woman. It was still happening now. That's why she was here, grooming herself for comfort, doing the domestic, while Spence went out in public to deal with the world. "I'll be taking to the veil next," she told the cat gloomily. And, indeed, there'd been times in the last few months when she'd have been glad to hide her head, to retire under a big thick blanket and never come out.

"What do I know about animal behavior, anyway?" she said aloud. "I'm a molecular biologist. Enough to impress Spence: that doesn't take much."

The yurt was too hot and the campsite outdoors was too empty. She took Ramone's essays into the utility room, where their washing was still going round, and sat on the cool tiled floor. The Burmese Temple Cat came with her, but couldn't settle. He paced and cried. "Poor thing," Anna sympathized. "Poor thing. They let you down, didn't they? They abandoned you, and you haven't an idea what you did wrong. Never mind, maybe we'll find them."

But his grief disturbed her. It was too close to her own.

Spence and Jake walked through the woods. Spence was wondering what the hell *is* the approved *Academie Française* term for "modem," anyhow? For God's sake, even the Vatican accepts "modem." If it's good enough for the Pope . . . He'd have to ask Anna. But he wasn't sure there had been any misunderstanding at the post office. It was possible the postmistress really had been telling him, *don't hang around.* He was still getting very strange vibes from that conversation with the *gardienne.* Maybe something final and terrible had happened. France and England had declared war on each other, and tourists were liable to be rounded up as undesirable aliens. He wasn't sure that war between two states of the European Union was technically possible. It would have to be a civil war.

No problem with that: a very popular global sport. In fact, he wouldn't be a bit surprised. The only problem would be for the French and English governments to handle anything so *organized*. Have to get the telecoms to work again first . . .

They had reached the dump. That smell surrounded them. Crowds of flies hummed and muttered, and the surface of the wide, garbage-filled hollow drew Spence's eyes. He was looking for something that he had seen last night in the twilight, seen and not quite registered. The flies buzzed. He had stopped walking. Jake was looking up at him, wrinkling his nose: puzzled that an adult could be so indifferent to the ripe stink.

He handed over his laptop. Jake was already carrying the bread.

"Go on back. I'll be along in a minute. I want to check something."

"But I want to see what you find!"

"I'm not going to find anything. I'm just going to take a leak."

"I want a wee too."

"No, you don't. Get going. Tell Anna I won't be long."

Spence waited until he was sure the child wasn't going to turn back. Then he went to investigate the buried wreckage. He found the remains of a caravan. It had been burned out, quite recently, having been stripped first (as far as he could tell) of identification. He crouched on the flank of a big plastic drum that had once contained fertilizer, and pondered. Someone had rolled a wrecked mobile home into this landfill, having removed the plates, and covered it over. What did that prove? It didn't prove anything except that he was letting himself get spooked. "I'm overtired," he said aloud, scowling. "Been on the road too long." But the garbage had shifted when he was clambering over it, and the dump refused to let him cling to his innocence. He climbed down from his perch, and discovered that the suggestive-looking bunch of twigs that he'd spotted really *was* a human hand.

It had been a woman's hand, not young. It was filthy, and the rats had been at it, but he could still see lumpy knuckles and the paler indentations left by her rings. He found a stick and pried at the surrounding layers of junk until he had uncovered her face. There wasn't much left of that. He squatted, looking down: remembering Father Moynihan in his coffin, like something carved out of yellow wax. His own father too, but he had no memory of that dead body. He'd been too young: not allowed to look.

"What did you do?" he whispered. "Too rich, too funny-looking? Wrong kind of car? Did you support the wrong football team? Was it because you didn't castrate your cat?"

The flies buzzed. Around him, beyond the thin woodland, stretched the great emptiness: all the parched, desolate, rural heartlands of Europe, where life was strained and desperate as in any foundering city. All the lost little towns starved of hope, where people turned into monsters without anything showing on the outside.

Anna groped for potatoes in the sack in the back of the car, brought out another that was too green to eat, and chucked it aside. He knows nothing. He hasn't a clue about the backbiting, the betrayals, all the internal politics. Spence admires my work in a romantic way, but in the end it's just something that keeps me away from home. Maybe he's my wife. She felt the descant of male to female, female to male, the slipping and sliding between identities that had been natural and accepted surely by most people, for years and years. It was Anna's boss who was crazy. How could anyone be *angry* about an arrangement of chemicals? The sack was nearly empty. *What's happening to my French beans? The lettuces will be shot.* She was pining for her garden. It was so difficult to get hold of good fresh vegetables on the road. The prepackaged stuff in the hypermarkets was an insult, but the farmers' markets weren't much better. Not when you were a stranger and didn't know your way around. We'll go home. I'll pull myself together, start fighting my corner the way I should have done at the start. We'll have to go back soon, she assured herself, knowing Spence's silent resistance. Jake has to go to school.

She saw him come out of the wood. He went straight to the sanitaires, vanished for several minutes, and slowly came toward her. He sat on the rim of the hatchback. There were drops of water in his hair, and his hands were wet.

"Where's Jake?"

"In the playground. What's the matter? You look sick."

"I found a body in the dump."

They both stared at the distant figure of the child. He was climbing on the knotted rope, singing a song from a French TV commercial. Anna felt claws of ice dig into her spine, as if something expected but ridiculously forgotten had jumped out *Boo!* from behind a door.

"You mean a human body?"

"Yes. I could only find one, but I think there must be two." He imagined a couple, a middle-aged early-retirement couple, modestly well-heeled, children, if any, long ago departed. Spending the summer *en plein air*, the way the French love to do: with their cat. "I covered it over again. I was afraid to root around, but there's a caravan too. I'm not joking. It's true."

"You'd better show me."

Spence gasped, and shook his head. "I can't."

"Why not?"

"Because we can't let Jake see that, and we can't leave him here alone."

Anna nodded. She went to the front of the car and started searching under the seats and in the door pockets.

"What are you looking for?"

"The camera." She brought it out. "I'll take pictures. Will it be easy for me to find?"

It was about the same time of day as it had been when they arrived. Shortly, Jake noticed that his father had returned and came running over. The Balinese Dancer ran along beside him.

"Where's Mummy?"

"She's gone to check something."

Jake's eyes narrowed. "Her too?" Spence had forgotten he'd used the exact same words at the dump, when he sent the kid on alone. "Is it something about my cat?"

Balinese Dancer looked up. Spence had a terrible, irrational feeling that the cat knew. He knew what Spence had seen, and that there was no hope anymore.

"Don't start getting ideas."

For most of the time that Anna was away, it didn't cross his mind that she was in danger. Then it did, and he spent a very unhappy quarter of an hour, playing Scrabble with Jake while racking his brains to recover every word he'd spoken in that town, especially in his rash interview with the *gardienne*: praying to God he'd said nothing to rouse anyone's suspicions. They washed the potatoes. Spence cut them up, chopped an onion and some garlic, opened a can of tomatoes and one of chickpeas. He put olives in a bowl, and spread the picnic table-cloth. He didn't light the stove until everything was ready, because they were running out of gas. At last, Anna came out of that grisly wood.

"Shall I start cooking?"

"I'm going to have a shower," she said.

While Anna put Jake to bed, Spence washed the dishes, and stored away the almost untouched potato stew. He checked the car over and gathered a few stray belongings from the shriveled grass. Their camp was compact. One modest green hatchback, UK plates, anonymous middle-class brand. One mushroom-shaped tent dwelling. No bicycles, no surfboards. No TV aerial dish, no patio furniture. The sky was overcast, but blurred with moon silver in the east. How often had they camped like this beside some still and secret little town? That place in Italy on the hilltop, most certainly a haunt of vampires. . . .

The cat wove at his ankles and followed him indoors. Inside, the yurt was a single conical space that could be divided by cunning foldaway partitions. It was furnished with nomad simplicity and comfort: their bed, rugs, books; small useful items of gear. There was no mere decoration, no more than if they'd been traveling on the steppes with Genghis Khan. Spence set down the wine bottle, two glasses, and the rest of the bread. Anna stepped out of Jake's section and sealed it behind her. They sat on the floor with the lamp turned low, and looked at the pictures she had taken. She'd uncovered the body further and taken several shots of the head and torso, the hands and wrists; and then the whole ensemble, the wrecked caravan. She had seen what she thought was the second corpse, burned to a black crisp inside the caravan, but hadn't been able to get a clear picture of that.

"You think it was locals?" she asked.

Spence told her about the postmistress, and the *gardienne*. A one-street town wrapped in guilty silence: "I'm sure they know about it. Maybe someone had an accident. Someone ran into them and wrecked them, found they were dead and got scared . . ."

"And took the woman's rings. And gouged out her eyes. And tied her up."

Anna touched the preview screen, advancing from shot to shot until she found the woman's face. She moved it into close-up, but their camera was not equal to this kind of work. The image blurred into a drab Halloween mask: crumpled plastic; black eye holes.

"That other couple must have picked up on something," she guessed. "That's why they left so quickly." She shivered.

"Well," said Spence, "it's been all around us. We finally managed to run right into it. The town that eats tourists. Of course, in the good old U.S. of A., we're cool about this kind of thing. Vampire towns, ghoul towns, whole counties run by serial-killer aliens. We take it for granted. Poor Balinese Dancer, I'm afraid your people definitely aren't coming back."

"You can't call him that," she said. "He's not a Balinese. He's a Birman. Don't you believe me? Hook up the CD-ROM, and we can look him up in Jake's encyclopedia—"

"I believe you. But why can't I *call* him Balinese?"

"Because you're doing it to annoy me. And . . . we don't need that."

In the direct look she gave him, the hostilities that had rumbled under their un-negotiated peace finally came to an end. Spence sighed. "Oh, okay. I won't."

"Is there any wine left?" asked Anna. He handed her the bottle. She poured some into their glasses, broke a chunk of bread, and ate it.

"So what are we going to do? Report our finds to the gendarmes?"

"Don't be stupid," said Anna.

"Not here, definitely not. But in Lyons, maybe."

"They wouldn't do anything. You know they wouldn't. City flics don't come looking for trouble in the *deserte rural*."

The rural desert. That was what the French called their prairie band. Mile upon mile of wheat and maize and sunflowers: all of it on death row as an economic activity, having lived just long enough to kill off most of the previous ecology. And destroy a lot of human lives.

"Okay, then we could stick around here and do a little investigation for ourselves."

The cat was sitting diffidently outside the circle of lamplight, his eyes moving from face to face. Spence's heart went out to him. "Try to find out who the cat's folks were, where they came from, why this happened to them. Uncover some fetid tale or other, maybe get one or other of ourselves tortured and killed as well; or maybe Jake—"

Anna grimaced wryly. "No thanks."

"Or we could do what they never do in the movies. Stop the thrilling plot before it starts. Walk on by."

She switched off the camera and stayed for a long time staring at the grey floor of the yurt, elbows on her knees and chin in her hands. She had turned the dead face from side to side, without flinching from her task. *This is the truth. It must be examined, described.* But no one wanted to be told. There would be no assessment, no judgment.

"Spence, I have a terrible feeling. It's about my paper. I started thinking this when I was looking at her, when I was recording her death. Suppose . . . suppose the tabloids *aren't* loopy and my boss *isn't* deranged? Suppose while we've been away, while we've been cut off from all the news, the world has finally been going over the edge, because of what I said?"

"The whole place was going mad before you published, kid. The end of the world as we know it started a long time ago."

"Yes, Spence dear. Exactly. That's what my paper says."

Spence took a slug from the wine bottle, neglecting the glass that was poured for him. That sweet tone of invincible intellectual superiority, *when it was friendly*, always made him go weak at the knees.

"Would you like to have sex?" he hazarded, across the tremulous lamplight.

"Like plague victims," said Anna huskily. "Rutting in the streets, death all around."

"Okay, but *would* you?"

Flash of white knickers in the twilight. Nothing's sure. Every time could be the last.

"Yes."

When they were both done, both satisfied, Spence managed to fall asleep. He dreamed that he was clinging to the side of a runaway train that was racing downhill in the dark. Anna was in his arms and Jake held between them. He knew that he had to leap from this train before it smashed, holding onto them both. But he was too terrified to let go.

They had pitched the yurt at dusk, in a service area campsite. The great road thundered by the scrubby expanse of red grit, where tents and trucks and vans stood cheek-by-jowl without a tree or a blade of grass in sight. The clientele was mixed. There were *gens de voyage*, with their pitches staked out in the traditional, aggressive washing lines; colorful New Age travelers trying to look like visitors from the stone age; respectable itinerant workers in their tidy camper vans; truck drivers asleep in their cabs. Among them were the tourists, people like Anna and Jake and Spence, turned back from the channel ports by the fishing-dispute blockade, who had wisely moved inland from the beaches.

Spence was removing the cassette player from the car, so he could refit the wide bandwidth receiver that would give them access to the great big world again. The dusk was no problem, as this campsite was lit by enormous gangling floodlights that seemed to have been bought secondhand from a football stadium. But the player had turned obstinate. He was lying on his back, legs in the yard and face squished in the leg space under the dashboard, struggling with some tiny recalcitrant screws. Chuck the cat, ever fascinated and helpful when there was work going on, was sitting on the passenger seat and patting the screws that *had* come out down into the crack at the back of the cushion.

Something thumped near Spence's head. He wriggled out. Anna had returned from her mission with a lumpy burlap sack.

"What's in there?"

"Potatoes, courgettes-I-mean-zucchini, and string beans. But the beans are pure string."

"Still, that's pretty good. What did you have to do?"

The channel tunnel had been down, so to speak, for most of the summer. This new interruption of the ferry services had compounded everyone's problems. Hypermarches along the coast had turned traitor, closing their doors to all but the local population. The more enterprising of the stranded travelers were resorting to barter.

"Nothing too difficult. First aid. Dietary advice to an incipient diabetic, she needs an implant but diet will help; and I'm attending to a septic cut."

"This is weird. You can't practice medicine!"

Anna rubbed her bare brown shoulder, where the sack had galled her, and shrugged. "Let me see. *First, do no harm.* Well, I have no antibiotics, no anti-malarials, no carrier viruses or steroids, so that's all right. I have aspirin, I know how to reduce a fracture, and I wash my hands a lot. What more can you ask?"

"My God." He groped for the screwdriver, which had escaped into camping-trip morass under the seat. "Could you give me some assistance for a moment? Since you're here?"

"No, because I don't want you to do that."

"But I'm doing it anyway."

"Good luck to you," she said, without rancor. "It's mostly pure noise, in my opinion."

At bedtime, Anna listened while Jake read to her the story of the Burmese Temple Cat called Sinh, who was an oracle. He lived with a priest called Mun-Ha, and they were both very miserable because Burma was being invaded. When Mun-Ha died, the goddess Tsun-Kyankse transfused Mun-Ha's spirit into Sinh. His eyes turned blue as sapphires, his nose and feet and tail turned dark as the sacred earth, and the rest of him turned gold, except for the tips of his paws— which were touching Mun-Ha's white hair at the moment the holy priest died. Then Sinh transfused his power into the rest of the priests, and they went and saved Burma.

"Do you know what an oracle is?"

"Yeah," he answered drowsily. "It's a little boat."

Coracle, oracle: a messenger from the gods and a little boat on a great big shoreless sea. Anna watched as the child fell deeper into sleep.

Spence finished his task and repaired to the bar. He ordered two *pression* and took them to a table by the doors that he already thought of as his and Anna's table, because that was where they sat when they came in for a drink before setting up. The large, dimly lit room was crowded, but not oppressively stuffed. Foosball in the games room, pizzas and frites and sandwiches readily available; absolutely no pretensions. Yes, he thought. It's our kind of joint. The clatter of conversation, mostly French, soon blended into a soothing, encompassing ocean roar: laughter or the clink of glassware springing up like spray.

We could live here, he decided. In this twilight. He imagined the blockade stretching into months and years; imagined that the actual no-kidding disintegration had begun—which of course was nonsense. Anna, armed with their home-medicine manual, could become a quack doctor. Maybe Spence could sell information? He dallied with the idea of describing Anna as a *wisewoman*, but rejected it. Call a spade a spade. This is not the dawning of some magical, nurturing female future. It's the same road we've been traveling for so long, going down into the dark. . . .

Chuck had followed him from the car and was sitting on the chair next to Spence, taking it all in with his usual assured and gentle gaze. The young woman from the bar came by with a tray of glasses. Spence had a moment's anxiety. Chuck was respectably vaccinated and tattooed now. They'd managed to get this done in the same town where they'd dispatched (this was the compromise they'd reached) an anonymous tip-off, and prints of Anna's photographs, to the police in the regional capital. But maybe he wasn't welcome in the bar.

But she'd only stopped to admire. "What do you call him?" she asked.

"Chuck Prophet."

The girl laughed, effortlessly balancing her tray on one thin muscular arm, and bending to rub the Birman's delectably soft, ruffled throat. "That's an unusual name for a cat."

"He's an unusual cat," explained Spence proudly.

She moved on. Chuck had accepted her caress the way he took any kind of attention: sweetly, but a little distracted, a little disappointed at the touch of a hand that was not the hand he waited for. The moment she was gone, he resumed his eager study of the crowd, his silver-blue eyes searching hopefully: ears alert for a voice and a step that he would never hear again. Still keeping the faith, still confident that normal service would be restored.

Marrow

ROBERT REED

Robert Reed is a frequent contributor to The Magazine of Fantasy & Science Fiction *and* Asimov's Science Fiction, *and has also sold stories to* Science Fiction Age, Universe, New Destinies, Tomorrow, Synergy, Starlight, *and elsewhere. His books include the novels* The Leeshore, The Hormone Jungle, Black Milk, The Remarkables, Down the Bright Way, *and* Beyond the Veil of Stars. *His most recent books are the novels* An Exaltation of Larks *and a sequel to* Beyond the Veil of Stars *titled* Beneath the Gated Sky, *and a new story collection is in the works. His stories have appeared in our Ninth, Tenth, Eleventh, Twelfth, Thirteenth, and Fourteenth Annual Collections. He lives in Lincoln, Nebraska.*

Reed is one of the most prolific of today's short fiction writers, seriously rivaled for the top position only by authors such as Stephen Baxter and Brian Stableford. And—also like Baxter and Stableford—he manages to keep up a very high standard of quality while being prolific, something that is not at all easy to do. Again this year, as has been true for the last several years, Reed produced at least three or four stories that were strong enough to have been sure choices for a best-of-the-year volume in another year, so that it became not a matter of whether or not I was going to use a Reed story, but rather which Reed story I was going to use. An embarrassment of riches!

In the end, I decided on the intricate and surprising novella that follows, a story mind-bogglingly vast in scope and scale even among examples of wide-screen SF, a story that shows us that right under our feet, unexpected and undiscovered, there might be a whole new world—one that we ought to think twice about visiting. . . .

MISSION YEAR 0.00:

Washen couldn't count all the captains spread out before her, and putting on her finest captainly smile, she joined them, trading the usual compliments, telling little stories about her travels, and with a genuine unease, asking if anyone knew why the Ship's Master would want to bring them here.

"She's testing us," one gray-eyed colleague ventured. "She's testing our obedience. Plus our security measures, too."

"Perhaps," Washen allowed.

Coded orders had found Washen through secure channels. Without explanation, the Master told her to abandon her post, discarding her uniform and taking on a suitable disguise. For the last seven days, she had played the role of dutiful tourist, wandering the vast ship, enjoying its wondrous sights, then after making triple-sure that she wasn't being monitored, boarding an anonymous tube-car that had brought her to this odd place.

"My name is Diu," said her companion, offering his hand and a wide smile.

She clasped the hand with both of hers, saying, "We met at the captains' banquet. Was it twenty years ago?"

"Twenty-five." Like most captains, Diu was tall for a human, with craggy features and an easy charm meant to instill trust in their human passengers. "It's kind of you to remember me. Thank you."

"You're most welcome."

The eyes brightened. "What do you think of the Master's tastes? Isn't this a bizarre place to meet?"

"Bizarre," Washen echoed. "That's a good word."

The leech once lived here. An obscure species, ascetic by nature, they had built their home inside the remote confines of one of the ship's enormous fuel tanks. Weaving together thick plastics, they had dangled this place from the tank's insulated ceiling. Its interior, following a leech logic, was a single room. Vast in two dimensions but with a glowing gray ceiling close enough to touch, the surroundings made every human feel claustrophobic. The only furnishings were hard gray pillows. The air was warm and stale, smelling of odd dusts and persistent pheromones. Colors were strictly forbidden. Even the gaudy tourists' clothes seemed to turn gray in the relentless light.

"I've been wondering," said Diu. "Whatever happened to the leech?"

"I don't know," Washen confessed. She had met the species when they came on board. But that was more than a thousand years before, and even a captain's memory was imperfect.

The leech could have simply reached their destination, disembarking without incident. Or they could have decided to build an even more isolated home, if that was possible. Or perhaps some disaster had struck, and they were dead. Shipboard extinctions were more common than any captain would admit. Some of their passengers proved too frail to endure any long journey. Mass suicides and private wars claimed others. Yet as Washen often reminded herself, for every failed species, a hundred others thrived, or at least managed to etch out some little corner of this glorious ship where they could hold their own.

"Wherever the leech are, I'm sure they're well."

"Of course they are," Diu replied, knowing what was polite. "Of course."

In the face of ignorance, captains should make positive sounds.

Washen noticed how even when standing still, Diu was moving, his flesh practically vibrating, as if the water inside him was ready to boil.

"So, madam . . . I'm dying to know what you think! What's our mission? What's so important that the Master pulls us all the way down here?"

"Yes," said a second voice. "What's your best bad guess, darling?"

Miocene had joined them. One of a handful of Submasters in attendance, she was rumored to be the Master's favorite. An imperious, narrow-faced woman, she was a full head taller than the others, dressed in rich robes, her brindle-colored hair brushing against the ceiling. Yet she stood erect, refusing to dip her head for the simple sake of comfort.

"Not that you know more than any of us," the Submaster persisted. "But what do you think the Master wants?"

The room seemed to grow quiet. Captains held their breath, secretly delighted that it was Washen who had to endure Miocene's attentions.

"Well," Washen began, "I can count several hundred clues."

A razor smile formed. "And they are?"

"Us." They were standing near one of the room's few windows—a wide slit of thick, distorting plastic. There was nothing outside but blackness and vacuum; an ocean of liquid hydrogen, vast and calm and brutally cold, lay some fifty kilometers below them. Nothing was visible in the window but their own murky reflections. Washen saw everyone at a glance. She regarded her own handsome, ageless face, black hair pulled back in a sensible bun and streaked with enough white to lend authority, her wide chocolate eyes betraying confidence with a twist of deserved pleasure. "The Master selected us, and we're the clues."

Miocene glanced at her own reflection. "And who are we?"

"The elite of the elite." Washen put names to the faces, listing bonuses and promotions earned over the last millennia. "Manka is a new second-grade. Aasleen was in charge of the last engine upgrade, which came in below budget and five months early. Saluki and Westfall have won the Master's award for duty ten times each." She gestured at the captain beside her, saying, "And there's Diu, of course. Already an eleventh-grade, which is astonishing. You came on board the ship—warn me if I'm wrong—as just another passenger."

The energetic man said, "True, madam. Thank you for remembering."

Washen grinned, then said, "And then there's you, Madam Miocene. You are one of three Submasters with first-chair status at the Master's table."

The tall woman nodded, enjoying the flattery. "But don't forget yourself, darling."

"I never do," Washen replied, earning a good laugh from everyone. And because nothing was more unseemly in a captain than false modesty, she admitted, "I've heard the rumors. I'm slated to become our newest Submaster."

Miocene grinned, but she made no comment about any rumors.

Instead she took an enormous breath, and in a loud voice asked, "Can you smell yourselves? Can you? That's the smell of ambition. No other scent is so tenacious, or in my mind, ever so sweet . . . !"

· · ·

No name but the ship was necessary. Ancient and spectacular, there was nothing else that could be confused with it, and everyone on board, from the Ship's Master to the most disreputable stowaway, was justifiably proud of their magnificent home.

The ship began as a jupiter-class world, but an unknown species had claimed it. Using its hydrogen atmosphere, they accelerated the core to a fraction of lightspeed. Then they built tunnels and compartments, plus chambers large enough to swallow small worlds. Premium hyperfibers lent strength and durability to the frame. And then, as with the leech's plastic abode, the builders suddenly and mysteriously abandoned their creation.

Billions of years later, humans stumbled across the ship. Most of its systems were in a diagnostic mode. Human engineers woke them, making repairs where necessary. Then the best human captains were hired, and every manner of passenger was ushered aboard, the ship's maiden voyage calling for a half-million year jaunt around the Milky Way.

Its undisputed ruler arrived a few hours later.

Accompanied by a melody of horns and angel-voiced humans, the Master strode into the room. Where other captains were disguised in civilian clothes, their leader wore a mirrored cap and uniform that suited her office, and for many reasons, her chosen body was broad and extraordinarily deep. It was status, in part. But a Master also needed bulk to give her augmented brain a suitable home, thousands of ship functions constantly monitored and adjusted, in the same unconscious way that the woman moved and breathed.

Gravity was weaker this deep inside the ship. With one vast hand skating along the ceiling, the Master deftly kept herself from bumping her head. A dozen of the low-grade captains offered greetings and hard cushions. Diu was among the supplicants, on his knees and smiling, even after she had passed.

"Thank you for coming," said that voice that always took Washen by surprise. It was a quiet, unhurried voice, perpetually amused by whatever the radiant brown eyes were seeing. "I know you're puzzled," she said, "and I hope you're concerned. So let me begin with my compelling reasons for this game, and what I intend for you."

A handful of guards stood in the distance; Washen saw their tiny armored silhouettes as the room's lights fell to nothing.

"The ship, please."

A real-time projection blossomed beside the Master, channeled through her own internal systems. The spherical hull looked slick and gray. A thousand lasers were firing from the bow, aiming at comets and other hazards. Mammoth engines rooted in the stern spat out hurricanes of plasma, incrementally adjusting their course and speed. And a tiny flare on the equator meant that another starship was arriving. With new passengers, presumably.

"Now," said the amused voice, "start peeling the onion. Please."

In a blink, the hyperfiber hull was removed. Washen could suddenly make out the largest high-deck chambers; she knew each by name and purpose, just as she knew every important place too small to be seen. Then another few hundred kilometers of rock and water, air and hyperfiber were erased, exposing more landmarks.

"This perfect architecture." The Master stepped closer to the shrinking projection, its glow illuminating a wide strong self-assured face—a face designed to inspire thousands of captains, and a crew numbering in the tens of millions. "In my mind, there's been no greater epic in history. I'm not talking about this journey of ours. I mean about the astonishing task of exploring our ancient starship. Imagine the honor: To be the first living organism to step into one of these chambers, the first sentient mind in billions of years to experience their vastness, their mystery. It was a magnificent time. And I'm talking first-hand, since I was one of the leaders of the first survey team . . ."

It was an old, honorable boast, and her prerogative.

"We did a superlative job," she assured. "I won't accept any other verdict. Despite technical problems and the sheer enormity of it, we mapped more than ninety-nine percent of the ship's interior. In fact, I was the first one to find my way through the plumbing above us, and the first to see the sublime beauty of the hydrogen sea below us . . ."

Washen hid a smile, thinking: A fuel tank is a fuel tank is a fuel tank.

"Here we are," the Master announced. The projection had shrunk by a third. The fuel tank was a fist-sized cavern; the leech habitat was far too small to be seen. Then in the next moment, they were gone, another layer removed without sound or fuss. Liquid hydrogen turned into a blackish solid, and deeper still, a transparent metal. "These seas have always been the deepest features," she commented. "Below them, there's nothing but iron and a stew of other metals squashed under fantastic pressures."

The ship had been reduced to a perfectly smooth black ball—the essential ingredient in a multitude of popular games.

"Until now, we knew nothing about the core." The Master paused for a moment, allowing herself a quick grin. "Evidence shows that when the ship was built, its core was stripped of its radionuclides, probably to help cool the metals and keep them relatively stiff. We don't know how the builders managed the trick. But there used to be narrow tunnels leading down, all reinforced with hyperfibers and energy buttresses, and all eventually crushed by time and a lack of repair." A second pause, then she said, "Not enough room left for a single microchine to pass. Or so we've always believed."

Washen felt herself breathing faster, enjoying the moment.

"There has never, ever been the feeblest hint of hidden chambers," the Master proclaimed. "I won't accept criticism on this matter. Every possible test was carried out. Seismic. Neutrino imaging. Even palm-of-the-hand calculations of mass and volume. Until fifty-three years ago, there was no reason to fear that our maps weren't complete."

A silence had engulfed the audience.

Quietly, smoothly, the Master said, "The full ship. Please."

The iron ball was again dressed in rock and hyperfiber.

"Now the impact. Please."

Washen stepped forward, anticipating what she would see. Fifty-three years ago, they passed through a dense swarm of comets. The captains had thrown gobs of antimatter into the largest hazards. Lasers fired without pause, evaporating trillions of tons of ice. But debris still peppered the hull, a thousand pinpricks of light dancing on its silver-gray projection, and then came a blistering white flash that dwarfed the other explosions and left the captains blinking, remembering that moment, and the shared embarrassment.

A chunk of nickel-iron had slipped through their defenses. The ship rattled with the impact, and for months afterwards, nervous passengers talked about little else. Even when the captains showed them all of the schematics and calculations, proving that they could have absorbed an even larger impact before anyone was in real danger . . . even then there people and aliens who insisted on being afraid.

With a palpable relish, the Master said, "Now the cross section, please."

Half of the ship evaporated. Pressure waves spread down and out from the blast site, then pulled together again at the stern, causing more damage before they bounced, and bounced back again, the diluted vibrations still detectable now, murmuring their way through the ship as well as through the captains' own bones.

"AI analysis. Please."

A map was laid over the cross section, every feature familiar. Save one.

"Madam," said a sturdy voice. Miocene's voice. "It's an anomaly, granted. But doesn't the feature seem rather . . . unlikely . . . ?"

"Which is why I thought it was nothing. And my trusted AI—part of my own neural net—agreed with me. This region is a change in composition. Nothing more." She paused for a long moment, watching her captains. Then with a gracious oversized smile, she admitted, "The possibility of a hollow core has to seem ludicrous."

Submasters and captains nodded with a ragged hopefulness.

Knowing they weren't ordered here because of an anomaly, Washen stepped closer. How large was it? Estimates were easy to make, but the simple math created some staggering numbers.

"Ludicrous," the Master repeated. "But then I thought back to when we were babies, barely a few thousand years old. Who would have guessed that a jupiter-class world could become a starship like ours?"

Just the same, thought Washen: Certain proposals will always be insane.

"But madam," said Miocene. "A chamber of those proportions would make us less massive. Assuming we know the densities of the intervening iron, of course . . ."

"And you're assuming, of course, that the core is empty." The Master grinned at her favorite officer, then at all of them. For several minutes, her expression was serene, wringing pleasure out of their confusion and ignorance.

Then she reminded everyone, "This began as someone else's vessel. We shouldn't forget: We don't understand why our home was built. For all we know, it was a cargo ship. A cargo ship, and here is its hold."

The captains shuddered at the idea.

"Imagine that something is inside this chamber. Like any cargo, it would have to be restrained. A series of strong buttressing fields might keep it from rattling around every time we adjusted our course. And naturally, if the buttressing fields were rigid enough, then they would mask whatever is down there—"

"Madam," shouted someone, "please, what's down there . . . ?"

Shouted Diu.

"A spherical object. It's the size of Mars, but considerably more massive." The Master grinned for a moment, then told the projection, "Please. Show them what I found."

The image changed again. Nestled inside the great ship was a world, black as iron and slightly smaller than the chamber surrounding it. The simple possibility of such an enormous, unexpected discovery didn't strike Washen as one revelation, but as many, coming in waves, making her gasp and shake her head as she looked at her colleagues' faces, barely seeing any of them.

"This world has an atmosphere," said the laughing voice, "with enough oxygen to be breathed, enough water for lakes and rivers, and all of the symptoms usually associated with a vigorous biosphere—"

"How do we know that?" Washen called out. Then, in a mild panic, "No disrespect intended, madam!"

"I haven't gone there myself, if that's what you're asking." She giggled like a child, telling them, "But after fifty years of secret work, using self-replicating drones to rebuild one of the old tunnels . . . after all that, I'm able to stand here and assure you that not only does this world exist, but that each of you are going to see it for yourselves . . ."

Washen glanced at Diu, wondering if her face wore that same wide smile.

"I have named the world, by the way. We'll call it Marrow." The Master winked and said, "For where blood is born, of course. And it's reserved for you . . . my most talented, trustworthy friends . . . !"

Wonders had been accomplished in a few decades. Mole-like drones had gnawed their way through beds of nickel and iron, repairing one of the ancient tunnels; fleets of tube-cars had plunged to where the tunnel opened into the mysterious chamber, assembling a huge stockpile of supplies directly above Marrow; then a brigade of construction drones threw together the captains' base camp—a sterile little city of dormitories, machine shops, and first-rate laboratories tucked within a transparent, airtight blister.

Washen was among the last to arrive. At the Master's insistence, she led a cleaning detail that stayed behind, erasing every trace of the captains' presence from the leech habitat. It was a security precaution, and it required exacting work. And some of her people considered it an insult. "We aren't janitors," they grumbled. To which Washen replied, "You're right. Professionals would have finished last week."

Diu belonged to her detail, and unlike some, the novice captain worked hard to endear himself. He was probably calculating that she would emerge from this mission as a Submaster and his benefactor. But there was nothing wrong in calculations, Washen believed—as long as the work was done, successes piled high and honors for everyone.

Only tiny, two passenger tube-cars could make the long fall to the base camp. Washen decided that Diu would provide comfortable company. He rewarded her with his life story, including how he came into the captains' ranks. "After a few thousand years of being a wealthy passenger, I realized that I was bored." He said it with a tone of confession, and amusement. "But you captains never look bored. Pissed, yes. And harried, usually. But that's what attracted me to you. If only because people expect it, captains can't help seem relentlessly, importantly busy."

Washen had to admit, it was a unique journey into the ship's elite.

At journey's end, their car pulled into the first empty berth. On foot, Diu and Washen conquered the last kilometer, stepping abruptly out onto the viewing platform, and not quite standing together, peering over the edge.

A tinted airtight blister lay between them and several hundred kilometers of airless, animated space. Force fields swirled through that vacuum, creating an array of stubborn, stable buttresses. The buttresses were visible as a brilliant blue-white light that flowed from everywhere, filling the chamber. The light never seemed to weaken. Even with the blister's protection, the glare was intense. Relentless. Eyes had to adapt—a physiological change that would take several ship-days—and even still, no one grew accustomed to the endless day.

Even inside her bedroom, windows blackened and the covers thrown over her head, a captain could feel the radiance piercing her flesh just so it could tickle her bones.

The chamber wall was blanketed with a thick mass of gray-white hyperfiber, and the wall was their ceiling, falling away on all sides until it vanished behind Marrow.

"Marrow," Washen whispered, spellbound.

On just the sliver of the world beneath them, the captain saw a dozen active volcanoes, plus a wide lake of bubbling iron. In cooler basins, hot-water streams ran into colorful, mineral-stained lakes. Above them, water clouds were gathering into enormous thunderheads. When the land wasn't exploding, it was a rugged shadowless black, and the blackness wasn't just because of the iron-choked soils. Vigorous, soot-colored vegetation basked in the endless day. And they were a blessing. From what the captains could see, the forests were acting as powerful filters, scrubbing the atmosphere until it was clean, at least to where humans, if conditioned properly, should be able to breathe, perhaps even comfortably.

"I want to get down there," Washen confessed.

"It's going to take time," Diu warned, pointing over her shoulder.

Above the blister, dormitories and machine shops were dangling from the hyperfiber, their roofs serving as foundations. Past them, at the blister's edge, the captains were assembling a silvery-white cylinder. It would eventually form a bridge to Marrow. There was no other way down. The buttress fields killed transports, and for many reasons, unprotected minds eroded in an instant, and died. To beat the challenge, their best engineer, Aasleen, had designed a shaft dressed in hyperfibers, its interior shielded with ceramics and superfluids. Theories claimed that the danger ended with Marrow's atmosphere, but just to be safe, several hundred immortal pigs and baboons were in cages, waiting to put those guesses to the test.

Washen was thinking about the baboons, and timetables.

A familiar voice broke her reverie.

"What are your impressions, darlings?"

Miocene stood behind them. In uniform, she was even more imposing, and more cold. Yet Washen summoned her best smile, greeting the mission leader, then adding, "I'm surprised. I didn't know it would be this beautiful."

"Is it?" The knife-edged face offered a smile. "Is there any beauty here, Diu?"

"A spartan kind of beauty," Diu replied.

"I wouldn't know. I don't have any feel for aesthetics." The Submaster smiled off into the distance. "Tell me. If this world proves harmless and beautiful, what do you think our passengers will pay for the chance to come here?"

"If it's a little dangerous," Washen ventured, "they would pay more."

Miocene's smile came closer, growing harder. "And if it's deadly, maybe we'll have to collapse the tunnel again. With us safely above, of course."

"Of course," the captains echoed.

Diu was grinning, with his face, and if possible, with his entire body.

Mirrors and antennae clung to hyperfiber, gazing at Marrow. He gestured at them, asking, "Have we seen any signs of intelligence, madam? Or artifacts of any sort?"

"No," said Miocene, "and no."

It would be a strange place for sentience to evolve, thought Washen. And if the builders had left ruins behind, they would have been destroyed long ago. The crust beneath them wasn't even a thousand years old. Marrow was an enormous forge, constantly reworking its face as well as the bones beneath.

"I can't help it," Diu confessed. "I keep dreaming that the builders are down there, waiting for us."

"A delirious dream," Miocene warned him.

But Washen felt the same way. She could almost see the builders slathering the hyperfiber, then building Marrow. This was a huge place, and they couldn't see more than a sliver of it from their tiny vantage point. Who knew what they would eventually find?

Diu couldn't stop talking. "This is fantastic," he said. "And an honor. I'm just pleased that the Master would include me."

The Submaster nodded, conspicuously saying nothing.

"Now that I'm here," Diu blubbered, "I can almost see the purpose of this place."

With a level glance, Washen tried to tell her companion, Shut up.

But Miocene had already tilted her head, eyeing their eleventh-grade colleague. "I'd love to hear your theories, darling."

Diu lifted his eyebrows.

An instant later, with bleak amusement, he remarked, "I think not." Then he looked at his own hands, saying, "Once spoken, madam, a thought hides inside at least one other."

MISSION YEAR 1.03:

Planetfall was exactly as the captains had planned—a routine day from the final five kilometers of bridge building to Miocene's first steps on the surface. And with success came cheers and singing, followed by ample late suppers served with bottomless glasses of well-chilled champagne, and congratulations from the distant Master.

Except for Washen, the day was just a little disappointing.

Watching from base camp, studying data harvests and live images, she saw exactly what she expected to see. Captains were administrators, not explorers; the historic moments were relentlessly organized. The landscape had been mapped until every bush and bug had a name. Not even tiny surprises could ambush the first teams. It was thorough and stifling, but naturally Washen didn't mention her disappointment, or even put a name to her emotions. Habit is habit, and she had been an exemplary captain for thousands of years. Besides, what sort of person would she be if she was offended that there were no injuries, or mistakes, or troubles of any kind?

And yet.

Two ship-days later, when her six-member team was ready to embark, Washen had to make herself sound like a captain. With a forced sincerity, she told the others, "We'll take our walk on the iron, and we'll exceed every objective. On schedule, if not before."

It was a swift, strange trip to Marrow.

Diu asked to ride with Washen, just as he'd requested to be part of her team. Their shielded tube-car retreated back up the access tunnel, then flung itself at Marrow, streaking through the buttress fields to minimize the exposure, a trillion electric fingers delicately playing with their sanity.

Then their car reached the upper atmosphere and braked, the terrific gees bruising flesh and shattering minor bones.

Artificial genes began weaving protein analogs, knitting their injuries.

The bridge was rooted into a hillside of cold iron and black jungle. The rest of the team and their supplies followed. Despite an overcast sky, the air was brilliant and furnace-hot, every breath tasting of metal and nervous sweat. As team leader, Washen gave orders that everyone knew by heart. Cars were linked, then reconfigured. The new vehicle was loaded, and tested, and the captains were tested by their autodocs: Newly implanted genes were helping their bodies adapt to the heat and metal-rich environment. Then Miocene, sitting in a nearby encampment, contacted them and gave her blessing, and Washen lifted off, steering towards the purely arbitrary north-northwest.

The countryside was broken and twisted, split by fault lines and raw mountains and volcanic vents. The vents had been quiet for a century or a decade, or in some cases, days. Yet the surrounding land was alive, adorned with jungle, pseudotrees reminiscent of mushrooms, all enormous, all pressed against one another, their lacquered black faces feeding on the dazzling blue-white light.

Marrow seemed as durable as the captains flying above it.

Growth rates were phenomenal, and for more reasons than photosynthesis. Early findings showed that the jungle also fed through its roots, chisel-like tips reaching down to where thermophilic bacteria thrived, Marrow's own heat supplying easy calories.

Were the aquatic ecosystems as productive?

It was Washen's question, and she'd selected a small, metal-choked lake for study. They arrived on schedule, and after circling the lake twice, as prescribed, she landed on a slab of bare iron. Then for the rest of the day they set up their lab and quarters, and specimen traps, and as a precaution, installed a defense perimeter—three paranoid AIs who did nothing but think the worst of every bug and spore that happened past.

Night was mandatory. Miocene insisted that each captain sleep at least four hours, and invest another hour in food and toiletries.

Washen's team went to bed on time, then lay awake until it was time to rise.

At breakfast, they sat in a circle and gazed at the sky. The chamber's wall was smooth and ageless, and infinitely bland. Base camp was a dark blemish visible only because the air was exceptionally clear. The bridge had vanished with the distance. If Washen was very careful, she could almost believe that they were the only people on this world. If she was lucky, she forgot for a minute or two that telescopes were watching her sitting on her aerogel chair, eating her scheduled rations.

Diu sat nearby, and when she glanced at him, he smiled wistfully, as if he could read her thoughts.

"I know what we need," Washen announced.

Diu said, "What do we need?"

"A ceremony. Some ritual before we can start." She rose and walked to one of the specimen traps, returning with one of their first catches. On Marrow, pseudoinsects filled almost every animal niche. Six-winged dragonflies were blue as gemstones and longer than a forearm. With the other captains watching, Washen stripped the dragonfly of its wings and tail, then eased the rest into their autokitchen. The broiling took a few seconds. With a dull thud, the carcass exploded inside the oven. Then she grabbed a lump of the blackish meat, and with a grimace, made herself bite and chew.

"We aren't supposed to," Diu warned, laughing gently.

Washen forced herself to swallow, then she told everyone, "And you won't want to do it again. Believe me."

There were no native viruses to catch, or toxins that their reinforced genetics couldn't handle. Miocene was simply being a cautious mother when she told them, "Except in emergencies, eat only the safe rations."

Washen passed out the ceremonial meat.

Last to take his share was Diu, and his first bite was tiny. But he didn't grimace, and with an odd little laugh, he told Washen, "It's not bad. If my tongue quit burning, I could almost think about enjoying it."

MISSION YEAR 1.22:

After weeks of relentless work, certain possibilities began to look like fact.

Marrow had been carved straight from the jupiter's heart. Its composition and their own common sense told the captains as much. The builders had first wrenched the uraniums and thoriums from the overhead iron, injecting them deep into the core. Then with the buttressing fields, the molten sphere was compressed, and the exposed chamber walls were slathered in hyperfiber. And billions of years later, without help from the vanished builders, the machinery was still purring along quite nicely.

But why bother creating such a marvel?

Marrow could be a dumping ground for radionuclides. Or it could have worked as an enormous fission reactor, some captains suggested. Except there were easier ways to create power, others pointed out, their voices not so gently dismissive.

But what if the world was designed to store power?

It was Aasleen's suggestion: By tweaking the buttresses, the builders could have forced Marrow to rotate. With patience—a resource they must have had in abundance—they could have given it a tremendous velocity. Spinning inside a vacuum, held intact by the buttresses, the iron ball would have stored phenomenal amounts of energy—enough to maintain the on board systems for billions of years, perhaps.

Washen first heard the flywheel hypothesis at the weekly briefing.

Each of the team leaders was sitting at the illusion of a conference table, in aerogel chairs, sweating rivers in Marrow's heat. The surrounding room was sculpted from light, and sitting at the head of the table was the Master's projection, alert but unusually quiet. She expected crisp reports and upbeat attitudes. Grand theories were a surprise. Finally, after a contemplative pause, she smiled, telling the captain, "That's an intriguing possibility. Thank you, Aasleen." Then to the others, "Considerations? Any?"

Her smile brought a wave of complimentary noise.

In private, Washen doubted they were inside someone's dead battery. But this wasn't the polite moment to list the troubles with flywheels. And besides, the bio-teams were reporting next, and she was eager to compare notes.

A tremor suddenly shook the captains, one after another, spreading out from its distant epicenter. Even for Marrow, that was a big jolt.

Compliments dissolved into an alert silence.

Then the Master lifted her wide hand, announcing abruptly, "We need to discuss your timetable."

What about the bio-teams?

"You're being missed, I'm afraid. Our cover story isn't clever enough, and the crew are suspicious." The Master lowered her hand, then said, "Before people are too worried, I want to bring you home."

Smiles broke out.

Some were tired of Marrow; other captains were tickled with the prospects of honors and promotions.

"Everyone, madam?" Washen dared.

"At least temporarily."

According to the ship's duty roster, the missing captains were visiting a nearby solar system, serving as travel agents to billions of potential passengers. And the truth told, there'd been boring moments when Washen found herself wishing that the fiction was real. But not today. Not when she was in the middle of something fascinating . . . !

As mission leader, it was Miocene's place to ask:

"Do you want us to cut our work short, madam?"

The Master squinted at the nearest window, gazing out at one of the ship's port facilities. For her, the room and its view were genuine, and her captains were illusions.

"Mission plans can be rewritten," she told them. "I want you to finish surveying the far hemisphere, and I want the critical studies wrapped up. Ten ship-days should be adequate. Then you'll come home, and we'll take our time deciding on our next actions."

Smiles wavered, but none crumbled.

Miocene whispered, "Ten days," with a tentative respect.

"Is that a problem?"

"Madam," the Submaster began, "I would feel much more comfortable if we were certain that Marrow isn't a threat."

There was a pause, and not just because the Master was thousands of kilometers removed from them. It was a lengthy, unnerving silence. Then captains' captain looked off into the distance, saying, "Considerations? Any?"

It would be a disruption. The other Submasters agreed with Miocene. To accomplish their work in ten days, with confidence, would require every captain, including those stationed with the support teams. Their base camp would have to be abandoned temporarily. That was an acceptable risk, perhaps. But mild words were obscured by clenched fists and distant, worried gazes.

Unsatisfied, the Master turned to her future Submaster. "Do you have any considerations to add?"

Washen hesitated as long as she dared.

"Marrow could have been a flywheel," she finally allowed. "Madam."

Brown eyes closed, opened. "I'm sorry," the Master responded, the voice devoid of amusement. "Aren't we discussing your timetable?"

"But if these buttresses ever weakened," Washen continued, "even for an instant, the planet would have expanded instantly. Catastrophically. The surrounding hyperfiber would have vaporized, and a shock wave would have passed through the entire ship, in moments." She offered simple calculations, then added, "Maybe this was an elaborate flywheel. But it also would have made an effective self-destruct mechanism. We don't know, madam. We don't know if the builders had enemies, real or imagined. But if we're going to find answers, I can't think of a better place to look."

The Master's face was unreadable, impenetrable.

Finally she shook her head, smiling in a pained manner. "Since my first moment on board this glorious vessel, I have nourished one guiding principle: The builders, whomever they were, would never endanger this marvelous creation."

Washen wished for the same confidence.

Then that apparition of light and sound leaned forward, saying, "You need a change of duty, Washen. I want you and your team in the lead. Help us explore the far hemisphere. And once the surveys are finished, everyone comes home. Agreed?"

"As you wish, madam," said Washen.

Said everyone.

Then Washen caught Miocene's surreptitious glance, something in the eyes saying, "Nice try, darling." And with that look, the faintest hint of respect.

Pterosaur drones had already drawn three maps of the region. Yet as Washen passed overhead, she realized that even the most recent map, drawn eight days ago, was too old to be useful.

Battered by quakes, the landscape had been heaved skyward, then torn open. Molten iron flowed into an oxbow lake, boiling water and mud, and columns of dirty steam rose skyward, then twisted to the east. As an experiment, Washen flew into the steam clouds. Samples were ingested through filters and sensors and simple lensing chambers. Riding with the steam were spores and eggs, encased in tough bioceramics and indifferent to the heat. Inside the tip of the needle flask, too small to see with the naked eye, were enough pond weeds and finned beetles to conquer ten new lakes.

Catastrophe was the driving force on Marrow.

That insight struck Washen every day, sometimes hourly, and it always arrived with a larger principle in tow:

In some flavor or another, disaster ruled every world.

But Marrow was the ultimate example. And as if to prove itself, the steam clouds dispersed suddenly, giving way to the sky's light, the chamber wall overhead, and far below, for as far as Washen could see, the stark black bones of a jungle.

Fumes and fire had incinerated every tree, every scrambling bug.

The carnage must have been horrific. Yet the blaze had passed days ago, and new growth was already pushing up from the gnarled trunks and fresh crevices, thousands of glossy black umbrella-like leaves shining in the superheated air.

Washen decided to blank the useless maps, flying on instinct.

"Twenty minutes, and we're as far from the bridge as possible," Diu promised, his smile wide and infectious.

No other team would travel as far.

Washen started to turn, intending to order chilled champagne for the occasion, her mouth opened and a distorted, almost inaudible voice interrupting her.

"Report ... all teams ...!"

It was Miocene's voice strained through a piercing electronic whistle.

"What do ... see ...?" asked the Submaster. "Teams ... report ...!"

Washen tried establishing more than an audio link, and failed.

A dozen other captains were chattering in a ragged chorus. Zale said, "We're on schedule." Kyzkee observed, "There's some com-interference ... otherwise, systems appear nominal." Then with more curiosity than worry, Aasleen inquired, "Why, madam? Is something wrong?"

There was a long, jangled hum.

Diu was hunched over sensor displays, and with a tight little voice, he said, "Shit."

"What—?" Washen cried out.

Then a shrill cry swept away every voice, every thought. And the day brightened and brightened, fat bolts of lightning flowing across the sky, then turning, moving with purpose, aiming for them.

From the far side of the world came a twisted voice:

"The bridge ... where is it ... do you see it ... where ...?"

The car bucked as if panicking, losing thrust and altitude, then its AIs. Washen deployed the manual controls, and centuries of drills made her concentrate, nothing existing but their tumbling vehicle, her syrupy reflexes, and an expanse of burnt forest.

The next barrage of lightning was purple-white, and brighter, nothing visible but its seething glare.

Washen flew blind, flew by memory.

Their car was designed to endure heroic abuse, the same as its passengers. But it was dead and its hull had been degraded, and when it struck the iron ground, the hull shattered. Restraining fields grabbed bodies, then failed. Nothing but mechanical belts and gas bags held the captains in their seats. Flesh was jerked and twisted, and shredded. Bones were shattered and wrenched from their sockets. Then the seats were torn free of the floor, and like useless wreckage, scattered across several hectares of iron and burnt stumps.

Washen never lost consciousness.

With numbed curiosity, she watched her own legs and arms break, and a thousand bruises spread into a single purple tapestry, every rib crushed to dust and her reinforced spine splintering until she was left without pain or a shred of mobility. Washen couldn't move her head, and her words were slow and watery, the sloppy mouth filled with cracked teeth and dying blood.

"Abandon," she muttered.

Then, "Ship," and she was laughing feebly. Desperately.

A gray sensation rippled through her body.

Emergency genes were already awake, finding their home in a shambles. They immediately protected the brain, flooding it with oxygen and anti-inflammatories, plus a blanket of comforting narcotics. Then they began to repair the vital organs and spine, cannibalizing meat for raw materials and energy, the captain's body wracked with fever, sweating salt water and blood, and after a little while, the body grew noticeably smaller.

An hour after the crash, a wrenching pain swept through Washen. It was a favorable sign. She squirmed and wailed, and with weak hands, freed herself from her ruined chair. Then with her sloppy rebuilt legs, she forced herself to stand.

Washen was suddenly twenty centimeters shorter, and frail. But she was able to limp over to Diu's body, finding him shriveled and in agony, but defiant—a fierce grin and a wink, then he told her, "You look gorgeous, madam. As always."

The others were alive, too. But not one machine in the wreckage would operate, not even well enough to say, "I'm broken."

The six captains healed within a day, and waited at the crash site, eating their rations to reclaim their size and vigor. No rescue team arrived. Whatever crippled their car must have done the same everywhere, they decided. Miocene was as powerless as them. And that left them with one viable option:

If Washen and the others wanted help, they were going to have to walk halfway around Marrow to find it.

MISSION YEAR 4.43:

The bridge resembled a rigid thread, silvery and insubstantial. Sheered off in the high stratosphere, it was far too short to serve as an escape route. But it made a useful landmark. Washen's team steered for the bridge during those last days, picking their way across the knife-like ridges and narrow valleys between. Wondering what they would find, whenever they rested—for a moment, now and again—they let themselves talk in hopeful tones, imagining the other captains' surprise when the six of them suddenly marched out of the jungle.

Except when they arrived at the bridge, there was no one to catch off guard. The main encampment had been abandoned. The hilltop where the bridge was rooted had been split open by quakes, and the entire structure tilted precariously toward the east. A simple iron post kept the main doors propped open, and there was a makeshift ladder in the shaft, but judging by the rust, nobody had used it for months. Or perhaps years.

A sketchy path led west. They followed, and after a long while, they came to a fertile river bottom and wider paths. With Washen at the lead, they were jogging, and it was Miocene who suddenly stepped into view, surprising them.

The Submaster was unchanged.

In uniform, she looked regal and well-chilled. "It took you long enough," she deadpanned. Then she smiled, adding, "It's good to see you. Honestly, we'd nearly given up hope."

Washen swallowed her anger.

The other captains bombarded Miocene with questions. Who else had survived? How were they making do? Did any machines work? Had the Master been in contact with them? Then Diu asked, "What kind of relief mission is coming?"

"It's a cautious relief mission," Miocene replied. "So cautious that it seems almost nonexistent."

Her captains had built telescopes from scratch, and at least one captain was always watching the base camp overhead. The transparent blister was intact. Every building was intact. But the drones and beacons were dead, which meant that the reactor was offline. A three kilometer stub of the bridge would make the perfect foundation for a new structure. But there wasn't any sign that captains or anyone was trying to mount any kind of rescue.

"The Master thinks we're dead," Diu offered, trying to be charitable.

"We aren't dead," Miocene countered. "And even if we were, she should be a little more interested in our bones, and answers."

Washen didn't talk. After three years of jogging, eating lousy food and forcing hope, she suddenly felt sickened and achingly tired.

The Submaster led them along a wide trail, working back through their questions.

"Every machine was ruined by the Event. That's our name for what happened. The Event left our cars and drones and sensors as fancy trash, and we can't fix them. And we can't decide why, either." Then she offered a distracted smile, adding, "But we're surviving. Wooden homes, with roofs. Iron tools. Pendulum clocks. Steam power when we go to the trouble, and enough homemade equipment, like the telescopes, that we can do some simple, simple science."

The jungle's understory had been cut down and beaten back, and the new encampment stretched out on all sides. Like anything built by determined captains, the place was orderly, perhaps to a fault. The houses were clean and in good repair. Paths were marked with logs, and someone had given each path its own name. Everyone was in uniform, and everyone was smiling, trying to hide the weariness in the eyes and their voices.

A hundred captains shouted, "Hello! Welcome!"

Washen stared at their faces, and counted, and finally forced herself to ask, "Who isn't here?"

Miocene recited a dozen names.

Eleven of them were friends or acquaintances of Washen's. The last name was Hazz—a Submaster and a voyage-long friend of Miocene's. "Two months ago," she explained, "he was exploring a nearby valley. A fissure opened up suddenly, without warning, and he was trapped by the flowing iron." Her eyes were distant, unreadable. "Hazz was perched on a little island that was melting. We tried to build a bridge, and tried to divert the current. Everything half-possible, we tried."

Washen stared at the narrow face, at the way the eyes had grown empty, and it was suddenly obvious that Miocene had been more than friends with the dead man.

"The island shrank," she told them, her voice too flat and slow. "It was a knob, if that. Hazz's boots dissolved, and his feet were boiling, and his flesh caught fire. But he managed to stand there. He endured it. He endured it and even managed to turn and take a step toward on us, on his boiling legs, and he fell forward, and that's when he finally died."

Washen had been mistaken. This wasn't the same Miocene.

"I have one goal," the Submaster confessed. "I want to find a way to get back to the Master, and I'll ask her why she sent us here. Was it to explore? Or was it just the best awful way to get rid of us . . . ?"

MISSION YEAR 6.55:

The iron crust rippled and tore apart under a barrage of quakes, and with its foundation shattered, the bridge pitched sideways with a creaking roar, then shattered, the debris field scattered over fifty kilometers of newborn mountains.

Its fall was inevitable, and unrecorded. Geysers of white-hot metal had already obliterated the captains' encampment, forcing them to flee with a minimum of tools and provisions. Lungs were seared. Tongues and eyes were blistered. But the captains eventually stumbled into a distant valley, into a grove of stately trees, where they collapsed, gasping and cursing. Then as if to bless them, the trees began releasing tiny balloons made from gold, and the shady, halfway cool air was filled with the balloons' glint and the dry music made by their brushing against one another.

Diu coined the name virtue tree.

Miocene set her captains to planning new streets and houses, several of the virtue trees already downed when the ground ripped open with an anguished roar.

Wearily, the captains fled again, and when they settled, finally, they built strong simple houses that could be rebuilt anywhere in a ship's day.

Nomadic blood took hold in them. When they weren't stockpiling food for the next migration, they were building lighter tools, and when they weren't doing either, they studied their world, trying to guess its fickle moods.

Washen assembled a team of twenty observant captains.

"Breeding cycles are key," she reported. Sitting in the meeting hall, looking up and down the iron table, she reported that virtue trees spun their golden balloons only when the crust turned unstable. "If we see another show like the last one," she promised, "we're screwed. We've got a day, or less, to get out of here."

Staff meetings were patterned after conferences with the Master, except they came on an irregular schedule, and Miocene presided, and despite her best intentions, the captains kept the atmosphere informal, even jocular, and because of the absence of soap, more than a little sour.

"How are our virtue trees acting?" asked Aasleen.

"As if they'll live forever," Washen replied. "They're still happy, still early in their growth cycle. As far as we can tell."

Miocene acted distant that day. Squinting at nothing, she repeated the word: "Cycles."

Everyone turned in their heavy chairs, and waited.

"Thank you, Washen." The Submaster rose and looked at each of them, then admitted, "This may be premature. I could be wrong for many reasons. But I think I've been able to find another cycle . . . one that's unexpected, at least for me . . ."

There was the distant droning of a hammerwing, and then, silence.

"Volcanic activity is escalating. I think that's obvious." The tall woman nodded for a moment, then asked, "But why? My proposal is that the buttresses have begun to relax their hold on Marrow. Not by much. Certainly nothing we can measure directly. But if it did happen, the metals under us are going to expand, and that's why, according to my careful computations, our home is growing larger."

Washen's first impulse was to laugh; it was a joke.

"Several kilometers larger," Miocene told the stunned faces. "I've gathered several lines of evidence. The buttresses' light has diminished by two or three percent. The horizon is a little more distant. And what's most impressive, I think: I've triangulated the distance to our base camp, and it's definitely closer than it was last year."

A dozen explanations occurred to Washen, but she realized that Miocene must have seen them, then discarded them.

"If Marrow isn't teasing us," said the Submaster, "and if the buttresses don't reverse the cycle, then you can see where we're going—"

Washen cried out, "How long will it take, madam?"

A dozen captains shouted the same question.

"The calculations aren't promising," Miocene replied. But she had to laugh in a soft, bitter way. "At the present rate, we'll be able to touch that three kilometer stub of the bridge in about five thousand years . . ."

MISSION YEAR 88.55:

It was time for the children to sleep.

Washen had come to check on them. But for some reason she stopped short of the nursery, eavesdropping on them, uncertain why it was important to remain hidden.

The oldest boy was telling a story.

"We call them the Builders," he said, "because they created the ship."

"The ship," whispered the other children, in one voice.

"The ship is too large to measure, and it is very beautiful. But when it was new, there was no one to share it with the Builders, and no one to tell them that it was beautiful. That's why they called out into the darkness, inviting others to come fill its vastness."

Washen leaned against the fragrant umbra wood, waiting.

"Who came from the darkness?" asked the boy.

"The Bleak," young voices answered, instantly.

"Was there anyone else?"

"No one."

"Because the universe was so young," the boy explained. "Only the Bleak and the Builders had already evolved."

"The Bleak," a young girl repeated, with feeling.

"They were a cruel, selfish species," the boy maintained, "but they always wore smiles and said the smartest words."

"They wanted the ship," the others prompted.

"And they stole it. In one terrible night, as the Builders slept, the Bleak attacked, slaughtering most of them in their beds."

Every child whispered, "Slaughtered."

Washen eased her way closer to the nursery door. The boy was sitting up on his cot, his face catching the one sliver of light that managed to slip through the ceiling. Till was his name. He looked very much like his mother for a moment, then he moved his head slightly, and he resembled no one else.

"Where did the survivors retreat?" he asked.

"To Marrow."

"And from here, what did they do?"

"They purified the ship."

"They purified the ship," he repeated, with emphasis. "They swept its tunnels and chambers free of the scourge. The Builders had no choice."

There was a long, reflective pause.

"What happened to the last of the Builders?" he asked.

"They were trapped here," said the others, on cue. "And one after another, they died here."

"What died?"

"Their flesh."

"But what else is there?"

"The spirit."

"What isn't flesh cannot die," said the young prophet.

Washen waited, wondering when she had last taken a breath.

Then in whisper, Till asked, "Where do their spirits live?"

With a palpable delight, the children replied, "They live inside us."

"We are the Builders now," the voice assured. "After a long lonely wait, we've finally been reborn . . . !"

MISSION YEAR 88.90:

Life on Marrow had become halfway comfortable and almost predictable. The captains weren't often caught by surprise eruptions, and they'd learned where the crust was likely to remain thick and stable for years at a time. With so much success, children had seemed inevitable; Miocene decided that every female captain should produce at least one. And like children anywhere, theirs filled many niches: They were fresh faces, and they were cherished distractions, and they were entertainment, and more than anyone anticipated, they were challenges to the captains' authority. But what Miocene wanted, first and always, were willing helpers. Till and his playmates were born so that someday, once trained, they could help their parents escape from Marrow.

The hope was that they could rebuild the bridge. Materials would be a problem, and Marrow would fight them. But Washen was optimistic. In these last eight decades, she'd tried every state of mind, and optimism far and away was the most pleasant.

And she tried to be positive everywhere: Good, sane reasons had kept them from being rescued. There was no one else the Master could trust like her favorite captains. Perhaps. Or she was thinking of the ship's well-being, monitoring Marrow from a distance. Or most likely, the access tunnel had totally collapsed during the Event, and digging them out was grueling, achingly slow work.

Other captains were optimistic in public, but in private, in their lovers' beds, they confessed to darker moods.

"What if the Master has written us off?" Diu posed the question, then offered an even worse scenario. "Or maybe something's happened to her. This was a secret mission. If she died unexpectedly, and if the First-chairs don't even know we're here . . ."

"Do you believe that?" Washen asked.

Diu shrugged his shoulders.

"There's another possibility," she said, playing the game. "What if everyone else on the ship has died?"

For a moment, Diu didn't react.

"The ship was a derelict," she reminded him. "No one knows what happened to its owners, or to anyone else who's used it since."

"What are you saying?" Diu sat up in bed, dropping his legs over the edge. "You mean the crew and the passengers . . . all of them have been killed . . . ?"

"Maybe the ship cleans itself out every hundred thousand years."

A tiny grin emerged. "So how did we survive?"

"Life on Marrow is spared," she argued. "Otherwise, all of this would be barren iron and nothing else."

Diu pulled one of his hands across his face.

"This isn't my story," she admitted, placing her hand on his sweaty back. Their infant son, Locke, was sleeping in the nearby crib, blissfully unaware of their grim discussion. In three years, he would live in the nursery. With Till, she was thinking. Washen had overheard the story about the Builders and the Bleak several months ago, but she never told anyone. Not even Diu. "Have you ever listened to the children?"

Glancing over his shoulder, he asked, "Why?"

She explained, in brief.

A sliver of light caught his gray eye and cheek. "You know Till," Diu countered. "You know how odd he can seem."

"That's why I never mention it."

"Have you heard him tell that story again?"

"No," she admitted.

Her lover nodded, looking at the crib. At Locke.

"Children are imagination machines," he warned. "You never know what they're going to think about anything."

He didn't say another word.

Washen was remembering her only other child—a long-ago foster child, only glancingly human—and with a bittersweet grin, she replied, "But that's the fun in having them . . . or so I've always heard . . ."

MISSION YEAR 89.09:

The boy was walking alone, crossing the public round with his eyes watching his own bare feet, watching them shuffle across the heat-baked iron.

"Hello, Till."

Pausing, he lifted his gaze slowly, a smile waiting to shine at the captain. "Hello, Madam Washen. You're well, I trust."

Under the blue glare of the sky, he was a polite, scrupulously ordinary boy. He had a thin face joined to a shorter, almost blockish body, and like most children, he wore as little as the adults let him wear. No one knew which of several captains was his genetic father. Miocene never told. She wanted to be his only parent, grooming him to stand beside her someday, and whenever Washen looked at Till, she felt a nagging resentment, petty as can be, and since it was directed at a ten year old, simply foolish.

With her own smile, Washen said, "I have a confession to make. A little while ago, I overheard you and the other children talking. You were telling each other a story."

The eyes were wide and brown, and they didn't so much as blink.

"It was an interesting story," Washen conceded.

Till looked like any ten year old who didn't know what to make of a bothersome adult. Sighing wearily, he shifted his weight from one brown foot to the other. Then he sighed again, the picture of boredom.

"How did you think up that story?" she asked.

A shrug of the shoulders. "I don't know."

"We talk about the ship. Probably too much." Her explanation felt sensible and practical. Her only fear was that she would come across as patronizing.

"Everyone likes to speculate. About the ship's past, and its builders, and all the rest. It has to be confusing. Since we're going to rebuild our bridge, with your help . . . it does make you into a kind of builder . . ."

Till shrugged again, his eyes looking past her.

On the far side of the round, in front of the encampment's shop, a team of captains had fired up their latest turbine—a primitive wonder built from memory and trial-and-error. Homebrewed alcohols combined with oxygen, creating a delicious roar. When it was working, the engine was powerful enough to do any job they could offer it, at least today. But it was dirty and noisy, and the sound of it almost obscured the boy's voice.

"I'm not speculating," he said softly.

"Excuse me?"

"I won't tell you that. That I'm making it up."

Washen had to smile, asking, "Aren't you?"

"No." Till shook his head, then looked back down at his toes. "Madam Washen," he said with a boy's fragile patience. "You can't make up something that's true."

MISSION YEAR 114.41:

Locke was waiting in the shadows—a grown man with a boy's guilty face and the wide, restless eyes of someone expecting trouble to come from every direction.

His first words were, "I shouldn't be doing this."

But a moment later, responding to an anticipated voice, he said, "I know, Mother. I promised."

Washen never made a sound.

It was Diu who offered second thoughts. "If this is going to get you in trouble . . . maybe we should go home . . ."

"Maybe you should," their son allowed. Then he turned and walked away, never inviting them to follow, knowing they wouldn't be able to help themselves.

Washen hurried, feeling Diu in her footsteps.

A young jungle of umbra trees and lambda bush dissolved into rugged bare iron: Black pillars and arches created an indiscriminate, infuriating maze. Every step was a challenge. Razored edges sliced at exposed flesh. Bottomless crevices threatened to swallow the graceless. And Washen's body was accustomed to sleep at this hour, which was why the old grove took her by surprise. Suddenly Locke was standing on the rusty lip of a cliff, waiting for them, gazing down at a narrow valley filled with black-as-night virtue trees.

It was lucky ground. When the world's guts began to pour out on all sides, that slab of crust had fallen into a fissure. The jungle had been burned but never killed. It could be a hundred years old, or older. There was a rich, eternal feel to the place, and perhaps that's why the children had chosen it.

The children. Washen knew better, but despite her best intentions, she couldn't think of them any other way.

"Keep quiet," Locke whispered, not looking back at them. "Please."

In the living shadows, the air turned slightly cooler and uncomfortably damp. Blankets of rotting canopy left the ground watery-soft. A giant daggerwing roared past, intent on some vital business, and Washen watched it vanish into the gloom, then reappear, tiny with the distance, its bluish carapace shining in a patch of sudden skylight.

Locke turned abruptly, silently.

A single finger lay against his lips. But what Washen noticed was his expression, the pain and worry so intense that she had to try and reassure him with a touch.

It was Diu who had wormed the secret out him.

The children were meeting in the jungle, and they'd been meeting for more than twenty years. At irregular intervals, Till would call them to some secluded location, and it was Till who was in charge of everything said and done. "What's said?" Washen had asked. "And what do you do?" But Locke refused to explain it, shaking his head and adding that he was breaking his oldest promise by telling any of it.

"Then why do it?" Washen pressed.

"Because," her son replied. "You have every right to hear what he's saying. So you can decide for yourselves."

Washen stood out of sight, staring at the largest virtue tree she had ever seen. Age had killed it, and rot had brought it down, splitting the canopy open as it crumbled. Adult children and their little brothers and sisters had assembled in that pool of skylight, standing in clumps and pairs, talking quietly. Till paced back and forth on the wide black trunk. He looked fully adult, ageless and decidedly unexceptional, wearing a simple breechcloth and nimble boots, his plain face showing a timid, self-conscious expression that gave Washen a strange little moment of hope.

Maybe Till's meetings were a just an old game that grew up into a social gathering.

Maybe.

Without a word or backward glance, Locke walked into the clearing, joining the oldest children up in the front.

His parents obeyed their promise, kneeling in the jungle.

A few more children filtered into view. Then with some invisible signal, the worshippers fell silent.

With a quiet voice, Till asked, "What do we want?"

"What's best for the ship," the children answered. "Always."

"How long is always?"

"Longer than we can count."

"And how far is always?"

"To the endless ends."

"Yet we live—"

"For a moment!" they cried. "If that long!"

The words were absurd, and chilling. What should have sounded silly to Washen wasn't, the prayer acquiring a muscular credibility when hundreds were speaking in one voice, with a practiced surety.

"What is best for the ship," Till repeated.

Except he was asking a question. His plain face was filled with curiosity, a genuine longing.

Quietly, he asked his audience, "Do you know the answer?"

In a muddled shout, the children said, "No."

"I don't either," their leader promised. "But when I'm awake, I'm searching. And when I'm sleeping, my dreams do the same."

There was a brief pause, then an urgent voice cried out, "We have newcomers!"

"Bring them up."

They were seven year olds—a twin brother and sister—and they climbed the trunk as if terrified. But Till offered his hands, and with a crisp surety, he told each to breathe deeply, then asked them, "What do you know about the ship?"

The little girl glanced at the sky, saying, "It's where we came from."

Laughter broke out in the audience, then evaporated.

Her brother corrected her. "The captains came from there. Not us." Then he added, "But we're going to help them get back there. Soon."

There was a cold, prolonged pause.

Till allowed himself a patient smile, patting both of their heads. Then he looked out at his followers, asking, "Is he right?"

"No," they roared.

The siblings winced and tried to vanish.

Till knelt between them, and with a steady voice said, "The captains are just the captains. But you and I and all of us here . . . we are the Builders."

Washen hadn't heard that nonsense in a quarter of a century, and hearing it now, she couldn't decide whether to laugh or explode in rage.

"We're the Builders reborn," Till repeated. Then he gave them the seeds of rebellion, adding, "And whatever our purpose, it is not to help these silly captains."

Miocene refused to believe any of it. "First of all," she told Washen, and herself, "I know my own child. What you're describing is ridiculous. Second of all, this rally of theirs would involve nearly half of our children—"

Diu interrupted. "Most of them are adults with their own homes." Then he added, "Madam."

"I checked," said Washen. "Several dozen of the younger children did slip out of the nurseries—"

"I'm not claiming that they didn't go somewhere." Then with a haughty expression, she asked, "Will the two of you listen to me? For a moment, please?"

"Go on, madam," said Diu.

"I know what's reasonable. I know how my son was raised and I know his character, and unless you can offer me some motivation for this . . . this shit . . . then I think we'll just pretend that nothing's been said here . . ."

"Motivation," Washen repeated. "Tell me what's mine."

With a chill delight, Miocene said, "Greed."

"Why?"

"Believe me, I understand." The dark eyes narrowed, silver glints in their corners. "If my son is insane, then yours stands to gain. Status, at least. Then eventually, power."

Washen glanced at Diu.

They hadn't mentioned Locke's role as the informant, and they would keep it secret as long as possible—for a tangle of reasons, most of them selfish.

"Ask Till about the Builders," she insisted.

"I won't."

"Why not?"

The woman took a moment, vainly picking spore cases from her new hand-made uniform. Then with a cutting logic, she said, "If it's a lie, he'll say it's a lie. If it's true and he lies, then it'll sound like the truth."

"But if he admits it—?"

"Then Till wants me to know. And you're simply a messenger." She gave them a knowing stare, then looked off into the distance. "That's not a revelation I want delivered at his convenience."

Three ship-days later, while the encampment slept, a great fist lifted the world several meters, then grew bored and flung it down again.

Captains and children stumbled into the open. The sky was already choked with golden balloons and billions of flying insects. In twelve hours, perhaps less, the entire region would blister and explode, and die. Like a drunken woman, Washen ran through the aftershocks, reaching a tidy home and shouting, "Locke," into its empty rooms. Where was her son? She moved along the round, finding all of the children's houses empty. A tall figure stepped out of Till's tiny house and asked, "Have you see mine?"

Washen shook her head. "Have you seen mine?"

Miocene said, "No," and sighed. Then she strode past Washen, shouting, "Do you know where I can find him?"

Diu was standing in the center of the round. Waiting.

"If you help me," the Submaster promised, "you'll help your own son."

With a little nod, Diu agreed.

Miocene and a dozen captains ran into the jungle. Left behind, Washen forced herself to concentrate, packing her household's essentials and helping the other worried parents. When they were finished, hours had passed. The quakes had shattered the crust beneath them, and the golden balloons had vanished, replaced with clouds of iron dust and the stink of burning jungle. The captains and remaining children stood in the main round, ready to flee. But the ranking

Submaster wouldn't give the order. "Another minute," he kept telling everyone, including himself. Then he would carefully hide his timepiece in his uniform's pocket, fighting the urge to watch the turning of its hands.

When Till suddenly stepped into the open, grinning at them, Washen felt a giddy, incoherent relief.

Relief collapsed into shock, then terror.

The young man's chest cavity had been opened up with a knife, the first wound partially healed but the second wound deeper, lying perpendicular to the first. Ripped, desiccated flesh tried desperately to knit itself back together. Till wasn't in mortal danger, but he wore his agony well. With an artful moan, he stumbled, then righted himself for a slippery instant. Then he fell sideways, slamming against the bare iron in the same instant that Miocene slowly, slowly stepped into view.

She was unhurt, and she was thoroughly, hopelessly trapped.

Spellbound, Washen watched the Submaster kneel beside her boy, gripping his straight brown hair with one hand while she stared into his eyes.

What did Till say to her in the jungle? How did he steer his mother into this murderous rage? Because that's what he must have done. As events played out, Washen realized that everything was part of an elaborate plan. That's why Locke took them to the meeting, and why he had felt guilty. When he said, "I know. I promised," he meant the promise he made to Till.

Miocene kept staring into her son's eyes.

Perhaps she was hunting for forgiveness, or better, for some hint of doubt. Or perhaps she was simply giving him a moment to contemplate her own gaze, relentless and cold. Then with both hands, she picked up a good-sized wedge of nickel-iron—the quakes had left the round littered with them—and with a calm fury, she rolled him over and shattered the vertebrae in his neck, then continued beating him, blood and shredded flesh flying, his head nearly cut free of his paralyzed body.

Washen and five other captains pulled Miocene off her son.

"Let go of me," she demanded. Then she dropped her weapon and raised her arms, telling everyone in earshot, "If you want to help him, help him. But if you do, you don't belong to our community. That's my decree. According to the powers of my rank, my office, and my mood . . . !"

Locke had stepped out of the jungle.

He was the first to come to Till's side, but only barely. More than two-thirds of the children gathered around the limp figure. A stretcher was found, and their leader was made comfortable. Then with a few possessions and virtually no food, the wayward children began to file away, moving north when the captains were planning to travel south.

Diu stood beside Washen; since when?

"We can't just let them get away," he whispered. "Someone needs to stay with them. To talk to them, and help them . . ."

She glanced at her lover, then opened her mouth.

"I'll go," she meant to say.

But Diu said, "You shouldn't, no. You'll help them more by staying close to Miocene." He had obviously thought it through, arguing, "You have rank. You have authority here. And besides, Miocene listens to you."

When it suited her, yes.

"I'll keep in contact," Diu promised. "Somehow."

Washen nodded, thinking that all of this would pass in a few years. Perhaps in a few decades, at most.

Diu kissed her, and they hugged, and she found herself looking over his shoulder. Locke was a familiar silhouette standing in the jungle. At that distance, through those shadows, she couldn't tell if her son was facing her or if she was looking at his back. Either way, she smiled and mouthed the words, "Be good." Then she took a deep breath and told Diu, "Be careful." And she turned away, refusing to watch either of her men vanish into the shadows and gathering smoke.

Miocene stood alone, speaking with a thin dry weepy voice.

"We're getting closer," she declared, lifting her arms overhead.

Closer?

Then she rose up on her toes, reaching higher, and with a low, pained laugh, she said, "Not close enough. Not yet."

MISSION YEARS 511.01–1603.73:

A dozen of the loyal grandchildren discovered the first artifact. Against every rule, they were playing beside a river of liquid iron, and suddenly a mysterious hyperfiber sphere drifted past. With their youngster's courage, they fished it out and cooled it down and brought it back to the encampment. Then for the next hundred years, the sphere lay in storage, under lock and key. But once the captains had reinvented the means, they split the hyperfiber, and inside it was an information vault nearly as old as the earth.

The device was declared authentic, and useless, its memories erased to gray by the simple crush of time.

There were attempts at secrecy, but the Waywards always had their spies. One night, without warning, Locke and his father strolled into the main round. Dressed in breechcloth and little else, they found Washen's door, knocked until she screamed, "Enter," then stepped inside, Diu offering a wry grin as Locke made the unexpected proposal: Tons of dried and sweetened meat in exchange for that empty vault.

Washen didn't have the authority. Four Submasters were pulled out of three beds, and at Miocene's insistence, they grudgingly agreed to the Waywards' terms.

But the negotiations weren't finished. Diu suddenly handed his ex-commanders wafers of pure sulfur, very rare and essential to the captains' fledgling industries. Then with a wink, he asked, "What would you give us in return for tons more?"

Everything, thought Washen.

Diu settled for a laser. As he made sure it had enough punch to penetrate hyperfiber, nervous voices asked how the Waywards would use it. "It's obvious," Diu replied, with easy scorn. "If your little group finds one artifact, by accident, how many more do you think that the Waywards could be sitting on?"

Afterwards, once or twice every century, the captains discovered new vaults. Most were dead and sold quickly to the Waywards for meat and sulfur. But it was ninth vault that still functioned, its ancient machinery full of images and data, and answers.

The elegant device was riding in Miocene's lap. She touched it lightly, lovingly, then confessed, "I feel nervous. Nervous, but exceptionally confident."

The Submaster never usually discussed her moods.

"With a little luck," she continued, "this treasure will heal these old rifts between them and us."

"With luck," Washen echoed, thinking it would take more than a little.

They arrived at the clearing at three in the morning, shiptime. Moments later, several thousand Waywards stepped from the jungle at the same moment, dressed in tool belts and little else, the men often carrying toddlers and their women pregnant, every face feral and self-assured, almost every expression utterly joyous.

Washen climbed out of the walker, and Miocene handed down the vault.

To the eye, it wasn't an impressive machine—a rounded lump of gray ceramics infused with smooth blue-white diamonds. Yet most of the Waywards stared at the prize. Till was the lone exception. Coming down the open slope, walking slowly, he watched Miocene, wariness mixed with other, less legible emotions.

Locke was following the Waywards' leader at a respectful distance. "How are you, Mother?" he called out. Always polite; never warm.

"Well enough," Washen allowed. "And you?"

His answer was an odd, tentative smile.

Where was Diu? Washen gazed at the crowd, assuming that he was somewhere close, hidden by the crush of bodies.

"May I examine the device?" asked Till.

Miocene took the vault from Washen so that she could hand it to her son. And Till covered the largest diamonds with his fingertips, blocking out the light, causing the machine to slowly, slowly awaken.

The clearing was a natural amphitheater, black iron rising on all sides. Washen couldn't count all the Waywards streaming out of the jungle above. Thousands had become tens of thousands. Some of them were her grandchildren and great-grandchildren. Diu would know which ones, perhaps. How many of her descendants lived with the Waywards? In the past, during their very occasional meetings, Diu had confided that the Waywards probably numbered in the millions—a distinct possibility since they'd inherited their parents' immortal genes, and since Till seemed to relish fecundity. In principle, this entire audience could be related to Washen. Not bad, she thought. Particularly for an old woman who for many fine reasons had only that one child of her own.

The vault began to hum softly, and Locke lifted an arm, shouting, "Now."

Suddenly the audience was silent, everyone motionless, a palpable anticipation hanging in the hot dry air.

The sky grew dark, and the clearing vanished.

Marrow swelled, nearly filling the chamber. Barren and smooth, it was covered in a worldwide ocean of bubbling, irradiated iron that lay just beneath the hyperfiber ceiling, and the audience stood on that ocean, unwarmed, watching an ancient drama play itself out.

Without sound or any warning, the Bleak appeared, squirming their way through the chamber's wall, through the countless access tunnels—insect-like cyborgs, enormous and cold and swift.

Like a swarm of wasps, they flowed toward Marrow, launching gobs of antimatter that slammed into the molten surface, scorching white-hot explosions rising up and up. The liquid iron swirled and lifted, then collapsed again. In the harsh light, Washen glanced at her son, trying to measure his face, his mood. He looked spellbound, eyes wide and his mouth ajar, his body shivering with an apocalyptic fever. Every face seemed to be seeing this for the first time. Washen remembered the last time she spoke to Diu, almost a decade ago. She asked about the vaults and the Waywards' beliefs, explaining that Miocene was pressing for details. In response, Diu growled, reminding her, "I'm their only nonbeliever, and they don't tell me much. I'm tolerated for my technical expertise, and just as important, because I long ago stopped kowtowing to Miocene and all the rest of you."

A hyperfiber dome suddenly burst from the iron, lasers firing, a dozen of the Bleak killed before the dome pulled itself under again.

The Bleak brought reinforcements, then struck again.

Hyperfiber missiles carried the antimatter deep into the iron. Marrow shook and twisted, then belched gas and fire. Perhaps the Bleak managed to kill the last of the Builders. Perhaps. Either way, the Builders' revenge was in place. Was waiting. In the middle of the attack, with the Bleak's forces pressing hard, the buttressing fields came on, bringing their blue-white glow. Suddenly the Bleak appeared tiny and frail. Then, before they could flee, the lightning storm swept across the sky, dissolving every wisp of matter into a plasma, creating a superheated mist that would persist for millions of years, cooling as Marrow cooled, gradually collecting on the warm, newborn crust.

Gradually, the Bleak's own carbon and hydrogen and oxygen became Marrow's atmosphere and its rivers, and those same precious elements slowly gathered themselves into butter bugs and virtue trees, then into the wide-eyed children standing in that clearing, weeping as they stared at the radiant sky.

The present reemerged gradually, almost reluctantly.

"There's much more," Miocene promised, her voice urgent. Motherly. "Other records show how the ship was attacked. How the Builders retreated to Marrow. This is where they made their last stand, whoever they were." She waited for a long moment, watching her son's unreadable face. Then with a genuine disappointment, she warned, "The Builders never show themselves. We understand a lot more now, but we're still not sure how they looked."

Till wasn't awestruck by what he had just witnessed. If anything, he was mildly pleased, grinning as if amused, but definitely not excited or surprised, or even particularly interested with what Miocene had to say.

"Listen to me," she snapped, unable to contain herself any longer. "Do you understand what this means? The Event that trapped us here is some kind of ancient weapon designed to kill the Bleak. And everything else on board the ship . . . perhaps . . ."

"Who's trapped?" Till replied with a smooth, unnerving calm. "I'm not. No believer is. This is exactly where we belong."

Only Miocene's eyes betrayed her anger.

Till continued with his explanation, saying, "You're here because the Builders called to you. They lured you here because they needed someone to give birth to us."

"That's insane," the Submaster snarled.

Washen was squinting, searching for Diu. She recognized his face and his nervous energy, but only in the children. Where was he? Suddenly it occurred to her that he hadn't been invited, or even worse—

"I know why you believe this nonsense." Miocene said the words, then took a long step toward Till, empty hands lifting into the air. "It's obvious. When you were a boy, you found one of these vaults. Didn't you? It showed you the war and the Bleak, and that's when you began all of this . . . this nonsense about being the Builders reborn . . . !"

Her son regarded her with an amused contempt.

"You made a mistake," said Miocene, her voice shrill. Accusing. "You were a child, and you didn't understand what you were seeing, and ever since we've had to pay for your ignorance. Don't you see . . . ?"

Her son was smiling, incapable of doubt.

Looking at the Waywards, Miocene screamed, "Who understands me?"

Silence.

"I didn't find any vault," Till claimed. "I was alone in the jungle, and a Builder's spirit appeared to me. He told me about the Ship and the Bleak. He showed me all of this. Then he made me a promise: As this day ends, in the coming twilight, I'll learn my destiny . . ."

His voice trailed away into silence.

Locke kneeled and picked up the vault. Then he looked at Washen, saying matter-of-factly, "The usual payment. That's what we're offering."

Miocene roared.

"What do you mean? This is the best artifact yet!"

No one responded, gazing at her as if she was insane.

"It functions. It remembers." The Submaster was flinging her arms into the air, telling them, "The other vaults were empty, or nearly so—"

"Exactly," said Till.

Then, as if it was beneath their leader to explain the obvious, Locke gave the two of them a look of pity, telling them, "Those vaults are empty because what they were holding is elsewhere now. Elsewhere."

Till and Locke touched their scalps.

Every follower did the same, fifty thousand arms lifting, a great ripple reaching the top of the amphitheater as everyone pointed at their minds. At their reborn souls.

Locke was staring at his mother.

A premonition made her mouth dry. "Why isn't Diu here?"

"Because he's dead," her son replied, an old sadness passing through his face. "I'm sorry. It happened eight years ago, during a powerful eruption."

Washen couldn't speak, or move.

"Are you all right, Mother?"

She took a breath, then lied. "Yes. I'm fine."

Then she saw the most astonishing sight yet in this long and astonishing day: Miocene had dropped to her knees, and with a pleading voice, she was begging for Till's forgiveness. "I never should have struck you," she said. She said, "Darling," with genuine anguish. Then as a last resort, she told him, "And I do love the ship. As much as you do, you ungrateful shit . . . !"

MISSION YEAR 4895.33:

From the very top of the new bridge, where the atmosphere was barely a sloppy vacuum, Marrow finally began to resemble a far away place.

The captains appreciated the view.

Whenever Washen was on duty, she gazed down at the city-like encampments and sprawling farms, the dormant volcanoes and surviving patches of jungle, feeling a delicious sense of detachment from it all. A soft gray twilight held sway. The buttresses had continued to shrivel and weaken over the last millennia, and if Miocene's model proved true, in another two centuries the buttresses would vanish entirely. For a few moments, or perhaps a few years, there would be no barrier between them and the ship. Marrow world would be immersed in a perfect blackness. Then the buttresses would reignite suddenly, perhaps accompanied by another Event. But by then the captains and their families, moving with a swift, drilled precision, would have escaped, climbing up this wondrously makeshift bridge, reaching the old base camp, then hopefully, returning to the ship, at last.

What they would find there, no one knew.

Or in a polite company, discussed.

In the last five thousand years, every remote possibility had been suggested, debated in depth, and finally, mercifully, buried in an unmarked grave.

Whatever was, was.

That was the mandatory attitude, and it had been for centuries now.

All that mattered was the bridge. The surviving captains—almost two-thirds of the original complement—lived for its completion. Hundreds of thousands of their descendants worked in distant mines or trucked the ore to the factories. Another half million were manufacturing superstrong alloys and crude flavors of hyperfiber, some of each added to the bridge's foundation, while the rest were spun together into hollow tubes. Washen's duty was to oversee the slow, rigorous hoisting of each new tube, then its final attachment. Compared to the original bridge, their contraption was inelegant and preposterously fat. Yet she felt a genuine pride all the same, knowing the sacrifices that went into its construction, and the enormous amounts of time, and when they didn't have any other choice, a lot of desperate, ad hoc inventiveness.

"Madam Washen?" said a familiar voice. "Excuse me, madam."

The captain blinked, then turned.

Her newest assistant stood in the doorway. An intense, self-assured man of no particular age, he was obviously puzzled—a rare expression—and with a mixture of curiosity and confusion, he announced, "Our shift is over."

"In fifty minutes," Washen replied, knowing the exact time for herself.

"No, madam." Nervous hands pressed at the crisp fabric of his technician's uniform. "I just heard. We're to leave immediately, using every tube but the Primary."

She looked at the displays on her control boards. "I don't see any orders."

"I know—"

"Is this another drill?" If the reinforced crust under them ever began to subside, they might have only minutes to evacuate. "Because if it is, we need a better system than having you walking about, tapping people's shoulders."

"No, madam. It's not a drill."

"Then what—?"

"Miocene," he blurted. "She contacted me directly. Following her instructions, I've already dismissed the others, and now I am to tell you to wait here. She is on her way." As proof, he gave the order's file code. Then with a barely restrained frustration, he added, "This is very mysterious. Everyone agrees. But the Submaster is such a secretive person, so I am assuming—"

"Who's with her?" Washen interrupted.

"I don't think anyone."

But the primary tube was the largest. Twenty captains could ride inside one of its cars, never brushing elbows with one another.

"Her car seems to have an extra thick hull," the assistant explained, "plus some embellishments that I can't quite decipher."

"What sorts of embellishments?"

He glanced at the time, pretending he was anxious to leave. But he was also proud of his cleverness, just as Washen guessed he would be. Cameras inside the tube let them observe the car. Its mass could be determined by the energy required to lift it. He pointed to the pipelike devices wrapped around its hull, making the car look like someone's ball of rope, and with a sudden dose of humility, he admitted, "I don't seem to quite understand that apparatus."

In other words, "Please explain it to me, madam."

But Washen didn't explain anything. Looking at her assistant—one of the most talented and loyal of the captains' offspring; a man who had proved himself on every occasion—she shrugged her shoulders, then lied.

She said, "I don't understand it, either."

Then before she took another breath, she suggested, "You should probably do what she wants. Leave. If Miocene finds you waiting here, she'll kick you down the shaft herself."

The Submaster had exactly the same face and figure that she had carried for millennia, but in the eyes and in the corners of her voice, she was changed. Transformed, almost. On those rare occasions when they met face to face, Washen marveled at all the ways life on Marrow had changed Miocene. And then she would wonder if it was the same for her—if old friends looked at Washen and thought to themselves, "She looks tired, and sad, and maybe a little profound."

They saw each other infrequently, but despite rank and Miocene's attitudes, it was difficult to remain formal. Washen whispered, "Madam," and then added, "Are you crazy? Do you really think it'll work?"

The face smiled, not a hint of joy in it. "According to my models, probably. With an initial velocity of five hundred meters per—"

"Accuracy isn't your problem," Washen told her. "And if you can slip inside your target—that three kilometer remnant of the old bridge, right?—you'll have enough time to brake your momentum."

"But my mind will have died. Is that what you intend to say?"

"Even as thin and weak as the buttresses are now . . . I would hope you're dead. Otherwise you'll have suffered an incredible amount of brain damage." Washen shook her head. "Unless you've accomplished a miracle, and that car will protect you for every millisecond of the way."

Miocene nodded. "It's taken some twenty-one hundred years, and some considerable secrecy on my part . . . but the results have been well worth it."

In the remote past—Washen couldn't remember when exactly—the captains toyed with exactly this kind of apparatus. But it was the Submaster who ordered them not to pursue it. "Too risky," was her verdict. Her lie. "Too many technical hurdles."

For lack of better, Washen smiled grimly and told her, "Good luck then."

Miocene shook her head, her eyes gaining an ominous light. "Good luck to both of us, you mean. The cabin's large enough for two."

"But why me?"

"Because I respect you," she reported. "And if I order you to accompany me, you will. And frankly, I need you. You're more gifted than me when it comes to talking to people. The captains and our halfway loyal descendants . . . well, let's just say they share my respect for you, and that could be an enormous advantage."

Washen guessed the reason, but she still asked, "Why?"

"I intend to explore the ship. And if the worst has happened—if it's empty and dead—then you're the best person, I believe, to bring home that terrible news . . ."

Just like that, they escaped from Marrow.

Miocene's car was cramped and primitive, and the swift journey brought little hallucinations and a wrenching nausea. But they survived with their sanity. Diving into the remains of the first bridge, the Submaster brought them to a bruising halt inside the assembly station, slipping into the first empty berth, then she took a moment to smooth her crude, homespun uniform with a trembling long hand.

Base camp had been without power for nearly five millennia. The Event had crippled every reactor, every drone. Without food or water, the abandoned lab animals had dropped into comas, and as their immortal flesh lost moisture, they mummified itself. Washen picked up one of the mandrill baboons—an enormous male weighing little more than a breath—and she felt its leathery heart beat, just once, just to tell her, "I waited for you."

She set it down, and left quietly.

Miocene was standing on the viewing platform, gazing expectantly at the horizon. Even at this altitude, they could only see the captains' realm. The nearest of the Wayward cities—spartan places with cold and simple iron buildings fitted together like blocks—were hundreds of kilometers removed from them. Which might as well have been hundreds of light years, as much as the two cultures interacted anymore.

"You look as if you're expecting someone," Washen observed.

The Submaster said nothing.

"The Waywards are going to find out that we're here, madam. If Till doesn't already know, it's only because he's got too many spies, and all of them are talking at once."

Miocene nodded absently, taking a deep breath.

Then she turned, and never mentioning the Waywards, she said, "We've wasted enough time. Let's go see what's upstairs."

The long access tunnel to the ship was intact.

Tube-cars remained in their berths, untouched by humans and apparently shielded from the Event by the surrounding hyperfiber. Their engines were charged, every system locked in a diagnostic mode. The com-links refused to work, perhaps because there was no one to maintain the dead ship's net. But by dredging the proper commands from memory, Washen got them under way, and every so often she would glance at Miocene, measuring the woman's stern profile, wondering which of them was more scared of what they would find.

The tunnel turned into an abandoned fuel line that spilled out into the leech habitat.

Everything was exactly as Washen's team had left it. Empty and dusty and relentlessly gray, the habitat welcomed them with a perfect silence.

Miocene gripped her belly, as if in pain.

Washen tried to link up with the ship's net, but every connection to the populated areas had been severed.

"We're going on," Miocene announced. "Now."

They pressed on, climbing out of the mammoth fuel tank and into the first of the inhabited quarters. Suddenly they were inside a wide, flattened tunnel, enormous and empty, and looking out at the emptiness, Miocene said, "Perhaps the passengers and crew . . . perhaps they were able to evacuate the ship . . . do you suppose . . . ?"

Washen began to say, "Maybe."

From behind, with a jarring suddenness, an enormous car appeared, bearing down on them until a collision was imminent, then skipping sideways with a crisp, AI precision. Then as the car was passing them, its sole passenger—an enormous whale-like entity cushioned within a salt water bath—winked at them with three of its black eyes, winking just as people did at each other, meaning nothing but the friendliest of greetings.

It was a Yawkleen. Five millennia removed from her post, yet Washen immediately remembered the species' name.

With a flat, disbelieving voice, Miocene said, "No."

But it was true. In the distance, they could just make out a dozen cars, the traffic light, but otherwise perfectly normal. Perfectly banal.

Pausing at the first waystation, they asked its resident AI about the Master's health.

With a smooth cheeriness, it reported, "She is in robust good health. Thank you for inquiring."

"Since when?" the Submaster pressed.

"For the last sixty thousand years, bless her."

Miocene was mute, a scalding rage growing by the instant.

One of the waystation's walls was sprinkled with com-booths. Washen stepped into the nearest booth, saying, "Emergency status. The captains' channel. Please, we need to speak to the Master."

Miocene followed, sealing the door behind them.

A modest office surrounded them, spun out of light and sound. Three captains and countless AIs served as the Master's staff and as buffers. It was the night staff, Washen realized; the clocks on Marrow were wrong by eleven hours. Not too bad after fifty centuries of little mistakes—

The human faces stared at the apparitions, while the AIs simply asked, "What is your business, please?"

"I want to see her!" Miocene thundered.

The captains tried to portray an appropriate composure.

"I'm Miocene! Submaster, First Chair!" The tall woman bent over the nearest captain, saying, "You've got to recognize me. Look at me. Something's very wrong—"

The AIs remembered them, and acted.

The image swirled and stabilized again.

The Master was standing alone in a conference room, watching the arrival of a small starship. She looked exactly as Washen remembered, except that her hair was longer and tied in an intricate bun. Preoccupied in ways that only a Ship's Master can be, she didn't bother to look at her guests. She wasn't paying attention to her AI's warnings. But when she happened to glance at the two captains—both dressed in crude, even laughable imitations of standard ship uniforms—a look of wonder and astonishment swept over that broad face, replaced an instant later with a piercing fury.

"Where have the two of you been?" the Master cried out.

"Where you sent us!" Miocene snapped. "Marrow!"

"Where . . . ?!" the woman spat.

"Marrow," the Submaster repeated. Then, in exasperation, "What sort of game are you playing with us?"

"I didn't send you anywhere . . . !"

In a dim, half-born way, Washen began to understand.

Miocene shook her head, asking, "Why keep our mission secret?" Then in the next breath, "Unless all you intended to do was imprison the best of your captains—"

Washen grabbed Miocene by the arm, saying, "Wait. No."

"My best captains? You?" The Master gave a wild, cackling laugh. "My best officers wouldn't vanish without a trace. They wouldn't take elaborate precautions to accomplish god-knows-what, keeping out of sight for how long? And without so much as a whisper from any one of them . . . !"

Miocene glanced at Washen with an empty face. "She didn't send us—"

"Someone did," Washen replied.

"Security!" the Master shouted. "Two ghosts are using this link! Track them! Hurry! Please, please!"

Miocene killed the link, giving them time.

The stunned ghosts found themselves standing inside the empty booth, trying to make sense out of pure insanity.

"Who could have fooled us . . . ?" asked Washen. Then in her next breath, she realized how easy it would have been: Someone with access and ingenuity sent orders in the Master's name, bringing the captains together in an isolated location. Then the same ingenious soul deceived them with a replica of the Master, sending them rushing down to the ship's core . . .

"I could have manipulated all of you," Miocene offered, thinking along the same seductive, extremely paranoid lines. "But I didn't know about Marrow's existence. None of us knew."

But someone had known. Obviously.

"And even if I possessed the knowledge," Miocene continued, "what could I hope to gain?"

An ancient memory surfaced of its own accord. Suddenly Washen saw herself standing before the window in the leech habitat, looking at the captains' reflections while talking amiably about ambition and its sweet, intoxicating stink.

"We've got to warn the Master," she told Miocene.

"Of what?"

She didn't answer, shouting instructions to the booth, then waiting for a moment before asking, "Are you doing what I said?"

The booth gave no reply.

Washen eyed Miocene, feeling a sudden chill. Then she unsealed the booth's door and gave it a hard shove, stepping warily out into the waystation.

A large woman in robes was calmly and efficiently melting the AI with a powerful laser.

Wearing a proper uniform, saying the expected words, she would be indistinguishable from the Master.

But what surprised the captains even more was the ghost standing nearby. He was wearing civilian clothes and an elaborate disguise, and Washen hadn't seen him for ages. But from the way his flesh quivered on his bones, and the way his gray eyes smiled straight at her, there was no doubt about his name.

"Diu," Washen whispered.

Her ex-lover lifted a kinetic stunner.

Too late and much too slowly, Washen attempted to tackle him.

Then she was somewhere else, and her neck had been broken, and Diu's face was hovering over her, laughing as it spoke, every word incomprehensible.

Washen closed her eyes. Another voice spoke, asking, "How did you find Marrow?" Miocene's voice?

"It's rather like your mission briefing. There was an impact. Some curious data were gathered. But where the Ship's Master dismissed the idea of a hollow core, I investigated. My money paid for the drones that eventually dug to this place, and I followed them here." There was soft laugh, a reflective pause. Then, "This happened tens of thousands of years ago. Of course. I wasn't a captain in those days. I had plenty of time and the wealth to explore this world, to pick apart its mysteries, and eventually formulate my wonderful plan . . ."

Washen opened her eyes again, fighting to focus.

"I've lived on Marrow more than twice as long as you, madam."

Diu was standing in the middle of the viewing platform, his face framed by the remnants of the bridge.

"I know its cycles," he said. "And all its many hazards, too."

Miocene was standing next to Washen, her face taut and tired but the eyes opened wide, missing nothing.

"How do you feel?" she inquired, glancing down at her colleague.

"Awful." Washen sat up, winced briefly, then asked, "How long have we been here?"

"A few minutes," Diu answered. "My associate, the false Master, was carrying both of you. But now it's gone ahead to check on my ship—"

"What ship?"

"That's what I was about to explain." The smile brightened, then he said, "Over the millennia, I've learned how to stockpile equipment in hyperfiber vaults. The vaults drift in the molten iron. In times of need, I can even live inside them. If I wanted to pretend my own death, for instance."

"For the Waywards," Miocene remarked.

"Naturally."

The Submaster pretended to stare at their captor. But she was looking past him, the dark eyes intense and unreadable, but in a subtle way, almost hopeful.

"What do you want?" asked Miocene.

"Guess," he told them.

Washen took a long breath and tried to stand. Miocene grabbed her by the arms, and they stood together like clumsy dancers, fighting for their balance.

"The ship," Washen managed.

Diu said nothing.

"The ultimate starship, and you want it for yourself." Washen took a few more breaths, testing her neck before she pulled free of Miocene's hands. "This scheme of yours is an elaborate mutiny. That's all it is, isn't it?"

"The Waywards are an army," said Miocene. "An army of religious fanatics being readied for a jihad. My son is the nominal leader. But who feeds him his visions? It's always been you, hasn't it?"

No response.

Washen found the strength to move closer to the railing, looking down, nothing to see but thick clouds of airborne iron kicked up by some fresh eruption.

Miocene took a sudden breath, then exhaled.

Strolling towards them, huge even at a distance, was the false Master. Knowing it was a machine made it look like one. It had a patient stride, even with its thick arms raised overhead, waving wildly.

"What about the Builders?" Miocene blurted.

Diu nearly glanced over his shoulder, then hesitated. "What are you asking?"

"Did they really fight the Bleak?"

Diu enjoyed the suspense, grinning at both of them before he admitted, "How the fuck should I know?"

"The artifacts—?" Miocene began.

"Six thousand years old," he boasted. "Built by an alien passenger who thought I was in the entertainment industry."

"Why pretend to die?" Miocene asked.

"For the freedom it gave me." There was a boy in his grin. "Being dead, I can see more. Being dead, I can disguise myself. I walk where I want. I make babies with a thousand different women, including some in the captains' realm."

There was silence.

Then for a moment, they could just begin to hear the machine's voice—a deep sound rattling between the dormitories, fading until it was a senseless murmur.

"We spoke to the Master," Washen blurted.

Miocene took the cue, adding, "She knows. We told her everything—"

"No, you told her almost nothing," Diu snapped.

"Are you certain?"

"Absolutely."

"But she'll be hunting for us," Washen said.

"She's been on that same hunt for five thousand years," he reminded them. "And even if she sniffs out the access tunnel this time, I won't care. Because on the way back down, I mined the tunnel. Patient one kilo charges of antimatter are ready to close things up tight. Excavating a new tunnel is going to take millennia, and probably much longer. Giving myself and my friends plenty of time to prepare."

"What if no one digs us out?" Washen asked.

Diu shrugged, grinning at her. "How does the old story play? It's better to rule in one realm than serve in another—?"

Then he hesitated, hearing a distant voice.

The Master's voice.

A laser appeared in his right hand, and he turned, squinting at his machine, puzzled by the frantic arm-waving.

"Another car," said the voice, diluted to a whisper. "It's in the berth next to yours . . . !"

"What car?" Diu muttered to himself.

"I believe I know," Miocene replied, eyes darting side to side. "I built two vessels, identical in every way. Including the fact that you never knew they existed."

Diu didn't seem to hear her.

Miocene took a step toward him, adding, "It's obvious, isn't it? Someone else is here. Or if they squeezed in together, two someones."

"So?" Diu replied. "A couple more captains lurking nearby—"

"Except," Miocene interrupted, "I didn't send my invitation to my captains."

Diu didn't ask to whom it was sent.

Washen remembered Miocene had stood on this platform, watching Marrow. Watching for Till, she realized. How long would it have taken him to move the car to the bridge? That was the only question. She had no doubts that once motivated, the Waywards could do whatever they wanted inside the captains' realm.

"I was hopeful," Miocene confessed. "I was hopeful that my son would be curious, that he would follow me back to the ship and see it for himself."

There was a sound, sharp and familiar.

The false Master stopped in mid-stride, then began to collapse in on itself. Then a thin column of light appeared in the smoke, betraying the laser's source.

Diu started to run.

Miocene followed, and Washen chased both of them.

Beside the platform, in easy earshot, stood a drone. A lone figure was kneeling beneath its ceramic body, wearing breechcloth and holding a crude laser drill against his shoulder, intent on reducing the machine to ash and gas.

Diu saw him, stopped and aimed.

At Locke.

Maybe he was hesitating, realizing it was his son. Or more likely, he simply was asking himself: Where's Till? Either way, he didn't fire. Instead, Diu started to turn, looking at his surroundings as if for the first time—

There was a clean hard crack.

A fat chunk of lead knocked Diu off his feet, opening his chest before it tore through his backside.

With the smooth grace of an athlete, Till climbed out from the meshwork beneath the platform. He seemed unhurried, empty of emotion. Strolling past Washen, he didn't give her the tiniest glance. It was like watching a soulless machine, right up until the moment when Miocene tried to block his way, saying, "Son," with a weak, sorrowful voice.

He shoved her aside, then ran toward Diu. Screaming. At the top of his lungs, screaming, "It's all been a lie—!"

Diu lifted his hand, reaching into a bloody pocket.

Moments later, the base camp began to shake violently. Dozens of mines were exploding simultaneously. But the enormous mass of the ship absorbed the blows, then counterattacked, pushing the access tunnel shut for its entire length, and as an afterthought, knocking everyone off their feet.

Diu grabbed his laser.

He managed to sit up.

Washen fought her way to her feet, but too late. She could only watch as Miocene managed to leap, grabbing Till by the head and halfway covering him as the killing blast struck her temple, and in half an instant, boiled away her brain.

Till rolled, using the body as a shield, discharging his weapon until it was empty. Then a burst of light struck him in the shoulder, removing his right arm and part of his chest even as it cauterized the enormous wound.

Using his drill, Locke quickly sliced his father into slivers, then burned him to dust.

Miocene lay dead at Washen's feet, and Till was beside her, oblivious to everything. There was a wasted quality to the face, a mark that went beyond any physical injury. "It's been a lie," he kept saying, without sound. "Everything. A monstrous lie."

Locke came to him, not to Washen, asking, "What is monstrous, Your Excellence?"

Till gazed up at him. With a careful voice, he said, "Nothing." Then after a long pause, he added, "We have to return home. Now."

"Of course. Yes, Your Excellence."

"But first," he said, "the ship must be protected from its foes!"

Locke knew exactly what was being asked of him. "I don't see why—?"

"The ship is in danger!" the prophet cried out. "I say it, which makes it so. Now prove your devotion, Wayward!"

Locke turned, looking at his mother with a weary, trapped expression.

Washen struck him on the jaw, hard and sudden.

She had covered almost a hundred meters before the laser drill bit into her calf, making her stumble. But she forced herself to keep running, slipping behind the drone with only two more burns cut deep into her back.

It was as if Locke was trying to miss.

Hours later, watching from the dormitory, Washen saw her son carrying four of the comatose baboons out into the courtyard, where he piled them up and turned the lasers on them. Then he showed the ashes to Till, satisfying him, and without a backward glance, the two walked slowly in the direction of the bridge.

Washen hid for several days, eating and drinking from the old stores.

When she finally crept into the bridge, she found Diu's sophisticated car cut into pieces, and Miocene's fused to its berth. But what startled her—what made her sick and sad—was Marrow itself. The captains' new bridge had been toppled. Wild fires and explosions were sweeping across the visible globe. A vast, incoherent rage was at work, erasing every trace of the despised captains, and attacking anyone that might pose any threat to a lost prophet.

In that crystalline moment of horror, Washen understood what she had to do. And without a wasted moment, she turned and began to make ready.

MISSION DATE—INCONSEQUENTIAL

At the ship's center, a seamless night has been born.

The figure moves by memory through the darkness, picking her way across a tangle of conduits and scrap parts. In a few moments, energy milked from hundreds of tube-cars will flow into an enormous projector, and for a fleeting instant or two, the darkness will be repelled. If her ink-and-paper calculations are correct, and if more than a century of singleminded preparation succeeds, a message of forgiveness and rebirth will skate along the chamber's wall, encircling and embracing the world.

But that is just the beginning.

Wearing a pressure suit and two bulky packs, she climbs over the railing and leaps, bracing for the impact.

Boom.

The blister is thick, but she began the hole decades ago. Tools wait in a neat pile. With a minimum of cuts, the hole opens, and a sudden wind blows past her, trying to coax her into joining it, nothing outside but Marrow's high cold stratosphere.

The buttresses have vanished, at least for the moment.

There's no time to waste. She obeys the wind, letting it carry her through the hole and downward in a wild tumbling spiral.

The sky behind her erupts in light.

In the colors of fire and hot iron, it cries out, "A BUILDER IS COMING. SHE COMES TO LEAD YOU OUT OF YOUR MISERY!"

The Builder grabs the cord of her parachute, then begins to scream.

Not out of fear. Not at all.

It's the full-throated, wonderstruck scream of a girl who has forgotten just how very much fun it is to fall.

Heart of whitenesse

HOWARD WALDROP

Howard Waldrop is widely considered to be one of the best short story writers in the business, and his famous story "The Ugly Chickens" won both the Nebula and the World Fantasy Awards in 1981. His work has been gathered in the collections: Howard Who?, All about Strange Monsters of the Recent Past: Neat Stories, *and* Night of the Cooters: More Neat Stories, *with more collections in the works. Waldrop is also the author of the novel* The Texas-Israeli War: 1999, *in collaboration with Jake Saunders, and of two solo novels,* Them Bones *and* A Dozen Tough Jobs. *He is at work on a new novel, tentatively titled* The Moon World. *His most recent book is a new collection,* Going Home Again. *His stories have appeared in our First, Third, Fourth, Fifth, Sixth, and Twelfth Annual Collections. A long-time Texan, Waldrop now lives in the tiny town of Arlington, Washington, outside Seattle, as close to a trout stream as he can possibly get without actually living in it. He does not have a computer or a phone but he has a Web site at http://www.sff.net/people/waldrop/.*

I'm not even going to try to describe the weird, vivid, and funny story that follows, except to say that no one but Howard would ever even have thought of it, let alone written it. So fasten your seat belt, take a deep breath, sit back, and enjoy the ride.

FOR JOHN CLUTE: THE HUM OF PLEROMA
"Doctor Faustus?—He's dead."

Down these mean cobbled lanes a man must go, methinks, especially when out before larkrise, if larks there still be within a thousand mile of this bone-breaking cold. From the Rus to Spain the world is locked in snow and ice, a sheet of blue glass. There was no summer to speak of; bread is dear, and in France we hear they are eating each other up, like the Carribals of the Western Indies.

It's bad enow I rehearse a play at the Rose, that I work away on the poem of the celebrated Hero and Leander, that life seems more like a jakes each day. Then some unseen toady comes knocking on the door and slips a note through the latchhole this early, the pounding fist matching that in my head.

I'd come up from the covers and poured myself a cup of malmsey you could have drowned a pygmy in, then dressed as best I could, and made my way out into this cold world.

Shoreditch was dismal in the best of times, and this wasn't it.

And what do I see on gaining the lane but a man making steaming water into the street-ditch from a great bull pizzle of an accouterment.

He sees me and winks.

I winks back.

His wink said I see you're interested.

My wink back says I'm usually interested but not at this instant but keep me in mind if you see me again.

He immediately smiles, then turns his picauventure beard toward the cold row of houses to his left.

Winking is the silent language full of nuance and detail: we are after all talking about the overtures to a capital offence.

I come to the shop on the note, I go in; though I've never been there before I know I can ignore the fellows working there (it is a dyer's, full of boiling vats and acrid smells and steam; at least it is *warm*) and go through a door up some rude steps, to go through another plated with strips of iron, and into the presence of a High Lord of the Realm.

He is signing something, he sees me and slides the paper under another; it is probably the names of people soon to decorate a bridge or fence.

This social interaction is, too, full of nuance; one of them is that we two pretend not to know who the other is. Sometimes *their* names are Cecil, Stansfield, Salisbury, sometimes not. Sometimes my name is Christopher, or Chris, familiar Kit, or the Poet, or plain Marlowe. We do pretend, though, we have no names, that we are the impersonal representatives of great ideas and forces, moved by large motives like the clockwork Heavens themselves.

"A certain person needs enquiring about," said the man behind the small table. "Earlier enquiries have proved . . . ineffectual. It has been thought best the next devolved to yourself. This person is beyond Oxford; make arrangements, go there quietly. Once in Oxford," he said, taking out of his sleeve a document with a wax seal upon it and laying it on the table, "you may open these, your instructions and knowledges; follow them to the letter. At a certain point, if you must follow them—thoroughly," he said, coming down hard upon the word, "we shall require a token of faith."

He was telling me without saying that I was to see someone, do something to change their mind, or keep them from continuing a present course. Failing that I was to bring back to London their heart, as in the old story of the evil step-queen, the huntsman, and the beautiful girl who ended up consorting with forest dwarves, eating poison, and so forth.

I nodded, which was all I was required to do.

But he had not as yet handed me the missive, which meant he was not through.

He leaned back in his chair.

"I said your name was put forth," he said, "for this endeavor. But not by me. I know you to be a godless man, a blasphemer, most probably an invert. I so hate that the business of true good government makes occasional use of such as *you*. But the awkward circumstances of this mission, shall we say, make some of your peccadilloes absolute necessities. *Only* this would make me have any dealings with you whatsoever. There will come a reckoning one fine day."

Since he had violated the unspoken tenets of the arrangement by speaking to me personally, and, moreover, telling the plain unvarnished truth, and he knew it, I felt justified in my answer. My answer was, "As you say, Lord____," and I used his name.

He clenched the arms of his chair, started up. Then he calmed himself, settled again. His eyes went to the other papers before him.

"I believe that is all," he said, and handed me the document.

I picked it up, turned and left.

Well, work on Hero and Leander's right out for a few days, but I betook me as fast as the icy ways would let, from my precincts in Shoreditch through the city. Normally it would mean going about over London Bridge, but as I was in a hurry I walked straight across the River directly opposite the Rose to the theatre itself in Southwark.

The River was, and had been for two months, frozen to a depth of five feet all the way to Gravesend. Small boys ran back and forth across the river. Here and there were set up booths with stiff frozen awnings; the largest concatenation of them was farther up past the town at Windsor, where Her Majesty the Queen had proclaimed a Frost Fair and set up a Royal Pavilion. A man with a bucket and axe was chopping the River for chunks of water. Others walked the ice and beat at limbs and timbers embedded in it—free firewood was free, in any weather. A thick pall of smoke hung over London town, every fire lit. A bank of heavy cloud hung farther north than that. There were tales that when the great cold had come, two months agone, flocks of birds in flight had fallen to the ground and shattered; cattle froze standing.

To make matters worse, the Plague, which had closed the theatres for three months this last, long-forgotten summer, had not gone completely away, as all hoped, and was still taking thirty a week on the bills of mortality. It would probably be back again this summer and close the Theater, the Curtain and the Rose once more. Lord Strange's and Lord Nottingham's Men would again have to take touring the provinces beyond seven mile from London.

But as for now, cold or no, at the Rose, we put on plays each afternoon without snow in the open-air ring. At the moment we do poor old Greene's *Friar Bacon and Friar Bungay*—Greene not dead these seven months, exploded from dropsy in a flop, they sold the clothes off him and buried him in a diaper with a wreath of laurel about his head—we rehearse mine own *Massacre at Paris*, and Shaxber's *Harry Sixt*, while we play his *T. Andronicus* alternate with Thomas Kyd's *Spanish Tragedy*, of which *Andronicus* is an overheated feeble Romanish imitation.

Shaxber's also writing a longish poem, his on the celebrated Venus and Adonis, which at this rate will be done before my Hero. This man, the same age as me, bears watching. Unlike when I did at Cambridge, I take no part in the Acting; Will Shaxber is forever being messenger, third murderer, courtier; he tugs ropes when engines are needed; he counts receipts, he makes himself useful withal.

No one here this early but Will Kemp; he snores as usual on his bed of straw and ticking in the 'tiring house above and behind the stage. He sounds the bear that's eaten All the dogs on a good day at the Pit. I find some ink (almost frozen) and leave a note for John Alleyn to take over for me, pleading urgent business *down* country, to throw off the scent, and make my way, this time over the Bridge, back to Shoreditch.

Shoreditch is the place actors live, since it was close to the original theatres, and so it is the place actors die. Often enough first news you hear on a morning is "another actor dead in Shoreditch." Never East Cheap, or Spital Fields, not even Southwark itself; always Shoreditch. At a tavern, at their lodgings, in the street itself. Turn them over; if it's not the Plague, it's another actor dead from a knife, fists, drink, pox, for all that matter cannonfire or hailstones in the remembered summers.

I make arrangements; I realign myself to other stations; my sword stays in its corner, my new hat, my velvet doublet all untied, hung on their hooks. I put on round slops, a leathern tunic, I cut away my beard; in place of sword a ten-inch poignard, a pointed slouch-hat, a large sack for my back.

In an hour I am back at River-side, appearing as the third of the three P's in John Heywood's *The Four PPPP's*, a 'pothecary, ready to make my way like him, at least as far as Oxenford.

The ferrymen are all on holiday, their boats put up on timbers above the ice. Here and there people skate, run shoed on the ice, slip and fall; the gaiety seems forced, not like the fierce abandon of the early days of the Great Frost. But I have been watching on my sojourn each day to and from the Rose, and I lick my finger and stick it up (the spit freezing almost at once) to test the wind, and as I know the wind, and I know my man, I walk about halfway out on the solid Thames and wait.

As I wait, I see two figures dressed much like the two Ambassadores From Poland in my *Massacre at Paris* (that is, not very well, one of them being Kemp) saunter toward me on the dull grey ice. I know them to be a man named Frizier and one named Skeres, Gram and Nicholas I believe, both to be bought for a shilling in any trial, both doing the occasional cony-catching, gulling and sharping; both men I have seen in taverns in Shoreditch, in Deptford, along the docks, working the theatres.

There is little way they can know me, so I assume they have taken me for a mark as it slowly becomes apparent they are approaching *me*. Their opening line, on feigning recognition, will be, "Ho, sir, are you not a man from (Hereford) (Cheshire) (Luddington) known to my Cousin Jim?"

They are closer, but they say to my surprise, "Seems the man is late this day, Ingo."

"That he be, Nick."

They are waiting for the same thing I am. They take no notice of me standing but twenty feet away.

"Bedamn me if it's not the fastest thing I ever seen," says one.

"I have seen the cheater-cat of Africa," says the other, "and this man would leave it standing."

"I believe you to be right."

And far down the ice, toward where the tide would be, I spy my man just before they do. If you do not know for what you look, you will think your eyes have blemished and twitched. For what comes comes fast and eclipses the background at a prodigious rate.

I drop my pack to the ground and slowly hold up a signal-jack and wave it back and forth.

"Bedamn me," says one of the men, "but he's turning this way."

"How does he stop it?" asks the other, looking for shelter from the approaching apparition.

And with a grating and a great screech and plume of powdered ice, the thing turns to us and slows. It is a ship, long and thin, up on high thin rails like a sleigh, with a mast amidships and a jib up front, and as the thing slows (great double booms of teethed iron have fallen from the stern where a keelboard should be) the sails luff and come down, and the thing stops three feet from me, the stinging curtain of ice falling around me.

"Who flies Frobisher's flag?" came a voice from the back. Then up from the hull comes a huge man and throws a round anchor out onto the frozen Thames.

"I," I said. "A man who's seen you come by here these last weeks punctually. A man who marvels at the speed of your craft. And," I said, "an apothecary who needs must get to Oxford, as quick as he can."

The huge man was bearded and wore furs and a round hat in the Russian manner of some Arctic beast. "So you spoil my tack by showing my old Admiral's flag? Who'd you sail with, man? Drake? Hawkins? Raleigh, Sir Walter Tobacco himself? You weren't with Admiral Martin, else I'd know you, that's for sure."

"Never a one," said I. "My brother was with Hawkins when he shot the pantaloons off Don Iago off Portsmouth. My cousin, with one good eye before the Armada, and one bad one after, was with Raleigh."

"So you're no salt?"

"Not whatsoever."

"Where's your brother and cousin now?"

"They swallowed the anchor."

He laughed. "That so? Retired to land, eh? Some can take the sea, some can't. Captain Jack Cheese, at your service. Where is it you need to go, Oxford? Hop in, I'll have you there in two hours."

"Did you hear that, Gram?" asked one of the men. "Oxford in two hours!"

"There's no such way he can do no such thing!" said the other, looking at Captain Cheese.

"Is that money I hear talking, or only the crackling of the ice?" asked Captain Jack.

"Well, it's as much money as we have, what be that, Gram? Two fat shillings you don't make no Oxford in no two hours. As against?"

"I can use two shillings," said Jack Cheese.

"But what's *your* bet, man?" asked the other.

"Same as you. Two shillings. If you'll kill me for two shillings," he said, pulling at his furry breeks and revealing the butts of two pistols the size of boarding cannons, "I'd do the same for you."

The two looked back and forth, then said, "Agreed!"

"Climb in," said Captain Jack. "Stay low, hang tight. Ship's all yar, I've got a following wind and a snowstorm crossing north from the west, and we'll be up on one runner most the time. Say your prayers now; for I don't stop for nothing nor nobody, and I don't go back for dead men nor lost bones."

The clock struck ten as we clambered aboard. My pack just hit the decking when, with a whoop, Jack Cheese jerked a rope, the jib sprang up; wind from nowhere filled it, the back of the boat screamed and wobbled to and fro. He jerked the anchor off the ice, pulled up the ice-brakes and jerked the mainsail up and full.

People scattered to left and right and the iceboat leapt ahead with a dizzy shudder. I saw the backward-looking eyes of Frizier and Skeres close tight as they hung onto the gunwales with whitened hands, buffeting back and forth like skittle-balls.

And the docks and quays became one long blur to left and right; then we stood still and the land moved to either side as if it were being paid out like a thick grey and white painted rope.

I looked back. Jack Cheese had a big smile on his face. His white teeth showed bright against his red skin and the brown fur; I swear he was humming.

Past Richmond we went, and Cheese steered out farther toward the leftward bank as the stalls, awnings, booths and bright red of the Royal Pavilion appeared, flung themselves to our right and receded behind.

Skizz was the only sound; we sat still in the middle of the noise and the objects flickering on and off, small then large then small again, side to side. Ahead, above the River, over the whiteness of the landscape and the ice, the dark line of cloud grew darker, thicker, lower.

Skeres and Frizier lay like dead men, only their grips on the hull showing them to be conscious.

I leaned my head closer to Captain Cheese.

"A word of warning," I said. "Don't trust those two."

"Hell and damn, son," he smiled, "I don't trust *you*! Hold tight," he said, pulling something. True to his word, in the stillness, one side of the iceboat rose up two feet off the level, we sailed along with the sound halved, slowly dropped back down to both iron runners, level. I looked up. The mainsail was tight as a pair of Italian leggings.

"There goes Hampton. Coming up on Staines!" he called out so the two men in front could have heard him if they'd chosen to.

A skater flashed by inches away. "Damn fool lubber!" said Jack Cheese. "I got sea-road rights-of-way!" A deer paused, flailed away, fell and was gone, untouched behind us.

And then we went into a wall of whiteness that peppered and stung. The whole world dissolved away. I thought for an instant I had gone blind from the speed of our progress. Then I saw Captain Cheese still sitting a foot or two away. Skeres and Frizier had disappeared, as had the prow and the jibsail. I could see nothing but the section of boat I was in, the captain, the edge of the mainsail above. No river, no people, no landmarks, just snow and whiteness.

"How can you see?"

"Can't," said the captain.

"How do you know where we are?"

"Ded reckoning," he said. "Kick them up front, tell 'em to hang tight," he said. I did. When Skeres and Frizier opened their eyes, they almost screamed.

Then Cheese dropped the jib and the main and let the ice-brakes go. We came to a stop in the middle of the swirling snow, as in the middle of a void. Snowflakes the size of thalers came down. Then I made out a bulking shape a foot or two beyond the prow of the icerunner.

"Everybody out! Grab the hull. Lift, that's right. Usually have to do this myself. Step sharp. You two, point the prow up. That's it. Push. Push."

In the driven snow, the indistinct shape took form. Great timbers, planking, rocks, chunks of iron were before us, covered with ice. The two men out front put the prow over one of the icy gaps fifteen feet apart. Cheese and I lifted the stern, then climbed over after it. "Settle in, batten down," said the captain. Once more we swayed sickeningly, jerked, the sails filled, and we were gone.

"What was that?" I asked.

"Reading Weir," he said. "Just where the Kennet comes in on the portside. If we'd have hit that, we'd of been crushed like eggs. You can go to sleep now if you want. It's smooth sailing all the way in now."

But of course I couldn't. There seemed no movement, just the white blank ahead, behind, to each side.

"That would have been Wallingford," he said once. Then, a little farther on, "Abingdon, just there." We sailed on. There was a small pop in the canvas. "Damn," he said, "the wind may go contrary; I might have to tack." He watched the sail awhile, then settled back. "I was wrong," he said.

Then, "Hold tight!" Frizier or Skeres moaned.

He dropped the sails. We lost motion. I heard the icebrakes grab, saw a small curtain of crystalline ice mix with the snow. The moving, roiling whiteness became a still, roiling whiteness. The anchor hit the ice.

And, one after the other, even with us, the bells of the Oxford Tower struck noon.

• • •

"Thanks be to you," I said, "Captain Jack Cheese."

"And to you—what was your name?"

"John," I said. "Johnny Factotum."

He looked at me, put his finger aside his nose. "Oh, then, Mr Factotum," he said. I shook his hand.

"You've done me a great service," I said.

"And you me," said Captain Jack. "You've made me the easiest three shillings ever."

"Three!" yelled the two men still in the boat. "The bet was two shillings!"

"The bet was two, which I shall now take." The captain held out his hand. "The fare back to London is one more, for you both."

"What? What fare?" they asked.

"The bet was two hours to here. Which I have just done, from the tower bells in London to the campanile of Oxford. To do this, I had perforce to take you here in the time allotted, which—" and Jack Cheese turned once more to me and laid his finger to nose, "I have just done, therefore, *quod erat demonstrandum*," he said. "The wager being forfeit, either I shall bid you adieu, and give to you the freedom of the River and the Roads, or I shall drop you off in your own footprints on the London ice for a further shilling."

The two looked at each other, their eyes pewter plates in the driven snow.

"But . . ." one began to say.

"These my unconditional, unimprovable terms," said Captain Jack.

We were drawing a crowd of student clerks and *magisters*, who marvelled at the iceboat.

"Very well," sighed one of the men.

"The bet?" It was handed over. "The downward fare?" It, too.

"Hunker down in front, keep your heads down," said Jack Cheese and took out one of his mutton-leg pistols and laid it in front of him. "And no Spanish sissyhood!" he said. "For going downriver we don't stop for Reading Weir, we take it at speed!"

"No!"

"Abaft, all ye!" yelled Jack Cheese to the crowd. "I go upstream a pace; I turn; I come back down. If you don't leave the River now, don't blame me for loss of life and limb. No stopping Jack Cheese!" he said. The sails snapped up, the icebrake lifted, they blurred away into the upper Thames-Isis.

We all ran fast as we could from the centre of the ice. I stopped; so did half the crowd who'd come to my side of the river. The blur of Captain Jack Cheese, the hull and sails, and the frightened popped eyes at gunwale level zipped by.

The laughter of Jack Cheese came back to us as they flashed into the closing downriver snow and were gone.

And here I had been worried about him with two sharpers aboard. Done as well as any Gamaliel Ratsy, and no Spanish sissyhood, for sure. I doubt the two would twitch till they got back to London Docks.

The students were marvelling among themselves. It reminded me of my days at Cambridge, bare seven years gone.

But my purposes lay elsewhere. I walked away from the crowd, unnoticed; they were as soon lost to me in the blowing whiteness as I, them.

I sat under a pine by the River-side. From my pack I took a snaphance and started a small fire in the great snowing chill, using needles of the tree for a fragrant combustion; I filled my pipe, lit it and took in a great calming lungful of Sir Walter's Curse.

I was no doubt in the middle of the great university. I didn't care. I finished one pipeful, lit another, took in half that, ate some saltbeef and hard bread (the only kind to be found in London). Then I took from the apothecary pack, with its compartments and pockets filled with simples, emetics, herbs and powders, the document with the seal.

I read it over, twice. Then per instructions, added it to the fire.

I finished my pipe, knocked the dottles into the flame, and put it away.

The man's name was Johan Faustus, a German of Wittenberg. He was suspected, of course, of the usual—blasphemy, treason, subornation of the judiciary, atheism. The real charge, of course, was that he consorted with known Catholics—priests, prelates, the Pope himself. But what most worried the government was that he consorted with known Catholics *here*, in this realm. I was to find if he were involved in any plot; if suspicions were true, to put an end to his part in it. These things were in the document itself.

To this I added a few things I knew. That he was a doctor of both law and medicine, as so many are in this our country; that he had spent many years teaching at Wittenberg (not a notorious stronghold of the Popish Faith); that he was a magician, a conjuror, an alchemist, and, in the popular deluded notion of the times, supposed to have trafficked with Satan. There were many tales from the Continent—that he'd gulled, dazzled, conjured to and for emperors and kings—whether with the usual golden leaden ruses, arts of ledgerdemain, or the Tarot cards or whatnot, I knew not.

Very well, then. But as benighted superstitious men had written my instructions, I had to ask myself—what would a man dealing with the Devil be doing in part of a Catholic plot? The Devil has his own devices and traps, all suppose, some of them, I think, involving designs on the Popish Church itself. Will he use one religion 'gainst 'nother? Why don't men stop and think when they begin convolving their minds as to motive? Were they all absent the day brains were forged?

And why would an atheist deal with the Devil? The very professors tie themselves in knotlets of logic over just such questions as these.

Well then: let's apply William of Ockham's fine razor to this Gordian knot of high senselessness. I'll trot up to him and ask him if he's involved in any treacherous plotting. Being an atheist, in league with *both* the Devil *and* the Pope (and for all I know the Turk), he'll tell me right out the truth. If treasonable, I shall cut off his head; if not . . . should I cut off his head to be safe?

Enough forethought; time for action. I reached into the bottom of my peddlar's pack and took out two long curved blades like scimitars, so long and thin

John Sincklo could have worn them Proportional, and attached them with thongs to the soles of my rude boots.

So equilibrized at the edge of the River I stood, and set out toward my destination which the letter had given me, Lotton near Cricklade, near the very source of the Thames-Isis.

And as I stood to begin my way norwestward the sun, as if in a poem by Chideock Tichbourne, showed itself for the first time in two long months through the overcast, as a blazing ball, flooding the sky, the snow and ice in a pure sheen of blinding light. I began to skate toward it, toward the Heart of Whitenesse itself.

Skiss skiss skiss the only sound from my skates, the pack swinging to and fro on my back; pure motion now, side to side, one arm folded behind me, the other out front as counterweight, into the blinded and blinding River before me. Past the mill at Lechlade, toward Kempsford, the sides of the Thames-Isis grew closer and rougher; past Kempsford to the edge of Cricklade itself, where the Roy comes in from the left just at the town, and turning then to right and north I go, up the River Churn, just larger than the Shoreditch in London itself. And a mile up and on the right, away from the stream, the outbuildings of a small town itself, and on a small hill beyond the town roofs, an old manor house.

I got off my skates, and unbound them and put them in the pack.

And now to ask leading questions of the rude common folk of the town.

I walked to the front of the manor house and stopped, and beheld a sight to make me furious.

Tied to a post in front of the place, a horse stood steaming in what must have been forty degrees below frost. Its coat was lathered, the foam beginning to freeze in clumps on its mane and legs. Steam came from its nostrils. That someone rode a horse like that and left it like that in weather like this made me burn. The animal regarded me with an unconcerned eye, without shivering.

I walked past it to the door of the manor house, where of course my man lived. The sun, once the bright white ball, was covered again, and going down besides. Dark would fall like a disgraced nobleman in a few moments.

I rang the great iron doorknocker three times, and three hollow booms echoed down an inner hallway. The door opened to reveal a hairy man, below the middle height. His beard flowed into his massive head of hair. His ears, which stuck out beyond that tangle, were thin and pointed. His smile was even, but two lower teeth stuck up from the bottom lip. His brows met in the middle to form one hairy ridge.

"That horse needs seeing to," I said.

He peered past me. "Oh, not *that* one," he said. "My master is expecting you, and cut the *merde*, he knows who you are and why you're here."

"To try to sell the Good Doctor simples and potions."

"Yeh, right," said the servant. "This way."

We walked down the hall. A brass head sitting on a shelf in a niche turned its eyes to follow me with its gaze as we passed. How very like Vergil.

We came to a closet doorway set at one side of the hallway.

"You can't just go in, though," said the servant, "without you're worthy. Inside this here room is a Sphinx. It'll ask you a question. You can't answer it, it eats you."

"What if I answer it?"

"Well, I guess you could eat *it*, if you've a mind to and she'll hold still. But mainly you can go through the next door; the Doctor's in."

"Have her blaze away," I said.

"Oh, that's a good one," said the servant. "I'll just stand behind the door here; she asks the first person she sees."

"You don't mind if I take out my knife, do you?"

"Take out a six-pounder cannon, for all the good it'll do you, you're not a wise man," he said.

I eased my knife from its sheath.

He opened the door. I expected either assassins, fright masks, jacks-in-boxes, some such. I stepped to the side, in case of mantraps or springarns. Nothing happened, nothing leapt out. I peered around the jamb.

Standing on a stone that led back into a cavern beyond was a woman to the waist, a four-footed leopard from there down; behind her back were wings. She was moulting, putting in new feathers here and there. She looked at me with the eyes of a cat, narrow vertical pupils. I dared not look away.

"What hassss," she asked, in a sibilant voice that echoed down the hall, "eleven fingers in the morning, lives in a high place at noon, and has no head at sundown?"

"The present Queen's late Mum," I said.

"Righto!" said the servant and closed the door. I heard a heavy weight thrash against it, the sound of scratching and tearing. The servant slammed his fist on the door. "Settle down, you!" he yelled. "There'll be plenty more dumb ones come this way."

He opened the door at the end of the hall, and I walked into the chamber of Doctor Faustus.

The room is dark but warm. A fire glows in the hearth, the walls are lined with books. There are dark marks on the high ceiling, done in other paint.

Doctor John Faust sits on a high stool before a reading stand; a lamp hangs above. I see another brass head is watching me from the wall.

"Ahem," says the servant.

"Oh?" says Faustus, looking up. "I thought you'd be alone, Wagner." He looks at me. "The others they sent weren't very bright. They barely got inside the house."

"I can imagine," I say. "Your lady's costume needs mending. The feathers aren't sewn in with double-loop stitches."

He laughs. "I am Doctor Johan Faustus."

"And I am—" I say, thinking of names.

"Please drop the mumming," he says. "I've read your *Tamerlane*—both parts."

I look around. "Can we be honest?" I ask.

"Only one of us," he says.

"I have been sent here—"

"Probably to find out to whom I owe *my* allegiance. And its treasonableness. And not being able to tell whether I'm lying, to kill me; better safe than sorry. Did you enjoy your ride on the ice?"

There is no way he could have known. I was not followed. Perhaps he is inducing; if he knows who I am, and that I was in London this morning, only one method could have gotten me here so fast. But no one else who saw—

I stopped. *This* is the way fear starts.

"Very much," I say.

"Your masters want to know if I plot for the Pope—excuse me, the Bishop of Rome. No. Or the Spaniard. No. Nor French, Jews, Turks, no. I do not plot even for myself. Now you can leave."

"And I am to take your word?" I ask.

"I'm taking yours."

"Easily enough done," I say. Wagner the servant has left the room. Faustus is very confident of himself.

"You haven't asked me if I serve the Devil," he says.

"No one serves the Devil," I say. "There is no Devil."

Faustus looks at me. "So they have finally stooped so high as to send an atheist. Then I shall have to deal with you on the same high level." He bows to me.

I bowed back.

"If you are a true atheist, and I convince you there's magic, will you take my word and go away?"

"All magic is mumbo-jumbo, sleight-of-hand, mists, leg-erdemain," I say.

"Oh, I think not," says Faustus.

"Blaze away," I say. "Convenient Wagner has gone. Next he'll no doubt appear as some smoke, a voice from a horn, a hand."

"Oh, Mr Marlowe," says Faustus. "What I serve is knowledge. I want it all. Knowledge is magic; other knowledge *leads* to magic. Where others draw back, I begin. I ask questions of Catholics, of Jews, of Spaniards, of Turks, if they have wisdom I seek. We'll find if you're a true atheist, a truly logical man. Look down."

I do. I am standing in a five-pointed star surrounded by a circle, written over with nonsense and names in Greek and Latin. Faustus steps off his stool. Onto another drawing on the floor. The room grows dark, then brighter, and much warmer as he waves his arms around like a conjuror before the weasel comes out the glove. Good trick, that.

"I tell you this as a rational man," he says. "Stay in the pentagram. Do not step out."

I felt hot breathing on the back of my neck that moved my hair.

"Do not look around," says Faustus, his voice calm and reasoned. "If you look around, you will scream. If you scream, you will jump. If you jump, you will leave the pentagram. If you leave it, the thing behind you will bite off your head; the Sphinx out yonder was but a dim stencil of what stands behind you. So do not look, no matter how much you want to."

"No," I said. "You've got it wrong. I won't look around, not because I am afraid I'll jump, but because the act of *looking* will be to admit you've touched a superstitious adytum of my brain, one left over from the savage state. I *look*, I am lost, no matter what follows."

Faust regards me anew.

"Besides," I said, "what is back there"— here whoever it was must have leaned even closer and blew hot breath down on me, though as I remember, Wagner was shorter, someone else then—"is another of your assistants. If they are going to kill me, they should have done it by now. On with your show. I am your attentive audience. Do you parade the wonders of past ages before me? Isis and Osiris and so forth? What of the past? Was Julius Caesar a redhead, as I have heard? How about Beauty? The Sphinx woman should have been able to change costumes by now?"

"You Cambridge men are always big on Homer. How about Helen of Troy?" asks Faustus.

"Is this the face that launched a thousand ships, etc.?" I ask. "I think not. Convince me, Faustus. Do your shilly-shally."

"You asked for it," he says. I expected the knife to go through my back. Whoever was behind me was breathing slowly, slowly.

Faustus waved his arms, his lips moved. He threw his arms downward. I expected smoke, sparkles, explosion. There is none.

It is fourteen feet tall. It has a head made of rocks and stones. Its body is brass; one leg of lead, the other of tin. I know this because the room was bright from the roaring fires that crackled with flame from each foot. This was more like it.

"Speak, spirit!" said Faustus.

"*Hissssk. Snarrrz. Skazzz,*" it said, or words to that effect.

And then it turned into the Queen, and the Queen turned into the King of Scotland. I don't mean someone who looked like him, I mean him. He shifted form and shape before me. He turns, his hair is longer, his nose thinner, his moustache flows. He changes to another version of himself, and his head jumped off bloodily to the floor. He turns into a huge sour-faced man, then back to someone who looks vaguely like the King of Scotland, then another; then a man and woman joined at the hip, another king, a woman, three fat Germans, a thin one, a small woman, a fat bearded man, a thin guy with a beard, a blip of light, another bearded man, a woman, a tall thin man, his son—

This was very good indeed. Would we had him at the Rose.

"Tell him of what lies before, Spirit."

"Tell him," I said to Faustus, "to tell me of plots."

"PLOTS!" the thing roared. "You want the truth?" It was back fourteen feet tall and afire, stooping under the ceiling. "You live by a government. Governments NEED plots! Else people ask why they die? Where's the bread? Human. Hu-man! You are the ones in torment! We here are FREE!

"PLOTS! BEware ESSEX!" Essex? The Queen's true right arm? Her lover? "BEWARE Guido and his dark SHINING lantern! BEWARE the House in the RYE-fields! Beware the papers in the TUB OF flour! Beware pillars! BEWARE POSTS! BeWARE the Dutch, the FRENCH, the colonists in VIRGINIA!" Virginia? They're lost? "BEWARE RUSSia and the zuLU and the DUTCHAFricans! Beware EVERYTHING! BEWARE EVERYboDY! AIIIiiiiiii!!!"

It disappears. Faustus slumps to the floor, sweating and pale.

The light comes back to normal.

"He'll be like that a few minutes," says Wagner, coming in the door with a jug of wine and three glasses. "He said malmsey's your favourite. Drink?"

We shook hands at the doorway early next morning.

"I was impressed," I said. "All that foofaraw just for me."

"If they're sending atheists, I had better get out of this country. No one will be safe."

"Goodbye," I said, putting the box in my pack. The door closed. I walked out past the hitching post. Tied to it with a leather-strap was a carpenter's sawhorse. Strapped about the middle of it, hanging under it, was a huge stoppered glass bottle filled with hay. *How droll of Wagner*, I thought.

I went to the river, put on my skates, and headed back out the Churn to the Thames-Isis, back to London, uneventfully, one hand behind me, the other counterweight, the pack swinging, my skates thin and sharp.

Skizz skizz skizz.

When I got back to my lodgings, there was a note for me in the locked room. I took the token of proof with me, and went by back ways and devious alleys to an address. There waiting was *another* high lord of the realm. He saw the box in my hand, nodded. He took the corner of my sleeve, pulled me to follow him. We went through several buildings, downward, through a long tunnel, turning, turning, and came to a roomful of guards beyond a door. Then we went upstairs, passing a few clerks and other stairwells that led down, from whence came screams. Too late to stop now.

"Someone wants to hear your report besides me," said the high lord. We waited outside a room from which came the sounds of high, indistinct conversation. The door opened; a man I recognised as the royal architect came out, holding a roll of drawings under his arm, his face reddened. "What a dump!" said a loud woman's voice from the room beyond.

"What a dump! What a dump!" came a high-pitched voice over hers.

I imagined a parrot of the red Amazonian kind.

"Shut up, you!" said the woman's voice.

"What a dump! What a dump!"

"Be sure to make a leg, man," said the high lord behind me, and urged me into the room.

There she was, Gloriana herself. From the waist down it looked as if she'd been swallowed by some huge spangled velvet clam while stealing from it the pearls that adorned her torso, arms, neck and hair.

"Your Majesty," I said, dropping to my knees.

The lord bowed behind me.

"What a dump!" said the other voice. I looked over. On a high sideboard, the royal dwarf, whose name I believed to be Monarcho, was dressed as a baby in a diaper and a bonnet, his legs dangling over the sides, four feet from the floor.

"Well?" asked the Queen. "(You look horrible without your face hair.) Well?"

I nodded toward the box under my arm.

"Oh, give that to someone else; I don't want to see those things." She turned her head away, then back, becoming the Queen again.

"Were we right?"

I looked her in the eyes, below her shaven brow and the painted-in browline, at the red wig, the pearls, the sparkling clamshell of a gown.

"His last words, Majesty," I said, "were of the Bishop of Rome, and of your late cousin."

"I knew it," she said. "I knew it!"

"I knew it!" yelled Monarcho.

The Queen threw a mirror at him. He jumped down with a thud and waddled off to torment the lapdog.

"You have been of great service," she said to me. "Reward him, my lord, but not overmuch. (Don't ever appear again in my presence without at least a moustache.)"

I made the knee again.

"Leave," she said to me. "You. Stay," she said to the lord. I backed out. The door swung. "Builders!" she was yelling. "What a dump!"

"What a dum—" said Monarcho, and the door closed with a thud.

So now it is another wet summer, in May, and I am lodging in Deptford, awaiting the pleasure of the Privy Council to question me.

At first I was sure it dealt with the business of this winter last, as rumour had come back to me that Faustus had been seen alive in France. If *I* had heard, other keener ears had heard a week before.

But no! The reason they sent the bailiff for me, while I was staying at Walsingham's place in Kent, was because of that noddy-costard Kyd.

For he and his friends had published a scurrilous pamphlet a month ago. Warrants had been sworn; searches made, and in Kyd's place they found some of my writings done, while we were both usually drunk, when we roomed together three years ago cobbling together old plays. I had, in some of them, been forthright and indiscreet. Kyd even more so.

So they took him downstairs, and just showed him the tongue-tongs, and he began to peach on his 104-years-old great naunt.

Of course, he'd said *all* the writings were mine.

And now I'm having to stay in Deptford (since I can get away to Kent if ever they are through with me) and await, every morning, and the last ten mornings, the vagaries of the Privy Council. And somewhat late of each May evening, a bailiff comes out, says, "You still here?" and "They're gone; be back here in the morning."

But not *this* morning. I come in at seven o' the clock, and the bailiff says, "They specifically and especially said they'd not get to you today, be back tomorrow." I thanked him.

I walked out. A day (and a night) of freedom awaited me.

And who do I spy coming at me but my companions in the adventure of the iceboat, Nick Skeres and Ingram Frizier, along with another real piece of work I know of from the theatres (people often reach for their purses and shake hands with him) named Robert Poley.

"What ho, Chris!" he says. "How's the playhouse dodge?"

"As right as rain till the Plague comes back," I say.

I watch, but neither Skeres nor Frizier seem to recognise me; I am dressed as a gentleman again; my beard and moustache new-waxed, my hat a perfect comet of colour and dash.

"Well, we're heading for Mrs Bull's place," says Poley. "She owes us each a drink from the cards last night; it is our good fortune, and business has been good," he says, holding up parts of three wallets. "How's about we stands you a few?"

"Thanks be," I say, "but I am at liberty for the first time in days, and needs be back hot on a poem, now that Shaxber's *Venus and Adonis* is printed."

"Well, then," says Poley, "one quick drink to fire the Muse?"

And then I see that Skeres is winking at me, but not one of the winks I know. Perhaps his eye is watering. Perhaps he is crying for the Frenchmen who we hear are once again eating each other up like cannibals. Perhaps not.

Oh well, I think, what can a few drinks with a bunch of convivial invert dizzards such as myself harm me? I have been threatened with the Privy Council; I walk away untouched and unfettered.

"Right!" I say, and we head off toward Deptford and Mrs Bull's, though I keep a tight hold on my purse. "A drink could be just what the doctors ordered."

The wisdom of old Earth
MichaEL SWANWiCK

Michael Swanwick made his debut in 1980 and has gone on to become one of the most popular and respected of all that decade's new writers. He has several times been a finalist for the Nebula Award, as well as for the World Fantasy Award and for the John W. Campbell Award, and has won the Theodore Sturgeon Award and the Asimov's Readers Award poll. In 1991, his novel Stations of the Tide *won him a Nebula Award as well, and in 1995 he won the World Fantasy Award for his story "Radio Waves." His other books include his first novel,* In the Drift, *which was published in 1985, a novella-length book,* Griffin's Egg, *1987's popular novel,* Vacuum Flowers, *and a critically acclaimed fantasy novel,* The Iron Dragon's Daughter, *which was a finalist for the World Fantasy Award and the Arthur C. Clarke Award. His short fiction has been assembled in* Gravity's Angels *and in a collection of his collaborative short work with other writers,* Slow Dancing Through Time. *His most recent books are a new novel,* Jack Faust, *a collection of critical essays titled* The Postmodern Archipelago, *and a new story collection,* A Geography of Unknown Lands. *He's had stories in our Second, Third, Fourth, Sixth, Seventh, Tenth, Thirteenth, and Fourteenth Annual Collections. Swanwick lives in Philadelphia with his wife, Marianne Porter, and their son, Sean, who, much to their annoyance, is now taller than either of them.*

Here he takes us to a bizarre and vividly realized far future to learn an ancient lesson: if you want wisdom, you must be prepared to pay for it. . . .

Judith Seize-the-Day was, quite simply, the best of her kind. Many another had aspired to the clarity of posthuman thought, and several might claim some rude mastery of its essentials, but she alone came to understand it as completely as any offworlder.

Such understanding did not come easily. The human mind is slow to generalize and even slower to integrate. It lacks the quicksilver apprehension of the posthuman. The simplest truth must be repeated often to imprint even the most primitive understanding of what comes naturally and without effort to the space-faring children of humanity. Judith had grown up in Pole Star City, where the shuttles slant down through the zone of permanent depletion in order to avoid further damage to the fragile ozone layer, and thus from childhood had associated extensively with the highly evolved. It was only natural that as a woman she would elect to turn her back on her own brutish kind and strive to bootstrap herself into a higher order.

Yet even then she was like an ape trying to pass as a philosopher. For all her laborious ponderings, she did not yet comprehend the core wisdom of posthumanity, which was that thought and action must be as one. Being a human, however, when she did comprehend, she understood it more deeply and thoroughly than the posthumans themselves. As a Canadian she could tap into the ancient and chthonic wisdoms of her race. Where her thought went, the civilized mind could not follow.

It would be expecting too much of such a woman that she would entirely hide her contempt for her own kind. She cursed the two trollish Ninglanders who were sweating and chopping a way through the lush tangles of kudzu, and drove them onward with the lash of her tongue.

"Unevolved bastard pigs!" she spat. "Inbred degenerates! If you ever want to get home to molest your dogs and baby sisters again, you'll put your backs into it!"

The larger of the creatures looked back at her with an angry gleam in his eye, and his knuckles whitened on the hilt of his machete. She only grinned humorlessly, and patted the holster of her *ankh*. Such weapons were rarely allowed humans. Her possession of it was a mark of the great respect in which she was held.

The brute returned to his labor.

It was deepest winter, and the jungle tracts of what had once been the mid-Atlantic coastlands were traversable. Traversable, that is, if one had a good guide. Judith was among the best. She had brought her party alive to the Flying Hills of southern Pennsylvania, and not many could have done that. Her client had come in search of the fabled bell of liberty, which many another party had sought in vain. She did not believe he would find it either. But that did not concern her.

All that concerned her was their survival.

So she cursed and drove the savage Ninglanders before her, until all at once they broke through the vines and brush out of shadow and into a clearing.

All three stood unmoving for an instant, staring out over the clumps and hillocks of grass that covered the foundations of what had once been factories, perhaps, or workers' housing, gasoline distribution stations, grist mills, shopping malls. . . . Even the skyline was uneven. Mystery beckoned from every ambiguous lump.

It was almost noon. They had been walking since sundown.

Judith slipped on her goggles and scanned the grey skies for navigation satellites. She found three radar beacons within range. A utility accepted their input and calculated her position: less than a hundred miles from Philadelphia. They'd made more distance than she'd expected. The empathic function mapped for her the locations of her party: three, including herself, then one, then two, then one, strung over a mile and a half of trail. That was wrong.

Very wrong indeed.

"Pop the tents," she ordered, letting the goggles fall around her neck. "Stay out of the food."

The Ninglanders dropped their packs. One lifted a refrigeration stick over his head like a spear and slammed it into the ground. A wash of cool air swept over them all. His lips curled with pleasure, revealing broken yellow teeth.

She knew that if she lingered, she would not be able to face the oppressive jungle heat again. So, turning, Judith strode back the way she'd come. Rats scattered at her approach, disappearing into hot green shadow.

The first of her party she encountered was Harry Work-to-Death. His face was pale and he shivered uncontrollably. But he kept walking, because to stop was to die. They passed each other without a word. Judith doubted he would live out the trip. He had picked up something after their disastrous spill in the Hudson. There were opiates enough in what survived of the medical kit to put him out of his misery, but she did not make him the offer.

She could not bring herself to.

Half a mile later came Leeza Child-of-Scorn and Maria Triumph-of-the-Will, chattering and laughing together. They stopped when they saw her. Judith raised her *ankh* in the air, and shook it so that they could feel its aura scrape ever so lightly against their nervous systems.

"Where is the offworlder?" The women shrank from her anger. "You abandoned him. You *dared*. Did you think you could get away with it? You were fools if you did!"

Wheedlingly, Leeza said, "The sky man knew he was endangering the rest of us, so he asked to be left behind." She and Maria were full-blooded Canadians, like Judith, free of the taint of Southern genes. They had been hired for their intelligence, and intelligence they had—a low sort of animal cunning that made them dangerously unreliable when the going got hard. "He insisted."

"It was very noble of him," Maria said piously.

"I'll give you something to be noble about if you don't turn around and lead me back to where you left him." She holstered her *ankh*, but did not lock it down. "Now!" With blows of her fists, she forced them down the trail. Judith was short, stocky, all muscle. She drove them before her like the curs that they were.

The offworlder lay in the weeds where he had been dropped, one leg twisted at an odd angle. The litter that Judith had lashed together for him had been flung into the bushes.

His clothes were bedraggled, and the netting had pulled away from his collar. But weak as he was, he smiled to see her. "I knew you would return for me." His hands fluttered up in a gesture indicating absolute confidence. "So I was careful to avoid moving. The fracture will have to be reset. But that's well within your capabilities, I'm sure."

"I haven't lost a client yet." Judith unlaced his splint and carefully straightened the leg. Posthumans, spending so much of their time in microgravity environments, were significantly less robust than their ancestral stock. Their bones broke easily. Yet when she reset the femur and tied up the splint again with lengths of nylon cord, he didn't make a sound. His kind had conscious control over their endorphin production. Judith checked his neck for ticks and chiggers, then tucked in his netting. "Be more careful with this. There are a lot of ugly diseases loose out here."

"My immune system is stronger than you'd suspect. If the rest of me were as strong, I wouldn't be holding you back like this."

As a rule, she liked the posthuman women better than their men. The men were hothouse flowers—flighty, elliptical, full of fancies and elaboration. Their beauty was the beauty of a statue; all sculptured features and chill affect. The offworlder, however, was not like that. His look was direct. He was as solid and straightforward as a woman.

"While I was lying here, I almost prayed for a rescue party."

To God, she thought he meant. Then saw how his eyes lifted briefly, involuntarily, to the clouds and the satellites beyond. Much that for humans required machines, a posthuman could accomplish with precisely tailored neural implants.

"They would've turned you down." This Judith knew for a fact. Her mother, Ellen To-the-Manner-Born, had died in the jungles of Wisconsin, eaten away with gangrene and cursing the wardens over an open circuit.

"Yes, of course, one life is nothing compared to the health of the planet." His mouth twisted wryly. "Yet still, I confess I was tempted."

"Put him back in the litter," she told the women. "Carry him gently." In the Québecois dialect, which she was certain her client did not know, she added, "Do this again, and I'll kill you."

She lagged behind, letting the others advance out of sight, so she could think. In theory she could simply keep the party together. In practice, the women could not both carry the offworlder and keep up with the men. And if she did not stay with the Ninglanders, they would not work. There were only so many days of winter left. Speed was essential.

An unexpected peal of laughter floated back to her, then silence.

Wearily, she trudged on. Already they had forgotten her, and her *ankh*. Almost she could envy them. Her responsibilities weighed heavily upon her. She had not laughed since the Hudson.

According to her goggles, there was a supply cache in Philadelphia. Once there, they could go back on full rations again.

The tents were bright mushrooms in the clearing. Work-to-Death lay dying within one of them. The women had gone off with the men into the bush. Even in this ungodly heat and humidity, they were unable or unwilling to curb their bestial lusts.

Judith sat outside with the offworlder, the refrigeration stick turned up just enough to take the edge off the afternoon heat. To get him talking, she asked, "Why did you come to Earth? There is nothing here worth all your suffering. Were I you, I'd've turned back long ago."

For a long moment, the offworlder struggled to gear down his complex thoughts into terms Judith could comprehend. At last he said, "Consider evolution. Things do not evolve from lower states to higher, as the ancients believed, with their charts that began with a fish crawling up upon the land and progressed on to mammals, apes, Neanderthals, and finally men. Rather, an organism evolves to fit its environment. An ape cannot live in the ocean. A human cannot brachiate. Each thrives in its own niche.

"Now consider posthumanity. Our environment is entirely artificial—floating cities, the Martian subsurface, the Venusian and Jovian bubbles. Such habitats require social integration of a high order. A human could survive within them, possibly, but she would not thrive. Our surround is self-defined, and therefore within it we are the pinnacle of evolution."

As he spoke, his hands twitched with the suppressed urge to amplify and clarify his words with the secondary emotive language offworlders employed in parallel with the spoken. Thinking, of course, that she did not savvy handsign. But as her facility with it was minimal, Judith did not enlighten him.

"Now imagine a being with more-than-human strength and greater-than-posthuman intellect. Such a creature would be at a disadvantage in the posthuman environment. She would be an evolutionary dead end. How then could she get any sense of herself, what she could do, and what she could not?"

"How does all apply to you personally?"

"I wanted to find the measure of myself, not as a product of an environment that caters to my strengths and coddles my weaknesses. I wanted to discover what I am in the natural state."

"You won't find the natural state here. We're living in the aftermath."

"No," he agreed. "The natural state is lost, shattered like an eggshell. Even if—when—we finally manage to restore it, gather up all the shards and glue them together, it will no longer be natural, but something we have decided to maintain and preserve, like a garden. It will be only an extension of our culture."

"Nature is dead," Judith said. It was a concept she had picked up from other posthumans.

His teeth flashed with pleasure at her quick apprehension. "Indeed. Even off Earth, where conditions are more extreme, its effects are muted by technology. I suspect that nature can only exist where our all-devouring culture has not yet reached. Still . . . here on Earth, in the regions where all but the simplest technologies are prohibited, and it's still possible to suffer pain and even death. . . . This is as close to an authentic state as can be achieved." He patted the ground by his side. "The past is palpable here, century upon century, and under that the strength of the soil." His hands involuntarily leapt. *This is so difficult,* they said. *This language is so clumsy.* "I am afraid I have not expressed myself very well."

He smiled apologetically then, and she saw how exhausted he was. But still she could not resist asking, "What is it like, to think as you do?" It was a question that she had asked many times, of many posthumans. Many answers had she received, and no two of them alike.

The offworlder's face grew very still. At last he said, "Lao-tzu put it best. 'The way that can be named is not the true way. The name that can be spoken is not the eternal name.' The higher thought is ineffable, a mystery that can be experienced but never explained."

His arms and shoulders moved in a gesture that was the evolved descendant of a shrug. His weariness was palpable.

"You need rest," she said, and, standing, "let me help you into your tent."

"Dearest Judith. What would I ever do without you?"

Ever so slightly, she flushed.

The next sundown, their maps, though recently downloaded, proved to be in-complete. The improbably named Skookle River had wandered, throwing off swamps that her goggles' topographical functions could not distinguish from solid land. For two nights the party struggled southward, moving far to the west and then back again so many times that Judith would have been entirely lost without the navsats.

Then the rains began.

There was no choice but to leave the offworlder behind. Neither he nor Harry Work-to-Death could travel under such conditions. Judith put Maria and Leeza in charge of them both. After a few choice words of warning, she left them her spare goggles and instructions to break camp and follow as soon as the rains let up.

"Why do you treat us like dogs?" a Ninglander asked her when they were under way again. The rain poured down over his plastic poncho.

"Because you are no better than dogs."

He puffed himself up. "I am large and shapely. I have a fine mustache. I can give you many orgasms."

His comrade was pretending not to listen. But it was obvious to Judith that the two men had a bet going as to whether she could be seduced or not.

"Not without my participation."

Insulted, he thumped his chest. Water droplets flew. "I am as good as any of your Canadian men!"

"Yes," she agreed, "unhappily, that's true."

When the rains finally let up, Judith had just crested a small hillock that her topographics identified as an outlier of the Welsh Mountains. Spread out before her was a broad expanse of overgrown twenty-first-century ruins. She did not bother accessing the city's name. In her experience, all lost cities were alike; she didn't care if she never saw another. "Take ten," she said, and the Ninglanders shrugged out of their packs.

Idly, she donned her goggles to make sure that Leeza and Maria were breaking camp, as they had been instructed to do.

And screamed with rage.

The goggles Judith had left behind had been hung, unused, upon the flap-pole of one of the tents. Though the two women did not know it, it was slaved to hers, and she could spy upon their actions. She kept her goggles on all the way back to their camp.

When she arrived, they were sitting by their refrigeration stick, surrounded by the discarded wrappings of half the party's food and all of its opiates. The stick was turned up so high that the grass about it was white with frost. Already there was an inch of ash at its tip.

Harry Work-to-Death lay on the ground by the women, grinning loopily, face frozen to the stick. Dead.

Outside the circle, only partially visible to the goggles, lay the offworlder, still strapped to his litter. He chuckled and sang to himself. The women had been generous with the drugs.

"Pathetic weakling," Child-of-Scorn said to the offworlder, "I don't know why you didn't drown in the rain. But I am going to leave you out in the heat until you are dead, and then I am going to piss on your corpse."

"I am not going to wait," Triumph-of-the-Will bragged. She tried to stand and could not. "In just—just a moment!"

The whoops of laughter died as Judith strode into the camp. The Ninglanders stumbled to a halt behind her, and stood looking uncertainly from her to the women and back. In their simple way, they were shocked by what they saw.

Judith went to the offworlder and slapped him hard to get his attention. He gazed up confusedly at the patch she held up before his face.

"This is a detoxifier. It's going to remove those drugs from your system. Unfortunately, as a side effect, it will also depress your endorphin production. I'm afraid this is going to hurt."

She locked it onto his arm, and then said to the Ninglanders, "Take him up the trail. I'll be along."

They obeyed. The offworlder screamed once as the detoxifier took effect, and then fell silent again. Judith turned to the traitors. "You chose to disobey me. Very well. I can use the extra food."

She drew her *ankh*.

Child-of-Scorn clenched her fists angrily. "So could we! Half-rations so your little pet could eat his fill. Work us to death carrying him about. You think I'm *stupid*. I'm not stupid. I know what you want with him."

"He's the client. He pays the bills."

"What are you to him but an ugly little ape? He'd sooner fuck a cow than you!"

Triumph-of-the-Will fell over laughing. "A cow!" she cried. "A fuh-fucking cow! Moo!"

Child-of-Scorn's eyes blazed. "You know what the sky people call the likes of you and me? Mud-women! Sometimes they come to the cribs outside Pole Star City to get good and dirty. But they always wash off and go back to their nice clean habitats afterward. Five minutes after he climbs back into the sky, he'll have forgotten your name."

"Moooo! Moooo!"

"You cannot make me angry," Judith said, "for you are only animals."

"I am not an animal!" Child-of-Scorn shook her fist at Judith. "I refuse to be treated like one."

"One does not blame an animal for being what it is. But neither does one trust an animal that has proved unreliable. You were given two chances."

"If I'm an animal, then what does that make *you?* Huh? What the fuck does that make *you*, goddamnit?" The woman's face was red with rage. Her friend stared blankly up at her from the ground.

"Animals," Judith said through gritted teeth, "should be killed without emotion."

She fired twice.

With her party thus diminished, Judith could not hope to return to Canada afoot. But there were abundant ruins nearby, and they were a virtual reservoir of chemical poisons from the days when humans ruled the Earth. If she set the *ankh* to its hottest setting, she could start a blaze that would set off a hundred alarms in Pole Star City. The wardens would have to come to contain it. She would be imprisoned, of course, but her client would live.

Then Judith heard the thunder of engines.

High in the sky, a great light appeared, so bright it was haloed with black. She held up a hand to lessen the intensity and saw within the dazzle a small dark speck. A shuttle, falling from orbit.

She ran crashing through the brush as hard and fast as she could. Nightmarish minutes later, she topped a small rise and found the Ninglanders standing there, the offworlder between them. They were watching the shuttle come to a soft landing in the clearing its thrusters had burned in the vegetation.

"You summoned it," she accused the offworlder.

He looked up with tears in his eyes. The detoxifier had left him in a state of pitiless lucidity, with nothing to concentrate on but his own suffering. "I had to, yes." His voice was distant, his attention turned inward, on the neural device that allowed him to communicate with the ship's crew. "The pain—you can't imagine what it's like. How it feels."

A lifetime of lies roared in Judith's ears. Her mother had died for lack of the aid that came at this man's thought.

"I killed two women just now."

"Did you?" He looked away. "I'm sure you had good reasons. I'll have it listed as death by accident." Without his conscious volition, his hands moved, saying, *It's a trivial matter, let it be.*

A hatch opened in the shuttle's side. Slim figures clambered down, white medkits on their belts. The offworlder smiled through his tears and stretched out welcoming arms to them.

Judith stepped back and into the shadow of his disregard. She was just another native now.

Two women were dead.

And her reasons for killing them mattered to no one.

She threw her head back and laughed, freely and without reserve. In that instant Judith Seize-the-Day was as fully and completely alive as any of the unworldly folk who walk the airless planets and work in the prosperous and incomprehensible habitats of deep space.

In that instant, had any been looking, she would have seemed not human at all.

The pipes of pan

BRIAN STABLEFORD

As the disturbing story that follows suggests, sooner or later, children grow up. Whether you try to stop them or not. . . .

Critically acclaimed British "hard science" writer Brian Stableford is the author of more than thirty books, including Cradle of the Sun, The Blind Worm, Days of Glory, In the Kingdom of the Beasts, Day of Wrath, The Halcyon Drift, The Paradox of the Sets, The Realms of Tartarus, *and the renowned trilogy consisting of* The Empire of Fear, The Angel of Pain, *and* The Carnival of Destruction. *His short fiction has been collected in* Sexual Chemistry: Sardonic Tales of the Genetic Revolution. *His nonfiction books include* The Sociology of Science Fiction *and, with David Langford,* The Third Millennium: A History of the World A.D. 2000–3000. *His most recent novel is* Serpent's Blood *and upcoming is* Inherit the Earth. *His acclaimed novella "Les Fleurs Du Mal" was a finalist for the Hugo Award in 1994. His stories have appeared in our Sixth (two separate stories), Seventh, Twelfth, and Thirteenth Annual Collections. A biologist and sociologist by training, Stableford lives in Reading, England.*

▼

In her dream Wendy was a pretty little girl living wild in a magical wood where it never rained and never got cold. She lived on sweet berries of many colors, which always tasted wonderful, and all she wanted or needed was to be happy.

There were other girls living wild in the dream-wood but they all avoided one another, because they had no need of company. They had lived there, untroubled, for a long time—far longer than Wendy could remember.

Then, in the dream, the others came: the shadow-men with horns on their brows and shaggy legs. They played strange music on sets of pipes which looked as if they had been made from reeds—but Wendy knew, without knowing how she knew or what sense there was in it, that those pipes had been fashioned out of the blood and bones of something just like her, and that the music they played was the breath of her soul.

After the shadow-men came, the dream became steadily more nightmarish, and living wild ceased to be innocently joyful. After the shadow-men came, life was all hiding with a fearful, fluttering heart, knowing that if ever she were found she would have to run and run and run, without any hope of escape—but wherever she hid, she could always hear the music of the pipes.

When she woke up in a cold sweat, she wondered whether the dreams her parents had were as terrible, or as easy to understand. Somehow, she doubted it.

There was a sharp rat-a-tat on her bedroom door.

"Time to get up, Beauty." Mother didn't bother coming in to check that Wendy responded. Wendy always responded. She was a good girl.

She climbed out of bed, took off her night-dress, and went to sit at the dressing-table, to look at herself in the mirror. It had become part of her morning ritual, now that her awakenings were indeed awakenings. She blinked to clear the sleep from her eyes, shivering slightly as an image left over from the dream flashed briefly and threateningly in the depths of her emergent consciousness.

Wendy didn't know how long she had been dreaming. The dreams had begun before she developed the sense of time which would have allowed her to make the calculation. Perhaps she had always dreamed, just as she had always got up in the morning in response to the summoning rat-a-tat, but she had only recently come by the ability to remember her dreams. On the other hand, perhaps the beginning of her dreams had been the end of her innocence.

She often wondered how she had managed not to give herself away in the first few months, after she first began to remember her dreams but before she attained her present level of waking self-control, but any anomalies in her behavior must have been written off to the randomizing factor. Her parents were always telling her how lucky she was to be thirteen, and now she was in a position to agree with them. At thirteen, it was entirely appropriate to be a little bit inquisitive and more than a little bit odd. It was even possible to get away with being too clever by half, as long as she didn't overdo it.

It was difficult to be sure, because she didn't dare interrogate the house's systems too explicitly, but she had figured out that she must have been thirteen for about thirty years, in mind and body alike. She was thirteen in her blood and her bones, but not in the privacy of her head.

Inside, where it counted, she had now been unthirteen for at least four months.

If it would only stay inside, she thought, *I might keep it a secret forever. But it won't. It isn't. It's coming out. Every day that passes is one day closer to the moment of truth.*

She stared into the mirror, searching the lines of her face for signs of maturity. She was sure that her face looked thinner, her eyes more serious, her hair less blonde. All of that might be mostly imagination, she knew, but there was no doubt about the other things. She was half an inch taller, and her breasts were getting larger. It was only a matter of time before that sort of thing attracted attention, and as soon as it was noticed the truth would be manifest. Measurements couldn't lie. As soon as they were moved to measure her, her parents would know the horrid truth.

Their baby was growing up.

"Did you sleep well, dear?" Mother said, as Wendy took her seat at the breakfast-table. It wasn't a trick question; it was just part of the routine. It wasn't even a matter of pretending, although her parents certainly did their fair share of that. It was just a way of starting the day off. Such rituals were part and parcel of what they thought of as *everyday life*. Parents had their innate programming too.

"Yes thank you," she replied, meekly.

"What flavor manna would you like today?"

"Coconut and strawberry please." Wendy smiled as she spoke, and Mother smiled back. Mother was smiling because Wendy was smiling. Wendy was supposed to be smiling because she was a smiley child, but in fact she was smiling because saying "strawberry and coconut" was an authentic and honest *choice*, an exercise of freedom which would pass as an expected manifestation of the randomizing factor.

"I'm afraid I can't take you out this morning, Lovely," Father said, while Mother punched out the order. "We have to wait in for the house-doctor. The waterworks still aren't right."

"If you ask me," Mother said, "the real problem's the water table. The taproots are doing their best but they're having to go down too far. The system's fine just so long as we get some good old-fashioned rain once in a while, but every time there's a dry spell the whole estate suffers. We ought to call a meeting and put some pressure on the landscape engineers. Fixing a water table shouldn't be too much trouble in this day and age."

"There's nothing wrong with the water table, dear," Father said, patiently. "It's just that the neighbors have the same indwelling systems that we have. There's a congenital weakness in the root-system; in dry weather the cell-terminal conduits in the phloem tend to get gummed up. It ought to be easy enough to fix—a little elementary somatic engineering, probably no more than a single-gene augment in the phloem—but you know what doctors are like; they never want to go for the cheap and cheerful cure if they can sell you something more complicated."

"What's phloem?" Wendy asked. She could ask as many questions as she liked, to a moderately high level of sophistication. That was a great blessing. She was glad she wasn't an eight-year-old, reliant on passive observation and a re-stricted vocabulary. At least a thirteen-year-old had the right equipment for thinking all set up.

"It's a kind of plant tissue," Father informed her, ignoring the tight-lipped look Mother was giving him because he'd contradicted her. "It's sort of equiv-alent to your veins, except of course that plants have sap instead of blood."

Wendy nodded, but contrived to look as if she hadn't really understood the answer.

"I'll set the encyclopedia up on the system," Father said. "You can read all about it while I'm talking to the house-doctor."

"She doesn't want to spend the morning reading what the encyclopedia has to say about phloem," Mother said, peevishly. "She needs to get out into the fresh air." That wasn't mere ritual, like asking whether she had slept well, but it wasn't pretense either. When Mother started talking about Wendy's supposed wants and needs she was usually talking about her own wants and supposed needs. Wendy had come to realize that talking that way was Mother's preferred method of criticizing Father; she was paying him back for disagreeing about the water table.

Wendy was fully conscious of the irony of the fact that she really did want to study the encyclopedia. There was so much to learn and so little time. Maybe she didn't *need* to do it, given that it was unlikely to make any difference in the long run, but she wanted to understand as much as she could before all the pretense had to end and the nightmare of uncertainty had to begin.

"It's okay, Mummy," she said. "Honest." She smiled at them both, attempting to bring off the delicate trick of pleasing Father by taking his side while simultaneously pleasing Mother by pretending to be as heroically long-suffering as Mother liked to consider herself.

They both smiled back. All was well, for now. Even though they listened to the news every night, they didn't seem to have the least suspicion that it could all be happening in their own home, to their own daughter.

It only took a few minutes for Wendy to work out a plausible path of icon selection which got her away from translocation in plants and deep into the heart of child physiology. Father had set that up for her by comparing phloem to her own circulatory system. There was a certain danger in getting into recent reportage regarding childhood diseases, but she figured that she could explain it well enough if anyone took the trouble to consult the log to see what she'd been doing. She didn't think anyone was likely to, but she simply couldn't help being anxious about the possibility—there were, it seemed, a lot of things one simply couldn't help being anxious about, once it was possible to be anxious at all.

"I wondered if I could get sick like the house's roots," she would say, if asked. "I wanted to know whether my blood could get clogged up in dry weather." She figured that she would be okay as long as she pretended not to have understood what she'd read, and conscientiously avoided any mention of the word *progeria*. She already knew that progeria was what she'd got, and the last thing she wanted was to be taken to a child-engineer who'd be able to confirm the fact.

She called up a lot of innocuous stuff about blood, and spent the bulk of her time pretending to study elementary material of no real significance. Every time she got hold of a document she really wanted to look at she was careful to move on quickly, so it would seem as if she hadn't even bothered to look at it if anyone did consult the log to see what she'd been doing. She didn't dare call up any extensive current affairs information on the progress of the plague or the fierce medical and political arguments concerning the treatment of its victims.

It must be wonderful to be a parent, she thought, *and not have to worry about being found out—or about anything at all, really.*

At first, Wendy had thought that Mother and Father really did have worries, because they talked as if they did, but in the last few weeks she had begun to see through the sham. In a way, they *thought* that they did have worries, but it was all just a matter of habit, a kind of innate restlessness left over from the olden days. Adults must have had authentic anxieties at one time, back in the days when everybody could expect to die young and a lot of people never even reached seventy, and she presumed that they hadn't quite got used to the fact that they'd changed the world and changed themselves. They just hadn't managed to lose the habit. They probably would, in the fullness of time. Would they still need children then, she wondered, or would they learn to do without? Were children just another habit, another manifestation of innate restlessness? Had the great plague come just in time to seal off the redundant umbilical cord which connected mankind to its evolutionary past?

We're just betwixts and betweens, Wendy thought, as she rapidly scanned a second-hand summary of a paper in the latest issue of *Nature* which dealt with the pathology of progeria. *There'll soon be no place for us, whether we grow older or not. They'll get rid of us all.*

The article which contained the summary claimed that the development of an immunoserum was just a matter of time, although it wasn't yet clear whether anything much might be done to reverse the aging process in children who'd already come down with it. She didn't dare access the paper itself, or even an abstract—that would have been a dead giveaway, like leaving a bloody thumbprint at the scene of a murder.

Wendy wished that she had a clearer idea of whether the latest news was good or bad, or whether the long-term prospects had any possible relevance to her now that she had started to show physical symptoms as well as mental ones. She didn't know what would happen to her once Mother and Father found out and notified the authorities; there was no clear pattern in the stories she glimpsed in the general news-broadcasts, but whether this meant that there was as yet no coherent social policy for dealing with the rapidly escalating problem she wasn't sure.

For the thousandth time she wondered whether she ought simply to tell her parents what was happening, and for the thousandth time, she felt the terror growing within her at the thought that everything she had might be placed in jeopardy, that she might be sent back to the factory or handed over to the researchers or simply cut adrift to look after herself. There was no way of knowing, after all, what really lay behind the rituals which her parents used in dealing with her, no way of knowing what would happen when their thirteen-year-old daughter was no longer thirteen.

Not yet, her fear said. *Not yet. Hang on. Lie low . . . because once you can't hide, you'll have to run and run and run and there'll be nowhere to go. Nowhere at all.*

She left the workstation and went to watch the house-doctor messing about in the cellar. Father didn't seem very glad to see her, perhaps because he was trying to talk the house-doctor round to his way of thinking and didn't like the way the house-doctor immediately started talking to her instead of him, so she went away again, and played with her toys for a while. She still enjoyed playing with her toys—which was perhaps as well, all things considered.

"We can go out for a while now," Father said, when the house-doctor had finally gone. "Would you like to play ball on the back lawn?"

"Yes please," she said.

Father liked playing ball, and Wendy didn't mind. It was better than the sedentary pursuits which Mother preferred. Father had more energy to spare than Mother, probably because Mother had a job that was more taxing physically. Father only played with software; his clever fingers did all his work. Mother actually had to get her hands inside her remote-gloves and her feet inside her big red boots and get things moving. "Being a ghost in a machine," she would often complain, when she thought Wendy couldn't hear, "can be bloody hard work." She never swore in front of Wendy, of course.

Out on the back lawn, Wendy and Father threw the ball back and forth for half an hour, making the catches more difficult as time went by, so that they could leap about and dive on the bone-dry carpet-grass and get thoroughly dusty.

To begin with, Wendy was distracted by the ceaseless stream of her insistent thoughts, but as she got more involved in the game she was able to let herself go a little. She couldn't quite get back to being thirteen, but she could get to a state of mind which wasn't quite so fearful. By the time her heart was pounding and she'd grazed both her knees and one of her elbows she was enjoying herself thoroughly, all the more so because Father was evidently having a good time. He was in a good mood anyhow, because the house-doctor had obligingly confirmed everything he'd said about the normality of the water-table, and had then backed down gracefully when he saw that he couldn't persuade Father that the house needed a whole new root-system.

"Those somatic transformations don't always take," the house-doctor had said, darkly but half-heartedly, as he left. "You might have trouble again, three months down the line."

"I'll take the chance," Father had replied, breezily. "Thanks for your time."

Given that the doctor was charging for his time, Wendy had thought, it should have been the doctor thanking Father, but she hadn't said anything. She already understood that kind of thing well enough not to have to ask questions about it. She had other matters she wanted to raise once Father collapsed on the baked earth, felled by healthy exhaustion, and demanded that they take a rest.

"I'm not as young as you are," he told her, jokingly. "When you get past a hundred and fifty you just can't take it the way you used to." He had no idea how it affected her to hear him say *you* in that careless fashion, when he really meant *we*: a *we* which didn't include her and never would.

"I'm bleeding," she said, pointing to a slight scratch on her elbow.

"Oh dear," he said. "Does it hurt?"

"Not much," she said, truthfully. "If too much leaks out, will I need injections, like the house's roots?"

"It won't come to that," he assured her, lifting up her arm so that he could put on a show of inspecting the wound. "It's just a drop. I'll kiss it better." He put his lips to the wound for a few seconds, then said: "It'll be as good as new in the morning."

"Good," she said. "I expect it'd be very expensive to have to get a whole new girl."

He looked at her a little strangely, but it seemed to Wendy that he was in such a light mood that he was in no danger of taking it too seriously.

"Fearfully expensive," he agreed, cheerfully, as he lifted her up in his arms and carried her back to the house. "We'll just have to take very good care of you, won't we?"

"Or do a somatic whatever," she said, as innocently as she possibly could. "Is that what you'd have to do if you wanted a boy for a while?"

He laughed, and there appeared to be no more than the merest trace of unease in his laugh. "We love you just the way you are, Lovely," he assured her. "We wouldn't want you to be any other way."

She knew that it was true. That was the problem.

She had ham and cheese manna for lunch, with real greens homegrown in the warm cellar-annex under soft red lights. She would have eaten heartily had she not been so desperately anxious about her weight, but as things were she felt it better to peck and pretend, and she surreptitiously discarded the food she hadn't consumed as soon as Father's back was turned.

After lunch, judging it to be safe enough, she picked up the thread of the conversation again. "Why did you want a girl and not a boy?" she asked. "The Johnsons wanted a boy." The Johnsons had a ten-year-old named Peter. He was the only other child Wendy saw regularly, and he had not as yet exhibited the slightest sign of disease to her eager eye.

"We didn't want *a girl*," Father told her, tolerantly. "We wanted *you*."

"Why?" she asked, trying to look as if she were just fishing for compliments, but hoping to trigger something a trifle more revealing. This, after all, was *the* great mystery. Why her? Why anyone? Why did adults think they needed children?

"Because you're beautiful," Father said. "And because you're Wendy. Some people are Peter people, so they have Peters. Some people are Wendy people, so they have Wendys. Your Mummy and I are definitely Wendy people—probably the Wendiest people in the world. It's a matter of taste."

It was all baby-talk, all gobbledygook, but she felt that she had to keep trying. Some day, surely, one of them would let a little truth show through their empty explanations.

"But you have different kinds of manna for breakfast, lunch and dinner," Wendy said, "and sometimes you go right off one kind for weeks on end. Maybe some day you'll go off me, and want a different one."

"No we won't, darling," he answered, gently. "There are matters of taste and matters of taste. Manna is fuel for the body. Variety of taste just helps to make the routine of eating that little bit more interesting. Relationships are something else. It's a different kind of need. We love you, Beauty, more than anything else in the world. Nothing could ever replace you."

She thought about asking about what would happen if Father and Mother ever got divorced, but decided that it would be safer to leave the matter alone for now. Even though time was pressing, she had to be careful.

They watched TV for a while before Mother came home. Father had a particular fondness for archive film of extinct animals—not the ones which the engineers had re-created but smaller and odder ones: weirdly shaped sea-dwelling creatures. He could never have seen such creatures even if they had still existed when he was young, not even in an aquarium; they had only ever been known to people as things on film. Even so, the whole tone of the tapes which documented their one-time existence was nostalgic, and Father seemed genuinely affected by a sense of personal loss at the thought of the sterilization of the seas during the last ecocatastrophe but one.

"Isn't it beautiful?" he said, of an excessively tentacled sea anemone which sheltered three vivid clown-fish while ungainly shrimps passed by. "Isn't it just *extraordinary?*"

"Yes," she said, dutifully, trying to inject an appropriate reverence into her tone. "It's lovely." The music on the sound-track was plaintive; it was being played on some fluty wind-instrument, possibly by a human player. Wendy had never heard music like it except on TV sound-tracks; it was as if the sound were the breath of the long-lost world of nature, teeming with undesigned life.

"Next summer," Father said, "I want us to go out in one of those glass-bottomed boats that take sight-seers out to the new barrier reef. It's not the same as the original one, of course, and they're deliberately setting out to create something modern, something new, but they're stocking it with some truly weird and wonderful creatures."

"Mother wants to go up the Nile," Wendy said. "She wants to see the sphinx, and the tombs."

"We'll do that the year after," Father said. "They're just ruins. They can wait. Living things . . ." He stopped. "Look at those!" he said, pointing at the screen. She looked at a host of jellyfish swimming close to the silvery surface, their bodies pulsing like great translucent hearts.

It doesn't matter, Wendy thought. *I won't be there. I won't see the new barrier reef or the sphinx and the tombs. Even if they find a cure, and even if you both want me cured, I won't be there. Not the real me. The real me will have died, one way or another, and there'll be nothing left except a girl who'll be thirteen forever, and a randomizing factor which will make it seem that she has a lively mind.*

Father put his arm around her shoulder, and hugged her fondly.

Father must really love her very dearly, she thought. After all, he had loved her for thirty years, and might love her for thirty years more, if only she could stay the way she was . . . if only she could be returned to what she had been before. . . .

The evening TV schedules advertised a documentary on progeria, scheduled for late at night, long after the nation's children had been put to bed. Wendy wondered if her parents would watch it, and whether she could sneak downstairs to listen to the sound-track through the closed door. In a way, she hoped that they wouldn't watch it. It might put ideas into their heads. It was better that they thought of the plague as a distant problem: something that could only affect other people; something with which they didn't need to concern themselves.

She stayed awake, just in case, and when the luminous dial of her bedside clock told her it was time she silently got up, and crept down the stairs until she could hear what was going on in the living room. It was risky, because the randomizing factor wasn't really supposed to stretch to things like that, but she'd done it before without being found out.

It didn't take long to ascertain that the TV wasn't even on, and that the only sound to be heard was her parents' voices. She actually turned around to go back to bed before she suddenly realized what they were talking about.

"Are you *sure* she isn't affected mentally?" Mother was saying.

"Absolutely, certain," Father replied. "I watched her all afternoon, and she's perfectly normal."

"Perhaps she hasn't got it at all," Mother said, hopefully.

"Maybe not the worst kind," Father said, in a voice that was curiously firm. "They're not sure that even the worst cases are manifesting authentic self-consciousness, and there's a strong contingent which argues that the vast majority of cases are relatively minor dislocations of programming. But there's no doubt about the physical symptoms. I picked her up to carry her indoors and she's a stone heavier. She's got hair growing in her armpits and she's got tangible tits. We'll have to be careful how we dress her when we take her to public places."

"Can we do anything about her food—reduce the calorific value of her manna or something?"

"Sure—but that'd be hard evidence if anyone audited the house records. Not that anyone's likely to, now that the doctor's been and gone, but you never know. I read an article which cites a paper in the latest *Nature* to demonstrate that a cure is just around the corner. If we can just hang on until then . . . she's a big girl anyhow, and she might not put on more than an inch or two. As long as she doesn't start behaving oddly, we might be able to keep it secret."

"If they do find out," said Mother, ominously, "there'll be hell to pay."

"I don't think so," Father assured her. "I've heard that the authorities are quite sympathetic in private, although they have to put on a sterner face for publicity purposes."

"I'm not talking about the bloody bureaucrats," Mother retorted, "I'm talking about the estate. If the neighbors find out we're sheltering a center of infection . . . well, how would you feel if the Johnsons' Peter turned out to have the disease and hadn't warned us about the danger to Wendy?"

"They're not certain how it spreads," said Father, defensively, "They don't know what kind of vector's involved—until they find out there's no reason to think that Wendy's endangering Peter just by living next door. It's not as if they spend much time together. We can't lock her up—that'd be suspicious in itself. We have to pretend that things are absolutely normal, at least until we know how this thing is going to turn out. I'm not prepared to run the risk of their taking her away—not if there's the slightest chance of avoiding it. I don't care what they say on the newstapes—this thing is getting out of control and I really don't know how it's going to turn out. I'm not letting Wendy go anywhere, unless I'm absolutely forced. She may be getting heavier and hairier, but *inside* she's still Wendy, and *I'm not letting them take her away.*"

Wendy heard Father's voice getting louder as he came toward the door, and she scuttled back up the stairs as fast as she could go. Numb with shock, she climbed back into bed. Father's words echoed inside her head: "I watched her all afternoon, and she's perfectly normal . . . *inside* she's still Wendy. . . ."

They were putting on an act too, and she hadn't known. She hadn't been able to tell. She'd been watching them, and they'd seemed perfectly normal . . . but *inside*, where it counted . . .

It was a long time before she fell asleep, and when she finally did, she dreamed of shadow-men and shadow-music, which drew the very soul from her even as she fled through the infinite forest of green and gold.

The men from the Ministry of Health arrived next morning, while Wendy was finishing her honey and almond manna. She saw Father go pale as the man in the gray suit held up his identification card to the door camera. She watched Father's lip trembling as he thought about telling the man in the gray suit that he couldn't come in, and then realized that it wouldn't do any good. As Father got up to go to the door he exchanged a bitter glance with Mother, and murmured: "That bastard house-doctor."

Mother came to stand behind Wendy, and put both of her hands on Wendy's shoulders. "It's all right, darling," she said. Which meant, all too clearly, that things were badly wrong.

Father and the man in the gray suit were already arguing as they came through the door. There was another man behind them, dressed in less formal clothing. He was carrying a heavy black bag, like a rigid suitcase.

"I'm sorry," the man in the gray suit was saying. "I understand your feelings, but this is an epidemic—a national emergency. We have to check out all reports, and we have to move swiftly if we're to have any chance of containing the problem."

"If there'd been any cause for alarm," Father told him, hotly, "I'd have called you myself." But the man in the gray suit ignored him; from the moment he had entered the room his eyes had been fixed on Wendy. He was smiling. Even though Wendy had never seen him before and didn't know the first thing about him, she knew that the smile was dangerous.

"Hello, Wendy," said the man in the gray suit, smoothly. "My name's Tom Cartwright. I'm from the Ministry of Health. This is Jimmy Li. I'm afraid we have to carry out some tests."

Wendy stared back at him as blankly as she could. In a situation like this, she figured, it was best to play dumb, at least to begin with.

"You can't do this," Mother said, gripping Wendy's shoulders just a little too hard. "You can't take her away."

"We can complete our initial investigation here and now," Cartwright answered, blandly. "Jimmy can plug into your kitchen systems, and I can do my part right here at the table. It'll be over in less than half an hour, and if all's well we'll be gone in no time." The way he said it implied that he didn't really expect to be gone in no time.

Mother and Father blustered a little more, but it was only a gesture. They knew how futile it all was. While Mr. Li opened up his bag of tricks to reveal an awesome profusion of gadgets forged in metal and polished glass Father came to stand beside Wendy, and like Mother he reached out to touch her.

They both assured her that the needle Mr. Li was preparing wouldn't hurt when he put it into her arm, and when it did hurt—bringing tears to her eyes in spite of her efforts to blink them away—they told her the pain would go away in a minute. It didn't, of course. Then they told her not to worry about the questions Mr. Cartwright was going to ask her, although it was as plain as the noses on their faces that they were terrified by the possibility that she would give the wrong answers.

In the end, though, Wendy's parents had to step back a little, and let her face up to the man from the Ministry on her own.

I mustn't play too dumb, Wendy thought. *That would be just as much of a giveaway as being too clever. I have to try to make my mind blank, let the answers come straight out without thinking at all. It ought to be easy. After all, I've been thirteen for thirty years, and unthirteen for a matter of months . . . it should be easy.*

She knew that she was lying to herself. She knew well enough that she had crossed a boundary that couldn't be re-crossed just by stepping backward.

"How old are you, Wendy?" Cartwright asked, when Jimmy Li had vanished into the kitchen to play with her blood.

"Thirteen," she said, trying to return his practiced smile without too much evident anxiety.

"Do you know *what* you are, Wendy?"

"I'm a girl," she answered, knowing that it wouldn't wash.

"Do you know what the difference between children and adults is, Wendy? Apart from the fact that they're smaller."

There was no point in denying it. At thirteen, a certain amount of self-knowledge was included in the package, and even thirteen-year-olds who never looked at an encyclopedia learned quite a lot about the world and its ways in the course of thirty years.

"Yes," she said, knowing full well that she wasn't going to be allowed to get away with minimal replies.

"Tell me what you know about the difference," he said.

"It's not such a big difference," she said, warily. "Children are made out of the same things adults are made of—but they're made so they stop growing at a certain age, and never get any older. Thirteen is the oldest—some stop at eight."

"Why are children made that way, Wendy?" Step by inexorable step he was leading her toward the deep water, and she didn't know how to swim. She knew that she wasn't clever enough—yet—to conceal her cleverness.

"Population control," she said.

"Can you give me a more detailed explanation, Wendy?"

"In the olden days," she said, "there were catastrophes. Lots of people died, because there were so many of them. They discovered how not to grow old, so that they could live for hundreds of years if they didn't get killed in bad accidents. They had to stop having so many children, or they wouldn't be able to feed everyone when the children kept growing up, but they didn't want to have a world with no children in it. Lots of people still wanted children, and couldn't stop wanting them—and in the end, after more catastrophes, those people who really wanted children a lot were able to have them . . . only the children weren't allowed to grow up and have more children of their own. There were lots of arguments about it, but in the end things calmed down."

"There's another difference between children and adults, isn't there?" said Cartwright, smoothly.

"Yes," Wendy said, knowing that she was supposed to have that information in her memory and that she couldn't refuse to voice it. "Children can't think very much. They have *limited self-consciousness*." She tried hard to say it as though it were a mere formula, devoid of any real meaning so far as she was concerned.

"Do you know why children are made with limited self-consciousness?"

"No." She was sure that *no* was the right answer to that one, although she'd recently begun to make guesses. It was so they wouldn't know what was happening if they were ever sent back, and so that they didn't *change* too much as they learned things, becoming un-childlike in spite of their appearance.

"Do you know what the word *progeria* means, Wendy?"

"Yes," she said. Children watched the news. Thirteen-year-olds were supposed to be able to hold intelligent conversations with their parents. "It's when children get older even though they shouldn't. It's a disease that children get. It's happening a lot."

"Is it happening to you, Wendy? Have you got progeria?"

For a second or two she hesitated between *no* and *I don't know*, and then realized how bad the hesitation must look. She kept her face straight as she finally said: "I don't think so."

"What would you think if you found out you *had* got progeria, Wendy?" Cartwright asked, smug in the knowledge that she must be way out of her depth by now, whatever the truth of the matter might be.

"You can't ask her that!" Father said. "She's thirteen! Are you trying to scare her half to death? Children can be scared, you know. They're not *robots*."

"No," said Cartwright, without taking his eyes off Wendy's face. "They're not. Answer the question, Wendy."

"I wouldn't like it," Wendy said, in a low voice. "I don't want anything to happen to me. I want to be with Mummy and Daddy. I don't want anything to happen."

While she was speaking, Jimmy Li had come back into the room. He didn't say a word and his nod was almost imperceptible, but Tom Cartwright wasn't really in any doubt.

"I'm afraid it has, Wendy," he said, softly. "It *has* happened, as you know very well.

"No she doesn't!" said Mother, in a voice that was halfway to a scream. "She doesn't know any such thing!"

"It's a very mild case," Father said. "We've been watching her like hawks. It's purely physical. Her behavior hasn't altered at all. She isn't showing any mental symptoms whatsoever."

"You can't take her away," Mother said, keeping her shrillness under a tight rein. "We'll keep her in quarantine. We'll join one of the drug-trials. You can monitor her *but you can't take her away*. She doesn't understand what's happening. She's just a little girl. It's only slight, only her body."

Tom Cartwright let the storm blow out. He was still looking at Wendy, and his eyes seemed kind, full of concern. He let a moment's silence endure before he spoke to her again.

"Tell them, Wendy," he said, softly. "Explain to them that it isn't slight at all."

She looked up at Mother, and then at Father, knowing how much it would hurt them to be told. "I'm still Wendy," she said, faintly. "I'm still your little girl. I . . ."

She wanted to say *I always will be*, but she couldn't. She had always been a good girl, and some lies were simply too difficult to voice.

I wish I was a randomizing factor, she thought, fiercely wishing that it could be true, that it might be true. *I wish I was . . .*

Absurdly, she found herself wondering whether it would have been more grammatical to have thought *I wish I were . . .*

It was so absurd that she began to laugh, and then she began to cry, helplessly. It was almost as if the flood of tears could wash away the burden of thought—almost, but not quite.

Mother took her back into her bedroom, and sat with her, holding her hand. By the time the shuddering sobs released her—long after she had run out of tears—Wendy felt a new sense of grievance. Mother kept looking at the door, wishing that she could be out there, adding her voice to the argument, because she didn't really trust Father to get it right. The sense of duty which kept her pinned to Wendy's side was a burden, a burning frustration. Wendy didn't like that.

Oddly enough, though, she didn't feel any particular resentment at being put out of the way while Father and the Ministry of Health haggled over her future. She understood well enough that she had no voice in the matter, no matter how unlimited her self-consciousness had now become, no matter what progressive leaps and bounds she had accomplished as the existential fetters had shattered and fallen away.

She was still a little girl, for the moment.

She was still Wendy, for the moment.

When she could speak, she said to Mother: "Can we have some music?"

Mother looked suitably surprised. "What kind of music?" she countered.

"Anything," Wendy said. The music she was hearing in her head was soft and fluty music, which she heard as if from a vast distance, and which somehow seemed to be the oldest music in the world, but she didn't particularly want it duplicated and brought into the room. She just wanted something to fill the cracks of silence which broke up the muffled sound of arguing.

Mother called up something much more liquid, much more upbeat, much more modern. Wendy could see that Mother wanted to speak to her, wanted to deluge her with reassurances, but couldn't bear to make any promises she wouldn't be able to keep. In the end, Mother contented herself with hugging Wendy to her bosom, as fiercely and as tenderly as she could.

When the door opened it flew back with a bang. Father came in first.

"It's all right," he said, quickly. "They're not going to take her away. They'll quarantine the house instead."

Wendy felt the tension in Mother's arms. Father could work entirely from home much more easily than Mother, but there was no way Mother was going to start protesting on those grounds. While quarantine wasn't exactly *all right* it was better than she could have expected.

"It's not generosity, I'm afraid," said Tom Cartwright. "It's necessity. The epidemic is spreading too quickly. We don't have the facilities to take tens of thousands of children into state care. Even the quarantine will probably be a short-term measure—to be perfectly frank, it's a panic measure. The simple truth is that the disease can't be contained no matter what we do."

"How could you let this happen?" Mother said, in a low tone bristling with hostility. "How could you let it get this far out of control? With all modern technology at your disposal you surely should be able to put the brake on a simple virus."

"It's not so simple," Cartwright said, apologetically. "If it really had been a freak of nature—some stray strand of DNA which found a new ecological niche—we'd probably have been able to contain it easily. We don't believe that any more."

"It was *designed*," Father said, with the airy confidence of the well-informed—though even Wendy knew that this particular item of wisdom must have been news to him five minutes ago. "Somebody cooked this thing up in a lab and let it loose *deliberately*. It was all planned, in the name of liberation . . . in the name of chaos, if you ask me."

Somebody did this to me! Wendy thought. *Somebody actually set out to take away the limits, to turn the randomizing factor into . . . into what, exactly?*

While Wendy's mind was boggling, Mother was saying: "Who? How? Why?"

"You know how some people are," Cartwright said, with a fatalistic shrug of his shoulders. "Can't see an apple-cart without wanting to upset it. You'd think the chance to live for a thousand years would confer a measure of maturity even on the meanest intellect, but it hasn't worked out that way. Maybe someday we'll get past all that, but in the meantime . . ."

Maybe someday, Wendy thought, *all the things left over from the infancy of the world will go. All the crazinesses, all the disagreements, all the diehard habits.* She hadn't known that she was capable of being quite so sharp, but she felt perversely proud of the fact that she didn't have to spell out—even to herself, in the brand new arena of her private thoughts—the fact that one of those symptoms of craziness, one of the focal points of those disagreements, and the most diehard of all those habits, was keeping children in a world where they no longer had any biological function—or, rather, keeping the *ghosts* of children, who weren't really children at all because they were *always* children.

"They call it liberation," Father was saying, "but it really is a disease, a terrible affliction. It's the destruction of *innocence*. It's a kind of mass murder." He was obviously pleased with his own eloquence, and with the righteousness of his wrath. He came over to the bed and plucked Wendy out of Mother's arms. "It's all right, Beauty," he said. "We're all in this together. We'll face it together. You're absolutely right. You're still our little girl. You're still Wendy. Nothing terrible is going to happen."

It was far better, in a way, than what she'd imagined—or had been too scared to imagine. There was a kind of relief in not having to pretend any more, in not having to keep the secret. That boundary had been crossed, and now there was no choice but to go forward.

Why didn't I tell them before? Wendy wondered. *Why didn't I just tell them, and trust them to see that everything would be all right?* But even as she thought it, even as she clutched at the straw, just as Mother and Father were clutching, she realized how hollow the thought was, and how meaningless Father's reassurances were. It was all just sentiment, and habit, and pretense. Everything couldn't and wouldn't be "all right," and never would be again, unless . . .

Turning to Tom Cartwright, warily and uneasily, she said: "Will I be an adult now? Will I live for a thousand years, and have my own house, my own job, my own . . . ?"

She trailed off as she saw the expression in his eyes, realizing that she was still a little girl, and that there were a thousand questions adults couldn't and didn't want to hear, let alone try to answer.

It was late at night before Mother and Father got themselves into the right frame of mind for the kind of serious talk that the situation warranted, and by that time Wendy knew perfectly well that the honest answer to almost all the questions she wanted to ask was: "Nobody knows."

She asked the questions anyway. Mother and Father varied their answers in the hope of appearing a little wiser than they were, but it all came down to the same thing in the end. It all came down to desperate pretense.

"We have to take it as it comes," Father told her. "It's an unprecedented situation. The government has to respond to the changes on a day-by-day basis. We can't tell how it will all turn out. It's a mess, but the world has been in a mess before—in fact, it's hardly ever been out of a mess for more than a few years at a time. We'll cope as best we can. *Everybody* will cope as best they can. With luck, it might not come to violence—to war, to slaughter, to ecocatastrophe. We're entitled to hope that we really are past all that now, that we really are capable of handling things *sensibly* this time."

"Yes," Wendy said, conscientiously keeping as much of the irony out of her voice as she could. "I understand. Maybe we won't just be sent back to the factories to be scrapped . . . and maybe if they find a cure, they'll ask us whether we want to be cured before they use it." *With luck*, she added, silently, *maybe we can all be* adult *about the situation*.

They both looked at her uneasily, not sure how to react. From now on, they would no longer be able to grin and shake their heads at the wondrous inventiveness of the randomizing factor in her programming. From now on, they would actually have to try to figure out what she *meant*, and what unspoken thoughts might lie behind the calculated wit and hypocrisy of her every statement. She had every sympathy for them; she had only recently learned for herself what a difficult, frustrating and thankless task that could be.

This happened to their ancestors once, she thought. *But not as quickly. Their ancestors didn't have the kind of head-start you can get by being thirteen for thirty years. It must have been hard, to be a thinking ape among unthinkers. Hard, but . . . well, they didn't ever want to give it up, did they?*

"Whatever happens, Beauty," Father said, "we love you. Whatever happens, you're our little girl. When you're grown up, we'll still love you the way we always have. We always will."

He actually believes it, Wendy thought. *He actually believes that the world can still be the same, in spite of everything. He can't let go of the hope that even though everything's changing, it will all be the same underneath. But it won't. Even if there isn't a resource crisis—after all, grown-up children can't eat much more than un-grown-up ones—the world can never be the same. This is the time in which the adults of the world have to get used to the fact that there can't be any more families, because from now on children will have to be rare and precious and strange. This is the time when the old people will have to recognize that the day of their silly stopgap solutions to imaginary problems is over. This is the time when we all have to grow up. If the old people can't do that by themselves, then the new generation will simply have to show them the way.*

"I love you too," she answered, earnestly. She left it at that. There wasn't any point in adding: "I always have," or "I can mean it now," or any of the other things which would have underlined rather than assuaged the doubts they must be feeling.

"And we'll be all right," Mother said. "As long as we love one another, and as long as we face this thing together, we'll be all right."

What a wonderful thing true innocence is, Wendy thought, rejoicing in her ability to think such a thing freely, without shame or reservation. *I wonder if I'd be able to cultivate it, if I ever wanted to.*

That night, bedtime was abolished. She was allowed to stay up as late as she wanted to. When she finally did go to bed she was so exhausted that she quickly drifted off into a deep and peaceful sleep—but she didn't remain there indefinitely. Eventually, she began to dream.

In her dream Wendy was living wild in a magical wood where it never rained. She lived on sweet berries of many colors. There were other girls living wild in the dream-wood but they all avoided one another. They had lived there for a long time but now the others had come: the shadow-men with horns on their brows and shaggy legs who played strange music, which was the breath of souls.

Wendy hid from the shadow-men, but the fearful fluttering of her heart gave her away, and one of the shadow-men found her. He stared down at her with huge baleful eyes, wiping spittle from his pipes onto his fleecy rump.

"Who are you?" she asked, trying to keep the tremor of fear out of her voice.

"I'm the devil," he said.

"There's no such thing," she informed him, sourly.

He shrugged his massive shoulders. "So I'm the Great God Pan," he said. "What difference does it make? And how come you're so smart all of a sudden?"

"I'm not thirteen anymore," she told him, proudly. "I've been thirteen for thirty years, but now I'm growing up. The whole world's growing up—for the first and last time."

"Not me," said the Great God Pan. "I'm a million years old and I'll *never* grow up. Let's get on with it, shall we? I'll count to ninety-nine. You start running."

Dream-Wendy scrambled to her feet, and ran away. She ran and she ran and she ran, without any hope of escape. Behind her, the music of the reed-pipes kept getting louder and louder, and she knew that whatever happened, her world would never fall silent.

When Wendy woke up, she found that the nightmare hadn't really ended. The meaningful part of it was still going on. But things weren't as bad as all that, even though she couldn't bring herself to pretend that it was all just a dream which might go away.

She knew that she had to take life one day at a time, and look after her parents as best she could. She knew that she had to try to ease the pain of the passing of their way of life, to which they had clung a little too hard and a little too long. She knew that she had to hope, and to trust, that a cunning combination of intelligence and love would be enough to see her and the rest of the world through—at least until the next catastrophe came along.

She wasn't absolutely sure that she could do it, but she was determined to give it a bloody good try.

And whatever happens in the end, she thought, *to live will be an awfully big adventure.*

crossing chao meng fu

G. DAVID NORDLEY

The determination to stick to a task until you complete it, to push through no matter what the odds or how overwhelming the problems you face, can be a positive quality—but, as the thriller that follows amply demonstrates, on the airless, sun-blasted surface of Mercury, with death only inches away at any moment, sometimes it may not be such a good idea. . . .

G. David Nordley is a retired U.S. Air Force officer and physicist who has become a frequent contributor to Analog *in the last couple of years as well as selling stories to* Asimov's Science Fiction, Tomorrow, *and elsewhere. He won* Analog's Analytical Laboratory *readers poll in 1992 for his story "Poles Apart" and also for his well-known story "Into the Miranda Rift," which appeared in our Eleventh Annual Collection; the story that follows is a "prequel" to it. He lives in Sunnyvale, California.*

> Begin a ghostly plain
> Dim white in pale starlight.
> Flat as far as you can see
> To where a distant black ridge
> Divides reality.
> Above the stars shine
> Below the ground crunches;
> Hillary, Byrd, Peary and Amundsen,
> Are your guides. It is beautiful.
> But you cannot stop long;
> The plain is life itself;
> Move on now, trod onward,
> Or stand and freeze, they say.
> —W. B.

▼

I am in the middle of a line of people walking determinedly across the most everything-forsaken boring waste in the Solar System. I am so sore and tired I could scream—if there were a warm bed around somewhere, I'd crawl in it to shudder. My attitude has hit rock bottom, but it is time to file my report and if I want anything good out of this pain, I'd best sound positive:

"I am Wojciech Bubka, college teacher, occasional poet and now your . . ." I take a breath of sterile suit air, ". . . guide to the natural universe, courtesy of the Solar System Astrographic Society and its many sponsors and members. Welcome to my personal journey through exotic, dangerous, and unusual places of the Solar System." I take another deep breath—got to keep up with everyone else. "Come with me while there are still such places to explore—for as we approach the twenty-third century, this frontier, too, is receding."

I try to gain a little ground to stop briefly and pan my helmet cam over the dirty ice field. Despite the exertion, the change of pace lifts my spirits a bit. But not even a ten-to-one vertical exaggeration will make this landscape interesting. Come on, Bubka. You're a poet? Find meaning.

"These are not robot explorations to be experienced in a video display, but personal ones. I seek authentic, not virtual, reality. I seek the *go there, see there,* and *be there* experience of the human explorer, not sterile pixels." Breathe deep. "There is nothing between me and the crunch of crampon spikes on this frozen mud, the strike of an axe into virgin scarps, the strain of muscles, the hiss of sliding ropes, and the sight of wonders. Such is the dream and the experience I seek to share with you here, today, on the frozen wastes of Chao Meng Fu crater on Mercury."

Said strain of muscles gets my attention as I start walking again, and I groan involuntarily. I am tired from the almost week of walking under a pack that brought my weight close to Earth normal—when what is normal for me is Mars. I wiggle my toes as hard as I can—despite vacuum insulation, thermistor environmental control and loose, fluffy socks, I think my feet are beginning to get cold.

"Come on, mate. Another hour will get us there." That is Ed Blake, a gentleman adventurer from New Zealand with Antarctic experience. Ed is my tentmate, lanky, mostly bald and prematurely gray, confident, competent, and reserved—unless he gets that kind of twinkle in his eye. Then beware a terrible pun. He's cheerful enough to me, but I sense a certain condescension.

Understandable, I think. What the frozen hell am I doing here?

I had been getting bored at Jovis Tholis University. Poetry, these days, includes video as well as text—something which would have delighted Will Shakespeare, I assure you—and has blended with drama so much that we distinguish the two by picking nits over length and symbolic content. But even in its media-inflated majesty, a dozen years of going over the same basic stuff while fighting battles with New Reformation censors and left-wing nihilists—neither of whom take kindly to the display of material contrary to their philosophies—has me well on my way to burnout.

JTU is in a dome over an ostensibly extinct volcano on Tharsis, roughly halfway to Olympus Mons from the tether tube terminal on Ascraeus. The location worked, and it became the biggest university on Mars—of which I was an increasingly small and out-of-step part.

As the politics of being an important academic became increasingly burdensome, my dreams of "out there" grew. I might teach at Saturn High Station with its magnificent view of the rings. Or I could compose random meter verse at Hyperion Institute, the lonely retreat of mathematical philosophers set on a detached mountain peak that careens about Saturn as metaphor of an uncertain future. Or I could volunteer to ride a comet and watch robots turn it into Martian air while writing my epics in the freedom of isolation as the comet fell for a decade into the inner Solar System. Or, and this was my most favorite, I might become a journalist in the old sense on the first expedition to Pluto and Charon.

Thus did I dream. But so, of course, dream millions of others. Only a chosen few can go anywhere the first time or do anything the first time. I dabbled at trail writing; journals of hikes and visits to parts of the vanishing "Red" Mars, but got little notice beyond a reasonably nice "been there, done that" rejection from the Solar System Astrographic Society. I needed an entree, a contact, an idea, something to lift me out of the background.

Then, last year (Martian year, everyone; almost two standard years ago), Miranda Lotati, the daughter of the man in charge of Solar System Astrographic Society's expeditions division, walked into my literature class at Jovis Tholis University, a junior transfer from Stanford on Earth. She looked to be a hard, vigorous, and exciting person but could barely choke two words out in succession—about as contrary to stereotype as one could be and still have breasts.

She was not really beautiful—too muscular, too thin in the face, too boyish a figure, but I saw the possibilities in that. Less competition, and perhaps a complement to my esthetic, well, softness, I told myself. I saw the romance of an attraction of opposites who themselves were opposites of conventionality, and I was looking for some romance somewhere—the women of my normal circles were hopeless and helpless in anything but words, and even seemed to take pride in that. I saw in her an invitation to beyond and away from here. If I played it right—and I resolved to do so.

It wasn't easy. Miranda was a rough-edged, prickly student, and her essays were condensed dullness, never more than the required length. A spoken sentence of more than a half dozen words was a rarity from her, and she sometimes seemed to speak a language so far evolved from today's English in its lack of articles and verbs that, had it been deliberate, would have been considered art in some circles. Nonetheless I was intent. I persisted in bringing her along. I bided my time.

I had to expend some moral capital, but convinced myself that she covered the ground on her final well enough to let me pass her. She liked me, I think. But I said nothing unethical to her, nor hinted at anything romantic while she was my student—I have my standards.

I saw her on the last day of classes of the winter semester, after the final grades were in.

"You're off to Mercury, I hear, to be along on your father's attempt to walk across Chao Meng Fu Crater?" Shielded from the Sun, that huge crater was an ice field—Mercury's Antarctica.

She nodded.

"Have you set the expedition membership?"

She shook her head, confirming what was known publicly.

"Will you have any journalists along? It would make a very exciting nature piece."

She smiled a bit. "Like your Ascraeus Mons hike piece? Dad liked that and sent me here."

He'd seen that? I tried to remember the rejection letter. I was flattered but a bit worried that it was a little light for a Lotati expedition. Then the alarm bells rang in my head. My competition for the position of expedition bard was standing in front of me.

I reached for a tone of professorial authority. "Randi, uh. You've come a long way in your composition . . ."

She shrugged. "Yeah. Thanks to you. Someone's got to do the article. Someone who fits on the team. Wish I wrote better."

"Randi, I suppose I shouldn't be obscure. Is there any chance I might come myself?"

Her eyes lit up for a moment, then she frowned. "Rough business, exploring."

"Then my accounts of it should draw interest, maybe enough to push Solar System Astrographic's allocation priorities a little further up." Not to mention that a single Astrographic article could bring in the equivalent in allocations of my entire Jovis Tholus University stipend for a year. A *Martian* year.

"Uh, huh." A doubtful assent on her part

"Might even help you get to your namesake, out by Uranus. Now there would be an angle that people would notice!"

That got her attention. "Dad's idea too. My name. Not that easy, though. No place for amateurs, out there."

I smiled at her. "I bet I'll make a good explorer. I'm observant, handy, and in reasonably good shape."

She gave me a somewhat skeptical look and a sigh. "Mercury first. Chao Meng Fu. Hundred fifty kilometer-wide. Never sees the Sun. Covered with granite-hard permafrost. Probably take us two, three weeks to walk it."

"Walk?"

She nodded. "Unassisted. Carry everything. Vacuum suits, tents, supplies, samples."

"Walk it? Uh, why?"

She looked at me as if I was born in some other cosmos. "Because we can."

There is this recklessness about me that allows me to throw words around without fully considering the consequences. "Well, I think I can too. I've done enough hiking around Tharsis—I even have a cinder cone named after me."

She looked skeptically at me. "Oh? How high?"

She had me there. I grinned sheepishly. "Well, 'Bubka Mons' is only a hundred meters above local mean. But it's kind of impressive because there's nothing else around it." And I knew someone in the Martian Geology Institute that was laying out the local real estate.

She giggled.

"It *is* registered, Randi. Anyway, my Ascraeus trip was solo, and by a new route."

She looked judiciously at me and sighed. "Lose ten kilos. Do fifty kilometers a day." We stood silent for a couple of seconds as I tried to digest that.

She turned away. "Physics final—see you." And she was gone, gliding easily down the hall.

Dreams are free; but realizing them has a price. And I resolved to pay it.

By the end of last semester, I had walked up a few Martian mountains and lost the ten kilos. I talked to her again and we arranged a checkout hike down to the base of Jovis Tholis and back up to the town again with full packs, breather gear, and by the most difficult route she could pick. She watched every move I made, and seemed satisfied enough to make another "date."

As this went on, I grew utterly fascinated with her. She was a busy woman. Reporters called her, outfitters called her. She was always meeting young women explorers who knew her reputation as a companion of her father, and old men explorers who had been somewhere with her father. My metaphor for Randi was a black hole; people and things seem to swirl around and accrete to her without any significant verbal effort on her part, as if her presence distorts space so that all roads simply lead to her and none away.

The week she was to leave Mars for Mercury she called me.

"You're in, Professor Bubka. Can you make the Shannon inbound? Friday?"

By moving heaven and Mars, I could, and did. I had, it seemed, been within her event horizon for some time now.

So, Mercury. Mercury gravity is the same as Mars gravity, which some say is more than a coincidence, but a coincidence as yet unexplained. The gravity here is exactly the same as on Mars, but I'm carrying three times my mass in supplies and vacuum survival equipment. I might as well be hiking in Antarctica with a light pack. Indeed, I could use the conditioning to visit Earth! Despite the extra mass, we try to keep up the fifty kilometers a day—a pace I must maintain.

There are eight of us strung out along the Chao Meng Fu crater floor, Dr. Lotati in the lead. Dr. Juanita Tierzo, a Harvard-trained geologist, follows him. Juanita is actually on the JTU faculty—in the Martian Geology Institute—but I had to come to Mercury to meet her. Randi follows her. Then come Ed, myself, and one of Dr. Tierzo's graduate students, Eloni Wakhweya, a slight Kenyan woman with a big grin. Solar System Astrographic expedition staffers Mike and Karen Svenson come last, pulling an equipment pallet on two large wire wheels.

They meant it; no robots, no powered vehicles, and in my now humbled opinion, no sense. If Mercury had a breathable atmosphere, they'd have done without the spacesuits and all their built-in communications and amenities, too. I'm exhausted, uncomfortable, and increasingly uneasy with this exercise in cosmic hubris.

The view is simple, unrelieved flatness, the kind of view that should reach one's soul in the way of all great expanses. The crater's stark lines go its name-sake's art one spareness better; the vertical dimension is almost absent. It too is painted in an ink of five colors, all gray. It is Aldrin's magnificent desolation, without relief. I appreciate it more in intellectual abstract than in person.

There is light to see: the tips of the peaks behind us blaze like distant arc lamps, and fill the bowl of Chao Meng Fu with a ghostly kind of moonlight. Small, rounded crater rims dot this frozen plane—very few higher than a man, for ice flows in time. The brighter stars shine down on us hard and free. Brilliant Earth hangs just over the horizon, a tiny dazzling blue-white star. Luna lies well away from it, a faint gray dot lost in Sagittarius.

Invisible to us in the Earth's glare is the beginning of Earth's Sunshield. This mammoth project will partly shade the heat-polluted atmosphere from the fires of Apollo's chariot someday. It is taking form at the Earth-Sun L-1 point, balanced there with the help of reflected light—they plan to reduce insolation by 1 percent. But more relevant to our endeavor is that it is the home of Solar System Astrographic's solar radio antenna, which we use to apprise the rest of the Solar System of the status of this madcap adventure. I look that way wondering why I ever left.

"Another five kilometers to the crevasse," Dr. Lotati tells us on the comnet.

This desolate flat sameness is an illusion; we have real work ahead. The crevasse is a major obstacle, or a major objective if you are a geologist. Halfway between the rim of Chao Meng Fu crater and its central peaks lies a huge crack in the permafrost caused, they think, by an almost infinitely slow lifting of the crater floor, still rebounding from the billion-year-old impact that formed the crater. To this poet, overhead views make the crevasse look like the mouth of the planet—and I worry about being devoured.

By noon, universal time, the mouth of Mercury yawns directly in front of us, an ugly black crack that makes the dark gray plain around us look silvery by comparison. We halt to plan our crossing. Juanita proposes that we simply go down into this thing, down into a darkness that has never known the Sun, and out again on the other side. That idea creates enough interest to scare me. But not now. A descent will take planning, and, in the meantime, I luxuriate in not having to move my body.

Yet, standing still, I forget my pain and become curious. The crevasse seems to run to the horizon to my right and left. The other side is the length of a football field away. I shudder—it is impossible to repress the thought that such darkness is not meant for human beings, that the laws of physics will become conscious and punish us for trying it. Perversely, the challenge of that danger attracts me.

Yet, there are reasons to go down beyond the simple thrill of it. Solar Astrographic's expedition is half stunt, half science—and here is where the other half gets its due. There is a mystery here and the root of it lies in a contrary mysticism of celestial dynamics. Here, a mere sixty million kilometers from its fiery photosphere, are surfaces that have not seen the Sun since the Caloris impact defined Mercury's final orientation.

This same counterintuitive magic then decrees that the ices of comets that orbit impossibly far—beyond even Pluto, Charon, and Persephone—are actually closer to the Sun, and Mercury, in the *energy* of their motion than anything in the inner Solar System. Something on Venus would have to be kicked at almost 11 km/s to reach Mercury, best case—but merely nudge a pair of Oort belt comets together and parts of them may fall into Mercury, decades hence. Sometimes these collisions give the planet a very temporary, tenuous atmosphere, which condenses in the deep freeze of Chao Meng Fu. Blame this on Kepler and Newton, not Ptolemy.

So near is far, and far is near, and the crevasse yawns from 'ere to 'ere. Does it have teeth? Do its open jaws reveal molecules from the beginning of time, such as measured in the Solar System? Lotati confers with his daughter, and Ed. Randi and Ed have a thing, I've found, and spend a fair amount of time touching helmets.

What great ideas I have! I despair of ever being able to itch again, let alone going to Miranda with its namesake. My rented vacuum gear fits like the skin of a hundred-year-old man; stretched taut digging into my flesh here, loose and bulging there. Randi says there's an art to it and I should take more time getting in. Next time I will.

I edge closer to the brink, attracted to the danger perhaps, or perhaps wanting to demonstrate courage to Randi. I gaze down. Here and there the dust has fallen from the sheer ice walls, and the layered structure is clear. There are Mercury's sediments. Each comet or meteor creates a temporary atmosphere for Mercury, and that which is not boiled away by the Sun condenses in the polar craters, mixed with ejecta dust. The bedrock lies perhaps a kilometer below us. After three days of the most physical labor I've done in decades, I now contemplate a rappel down to the bottom of a bottomless crevasse and the climb back up again.

I look away as though by not observing it, I can create the possibility that it does not exist.

But I have my journalist's duty. At my command, my helmet camera plays back the view, and it floats, reflected off my face plate, against the stars. It doesn't fit in the standard field of view, I realize, so I look over the edge again and slowly turn my head from horizon to horizon. An object of professional interest now, it begins to lose some of its scariness for me.

Bubka's prescription for fear of something—study the hell out of it.

How long and wide! Then I turn off all my lights, let my eyes relax, and turn back to see the solar corona, a peacock's tail of icy fire spreading from the Sun that sits just under those utterly black mountains that ring our horizon. If Chao Meng Fu did not flatten Mercury's globe here, we would not be able to see those mountains this far into the trek, so close is Mercury's horizon—but we have been heading ever so slightly inward, downhill, as well as south.

The furthest streamers of the corona glow far above that rim behind, looking almost like the aurora borealis back on Earth. Awed, I step back, and back again to catch my balance.

I happen to glance down—my boot is barely centimeters from the edge of the chasm.

"Bubka, freeze." Randi's voice echoes in my helmet.

I am already frozen.

"Now. Raise right hand," she continues.

I am carrying a strobe lamp in my right hand so I automatically start to raise my left—

"Your other right!" she snaps, instantly.

This time I get it right, raising both my arm and the strobe lamp.

"Now lean *that* way. Walk slowly. Away from edge."

I understand now: if I teeter, she wants me to teeter in the direction of safety. I walk away from the edge with as much dignity as I can muster, as if there were nothing at all wrong, knowing that anyone monitoring my heartbeat will know that I am anything but calm.

She detaches herself from the management group and strides toward me, ghostly dust glittering in my helmet light behind her footsteps. She halts in a cloud of fairy sparkles, grabs my hand, and leads me well away from the edge of the crevasse.

"Professor Bubka, near crevasses, tether. Always, always, tether."

"Professor" hangs in my mind dripping with irony. On Mars, I taught her literature. Here, I am her student—and I had just come close to failing a test where failure is judged somewhat more harshly than at Jovis Tholis University.

Nodding ruefully, I pull a piton gun from my pack and harpoon the planet. A test pull shows that it's secure, and I clip the line to my belt. Randi fires a piton in too, clips on, then clips another line between her belt and mine. "Ed, some baby-sitter you'd make! Going to take a look."

"Sorry, mate. Watching, Randi."

Baby-sitter?

"Now, Professor Bubka. Let's go look." Dark eyes, on a tanned face with a snub nose, twinkle at me behind the clear, non-reflecting visor.

We retrace my footprints together. We walk to the edge together. This time, I think to clip my strobe light to my belt as well.

One of the things I see is half a footprint at the edge of the crevasse. The toe half. Mine.

What I had done was, I realize, foolish, but I think I am forgiven. She pulls on her line, then actually leans out over the cut, to inspect its near side.

"Light." The word is a request and a command. Crystals from far down glitter in response.

Nervously, wrapping my line around my left hand and playing it out through a "smart slot" belay device, centimeter by centimeter, I lean out with her and shine my strobe on the wall under us. On a clean vertical, the layering resembles a diffraction grating—fine thin grooves, perfectly horizontal, broken occasionally by what must be the sections of ancient buried craters.

The strobe light looks continuous, but contains off-pulses for range—it times a journey of the absence of light. So. The crack goes down, a hundred meters, two hundred, three hundred. At five hundred, I can no longer see the light returning, but it can. I swing it slowly from side to side, as my helmet display paints a graph of angle and range. The walls seem to almost converge about twelve hundred meters below us here, with some flatness between them. I move the beam a bit to the left.

There is something across the chasm at eight hundred meters, just to our left. "Randi?"

"I see it. Bridge. Dad, channel seven."

"I have it, Randi! I'll think that is a billion years down if it's a day! What do you say, Juanita, my Randi's found a bridge!"

There seemed no point in immediately explaining that I'd found it.

"Eight hundred meters down and all the way across! Can we do it?" Juanita answers, thrill in her voice. "Do we have enough line?"

"Yes and yes," Randi's father answers after a moment of thought. Then he points to a slight dip almost above the bridge. "Probably half of an old crater, broken by the crack. That will get us a few meters closer. We could rappel down from there. Perhaps two billion years down, if the crevasse goes to the bottom of Chao Meng Fu. Do you want the bottom, Juanita?"

"God, yes, Emilio, if it isn't too dangerous."

Dr. Lotati shrugs. "It has been this way for millions of years of impacts; the walls should tolerate a few ants crawling on them. We'll go ourselves, instead of waiting for some robots to do it."

I look across the chasm for the other half of the ancient crater, but, like the other half of my footprint, there is no sign of it. Where did it go? I feel a curiosity as powerful as any hunger. What formed the bridge? What lies at the bottom? We shall find out, if the Laws of the Universe let us.

We all have some climbing experience, but only the Lotatis and Ed have very much. It is, however, a very easy climb down in 38 percent gravity. The ropes are well secured to the plain above, the slope is usually less than vertical. Mike and Karen Svenson will remain on the rim with the bulk of the equipment until we are all safely down. They call themselves the "human robots" and have been in excellent humor. When Randi and Dr. Lotati scale the other wall, they will fire a rope across. The Lotatis will then pull over a larger rope on which a tram will carry the equipment. Meanwhile, at the bottom, Dr. Tierzo will supervise sample gathering by the rest of us. That is the plan.

It becomes dark quickly as we descend. The sky contracts to a starry band overhead, one edge of which glows a faint, frozen, shadowy pearl, a reflection lit by a reflection of sunlight on distant peaks. We turn on our helmet lights, and their glare banishes any other source of illumination. They spread sparkly pools of light on the wall—tiny crystals everywhere. I am conscious of a fine mist or fog, just on the edge of the perceivable. Our suits allow the skin's waste gases to diffuse slowly outward, our footsteps create microscopic dust clouds on which it may condense, our helmet lights evaporate hydrogen gas that has condensed on the wall. Our progress appears tinged with the ethereal.

We are three hundred meters down: a football field on end. The descent is easy, simple, routine. You ease rope out under friction, take a pair of steps down, and ease out some more. This descent is demanding and terrifying. You dare not lose concentration. Pitons can pull out, crampons can slip, and you will be just as dead from a fall of a kilometer in Mercury's gravity as Earth's. Yes, it will take a few seconds longer and an academic might note that you hit with less velocity—only about five times instead of fifteen times what is needed to smash your helmet and the skull within it.

You dare not cause problems for everyone else. One foot after another.

A person in fear of his or her life needs no more excitement—but if you want it, you glance at the wall in front of you, at layers of ice laid down when dinosaurs were young. This is not on a screen, not a simulation, but never-seen-before reality that puts ice hard in front of your own eyes.

"Ed," I ask, "do you wonder if anyone might have been here a billion years ago?"

"Eh? Interesting thought, that. The feature would attract someone with enough curiosity to build spaceships, I should think. But the crack itself wouldn't be that old, now, would it?"

"No, I guess not." When the layers were laid down, of course, this had been a part of the plain.

Still, my eyes scan every layer, hoping.

"Has everyone got positive pressure in their suits?" Dr. Lotati asks, and receives chuckles. "There is," he continues, "a significant build-up of nitrogen gas, and a bare trace of nitrogen tri-flouride, which I would not recommend breathing."

I call up a temp display and find that it is cold in the crack—about eighty kelvins, versus a hundred twenty at the surface. As I think about it, I notice traces of frost on the outside of my gloves: our insulation is that good. I have no idea what the biological implications of nitrogen tri-fluoride are, but I would rather someone else perform the experiments. A drop rolls down my face plate.

"Watch your footing, Juanita," Dr. Lotati says. "It's slippery here."

So far, my crampons dig into the dirty clathrate walls with ease, but I can tell it is wet. The wall is mostly ice, but ice that is heavily mixed with crater ejecta, pocked with more volatile ices, and stiffened far harder than anything on Earth by cryogenic temperatures. Dr. Lotati says it's something like sandstone, but if it weren't for the gas in the ice, it would be like concrete. There are few cracks, but the piton gun works well, as does the ax.

"Nitrogen trifluoride data," I ask. Floating in the wall, by virtue of my helmet display hardware, are glowing numbers telling me that nitrogen tri-fluoride is liquid over a range of about 80 kelvins—from about 77 up to 145—which is over 120 Celsius degrees below the freezing point of water. Somehow, stating such temperatures in kelvins above absolute zero is less scary than using negative Celsius degrees below freezing. The vapor pressure of this big, heavy molecule is almost nil at the low end of this temperature range—a wet vacuum.

A hundred meters to go, and I can see the bridge clearly in the shifting pools of our helmet lights.

"A sliver of wall appears to have detached itself and slid down until it jammed," Dr. Tierzo tells us. "The top is a jumble with, here and there, flat spaces that may have been part of the original surface, including part of a crater. I wonder if that's what knocked it down?"

"Hello down there," Karen Svenson calls. "Yes, that crater would explain what looks like a ray network around where you went down. Now that I know what I'm looking at, this spiderweb network of cracks is a real giveaway."

I hadn't remembered any cracks. I ask my suit to play back my recording of our approach to the side. The surface in the depression was smooth. My pulse races. "Playback two hours ago," I command. In a ghostly video window, my suit shows me almost falling in to the crevasse, but . . .

"Hey, everyone!" I shout. "Those cracks weren't there before. Dr. Lotati, I've got it on channel six."

There is a moment of silence.

"Quickly now," Dr. Lotati speaks briefly and very businesslike. "Those of you still on the wall come down as quickly as possible without panic and without yanking on anything. Mike and Karen, set another belay well back of the cracked area."

I have my full attention on climbing down, gingerly as possible. Dr. Tierzo is off belay just below me. I remember to lock my crampon spikes *out*—the bridge is slippery.

Meanwhile, Dr. Lotati has set an ice bolt in at the far end of our bridge. Dr. Tierzo sets another one in the biggest hunk of bridge she can find at our end and pulls the line tight.

Then I am off the wall. I quickly clip my line to the bridge line and release myself from the wall ropes. "Off belay."

Miranda Lotati and the grad student, Eloni, are still on the wall.

I hear, I think, at very low frequency, a kind of groan.

"We have the protection in," Karen says. "The cracks are larger!"

"Wojciech can get your line, Ed," Dr. Lotati says, "release from the wall immediately!"

"No worry. Here." He tosses me the end of his spare line and I hit it with the loop of a smart 'biner, which opens, takes the line, and shuts faster than I can see—like that old magic trick with hoops. I take up the slack.

Ed releases and scrambles off the wall, holding the taut line for balance until he reaches me. We move further down the bridge.

"Come on, Eloni," Ed says encouragingly. The young Kenyan woman is the least experienced of our group—she descends slowly, but flawlessly, a few meters right of where Ed came down. "Toss me the end of your spare line."

She stops to find it. Miranda Lotati's feet are but a few meters above her. I hear another groan.

"Come on . . ." Ed says again.

Finally, Eloni tosses a coiled line toward Ed. It jerks short and dangles below her, a hopeless tangle.

"Sorry, I try to do this too fast."

"That's OK, mate," Ed says. "Just come on down now. We'll improvise."

We feel a slight tremor. She freezes.

"Down, Eloni. Fast," Randi says.

Eloni starts moving again. I can see her tremble.

"Ice!" Karen shouts. Our radios level amplitude, magnifying whispers and buffering shouts—that shout was well buffered.

Eloni freezes.

"Go," Randi snaps, and clips Eloni's helmet with the side of her boot. "Get going!"

Galvanized, Eloni half scrambles and half falls the remaining fifty meters, landing on her seat where the bridge butts against the wall. She starts fumbling with the 'biner holding her line to the wall belay line. Ed, clipped to a line, moves to help her—I think he has a knife in his hand. Heedless, I follow him using crampons and ax. Ed reaches Eloni.

I look up and see the sky falling.

Randi releases and leaps from almost twenty meters up on the wall, unbelayed, right at me. "Catch," she shouts.

I have time to set my crampon spikes and open my arms. She hits hard, and various pieces of her gear dig into my chest. I grab her as the boots tear free and we skitter together down the side of the bridge. My line stops us after a three-meter slide.

Ten meters from us, with a roar clearly conducted through the ice we lie against, an avalanche of clathrate pours down. There is no sign of Ed and Eloni.

Randi clips a line to my belt, rolls off, and starts to scramble back to the top of the bridge, ice dust streaming around her.

"Ed!" she shouts. "Eloni!"

The fall increases, becoming a white wall. Randi scrambles into it. I follow and am enveloped in a stream of pulverized clathrate, and I can see nothing. It flows over me, not like sand or water, but something in between—not dense, but still exerting pressure.

I wait. My helmet is filled with the sound of my breathing.

"Ed!" Randi shouts again.

"We're alive." Ed's voice is hoarse and strained. "Trapped next to the wall. The fall created a bit of a pocket. No injuries, but it's getting somewhat cold."

In spacesuits with rebreathers and plenty of energy, we are in no danger of suffocating. But under our coveralls we wear skintight vacuum suits that depend on a surrounding vacuum for much of their thermal control and the fabric of the vacuum suits, while smart and extremely tough, is necessarily thin. Conduction of heat could quickly freeze Ed and Eloni. But, clinging to the side of the bridge with the landslide still in progress, there is nothing I can do to reach them.

"Got you on locator. Can move." That is Randi Lotati, for me. Move? How?

I roll over prone to the face of the bridge, reach forward into the flow with my hands, and find purchase. With both arms and legs, I find I can edge forward, too.

"Solid piece—here," Randi says. "Ice boulder. Think you're on other side."

"S—sounds that w—way," Ed replies.

"Line charge. My side. Push like hell when I say."

"No, Randi," Ed pleads, "too dangerous—"

"Push, damn it! Now!"

I hear the crack of the detonation.

"Randi?" I call, and claw my way toward the signals, white sand and occasional rocks still streaming by me. Somehow, though, it seems a bit easier. "Randi, Ed?"

"Wojciech, Ed. We—we're free. At—at least the rock's split. Need help with Eloni."

"I'm trying." I pant. "Where's Randi?" I am exhausted struggling against the continuing stream of material from above. I reach forward with my hand and hit flesh. Someone there. The world is gray in my helmet lamp; I can see nothing. "Ed, is that you?"

"Not me, mate. It's slackening a little. I've got some space."

The someone moans. The groan is female.

"Eloni?" I push the person in front of me again, harder.

"She's with me, Wojciech," Ed says.

"Randi?"

She grunts. "Wojciech. I'm OK. I'm just . . . stuck. Legs won't move." I feel a hand brush mine, then lock with mine. "Drag me back."

"I'll try." Trusting the precarious hand link, I sit up into the flow of clathrate mud. It tries to take me away with tremendous force, but my line holds me. Slowly I get my legs around in front of me and pull as hard as I dare. She doesn't move.

"It's no good. I'll hurt you if I pull any harder."

"Freezing's worse. Hurt me. Pull."

God knows how much force I put on her arm, but something seems to unstick, and she comes toward me, slowly at first; then something breaks free and we scoot back about four meters. I can see through whirls of snow here. I can see my clip still on the bridge line, see Randi strung out at the end of my arm.

"Dr. Lotati, she's out. Over here."

"What? Wojciech? Where? . . . There, I have you! I'll be right over."

He is there in a moment. "Had you on the other side of the bridge for a moment—propagation freak, I think. Randi, will you be all right for a few minutes?"

"Hurts like hell, Dad, but yes. Thanks, Wojciech."

Dr. Lotati gives her a pat and plunges into the remains of the ice fall. Minutes later, he and Ed emerge, carrying Eloni between them. "Mike, Karen, this is Emilio," he says. "We're all out of the avalanche. I don't know in what shape yet, but we're all out."

"Roger. We suggest all of you rest a bit until this plays itself out."

"Mike . . ." He pauses, catching his breath. "We'll consider that."

There are several rueful chuckles, and we spend the next five minutes or so watching the river of white dust slowly come to a halt.

Finally the ice fall abates entirely and we take stock. Randi reports a severe sprain in her right shoulder. Ed is recovering from hypothermia and is severely bruised as well. Eloni is better, physically, but appears to be in some kind of psychological shock. The rest of us have minor bruises.

The side of the crevasse looks like a giant took a huge, semicircular bite out of it. Karen and Mark wave at us from an edge that is now at least fifty meters back from where it was. We lost two long lines, buried in the debris. The avalanche has buried half the bridge and I worry that it could start again at any time and bury us along with the other half. I try to do some mental calculations on how long it would take a suborbital hopper to get here and pull us out.

"I think we are here for a while," Dr. Lotati says, "at least until we're all up to climbing out again. We might overnight on the bridge." If he's worried about the avalanche restarting, he isn't saying so.

"We'll need to revise the schedule a bit," Ed adds. "Another five kilometers per day would do it, I should think. Now, how do we get the gear down here?"

"Toboggan the big tent down to us," Randi says. "Meantime, collect data."

I stare at Randi, stupefied.

"Are you OK, Eloni?" I ask, mainly out of concern but perhaps with a secondary agenda of reminding people of something.

Eloni raises her head and looks around in wonder. If she expects a chewing out, it seems she is in the wrong group. I lay a hand very gently on her shoulder, and, as if I touched some kind of hidden button, she leans into me and lets out a very long sigh, which I hear clearly where my helmet touches her. Randi is looking right at us, but in the glare of our headlights, her face is unreadable. Warning bells ring in my head.

"My mistake, Eloni," Ed says, "pressuring you like that for something that's not automatic. You needed to think it through, and with me talking at you like that, you couldn't. My mistake."

"Eloni," Dr. Lotati asks, "can you help Juanita get her samples tomorrow?"

Eloni takes a breath and slips away from me. "I—I can do that." A smile of relief creases the young woman's features.

"That a way!"

"Randi?" I ask, dumbfounded. "Your arm?"

"I'll live. Still go for the bottom, Juanita?"

"There may be a pond of liquid nitrogen trifluoride down there—it's unprecedented."

"Ed?"

He looks down, then at the crevasse sides. "Why don't I help Randi with the camp and prepare for climbing out of here?"

Apparently, we *will* sleep here—under the sword of Damocles.

"Wojciech?" Dr. Lotati asks.

I am at a loss for words. I am more tired and sore than I have ever been. How much more tired and sore can I be before I am a danger, I wonder? Everyone has been pummeled and challenged. But these people, these comrades of mine, will not admit disaster. They will press on. It is a collective decision—a spontaneous informal vote of voices that is already a majority. Voicing misgivings on my part would do no good at all, and my fate is tied to theirs. But I wonder that such things can still be in this age of robots. May the ghosts of Byrd, Amundsen, Lewis and Clark, and Bering fill my mind with whatever it is that gets one through. I came here to prove myself worthy and now the question is upon me. I look at the crevasse sides and down into its deep.

"Three climbers would be best," Dr. Lotati says.

"I'm . . . I can go with a little rest."

Dr. Lotati nods. "We can all use some. It's only 1100. We'll set up on the bridge. Mike and Karen, we'll take the big tent—you can probably slide it down on ropes."

This only takes a few minutes. We anchor the large vacuum tent to the bridge. It fits with about a meter to spare in width—with the door toward the intact wall. Room in the tent is limited. It was meant to sleep four and it is crowded with six of us. Our body odors again mingle in a forgettable stew of smells, and the drop curtain for its tiny commode is woefully inadequate for privacy. But we are relieved and happy—we have been through a memorable adventure and nobody has gotten killed.

Ed is quiet, eats quickly, and is asleep in his sack, fully clothed, in minutes. He says nothing. We will take a very real risk shortly, far, far, from help—for the sake of samples that could easily be gathered by robots a month from now.

As a certified—and some might say certifiable—poet, suicidal undertakings are perhaps in my nature. But the milieu of the Gentleman Adventurer requires that one return from the adventure to recount it. While Ed was gallant in the crisis, the closeness of his brush with death might only now be sinking into him. I, with far less experience, accepted a challenge he did not—does he resent this? No, I tell myself, he is just exhausted.

I have to make myself eat—I'm hungry, but more tired. A warm sleep-sack never felt so good, I realize. It seems I have barely closed my eyes when Dr. Lotati is gently rocking me awake.

"It's 1400," he says. "Time to go."

The trip to the bottom of the crevasse is a straightforward rappel. With Randi resting her arm, Eloni and I head for the bottom with Juanita in the lead.

"This could be Calorian clathrate—proof that Chao Meng Fu is older."

"But doesn't its flatness mean it's young?" I ask. Old surfaces are heavily cratered.

"Watch for a hollow to your left. No, the surface is young due to deposition—the crater itself is ancient. I'd guess we're about 3.8 billion years down, below the original crater floor. The walls are shock-fractured rock, not exposed sediment layers. No strata—" a swing of her ax tears a rough section of about a square meter from the wall "—underneath."

"Look, more signs of erosion," she adds later.

"Erosion?" The wall is a rough breccia, a compressed clathrate and gravel mixture. The larger stones are sharp, not rounded.

"There is evidence of atmosphere all around us—you can see icicles in the hollows, and a cold glistening wetness on the walls."

I turn off my radio. "Can you hear me?" I shout.

There is no answer—the vapor is still too thin, even at the bottom, to conduct sound.

We hang from the wall and gaze into the utterly still pool of nitrogen trifluoride in the circles of our helmet lamps below us. Unable to resist the temptation, I reach into one of Mercury's nostrils and break off an icicle and toss it into the pool. It ripples like oily water.

"Wojciech," Eloni says in a mildly scolding voice, "have some respect! That pool has been built up, molecule by molecule, probably over billions of years."

"How?" Juanita asks, gently. "Even if the crater is that old, the crevasse isn't."

Eloni is silent, then says, "Oh, of course. But where does it come from then?"

"The pool is a mystery, for now," Juanita says. "Perhaps some comet with an unusual concentration of fluorine ices struck not too long ago. Or something else." She laughs. "Fortunately, not all mysteries can be solved now. We would run out of things to do!"

I envision tentacles reaching out of that deep to pluck us from the crevasse wall. "Could something have evolved to base its blood on that, the way we use seawater?"

"Not my field," Juanita answers. "But let's take a sample."

She is closest, and deftly dips a sample capsule into the liquid. Nothing emerges to bite her hand off—so much for that fantasy. I might not have had the nerve. Then I have a moment of insight; to do this requires the right balance of imagination and nerve.

"I do not think," Eloni offers, "that there would be enough energy for life. If there were, the liquid would boil away. Hydrocarbons at these temperatures would be frozen solid, so what could one use to build life molecules? How could anything that would work at these temperatures get here without being destroyed by the Sun first? Still, it is an interesting thought, Wojciech."

"If the crack could go down a hundred kilometers or so," Juanita remarks, "it would be warm enough to evaporate everything, possibly warm enough to walk around with the right atmosphere. But Mercury would close a crack that deep; its crust is surprisingly thin, even now. This is not Mars."

She sounds like my fifth-year teacher back in Krakow. I suddenly feel far, far over my head. These people understand where they are and what they are doing: it holds no terror for them, no fear of sticking a hand where it might not come back. But for me, my overripe literary imagination haunts my mind like the tale of the bogeyman that kept me out of grandfather's basement until I was seven. I am not comfortable here—but, I tell myself, I will enjoy having been here *more* when, and if—always if—we get back.

"It's time to go back," Juanita says, her vials filled. "Climbing."

"Climbing," we all say.

"Belay on," Dr. Lotati says, from far above us.

The climb back up to the bridge is slow. Once we hit the layered material, we stop to take half-meter cores, drilled slantwise, at those layers which Juanita estimates to have been laid down during the great events of the inner Solar System: layers that may contain glass beads from the Imbrium impact on Luna, Caloris here, Hellas on Mars, and, just possibly, a few grains with the right isotope ratios to be from the K-T impact on Earth. If we find these, we can bring the geological history of the planets together. If, the paradigm goes, we understand better why the Solar System is the way it is, we will understand better why we are the way we are—the forces that have shaped our evolution and those of other sentient races. But we won't know if the samples contain what we suspect for many months, by which time we will have scattered to the nether ends of the Solar System.

We are tired and bruises remind us of yesterday's avalanche with each bump, but there is a sense of elation about us. We are the first people to see a pool of liquid on an alien planet in its natural state. And no machine saw it first.

When we arrive back at the ice bridge, Juanita sees me staring nervously at the slide.

"I've calculated the slope and the coefficient of friction, Wojciech—I think it's fully relaxed. It may stay that way for a billion years."

"Now you tell me!" But would the trip have been as thrilling if she had? "What caused it to go in the first place?"

"Our weight, I think, plus an accumulation of stresses. I'm beginning to think the crevasse is fairly young—otherwise a meteor impact would have caused the slump before we did."

"There could be more than physical tension," Eloni says. "Near the surface, over many years, radiation will cause chemical changes and produce unstable molecules in crystalline ice. A physical shock, such as an ax, might release these energies."

"Possibly," Juanita says.

I look down at the ice bridge under me. If the crevasse is fairly recent, this would be even more recent—and not, I hope, have had time to accumulate radiation "energies."

We are physically tired but the midday nap and the feeling of accomplishment leave us too hyper to sleep immediately. After rations, I suggest the idea that had led me to join their expedition in the first place.

"Randi?" I ask. "Dr. Lotati?"

They turn their heads to me.

"Are you aware of the theories of a Dr. Nikhil Ray?"

Dr. Lotati purses his lips as if he had something to say, then thought better of it.

Juanita answers. "He tries to explain the low density of Miranda and some other outer satellites, by making them a sponge of caverns. It is an innovative idea, but, I'm afraid, not well accepted."

Dr. Lotati grunts. "I've met the man. His theories are unorthodox and he has this infuriatingly superior manner about him. . . . Well, we'll know soon enough anyway. The IPA is finally getting around to dropping sonography stations on the major Uranian satellites."

As "free" robot-produced resources grew exponentially, so did the Interplanetary Association's influence on who goes where and does what. The IPA, whose main members are the United Nations of Earth, the Mars Council, and the Cislunar Republic, responds, in large measure, to politicians. They in turn respond to the media and the public—I am counting on this.

"I was," I venture, "thinking that it might be time to visit Miranda—and that, with the coincidence in their names, Randi might be the one to do it. It would certainly be an interesting angle. Especially if Dr. Ray could be persuaded to come."

Dr. Lotati frowns. "That would be rather commercial, wouldn't it?" Ed contributes with a wink in my direction. He is not taking this too seriously.

"Finish school," Randi says, "do some low g work in the asteroids, Saturn, then maybe." She grins at me. "My world. Caves?"

"There are certainly caves there," Juanita says with a grin, "but if they are big ones, you might be sorry about taking Nikhil. He's already insufferable with the issue in doubt. God help us if he's right!"

Dr. Lotati and Ed laugh heartily. Randi shrugs, and a flicker of pain crosses her face at the gesture. The shoulder hurts more than she wants us to know, I suspect.

"You can make too much of that," Ed says. "He's not a monster, Juanita. He can be very much the gentleman, and his conversation is always interesting. I sometimes wonder if the personality conflicts don't have more to do with his peer review problems than the merits of his work."

Dr. Lotati turns and tugs on his beard. "Uranus is the frontier," he finally says. "There's only one small inhabited scientific station in the Uranus system, in its outer satellite, Mustardseed. Within the Uranian magnetosphere, radiation is a concern." He stares briefly at me, then Randi. "Also, I don't want to associate the Society with Ray's claims just yet. Let's see what happens with the seismic study. And let's see how well Wojciech's presentation of this expedition is received."

I glance at Randi. She stares back at me, intently, and the ghost of a smile crosses her face as she wrinkles her nose.

"I could use a shower," I say—humorously. There will be no showers for several days yet.

But Randi hands me a silver foil wrapper. Her nose has decided that it's bath time—understandable in view of our exertions. The foil contains a light towelette soaked in a cleaning solution that does not have to be rinsed. She offers them to the others, removes her coveralls, and then releases the seam of her vacuum suit. Her father turns his back to us and, facing the wall of the tent, does the same. Eloni also turns to the wall of the tent. Ed watches Randi, and they exchange a brief smile.

We are a cross section of the Solar System, and a cross section of attitudes about our bodies. I still feel a slight twinge, as if in nostalgia for an old cultural taboo, but the observer of people in me rejoices in the passing of taboos. Ed, surprisingly, seems the one uncomfortable with communal bathing.

Juanita, whose family left Earth a century ago, is already sponging, oblivious to anything else. She is a well-endowed woman in excellent condition, as is everyone on this kind of endeavor. Her hair, unbound, hangs to her shoulders. It is almost all white and makes her skin look darker than it is in contrast. Her only other concessions to her fifty standard years are a slight gut and a bit of looseness on her neck and under her arms.

Randi is still watching Ed watch her, as if she enjoys it. She is a rangy young woman of jet-black hair and well defined, though not exaggerated muscles. Her female features seem like the afterthoughts of a god who in making an athlete decided at the last minute to make a woman, too. There is an intriguing hardness about the rest of her, including an untouched scar on her side. But her face, her smile, and her manner are womanly.

Embarrassed at myself for staring, I turn around like Dr. Lotati and finish undressing—applying the cleaning cloth to my body. But I love women too much to resist another look. When I do, both Eloni and Juanita are looking at me. Our eyes meet, we smile and I relax. My feelings as they watch me bathe are hard to describe—would it make sense to say that I felt first forgiven? I feel something of a sense of camaraderie.

Then Eloni reaches with both hands and turns me to the side of the tent. Its drum-tight bulge instantly reminds me of the vacuum, just beyond that milli-meter of tough, impervious fabric.

I feel a damp cloth on my back, up and down, hitting every needful spot. When she is done, I return the favor. She sighs just on the edge of audibility. Almost like a purr.

I feel suddenly very good, and useful—should poetry and nature writing fail me completely, I could do this for a living. Well, maybe.

Dr. Lotati turns to crawl into his sleeping bag, and I accidentally get a brief glimpse of injuries he has chosen not to show the rest of us. Gunshot wounds? Before he can seal the side, Juanita touches his shoulder and crawls in with him.

Eloni turns from the wall then and sees Randi and me, not yet in our sleeping bags. She looks down, then looks up again, then crawls into her sleeping bag. I can't read the expression on her face.

I get into my bag, pull my suit and helmet in with me, and seal the hood behind me. Its flaps will close and hold pressure if there is an accident while I sleep.

"Lights off," Randi says, and the tent complies. It is utterly, totally dark. There is movement. As my eyes adapt, I glance in her direction, but her sleeping bag is empty. She is probably not sleeping with Eloni, which leaves Ed. I feel a twinge of jealousy, though I know Ed has known the Lotatis for many years, and gone on several expeditions with them.

The exhaustion of this day does not permit sexual regrets, however. It seems like only a moment, and then I awake to light, discussions about the ascent, and the smell of freshly opened breakfast bars. The discussion is between Ed and Emilio, and it concerns who is to go up the wall with Randi, to set the ropes for the rest of us.

"We need to make time," Dr. Lotati says.

"All the more reason for you to go with Randi. You're a team."

"Thank you, friend, but I am sixty-two years old and you are thirty-eight. You and Randi climb well together." There is a slight hint of humor in Emilio's voice to suggest to my perhaps oversensitive mind that he knows they do more than climb well together.

"It's only a kilometer, mate. You're as good as ever."

"I'll second that," Juanita says.

Dr. Lotati smiles and shakes his head. "The group comes first."

Randi embraces her father, wordlessly, but I can see her eyes glisten. Then Dr. Lotati reaches over to Ed and they grasp hands.

Something has passed, I realize, and who am I to witness such a passing? More than ever, I feel an ambitious interloper. I look over at Eloni. She is looking at me. Wistfully? I smile back.

We pack quickly and efficiently, filling the soft pressure packs first with the things that can stand vacuum, then the hard ones. When the tent is bare, the last pack is sealed and we take it down to a tenth of an atmosphere. We check each other's seals and fit. Randi frowns at mine, and has me depressurize to readjust my fit. If the pressure were much lower, I think, my blood would boil. We normally breathe a fifty-fifty oxygen-nitrogen mix at four-tenths atmosphere, so I still have a quarter of Earth normal oxygen partial pressure. I try not to get excited.

Randi treats this like an everyday event. She tugs, pulls, and smooths all my joint areas. She is utterly clinical about this, but happens to glance up with a wink when she adjusts my leg seams. "It's all in the family," her look seems to say.

I find myself slipping as if to an event horizon. Do I want to befriend this woman to pursue fame and fortune on her distant namesake moon, or has my idea for an expedition to the moon become an excuse to be near the woman? I suddenly realize that I am very, very taken by her.

She reseals my suit and I tell it to bring its pressure up again. She has indeed worked wonders, and I am much more comfortable than I was the day before. She apparently likes what she sees, grins, and squeezes my arm, then turns to the business at hand.

The tent finishes taking itself down to near vacuum. When the sides are noticeably softer, we open the main seal, and the tent ripples as the remaining millibar or so of air escapes. We turn our helmet lights on and emerge into the crevasse again.

The wall is suddenly lit with flood-lights—Mike and Karen have seen us emerge. It is one kilometer of gray-banded dirty clathrate, vertical, except for the parts that are more than vertical.

Randi leads; if she falls, she is less weight on the bolts and pitons that hold our ropes.

"This stuff is like soft sandstone," Ed says. "I can almost push a piton in by hand, here and there."

"Use more," Randi says. "Angle down."

"OK." He is silent for a while. "There. I suggest we do this before I lose my nerve. Belay on."

"Climbing," Randi answers. They proceed upward carefully but steadily, taking turns.

I happen to be looking up when it happens. Randi is climbing when her foothold crumbles. She grabs for a line, says, "Damn!" then, "Falling." Her effort to grab has pushed her out from the wall, and when the rope goes taut, one of the pitons pops out of the wall with a shower of dust and ice. After a brief hesitation, the other two follow, and Ed yells, "Slack!"

Desperately, Randi tries to slow her fall by digging her hands and crampons into the wall beside her, throwing up a wake of dust. The smoothness of the wall helps; it is not completely vertical, and there are no bumps to throw her out.

The next set of pitons catches her rope, and for half a second it looks like it might hold. But before she comes to a complete halt, they pull out too and she starts to slide down again. Now, only Ed's own precarious hold on the wall stands between them and a five hundred-meter fall. He is furiously trying to hammer in more pitons, but there is little rope left between him and Randi.

They need another secure line. Why, with six other more experienced explorers present, I am the one to think of something is a mystery. Perhaps it has something to do with creativity, or with not having a mind full of the knowledge of things that wouldn't work.

"Mike, Wojciech. Can you fire a rocket line right into the wall above them? It ought to penetrate that stuff and anchor itself."

He doesn't take time to answer me. There is a flash from overhead and an impact ten meters above Ed. The line it carries is much thinner than climbing rope, but drapes down beside them quickly in the vacuum. It continues to play out, draping all the way down to our little camp.

The line between Randi and Ed snaps tight, and his foot and arm come free in a shower of ice. He should hit the release, I think. Better one death than two, but he tries to hold on to the wall. He doesn't dare let go and reach for the new, untested line, hanging less than a meter away.

It almost works. Randi, caught short, manages to reach her ax and digs into the wall like a desperate fly. Working with her right hand, she sets one piton and then another, hammering them in with her fist.

Above her, the rest of the ice holding Ed begins to give way as he tries to regain his handhold. "Can't hold, falling!" He flails for the new line as he starts to slip, but it is out of reach.

They, would, I think, be dead on Earth—but Mercury gravity is more forgiving. Working as Ed slides, Randi reaches the new line and yanks hard on it. She yanks hard again—it must not have been firmly set. Another hard pull and she seems satisfied. Ed slides down beside her in a plume of dust and ice, barely in contact with the wall.

Quickly Randi connects the new line to the line that still connects them, slack now, and loops it around the piton she has just set. "Protection in!"

Thirty meters below her, Ed bounces as the line pulls taut and pops the piton out of the wall in another shower of debris. Ed's weight pulls Randi free of her holds as well.

They both slide another ten meters, but now the slack in the line from the rocket has been taken up. They slide some more as it stretches, then, finally, stop. All told, Randi has fallen about a hundred meters and Ed perhaps fifty.

"Jupiter!" Karen, on the crevasse rim, exclaims. "Randi, Ed, set yourselves if you can. I can see the rocket: it's wedged itself vertically in the hole it made when it hit the wall, only about ten centimeters from the face. Try to hold tight while we think of something."

"OK," Ed says. "But don't take too long. I think I'm about at the end of my rope about this."

The laughter, fueled by relief, is perhaps a little too loud for the quality of the pun. Ed quickly starts hammering in additional protection. Randi, however, is simply hanging passively in her harness.

"Randi?" Mike calls.

"Injured. Both arms." Her voice attempts calm, but I can hear the pain in it.

"Can you climb?" Mike asks.

Randi tries to lift an arm up to her rope and gasps. "Not now."

"Descending," Ed says. "I'd like another belay if you can think of something."

What we think of is setting our remaining line rocket for maximum range and steering it about six meters under the far edge of the crevasse. It slams in hard, burying itself too far in for Karen to see. "Ice," Mike says, instantly, as a patch of icy regolith loosened by the rocket impact snows down left of the climbers. The upper layers, as we know, are softer. They pull the line from the far edge until it sets hard—ten kilonewtons tension, Mike estimates. Then they let the line drape down to us, and we walk it over to where Ed can reach it.

He connects the lines, and continues down.

Randi tries to descend. We hear the slightest hint of a cry of pain over the radio, then a loud "Damn! Dad, I can't lift my hands over my shoulders. Both shoulders shot."

"That's all right, Randi, I'm coming." Dr. Lotati turns and looks at me. "Come on, Wojciech. I want your head on that wall."

Juanita gives me a pat on the rear, and surprisingly, Eloni gives me a silent hug. Inside her visor, her dark eyes are glistening. I think of how frightened the Kenyan student must be, but she has just contributed in the only way she could think of.

"Thanks, team," I say, and squeeze her hand.

I clip my ascent ratchet on and start climbing. There are no problems and we reach Randi and Ed in half an hour.

Randi is calm. "Right arm. Won't go above shoulder. Maybe dislocated. Left arm works, sort of. But hurts too much. Might faint. OK as long as I keep my hands down."

"I'll take you down, papoose-style," Ed offers. "Then we'll ride the elevator up."

Dr. Lotati touches Randi. "OK?"

"I'll make it, Dad."

"Good, Wojciech and I will go up then, and set the anchor," Dr. Lotati decides. His voice crackles with leadership and confidence. I smile. Everyone, including him, has forgotten about his age. It won't be obvious on this climb; if anything, I will slow *him* down.

We replace Ed's backpack with Randi, tying her to his shoulder harness, and help guide them down. When they are safe below, Dr. Lotati nods to me, and says, "We have to consider everything we put into this surface to be hazardous, no?"

I nod. We are leaning out from a wall almost half a kilometer above a bridge about half a kilometer above a pool of cryogenic nitrogen trifluoride, talking about how the various things that hold our ropes to said wall may give way at any time.

"OK. We use four pitons, or bolts, or a combination, on each belay, and arrange the ropes like so." He demonstrates, creating what looks at first glance to be a cat's cradle of ropes between carabiners and pitons. "This equalizes forces among the pitons and minimizes the shock if one lets go."

It takes me a couple of tries to get it right. He finally pats me on the shoulder, and without further ado says, "Climbing."

"On belay," I answer, wondering about people who seem to come alive only when staring death in the face. He ascends deliberately, and deceptively fast.

Actually, I keep up, but exhaust myself in the process. Dr. Lotati is only a centimeter or two taller than his daughter, and hardly much heavier. He is wiry strong; occasional rest stops are the only concession he makes to age—and I need them more than he does. We stop where the second line-bearing rocket buried itself in the fragile clathrate, six meters below the crater floor. The ledge is overhung by about a meter, more where the rocket impact dislodged a large hunk of wall.

"Can you stand a short fall?" he asks me. "I think we'll need several tries to get around that edge." I've never fallen on a belay line before. I want to impress Emilio; my Mirandas, moon and woman, are at stake. But the idea of trying to scramble almost upside down and free-falling six to ten meters, with only a questionable anchor to stop me if I slip, scares the crap out me. If there were any other way . . .

"Wojciech?"

"Yes." Then, perhaps because my mind works best in an emergency, or under a deadline, the idea comes to me. "Dr. Lotati—this is fairly soft stuff. You don't suppose we could just tunnel through it, up to the surface?"

He looks down at me. "Perhaps! I wouldn't consider desecrating an Earth climb like that, but I think we will be forgiven here. I knew your head would be good for something!" Then he takes an ax from his belt and swings it into the ice overhead. A good sized hunk falls and shatters into tiny chips on my helmet.

"Ice!" He looks at his handiwork, says, "Sì," and swings again, and again, cutting a notch more than a tunnel as it turns out. We are through and up to the crater floor in less than an hour.

There is a round of cheers when we say, "On top!" Mike and Karen wave from the other side of the crevasse—only a hundred meters away. It has taken us two days to go that hundred meters.

I help set the next set of anchors a hundred meters back from the edge, in firm regolith. The rest is ropes, ascenders and pulleys. Mike and Karen send the remaining gear, and themselves, across in an ersatz tram, and help us hoist the rest of the party. Juanita is the last one to emerge from the crevasse and we all cheer, intoxicated with our close call and our final victory. By the time everything is up or over, we have been awake for thirty hours. Dr. Lotati decides to set up camp immediately.

We have four two-person tents in addition to the large one. They can be independent or their entrances can be sealed to connecting ports in the large tent, forming a mini-base looking something like an inflated starfish minus an arm. That way, early risers can let others sleep.

Randi's left shoulder is bad—a possible separation—and we have at least three days' march ahead of us to our pickup point. We discuss an evacuation, but she won't hear of it. Mike and Ed both have field medical training but Mike has more practice, so he is the closest thing to a doctor we have, and he consults with Earth. It turns out that our optical scattering imager is good enough to build up a picture of the injury; Randi's humerus is not quite in its socket.

Earth recommends evacuation. Randi says no. Dr. Lotati supports her—we are in an age where injuries can be healed if they can be endured, but the opportunities to do something more significant than entertain oneself and collect one's automation stipend are few and far between.

Randi, Ed told me several nights ago, is Dr. Lotati's only son. I laughed and asked Ed what that made him. "The gayest man on Mercury," he answered— and threw such a convincing leer at me that it took me an unsettling second to get the joke. But the humor disguises a poignant situation—a young woman trying to be, for her father, the son he could never have. How much was from her nature, how much was from her love? Or was there a difference? And what of her mother? Randi's mother was never mentioned by anyone, and the only public biographical info was that Emilio had divorced her when Randi was six and never married again.

Following instructions from the doctors on Earth, Mike resets the shoulder. It takes him two tries. Randi shuts her eyes and gasps—that is all. Then it is in. Painkillers, anti-inflammatory drugs, and reconstructive stimulants we have— she will be sore, but as good as new in a few months. Climbing is out, but she can walk the rest of the way.

Ed and Randi retire together, her arm immobilized to her body with tape.

Juanita decides to sleep with Emilio. Mike and Karen are a given.

Eloni is looking at me with dark pools of eyes and what could be a hopeful smile on her face. I look at the shy graduate student who had given me a hug to send me up a treacherous wall that had just come within the width of an idea of killing two people. I shrug and reach a hand out to her and she comes and sits by me with the widest grin on her face I have ever seen.

"You wish I were Randi, don't you?" Eloni asks me.

"That's not your fault."

Her smile fades. "I almost got us all killed by being too slow. That was my fault."

There are times when sympathy can do things lust cannot. I have my arms around her in a second. "No one blames you. You're part of us, now. Time to enjoy it."

She kind of melts into me and gently pushes me down onto my back on my sleepsack. She has a low, incredibly sexy voice. "That is about as much as I can enjoy. I hope I do not disappoint you."

Tired as I am, I'm relieved; and confused. "Eloni, I write about the male and female thing, more from reading than experience, I'm afraid. I may sigh, but disappointment would be putting things a bit strong. But I'm curious. Do you believe in abstinence, and if so, can you tell me why?"

No contraception, I speculate? In this day, I find that hard to believe—but she is studying at Jovis Tholis on Mars, I remind myself, in the middle of the New Reformation.

A certain hardness comes over her face. "You want to know? I spoke literal truth. Abstinence has nothing to do with it. I was mutilated so I cannot enjoy what most women can enjoy. So I hike across glaciers and climb mountains instead," she smiles wryly. "That is how I get high. Try to understand. I am not Kenyan by birth. Kenya is a civilized nation."

I have it then. Female circumcision. Back on Earth, the villages all have nice premanufactured houses, with bathrooms, electricity, diagnostic comm ports, and regular food deliveries. But here and there, otherwise gentle people protect primitive cultures from "western interference," and so we still permit this to be done to children.

"How old were you?"

"Ten. They were very thorough. But in a few years, doctors will be able to fix it, I think. Regenerate the tissue that was taken from me. That's a spin-off from the interstellar project. They needed to solve tissue regeneration to do cold sleep reliably. For now, I must enjoy giving and being enjoyed while I fantasize what it might really be like."

What can one say? I take her hand and she squeezes it.

"Oh, yes." Her voice is low and throaty. "They mutilated me, they tried to keep me barefoot and stupid to carry on their primitive culture. They even tried to keep me from school. But they could not shut off my mind. And here I am, yes, here I am where they thought I could never go doing what they thought to keep from me forever. So I am a space person now, part of another tribe."

Eloni and I are both, I realize, refugees from cultures that do not want who we are. Hers a primitive one, mine too sophisticated to see itself. I only want to hold her, smother her hurt, and bring a smile to her face. I try to kiss her.

She holds me off. "Someday I have to go back there and try to change what the people do to each other there. I cannot be a space person forever. Do you understand?" She buries her face in my shoulder. "For now. Just for now."

I understand. This is for now—and whatever our feelings for each other now, our destinies lie in different directions. I nod and she is in my arms. Our lips touch again and the future vanishes. "What do you do want me to do?" I ask.

In answer, she releases the seal of my tight suit.

We remove each other's remaining clothes and slip into my sleep sack. She wriggles against me and we do kiss, and our hands do stroke and caress, and begin to defy the cold dead gray cruelty outside our bubble with yet another act of life.

But there really isn't very much room and we are both very tired. So, in each other's arms, we fall asleep, content with a mostly symbolic defiance.

The remaining walk toward the center of Chao Meng Fu is two by two, the time filled mostly with conversations that share what we are and what we know, but sometimes with those comfortable silences in which your mind digests what you have learned, playing this way and that with it. There are more crevasses to cross, but we do so expeditiously.

During one of these crossings, I say, "On belay, Dr. Lotati."

"Climbing. Wojciech, call me Emilio, it's quicker."

A small thing, but it suggests to me a future more interesting than correcting undergraduate papers.

Juanita suggests we share a piece of music for our final approach to the central depot. It is by a twentieth-century composer named Alan Hovhaness, a symphony called "City of Light." She says it is his symphony number twenty-two.

"Twenty-two?" I ask. "Did I hear you right? I know Haydn wrote over a hundred, but that was when they were short and highly formatted. Beethoven wrote only nine. Tchaikovsky, six. I thought they'd pretty much stopped doing symphonies by the twenty-first century."

Juanita laughed. "We geologists call Hovhaness our patron composer because he actually wrote a symphony about a volcano—and that was number *fifty*. By the mid-twenty-first century, they were calling him 'the American Haydn.' Now let's just listen."

As we approach the brilliant peaks of the Chao Meng Fu central crown—great massive round Sun-gilded domes that speak of power and eternity—I am incapable of understanding why I once thought of this expedition as a stunt. I feel like a piece of steel, bent, hammered, bent and hammered again in the fire with greater strength and balance than I have ever known before.

It is a feeling I want to have again, if I must pursue it to the ends of the Solar System. Perhaps I am not in a class with Ed Blake and perhaps any fantasies I had of a match with Randi must remain fantasies, but I have found in my own backyard a delicate and precious union with Eloni and a friend and colleague in Juanita. And I think I have succeeded in my main objective—I have, I think, the friendship and respect of the people who could bring me out to the frontier which calls my spirit.

As I walk I feel the voices of a more broad-shouldered century calling me; Stanley, Peary, Scott, Teddy Roosevelt, and among poets, of course, Kipling. As I trudge, I amuse myself with a doggerel: Perhaps those prudent people—

Who never risk the pit,
Also never know the joy
Of coming out of it.

Not prize material, perhaps, but sums my experience, and in my present state of deranged ecstasy, I am no critic!

And if my words fail you—as they fail many others of highly educated tastes— then listen to the finale of Hovhaness' symphony. For if you cannot understand after hearing *that*, you have left the human race. What I learned, in the crossing of Chao Meng Fu, was that such things still can be, in any age, for anyone who will do them.

yeyuka

GREG EGAN

Here's another intense and powerful story by Greg Egan, whose "Reasons to Be Cheerful" appears elsewhere in this anthology. In this one, he asks the question: No matter how well-intentioned you are, just how much are you really willing to sacrifice in order to help those who really need it? Are you sure?

On my last day in Sydney, as a kind of farewell, I spent the morning on Bondi Beach. I swam for an hour, then lay on the sand and stared at the sky. I dozed off for a while, and when I woke there were half a dozen booths set up among the sun-bathers, dispensing the latest fashion: solar tattoos. On a touch-screen the size of a full-length mirror you could choose a design and customize it or create one from scratch with software assistance. Computer-controlled jets sprayed the undeveloped pigments onto your skin, then an hour of UV exposure brought out the colours.

As the morning wore on, I saw giant yellow butterflies perched between shoulder blades, torsos wrapped in green-and-violet dragons, whole bodies wreathed in chains of red hibiscus. Watching these images materialize around me, I couldn't help thinking of them as banners of victory. Throughout my childhood, there'd been nothing more terrifying than the threat of melanoma, and by the turn of the millennium, nothing more hip than neck-to-knee lycra. Twenty years later, these elaborate decorations were designed to encourage, *to boast of,* irradiation. To proclaim, not that the sun itself had been tamed, but that our bodies had. To declare that cancer had been defeated.

I touched the ring on my left index finger and felt a reassuring pulse. Blood flowed constantly around the hollow core of the device, diverted from a vein in my finger. The ring's inner surface was covered with billions of tiny sensors, spring-loaded, funnel-shaped structures like microscopic Venus fly-traps, each just a few hundred atoms wide. Every sizeable molecule in my bloodstream that collided with one of these traps was seized, shrink-wrapped and held long enough to determine its shape and chemical identity before it was released.

So the ring knew exactly what was in my blood. It also knew what belonged and what didn't. Under its relentless scrutiny, the biochemical signature of a viral or bacterial infection, or even a microscopic tumour far downstream, could never escape detection for long—and once a diagnosis was made, treatment was almost instantaneous. Planted alongside the sensors were programmable catalysts, versatile molecules that could be reshaped under computer control. The ring could manufacture a wide range of drugs from raw materials circulating in the blood, just by choosing the right sequence of shapes for these catalysts—trapping the necessary ingredients together in nooks and crannies moulded to fit like plaster casts around their combined outlines.

With medication delivered within minutes or seconds, infections were wiped out before they could take hold, tiny clusters of cancer cells destroyed before they could grow or spread. Linked by satellite to a vast array of medical databases, and as much additional computing power as it required, the ring gave me a kind of electronic immune system, fast enough and smart enough to overcome any adversary.

Not everyone on the beach that morning would have had their own personal HealthGuard, but a weekly session on a shared family unit or even a monthly check-up at the local GP would have been enough to reduce their risk of cancer dramatically. And though melanoma was the least of my worries (fair-skinned, I was covered in sunscreen as usual; fatal or not, getting burnt was painful) with the ring standing guard against ten thousand other possibilities, I'd come to think of it as a vital part of my body. The day I'd installed it my life expectancy had risen by fifteen years. And no doubt my bank's risk-assessment software had assumed a similar extension to my working life, since I'd be paying off the loan I'd needed to buy the thing well into my sixties.

I tugged gently at the plain metal band, until I felt a sharp warning from the needle-thin tubes that ran deep into the flesh. This model wasn't designed to be slipped on and off in an instant like the shared units, but it would only take a five-minute surgical procedure under local anaesthetic to remove it. In Uganda, a single HealthGuard machine served 40 million people—or rather, the lucky few who could get access to it. Flying in wearing my own personal version seemed almost as crass as arriving with a giant solar tattoo. Where I was headed, cancer had very definitely not been defeated.

Nor had malaria, typhoid, yellow fever, schistosomiasis. I could have the ring immunize me against all of these and more, before removing it. But the malaria parasite was notoriously variable, so constant surveillance would provide far more reliable protection. I'd be no use to anyone lying in a hospital bed for half my stay. Besides, the average villager or shanty-town dweller probably wouldn't even recognize the thing, let alone resent it. I was being hypersensitive.

I gathered up my things and headed for the cycle rack. Looking back across the sand, I felt the kind of stab of regret that came upon waking from a dream of impossible good fortune and serenity, and for a moment I wanted nothing more than to close my eyes and rejoin it.

Lisa saw me off at the airport.

I said "It's only three months. It'll fly past." I was reassuring myself, not her.

"It's not too late to change your mind." She smiled calmly; no pressure, it was entirely my decision. In her eyes, I was clearly suffering from some kind of disease—a very late surge of adolescent idealism, or a very early mid-life crisis—but she'd adopted a scrupulously nonjudgmental bedside manner. It drove me mad.

"And miss my last chance ever to perform cancer surgery?" That was a slight exaggeration; a few cases would keep slipping through the HealthGuard net for years. Most of my usual work was trauma, though, which was going through changes of its own. Computerized safeguards had made traffic accidents rare, and I suspected that within a decade no one would get the chance to stick their hand in a conveyor belt again. If the steady stream of gunshot and knife wounds ever dried up, I'd have to retrain for nose jobs and reconstructing rugby players. "I should have gone into obstetrics, like you."

Lisa shook her head. "In the next twenty years, they'll crack all the molecular signals, within and between mother and foetus. There'll be no premature births, no Caesarians, no complications. The HealthGuard will smooth my job away, too." She added, deadpan, "Face it, Martin, we're all doomed to obsolescence."

"Maybe. But if we are . . . it'll happen sooner in some places than others."

"And when the time comes, you might just head off to some place where you're still needed?"

She was mocking me, but I took the question seriously. "Ask me that when I get back. Three months without mod cons and I might be cured for life."

My flight was called. We kissed goodbye. I suddenly realized that I had no idea why I was doing this. The health of distant strangers? Who was I kidding? Maybe I'd been trying to fool myself into believing that I really was that self-less—hoping all the while that Lisa would talk me out of it, offering some face-saving excuse for me to stay. I should have known she'd call my bluff instead.

I said plainly "I'm going to miss you. Badly."

"I should hope so."

She took my hand, scowling, finally accepting the decision. "You're an idiot, you know. Be careful."

"I will." I kissed her again, then slipped away.

I was met at Entebbe airport by Magdalena Iganga, one of the oncologists on a small team put together by Médécins sans Frontières to help overburdened Ugandan doctors tackle the growing number of Yeyuka cases. Iganga was Tanzanian, but she'd worked throughout eastern Africa, and as she drove her battered, ethanol-powered car the thirty kilometres into Kampala, she recounted some of her brushes with the World Health Organization in Nairobi.

"I tried to persuade them to set up an epidemiological database for Yeyuka. Good idea, they said. Just put a detailed proposal to the cancer epidemiology expert committee. So I did. And the committee said, we like your proposal, but oh dear, Yeyuka is a contagious disease, so you'll have to submit this to the contagious diseases expert committee instead—whose last annual sitting I'd just missed by a week." Iganga sighed stoically. "Some colleagues and I ended up doing it ourselves on an old 386 and a borrowed phone line."

"Three eight what?"

She shook her head. "Palaeocomputing jargon, never mind."

Though we were dead on the equator and it was almost noon, the temperature must have been 30 at most; Kampala was high above sea level. A humid breeze blew off Lake Victoria, and low clouds rolled by, gathering threateningly and then dissipating, again and again. I'd been promised that it would be the dry season; at worst there'd be occasional thunderstorms.

On our left, between patches of marshland, small clusters of shacks began to appear. As we drew closer to the city, we passed through rings of shanty towns, the older and more organized verging on a kind of bedraggled suburbia, others looking more like out-and-out refugee camps. The tumours caused by the Yeyuka virus tended to spread fast but grow slowly, often partially disabling people for years before killing them, and when they could no longer manage heavy, rural labour they usually headed for the nearest city in the hope of finding work. Southern Uganda had barely recovered from HIV when Yeyuka cases began to appear around 2013; in fact, some virologists believed that Yeyuka had arisen from a less virulent ancestor after gaining a foothold within the immune-suppressed population. And though Yeyuka wasn't as contagious as cholera or tuberculosis, crowded conditions, poor sanitation and chronic malnutrition set up the shanty towns to bear the brunt of the epidemic.

As we drove north between two hills, the centre of Kampala appeared ahead of us, draped across a hill of its own. Compared with Nairobi, which I'd flown over a few hours before, Kampala looked uncluttered. The streets and low buildings were laid out in a widely spaced plan, neatly organized but lacking any rigid geometry of grid lines or concentric circles. There was plenty of traffic around us, both cycles and cars, but it flowed smoothly enough and for all the honking and shouting going on the drivers seemed remarkably good-humoured.

Iganga took a detour to the east, skirting the central hill. There were lush, green sports grounds and golf courses on our right, colonial-era public buildings and high-fenced foreign embassies on our left. There were no high-rise slums in sight, but there were makeshift shelters and even vegetable gardens on some stretches of parkland, traces of the shanty towns spreading inwards.

In my jet-lagged state, it was amazing to find that this abstract place I'd been imagining for months had solid ground, actual buildings, real people. Most of my second-hand glimpses of Uganda had come from news clips set in war zones and disaster areas; from Sydney, it had been almost impossible to conceive of the country as anything more than a frantically edited video sequence full of soldiers, refugees and fly-blown corpses. In fact, rebel activity was confined to a shrinking zone in the country's far north, most of the last wave of Zairean refugees had gone home a year ago, and while Yeyuka was a serious problem, people weren't exactly dropping dead in the streets.

Makerere University was in the north of the city; Iganga and I were both staying at the guest-house there. A student showed me to my room, which was plain but spotlessly clean; I was almost afraid to sit on the bed and rumple the sheets. After washing and unpacking, I met up with Iganga again and we walked across the campus to Mulago Hospital, which was affiliated with the university medical school. There was a soccer team practising across the road as we went in, a reassuringly mundane sight.

Iganga introduced me to nurses and porters left and right; everyone was busy but friendly, and I struggled to memorize the barrage of names. The wards were all crowded, with patients spilling into the corridors, a few in beds but most on mattresses or blankets. The building itself was dilapidated and some of the equipment must have been thirty years old, but there was nothing squalid about the conditions; all the linen was clean, and the floor looked like you could do surgery on it.

In the Yeyuka ward, Iganga showed me the six patients I'd be operating on the next day. The hospital did have a CAT scanner, but it had been broken for the past six months, waiting for money for replacement parts, so flat X-rays with cheap contrast agents like barium were the most I could hope for. For some tumours, the only guide to location and extent was plain old palpation. Iganga guided my hands, and kept me from applying too much pressure; she'd had a great deal more experience at this than I had, and an overzealous beginner could do a lot of damage. The world of three-dimensional images spinning on my workstation while the software advised on the ideal incision had receded into fantasy. Stubbornly, though, I did the job myself, gently mapping the tumours by touch, picturing them in my head, marking the X-rays or making sketches.

I explained to each patient where I'd be cutting, what I'd remove, and what the likely effects would be. Where necessary, Iganga translated for me—either into Swahili or what she described as her "broken Luganda". The news was always only half good, but most people seemed to take it with a kind of weary optimism. Surgery was rarely a cure for Yeyuka, usually just offering a few years' respite, but it was currently the only option. Radiation and chemotherapy were useless, and the hospital's sole HealthGuard machine couldn't generate custom-made molecular cures; seven years into the epidemic Yeyuka wasn't yet well enough understood for anyone to have written the necessary software.

By the time I was finished it was dark outside. Iganga asked "Do you want to look in on Ann's last operation?" Ann Collins was the Irish volunteer I was replacing.

"Definitely." I'd watched a few operations performed here on video back in Sydney, but no VR scenarios had been available for proper "hands on" rehearsals, and Collins would only be around to supervise me for a few more days. It was a painful irony: foreign surgeons were always going to be inexperienced, but no one else had so much time on their hands. Ugandan medical students had to pay a small fortune in fees—the World Bank had put an end to the new government's brief flirtation with state-subsidized training—and it looked like there'd be a shortage of qualified specialists for at least another decade.

We donned masks and gowns. The operating theatre was like everything else, clean but outdated. Iganga introduced me to Collins, the anaesthetist Eriya Okwera and the trainee surgeon Balaki Masika.

The patient, a middle-aged man, was covered in orange Betadine-soaked surgical drapes, arranged around a long abdominal incision. I stood beside Collins and watched, entranced. Growing within the muscular wall of the small intestine was a grey mass the size of my fist, distending the organ's translucent skin almost to bursting point. It would certainly have been blocking the passage of food; the patient must have been on liquids for months.

The tumour was very loose, almost like a giant discoloured blood clot; the hardest thing would be to avoid dislodging any cancerous cells in the process of removing it, sending them back into circulation to seed another tumour. Before making a single cut in the intestinal wall, Collins used a laser to cauterize all the blood vessels around the growth, and she didn't lay a finger on the tumour itself at any time. Once it was free, she lifted it away with clamps attached to the surrounding tissue, as fastidiously as if she was removing a leaky bag full of some fatal poison. Maybe other tumours were already growing unseen in other parts of the body, but doing the best possible job, here and now, might still add three or four years to this man's life.

Masika began stitching the severed ends of the intestine together. Collins led me aside and showed me the patient's X-rays on a lightbox. "This is the site of origin." There was a cavity clearly visible in the right lung, about half the size of the tumour she'd just removed. Ordinary cancers grew in a single location first, and then a few mutant cells in the primary tumour escaped to seed growths in the rest of the body. With Yeyuka there were no "primary tumours"; the virus itself uprooted the cells it infected, breaking down the normal molecular adhesives that kept them in place, until the infected organ seemed to be melting away. That was the origin of the name: *yeyuka*, to melt. Once set loose into the bloodstream, many of the cells died of natural causes, but a few ended up lodged in small capillaries—physically trapped, despite their lack of stickiness—where they could remain undisturbed long enough to grow into sizeable tumours.

After the operation, I was invited out to a welcoming dinner in a restaurant down in the city. The place specialized in Italian food, which was apparently hugely popular in Kampala. Iganga, Collins and Okwera, old colleagues by now, unwound noisily. Okwera, a solid man in his forties, grew mildly but volubly intoxicated and told medical horror stories from his time in the army. Masika, the trainee surgeon, was very softly spoken and reserved. I was something of a zombie from jet lag and didn't contribute much to the conversation, but the warm reception put me at ease.

I still felt like an impostor, here only because I hadn't had the courage to back out, but no-one was going to interrogate me about my motives. No one cared. It wouldn't make the slightest difference whether I'd volunteered out of genuine compassion or just a kind of moral insecurity brought on by fears of obsolescence. Either way, I'd brought a pair of hands and enough general surgical experience to be useful. If you'd ever had to be a saint to heal someone, medicine would have been doomed from the start.

I was nervous as I cut into my first Yeyuka patient, but by the end of the operation, with a growth the size of an orange successfully removed from the right lung, I felt much more confident. Later the same day, I was introduced to some of the hospital's permanent surgical staff—a reminder that even when Collins left, I'd hardly be working in isolation. I fell asleep on the second night exhausted but reassured. I could do this, it wasn't beyond me. I hadn't set myself an impossible task.

I drank too much at the farewell dinner for Collins, but the HealthGuard magicked the effects away. My first day solo was anticlimactic; everything went smoothly, and Okwera, with no high-tech hangover cure, was unusually subdued, while Masika was as quietly attentive as ever.

Six days a week the world shrank to my room, the campus, the ward, the operating theatre. I ate in the guest-house and usually fell asleep an hour or two after the evening meal; with the sun diving straight below the horizon, by eight o'clock it felt like midnight. I tried to call Lisa every night, though I often finished in the theatre too late to catch her before she left for work, and I hated leaving messages or talking to her while she was driving.

Okwera and his wife invited me to lunch the first Sunday, Masika and his girlfriend the next. Both couples were genuinely hospitable, but I felt that I was intruding on their one day together. The third Sunday, I met up with Iganga in a restaurant, then we wandered through the city on an impromptu tour.

There were some beautiful buildings in Kampala, many of them war-scarred but lovingly repaired. I tried to relax and take in the sights, but I kept thinking of the routine—six operations, six days a week—stretching out ahead of me until the end of my stay. When I mentioned this to Iganga, she laughed. "All right. You want something more than assembly-line work? I'll line up a trip to Mubende for you. They have patients there who are too sick to be moved. Multiple tumours, all nearly terminal."

"Okay." Me and my big mouth; I knew I hadn't been seeing the worst cases, but I hadn't given much thought to where they all were.

We were standing outside the Sikh temple, beside a plaque describing Idi Amin's expulsion of Uganda's Asian community in 1972. Kampala was dotted with memorials to atrocities, and though Amin's reign had ended more than forty years ago, it had been a long path back to normality. It seemed unjust beyond belief that even now, in an era of relative political stability, so many lives were being ruined by Yeyuka. No more refugees marching across the countryside, no more forced expulsions—but cells cast adrift could bring just as much suffering.

I asked Iganga, "So why did you go into medicine?"

"Family expectations. It was either that or the law. Medicine seemed less arbitrary; nothing in the body can be overturned by an appeal to the High Court. What about you?"

I said "I wanted to be in on the revolution. The one that was going to banish all disease."

"Ah, that one."

"I picked the wrong job, of course. I should have been a molecular biologist."

"Or a software engineer."

"Yeah. If I'd seen the HealthGuard coming fifteen years ago, I might have been right at the heart of the changes. And I'd never have looked back. Let alone sideways."

Iganga nodded sympathetically, quite unfazed by the notion that molecular technology might capture the attention so thoroughly that little things like Yeyuka epidemics would vanish from sight altogether. "I can imagine. Seven years ago, I was all set to make my fortune in one of the private clinics in Dar es Salaam. Rich businessmen with prostate cancer, that kind of thing. I was lucky in a way; before that market vanished completely, the Yeyuka fanatics were nagging me, bullying me, making little deals." She laughed. "I've lost count of the number of times I was promised I'd be coauthor of a ground-breaking paper in *Nature Oncology* if I just helped out at some field clinic in the middle of nowhere. I was dragged into this, kicking and screaming, just when all my old dreams were going up in smoke."

"But now Yeyuka feels like your true vocation?"

She rolled her eyes. "Spare me. My ambition now is to retire to a highly paid consulting position in Nairobi or Geneva."

"I'm not sure I believe you."

"You should." She shrugged. "Sure, what I'm doing now is a hundred times more useful than any desk job, but that doesn't make it any easier. You know as well as I do that the warm inner glow doesn't last for a thousand patients. If you fought for them all as if they were your own family or friends, you'd go insane . . . So, they become a series of clinical problems, which just happen to be wrapped in human flesh. And it's a struggle to keep working on the same problems over and over, even if you're convinced that it's the most worthwhile job in the world."

"So why are you in Kampala right now, instead of Nairobi or Geneva?"

Iganga smiled. "Don't worry, I'm working on it. I don't have a date on my ticket out of here like you do, but when the chance comes, believe me, I'll grab it just as fast as I can."

It wasn't until my sixth week, and my two-hundred-and-fourth operation, that I finally screwed up.

The patient was a teenaged girl with multiple infestations of colon cells in her liver. A substantial portion of the organ's left lobe would have to be removed, but her prognosis seemed relatively good; the right lobe appeared to be completely clean, and it was not beyond hope that the liver, directly downstream from the colon, had filtered all the infected cells from the blood before they could reach any other part of the body.

Trying to clamp the left branch of the portal vein, I slipped, and the clamp closed tightly on a swollen cyst at the base of the liver, full of grey-white colon cells. It didn't burst open, but it might have been better if it had. I couldn't see where the contents were squirted, but I could imagine the route very clearly: back as far as the Y-junction of the vein, where the blood flow would carry cancerous cells into the previously unaffected right lobe.

I swore for ten seconds, enraged by my own helplessness. I had none of the emergency tools I was used to: there was no drug I could inject to kill off the spilt cells while they were still more vulnerable than an established tumour, no vaccine on hand to stimulate the immune system into attacking them.

Okwera said "Tell the parents you found evidence of leakage, so she'll need to have regular follow-up examinations."

I glanced at Masika, but he was silent.

"I can't do that."

"You don't want to cause trouble."

"It was an accident!"

"Don't tell her, and don't tell her family." Okwera regarded me sternly, as if I was contemplating something both dangerous and self-indulgent. "It won't help anyone if you dive into the shit for this. Not her, not you. Not the hospital. Not the volunteer program."

The girl's mother spoke English. I told her there were signs that the cancer might have spread. She wept and thanked me for my good work.

Masika didn't say a word about the incident, but by the end of the day I could hardly bear to look at him. When Okwera departed, leaving the two of us alone in the locker room, I said "In three or four years there'll be a vaccine. Or even HealthGuard software. It won't be like this forever."

He shrugged, embarrassed. "Sure."

"I'll raise funds for the research when I get home. Champagne dinners with slides of photogenic patients, if that's what it takes." I knew I was making a fool of myself, but I couldn't shut up. "This isn't the nineteenth century. We're not helpless any more. Anything can be cured, once you understand it."

Masika eyed me dubiously, as if he was trying to decide whether or not to tell me to save my platitudes for the champagne dinners. Then he said "We do understand Yeyuka. We have HealthGuard software written for it, ready and waiting to go. But we can't run it on the machine here. So we don't need funds for research. What we need is another machine."

I was speechless for several seconds, trying to make sense of this extraordinary claim. "The hospital's machine is broken?"

Masika shook his head. "The software is unlicensed. If we used it on the hospital's machine, our agreement with HealthGuard would be void. We'd lose the use of the machine entirely."

I could hardly believe that the necessary research had been completed without a single publication, but I couldn't believe Masika would lie about it either. "How long can it take HealthGuard to approve the software? When was it submitted to them?"

Masika was beginning to look like he wished he'd kept his mouth shut, but there was no going back now. He admitted warily "It hasn't been submitted to them. It can't be—that's the whole problem. We need a bootleg machine, a decommissioned model with the satellite link disabled, so we can run the Yeyuka software without their knowledge."

"Why? Why can't they find out about it?"

He hesitated. "I don't know if I can tell you that."

"Is it illegal? Stolen?" But if it was stolen, why hadn't the rightful owners licensed the damned thing, so people could use it?

Masika replied icily, "Stolen *back*. The only part you could call 'stolen' was stolen back." He looked away for a moment, actually struggling for control. Then he said, "Are you sure you want to know the whole story?"

"Yes."

"Then I'll have to make a phone call."

Masika took me to what looked like a boarding house, student accommodation in one of the suburbs close to the campus. He walked briskly, giving me no time to ask questions, or even orient myself in the darkness. I had a feeling he would have liked to blindfold me, but it would hardly have made a difference; by the time we arrived I couldn't have said where we were to the nearest kilometre.

A young woman, maybe nineteen or twenty, opened the door. Masika didn't introduce us, but I assumed she was the person he'd phoned from the hospital, since she was clearly expecting us. She led us to a ground-floor room; someone was playing music upstairs, but there was no one else in sight.

In the room, there was a desk with an old-style keyboard and computer monitor, and an extraordinary device standing on the floor beside it: a rack of electronics the size of a chest of drawers, full of exposed circuit boards, all cooled by a fan half a metre wide.

"What is that?"

The woman grinned. "We modestly call it the Makerere supercomputer. Five hundred and twelve processors, working in parallel. Total cost, fifty thousand shillings."

That was about fifty dollars. "How—?"

"Recycling. Twenty or thirty years ago, the computer industry ran an elaborate scam: software companies wrote deliberately inefficient programs, to make people buy newer, faster computers all the time—then they made sure that the faster computers needed new software to work at all. People threw out perfectly good machines every three or four years, and though some ended up as landfill, millions were saved. There's been a worldwide market in discarded processors for years, and the slowest now cost about as much as buttons. But all it takes to get some real power out of them is a little ingenuity."

I stared at the wonderful contraption. "And you wrote the Yeyuka software on this?"

"Absolutely." She smiled proudly. "First, the software characterizes any damaged surface adhesion molecules it finds—there are always a few floating freely in the bloodstream, and their exact shape depends on the strain of Yeyuka, and the particular cells that have been infected. Then drugs are tailor-made to lock onto those damaged adhesion molecules and kill the infected cells by rupturing their membranes." As she spoke, she typed on the keyboard, summoning up animations to illustrate each stage of the process. "If we can get onto a real machine we'll be able to cure three people a day."

Cure. Not just cut them open to delay the inevitable.

"But where did all the raw data come from? The RNA sequencing, the X-ray diffraction studies . . . ?"

The woman's smile vanished. "An insider at HealthGuard found it in the company archives, and sent it to us over the Net."

"I don't understand. When did HealthGuard do Yeyuka studies? Why haven't they published them? Why haven't they written software themselves?"

She glanced uncertainly at Masika. He said "HealthGuard's parent company collected blood from five thousand people in southern Uganda in 2013, supposedly to follow up on the effectiveness of their HIV vaccine. What they actually wanted, though, was a large sample of metastasizing cells so they could perfect the biggest selling point of the HealthGuard: cancer protection. Yeyuka offered them the cheapest, simplest way to get the data they needed."

I'd been half expecting something like this since Masika's comments back in the hospital, but I was still shaken. To collect the data dishonestly was bad enough, but to bury information that was halfway to a cure, just to save paying for what they'd taken, was unspeakable.

I said "Sue the bastards! Get everyone who had samples taken together for a class action: royalties plus punitive damages. You'll raise hundreds of millions of dollars. Then you can buy as many machines as you want."

The woman laughed bitterly. "We have no proof. The files were sent anonymously, there's no way to authenticate their origin. And can you imagine how much HealthGuard would spend on their defence? We can't afford to waste the next twenty years in a legal battle just for the satisfaction of shouting the truth from the rooftops. The only way we can be sure of making use of this software is to get a bootleg machine and do everything in silence."

I stared at the screen, at the cure being played out in simulation that should have been happening three times a day in Mulago hospital. She was right, though. However hard it was to stomach, taking on HealthGuard directly would be futile.

Walking back across the campus with Masika, I kept thinking of the girl with the liver infestation, and the possibility of undoing the moment of clumsiness that would otherwise almost certainly kill her. I said "Maybe I can get hold of a bootleg machine in Shanghai. If I knew where to ask, where to look." They'd certainly be expensive, but they'd have to be much cheaper than a commissioned model, running without the usual software and support.

My hand moved almost unconsciously to check the metal pulse on my index finger. I held the ring up in the starlight. "I'd give you this, if it was mine to give. But that's thirty years away." Masika didn't reply, too polite to suggest that if I'd owned the ring outright I wouldn't even have raised the possibility.

We reached University Hall; I could find my way back to the guest-house now. But I couldn't face another six weeks of surgery unless I knew something was going to come of the night's revelations. I said "Look, I don't have connections to any black market, I don't have a clue how to go about getting a machine. But if you can find out what I have to do, and it's within my power . . . I'll do it."

Masika smiled, and nodded thanks, but I could tell that he didn't believe me. I wondered how many other people had made promises like this, then vanished back into the world-without-disease while the Yeyuka wards kept overflowing.

As he turned to go, I put a hand on his shoulder to stop him. "I mean it. Whatever it takes, I'll do it."

He met my eyes in the dark, trying to judge something deeper than this easy protestation of sincerity. I felt a sudden flicker of shame; I'd completely forgotten that I was an impostor, that I'd never really meant to come here, that two months ago a few words from Lisa would have seen me throw away my ticket, gratefully.

Masika said quietly "Then I'm sorry that I doubted you. And I'll take you at your word."

Mubende was a district capital, half a day's drive west of Kampala. Iganga delayed our promised trip to the Yeyuka clinic there until my last fortnight, and once I arrived I could understand why. It was everything I'd feared: starved of funds, understaffed and overcrowded. Patients' relatives were required to provide and wash the bedclothes, and half of them also seemed to be bringing in painkillers and other drugs bought at the local markets—some genuine, some rip-offs full of nothing but glucose or magnesium sulphate.

Most of the patients had four or five separate tumours. I treated two people a day, with operations lasting six to eight hours. In ten days, seven people died in front of me; dozens more died in the wards, waiting for surgery.

I shared a crowded room at the back of the clinic with Masika and Okwera, but even on the rare occasions when I caught Masika alone, he seemed reluctant to discuss the issue of a bootleg HealthGuard. He said "Right now, the less you know the better. When the time comes, I'll fill you in."

The ordeal of the patients was overwhelming, but I felt more for the clinic's sole doctor and two nurses; for them, it never ended. The morning we packed our equipment into the truck and headed back for Kampala, I felt like a deserter from some stupid, pointless war: guilty about the colleagues I was leaving behind, but almost euphoric with relief to be out of it myself. I knew I couldn't have stayed on here—or even in Kampala—month after month, year after year. However much I wished that I could have been that strong, I understood now that I wasn't.

There was a brief, loud stuttering sound, then the truck squealed to a halt. The four of us were in the back, guarding the equipment against potholes, with the tarpaulin above us blocking everything but a narrow rear view. I glanced at the others; someone outside shouted in Luganda at Akena Ibingira, the driver, and he started shouting back.

Okwera said "Bandits."

I felt my heart racing. "You're kidding!"

There was another burst of gunfire. I heard Ibingira jump out of the cab, still muttering angrily.

Everyone was looking at Okwera for advice. He said "Just cooperate, give them what they want." I tried to read his face; he seemed grim but not desperate—he expected unpleasantness, but not a massacre. Iganga was sitting on the bench beside me; I reached for her hand almost without thinking. We were both trembling. She squeezed my fingers for a moment, then pulled free.

Two tall, smiling men in dirty, brown camouflage appeared at the back of the truck, gesturing with automatic weapons for us to climb out. Okwera went first, but Masika, who'd been sitting beside him, hung back. Iganga was nearer to the exit than me, but I tried to get past her; I had some half-baked idea that this would somehow lessen her risk of being taken off and raped. When one of the bandits blocked my way and waved her forward, I thought this fear had been confirmed.

Masika grabbed my arm, and when I tried to break free, he tightened his grip and pulled me back into the truck. I turned on him angrily, but before I could say a word he whispered "She'll be all right. Just tell me: do you want them to take the ring?"

"What?"

He glanced nervously towards the exit, but the bandits had moved Okwera and Iganga out of sight. "I've paid them to do this. It's the only way. But say the word now and I'll give them the signal, and they won't touch the ring."

I stared at him, waves of numbness sweeping over my skin as I realized exactly what he was saying.

"You could have taken it off under anaesthetic."

He shook his head impatiently. "It's sending data back to HealthGuard all the time: cortisol, adrenaline, endorphins, prostaglandins. They'll have a record of your stress levels, fear, pain . . . if we took it off under anaesthetic, they'd *know* you'd given it away freely. This way, it'll look like a random theft. And your insurance company will give you a new one."

His logic was impeccable; I had no reply. I might have started protesting about insurance fraud, but that was all in the future, a separate matter entirely. The choice, here and now, was whether or not I let him have the ring by the only method that wouldn't raise suspicion.

One of the bandits was back, looking impatient. Masika asked plainly, "Do I call it off? I need an answer." I turned to him, on the verge of ranting that he'd wilfully misunderstood me, abused my generous offer to help him, and put all our lives in danger.

It would have been so much bullshit, though. He hadn't misunderstood me. All he'd done was taken me at my word.

I said "Don't call it off."

The bandits lined us up beside the truck, and had us empty our pockets into a sack. Then they started taking watches and jewellery. Okwera couldn't get his wedding ring off, but stood motionless and scowling while one of the bandits applied more force. I wondered if I'd need a prosthesis, if I'd still be able to do surgery, but as the bandit approached me I felt a strange rush of confidence.

I held out my hand and looked up into the sky. I knew that anything could be healed, once it was understood.

frost painting

CAROLYN IVES GILMAN

New writer Carolyn Ives Gilman has sold stories to The Magazine of Fantasy & Science Fiction, Interzone, Universe, Full Spectrum, Realms of Fantasy, Bending the Landscape, *and elsewhere. She is the author of five nonfiction books on frontier and American Indian history and recently published her first novel,* Halfway Human. *She lives in Saint Louis, where she works as a museum exhibition developer.*

In the deceptively quiet story that follows, she shows us that the hardest thing to let go of is something that you never really had. . . .

Soon after Galena Pittman's plane landed in Williston, North Dakota, she began to pick up nuggets of valuable information. To wit:

1. They really listen to Country Western music in the country west. Monotonous, whining hours of it, in fact.

2. Edible vegetables are as rare there as art critics.

3. Don't depend on public transportation if you want to get somewhere before dehydration sets in.

"I'll just catch a cab," she said to the woman at the ticket counter in the one-room Williston airport. The woman was dressed in the polyester pant suit all small-town females seemed required to wear, and she had that rural look of certainty that she knew how the land lay. Right now she was regarding Galena as if she were a six-year-old who needed life explained to her.

"The cab drivers will both be at home," she said.

"*Both?*" Galena said.

"It's suppertime," the ticket woman said, efficiently piling up papers.

She cast an eye over Galena, taking in the stylish bolo tie with the ceramic cactus pin, the wide-brimmed hat with the quail feather, the hand-painted cowboy boots. Her eyebrow rose.

"How am I supposed to get to the motel, then?" Galena said. Outside, there was nothing in sight but range land. It was going to be a long walk.

At last the woman sighed. "I'll give you a lift."

Climbing into the woman's pickup, it occurred to Galena that the context had changed the message of her clothing since she had left Chicago that morning. Normally, she took pride in dressing with the kind of riskiness that said to onlookers, "This is a trained professional. Do not try this at home." But here the cultural referents were different.

"I suppose you think I'm intending to be satirical," she said as the truck thudded across cattle grates onto the highway, bouncing her off the seat. "Actually, I'm making a kind of reflexive commentary on the banalization of the Western motif in the mass market."

No reaction.

"It's a statement on Eastern use of Western symbols. I'm satirizing us, not you."

"You heading for the Windrow Mountains?" the woman said.

"Yes." Galena was surprised to be found out so quickly.

"I figured. You're the type."

The type? Galena would admit to being many things, but not a *type*.

"We've been getting a lot of you through here," the woman went on. "Arty types."

Kooks. Weirdos. Galena could almost hear the woman thinking the words. "I'm not going there to stay," she said. "Joining a hive-mind's not my thing. I'm not a Californian."

"Uh-huh," the woman said.

There was something like a siren that went off in Galena's mind at times like this. It was whooping, *wrong, wrong*. She had made a fool of herself again. It was like a career.

The next morning when Galena picked up the white rental Hyundai at the Chevrolet dealership, the boots and bolo were gone. Even so, the car dealer spotted her right away. Guessing where she was bound, he turned suddenly reluctant to rent her the car.

"Look, I'm just going there to see a friend," Galena said reasonably. "I'll be back Sunday."

"So you say."

"You want to see my plane ticket?"

"You all have plane tickets."

Exasperated, Galena said, "Have they ever heard of tolerance in this town?"

"It's easy for you East-Coasters to be tolerant," the man said. "You don't have to live near them. I'll tell you this: If those weirdos ever decide to come out of the mountains, we're going to be ready for them. That is, if you liberals haven't taken away our guns by then, too."

Galena would have gladly gotten into a scrap with the man, but there was no time. She ended up leaving a signed credit-card slip with him to cover the cost of retrieving the car, if necessary.

Unfolding the map on her dashboard, she saw that south and west of Williston was nothing but blank space with anemic gray lines wandering through it. "Road condition unknown," the map said helpfully. "Hi ho Silver," Galena said to the Hyundai. Then she put on her sunglasses and prepared to cross the Great Plains in a Japanese rattletrap.

"I hope you appreciate this, Thea," she said.

. . .

"Galena Pittman," a rival columnist had once written, "is aptly named for a poisonous mineral." The phrase had amused Galena's colleagues so annoyingly that she had adopted it, mentioning it so often and laughing so hard that everyone began to realize it stung her.

In fact, Galena had been stinging since she was born. Long ago she had realized she was the world's pincushion, a target for every petty mortification, every nettling slight the world could invent. She could chew her cuticles raw thinking of the condescensions she had to endure in a given day, the premeditated cruelties of cabmen and bureaucrats. The only defense was to attack earlier and more wittily, to wear a coat of banter thick enough to keep the pins away. It rarely worked.

Her mother had a favorite saying: "If you make a bed of nails for yourself, you'd better lie on it, and like it." Galena had spent a lifetime casting barbs at that slogan, trying to find ways to disprove it.

In college, she had wanted to be an artist; but she had soon learned that she couldn't bear to see others looking at her work, thinking thoughts she couldn't control. She had tried to explain herself so intrusively, and annoyed so many people, that it finally dawned on her that the explaining was all she was really good at. So, unable to be criticized, she became a critic.

Galena had actually fallen in love with Thea Nodine's art several minutes before she fell in love with the artist herself. It had happened on a day when her landlord had decided to repair the plaster without any notice, and she had spent most of an hour calling everyone she knew to come help her move furniture, receiving only one recorded message after another. At last, where friendship failed money had to take over. The people at Hank's Hauling had been only too happy to help, once they had taken her Visa number hostage. By evening her apartment was in chaos and Galena was in a state of advanced disappointment with the world. She wouldn't have gone to the opening if she hadn't been paid to cover it for the *North Side Review*.

Standing there in a haze induced by exhaustion, cheap chablis, and whatever nutrition came from brie on rice cakes, Galena saw her first frost painting. It was a feathery, crystalline abstraction on glass—almost an image, like an elusive memory. It had been taken from its refrigeration box and set in a wooden stand for display, and the overheated gallery air was beginning to melt it. She stood and watched as the painting slowly turned to water from the outside in. She couldn't figure out why she found it so moving till someone behind her said, "That's how I feel." Galena realized it was how *she* felt, too—like a fragile thing aging and perishing as everyone stood and watched. She stared until the painting was no more than a sheet of glass covered with tears, and all that was left was a memory of beauty that had changed and passed on, like time and lost youth.

She asked the gallery owner about the artist, and he said, "Oh, you've *got* to meet Thea. She's simply an angel. All her work is perishable, you know. She works with the craziest things—sand, smoke, ice, sparks."

Thea was dressed in an oversized lumberjack shirt and jeans, her tangled brown hair falling around her shoulders. At first Galena wondered what kind of schtick this was—but a look at Thea's young face immediately told her that it was no schtick—the girl was simply unaware of the impression she made. Galena was suddenly seized with an urge to cherish this wisp of smoke, to protect it from all the winds that might dissipate it, to keep it young forever.

She gave Thea a ride home that night. The artist was living in a squalid, firetrap loft with five others, sleeping on old mattresses and cooking on a portable grill. The next morning, Galena bustled to the rescue, transplanting Thea into her apartment. The girl came willingly enough, but without the gratitude Galena expected. She had yet to learn that Thea was oblivious to her environment, existing like an air plant with no soil, just on sunlight and inspiration.

Galena made the nest, brought in the money, and kept out the world. Thea brought into her life almost-forgotten pleasures like scented soaps and silk pajamas, pearly Christmas ornaments and pomegranate seeds. Their relationship had all the hallmarks of permanence: an adopted cat, Chinese takeout in front of the television, Saturday morning errands, repainting the bedroom. Life was so normal, so trustworthy, it lulled Galena into forgetfulness. She almost became amiable.

She missed the signs of Thea's restlessness at first. In hindsight, the whole shift to wind sculpture had been part of it—a yearning attempt to grasp impermanence again. In that sunny spring Galena would come home to find her staring at the vortexes formed in Plexiglas tubes by the wind machines. They were like miniature, multicolored tornadoes, made visible by smoke or sand or bubbles. They had never looked strong enough to sweep any Dorothys off to Oz. Or Montana.

GAS—CASINO—ALIEN CURIOS, said the hand-painted roadside sign. Galena lifted the sunglasses onto her forehead; in the rearview mirror she saw they had left white circles in the dust on her face. Without the green tint of the lenses, the landscape looked bleached into shades of gray. Eroded hills, tufted with buckbrush and jackpine, cooked under the glaring sky. Ahead, hovering above the distant horizon, was a brushstroke of white—not clouds, but the snow capping unseen mountains.

She turned the Hyundai into the gravel parking lot in front of the gas station. The air conditioner sighed wearily as she killed the engine. As she twisted to get out, a sharp pain caught her unawares. She waited, sweaty, till it was gone, thinking: *Serves you right for growing up.*

Outside, the heat radiated off the yellow ground. In a dust-caked pickup by the gas pumps, a young woman waited with a child, her wispy blond hair blowing in the dry wind. The bumper sticker on the truck said, IF YOU DON'T WANT HEMORRHOIDS, GET OFF YOUR ASS. A Western sentiment, Galena presumed.

A wiry, bowlegged man was buying cigarettes at the counter inside. Galena wandered down the aisle of dusty tourist trinkets: rubber tomahawks, dribble glasses, ashtrays with toilet humor on them.

The door closed and Galena became aware of someone watching her. The woman stood motionless at the head of the aisle, not unlike one of the rock formations outside: a wind-scoured, lumpy shape with a cracked complexion that looked hard to the touch.

"Where are the alien curios?" Galena asked, thinking that the woman herself looked a little like one.

The woman pointed to a tabletop display case at the end of the aisle. Galena had to wipe the dust off the glass to see inside. She had expected plastic E.T.'s, but instead saw an assortment of lumpy concretions like fossilized organs. The shop's proprietor eased in behind the case, moving her bulk with uncanny silence. Without asking, she opened the case, took out one of the rocks, and handed it over. It was translucent, like onyx, and threaded through with red-brown veins. Galena suddenly had the feeling she was holding a giant eyeball, and put it down on the counter, a little revolted.

"How do you know it's alien?" she said to play along.

"It sure's hell ain't natural," the woman said. She had a breathy cigarette-voice.

"So what is it? A transdimensional doo-dad?"

"One of the things the Dirigo leave behind."

Galena said, "I thought the Dirigo looked like strings of Christmas lights." That was how *Unsolved Mysteries* had it, at any rate. "No one ever said they left turds."

The woman drew another object from the case and cradled it in her palm. It was the color of a kidney, and shaped a little like one. Its surface was slick, as if wet. "The aliens didn't leave these. The people that let them take over did."

So this was the much-publicized art created by the Windrow Mountain colony. It was not up to Thea's standards. Galena felt partly relief, partly anger that Thea could have been hoodwinked into participating in this travesty.

The woman's mineralized skin did not show a flicker of emotion. "You going up there?" she said.

"Yes. I've got a friend there."

"You think. There's nothing human living up there."

There's nothing much human down here either, Galena wanted to say; but she curbed her tongue.

When she emerged from the shop, a wind brushed by, scented with sage. She turned to look south, where the Windrow Mountains still hovered like an unkept promise on the horizon. "Don't leave, kid," she whispered. "I'm coming."

The reports from Montana had fascinated Thea from the start. There were many versions at first: Remote Montana community taken over by aliens. Demonic possession in Montana wasteland. Mystery Montana disease baffles scientists. Galena scoffed at it all.

After anthropologists at the University of Montana began to investigate, the explanations still metamorphosed to suit every paranoia. It was a type of mass hysteria. It was a scandalous case of environmental contamination. It was genetic inbreeding. It was a secret government experiment. One debunking journalist concluded that the "victims" were in fact members of a harmless New Age religious community who were being stigmatized by society as "ill" for their nonconformity.

The explanation of the victims themselves never changed. The Dirigo, they said, were enabling them to create art of a type never before imagined.

It was the art that riveted Thea's attention. As pictures finally filtered out, Thea bought all the magazines and pored over them. "Just think," she said, "I could work in real wind, real lightning, if I had their inspiration."

"If you had their inspiration, you'd be in a looney bin," Galena said.

But it did seem as if Thea's creativity was lagging that spring. Her studio was cluttered with unfinished work; it was over a year since she had held one of her famous shows that drew such crowds to see the self-destroying art. As her comfort increased it seemed her drive faded. Galena worried that her own happiness was poisoning the well from which it sprang.

One morning when Galena, ready to leave for work, leaned over the bed to kiss her partner goodbye, Thea looked up out of the rumpled bedclothes and said, "I'm going to Montana." Galena laughed, brushed the scattered hair out of Thea's face, and said, "Ride 'em, cowboy."

When she got home that evening, Thea's suitcase and backpack were waiting by the door. The truth smashed all the elaborate structure of Galena's security. Contentment had come to her so late, so unexpectedly, that she had never thought it, too, could be perishable. She followed Thea around the house, asking questions in a voice like a lost child.

"How can I get in touch with you?"

"What are you going to do there?"

"How long will you be gone?"

"Why are you doing this?"

"When will you know?"

"What about me?"

"What about me?"

To which Thea could only answer again and again, "I don't know."

And that was all Galena had ever gotten out of her. She consented to drop Thea off at the airport, but wouldn't go in with her, and they didn't part with a kiss, or even a handshake.

The road deteriorated as it began to climb. The shoulders were first to go, then the paint, till all that was left was a line of asphalt about as flat as a strip of cooked bacon. Galena's stomach was running on empty, but a touch of nervous nausea kept her from stopping to eat the granola bars she had brought. She didn't know how she was going to find Thea, and she didn't want to be wandering the Windrow Mountains all night.

The mountains wore a skirt of pine forest. The road veered to and fro through the still trunks till Galena began to suspect it didn't know where it was going. Down under the canopy of needles the air was dark as twilight, though the sun had to be in the sky, somewhere.

She rounded a corner and laid on the brakes. Ahead, the road was blocked by a fallen tree. A large yellow sign said, PRIVATE PROPERTY. TRESPASSERS WILL BE PROSECUTED. The sign was pockmarked with bullet holes.

She got out to survey the problem. The air was surprisingly cool; she must have climbed in altitude. The tree turned out to be just a poplar sapling, more leaves than trunk, felled by a chain saw. She seized a branch and dragged it across the asphalt, out of the way.

"If you want to keep me out, you'll have to try harder than this," Galena said to the unknown woodsman.

The effort had winded her, and she sat sideways in the driver's seat a while, her door open on the chill, quiet air. At first she thought that her tired eyes were playing tricks; but no, the shifting points of light were real. Off in the forest, down the winding corridors of pines, some people were carrying candles, or flashlights.

"Excuse me," Galena called out, getting up. "Can you give me some directions?"

The lights winked out. Piney silence surrounded her. Only then did Galena remember the reports—floating strings of lights sighted; gauzy veils, unexplained. She realized she was standing with one arm outstretched, as if hailing a cab. With a nervous laugh at her own absurdity, she headed back to the car and the security of self-examination. One's first brush with the paranormal ought to have more dignity than this, she decided. In her mind she composed the headlines. CHICAGOAN TRIES TO CATCH RIDE ON UFO: "I THOUGHT IT WAS A CAB," CITY SLICKER SAYS.

The road plunged down a ravine, then abruptly emerged from the trees into a barren valley. The setting sun touched the sandstone cliffs, a vivid orange. Lines of erosion made the rock face look like an ancient bas-relief, so worn away that the original sculpture was barely visible. Galena stopped the car to study it. She could almost see figures in motion—no, an inscription in flowing characters. It reminded her vividly of something. It was on the tip of her tongue: she would remember in a second.

It was just a cliff. Frowning at the illusion that had drawn her briefly out of herself, she put the car in Drive again and followed the winding road down into the heart of the valley. Rock formations rose on either side: twisted sandstone pillars that looked like figures hidden in stone cocoons, their protolimbs still obscure beneath the surface. They drew her eyes, as if subconsciously she knew what shapes lay beneath. The valley floor held an army of them in a thousand poses, straining to free themselves. Galena sped through them; they towered over the little car, their shadows lying like barriers across the road.

At last the forest enclosed her again. It was dark now; she turned on the headlights. There was still no sign of any colony—no sign of humans at all. She had passed the last motel just after noon.

At last, a light shone through the trees. She slowed, then spotted the driveway—just a dirt track, really. As she drove up it, the tall grass swished against the car's undercarriage.

It was a log house, probably built as a hunter's lodge. Leaving the headlights on, Galena skirted the stack of firewood and climbed three board steps onto the porch. The screen door creaked when she opened it to knock. It was several seconds before there was any response. Then, hesitantly, the door opened a crack and someone peered out.

It was Thea. "Hi there, kid," Galena said, as if she'd known it was going to be her.

Thea stood staring. "Galena," she said.

Her long brown hair fell in curly tendrils, uncombed but fetching. She looked more thin and waiflike than ever in a flannel shirt and jeans. Her feet were bare. Galena wanted to hug her to make sure that everything was all right, but there was something in her manner—a slight shrinking back, a wariness.

Thea held the door open. "Come in."

The kitchen table was soon strewn with the snapshots Galena had brought—mostly their cat, Pesto, doing assorted catlike things. Thea stared for a long time at one where the flashbulb made the cat's eyes light up like headlights.

"He's gotten to be a real sentimental slob," Galena said. "After you left, he wandered around the house and cried for a few days." So did I, she didn't say.

She continued the patter she'd tried to keep up ever since entering, afraid of what silence might mean. "Mr. Garavelli at the dry cleaners told me to say hi to you. They've been repaving the street out front and it's been unbearable all summer: nothing but dust and noise. Workers leaving their shirts on the bushes. Manly sweat everywhere." She took a sip of the tea that was virtually all Thea could offer her; the refrigerator was almost empty. "I had to go in to Dr. Hamer for a biopsy last week. I find out the results Tuesday."

At last Thea's eyes focused on her. "What's wrong?" she asked.

"Getting old, that's what's wrong." *Getting old alone*, she thought. *No one to tell how it feels, no one to give a damn.* "Never mind," she said.

At last silence fell. Inside the wood stove, a log settled with a brittle sound.

"Galena, I can't come back," Thea said. Her voice sounded like a guilty child confessing. "I've made the commitment here."

"Sure. I understand," Galena said, barely hearing the words. "What's important is your work. How's it going?" She glanced around the cabin. There was not a sign of artistry anywhere, just worn Salvation Army furniture.

"I'm working outside now," Thea said. "I'll show you tomorrow, if you want."

"Yes. I want."

Silence again.

"I'd better get my suitcase out of the car," Galena said. There was a twinge of pain as she rose, mocking her. *Think you're brave, do you?* it said. She took care not to react. She couldn't bear to seem vulnerable.

"Sure. You can sleep on the couch," Thea said.

Galena looked at her silently. Thea wouldn't meet her eyes. "What is this, Montana morality?" Galena asked.

"No." Thea's voice was pleading. "I just can't, Galena. I don't want you to lure me back. It will be too hard."

Too hard on whom? Galena wondered. "Okay," she said slowly. "You make the rules."

Suddenly, Thea gave her an impulsive hug. "Thank you," she whispered. As she disappeared behind the bedroom door she glanced back. The light caught her eyes with an odd glint, as if the retinas were brushed metal. For a moment she looked utterly alien.

That night Galena lay alone on the lumpy couch, kept awake by wind in the branches outside, the skittering of small feet across the roof, insect wings on the window screen. None of the soporific sounds she was used to—the roar of garbage trucks, the wail of sirens. No comforting weight of possessive cat on her feet. She wondered if Thea were awake.

This desire to be held and comforted was childish, she told herself. *You're an adult now. You know how to survive.*

Lying in the dark, she imagined a tumor growing inside her, a living thing that wasn't her, like the child she never had nor wanted. Nature had a way of getting back at people who didn't follow its rules. And reproduction was the first rule, the evolutionary imperative.

She had never made a decision to swear off men—just drifted into it, the path of least resistance. Her last attempt at a straight relationship had been a madcap fling with a sculptor. The only time they had had sex together, while she was still basking in the afterglow, he had smiled at her and said, "You look like a woman who's just been fucked."

The statement had jarred her. Why was it *she* that had just been fucked, and not *him*? He had slipped, and revealed the real reason he had done it—not for the enjoyment, no strings attached, but in order to transform her into something she hadn't been before, as if she had been raw material he had made into something. As if he had put his mark on her, like a dog pissing on a lamppost.

From that moment she knew that for men, sex was inextricably connected to power, and always would be. No matter what they said, or how enlightened they acted, sex was dominance to them, on such an instinctual, hardwired brainstem level they could never overcome it. And she had far too vivid a sense of her own individuality to ever imagine herself as a thing marked as a man's territory.

Thea's love had always been free of other agendas. It had never been mixed up with power, or pride, or self. It had been a spontaneous gift, unpremeditated, as if it sprang from the air between them. Galena had never had to give up being who she was in order to be who Thea loved.

She hugged the pillow to the hollow feeling in her body, wondering if loneliness caused cancer.

•   •   •

In the morning, Galena ate a breakfast of granola bars and tea; Thea was not hungry. By daylight, the cabin looked more dilapidated than ever. One of the kitchen windows was broken, and there was an old mouse nest in a corner. "How did you find this place?" Galena asked.

"Everyone stays here when they first come," Thea answered. "It's where you wait."

"Wait for what?"

"For the Dirigo. I'll be moving on soon."

"On to where?"

"The colony. I'm almost ready."

"Will you show me the colony?"

"If you want."

Thea set out as if to walk, but Galena asked how far it was, then persuaded her to take the car. Thea looked at the Hyundai as if she'd forgotten how they worked, then opened the door awkwardly. Galena watched her carefully, suspicious.

"What do you want to see first?" Thea asked.

"What's the choice?"

"There are work sites all around us. The Wind Clock, the Haunt, Nostra Knob."

"What have you been working on?"

"The Flens."

"Let's see it, then."

A few miles down the road, Thea suddenly exclaimed, "Stop! Stop here!"

Galena pulled over. They were high on the mountainside; on their right hand was a steep dropoff, giving them a wide view of a wooded valley that wound into blue distance, interrupted by the outthrusting roots of mountains on either side.

"Look out there," Thea said. "Do you see the painting?"

The vegetation on north slopes, south slopes, and valley floor was a pattern of green, teal, and umber. It was as if someone had taken a giant brush and painted the land to form an abstract of overlapping tints. "Isn't that natural?" Galena said.

"Of course not. This was one of the first landscape paintings the colony did. Here, let me drive so you can watch."

A little reluctantly, Galena got out and went to the passenger side. Thea said, "Unfocus your eyes just a little the first time," then started the car slowly forward.

At first Galena saw a complex patchwork of sunny streaks. Then, as her perspective changed, a dark, spear-shaped wedge began to push its way into the foliage colors. As it touched each band of color, that area went suddenly dark, drab, and uniform. It had almost reached the opposite side when a cascade of rusts, siennas, and lemons erupted from the speartip and turned the landscape bright again.

The car stopped. Galena blinked out at the view, which had been transformed by traveling 300 feet along the road. "How did they do that?" she asked. "By painting the back side of every leaf?"

"I don't know," Thea said. "It looks different at every time of day, and every type of weather."

Galena shook her head. "Landscape painting. I see what you mean. Not painting the landscape, but *painting the landscape*. How many people did it take?"

"I don't know," Thea said again.

As they continued on, Galena looked on every prospect around her with new attention, to find more *trompes l'oeil* hidden in the leaves.

They arrived at the Flens down a rocky path. At first, it looked like a range of rampart cliffs, formed into organ-pipe pillars of a thousand dimensions. A swarm of people was at work on the cliff face, some on scaffolding anchored into the rock, some swinging on ropes. Though she tried from several angles, Galena could not tell what the sculpture was going to be.

When she asked, Thea laughed. "The sculpture is not in the rock," she said. "The medium we are working in is wind. At sunset, the mountain above us cools faster than the valley, and a wind rushes down the slope. The Flens will catch it in a thousand fissures, and part it, till it forms a shape. We will know we have gotten it right when the rock pipes sing. It's almost done; we are tuning it now."

"You are making an organ from the mountain," Galena said, struck by the strangeness of the concept.

"An organ only the wind can play," Thea answered.

As Galena watched, the workers vacated one area. There was a puff of smoke, then an echoing explosion.

"They use dynamite?" Galena asked.

"We use anything that will do the job," Thea answered.

The workers moved back into the dynamited area, their movements efficient and coordinated. Galena could see no one in charge, hear no shouted orders.

"Who designs the artworks?" she asked. "Who is in charge?"

Thea looked at the ground and shrugged.

"Thea?" Galena said.

"You will just misinterpret it," Thea said.

"Try me. Come on."

"The colonists just *know* what to do. They feel what's right. Imagine having the skill to produce each effect deliberately. Imagine thinking, 'I need pathos here, or an ominous effect,' and knowing exactly what you have to do to create it, as if it were being whispered in your ear. And everyone else knows the same."

"Kind of like having a muse?"

"That's right. The Dirigo are our muses."

Gently, Galena said, "You never needed to use anyone else's inspiration before. You never worked by anyone else's plan. That's what made you so good."

Nervously, Thea brushed a strand of hair behind her ear. "I was never as good as you thought I was."

Galena was about to protest strenuously, but Thea said, "You blew me up so big, nothing I could do would ever justify it. Everyone's expectations were so high."

"Thea, kid, you deserved it!" Galena said.

"You see what I mean," Thea said, then turned back toward the car.

"So is that my sin?" Galena shouted after her. "Having faith in you?"

Thea didn't stop or answer. When they both got back to the car they sat a while in silence. Galena considered, and rejected, half a dozen strategies: conciliatory, wounded, encouraging, authoritative. None of them were sufficient to the way she felt.

When Thea finally spoke, it wasn't about Galena at all. "Here, no one makes the art for any reason but because we want to."

They drove on to other sites. The art was everywhere. It was fashioned from streams and sand, shadows, lichen, and rain. In one place a flight of swallows was an intermittent part of the sculpture. After a while it was impossible to see the landscape as a backdrop, an accidental thing.

"Supposing these Dirigo were real—" Galena started.

"They *are* real," Thea said.

"Okay, okay. Are they trying to tell us something?"

"I don't know. You're the one who gets messages from art."

"Do they talk to you?"

"No. Not the way you mean. We don't know what they want. We're not even sure they know we're any different from the trees and rocks. Except—"

"Yes?"

"Some people feel they're trying to remember something. Something they once knew long, long ago, but now they've forgotten."

"Like us all," Galena said.

The last site they visited was what Thea called the Pivotary. They drove up a long gravel road that climbed past the trees into a cold, bleached world where the very air seemed purified and rare. Through the afternoon an ache had been growing somewhere between Galena's back and gut; when they reached the end of the road she parked and sat a while, waiting for it to subside. The sun was low, but above them the sky was still bright.

They walked side by side up a gravelly path that curved between two spurs standing out from the mountain like rock gates. Beyond them, in a sheer-sided bowl, lay a mountain lake, its surface so perfectly still it mirrored every rock around it. When they came to a halt beside it, and their footsteps ceased, silence settled in. The air seemed so crystalline it might break at a touch.

In a hushed voice, Thea said, "This is where the Dirigo live. They've been here for eons, maybe since the beginning. It's possible that the Blackfeet Indians knew about them. We think other humans may have known, once, in other times and places. We come here to invite them in. Don't worry, they can't inhabit anyone who is unwilling. You would have to go into the lake to make them part of your life."

"Like a baptism?" Galena said.

"That's right."

There was a silence. At last Thea said hesitantly, "You could do it, too. You could join us."

"Oh, Thea. When will you learn? I don't have the talent for art."

"You could. There are people in the colony who never made a thing before coming here."

"So that's what the Dirigo offer? Instant talent?"

"Vision. Creativity. A feel for the elements. If that's talent."

"What a deal," Galena said, stirring a pebble at her feet. "You'd have to be crazy to turn it down." She glanced sidelong at Thea. "But what's the catch?"

"There are only catches in a human context. Catches belong to the outside world."

"The human world, you mean. Catches are part of being human."

"All right," Thea said. "The catch is, I have to hurt you, by leaving you behind."

They stood looking at each other then—communicating, Galena thought, for the first time, though not a word was said. *I need to say it aloud*, Galena thought. *I have to admit how badly I need her.*

As the light shifted with the setting sun, it caught Thea's eyes, and the retinas reflected through, opaque as mirrors, beautiful as gemstones. A chill went down Galena's spine. She grasped. Thea's hand. It felt cold.

"Have you already gone into the lake?" she asked.

Thea nodded. "Three weeks ago."

"Can you still back out?"

"I don't want to."

She was the same, but unknowable. Unchanged, yet wholly different. "What did I do to make you want this?" Galena said.

"It has nothing to do with you."

It couldn't be true, Galena thought. Somehow, this was her fault.

"Look!" Thea said, pointing out over the lake. "They've come."

The sun had set, and darkness leaped up from the ground. But the sky was still light, and the lake, reflecting it, glowed azure in the twilight. Above it, a constellation of sparks danced, firefly lights cavorting. Around them the air shimmered as with heat waves. Galena glimpsed something like a shred of iridescent gauze, gone as soon as she focused on it.

"What are they doing here?" Galena whispered. "What do they want?"

"The art," Thea said. "It's all they want. To make beautiful things. They can't do it themselves; they need our hands, our ingenuity."

She was gazing at them entranced. *I am losing her*, Galena thought.

The valley was growing dark; now faint streaks of colored light flashed and disappeared above the lake, like an aurora, or a reflection from a light that wasn't there.

Galena took Thea's hand firmly in hers. "Come on," she said, "I'll drive you home."

Following the headlights down the steep road, Galena remembered how, in the days when Thea had still gone down to her old studio to work, Galena had picked her up after work, to drive her home. Sometimes she would climb the steps and hear the artists who shared the space laughing together uproariously, like teenagers. When she entered the room, the laughter would cut off self-consciously. Even if she told them to go on talking, the atmosphere would turn stiff and formal, as if Teacher were watching. It had made Galena hate to go there after a while, and feel out of place, unwanted.

There was an ache in her gut that said, *No more future, no more chances.* Always the future had been there, a sketchbook where she could try out new scenarios. Now experimentation was done; only action was left.

She came to the main road, then retraced the way back past the turnoff to the Flens, past the landscape painting, speeding faster with every mile. As pine trunks flashed by in the darkness, Thea said, "That was the turnoff to the house. You missed it."

"I know," Galena said.

The road curved and plunged downward, into the valley of the stone shapes. Thea said tensely, "Stop, Galena. I can't leave."

"Yes, you can," Galena said. "And I think you'd better, before they brainwash you completely."

She pressed down on the gas, wanting to get past the rock formations that loomed in frozen motion over the road. The passenger side door opened, and Galena heard the pavement rushing past. She reached over to grab Thea's arm, only to feel it pull away. The loony girl was actually going to jump. Galena braked hard, and the car slewed around on loose gravel. For a moment she had a terrifying out-of-control feeling. Then the car came to rest in the roadway, facing back the way it had come. The headlight beams pointed crookedly into the dust and exhaust. The passenger seat was empty.

Galena left the car door open and walked down the harsh beams of light, searching the shoulders for a sign, her stomach muscles clenched. Then, ahead on the roadway, she saw Thea's silhouette, walking steadily away from her. She sprinted to catch up.

"Thea!" She grasped the girl's arm and forced her to turn around. "Are you—" The headlights caught Thea's eyes and they shone back, bright and preternatural.

Instinctively, Galena stepped back. Then a desperate sense that she was losing overcame her, and she grasped Thea by the shoulders. "Fight them, Thea! Be yourself. Don't surrender, don't let them control you."

A wan smile crossed Thea's face, too wise and knowing for her young features. "Myself?"

"Yes." Galena clutched her tight. "The Thea I knew."

Thea's voice was maddeningly adult. "The Thea you invented, you mean. I know all about being dominated, Galena."

Galena loosed her grip, deeply stung. "That's not true! All I ever wanted was for you to be yourself."

"Then let me go," Thea said.

"Not to give up your freedom," Galena said stubbornly. "Not to become something that's not even human."

"The only humanity I lose is the ability to make things ugly."

"Oh, isn't that great," Galena said, bitingly sarcastic. "Why don't we all join the Dirigo, then, and have a world of people who want nothing but beauty. A world of saints and artists."

"Why not?" Thea said.

There was a cloud of sparks around her head, like a halo in a medieval painting, but they cast no light on her features. Half to them and half to her Galena said, "Because it wouldn't be a human world, Thea."

There was a silence. The rock shapes around them seemed to be listening. "Then I don't want to be human," Thea said.

She was leaving her face, retreating back behind those eyes that revealed nothing. When she turned again to walk into the dark, there was no one left to stop.

The shoal of silver slivers that had hung above Thea's head did not leave with her. They still hung in the air, darting about in school formation.

Galena knew that she too could wear a halo of stars if she only consented. There was a heavy lump inside her gut—her own inhabiting being, eating her away from inside.

"Get out of here!" she shouted at the pinprick lights above her. "Let us be! You've got no business trying to make us better than we are."

Her footsteps sounded heavy and corporeal as she walked back to the car. When she had turned it around she paused with her foot on the brake, caught on a snag of grief. For a moment she rested her forehead on the steering wheel, then shifted blindly into Drive.

She had her comebacks ready by the time she got to Williston. When the car dealer's eyebrows cast aspersions her way, she said, "The Dirigo didn't want me. I guess they saw I was already alienated enough."

She would have been ashamed to commit a pun in Chicago, but this was North Dakota.

The sweaty, overly familiar salesman in the seat next to her on the plane found out where she had been and said jocularly, "Did you see any aliens?"

"Not as many as I've seen since coming back," Galena retorted.

As they circled high above the fumes and grime of O'Hare, caught in traffic, she looked down at the barren mess humanity had made of the landscape, and imagined it all melting away like one of Thea's frost paintings.

It would never happen. If humanity were offered salvation on a silver platter, someone would probably just mug the messenger.

She shifted, feeling the bed of nails beneath her.

Lethe

WALTER JON WILLIAMS

Walter Jon Williams was born in Minnesota and now lives in Albuquer-que, New Mexico. His short fiction has appeared frequently in Asimov's Science Fiction, *as well as in* The Magazine of Fantasy & Science Fic-tion, Wheel of Fortune, Global Dispatches, Alternate Outlaws, *and other markets, and has been gathered in the collection* Facets. *His novels include* Ambassador of Progress, Knight Moves, Hardwired, The Crown Jewels, Voice of the Whirlwind, House of Shards, Days of Atonement, *and* Aristoi. *His novel* Metropolitan *garnered wide critical acclaim in 1996 and was one of the most talked about books of the year. His most recent books are a sequel to* Metropolitan, City on Fire, *and a new short story collection,* Frankensteins and Foreign Devils. *His stories have ap-peared in our Third, Fourth, Fifth, Sixth, Ninth, Eleventh, Twelfth, and Fourteenth Annual Collections. He has a Web site at http:// www.thuntek.net/~walter/.*

In the pyrotechnic tale that follows, he tells the story of an explorer who returns from a voyage to the stars obsessed with the past that he's lost. . . .

D avout had himself disassembled for the return journey. He had already been torn in half, he felt: the remainder, the dumb beast still alive, did not matter. The captain had ruled, and Katrin would not be brought back. Dav-out did not want to spend the years between the stars in pain, confronting the gap-ing absence in his quarters, surrounded by the quiet sympathy of the crew.

Besides, he was no longer needed. The terraforming team had done its work, and then, but for Davout, had died.

Davout lay down on a bed of nano and let the little machines take him apart piece by piece, turn his body, his mind, and his unquenchable longing into long strings of numbers. The nanomachines crawled into his brain first, mapping, recording, and then shut down his mind piece by piece, so that he would feel no discomfort during what followed, or suffer a memory of his own body being taken apart.

Davout hoped that the nanos would shut down the pain before his conscious-ness failed, so that he could remember what it was like to live without the anguish that was now a part of his life, but it didn't work out that way. When his consciousness ebbed, he was aware, even to the last fading of the light, of the knife-blade of loss still buried in his heart.

The pain was there when Davout awoke, a wailing voice that cried, a pure contralto keen of agony, in his first dawning awareness. He found himself in an early-Victorian bedroom, blue-striped wallpaper, silhouettes in oval frames, silk flowers in vases. Crisp sheets, light streaming in the window. A stranger—shoulder-length hair, black frock coat, cravat carelessly tied—looked at him from a gothic-revival armchair. The man held a pipe in the right hand and tamped down tobacco with the prehensile big toe of his left foot.

"I'm not on the *Beagle*," Davout said.

The man gave a grave nod. His left hand formed the mudra for <correct>. "Yes."

"And this isn't a virtual?"

<Correct> again. "No."

"Then something has gone wrong."

<Correct> "Yes. A moment, sir, if you please." The man finished tamping, slipped his foot into a waiting boot, then lit the pipe with the anachronistic lighter in his left hand. He puffed, drew in smoke, exhaled, put the lighter in his pocket, and settled back in the walnut embrace of his chair.

"I am Dr. Li," he said. <Stand by> said the left hand, the old finger position for a now-obsolete palmtop computer, a finger position that had once meant *pause*, as <correct> had once meant *enter*, enter because it was correct. "Please remain in bed for a few more minutes while the nanos doublecheck their work. Redundancy is frustrating," puffing smoke, "but good for peace of mind."

"What happens if they find they've made a mistake?"

<Don't be concerned.> "It can't be a very large mistake," said Li, "or we wouldn't be communicating so rationally. At worst, you will sleep for a bit while things are corrected."

"May I take my hands out from under the covers?" he asked.

"Yes."

Davout did so. His hands, he observed, were brown and leathery, hands suitable for the hot, dry world of Sarpedon. They had not, then, changed his body for one more suited to Earth, but given him something familiar.

If, he realized, they were on Earth.

His right fingers made the mudra <thank you>.

<Don't mention it> signed Li.

Davout passed a hand over his forehead, discovered that the forehead, hand, and gesture itself were perfectly familiar.

Strange, but the gesture convinced him that he was, in a vital way, still himself. Still Davout.

Still alive, he thought. Alas.

"Tell me what happened," he said. "Tell me why I'm here."

Li signed <stand by>, made a visible effort to collect himself. "We believe," he said, "that the *Beagle* was destroyed. If so, you are the only survivor."

Davout found his shock curiously veiled. The loss of the other lives—friends, most of them—stood muted by the precedent of his own earlier, overriding grief. It was as if the two losses were weighed in a balance, and the *Beagle* found wanting.

Li, Davout observed, was waiting for Davout to absorb this information before continuing.

<Go on> Davout signed.

"The accident happened seven light-years out," Li said. "*Beagle* began to yaw wildly, and both automatic systems and the crew failed to correct the maneuver. *Beagle*'s automatic systems concluded that the ship was unlikely to survive the increasing oscillations, and began to use its communications lasers to download personality data to collectors in Earth orbit. As the only crew member to elect disassembly during the return journey, you were first in the queue. The others, we presume, ran to nano disassembly stations, but communication was lost with the *Beagle* before we retrieved any of their data."

"Did Katrin's come through?"

Li stirred uneasily in his chair. <Regrettably> "I'm afraid not."

Davout closed his eyes. He had lost her again. Over the bubble of hopelessness in his throat he asked, "How long has it been since my data arrived?"

"A little over eight days."

They had waited eight days, then, for *Beagle*—for the *Beagle* of seven years ago—to correct its problem and reestablish communication. If *Beagle* had re-sumed contact, the mass of data that was Davout might have been erased as redundant.

"The government has announced the loss," Li said. "Though there is a remote chance that the *Beagle* may come flying in or through the system in eleven years as scheduled, we have detected no more transmissions, and we've been unable to observe any blueshifted deceleration torch aimed at our system. The govern-ment decided that it would be unfair to keep sibs and survivors in the dark any longer."

<Concur> Davout signed.

He envisioned the last moments of the *Beagle*, the crew being flung back and forth as the ship slammed through increasing pendulum swings, the desperate attempts, fighting wildly fluctuating gravity and inertia, to reach the emergency nanobeds . . . no panic, Davout thought, Captain Moshweshwe had trained his people too well for that. Just desperation, and determination, and, as the oscil-lations grew worse, an increasing sense of futility, and impending death.

No one expected to die anymore. It was always a shock when it happened near you. Or *to* you.

"The cause of the *Beagle*'s problem remains unknown," Li said, the voice far away. "The Bureau is working with simulators to try to discover what happened."

Davout leaned back against his pillow. Pain throbbed in his veins, pain and loss, knowledge that his past, his joy, was irrecoverable. "The whole voyage," he said, "was a catastrophe."

<I respectfully contradict> Li signed. "You terraformed and explored two worlds," he said. "Downloads are already living on these worlds, hundreds of

thousands now, millions later. There would have been a third world added to our commonwealth if your mission had not been cut short due to the, ah, first accident . . ."

<Concur> Davout signed, but only because his words would have come out with too much bitterness.

<Sorry>, a curt jerk of Li's fingers. "There are messages from your sibs," Li said, "and downloads from them also. The sibs and friends of Beagle's crew will try to contact you, no doubt. You need not answer any of these messages until you're ready."

<Understood.>

Davout hesitated, but the words were insistent; he gave them tongue. "Have Katrin's sibs sent messages?" he asked.

Li's grave expression scarcely changed. "I believe so." He tilted his head. "Is there anything I can do for you? Anything I can arrange?"

"Not now, no," said Davout. <Thank you> he signed. "Can I move from the bed now?"

Li's look turned abstract as he scanned indicators projected somewhere in his mind. <Yes> "You may," he said. He rose from his chair, took the pipe from his mouth. "You are in a hospital, I should add," he said, "but you do not have the formal status of patient, and may leave at any time. Likewise, you may stay here for the foreseeable future, as long as you feel it necessary."

<Thank you> "Where is this hospital, by the way?"

"West Java. The city of Bandung."

Earth, then. Which Davout had not seen in seventy-seven years. Memory's gentle fingers touched his mind with the scent of durian, of ocean, of mace, cloves, and turmeric.

He knew he had never been in Java before, though, and wondered whence the memory came. From one of his sibs, perhaps?

<Thank you> Davout signed again, putting a touch of finality, a kind of dismissal, into the twist of his fingers.

Dr. Li left Davout alone, in his new/old body, in the room that whispered of memory and pain.

In a dark wood armoire, Davout found identification and clothing, and a record confirming that his account had received seventy-eight years' back pay. His electronic inbox contained downloads from his sibs and more personal messages than he could cope with—he would have to construct an electronic personality to answer most of them.

He dressed and left the hospital. Whoever supervised his reassembly—Dr. Li perhaps—had thoughtfully included a complete Earth atlas in his internal ROM, and he accessed it as he walked, making random turnings but never getting lost. The furious sun burned down with tropical intensity, but his current body was constructed to bear heat, and a breeze off the mountains made pleasant even the blazing noontide.

The joyful metal music of the gamelans clattered from almost every doorway.

People in bright clothing, agile as the siamang of near Sumatra, sped overhead along treeways and ropeways, arms and hands modified for brachiation. Robots, immune to the heat, shimmered past on silent tires. Davout found it all strangely familiar, as if he had been here in a dream.

And then he found himself by the sea, and a pang of familiarity knifed through his heart. *Home!* cried his thoughts. Other worlds he had built, other beauties he had seen, but he had never beheld *this* blue, *this* perfection, anywhere else but on his native sphere. Subtle differences in atmospherics had rendered this color unnatural on any other world.

And with the cry of familiarity came a memory: it had been Davout the Silent who had come here, a century or more ago, and Katrin had been by his side.

But Davout's Katrin was dead. And as he looked on Earth's beauty, he felt his world of joy turn to bitter ashes.

<Alas!> His fingers formed the word unbidden. <Alas!>

He lived in a world where no one died, and nothing was ever lost. One understood that such things occasionally occurred, but never—hardly ever—to anyone that one knew. Physical immortality was cheap and easy, and was supported by so many alternate systems: backing up the mind by downloading, or downloading into a virtual reality system or into a durable machine. Nanosystems duplicated the body or improved it, adapted it for different environments. Data slumbered in secure storage, awaiting the electron kiss that returned it to life. Bringing a child to term in the womb was now the rarest form of reproduction, and bringing a child to life in a machine womb the next rarest.

It was so much easier to have the nanos duplicate you as an adult. Then, at least, you had someone to talk to.

No one died, and nothing was ever lost. But Katrin died, Davout thought, and now I am lost, and it was not supposed to be this way.

<Alas!> Fingers wailed the grief that was stopped up in Davout's throat. <Alas!>

Davout and Katrin had met in school, members of the last generation in which womb-breeding outnumbered the alternatives. Immortality whispered its covenant into their receptive ears. On their first meeting, attending a lecture (Dolphus on "Reinventing the Humboldt Sea") at the College of Mystery, they looked at each other and *knew*, as if angels had whispered into their ears, that there was now one less mystery in the world, that each served as an answer to another, that each fitted neatly into a hollow that the other had perceived in his or her soul, dropping into place as neatly as a butter-smooth piece in a finely made teak puzzle—or, considering their interests, as easily as a carbolic functional group nested into place on an indole ring.

Their rapport was, they freely admitted, miraculous. Still young, they exploded into the world, into a universe that welcomed them.

He could not bear to be away from her. Twenty-four hours was the absolute limit before Davout's nerves began to beat a frustrated little tattoo, and he found himself conjuring a phantom Katrin in his imagination, just to have someone to share the world with—he *needed* her there, needed this human lens through which he viewed the universe.

Without her, Davout found the cosmos veiled in a kind of uncertainty. While it was possible to apprehend certain things (the usefulness of a coenocytic arrangement of cells in the transmission of information-bearing proteins and nuclei, the historical significance of the Yucatán astrobleme, the limitations of the Benard cell model in predicting thermic instabilities in the atmosphere), these things lacked *nóesis*, existed only as a series of singular, purposeless accidents. Reflected through Katrin, however, the world took on brilliance, purpose, and genius. With Katrin he could feast upon the universe; without her the world lacked savor.

Their interests were similar enough for each to generate enthusiasm in the other, diverse enough that each was able to add perspective to the other's work. They worked in cozy harmony, back to back, two desks set in the same room. Sometimes Davout would return from a meeting, or a coffee break, and find that Katrin had added new paragraphs, sometimes an entire new direction, to his latest effort. On occasion he would return the favor. Their early work— eccentric, proliferating in too many directions, toward too many specialties— showed life and promise and more than a hint of brilliance.

Too much, they decided, for just the two of them. They wanted to do too much, and all at once, and an immortal lifetime was not time enough.

And so, as soon as they could afford it, Red Katrin, the original, was duplicated—with a few cosmetic alterations—in Dark Katrin and later Katrin the Fair; and nanomachines read Old Davout, blood and bone and the long strands of numbers that were his soul, and created perfect copies in Dangerous Davout, later called the Conqueror, and Davout the Silent.

Two had become six, and half a dozen, they now agreed, was about all the universe could handle for the present. The wild tangle of overlapping interests was parceled out between the three couples, each taking one of the three most noble paths to understanding. The eldest couple chose History as their domain, a part of which involved chronicling the adventures of their sibs; the second couple took Science; the third Psyche, the exploration of the human mind. Any developments, any insights, on the part of one of the sibs could be shared with the others through downloads. In the beginning they downloaded themselves almost continually, sharing their thoughts and experiences and plans in a creative frenzy. Later, as separate lives and more specialized careers developed, the downloads grew less frequent, though there were no interruptions until Dangerous Davout and Dark Katrin took their first voyage to another star. They spent over fifty years away, though to them it was less than thirty; and the downloads from Earth, pulsed over immense distances by communications lasers, were less frequent, and less frequently resorted to. The lives of the other couples, lived at what seemed speeded-up rates, were of decreasing relevance to their own existence, as if they were lives that dwelled in a half-remembered dream.

<Alas!> the fingers signed. <Alas!> for the dream turned to savage nightmare.

The sea, a perfect terrestrial blue, gazed back into Davout's eyes, indifferent to the sadness frozen into his fingers.

. . .

"Your doctors knew that to wake here, after such an absence, would result in a feeling of anachronism," said Davout's sib, "so they put you in this Victorian room, where you would at least feel at ease with the kind of anachronism by which you are surrounded." He smiled at Davout from the neo-gothic armchair. "If you were in a modern room, you might experience a sensation of obsolescence. But everyone can feel superior to the Victorians, and besides, one is always more comfortable in one's past."

"Is one?" Davout asked, fingers signing <irony>. The past and the present, he found, were alike a place of torment.

"I discover," he continued, "that my thoughts stray for comfort not to the past, but to the future."

"Ah." A smile. "That is why we call you Davout the Conqueror."

"I do not seem to inhabit that name," Davout said, "if I ever did."

Concern shadowed the face of Davout's sib. <Sorry> he signed, and then made another sign for <profoundly>, the old *multiply* sign, multiples of sorrow in his gesture.

"I understand," he said. "I experienced your last download. It was . . . intensely disturbing. I have never felt such terror, such loss."

"Nor had I," said Davout.

It was Old Davout whose image was projected into the gothic-revival armchair, the original, womb-born Davout of whom the two sibs were copies. When Davout looked at him it was like looking into a mirror in which his reflection had been retarded for several centuries, then unexpectedly released—Davout remembered, several bodies back, once possessing that tall forehead, the fair hair, the small ears flattened close to the skull. The grey eyes he had still, but he could never picture himself wearing the professorial little goatee.

"How is our other sib?" Davout asked.

The concern on Old Davout's face deepened. "You will find Silent Davout much changed. You haven't uploaded him, then?"

<No> "Due to the delays, I'm thirty years behind on my uploading."

"Ah." <Regret> "Perhaps you should speak to him, then, before you upload all those years."

"I will." He looked at his sib and hoped the longing did not burn in his eyes. "Please give my best to Katrin, will you?"

"I will give her your *love*," said Old Davout, wisest of the sibs.

The pain was there when Davout awoke next day, fresh as the moment it first knifed through him, on the day their fifth child, the planet Sarpedon, was christened. Sarpedon had been discovered by astronomers a couple of centuries before, and named, with due regard for tradition, after yet another minor character in Homer; it had been mapped and analyzed by robot probes; but it had been the *Beagle*'s terraforming team that had made the windswept place, with its barren mountain ranges and endless deserts, its angry radiation and furious dust storms, into a place suitable for life.

Katrin was the head of the terraforming team. Davout led its research division. Between them, raining nano from Sarpedon's black skies, they nursed the planet to life, enriched its atmosphere, filled its seas, crafted tough, versatile vegetation capable of withstanding the angry environment. Seeded life by the tens of millions, insects, reptiles, birds, mammals, fish, and amphibians. Re-created themselves, with dark, leathery skin and slit pupils, as human forms suitable for Sarpedon's environment, so that they could examine the place they had built.

And—unknown to the others—Davout and Katrin had slipped bits of their own genetics into almost every Sarpedan life-form. Bits of redundant coding, mostly, but enough so that they could claim Sarpedon's entire world of creatures as their children. Even when they were junior terraformers on the *Cheng Ho's* mission to Rhea, they had, partly as a joke, partly as something more calculated, populated their creations with their genes.

Katrin and Davout spent the last two years of their project on Sarpedon among their children, examining the different ecosystems, different interactions, tinkering with new adaptations. In the end, Sarpedon was certified as suitable for human habitation. Preprogrammed nanos constructed small towns, laid out fields, parks, and roads. The first human Sarpedans would be constructed in nanobeds, and their minds filled with the downloaded personalities of volunteers from Earth. There was no need to go to the expense and trouble of shipping out millions of warm bodies from Earth, running the risks of traveling for decades in remote space. Not when nanos could construct them all new on site.

The first Sarpedans—bald, leather-skinned, slit-eyed—emerged blinking into their new red dawn. Any further terraforming, any attempts to fine-tune the planet and make it more Earthlike, would be a long-term project and up to them. In a splendid ceremony, Captain Moshweshwe formally turned the future of Sarpedon over to its new inhabitants. Davout had a few last formalities to perform, handing certain computer codes and protocols over to the Sarpedans, but the rest of the terraforming team, most fairly drunk on champagne, filed into the shuttle for the return journey to the *Beagle*. As Davout bent over a terminal with his Sarpedan colleagues and the *Beagle's* first officer, he could hear the roar of the shuttle on its pad, the sustained thunder as it climbed for orbit, the thud as it crashed through the sound barrier, and then he saw out of the corner of his eye the sudden red-gold flare . . .

When he raced outside, it was to see the blazing poppy unfolding in the sky, a blossom of fire and metal falling slowly to the surface of the newly christened planet.

There she was—her image anyway—in the neo-gothic armchair: Red Katrin, the green-eyed lady with whom he in memory, and Old Davout in reality, had first exchanged glances two centuries ago while Dolphus expanded on what he called his "lunaforming."

Davout had hesitated about returning her call of condolence. He did not know whether his heart could sustain *two* knife-thrusts, both Katrin's death and the sight of her sib, alive, sympathetic, and forever beyond his reach.

But he couldn't *not* call her. Even when he was trying not to think about her, he still found Katrin on the edge of his perceptions, drifting though his thoughts like the persistent trace of some familiar perfume.

Time to get it over with, he thought. If it was more than he could stand, he could apologize and end the call. But he had to *know* . . .

"And there are no backups?" she said. A pensive frown touched her lips.

"No *recent* backups," Davout said. "We always thought that, if we were to die, we would die together. Space travel is hazardous, after all, and when catastrophe strikes it is not a *small* catastrophe. We didn't anticipate one of us surviving on Earth, and the other dying light-years away." He scowled.

"Damn Mosheshwe anyway! There were recent backups on the *Beagle*, but with so many dead from an undetermined cause, he decided not to resurrect anyone, to cancel our trip to Astoreth, return to Earth, and sort out all the complications once he got home."

"He made the right decision," Katrin said. "If my sib had been resurrected, you both would have died together."

<Better so> Davout's fingers began to form the mudra, but he thought better of it, made a gesture of negation.

The green eyes narrowed. "There are older backups on Earth, yes?"

"Katrin's latest surviving backup dates from the return of the *Cheng Ho*."

"Almost ninety years ago." Thoughtfully. "But she could upload the memories she has been sending me . . . the problem does not seem insurmountable."

Red Katrin clasped her hands around one knee. At the familiar gesture, memories rang through Davout's mind like change-bells. Vertigo overwhelmed him, and he closed his eyes.

"The problem is the instructions Katrin—we both—left," he said. "Again, we anticipated that if we died, we'd die together. And so we left instructions that our backups on Earth were not to be employed. We reasoned that we had two sibs apiece on Earth, and if they—you—missed us, you could simply duplicate yourselves."

"I see." A pause, then concern. "Are you all right?"

<No> "Of course not," he said. He opened his eyes. The world eddied for a moment, then stilled, the growing calmness centered on Red Katrin's green eyes.

"I've got seventy-odd years' back pay," he said. "I suppose that I could hire some lawyers, try to get Katrin's backup released to my custody."

Red Katrin bit her nether lip. "Recent court decisions are not in your favor."

"I'm very persistent. And I'm cash-rich."

She cocked her head, looked at him. "Are you all right talking to me? Should I blank my image?"

<No.> He shook his head. "It helps, actually, to see you."

He had feared agony in seeing her, but instead he found a growing joy, a happiness that mounted in his heart. As always, his Katrin was helping him to understand, helping him to make sense of the bitter confusion of the world.

An idea began to creep into his mind on stealthy feet.

"I worry that you're alone there," Red Katrin said. "Would you like to come stay with us? Would you like us to come to Java?"

<No, thanks> "I'll come see you soon," Davout said. "But while I'm in the hospital, I think I'll have a few cosmetic procedures." He looked down at himself, spread his leathery hands. "Perhaps I should look a little more Earthlike."

After his talk with Katrin ended, Davout called Dr. Li and told him that he wanted a new body constructed.

Something familiar, he said, already in the files. His own, original form.

Age twenty or so.

"It is a surprise to see you . . . as you are," said Silent Davout.

Deep-voiced, black-skinned, and somber, Davout's sib stood by his bed.

"It was a useful body when I wore it," Davout answered. "I take comfort in . . . familiar things . . . now that my life is so uncertain." He looked up. "It was good of you to come in person."

"A holographic body," he said, taking Davout's hand, "however welcome, however familiar, is not the same as a real person."

Davout squeezed the hand. "Welcome, then," he said. Dr. Li, who had supervised in person through the new/old body's assembly, had left after saying the nanos were done, so it seemed appropriate for Davout to stand and embrace his sib.

The youngest of the sibs was not tall, but he was built solidly, as if for permanence, and his head seemed slightly oversized for his body. With his older sibs, he had always maintained a kind of formal reserve that had resulted in his being nicknamed "the Silent." Accepting the name, he remarked that the reason he spoke little when the others were around was that his older sibs had already said everything that needed saying before he got to it.

Davout stepped back and smiled. "Your patients must think you a tower of strength."

"I have no patients these days. Mostly I work in the realm of theory."

"I will have to look up your work. I'm so far behind on uploads—I don't have any idea what you and Katrin have been doing these last decades."

Silent Davout stepped to the armoire and opened its ponderous mahogany doors. "Perhaps you should put on some clothing," he said. "I am feeling chill in this conditioned air, and so must you."

Amused, Davout clothed himself, then sat across the little rosewood side table from his sib. Davout the Silent looked at him for a long moment—eyes placid and thoughtful—and then spoke.

"You are experiencing something that is very rare in our time," he said. "Loss, anger, frustration, terror. All the emotions that in their totality equal *grief*."

"You forgot sadness and regret," Davout said. "You forgot memory, and how the memories keep replaying. You forgot *imagination*, and how imagination only makes those memories worse, because imagination allows you to write a different ending, but the world will not."

Silent Davout nodded. "People in my profession," fingers forming <irony>, "anyway those born too late to remember how common these things once were, must view you with a certain clinical interest. I must commend Dr. Li on his restraint."

"Dr. Li is a shrink?" Davout asked.

<Yes.> A casual press of fingers. "Among other things. I'm sure he's watching you very carefully and making little notes every time he leaves the room."

"I'm happy to be useful." <Irony> in his hand, bitterness on his tongue. "I would give those people my memories, if they want them so much."

<Of course> "You can do that."

Davout looked up in something like surprise.

"You know it is possible," his sib said. "You can download your memories, preserve them like amber or simply hand them to someone else to experience. And you can erase them from your mind completely, walk on into a new life, *tabula rasa* and free of pain."

His deep voice was soft. It was a voice without affect, one he no doubt used on his patients, quietly insistent without being officious. A voice that made suggestions, or presented alternatives, but which never, ever, gave orders.

"I don't want that," Davout said.

Silent Davout's fingers were still set in <of course>. "You are not of the generation that accepts such things as a matter of course," he said. "But this, this *modular* approach to memory, to being, constitutes much of my work these days."

Davout looked at him. "It must be like losing a piece of yourself, to give up a memory. Memories are what make you."

Silent Davout's face remained impassive as his deep voice sounded through the void between them. "What forms a human psyche is not a memory, we have come to believe, but a pattern of thought. When our sib duplicated himself, he duplicated his pattern in us; and when we assembled new bodies to live in, the pattern did not change. Have you felt yourself to be a different person when you took a new body?"

Davout passed a hand over his head, felt the fine blond hair covering his scalp. This time yesterday, his head had been bald and leathery. Now he felt subtle differences in his perceptions—his vision was more acute, his hearing less so— and his muscle memory was somewhat askew. He remembered having a shorter reach, a slightly different center of gravity.

But as for *himself*, his essence—no, he felt himself unchanged. He was still Davout.

<No> he signed.

"People have more choices than ever before," said Silent Davout. "They choose their bodies, they choose their memories. They can upload new knowledge, new skills. If they feel a lack of confidence, or feel that their behavior is too impulsive, they can tweak their body chemistry to produce a different effect. If they find themselves the victim of an unfortunate or destructive compulsion, the compulsion can be edited from their being. If they lack the power to change their circumstances, they can at least elect to feel happier about them. If a memory cannot be overcome, it can be eliminated."

"And you now spend your time dealing with these problems?" Davout asked.

"They are not *problems*," his sib said gently. "They are not *syndromes* or *neuroses*. They are *circumstances*. They are part of the condition of life as it exists today. They are environmental." The large, impassive eyes gazed steadily at Davout. "People choose happiness over sorrow, fulfillment over frustration. Can you blame them?"

<Yes> Davout signed. "If they deny the evidence of their own lives," he said. "We define our existence by the challenges we overcome, or those we don't. Even our tragedies define us."

His sib nodded. "That is an admirable philosophy—for Davout the Conqueror. But not all people are conquerors."

Davout strove to keep the impatience from his voice. "Lessons are learned from failures as well as successes. Experience is gained, life's knowledge is applied to subsequent occurrence. If we deny the uses of experience, what is there to make us human?"

His sib was patient. "Sometimes the experiences are negative, and so are the lessons. Would you have a person live forever under the shadow of great guilt, say for a foolish mistake that resulted in injury or death to someone else; or would you have them live with the consequences of damage inflicted by a sociopath, or an abusive family member? Traumas like these can cripple the whole being. Why should the damage not be repaired?"

Davout smiled thinly. "You can't tell me that these techniques are used only in cases of deep trauma," he said. "You can't tell me that people aren't using these techniques for reasons that might be deemed trivial. Editing out a foolish remark made at a party, or eliminating a bad vacation or an argument with the spouse."

Silent Davout returned his smile. "I would not insult your intelligence by suggesting these things do not happen."

<Q.E.D.> Davout signed. "So how do such people mature? Change? Grow in wisdom?"

"They cannot edit out *everything*. There is sufficient friction and conflict in the course of ordinary life to provide everyone with their allotted portion of wisdom. Nowadays our lives are very, very long, and we have a long time to learn, however slowly. And after all," he said, smiling, "the average person's capacity for wisdom has never been so large as all *that*! I think you will find that as a species we are far less prone to folly than we once were."

Davout looked at his sib grimly. "You are suggesting that I undergo this technique?"

"It is called Lethe."

"That I undergo Lethe? Forget Katrin? Or forget what I feel for her?"

Silent Davout slowly shook his grave head. "I make no such suggestion."

"Good."

The youngest Davout gazed steadily into the eyes of his older twin. "Only you know what you can bear. I merely point out that this remedy exists, should you find your anguish beyond what you can endure."

"Katrin deserves mourning," Davout said.

Another grave nod. "Yes."

"She deserves to be remembered. Who will remember her if I do not?"

"I understand," said Silent Davout. "I understand your desire to feel, and the necessity. I only mention Lethe because I comprehend all too well what you endure now. Because"—he licked his lips—"I, too, have lost Katrin."

Davout gaped at him. "You—" he stammered. "She is—she was killed?"

<No.> His sib's face retained its remarkable placidity. "She left me, sixteen years ago."

Davout could only stare. The fact, stated so plainly, was incomprehensible.

"I—" he began, and then his fingers found another thought. <What happened?>

"We were together for a century and a half. We grew apart. It happens."

Not to us it doesn't! Davout's mind protested. *Not to Davout and Katrin!*

Not to the two people who make up a whole greater than its parts. Not to *us.* Not ever.

But looking into his sib's accepting, melancholy face, Davout knew that it had to be true.

And then, in a way he knew to be utterly disloyal, he began to hope.

"Shocking?" said Old Davout. "Not to us, I suppose."

"It was their downloads," said Red Katrin. "Fair Katrin in particular was careful to edit out some of her feelings and judgments before she let me upload them, but still I could see her attitudes changing. And knowing her, I could make guesses by what she left out . . . I remember telling Davout three years before the split that the relationship was in jeopardy."

"The Silent One was still surprised, though, when it happened," Old Davout said. "Sophisticated though he may be about human nature, he had a blind spot where Katrin was concerned." He put an arm around Red Katrin and kissed her cheek. "As I suppose we all do," he added.

Katrin accepted the kiss with a gracious inclination of her head, then asked Davout, "Would you like the blue room here, or the green room upstairs? The green room has a window seat and a fine view of the bay, but it's small."

"I'll take the green room," Davout said. I do not need so much room, he thought, now that I am alone.

Katrin took him up the creaking wooden stair and showed him the room, the narrow bed of the old house. Through the window, he could look south to a storm on Chesapeake Bay, bluegray cloud, bright eruptions of lightning, slanting beams of sunlight that dropped through rents in the storm to tease bright winking light from the foam. He watched it for a long moment, then was startled out of reverie by Katrin's hand on his shoulder, and a soft voice in his ear.

"Are there sights like this on other worlds?"

"The storms on Rhea were vast," Davout said, "like nothing on this world. The ocean area is greater than that on Earth, and lies mostly in the tropics— the planet was almost called Oceanus on that account. The hurricanes built up around the equatorial belts with nothing to stop them, sometimes more than a thousand kilometers across, and they came roaring into the temperate zones like multi-armed demons, sometimes one after another for months. They spawned waterspots and cyclones in their vanguard, inundated whole areas with a storm surge the size of a small ocean, dumped enough rain to flood an entire province away. . . . We thought seriously that the storms might make life on land untenable."

He went on to explain the solution he and Katrin had devised for the enormous problem: huge strings of tall, rocky barrier islands built at a furious rate by nanomachines, a wall for wind and storm surge to break against; a species of silvery, tropical floating weed, a flowery girdle about Rhea's thick waist, that radically increased surface albedo, reflecting more heat back into space. Many species of deep-rooted, vinelike plants to anchor slopes and prevent erosion, other species of thirsty trees, adaptations of cottonwoods and willows, to line streambeds and break the power of flash floods.

Planetary engineering on such an enormous scale, in such a short time, had never been attempted, not even on Mars, and it had been difficult for Katrin and Davout to sell the project to the project managers on the *Cheng Ho*. Their superiors had initially preferred a different approach, huge equatorial solar curtains deployed in orbit to reflect heat, squadrons of orbital beam weapons to blast and disperse storms as they formed, secure underground dwellings for the inhabitants, complex lock and canal systems to control flooding . . . Katrin and Davout had argued for a more elegant approach to Rhea's problems, a reliance on organic systems to modify the planet's extreme weather instead of assaulting Rhea with macro-tech and engineering. Theirs was the approach that finally won the support of the majority of the terraforming team, and resulted in their subsequent appointment as heads of *Beagle*'s terraforming team.

"Dark Katrin's memories were very exciting to upload during that time," said Katrin the Red. "That delirious explosion of creativity! Watching a whole globe take shape beneath her feet!" Her green eyes look up into Davout's. "We were jealous of you then. All that abundance being created, all that talent going to shaping an entire world. And we were confined to scholarship, which seemed so lifeless by comparison."

He looked at her. <Query> "Are you sorry for the choice you made? You two were senior: you could have chosen our path if you'd wished. You still could, come to that."

A smile drifts across her face. "You tempt me, truly. But Old Davout and I are happy in our work—and besides, you and Katrin needed someone to provide a proper record of your adventures." She tilted her head, and mischief glittered in her eyes. "Perhaps you should ask Blonde Katrin. Maybe she could use a change."

Davout gave a guilty start: she was, he thought, seeing too near, too soon. "Do you think so?" he asked. "I didn't even know if I should see her."

"Her grudge is with the Silent One, not with you."

"Well." He managed a smile. "Perhaps I will at least call."

· · ·

Davout called Katrin the Fair, received an offer of dinner on the following day, accepted. From his room, he followed the smell of coffee into his hosts' office, and felt a bubble of grief lodge in his heart: two desks, back-to-back, two computer terminals, layers of papers and books and printout and dust . . . he could imagine himself and Katrin here, sipping coffee, working in pleasant compatibility.

<How goes it?> he signed.

His sib looked up. "I just sent a chapter to Sheol," he said. "I was making *Maxwell* far too wise." He fingered his little goatee. "The temptation is always to view the past solely as a vehicle that leads to our present grandeur. These people's sole function was to produce *us*, who are of course perfectly wise and noble and far superior to our ancestors. So one assumes that these people had *us* in mind all along, that we were what they were working toward. I have to keep reminding myself that these people lived amid unimaginable tragedy, disease and ignorance and superstition, vile little wars, terrible poverty, and *death* . . ."

He stopped, suddenly aware that he'd said something awkward—Davout felt the word vibrate in his bones, as if he were stranded inside a bell that was still singing after it had been struck—but he said, "Go on."

"I remind myself," his sib continued, "that the fact that we live in a modern culture doesn't make us better, it doesn't make us superior to these people—in fact it enlarges *them*, because they had to overcome so much more than we in order to realize themselves, in order to accomplish as much as they did." A shy smile drifted across his face. "And so a rather smug chapter is wiped out of digital existence."

"*Lavoisier* is looming," commented Red Katrin from her machine.

"Yes, that too," Old Davout agreed. His *Lavoisier and His Age* had won the McEldowney Prize and been shortlisted for other awards. Davout could well imagine that bringing *Maxwell* up to *Lavoisier*'s magisterial standards would be intimidating.

Red Katrin leaned back in her chair, combed her hair back with her fingers. "I made a few notes about the *Beagle* project," she said. "I have other commitments to deal with first, of course."

She and Old Davout had avoided any conflicts of interest and interpretation by conveniently dividing history between them: she would write of the "modern" world and her near-contemporaries, while he wrote of those securely in the past. Davout thought his sib had the advantage in this arrangement, because her subjects, as time progressed, gradually entered his domain, and became liable to his reinterpretation.

Davout cleared away some printout, sat on the edge of Red Katrin's desk. "A thought keeps bothering me," he said. "In our civilization we record everything. But the last moments of the crew of the *Beagle* went unrecorded. Does that mean they do not exist? Never existed at all? That death was *always* their state, and they returned to it, like virtual matter dying into the vacuum from which it came?"

Concern darkened Red Katrin's eyes. "They will be remembered," she said. "I will see to it."

"Katrin didn't download the last months, did she?"

<No> "The last eight months were never sent. She was very busy, and—"

"Virtual months, then. Gone back to the phantom zone."

"There are records. Other crew sent downloads home, and I will see if I can gain access either to the downloads, or to their friends and relations who have experienced them. There is *your* memory, your downloads."

He looked at her. "Will you upload my memory, then? My sib has everything in his files, I'm sure." Glancing at Old Davout.

She pressed her lips together. "That would be difficult for me. *Me* viewing *you* viewing *her.* . . ." She shook her head. "I don't dare. Not now. Not when we're all still in shock."

Disappointment gnawed at his insides with sharp rodent teeth. He did not want to be so alone in his grief; he didn't want to nourish all the sadness by himself.

He wanted to share it with *Katrin*, he knew, the person with whom he shared everything. Katrin could help him make sense of it, the way she clarified all the world for him. Katrin would comprehend the way he felt.

<I understand> he signed. His frustration must have been plain to Red Katrin, because she took his hand, lifted her green eyes to his.

"I will," she said. "But not now. I'm not ready."

"I don't want *two* wrecks in the house," called Old Davout over his shoulder.

Interfering old bastard, Davout thought. But with his free hand he signed, again, <I understand>.

Katrin the Fair kissed Davout's cheek, then stood back, holding his hands, and narrowed her grey eyes. "I'm not sure I approve of this youthful body of yours," she said. "You haven't looked like this in—what—over a century?"

"Perhaps I seek to evoke happier times," Davout said.

A little frown touched the corners of her mouth. "*That* is always dangerous," she judged. "But I wish you every success." She stepped back from the door, flung out an arm. "Please come in."

She lived in a small apartment in Toulouse, with a view of the Allée Saint-Michel and the rose-red brick of the Vieux Quartier. On the white-washed walls hung terra-cotta icons of Usil and Tiv, the Etruscan gods of the sun and moon, and a well cover with a figure of the demon Charun emerging from the underworld. The Etruscan deities were confronted, on another wall, by a bronze figure of the Gaulish Rosmerta, consort of the absent Mercurius.

Her little balcony was bedecked with wrought iron and a gay striped awning. In front of the balcony a table shimmered under a red-and-white checked tablecloth: crystal, porcelain, a wicker basket of bread, a bottle of wine. Cooking scents floated in from the kitchen.

"It smells wonderful," Davout said.

<Drink?> Lifting the bottle.

\<Why not?\>

Wine was poured. They settled onto the sofa, chatted of weather, crowds, Java. Davout's memories of the trip that Silent Davout and his Katrin had taken to the island were more recent than hers.

Fair Katrin took his hand. "I have uploaded Dark Katrin's memories, so far as I have them," she said. "She loved you, you know—absolutely, deeply." \<Truth.\> She bit her lip. "It was a remarkable thing."

\<Truth\> Davout answered. He touched cool crystal to his lips, took a careful sip of his cabernet. Pain throbbed in the hollows of his heart.

"Yes," he said. "I know."

"I felt I should tell you about her feelings. Particularly in view of what happened with me and the Silent One."

He looked at her. "I confess I do not understand that business."

She made a little frown of distaste. "We and our work and our situation grew irksome. Oppressive. You may upload his memories if you like—I daresay you will be able to observe the signs that he was determined to ignore."

\<I am sorry.\>

Clouds gathered in her grey eyes. "I, too, have regrets."

"There is no chance of reconciliation?"

\<Absolutely not\>, accompanied by a brief shake of the head. "It was over." \<Finished\> "And, in any case, Davout the Silent is not the man he was."

\<Yes?\>

"He took Lethe. It was the only way he had of getting over my leaving him."

Pure amazement throbbed in Davout's soul. Fair Katrin looked at him in surprise.

"You didn't know?"

He blinked at her. "I *should* have. But I thought he was talking about *me*, about a way of getting over . . ." Aching sadness brimmed in his throat. "Over the way my Dark Katrin left me."

Scorn whitened the flesh about Fair Katrin's nostrils. "That's the Silent One for you. He didn't have the nerve to tell you outright."

"I'm not sure that's true. He may have thought he was speaking plainly enough—"

Her fingers formed a mudra that gave vent to a brand of disdain that did not translate into words. "He knows his effects perfectly well," she said. "He was trying to suggest the idea without making it clear that this was his *choice* for you, that he wanted you to fall in line with his theories."

Anger was clear in her voice. She rose, stalked angrily to the bronze of Rosmerta, adjusted its place on the wall by a millimeter or so. Turned, waved an arm.

\<Apologies\>, flung to the air. "Let's eat. Silent Davout is the last person I want to talk about right now."

"I'm sorry I upset you." Davout was not sorry at all: he found this display fascinating. The gestures, the tone of voice, were utterly familiar, ringing like chimes in his heart; but the *style*, the way Fair Katrin avoided the issue, was different. Dark Katrin never would have fled a subject this way: she would have knit her brows and confronted the problem direct, engaged with it until she'd reached either understanding or catastrophe. Either way, she'd have laughed, and tossed her dark hair, and announced that now she understood.

"It's peasant cooking," Katrin the Fair said as she bustled to the kitchen, "which of course is the best kind."

The main course was a ragoût of veal in a velouté sauce, beans cooked simply in butter and garlic, tossed salad, bread. Davout waited until it was half consumed, and the bottle of wine mostly gone, before he dared to speak again of his sib.

"You mentioned the Silent One and his theories," he said. "I'm thirty years behind on his downloads, and I haven't read his latest work—what is he up to? What's all this theorizing about?"

She sighed, fingers ringing a frustrated rhythm on her glass. Looked out the window for a moment, then conceded. "Has he mentioned the modular theory of the psyche?"

Davout tried to remember. "He said something about modular *memory*, I seem to recall."

<Yes> "That's a part of it. It's a fairly radical theory that states that people should edit their personality and abilities at will, as circumstances dictate. That one morning, say, if you're going to work,' you upload appropriate memories, and work skills, along with a dose of ambition, of resolution, and some appropriate emotions like satisfaction and eagerness to solve problems, or endure drudgery, as the case may be."

Davout looked at his plate. "Like cookery, then," he said. "Like this dish—veal, carrots, onions, celery, mushrooms, parsley."

Fair Katrin made a mudra that Davout didn't recognize. <Sorry?> he signed.

"Oh. Apologies. That one means, roughly, 'har-de-har-har.' " Fingers formed <laughter>, then <sarcasm>, then slurred them together. "See?"

<Understood.> He poured more wine into her glass.

She leaned forward across her plate. "Recipes are fine if one wants to be *consumed*," she said. "Survival is another matter. The human mind is more than just ingredients to be tossed together. The atomistic view of the psyche is simplistic, dangerous, and *wrong*. You cannot *will* a psyche to be whole, no matter how many *wholeness* modules are uploaded. A psyche is more than the sum of its parts."

Wine and agitation burnished her cheeks. Conviction blazed from her eyes. "It takes *time* to integrate new experience, new abilities. The modular theorists claim this will be done by a 'conductor,' an artificial intelligence that will be able to judge between alternate personalities and abilities and upload whatever's needed. But that's such *rubbish*, I—" She looked at the knife she was waving, then permitted it to return to the table.

"How far are the Silent One and his cohorts toward realizing this ambition?" Davout said.

<Beg pardon?> She looked at him. "I didn't make that clear?" she said. "The technology is already here. It's happening. People are fragmenting their psyches deliberately and trusting to their conductors to make sense of it all. And

they're *happy* with their choices, because that's the only emotion they permit themselves to upload from their supply." She clenched her teeth, glanced angrily out the window at the Vieux Quartier's sunset-burnished walls. "All traditional psychology is aimed at integration, at wholeness. And now it's all to be *thrown away*. . . ." She flung her hand out the window. Davout's eyes automatically followed an invisible object on its arc from her fingers toward the street.

"And how does this theory work in practice?" Davout asked. "Are the streets filled with psychological wrecks?"

Bitterness twisted her lips. "Psychological imbeciles, more like. Executing their conductors' orders, docile as well-fed children, happy as clams. They upload passions—anger, grief, loss—as artificial experiences, secondhand from someone else, usually so they can tell their conductor to avoid such emotions in the future. They are not *people* any more, they're . . ." Her eyes turned to Davout.

"You saw the Silent One," she said. "Would you call him a *person?*"

"I was with him for only a day," Davout said. "I noticed something of a . . ." <Stand by> he signed, searching for the word.

"Lack of affect?" she interposed. "A demeanor marked by an extreme placidity?"

<Truth> he signed.

"When it was clear I wouldn't come back to him, he wrote me out of his memory," Fair Katrin said. "He replaced the memories with *facts*—he knows he was married to me, he knows we went to such-and-such a place or wrote such-and-such a paper—but there's nothing else there. No feelings, no real memories good or bad, no understanding, nothing left from almost two centuries together." Tears glittered in her eyes. "I'd rather he felt anything at all—I'd rather he hated me than feel this apathy!"

Davout reached across the little table and took her hand. "It is his decision," he said, "and his loss."

"It is *all* our loss," she said. Reflected sunset flavored her tears with the color of roses. "The man we loved is gone. And millions are gone with him—millions of little half-alive souls, programmed for happiness and unconcern." She tipped the bottle into her glass, received only a sluicing of dregs.

"Let's have another," she said.

When he left, some hours later, he embraced her, kissed her, let his lips linger on hers for perhaps an extra half-second. She blinked up at him in wine-muddled surprise, and then he took his leave.

"How did you find my sib?" Red Katrin asked.

"Unhappy," Davout said. "Confused. Lonely, I think. Living in a little apartment like a cell, with icons and memories."

<I know> she signed, and turned on him a knowing green-eyed look.

"Are you planning on taking her away from all that? To the stars, perhaps?"

Davout's surprise was brief. He looked away and murmured, "I didn't know I was so transparent."

A smile touched her lips. <Apologies> she signed. "I've lived with Old

Davout for nearly two hundred years. You and he haven't grown so very far apart in that time. My fair sib deserves happiness, and so do you . . . if you can provide it, so much the better. But I wonder if you are not moving too fast, if you have thought it all out."

Moving fast, Davout wondered. His life seemed so very slow now, a creeping dance with agony, each move a lifetime.

He glanced out at Chesapeake Bay, saw his second perfect sunset in only a few hours—the same sunset he'd watched from Fair Katrin's apartment, now radiating its red glories on the other side of the Atlantic. A few water-skaters sped toward home on their silver blades. He sat with Red Katrin on a porch swing, looking down the long green sward to the bayfront, the old wooden pier, and the sparkling water, that profound, deep blue that sang of home to Davout's soul. Red Katrin wrapped herself against the breeze in a fringed, autumn-colored shawl. Davout sipped coffee from gold-rimmed porcelain, set the cup into its saucer.

"I wondered if I was being untrue to *my* Katrin," he said. "But they are really the same person, aren't they? If I were to pursue some other woman now, I would know I was committing a betrayal. But how can I betray Katrin with herself?"

An uncertain look crossed Red Katrin's face. "I've downloaded them both," she said hesitantly, "and I'm not certain that the Dark and Fair Katrins are quite the same person. Or ever were."

Not the same—of course he knew that. Fair Katrin was not a perfect copy of her older sib—she had flaws, clear enough. She had been damaged, somehow. But the flaws could be worked on, the damage repaired. Conquered. There was infinite time. He would see it done.

<Question> "And how do your sibs differ, then?" he asked. "Other than obvious differences in condition and profession?"

She drew her legs up and rested her chin on her knees. Her green eyes were pensive. "Matters of love," she said, "and happiness."

And further she would not say.

Davout took Fair Katrin to Tangier for the afternoon and walked with her up on the old palace walls. Below them, white in the sun, the curved mole built by Charles II cleaved the Middle Sea, a thin crescent moon laid upon the perfect shimmering azure. (Home! home!, the waters cried.) The sea breeze lashed her blonde hair across her face, snapped little sonic booms from the sleeves of his shirt.

"I have sampled some of the Silent One's downloads," Davout said. "I wished to discover the nature of this artificial tranquility with which he has endowed himself."

Fair Katrin's lips twisted in distaste, and her fingers formed a scatologue.

"It was . . . interesting," Davout said. "There was a strange, uncomplicated quality of bliss to it. I remember experiencing the download of a master sitting zazen once, and it was an experience of a similar cast."

"It may have been the exact same sensation." Sourly. "He may have just copied the Zen master's experience and slotted it into his brain. That's how *most* of the vampires do it—award themselves the joy they haven't earned."

"That's a Calvinistic point of view," Davout offered. "That happiness can't just happen, that it has to be earned."

She frowned out at the sea. "There is a difference between real experience and artificial or recapitulative experience. If that's Calvinist, so be it."

<Yes> Davout signed. "Call me a Calvinist sympathizer, then. I have been enough places, done enough things, so that it matters to me that I was actually there and not living out some programmed dream of life on other worlds. I've experienced my sibs' downloads—lived significant parts of their lives, moment by moment—but it is not the same as *my life*, as *being me*. I am," he said, leaning elbows on the palace wall, "I am myself, I am the sum of everything that happened to me, I stand on this wall, I am watching this sea, I am watching it with you, and no one else has had this experience, nor ever shall, it is *ours*, it belongs to *us* . . ."

She looked up at him, straw-hair flying over an unreadable expression. "Davout the Conqueror," she said.

<No> he signed. "I did not conquer alone."

She nodded, holding his eyes for a long moment. "Yes," she said. "I know."

He took Katrin the Fair in his arms and kissed her. There was a moment's stiff surprise, and then she began to laugh, helpless peals bursting against his lips. He held her for a moment, too surprised to react, and then she broke free. She reeled along the wall, leaning for support against the old stones. Davout followed, babbling, "I'm sorry, I didn't mean to—"

She leaned back against the wall. Words burst half-hysterical from her lips, in between bursts of desperate, unamused laughter. *"So that's* what you were after! My God! As if I hadn't had enough of you all after all these years!"

"I apologize," Davout said. "Let's forget this happened. I'll take you home."

She looked up at him, the laughter gone, blazing anger in its place. "The Silent One and I would have been all right if it hadn't been for you—*for our sibs!*" She flung her words like daggers, her voice breaking with passion. "You lot were the eldest, you'd already parceled out the world between you. You were only interested in psychology because my damned Red sib and your Old one wanted insight into the characters in their histories, and because you and your dark bitch wanted a theory of the psyche to aid you in building communities on other worlds. We only got created because *you were too damned lazy to do your own research!*"

Davout stood, stunned. <No> he signed, "That's not—"

"We were *third*," she cried. "We were *born in third place*. We got the jobs you wanted *least*, and while you older sibs were winning fame and glory, we were stuck in work that didn't suit, that you'd *cast off*, awarded to us as if we were charity cases—" She stepped closer, and Davout was amazed to find a white-knuckled fist being shaken in his face. "My husband was called The Silent because his sibs had already used up all the words! He was third-rate and *knew* it!

It *destroyed* him! Now he's plugging artificial satisfaction into his head because it's the only way he'll ever feel it."

"If you didn't like your life," Davout said, "you could have changed it. People start over all the time—we'd have helped." He reached toward her. "I can help you to the stars, if that's what you want."

She backed away. "The only help we ever needed was to *get rid of you!*" A mudra, <har-de-har-har>, echoed the sarcastic laughter on Fair Katrin's lips. "And now there's another gap in your life, and you want me to fill it—*not this time.*"

<Never> her fingers echoed. <Never.> The laughter bubbled from her throat again.

She fled, leaving him alone and dazed on the palace wall, as the booming wind mocked his feeble protests.

"I am truly sorry," Red Katrin said. She leaned close to him on the porch swing, touched soft lips to his cheek. "Even though she edited her downloads, I could tell she resented us—but I truly did not know how she would react."

Davout was frantic. He could feel Katrin slipping farther and farther away, as if she were on the edge of a precipice and her handholds were crumbling away beneath her clawed fingers.

"Is what she said true?" he asked. "Have we been slighting them all these years? Using them, as she claims?"

"Perhaps she had some justification once," Red Katrin said. "I do not remember anything of the sort when we were young, when I was uploading Fair Katrin almost every day. But now . . ." Her expression grew severe. "These are mature people, not without resources or intelligence—I can't help but think that surely after a person is a century old, any problems that remain are *her* fault."

As he rocked on the porch swing he could feel a wildness rising in him. *My God*, he thought, *I am going to be* alone.

His brief days of hope were gone. He stared out at the bay—the choppy water was too rough for any but the most dedicated water-skaters—and felt the pain pressing on his brain, like the two thumbs of a practiced sadist digging into the back of his skull.

"I wonder," he said. "Have you given any further thought to uploading my memories?"

She looked at him curiously. "It's scarcely time yet."

"I feel a need to share . . . some things."

"Old Davout has uploaded them. You could speak to him."

This perfectly intelligent suggestion only made him clench his teeth. He needed *sense* made of things, he needed things put in *order*, and that was not the job of his sib. Old Davout would only confirm what he already knew.

"I'll talk to him, then," he said.

And then never did.

· · ·

The pain was worst at night. It wasn't the sleeping alone, or merely Katrin's absence: it was the knowledge that she would *always* be absent, that the empty space next to him would be there forever. It was then that the horror fully struck him, and he would lie awake for hours, eyes staring into the terrible void that wrapped him in its dark cloak, while fits of trembling sped through his limbs.

I will go mad, he sometimes thought. It seemed something he could choose, as if he were a character in an Elizabethan drama who turns to the audience to announce that he will be mad now, and then in the next scene is found gnawing bones dug out of the family sepulcher. Davout could see himself being found outside, running on all fours and barking at the stars.

And then, as dawn crept across the windowsill, he would look out the window and realize, to his sorrow, that he was not yet mad, that he was condemned to another day of sanity, of pain, and of grief.

Then, one night, he *did* go mad. He found himself squatting on the floor in his nightshirt, the room a ruin around him: mirrors smashed, furniture broken. Blood was running down his forearms.

The door leapt off its hinges with a heave of Old Davout's shoulder. Davout realized, in a vague way, that his sib had been trying to get in for some time. He saw Red Katrin's silhouette in the door, an aureate halo around her auburn hair in the instant before Old Davout snapped on the light.

Afterward Katrin pulled the bits of broken mirror out of Davout's hands, washed and disinfected them, while his sib tried to reconstruct the green room and its antique furniture.

Davout watched his spatters of blood stain the water, threads of scarlet whirling in coreolis spirals. "I'm sorry," he said. "I think I may be losing my mind."

"I doubt that." Frowning at a bit of glass in her tweezers.

"I want to *know*."

Something in his voice made her look up. "Yes?"

He could see his staring reflection in her green eyes. "Read my downloads. Please. I want to know if . . . I'm reacting normally in all this. If I'm lucid or just . . ." He fell silent. *Do it*, he thought. *Just do this one thing.*

"I don't upload other people. Davout can do that. *Old* Davout, I mean."

No, Davout thought. His sib would understand all too well what he was up to.

"But he's me!" he said. "He'd think I'm normal!"

"Silent Davout, then. Crazy people are his specialty."

Davout wanted to make a mudra of scorn, but Red Katrin held his hands captive. Instead he gave a laugh. "He'd want me to take Lethe. Any advice he gave would be . . . in that direction." He made a fist of one hand, saw drops of blood well up through the cuts. "I need to know if I can stand this," he said. "If—something drastic is required."

She nodded, looked again at the sharp little spear of glass, put it deliberately on the edge of the porcelain. Her eyes narrowed in thought—Davout felt his heart vault at that look, at the familiar lines forming at the corner of Red Katrin's right eye, each one known and adored.

Please do it, he thought desperately.

"If it's that important to you," she said, "I will."

"Thank you," he said.

He bent his head over her and the basin, raised her hand, and pressed his lips to the flesh beaded with water and streaked with blood.

It was almost like conducting an affair, all clandestine meetings and whispered arrangements. Red Katrin did not want Old Davout to know she was uploading his sib's memories—"I would just as soon not deal with his disapproval"—and so she and Davout had to wait until he was gone for a few hours, a trip to record a lecture for Cavor's series on *Ideas and Manners.*

She settled onto the settee in the front room and covered herself with her fringed shawl. Closed her eyes. Let Davout's memories roll through her.

He sat in a chair nearby, his mouth dry. Though nearly thirty years had passed since Dark Katrin's death, he had experienced only a few weeks of that time; and Red Katrin was floating through these memories at speed, tasting here and there, skipping redundancies or moments that seemed inconsequential . . .

He tried to guess from her face where in his life she dwelt. The expression of shock and horror near the start was clear enough, the shuttle bursting into flames. After the shock faded, he recognized the discomfort that came with experiencing a strange mind, and flickering across her face came expressions of grief, anger, and here and there amusement; but gradually there was only a growing sadness, and lashes wet with tears. He crossed the room to kneel by her chair and take her hand. Her fingers pressed his in response . . . she took a breath, rolled her head away . . . he wanted to weep not for his grief, but for hers.

The eyes fluttered open. She shook her head. "I had to stop," she said. "I couldn't take it—" She looked at him, a kind of awe in her wide green eyes. "My God, the sadness! And the *need*. I had no idea. I've never felt such need. I wonder what it is to be needed that way."

He kissed her hand, her damp cheek. Her arms went around him. He felt a leap of joy, of clarity. The need was hers, now.

Davout carried her to the bed she shared with his sib, and together they worshipped memories of his Katrin.

"I will take you there," Davout said. His finger reached into the night sky, counted stars, *one, two, three*. . . . "The planet's called Atugan. It's boiling hot, nothing but rock and desert, sulphur and slag. But we can make it home for ourselves and our children—all the species of children we desire, fish and fowl." A bubble of happiness filled his heart. "Dinosaurs, if you like," he said. "Would you like to be parent to a dinosaur?"

He felt Katrin leave the shelter of his arm, step toward the moonlit bay. Waves rumbled under the old wooden pier. "I'm not trained for terraforming," she said. "I'd be useless on such a trip."

"I'm decades behind in my own field," Davout said. "You could learn while I caught up. You'll have Dark Katrin's downloads to help. It's all possible."

She turned toward him. The lights of the house glowed yellow off her pale face, off her swift fingers as she signed.

<Regret> "I have lived with Old Davout for near two centuries," she said.

His life, for a moment, seemed to skip off its internal track; he felt himself suspended, poised at the top of an arc just before the fall.

Her eyes brooded up at the house, where Old Davout paced and sipped coffee and pondered his life of Maxwell. The mudras at her fingertips were unreadable in the dark.

"I will do as I did before," she said. "I cannot go with you, but my other self will."

Davout felt his life resume. "Yes," he said, because he was in shadow and could not sign. "By all means." He stepped nearer to her. "I would rather it be you," he whispered.

He saw wry amusement touch the corners of her mouth. "It *will* be me," she said. She stood on tiptoe, kissed his cheek. "But now I am your sister again, yes?" Her eyes looked level into his. "Be patient. I will arrange it."

"I will in all things obey you, madam," he said, and felt wild hope singing in his heart.

Davout was present at her awakening, and her hand was in his as she opened her violet eyes, the eyes of his Dark Katrin. She looked at him in perfect comprehension, lifted a hand to her black hair; and then the eyes turned to the pair standing behind him, to Old Davout and Red Katrin.

"Young man," Davout said, putting his hand on Davout's shoulder, "allow me to present you to my wife." And then (wisest of the sibs), he bent over and whispered, a bit pointedly, into Davout's ear, "I trust you will do the same for me, one day."

Davout concluded, through his surprise, that the secret of a marriage that lasts two hundred years is knowing when to turn a blind eye.

"I confess I am somewhat envious," Red Katrin said as she and Old Davout took their leave. "I envy my twin her new life."

"It's your life as well," he said. "She *is* you." But she looked at him soberly, and her fingers formed a mudra he could not read.

He took her on honeymoon to the Rockies, used some of his seventy-eight years' back pay to rent a sprawling cabin in a high valley above the headwaters of the Rio Grande, where the wind rolled grandly through the pines, hawks spun lazy high circles on the afternoon thermals, and the brilliant clear light blazed on white starflowers and Indian paintbrush. They went on long walks in the high hills, cooked simply in the cramped kitchen, slept beneath scratchy trade blankets, made love on crisp cotton sheets.

He arranged an office there, two desks and two chairs, back-to-back. Katrin applied herself to learning biology, ecology, nanotech, and quantum physics— she already had a good grounding, but a specialist's knowledge was lacking. Davout tutored her, and worked hard at catching up with the latest developments in the field. She—they did not have a name for her yet, though Davout thought of her as "New Katrin"—would review Dark Katrin's old downloads, concentrating on her work, the way she visualized a problem.

Once, opening her eyes after an upload, she looked at Davout and shook her head. "It's strange," she said. "It's *me*, I know it's me, but the way she *thinks*—" <I don't understand> she signed. "It's not memories that make us, we're told, but patterns of thought. We are who we are because we think using certain patterns . . . but I do not seem to think like her at all."

"It's habit," Davout said. "Your habit is to think a different way."

<Possibly> she conceded, brows knit.

<Truth> "You—Red Katrin—uploaded Dark Katrin before. You had no difficulty in understanding her then."

"I did not concentrate on the technical aspects of her work, on the way she visualized and solved problems. They were beyond my skill to interpret—I paid more attention to other moments in her life." She lifted her eyes to Davout. "Her moments with you, for instance. Which were very rich, and very intense, and which sometimes made me jealous."

"No need for jealousy now."

<Perhaps> she signed, but her dark eyes were thoughtful, and she turned away.

He felt Katrin's silence after that, an absence that seemed to fill the cabin with the invisible, weighty cloud of her somber thought. Katrin spent her time studying by herself or restlessly paging through Dark Katrin's downloads. At meals and in bed, she was quiet, meditative—perfectly friendly, and, he thought, not unhappy—but keeping her thoughts to herself.

She is adjusting, he thought. *It is not an easy thing for someone two centuries old to change.*

"I have realized," she said ten days later at breakfast, "that my sib—that Red Katrin—is a coward. That I am created—and the other sibs, too—to do what she would not, or dared not." Her violet eyes gazed levelly at Davout. "She wanted to go with you to Atugan, she wanted to feel the power of your desire . . . but something held her back. So I am created to do the job for her. It is my purpose . . . to fulfill *her* purpose."

"It's her loss, then," Davout said, though his fingers signed <surprise>.

<Alas!> she signed, and Davout felt a shiver caress his spine. "But I am a coward, too!" Katrin cried. "I am *not* your brave Dark Katrin, and I cannot become her!"

"Katrin," he said. "You are the same person—you *all* are!"

She shook her head. "I do not think like your Katrin. I do not have her courage. I do not know what liberated her from her fear, but it is something I do not have. And—" She reached across the table to clasp his hand. "I do not have the feelings for you that she possessed. I simply do not. I have tried, I have had that world-eating passion read into my mind, and I compare it with what I feel, and—what I have is as nothing. I *wish* I felt as she did, I truly do. But if I love anyone, it is Old Davout. And . . ." She let go his hand, and rose from the table. "I am a coward, and I will take the coward's way out. I must leave."

<No> his fingers formed, then <please>. "You can change that," he said. He followed her into the bedroom. "It's just a switch in your mind, Silent Davout can throw it for you, we can love each other forever...." She made no answer. As she began to pack, grief seized him by the throat and the words dried up. He retreated to the little kitchen, sat at the table, held his head in his hands. He looked up when she paused in the door, and froze like a deer in the violet light of her eyes.

"Fair Katrin was right," she said. "Our elder sibs are bastards—they use us, and not kindly."

A few moments later he heard a car drive up, then leave. <Alas!> his fingers signed. <Alas!>

He spent the day unable to leave the cabin, unable to work, terror shivering through him. After dark, he was driven outside by the realization that he would have to sleep on sheets that were touched with Katrin's scent. He wandered by starlight across the high mountain meadow, dry soil crunching beneath his boots, and when his legs began to ache he sat down heavily in the dust.

I am weary of my groaning ... he thought.

It was summer, but the high mountains were chill at night, and the deep cold soaked his thoughts. The word *Lethe* floated through his mind. Who would not choose to be happy? he asked himself. It is a switch in your mind, and someone can throw it for you.

He felt the slow, aching droplets of mourning being squeezed from his heart, one after the other, and wondered how long he could endure them, the relentless moments, each striking with the impact of a hammer, each a stunning, percussive blow....

Throw a switch, he thought, and the hammerblows would end.

"Katrin deserves mourning," he had told Davout the Silent, and now he had so many more Katrins to mourn, Dark Katrin and Katrin the Fair, Katrin the New and Katrin the Old. All the Katrins webbed by fate, alive or dead or merely enduring. And so he would, from necessity, endure.... *So long lives this, and this gives life to thee.*

He lay on his back, on the cold ground, gazed up at the world of stars, and tried to find the worlds, among the glittering teardrops of the heavens, where he and Katrin had rained from the sky their millions of children.

winter fire

GEOFFREY A. LANDIS

A physicist who works for NASA, Geoffrey A. Landis is a frequent con-
tributor to Analog *and to* Asimov's Science Fiction, *and has also sold*
stories to markets such as Interzone, Amazing, *and* Pulphouse. *Landis is*
not a prolific writer, by the high-production standards of the genre, but
he is popular. His story "A Walk in the Sun," which appeared in our
Ninth Annual Collection, won him a Nebula and a Hugo Award; his story
"Ripples in the Dirac Sea" won him a Nebula Award; and his story "El-
emental" was on the Final Hugo Ballot a few years back. His first book
was the collection Myths, Legends, *and* True History. *He lives in Brook*
Park, Ohio.

In the eloquent story that follows, he takes us to an embattled future
Salzburg for a compelling study of human courage and the persistence of
love even under the most appalling and dehumanizing of conditions. . . .

▼

I am nothing and nobody; atoms that have learned to look at themselves;
dirt that has learned to see the awe and the majesty of the universe.

The day the hover-transports arrived in the refugee camps, huge windowless shells of titanium floating on electrostatic cushions, the day faceless men
took the ragged little girl that was me away from the narrow, blasted valley
that had once been Salzburg to begin a new life on another continent: that is
the true beginning of my life. What came before then is almost irrelevant, a
sequence of memories etched as with acid into my brain, but with no meaning to real life.

Sometimes I almost think that I can remember my parents. I remember them
not by what was, but by the shape of the absence they left behind. I remember
yearning for my mother's voice, singing to me softly in Japanese. I cannot remember her voice, or what songs she might have sung, but I remember so vividly
the missing of it, the hole that she left behind.

My father I remember as the loss of something large and warm and infinitely
strong, smelling of—of what? I don't remember. Again, it is the loss that remains
in my memory, not the man. I remember remembering him as more solid than
mountains, something eternal; but in the end he was not eternal, he was not
even as strong as a very small war.

I lived in the city of music, in Salzburg, but I remember little from before the siege. I do remember cafés (seen from below, with huge tables and the legs of waiters and faces looming down to ask me if I would like a sweet). I'm sure my parents must have been there, but that I do not remember.

And I remember music. I had my little violin (although it seemed so large to me then), and music was not my second language but my first. I thought in music before ever I learned words. Even now, decades later, when I forget myself in mathematics I cease to think in words, but think directly in concepts clear and perfectly harmonic, so that a mathematical proof is no more than the inevitable majesty of a crescendo leading to a final, resolving chord.

I have long since forgotten anything I knew about the violin. I have not played since the day, when I was nine, I took from the rubble of our apartment the shattered cherry-wood scroll. I kept that meaningless piece of polished wood for years, slept with it clutched in my hand every night until, much later, it was taken away by a soldier intent on rape. Probably I would have let him, had he not been so ignorant as to think my one meager possession might be a weapon. Coitus is nothing more than the natural act of the animal. From songbirds to porpoises, any male animal will rape an available female when given a chance. The action is of no significance except, perhaps, as a chance to contemplate the impersonal majesty of the chain of life and the meaninglessness of any individual's will within it.

When I was finally taken away from the city of music, three years later and a century older, I owned nothing and wanted nothing. There was nothing of the city left. As the hoverjet took me away, just one more in a seemingly endless line of ragged survivors, only the mountains remained, hardly scarred by the bomb craters and the detritus that marked where the castle had stood, mountains looking down on humanity with the gaze of eternity.

My real parents, I have been told, were rousted out of our apartment with a tossed stick of dynamite, and shot as infidels as they ran through the door, on the very first night of the war. It was probably fanatics of the New Orthodox Resurgence that did it, in their first round of ethnic cleansing, although nobody seemed to know for sure.

In the beginning, despite the dissolution of Austria and the fall of the federation of free European states, despite the hate-talk spread by the disciples of Dragan Vukadinović, the violent cleansing of the Orthodox church, and the rising of the Pan-Slavic unity movement, all the events that covered the news-nets all through 2081, few people believed there would be a war, and those that did thought that it might last a few months. The dissolution of Austria and eastern Europe into a federation of free states was viewed by intellectuals of the time as a good thing, a recognition of the impending irrelevance of governments in the post-technological society with its burgeoning sky-cities and prospering free-trade zones. Everyone talked of civil war, but as a distant thing; it was an awful mythical monster of ancient times, one that had been thought dead, a thing that ate people's hearts and turned them into inhuman gargoyles of stone. It would not come here.

Salzburg had had a large population of Asians, once themselves refugees from the economic and political turmoil of the twenty-first century, but now prosperous citizens who had lived in the city for over a century. Nobody thought about religion in the Salzburg of that lost age; nobody cared that a person whose family once came from the Orient might be a Buddhist or a Hindu or a Confucian. My own family, as far as I know, had no religious feelings at all, but that made little difference to the fanatics. My mother, suspecting possible trouble that night, had sent me over to sleep with an old German couple who lived in a building next door. I don't remember whether I said good-bye.

Johann Achtenberg became my foster father, a stocky old man, bearded and forever smelling of cigar smoke. "We will stay," my foster father would often say, over and over. "It is *our* city; the barbarians cannot drive us out." Later in the siege, in a grimmer mood, he might add, "They can kill us, but they will never drive us out."

The next few months were full of turmoil, as the Orthodox Resurgence tried, and failed, to take Salzburg. They were still disorganized, more a mob than an army, still evolving toward the killing machine that they would eventually become. Eventually they were driven out of the city, dynamiting buildings behind them, to join up with the Pan-Slavic army rolling in from the devastation of Graz. The roads in and out of the city were barricaded, and the siege began.

For that summer of 2082, the first summer of the siege, the life of the city hardly changed. I was ten years old. There was still electricity, and water, and stocks of food. The cafés stayed open, although coffee became hard to obtain, and impossibly expensive when it was available, and at times they had nothing to serve but water. I would watch the pretty girls, dressed in colorful Italian suede and wearing ornately carved Ladakhi jewelry, strolling down the streets in the evenings, stopping to chat with T-shirted boys, and I would wonder if I would ever grow up to be as elegant and poised as they. The shelling was still mostly far away, and everybody believed that the tide of world opinion would soon stop the war. The occasional shell that was targeted toward the city caused great commotion, people screaming and diving under tables even for a bird that hit many blocks away. Later, when civilians had become targets, we all learned to tell the caliber and the trajectory of a shell by the sound of the song it made as it fell.

After an explosion, there is silence for an instant, then a hubbub of crashing glass and debris as shattered walls collapse, and people gingerly touch each other, just to verify that they are alive. The dust would hang in the air for hours.

Toward September, when it became obvious that the world powers were stalemated, and would not intervene, the shelling of the city began in earnest. Tanks, even modern ones with electrostatic hover and thin coilguns instead of heavy cannons, could not maneuver into the narrow alleys of the old city and were stymied by the steep-sided mountain valleys. But the outer suburbs and the hilltops were invaded, crushed flat, and left abandoned.

I did not realize it at the time, for a child sees little, but with antiquated equipment and patched-together artillery, my besieged city clumsily and painfully fought back. For every fifty shells that came in, one was fired back at the attackers.

There was an international blockade against selling weapons to the Resurgence, but that seemed to make no difference. Their weapons may not have had the most modern of technology, but they were far better than ours. They had superconducting coilguns for artillery, weapons that fired aerodynamically shaped slugs—we called them birds—that maneuvered on twisted arcs as they moved. The birds were small, barely larger than my hand, but the metastable atomic hydrogen that filled them held an incredible amount of explosive power.

Our defenders had to rely on ancient weapons, guns that ignited chemical explosives to propel metal shells. These were quickly disassembled and removed from their position after each shot, because the enemy's computers could backtrail the trajectory of our shells, which had only crude aeromaneuvering, to direct a deadly rain of birds at the guessed position. Since we were cut off from regular supply lines, each shell was precious. We were supplied by ammunition carried on mules whose trails would weave through the enemy's wooded territory by night and by shells carried one by one across dangerous territory in backpacks.

But still, miraculously, the city held. Over our heads, the continuous shower of steel eroded the skyline. Our beautiful castle Hohensalzburg was sandpapered to a hill of bare rock; the cathedral towers fell and the debris by slow degrees was pounded into gravel. Bells rang in sympathy with explosions until at last the bells were silenced. Slowly, erosion softened the profiles of buildings that once defined the city's horizon.

Even without looking for the craters, we learned to tell from looking at the trees which neighborhoods had had explosions in them. Near a blast, the city's trees had no leaves. They were all shaken off by the shock waves. But none of the trees lasted the winter anyway.

My foster father made a stove by pounding with a hammer on the fenders and door panels of a wrecked automobile, with a pipe made of copper from rooftops and innumerable soft-drink cans. Floorboards and furniture were broken to bits to make fuel for us to keep warm. All through the city, stovepipes suddenly bristled through exterior walls and through windows. The fiberglass sides of modern housing blocks, never designed for such crude heating, became decorated with black smoke trails like unreadable graffiti, and the city parks became weirdly empty lots crossed by winding sidewalks that meandered past the craters where the trees had been.

Johann's wife, my foster mother, a thin, quiet woman, died by being in the wrong building at the wrong time. She had been visiting a friend across the city to exchange chat and a pinch of hoarded tea. It might just as easily have been the building I was in where the bird decided to build its deadly nest. It took some of the solidity out of Johann. "Do not fall in love, little Leah," he told me, many months later, when our lives had returned to a fragile stability. "It hurts too much."

In addition to the nearly full-time job of bargaining for those necessities that could be bargained for, substituting or improvising those that could not, and hamstering away in basements and shelters any storable food that could be found, my foster father Johann had another job, or perhaps an obsession. I only learned this slowly. He would disappear, sometimes for days. One time I followed him as far as an entrance to the ancient catacombs beneath the bird-pecked ruins of the beautiful castle Hohensalzburg. When he disappeared into the darkness, I dared not follow.

When he returned, I asked him about it. He was strangely reluctant to speak. When he did, he did not explain, but only said that he was working on the molecular still, and refused to say anything further, or to let me mention it to anyone else.

As a child, I spoke a hodgepodge of languages; the English of the foreigners, the French of the European Union, the Japanese that my parents had spoken at home, the book-German of the schools, and the Austrian German that was the dominant tongue of the culture I lived in. At home, we spoke mostly German, and in German, "Still" is a word which means quietude. Over the weeks and months that followed, the idea of a molecular still grew in my imagination into a wonderful thing, a place that is quiet even on the molecular level, far different from the booming sounds of war. In my imagination, knowing my foster father was a gentle man who wanted nothing but peace, I thought of it as a reverse secret weapon, something that would bring this wonderful stillness to the world. When he disappeared to the wonderful molecular still, each time I would wonder whether this would be the time that the still would be ready, and peace would come.

And the city held. "Salzburg is an idea, little Leah," my foster father Johann would tell me, "and all the birds in the world could never peck it away, for it lives in our minds and in our souls. Salzburg will stand for as long as any one of us lives. And, if we ever abandon the city, then Salzburg has fallen, even if the city itself still stands."

In the outside world, the world I knew nothing of, nations quarreled and were stalemated with indecision over what to do. Our city had been fragilely connected to the western half of Europe by precarious roads, with a series of tunnels through the Alps and long arcing bridges across narrow mountain valleys. In their terror that the chaos might spread westward, they dynamited the bridges, they collapsed the tunnels. Not nations, but individuals, did it. They cut us off from civilization, and left us to survive, or die, on our own.

Governments had become increasingly unimportant in the era following the opening of the resources of space by the free-trade zones of the new prosperity, but the trading consortia that now ruled America and the far east in the place of governments had gained their influence only by assiduously signing away the capacity to make war, and although the covenants that had secured their formation had eroded, that one prohibition still held. Only governments could help us, and the governments tried negotiation and diplomacy as Dragan Vukadinović made promises for the New Orthodox Resurgence and broke them.

High above, the owners of the sky-cities did the only thing that they could, which was to deny access to space to either side. This kept the war on the ground, but hurt us more than it hurt the armies surrounding us. They, after all, had no need for satellites to find out where *we* were.

To the east, the Pan-Slavic army and the New Orthodox Resurgence were pounding against the rock of the Tenth Crusade; farther south they were skirmishing over borders with the Islamic Federation. Occasionally the shelling would stop for a while, and it would be safe to bring hoarded solar panels out into the sunlight to charge our batteries—the electric grid had gone long ago, of course—and huddle around an antique solar-powered television set watching the distant negotiating teams talk about our fate. Everybody knew that the war would be over shortly; it was impossible that the world would not act.

The world did not act.

I remember taking batteries from wrecked cars to use a headlight, if one happened to survive unbroken, or a taillight, to allow us to stay up past sunset. There was a concoction of boiled leaves that we called "tea," although we had no milk or sugar to put in it. We would sit together, enjoying the miracle of light, sipping our "tea," perhaps reading, perhaps just sitting in silence.

With the destruction of the bridges, Salzburg had become two cities, connected only by narrow-beam microwave radio and the occasional foray by individuals walking across the dangerous series of beams stretched across the rubble of the Old Stone Bridge. The two Salzburgs were distinct in population, with mostly immigrant populations isolated in the modern buildings on the east side of the river, and the old Austrians on the west.

It is impossible to describe the Salzburg feeling, the aura of a sophisticated ancient city, wrapped in a glisteningly pure blanket of snow, under siege, faced with the daily onslaught of an unseen army that seemed to have an unlimited supply of coilguns and metastable hydrogen. We were never out of range. The Salzburg stride was relaxed only when protected by the cover of buildings or specially constructed barricades, breaking into a jagged sprint over a stretch of open ground, a cobbled forecourt of crossroads open to the rifles of snipers on distant hills firing hypersonic needles randomly into the city. From the deadly steel birds, there was no protection. They could fly in anywhere, with no warning. By the time you heard their high-pitched song, you were already dead, or, miraculously, still alive.

Not even the nights were still. It is an incredible sight to see a city cloaked in darkness suddenly illuminated with the blue dawn of a flare sent up from the hilltops, dimming the stars and suffusing coruscating light across the glittering snow. There is a curious, ominous interval of quiet: the buildings of the city dragged blinking out of their darkness and displayed in a fairy glow, naked before the invisible gunners on their distant hilltops. Within thirty seconds, the birds would begin to sing. They might land a good few blocks away, the echo of their demise ringing up and down the valley, or they might land in the street below, the explosion sending people diving under tables, windows caving in across the room.

They could, I believe, have destroyed the city at any time, but that did not serve their purposes. Salzburg was a prize. Whether the buildings were whole or in parts seemed irrelevant, but the city was not to be simply obliterated.

In April, as buds started to bloom from beneath the rubble, the city woke up, and we discovered that we had survived the winter. The diplomats proposed partitioning the city between the Slavs and the Germans—Asians and other ethnic groups, like me, being conveniently ignored—and the terms were set, but nothing came of it except a cease-fire that was violated before the day was over.

The second summer of the siege was a summer of hope. Every week we thought that this might be the last week of the siege; that peace might yet be declared on terms that we could accept, that would let us keep our city. The defense of the city had opened a corridor to the outside world, allowing in humanitarian aid, black-market goods, and refugees from other parts of the war. Some of the people who had fled before the siege returned, although many of the population who had survived the winter used the opportunity to flee to the west. My foster father, though, swore that he would stay in Salzburg until death. It is civilization, and if it is destroyed, nothing is worthwhile.

Christians of the Tenth Crusade and Turks of the Islamic Federation fought side by side with the official troops of the Mayor's Brigade, sharing ammunition but not command, to defend the city. High above, cities in the sky looked down on us, but, like angels who see everything, they did nothing.

Cafés opened again, even those that, without black-market connections, could only serve water, and in the evenings there were night-clubs, the music booming even louder than the distant gunfire. My foster father, of course, would never let me stay up late enough to find out what went on in these, but once, when he was away tending his molecular still, I waited for darkness and then crept through the streets to see.

One bar was entirely Islamic Federation Turks, wearing green turbans and uniforms of dark maroon denim, with spindly railgun-launchers slung across their backs and knives and swords strung on leather straps across their bodies. Each one had in front of him a tiny cup of dark coffee and a clear glass of whisky. I thought I was invisible in the doorway, but one of the Turks, a tall man with a pocked face and a dark moustache that drooped down the side of his mouth, looked up and, without smiling, said, "Hoy, little girl, I think that you are in the wrong place."

In the next club, mercenaries wearing cowboy hats, with black uniforms and fingerless leather gloves, had parked their guns against the walls before settling in to pound down whisky in a bar where the music was so loud that the beat reverberated across half the city. The one closest to the door had a shaven head, with a spiderweb tattooed up his neck, and daggers and weird heraldic symbols tattooed across his arms. When he looked up at me, standing in the doorway, he smiled, and I realized that he had been watching me for some time, probably ever since I had appeared. His smile was far more frightening than the impassive face of the Turk. I ran all the way home.

In the daytime, the snap of a sniper's rifle might prompt an exchange of heavy machine-gun fire, a wild, rattling sound that echoed crazily from the hills. Small-arms fire would sound, tak, tak, tak, answered by the singing of small railguns, tee, tee. You can't tell the source of rifle fire in an urban environment; it seems to come from all around. All you can do is duck, and run. Later that summer, the first of the omniblasters showed up, firing a beam of pure energy with a silence so loud that tiny hairs all over my body would stand up in fright.

Cosmetics, baby milk, and whisky were the most prized commodities on the black market.

I had no idea what the war was about. Nobody was able to explain it in terms that an eleven-year-old could understand; few even bothered to try. All I knew was that evil people on hilltops were trying to destroy everything I loved, and good men like my foster father were trying to stop them.

I slowly learned that my foster father was, apparently, quite important to the defense. He never talked about what he did, but I overheard other men refer to him with terms like "vital" and "indispensable," and these words made me proud. At first I simply thought that they merely meant that the existence of men like him, proud of the city and vowing never to leave, was the core of what made the defense worthwhile. But later I realized that it must be more than this. There were thousands of men who loved the city.

Toward the end of the summer, the siege closed around the city again. The army of the Tenth Crusade arrived and took over the ridgetops just one valley to the west; the Pan-Slavic army and the Orthodox Resurgence held the ridges next to the city and the territory to the east. All that autumn the shells of the Tenth Crusade arced over our heads toward the Pan-Slavs, and beams of purple fire from pop-up robots with omniblasters would fire back. It was a good autumn; mostly only stray fire hit the civilians. But we were locked in place, and there was no way out.

There was no place to go outside; no place that was safe. The sky had become our enemy. My friends were books. I had loved storybooks when I had been younger, in the part of my childhood before the siege that even then I barely remembered. But Johann had no storybooks; his vast collection of books were all forbidding things, full of thick blocks of dense text and incomprehensible diagrams that were no picture of anything I could recognize. I taught myself algebra, with some help from Johann, and started working on calculus. It was easier when I realized that the mathematics in the books was just an odd form of music, written in a strange language. Candles were precious, and so in order to keep on reading at night, Johann made an oil lamp for me, which would burn vegetable oil. This was nearly as precious as candles, but not so precious as my need to read.

A still, I had learned from my reading—and from the black market—was a device for making alcohol, or at least for separating alcohol from water. Did a molecular still make molecules?

"That's silly," Johann told me. "Everything is made of molecules. Your bed, the air you breathe, even you yourself, nothing but molecules."

In November, the zoo's last stubborn elephant died. The predators, the lions, the tigers, even the wolves, were already gone, felled by simple lack of meat. The zebras and antelopes had gone quickly, some from starvation-induced illness, some killed and butchered by poachers. The elephant, surprisingly, had been the last to go, a skeletal apparition stubbornly surviving on scraps of grass and bits of trash, protected against ravenous poachers by a continuous guard of armed watchmen. The watchmen proved unable, however, to guard against starvation. Some people claim that kangaroos and emus still survived, freed from their hutches by the shelling, and could be seen wandering free in the city late at night. Sometimes I wonder if they survive still awkward birds and bounding marsupials, hiding in the foothills of the Austrian Alps, the last survivors of the siege of Salzburg.

It was a hard winter. We learned to conserve the slightest bit of heat, so as to stretch a few sticks of firewood out over a whole night. Typhus, dysentery, and pneumonia killed more than the shelling, which had resumed in force with the onset of winter. Just after New Year, a fever attacked me, and there was no medicine to be had at any price. Johann wrapped me in blankets and fed me hot water mixed with salt and a pinch of precious sugar. I shivered and burned, hallucinating strange things, now seeing kangaroos and emus outside my little room, now imagining myself on the surface of Mars, strangling in the thin air, and then instantly on Venus, choking in heat and darkness, and then floating in interstellar space, my body growing alternately larger than galaxies, then smaller than atoms, floating so far away from anything else that it would take eons for any signal from me to ever reach the world where I had been born.

Eventually the fever broke, and I was merely back in my room, shivering with cold, wrapped in sheets that were stinking with sweat, in a city slowly being pounded into rubble by distant soldiers whose faces I had never seen, fighting for an ideology that I could never understand.

It was after this, at my constant pleading, that Johann finally took me to see his molecular still. It was a dangerous walk across the city, illuminated by the glow of the Marionette Theater, set afire by incendiary bombs two days before. The still was hidden below the city, farther down even than the bomb shelters, in catacombs that had been carved out of rock over two thousand years ago. There were two men there, a man my foster father's age with a white moustache, and an even older Vietnamese-German man with one leg, who said nothing the whole time.

The older man looked at me and said in French, which perhaps he thought I wouldn't understand, "This is no place to bring a little one."

Johann replied in German, "She asks many questions." He shrugged, and said, "I wanted to show her."

The other said, still in French, "She couldn't understand." Right then I resolved that I would make myself understand, whatever it was that they thought I could not. The man looked at me critically, taking in, no doubt, my straight black hair and almond eyes. "She's not yours, anyway. What is she to you?"

"She is my daughter," Johann said.

The molecular still was nothing to look at. It was a room filled with curtains of black velvet, doubled back and forth, thousands and thousands of meters of blackness. "Here it is," Johann said. "Look well, little Leah, for in all the world, you will never see such another."

Somewhere there was a fan that pushed air past the curtains; I could feel it on my face, cool, damp air moving sluggishly past. The floor of the room was covered with white dust, glistening in the darkness. I reached down to touch it, and Johann reached out to still my hand. "Not to touch," he said.

"What is it?" I asked in wonder.

"Can't you smell it?"

And I could smell it, in fact, I had been nearly holding my breath to avoid smelling it. The smell was thick, pungent, almost choking. It made my eyes water. "Ammonia," I said.

Johann nodded, smiling. His eyes were bright. "Ammonium nitrate," he said.

I was silent most of the way back to the fortified basement we shared with two other families. There must have been bombs, for there were always the birds, but I do not recall them. At last, just before we came to the river, I asked, "Why?"

"Oh, my little Leah, think. We are cut off here. Do we have electrical generators to run coilguns like the barbarians that surround us? We do not. What can we do, how can we defend ourselves? The molecular still sorts molecules out of the air. Nitrogen, oxygen, water; this is all that is needed to make explosives, if only we can combine them correctly. My molecular still takes the nitrogen out of the air, makes out of it ammonium nitrate, which we use to fire our cannons, to hold the barbarians away from our city."

I thought about this. I knew about molecules by then, knew about nitrogen and oxygen, although not about explosives. Finally something occurred to me, and I asked, "But what about the energy? Where does the energy come from?"

Johann smiled, his face almost glowing with delight. "Ah, my little Leah, you know the right questions already. Yes, the energy. We have designed our still to work by using a series of reactions, each one using no more than a gnat's whisker of energy. Nevertheless, you are right, we must needs steal energy from somewhere. We draw the thermal energy of the air. But old man entropy, he cannot be cheated so easily. To do this we need a heat sink."

I didn't know then enough to follow his words, so I merely repeated his words dumbly: "A heat sink?"

He waved his arm, encompassing the river, flowing dark beneath a thin sheet of ice. "And what a heat sink! The barbarians know we are manufacturing arms; we fire the proof of that back at them every day, but they do not know where! And here it is, right before them, the motive power for the greatest arms factory of all of Austria, and they cannot see it."

Molecular still or not, the siege went on. The Pan-Slavics drove back the Tenth Crusade, and resumed their attack on the city. In February the armies entered the city twice, and twice the ragged defenders drove them back. In April, once more, the flowers bloomed, and once more, we had survived another winter.

It had been months since I had had a bath; there was no heat to waste on mere water, and in any case, there was no soap. Now, at last, we could wash, in water drawn directly from the Salzach, scrubbing and digging to get rid of the lice of winter.

We stood in line for hours waiting for a day's ration of macaroni, the humanitarian aid that had been air-dropped into the city, and hauled enormous drums across the city to replenish our stockpile of drinking water.

Summer rain fell, and we hoarded the water from rain gutters for later use. All that summer the smell of charred stone hung in the air. Bullet-riddled cars, glittering shards of glass, and fragments of concrete and cobblestone covered the streets. Stone heads and gargoyles from blasted buildings would look up at you from odd corners of the city.

Basements and tunnels under the city were filled out with mattresses and camp beds as makeshift living quarters for refugees, which became sweaty and smelly during summer, for all that they had been icy cold in winter. Above us, the ground would shake as the birds flew in, and plaster dust fell from the ceiling.

I was growing up. I had read about sex, and knew it was a natural part of the pattern of life, the urging of chromosomes to divide and conquer the world. I tried to imagine it with everybody I saw, from Johann to passing soldiers, but couldn't ever make my imagination actually believe in it. There was enough sex going on around me—we were packed together tightly, and humans under stress copulate out of desperation, out of boredom, and out of pure instinct to survive. There was enough to see, but I couldn't apply anything of what I saw to myself.

I think, when I was very young, I had some belief that human beings were special, something more than just meat that thought. The siege, an unrelenting tutor, taught me otherwise. A woman I had been with on one day, cuddled in her lap and talking nonsense, the next day was out in the street, bisected by shrapnel, reduced to a lesson in anatomy. If there was a soul it was something intangible, something so fragile that it could not stand up to the gentlest kiss of steel.

People stayed alive by eating leaves, acorns, and, when the humanitarian aid from the sky failed, by grinding down the hard centers of corn cobs to make cakes with the powder.

There were developments in the war, although I did not know them. The Pan-Slavic Army, flying their standard of a two-headed dragon, turned against the triple cross of the New Orthodox Resurgence, and to the east thousands of square kilometers of pacified countryside turned in a day into flaming ruin, as the former allies savaged each other. We could see the smoke in the distance, a huge pillar of black rising kilometers into the sky.

It made no difference to the siege. On the hilltops, the Pan-Slavic Army drove off the New Orthodox Resurgence, and when they were done, the guns turned back on the city. By the autumn, the siege had not lifted, and we knew we would have to face another winter.

Far over our heads, through the ever-present smoke, we could see the lights of freedom, the glimmering of distant cities in the sky, remote from all of the trouble of Earth. "They have no culture," Johann said. "They have power, yes, but they have no souls, or they would be helping us. Aluminum and rock, what do they have? Life, and nothing else. When they have another thousand years, they will still not have a third of the reality of our city. Freedom, hah! Why don't they *help* us, eh?"

The winter was slow frozen starvation. One by one, the artillery pieces that defended our city failed, for we no longer had the machine shops to keep them in repair, nor the tools to make shells. One by one the vicious birds fired from distant hilltops found the homes of our guns and ripped them apart. By the middle of February, we were undefended.

And the birds continued to fall.

Sometimes I accompanied Johann to the molecular still. Over the long months of siege, they had modified it so that it now distilled from air and water not merely nitrate, but finished explosive ready for the guns, tons per hour. But what good was it now, when there were no guns left for it to feed? Of the eight men who had given it birth, only two still survived to tend it, old one-legged Nguyen, and Johann.

One day Nguyen stopped coming. The place he lived had been hit, or he had been struck in transit. There was no way I would ever find out.

There was nothing left of the city to defend, and almost nobody able to defend it. Even those who were willing were starved too weak to hold a weapon.

All through February, all through March, the shelling continued, despite the lack of return fire from the city. They must have known that the resistance was over. Perhaps, Johann said, they had forgotten that there was a city here at all, they were shelling the city now for no other reason than that it had become a habit. Perhaps they were shelling us as a punishment for having dared to defy them.

Through April, the shelling continued. There was no food, no heat, no clean water, no medicine to treat the wounded.

When Johann died, it took me four hours to remove the rubble from his body, pulling stones away as birds falling around me demolished a building standing a block to the east, one two blocks north. I was surprised at how light he was, little more than a feather pillow. There was no place to bury him; the graveyards were all full. I placed him back where he had lain, crossed his hands, and left him buried in the rubble of the basement where we had spent our lives entwined.

I moved to a new shelter, a tunnel cut out of the solid rock below the Mönchsberg, an artificial cavern where a hundred families huddled in the dark, waiting for an end to existence. It had once been a parking garage. The moisture from three hundred lungs condensed on the stone ceiling and dripped down on us.

At last, at the end of April, the shelling stopped. For a day there was quiet, and then the victorious army came in. There were no alleys to baffle their tanks now. They came dressed in plastic armor, faceless soldiers with railguns and omniblasters thrown casually across their backs; they came flying the awful standard of the Pan-Slavic Army, the two-headed dragon on a field of blue crosses. One of them must have been Dragan Vukadinović, Dragan the Cleanser, the Scorpion of Bratislava, but in their armor I could not know which one. With them were the diplomats, explaining to all who would listen that peace had been negotiated, the war was over, and our part of it was that we would agree to leave our city and move into camps to be resettled elsewhere.

Would the victors write the history, I wondered? What would they say, to justify their deeds? Or would they, too, be left behind by history, a minor faction in a minor event forgotten against the drama of a destiny working itself out far away?

It was a living tide of ragged humans that met them, dragging the crippled and wounded on improvised sledges. I found it hard to believe that there could be so many left. Nobody noticed a dirty twelve-year-old girl, small for her age, slip away. Or if they did notice, where could she go?

The molecular still was still running. The darkness, the smell of it, hidden beneath a ruined, deserted Salzburg, was a comfort to me. It alone had been steadfast. In the end, the humans who tended it had turned out to be too fragile, but it had run on, alone in the dark, producing explosives that nobody would ever use, filling the caverns and the dungeons beneath a castle that had once been the proud symbol of a proud city. Filling it by the ton, by the thousands of tons, perhaps even tens of thousands of tons.

I brought with me an alarm clock, and a battery, and I sat for a long time in the dark, remembering the city.

And in the darkness, I could not bring myself to become the angel of destruction, to call down the cleansing fire I had so dreamed of seeing brought upon my enemies. In order to survive, you must become tough, Johann had once told me; you must become hard. But I could not become hard enough. I could not become like *them*.

And so I destroyed the molecular still, and fed the pieces into the Salzach. For all its beauty and power, it was fragile, and when I had done, there was nothing left by which someone could reconstruct it, or even understand what it had been. I left the alarm clock and the battery, and ten thousand tons of explosives, behind me in the catacombs.

Perhaps they are there still.

It was, I am told, the most beautiful, the most civilized, city in the world. The many people who told me that are all dead now, and I remember it only through the eyes of a child, looking up from below and understanding little.

Nothing of that little girl remains. Like my civilization, I have remade myself anew. I live in a world of peace, a world of mathematics and sky-cities, the opening of the new renaissance. But, like the first renaissance, this one was birthed in fire and war.

I will never tell this to anybody. To people who were not there, the story is only words, and they could never understand. And to those who *were* there, we who lived through the long siege of Salzburg and somehow came out alive, there is no need to speak.

In a very long lifetime, we could never forget.

IAN R. MACLEOD

British writer Ian R. MacLeod has been one of the hottest new writers of the nineties to date, and, as the decade progresses, his work continues to grow in power and deepen in maturity. MacLeod has published a slew of strong stories in the first years of the nineties in Interzone, Asimov's Science Fiction, Weird Tales, Amazing, *and* The Magazine of Fantasy & Science Fiction, *among other markets. Several of these stories made the cut for one or another of the various "Best of the Year" anthologies; in 1990, in fact, he appeared in three different Best of the Year anthologies with three different stories, certainly a rare distinction. His stories have appeared in our Eighth, Ninth, Tenth, Eleventh, and Thirteenth Annual Collections. His first novel,* The Great Wheel, *was published in 1997, followed by a major collection of his short work,* Voyages by Starlight. *MacLeod lives with his wife and young daughter in the West Midlands of England.*

Here, in a stylish and compelling look at a decadent modern world that ought to be Utopia, he proves once again that Art—like Passion—is in the eye of the beholder.

N ow that he couldn't afford to buy enough reality, Gustav had no option but to paint what he saw in his dreams. With no sketchpad to bring back, no palette or cursor, his head rolling up from the pillow and his mouth dry and his jaw aching from the booze he'd drunk the evening before—which was the cheapest means he'd yet found of getting to sleep—he was left with just that one chance, and a few trailing wisps of something that might once have been beautiful before he had to face the void of the day.

It hadn't started like this, but he could see by now that this was how it had probably ended. Representational art had had its heyday, and for a while he'd been feted like the bright new talent he'd once been sure he was. And big lumpy actuality that you could smell and taste and get under your fingernails would probably come back into style again—long after it had ceased to matter to him.

So that was it. Load upon load of self-pity falling down upon him this morning from the damp-stained ceiling. What *had* he been dreaming? Something—surely something. Otherwise, being here and being Gustav wouldn't come as this big a jolt. He should've got more used to it than this by now . . . Gustav scratched himself, and discovered that he also had an erection, which was another sign—hadn't he read once, somewhere?—that you'd been dreaming dreams of the old-fashioned kind, unsimulated, unaided. A sign, anyway, of a kind of biological optimism. The hope that there might just be a hope.

Arthritic, cro-magnon, he wandered out from his bed. Knobbled legs, knobbled veins, knobbled toes. He still missed the habit of fiddling with the controls of his window in the pockmarked far wall, changing the perspectives and the light in the dim hope that he might stumble across something better. The sun and the moon were blazing down over Paris from their respective quadrants, pouring like mercury through the nanosmog. He pressed his hand to the glass, feeling the watery wheeze of the crack that now snaked across it. Five stories up in these scrawny empty tenements, and a long, long way down. He laid his forehead against its coolness as the sour thought that he might try to paint this scene speeded through him. He'd finished at least twenty paintings of foreal Paris; all reality engines and cabled ruins in gray, black, and white. Probably done, old Vincent had loved his cadmiums and chromes! And never sold one single fucking painting in his entire life.

"What—what I told you was true," Elanore said, stumbling slightly over these little words, sounding almost un-Elanore-like for a moment; nearly uneasy. "I mean, about Marcel in Venice and Francine across the sky. And, yes, we *did* talk about a reunion. But you know how these things are. Time's precious, and, at the end of the day it's been so long that these things really do take a lot of nerve. So it didn't come off. It was just a few promises that no one really imagined they'd keep. But I thought—well, I thought that it would be nice to see *you* anyway. At least one more time."

"So all of this is just for me. *Jesus*, Elanore, I knew you were rich, but . . ."

"Don't be like that, Gustav. I'm not trying to impress you or depress you or whatever. It was just the way it came out."

He poured more of the wine, wondering as he did so exactly what trick it was that allowed them to share it.

"So, you're still painting?"

"Yep."

"I haven't seen much of your work about."

"I do it for private clients," Gustav said. "Mostly."

He glared at Elanore, daring her to challenge his statement. Of course, if he really *was* painting and selling, he'd have some credit. And if he had *credit*, he wouldn't be living in that dreadful tenement she'd tracked him down to. He'd have paid for all the necessary treatments to stop himself becoming the frail old man he so nearly was. *I can help, you know*, Gustav could hear Elanore saying because he'd heard her say it so many times before. *I don't need all this wealth. So let me give you just a little help. Give me that chance* . . . But what she actually *said* was even worse.

"Are you recording yourself, Gus?" Elanore asked. "Do you have a librarian?"

Now, he thought, now is the time to walk out. Pull this whole thing down and go back into the street—the foreal street. And forget.

"Did you know," he said instead, "that the word reality once actually *meant* foreal—not the projections and the simulations, but proper actuality. But then along came *virtual* reality, and of course, when the *next* generation of products was developed, the illusion was so much better that you could walk right into it instead of having to put on goggles and a suit. So they had to think of an improved phrase, a super-word for the purposes of marketing. And someone must have said, *Why don't we just call it reality?*"

"You don't have to be hurtful, Gus. There's no rule written down that says we can't get on."

"I thought that that was exactly the problem. It's in my head, and it was probably there in yours before you died. Now it's . . ." He'd have said more. But he was suddenly, stupidly, near to tears.

"What exactly *are* you doing these days, Gus?" she asked as he cleared his throat and pretended it was the wine that he'd choked on. "What are you painting at the moment?"

"I'm working on a series," he was surprised to hear himself saying. "It's a sort of a journey-piece. A sequence of paintings which begin here in Paris and then . . ." He swallowed. ". . . Bright, dark colors . . ." A nerve began to leap beside his eye. Something seemed to touch him, but was too faint to be heard or felt or seen.

"Sounds good, Gus," Elanore said, leaning toward him across the table. And Elanore smelled of Elanore, the way she always did. Her pale skin was freckled from the sunlight of whatever warm and virtual place she was living. Across her cheeks and her upper lip, threaded gold, lay the down that he'd brushed so many times with the tips of his fingers. "I can tell from that look in your eyes that you're into a really good phase . . ."

After that, things went better. They shared a second bottle of *vin ordinaire.* They made a little mountain of the butts of her Disc Bleu in the ashtray. This ghost—she really *was* like Elanore. Gustav didn't even object to her taking his hand across the table. There was a kind of abandon in all of this—new ideas mixed with old memories. And he understood more clearly now what van Gogh had meant about this café being a place where you could ruin yourself, or go mad, or commit a crime.

The few other diners faded. The virtual waiters, their aprons a single assured gray-white stroke of the palette knife, started to tip the chairs against the tables. The aromas of the Left Bank's ever-unreliable sewers began to override those of cigarettes and people and horse dung and wine. At least, Gustav thought, *that* was still foreal . . .

"I suppose quite a lot of the others have died by now," Gustav said. "All that facile gang you seem to so fondly remember."

"People still change, you know. Just because we've passed on, doesn't mean we can't *change.*"

By now, he was in a mellow enough mood just to nod at that. And how have *you* changed, Elanore? he wondered. After so long, what flicker of the electrons made you decide to come to me now?

"You're obviously doing well."

"I am . . ." She nodded, as if the idea surprised her. "I mean, I didn't expect—"

"—And you look—"

"—And *you*, Gus, what I said about you being—"

"—That project of mine—"

"—I know, I—"

They stopped and gazed at each other. Then they both smiled, and the moment seemed to hold, warm and frozen, as if from a scene within a painting. It was almost . . .

"Well . . ." Elanore broke the illusion first as she began to fumble in the small sequined purse she had on her lap. Eventually, she produced a handkerchief and blew delicately on her nose. Gustav tried not to grind his teeth—although this was *exactly* the kind of affectation he detested about ghosts. He guessed, anyway, from the changed look on her face, that she knew what he was thinking. "I suppose that's it, then, isn't it, Gus? We've met—we've spent the evening together without arguing. Almost like old times."

"Nothing will ever be like old times."

"No . . ." Her eyes glinted, and he thought for a moment that she was going to become angry—goaded at last into something like the Elanore of old. But she just smiled. "Nothing ever will be like old times. That's the problem, isn't it? Nothing ever was, or ever will be . . ."

Elanore clipped her purse shut again. Elanore stood up. Gustav saw her hesitate as she considered bending down to kiss him farewell, then decide that he would just regard that as another affront, another slap in the face.

Elanore turned and walked away from Gustav, fading into the chiaroscuro swirls of lamplight and gray.

Elanore, as if Gustav needed reminding, had been alive when he'd first met her. In fact, he'd never known anyone who was *more* so. Of course, the age difference between them was always huge—she'd already been past a hundred by then, and he was barely forty—but they'd agreed on that first day that they met, and on many days after, that there was a corner in time around which the old eventually turned to rejoin the young.

In another age, and although she always laughingly denied it, Gustav always suspected that Elanore would have had her sagging breasts implanted with silicone, the wrinkles stretched back from her face, her heart replaced by a throbbing steel simulacrum. But she was lucky enough to exist at a time when effective anti-aging treatments were finally available. As a post-centenarian, wise and rich and moderately, pleasantly, famous, Elanore was probably more fresh and beautiful than she'd been at any other era in her life. Gustav had met her at a party beside a Russian lake—guests wandering amid dunes of snow. Foreal had been a fashionable option then; although for Gustav, the grounds of this pillared ice-crystalled palace that Catherine the Great's Scottish favorite Charles Cameron had built seemed far too gorgeous to be entirely true. But it *was* true—foreal, actual, concrete, genuine, unvirtual—and such knowledge was what had driven him then. That, and the huge impossibility of ever really managing to convey any of it as a painter. That, and the absolute certainty that he would *try*.

Elanore had wandered up to him from the forest dusk dressed in seal furs. The shock of her beauty had been like all the rubbish he'd heard other artists talk about and thus so detested. And he'd been a stammering wreck, but somehow that hadn't mattered. There had been—and here again the words became stupid, meaningless—a dazed physicality between them from that first moment that was so intense it was spiritual.

Elanore told Gustav that she'd seen and admired the series of triptychs he'd just finished working on. They were painted directly onto slabs of wood, and depicted totemistic figures in dense blocks of color. The critics had generally dammed them with faint praise—had talked of Cubism and Mondrian—and were somehow unable to recognize Gustav's obvious and grateful debt to Gauguin's Tahitian paintings. But Elanore had seen and understood those bright muddy colors. And, yes, she'd dabbled a little in painting herself—just enough to know that truly creative acts were probably beyond her . . .

Elanore wore her red hair short in those days. And there were freckles, then as always, scattered across the bridge of her nose. She showed the tips of her teeth when she smiled, and he was conscious of her lips and her tongue. He could smell, faint within the clouds of breath that entwined them, her womanly scent.

A small black cat threaded its way between them as they talked, then, barely breaking the crust of the snow, leaped up onto a bough of the nearest pine and crouched there, watching them with emerald eyes.

"That's Metzengerstein," Elanore said, her own even greener eyes flickering across Gustav's face, but never ceasing to regard him. "He's my librarian."

When they made love later on in the agate pavilion's frozen glow, and as the smoke of their breath and their sweat clouded the winter twilight, all the disparate elements of Gustav's world finally seemed to join. He carved Elanore's breasts with his fingers and tongue, and painted her with her juices, and plunged into her sweet depths, and came, finally, finally, and quite deliciously, as her fingers slid around and he in turn was parted and entered by her.

Swimming back up from that, soaked with Elanore, exhausted, but his cock amazingly still half-stiff and rising, Gustav became conscious of the black cat that all this time had been threading its way between them. Its tail now curled against his thigh, corrugating his scrotum. Its claws gently kneaded his belly.

Elanore had laughed and picked Metzengerstein up, purring herself as she laid the creature between her breasts.

Gustav understood. Then or later, there was never any need for her to say more. After all, even Elanore couldn't live forever—and she needed a librarian with her to record her thoughts and actions if she was ever to pass on. For all its myriad complexities, the human brain had evolved to last a single lifetime; after that, the memories and impressions eventually began to overflow, the data became corrupted. Yes, Gustav understood. He even came to like the way Metzengerstein followed Elanore around like a witch's familiar, and, yes, its soft sharp cajolings as they made love.

Did they call them ghosts then? Gustav couldn't remember. It was a word, anyway—like spic, or nigger—that you never used in front of them. When he and Elanore were married, when Gustav loved and painted and loved and painted her, when she gave him her life and her spirit and his own career somehow began to take off as he finally mastered the trick of getting some of the passion he felt down onto the lovely, awkward canvas, he always knew that part of the intensity between them came from the age gap, the difference, the inescapable fact that Elanore would soon have to die.

It finally happened, he remembered, when he was leaving Gauguin's tropic dreams and nightmares behind and toying with a more straightforwardly Impressionist phase. Elanore was modeling for him nude as Manet's *Olympia*. As a concession to practicalities and to the urgency that then always possessed him when he was painting, the black maidservant bearing the flowers in his lavish new studio on the Boulevard des Capucines was a projection, but the divan and all the hangings, the flowers, and the cat, of course—although by its programmed nature, Metzengerstein was incapable of looking quite as scared and scrawny as Manet's original—were all foreal.

"You know," Elanore said, not breaking pose, one hand toying with the hem of the shawl on which she was lying, the other laid negligently, possessively, without modesty, across her pubic triangle, "we really should reinvite Marcel over after all he's done for us lately."

"Marcel?" In honesty, Gustav was paying little attention to anything at that moment other than which shade to swirl into the boudoir darkness. He dabbed again onto his testing scrap. "Marcel's in San Francisco. We haven't seen him in months."

"Of course . . . Silly me."

He finally glanced up again, what could have been moments or minutes later, suddenly aware that a cold silence that had set in. Elanore, being Elanore, never forgot anything. Elanore was light and life. Now, all her *Olympia*-like poise was gone.

This wasn't like the decay and loss of function that affected the elderly in the days before recombinant drugs. Just like her heart and her limbs, Elanore's physical brain still functioned perfectly. But the effect was the same. Confusions and mistakes happened frequently after that, as if consciousness drained rapidly once the initial rent was made. For Elanore, with her exquisite dignity, her continued beauty, her companies and her investments and the contacts that she needed to maintain, the process of senility was particularly terrible. No one, least of all Gustav, argued against her decision to pass on.

Back where reality ended, it was past midnight and the moon was blazing down over the Left Bank's broken rooftops through the grayish brown nanosmog. And exactly where, Gustav wondered, glaring up at it through the still-humming gantries of the reality engine that had enclosed him and Elanore, is Francine across the sky? How much do you have to pay to get the right decoders in your optic nerves to see the stars entwined in some vast projection of her? How much of your life do you have to give away?

The mazy streets behind St-Michael were rotten and weed-grown in the bilious fog, the dulled moonlight. No one but Gustav seemed to live in the half-supported ruins of the Left Bank nowadays. It was just a place for posing in and being seen—although in that respect, Gustav reflected, things really hadn't changed. To get back to his tenement, he had to cross the Boulevard St. Germain through a stream of buzzing robot cars that, no matter how he dodged them, still managed to avoid him. In the busier streets beyond, the big reality engines were still glowing. In fact, it was said that you could now go from one side of Paris to the other without having to step out into foreal. Gustav, as ever, did his best to do the opposite, although he knew that, even without any credit, he would still be freely admitted to the many realities on offer in these generous, carefree days. He scowled at the shining planes of the powerfields that stretched between the gantries like bubbles. Faintly from inside, coming at him from beyond the humming of the transformers that tamed and organized the droplets of nanosmog into shapes you could feel, odors you could smell, chairs you could sit on, he could hear words and laughter, music, the clink of glasses. He could even just make out the shapes of the living as they postured and chatted. It was obvious from the way that they were grouped that the living were outnumbered by the dead these days. Outside, in the dim streets, he passed figures like tumbling decahedrons who bore their own fields with them as they moved between realities. They were probably unaware of him as they drifted by, or perhaps saw him as some extra enhancement of whatever dream it was they were living. Flick, flick. Scheherazade's Baghdad. John Carter's Mars. It really didn't matter that you were still in Paris, although Elanore, of course, had showed sensitivity in the place she had selected for their meeting.

Beyond the last of the reality engines, Gustav's own cheap unvirtual tenement loomed into view. He picked his way across the tarmac toward the faint neon of the foreal Spar store beside it. Inside, there were the usual gray slabs of packaging with tiny windows promising every possible delight. He wandered up the aisles and activated the homely presence of the woman who served the dozen or so anachronistic places that were still scattered around Paris. She smiled at him—a living ghost, really; but then, people seemed to prefer the illusion of the personal touch. Behind her, he noticed, was an antiquated cigarette machine. He ordered a packet of Disc Bleu, and palmed what were probably the last of his credits—which amounted to half a stick of charcoal or two squeezes' worth of Red Lake. It was a surprise to him, in fact, that he even had enough for these cigarettes.

Outside, ignoring the health warning that flashed briefly before his eyes, he lighted a Disc Bleu, put it to his lips, and deeply inhaled. A few moments later, he was in a nauseous sweat, doubled up and gasping.

Another bleak morning, timeless and gray. This ceiling, these walls. And Elanore . . . Elanore was dead. Gone.

Gustav belched on the wine he was sure that he'd drunk, and smelled the sickness and the smoke of that foreal Disc Bleu still clinging to him. But there was no trace of Elanore. Not a copper strand of hair on his shoulder or curled around his cock, not her scent riming his hands.

He closed his eyes and tried to picture a woman in a white chemise bathing in a river's shallows, two bearded men talking animatedly in a grassy space beneath the trees, and Elanore sitting naked close by, although she watches rather than joins in their conversation . . .

No. That wasn't it.

Somehow getting up, pissing cloudily into the appropriate receptacle, Gustav finally grunted in unsurprise when he noticed a virtual light flickering through the heaped and broken frames of his easels. Unlike the telephone, he was sure that the company had disconnected his terminal long ago. His head fizzing, his groin vaguely tumescent, some lost bit of the night nagging like a stray scrap of meat between his teeth, he gazed down into the spinning options that the screen offered.

It was Elanore's work, of course—or the ghost of entangled electrons that Elanore had become. Hey, presto!—Gustav was back on line; granted this shimmering link into the lands of the dead and the living. He saw that he even had positive credit, which explained why he'd been able to buy that packet of Disc Bleu. He'd have slammed his fist down into the thing if it would have done any good.

Instead, he scowled at his room, the huddled backs of the canvases, the drifts of discarded food and clothing, the heap of his bed, wondering if Elanore was watching him now, thrusting a spare few gigabytes into the sensors of some nano-insect that was hovering close beside him. Indeed, he half expected the thin partitions and dangling wires, all the mocking rubbish of his life, to shudder and change into snowy Russian parkland, a wooded glade, even Paris again, 1890. But none of that happened.

The positive credit light still glowed enticingly within the terminal. In the almost certain knowledge that he would regret it, but quite unable to stop himself, Gustav scrolled through the pathways that led him to the little-frequented section dealing with artist's foreal requisites. Keeping it simple—down to fresh brushes, and Lefranc and Bourgeois's extra-fine Flake White, Cadmium Yellow, Vermilion, Deep Madder, Cobalt Blue, and Emerald Green—and still waiting as the cost all of that clocked up for the familiar credit-expired sign to arrive, he closed the screen.

The materials arrived far quicker than he'd expected, disgorging themselves into a service alcove in the far corner with a *whoosh* like the wind. The supplier had even remembered to include the fresh bottles of turpentine he'd forgotten to order—he still had plenty of clean stretched canvases anyway. So here (the feel of the fat new tubes, the beautiful, haunting names of the colors, the faint stirring sounds that the brushes made when he tried to lift them) was everything he might possibly need.

Gustav was an artist.

• • •

The hours did funny things when Gustav was painting—or even thinking about painting. They ran fast or slow, passed by on a fairy breeze, or thickened and grew huge as megaliths, then joined up and began to dance lumberingly around him, stamping on every sensibility and hope.

Taking fierce drags of his last Disc Bleu, clouding his tenement's already filmy air, Gustav finally gave up scribbling on his pad and casting sidelong glances at the canvas as the blazing moon began to flood Paris with its own sickly version of evening. As he'd always known he'd probably end up doing, he then began to wander the dim edges of his room, tilting back and examining his old, unsold, and generally unfinished canvases. Especially in this light, and seen from upside down, the scenes of foreal Paris looked suitably wan. There was so little to them, in fact, such a thinness and lack of color, that they could easily be re-used. But here in the tangled shadows of the farthest corner, filled with colors that seemed to pour into the air like a perfume, lay his early attempts at Symbolism and Impressionism . . . Amid those, he noticed something paler again. In fact, unfinished—but from an era when, as far as he could recall, he'd finished everything. He risked lifting the canvas out, and gazed at the outlines, the dabs of paint, the layers of wash. He recognized it now. It had been his attempt at Manet's *Olympia.*

After Elanore had said her good-byes to all her friends, she retreated into the white virtual corridors of a building near the Cimetière du Père Lachaise that might once have been called a hospital. There, as a final fail-safe, her mind was scanned and stored, the lineaments of her body were recorded. Gustav was the only person Elanore allowed to visit her during those last weeks; she was perhaps already too confused to understand what seeing her like this was doing to him. He'd sit amid the webs of sliver monitoring wires as she absently stroked Metzengerstein, and the cat's eyes, now far greener and brighter than hers, regarded him. She didn't seem to want to fight this loss of self. That was probably the thing that hurt him most. Elanore, the proper foreal Elanore, had always been searching for the next river to cross, the next challenge; it was probably the one characteristic that they had shared. But now she accepted death, this loss of Elanore, with nothing but resignation. *This is the way it is for all us,* Gustav remembered her saying in one of the last cogent periods before she forgot his name. *So many of our friends have passed on already. It's just a matter of joining them . . .*

Elanore never quite lost her beauty, but she became like a doll, a model of herself, and her eyes grew vacant as she sat silent or talked ramblingly. The freckles faded from her skin. Her mouth grew slack. She began to smell sour. There was no great fuss made when they finally turned her off, although Gustav still insisted that he be there. It was a relief, in fact, when Elanore's eyes finally closed and her heart stopped beating, when the hand he'd placed in his turned even more flaccid and cold. Metzengerstein gave Gustav one final glance before it twisted its way between the wires, leaped off the bed, and padded from the room, its tail raised. For a moment, Gustav considered grabbing the thing, slamming it down into a pulp of memory circuits and flesh and metal. But it had already been deprogrammed. Metzengerstein was just a shell; a comforter for Elanore in her last dim days. He never saw the creature again.

Just as the living Elanore had promised, her ghost only returned to Gustav after a decent interval. And she made no assumptions about their future at that first meeting on the neutral ground of a shorefront restaurant in virtual Balbec. She clearly understood how difficult all this was for him. It had been a windy day, he remembered, and the tablecloths flapped, the napkins threatened to take off, the lapel of the cream brocade jacket she was wearing kept lying across her throat until she pinned it back with a brooch. She told him that she still loved him, and that she hoped they would be able to stay together. A few days later, in a room in the same hotel overlooking the same windy beach, Elanore and Gustav made love for the first time since she had died.

The illusion, Gustav had to admit, then and later, was always perfect. And, as the dying Elanore had pointed out, they both already knew many ghosts. There was Marcel, for instance, and there was Jean, Gustav's own dealer and agent. It wasn't as if Elanore had even been left with any choice. In a virtual, ghostly daze himself, Gustav agreed that they should set up home together. They chose Brittany, because it was new to them—unloaded with memories—and the scenery was still often decent and visible enough to be worth painting.

Foreal was going out of style by then. For many years, the technologies of what was called reality had been flawless. But now, they became all-embracing. It was at about this time, Gustav supposed, although his memory once was again dim on this matter, that they set fire to the moon. The ever-bigger reality engines required huge amounts of power—and so it was that the robot ships set out, settled into orbit around the moon, and began to spray the surface with antimatter, spreading their wings like hands held out to a fire to absorb and then transmit back to earth the energies this iridescence gave. The power the moon now provided wasn't quite limitless, but it was near enough. With so much alternative joy and light available, the foreal world, much like a garden left untended, soon began to assume a look of neglect.

Ever considerate to his needs, Elanore chose and had refurbished a gabled clifftop mansion near Locronan, and ordered graceful and foreal furniture at huge extra expense. For a month or so, until the powerlines and transformers of the reality engines had been installed, Gustav and Elanore could communicate with each other only by screen. He did his best to tell himself that being unable to touch her was a kind of tease, and kept his thoughts away from such questions as where exactly Elanore was when she wasn't with him, and if she truly imagined she was the seamless continuation of the living Elanore that she claimed herself to be.

The house smelled of salt and old stone, and then of wet plaster and new carpets, and soon began to look as charming and eccentric as anything Elanore had organized in her life. As for the cost of all this forgotten craftsmanship, which, even in these generous times, was quite daunting, Elanore had discovered, like many of the ghosts who had gone before her, that her work—the dealing in stocks, ideas, and raw megawatts in which she specialized—was suddenly much easier. She could flit across the world, make deals based on long-term calculations that no living person could ever hope to understand.

Often, in the early days when Elanore finally reached the reality of their clifftop house in Brittany, Gustav would find himself gazing at her, trying to catch her unawares, or, in the nights when they made love with an obsessive frequency and passion, he would study her while she was sleeping. If she seemed distracted, he put it down to some deal she was cooking, a new antimatter trail across the Sea of Storms, perhaps, or a business meeting in Capetown. If she sighed and smiled in her dreams, he imagined her in the arms of some long-dead lover.

Of course, Elanore always denied such accusations. She even gave a good impression of being hurt. She was, she insisted, configured to ensure that she was always exactly where she appeared to be, except for brief times and in the gravest of emergencies. In the brain or on the net, human consciousness was a fragile thing—permanently in danger of dissolving. *I really* am *talking to you now, Gustav.* Otherwise, Elanore maintained, she would unravel, she would cease to be Elanore. As if, Gustav thought in generally silent rejoinder, she hadn't ceased to be Elanore already.

She'd changed, for a start. She was cooler, calmer, yet somehow more mercurial. The simple and everyday motions she made, like combing her hair or stirring coffee, began to look stiff and affected. Even her sexual preferences had changed. And passing over *was* different. Yes, she admitted that, even though she could feel the weight and presence of her own body just as she could feel his when he touched her. Once, as the desperation of their arguments increased, she even insisted on stabbing herself with a fork, just so that he might finally understand that she felt pain. But for Gustav, Elanore wasn't like the many other ghosts he'd met and readily accepted. They weren't *Elanore.* He'd never loved and painted *them.*

Gustav soon found that he couldn't paint Elanore now, either. He tried from sketches and from memory; once or twice he got her to pose. But it didn't work. He couldn't quite loose himself enough to forget what she was. They even tried to complete that *Olympia,* although the memory was painful for both of them. She posed for him as Manet's model, who in truth she did look a little like; the same model who'd posed for that odd scene by the river, *Dejéuner sur l'Herbe.* Now, of course, the cat as well as the black maid had to be a projection, although they did their best to make everything else the same. But there was something lost and wan about the painting as he tried to develop it. The nakedness of the woman on the canvas no longer gave off strength and knowledge and sexual assurance. She seemed pliant and helpless. Even the colors grew darker; it was like fighting something in a dream.

Elanore accepted Gustav's difficulties with what he sometimes found to be chillingly good grace. She was prepared to give him time. He could travel. She could develop new interests, burrow within the net as she'd always promised herself, and live in some entirely different place.

Gustav began to take long walks away from the house, along remote clifftop paths and across empty beaches, where he could be alone. The moon and the sun sometimes cast their silver ladders across the water. Soon, Gustav thought sourly, there'll be nowhere left to escape *to*. Or perhaps we will *all* pass on, and the gantries and the ugly virtual buildings that all look like the old Pompidou Centre will cease to be necessary; but for the glimmering of a few electrons, the world will revert to the way it was before people came. We can even extinguish the moon.

He also started to spend more time in the few parts of their rambling house that, largely because much of the stuff they wanted was handbuilt and took some time to order, Elanore hadn't yet had fitted out foreal. He interrogated the house's mainframe to discover the codes that would turn the reality engines off and on at will. In a room filled with tapestries, a long oak table, a vase of hydrangeas, pale curtains lifting slightly in the breeze, all it took was the correct gesture, a mere click of his fingers, and it would shudder and vanish, to be replaced by nothing but walls of mildewed plaster, the faint tingling sensation that came from the receding powerfield. There—then gone. Only the foreal view at the window remained the same. And now, click, and it all came *back* again. Even the fucking vase. The fucking flowers.

Elanore sought him out that day. Gustav heard her footsteps on the stairs, and knew that she'd pretend to be puzzled as to why he wasn't working in his studio.

"*There* you are," she said, appearing a little breathless after her climb up the stairs. "I was thinking—"

Finally scratching the itch that he realized had been tickling him for some time, Gustav clicked his fingers. Elanore—and the whole room, the table, the flowers, the tapestries—flickered off.

He waited—several beats, he really didn't know how long. The wind still blew in through the window. The powerfield hummed faintly, waiting for its next command. He clicked his fingers. Elanore and the room took shape again.

"I thought you'd probably override that," he said. "I imagined you'd given yourself a higher priority than the furniture."

"I could if I wished," she said. "I didn't think I'd need to do such a thing."

"No. I mean, you can just go somewhere else, can't you? Some other room in this house. Some other place. Some other continent . . ."

"I keep telling you. It isn't like that."

"I know. Consciousness is fragile."

"And we're really not that different, Gus. I'm made of random droplets held in a force field—but what are *you*? Think about it. You're made of atoms, which are just quantum flickers in the foam of space, particles that aren't even particles at all . . ."

Gustav stared at her. He was remembering—he couldn't help it—that they'd made love the previous night. Just two different kinds of ghost; entwined, joining—he supposed that that was what she was saying. And what about my *cock*, Elanore, and all the stuff that gets emptied into you when we're fucking? What the hell do you do with *that*?

"Look, Gus, this isn't—"

"—And what do you dream at night, Elanore? What is it that you do when you pretend you're sleeping?"

She waved her arms in a furious gesture that Gustav almost recognized from the Elanore of old. "What the hell do you *think* I do, Gus? I *try* to be human. You think it's easy, do you, hanging on like this? You think I enjoy watching *you* flicker in and out?—which is basically what it's like for me every time you step outside these fields? Sometimes I just wish I . . ."

Elanore trailed off there, glaring at him with emerald eyes. Go on, Gustav felt himself urging her. *Say* it, you phantom, shade, wraith, ghost. Say you wish you'd simply died. But instead, she made some internal command of her own, and blanked the room—and vanished.

It was the start of the end of their relationship.

Many guests came to visit their house in the weeks after that, and Elanore and Gustav kept themselves busy in the company of the dead and the living. All the old crowd, all the old jokes. Gustav generally drank too much, and made his presence unwelcome with the female ghosts as he decided that once he'd fucked the nano-droplets in one configuration, he might as well try fucking them in another. What the hell was it, Gus wondered, that made the living so reluctant to give up the dead, and the dead to give up the living?

In the few hours that they did spend together and alone at that time, Elanore and Gustav made detailed plans to travel. The idea was that they (meaning Elanore, with all the credit she was accumulating) would commission a ship, a sailing ship, traditional in every respect apart from the fact that the sails would be huge power receptors driven directly by the moon, and the spars would be the frame of a reality engine. Together, they would get away from all of this, and sail across the foreal oceans, perhaps even as far as Tahiti. Admittedly, Gustav was intrigued by the idea of returning to the painter who by now seemed to be the initial wellspring of his creativity. He was certainly in a suitably grumpy and isolationist mood to head off, as the poverty-stricken and desperate Gauguin had once done, in search of inspiration in the South Seas; and ultimately to his death from the prolonged effects of syphilis. But they never actually discussed what Tahiti would be *like*. Of course, there would be no tourists there now— only eccentrics bothered to travel foreal these days. Gustav liked to think, in fact, that there would be none of the tall ugly buildings and the huge Coca-Cola signs that he'd once seen in an old photograph of Tahiti's main town of Papeete. There might—who knows?—not be any reality engines, even, squatting like spiders across the beaches and jungle. With the understandable way that the birth rate was now declining, there would be just a few natives left, living as they had once lived before Cook and Bligh and all the rest—even Gauguin with his art and his myths and his syphilis—had ruined it for them. That was how Gustav wanted to leave Tahiti.

Winter came to their clifftop house. The guests departed. The wind raised white crests across the ocean. Gustav developed a habit, which Elanore pretended not to notice, of turning the heating down; as if he needed chill and discomfort to make the place seem real. Tahiti, that ship of theirs, remained an impossibly long way off. There were no final showdowns—just this gradual drifting apart. Gustav gave up trying to make love to Elanore, just as he had given up trying to paint her. But they were friendly and cordial with each other. It seemed that neither of them wished to pollute the memory of something that had once been wonderful. Elanore was, Gustav knew, starting to become concerned about his failure to have his increasing signs of age treated, and his refusal to have a librarian; even his insistence on pursuing a career that seemed only to leave him depleted and damaged. But she never said anything.

They agreed to separate for a while. Elanore would head off to explore pure virtuality. Gustav would go back to foreal Paris and try to rediscover his art. And so, making promises they both knew they would never keep, Gustav and Elanore finally parted.

Gustav slid his unfinished *Olympia* back down amid the other canvases. He looked out of the window, and saw from the glow coming up through the gaps in the houses that the big reality engines were humming. The evening, or whatever other time and era it was, was in full swing.

A vague idea forming in his head, Gustav pulled on his coat and headed out from his tenement. As he walked down through the misty, smoggy streets, it almost began to feel like inspiration. Such was his absorption that he didn't even bother to avoid the shining bubbles of the reality engines. Paris, at the end of the day, still being Paris, the realities he passed through mostly consisted of one or another sort of café, but there were set amid dazzling souks, dank medieval alleys, yellow and seemingly watery places where swam strange creatures that he couldn't think to name. But his attention wasn't on it anyway.

The Musée D'Orsay was still kept in reasonably immaculate condition beside the faintly luminous and milky Seine. Outside and in, it was well lit, and a trembling barrier kept in the air that was necessary to preserve its contents until the time came when they were fashionable again. Inside, it even *smelled* like an art gallery, and Gustav's footsteps echoed on the polished floors, and the robot janitors greeted him; in every way, and despite all the years since he'd last visited, the place was the same.

Gustav walked briskly past the statues and the bronze casts, past Ingres's big, dead canvases of supposedly voluptuous nudes. Then Moreau, early Degas, Corot, Millet . . . Gustav did his best to ignore them all. For the fact was that Gustav hated art galleries—he was still, at least, a painter in that respect. Even in the years when he'd gone deliberately to such places, because he knew that they were good for his own development, he still liked to think of himself as a kind of burglar—get in, grab your ideas, get out again. Everything else, all the ahhs and the oohs, was for mere spectators . . .

He took the stairs to the upper floor. A cramp had worked its way beneath his diaphragm and his throat felt raw, but behind all of that there was this feeling, a tingling of power and magic and anger—a sense that perhaps . . .

Now that he was up amid the rooms and corridors of the great Impressionist works, he forced himself to slow down. The big gilt frames, the pompous marble, the names and dates of artists who had often died in anonymity, despair, disease, blindness, exile, near-starvation. Poor old Sisley's *Misty Morning*. Vincent van Gogh in a self-portrait formed from deep, sensuous, three-dimensional oils. Genuinely great art was, Gustav thought, pretty depressing for would-be great artists. If it hadn't been for the invisible fields that were protecting these paintings, he would have considered ripping the things off the walls, destroying them.

His feet led him back to the Manets, that woman gazing out at him from *Dejéuner sur l'Herbe*, and then again from *Olympia*. She wasn't beautiful, didn't even look much like Elanore . . . But that wasn't the point. He drifted on past the clamoring canvases, wondering if the world had ever been this bright, this new, this wondrously chaotic. Eventually, he found himself face-to-face with the surprisingly few Gauguins that the Musée D'Orsay possessed. Those bright slabs of color, those mournful Tahitian natives, which were often painted on raw sacking because it was all Gauguin could get his hands on in the hot stench of his tropical hut. He became wildly fashionable after his death, of course; the idea of destitution on a faraway isle suddenly stuck everyone as romantic. But it was too late for Gauguin by then. And too late—as his hitherto worthless paintings were snapped up by Russians, Danes, Englishmen, Americans—for these stupid, habitually arrogant Parisians. Gauguin was often poor at dealing with his shapes, but he generally got away with it. And his sense of color was like no one else's. Gustav remembered vaguely now that there was a nude that Gauguin had painted as his own lopsided tribute to Manet's *Olympia*—had even pinned a photograph of it to the wall of his hut as he worked. But, like most of Gauguin's other really important paintings, it wasn't here at the Musée D'Orsay, this supposed epicenter of Impressionist and Symbolist art. Gustav shrugged and turned away. He hobbled slowly back down through the galley.

Outside, beneath the moonlight, amid the nanosmog and the buzzing of the powerfields, Gustav made his way once again through the realities. An English tea house circa 1930. A Guermantes salon. If they'd been foreal, he'd have sent the cups and the plates flying, bellowed in the self-satisfied faces of the dead and living. Then he stumbled into a scene he recognized from the Musée D'Orsay, one, in fact, that had once been as much a cultural icon as Madonna's tits or a Beatles tune. *Le Moulin de la Galette*. He was surprised and almost encouraged to see Renoir's Parisian figures in their Sunday-best clothing, dancing under the trees in the dappled sunlight, or chatting at the surrounding benches and tables. He stood and watched, nearly smiling. Glancing down, saw that he was dressed appropriately in a rough woollen navy suit. He studied the figures, admiring their animation, the clever and, yes, convincing way that, through some trick of reality, they were composed. . . . Then he realized that he recognized some of the faces, and that they had also recognized him. Before he could turn back, he was called to and beckoned over.

"Gustav," Marcel's ghost said, sliding an arm around him, smelling of male sweat and Pernod. "Grab a chair. Sit down. Long time no see, eh?"

Gustav shrugged and accepted the brimming tumbler of wine that was offered. If it was foreal—which he doubted—this and a few more of the same might help him sleep tonight. "I thought you were in Venice," he said. "As the Doge."

Marcel shrugged. There were breadcrumbs on his mustache. "That was *ages* ago. Where have you been, Gustav?"

"Just around the corner, actually."

"Not still *painting* are you?"

Gustav allowed that question to be lost in the music and the conversation's ebb and flow. He gulped his wine and looked around, expecting to see Elanore at any moment. So many of the others were here—it was almost like old times. There, even, was Francine, dancing with a top-hatted man—so she clearly wasn't across the sky. Gustav decided to ask the girl in the striped dress who was nearest to him if she'd seen Elanore. He realized as he spoke to her that her face was familiar to him, but he somehow couldn't recollect her name—even whether she was living or a ghost. She shook her head, and asked the woman who stood leaning behind her. But she, also, hadn't seen Elanore; not, at least, since the times when Marcel was in Venice and when Francine was across the sky. From there, the question rippled out across the square. But no one, it seemed, knew what had happened to Elanore.

Gustav stood up and made his way between the twirling dancers and the lantern-strung trees. His skin tingled as he stepped out of the reality, and the laughter and the music suddenly faded. Avoiding any other such encounters, he made his way back up the dim streets to his tenement.

There, back at home, the light from the setting moon was bright enough for him to make his way through the dim wreckage of his life without falling—and the terminal that Elanore's ghost had reactivated still gave off a virtual glow. Swaying, breathless, Gustav paged down into his accounts, and saw the huge sum—the kind of figure that he associated with astronomy, with the distance of the moon from the earth, the earth from the sun—that now appeared there. Then he passed back through the terminal's levels, and began to search for Elanore.

But Elanore wasn't there.

Gustav was painting. When he felt like this, he loved and hated the canvas in almost equal measures. The outside world, foreal or in reality, ceased to exist for him.

A woman, naked, languid, and with a dusky skin quite unlike Elanore's, is lying upon a couch, half-turned, her face cupped in her hand that lies upon the primrose pillow, her eyes gazing away from the onlooker at something far off. She seems beautiful but unerotic, vulnerable yet clearly available, and self-absorbed. Behind her—amid the twirls of bright yet gloomy decoration—lies a glimpse of stylized rocks under a strange sky, while two oddly disturbing figures are talking, and a dark bird perches on the lip of a balcony; perhaps a raven . . .

Although he detests plagiarism, and is working solely from memory, Gustav finds it hard to break away from Gauguin's nude on this canvas he is now painting. But he really isn't fighting that hard to do so, anyway. In this above all of Gauguin's great paintings, stripped of the crap and the despair and the self-justifying symbolism, Gauguin was simply *right*. So Gustav still keeps work-ing, and the paint sometimes almost seems to want to obey him. He doesn't know or care at the moment what the thing will turn out like. If it's good, he might think of it as his tribute to Elanore; and if it isn't . . . Well, he knows that, once he's finished this painting, he will start another one. Right now, that's all that matters.

Elanore was right, Gustav decides, when she once said that he was entirely selfish, and would sacrifice everything—himself included—just so that he could continue to paint. She was eternally right and, in her own way, she too was always searching for the next challenge, the next river to cross. Of course, they should have made more of the time that they had together, but as Elanore's ghost admitted at that van Gogh café when she finally came to say good-bye, nothing could ever quite be the same.

Gustav stepped back from his canvas and studied it, eyes half-closed at first just to get the shape, then with a more appraising gaze. Yes, he told himself, and reminded himself to tell himself again later when he began to feel sick and miserable about it, this is a true work. This is worthwhile.

Then, and although there was much that he still had to do, and the oils were still wet, and he knew that he should rest the canvas, he swirled his brush in a blackish puddle of palette-mud and daubed the word NEVERMORE across the top, and stepped back again, wondering what to paint *next*.

open veins
SİMON İNGS

British writer Simon Ings is the author of four novels, City of the Iron Fish, Hot Head, Hotwired, *and, most recently,* Headlong. *His short fiction has appeared in* Interzone, New Worlds, Omni Online, *and various anthologies both in and out of the genre, and he reviews regularly for* New Scientist. *He has recently completed* Painkillers, *a crime novel about autism set in London, where he lives and works.*

In the unsettling story that follows, a government troubleshooter investigating a grisly and mysterious death learns that you can have too much of anything—*even intimacy.*

T hey told me she had died inside a sensory deprivation tank; the sort the hotwired use, twisting their sense of shape till they corkscrew into the virtual world. They told me, when they got to her, her lungs were full of brine pinked with her own blood. And they told me to erase it all.

They'd already bagged her up by the time I got there. I wanted to see her face, but I didn't say anything; just watched as they lifted her into the ambulance. It was pointless; you can't learn anything from a shroud.

They closed the doors and turned the vehicle around. Behind the driver's cab there were no windows, no name of any hospital, no red cross; just army drab, and hazard lights front and rear. It looked like one of those unmarked vehicles you see on highways sometimes, bearing toxins from one nameless compound to another. It was slung so low, pebbles and splinters of driftwood pinged and scraped its belly. It disappeared a moment behind the hangar and turned away, up the long route past the power station. You could watch it go for miles if you wanted to, it was so flat here, and the sky was grey like God had forgot it.

Up until three years ago this site was an army listening post. When the army moved out a married couple, Laura and Peter Lewis, bought the site and set up an outbound school: sea scuba and some gliding. But it was winter now, January 10, there were no guests, and we had descended like army ghosts on this place, reclaiming it for our own. Forensics in paper jumpsuits skirted around each other as though rehearsing some intricate, ugly dance. Observers kicked stones and muttered into their cell phones. There were even some soldiers, throat-miked, wrap-shaded: they looked well pissed, given nothing to do.

I looked for someone I knew and found Morley. I'd last met him in summer; with enough red wine inside him he'd passed for chubby. Out of season he wrapped himself up in an ugly sheep-skin car coat; he turned to me looking like something spat out of a tank and said, "Joanne Rynard. Thirty-one years old. Five-foot-seven, brown hair."

"One of ours?"

"Flight lieutenant, retired eight months ago."

"Was she hotwired?"

"There's a jack in her neck big enough, you could plug her into a battleship."

"Where's the battleship?"

"No ship. But there's a hotwire feed in the hangar."

"Bootleg?"

"No, it's legit. A stray. It wasn't in the building specs and it got overlooked when the army stripped it."

"How'd she know about it?"

"God knows. First we knew it was here was this morning."

"She ring any presidents? Fire any missiles?"

Morley looked around, counting the army ghosts, muttering: "Whatever she did, she sure touched a nerve."

"How'd she die?"

"She slashed her wrists diagonally with a scalpel and bound the cuts with bandages."

"She was backing off?"

He shook his head. "Each hour or so she'd undo the dressing, let out more blood."

"Slow way to die."

"What she wanted."

"Know why?"

He shook his head.

"She have help?" I asked him.

"What for?"

"The bandages. Retying them can't have been easy."

"You met the Lewises?" he said. "There's nobody else around. If it was anyone it was them."

I remembered, it was Mrs. Lewis who had called the police, who in turn had called us. But why had she called the police? Most people find a body they call an ambulance, not a policeman. The Lewises were somewhere about. I was supposed to introduce myself, but I didn't feel ready. I'd been brought in to reassure this frightened couple, convince them to unsee what they had seen, unhear the things they'd heard, and, if they'd got involved somehow, to tell them it was over; all was fine.

The trouble was, Laura and Peter Lewis weren't frightened.

Each hour she undid the dressing and let out more blood. Had they helped her?

If so, why? Until I had those answers, I knew I could not begin to erase what had happened here.

I thought over what I knew. She'd been in the tank. She'd been floating— "She was plugged in to the hotwire feed when you found her?"

"Yes."

"Doing what?"

"Nobody knows, or if they do nobody wants to say."

Once you're plugged into a hotwire feed you can surf the world: control in real-time the trajectory of a satellite, lower or raise the price of corn on the Nippon Exchange, read teletext in Urdu, or fire an automated gun on the Iran-Iraq border. There's a price tag to this virtual joyride: the surveillance they put you under is hardly less invasive than the surgery. So how had Joanne Rynard slipped our net? Fortunately, that wasn't my problem. My problem was how to erase the evidence.

"And something else." Morley reached into his coat and pulled out a blister-pack. The stiff, clear plastic was heat-sealed around three slender hypodermics, each containing maybe thirty CCs of red liquid. "This was stolen from an army pharmacy three months ago. We found a stash of it beside the tank."

"What is it?"

"Rose Red."

"What's it do?"

"Cripples your immune system."

I stared at the hypodermics. "Well, who would want that?"

Morley shrugged and walked off, ramming the packet quickly back into his coat. I realized he had told me things even he was not supposed to know.

I wandered around the base awhile, waiting for people to leave.

The site bore little mark of its military past. The hardened bunkers, the offices and barracks, had been ripped out years ago. The radar arrays and satellite dishes had all been dismantled, leaving large, low concrete platforms, their smooth grey surfaces punctuated by rusted spars, irregular brick walls, depressions and score-marks: the tracks and spoor and burrow-mounds of artificial life. The single concrete runway was crazed and weed-lined and there were shreds of cable rotting in the verges.

I was still avoiding the Lewises, and it wasn't easy: their stone cottage was the only house in sight; the only building the army had left standing when they quit. That and the tin hangar.

I tried the hangar door. It was open.

There was a row of gliders in front, their clean lines blurred and broken beneath shrouds of clear blue plastic. Beyond them the hangar was empty. Just concrete, and puddles, and the sight of my own breath.

Two flights of grille stairs led to a scaffold mezzanine that ran the length of the back wall. I climbed and walked along it till I came to the booth where she'd died. Plastic hung off the plasterboard and perspex partitions in shreds: the remains of her sterile tent. Morley's team had had to trash it, stripping out what they could of her gear.

There was still the tank of course, its glass sides fogged with salt and grease. Beside it there was a medical stand draped with wires. I fed them through my hands. One of them was thicker than the rest. It ended in a jack. It was this that had plugged into the socket at the base of Rynard's neck.

I passed the hotwire feed twice before I recognized it. It looked innocent enough. Easy to mistake it for an IBCN socket: plug a phone into it, you wouldn't get a tone; you'd think it was disconnected. But Rynard could have jacked into just about anything on the system.

I leaned against the side of the tank and looked in. Most of the water had been drained off but there was a puddle left in the bottom, purple with a dark scum: brine and old blood.

This wasn't suicide. It was something else, something more. What, I didn't know.

The beaches here were shingle. For sand you had to drive two miles up the coast, past the power station, but I prefer stones, I like the sound they make. I leaned back against a breakwater and watched the sea roll in awhile and when I got bored I phoned in.

They had little enough for me. Peter first: "He graduated from Central St Martin's twelve years back. No employment record."

"None?"

"An exhibition in Karsten Schubert every couple of years, a few sales, that's all."

"Where's his money come from?"

"Rich family. Landowners. Nothing to tell."

"He have any political affiliations?"

"He subscribed for one year to *Marxism Today*."

"Naturally. Movements?"

"Bradford, Bristol, London. Iain, he's clean. I've nothing to give. There's a roomful on Laura—"

But I learned little from it. Laura Lewis's record was long but inconclusive. She'd belonged to a lot of organizations but she'd made the grade in none of them. Her politics were unformed; she was happier on protests than in political meetings. There she was in all weathers, before bulldozers and lines of mounted police and even soldiers once or twice, one week chained to a tree, the next roughing it in some school hall due for demolition. She was a regular at county courts, consistently refusing to plead in cases involving trespass, criminal damage, even assault. She'd spent about four years in prison between the ages of seventeen and twenty-six. After that her record was clean. She was thirty-one, the same age as Joanne Rynard.

I thought, Laura Lewis's politics wouldn't favor the virtual world. That unaccountable space was open to so few, and yet it was there that all the big decisions affecting people got made. Did that mean she'd help someone use a hotwire illegally? Was this why Rynard had been made welcome here? Was she trying to damage some part of the virtual world? Had she turned saboteur?

I was heading back up the beach when I heard the car. I topped the bank and saw a 4X4 shoot past, rocking heavily from side to side. The back door was off, and through the empty cabin I caught a glimpse of black hair, woven by the wind. The tresses curled in on themselves like storm eddies, a hurricane of ink.

I wondered where she was going. Was she trying to break the cordon? If so, we would steer her back: we've had practice. I wondered whether to wait for her here, to flag her down and speak to her before she reached home, familiar territory, known space. But it got so cold waiting I gave it up and walked back to the grey house.

Peter Lewis was tall and skinny and his mouth was hidden by an overgrown oval of beard. He was balding; wisps of ginger hair stood out like wings above each ear. I wanted in out of the cold but he stood blocking the door, staring out at me from under his pale eyebrows like an indignant owl. "I thought you'd all left," he said.

I shrugged. Time was on my side, and so was he, though he didn't know it yet. He sighed and let me in. "Peter Lewis."

"Iain Prior."

His handshake was warm and wet. "Sit down."

The door gave straight onto the kitchen, a city folk's dream of a country parlour: Aga stove, blue check curtains at the windows, stripped pine cabinets with diamond panes of blue and red glass, terracotta tiled floor.

"Coffee?"

"Something stronger?"

"Sure." He handed me a finger of scotch and sat opposite me across the table. "What do you do, then?"

I erase things. A death's more than a body: it's witnesses, loved ones, memories. An eraser is more than a detective: he has to dig deeper than facts, and he has to know how to bury it all afterward. "Your wife's in trouble," I said. "I'm here to help her."

"Trouble?"

"A woman died here. We know she had help doing it. We think your wife helped her."

He blustered for a while. The Lewises had been assured there would be no police here after us, no inquest, no charges, that all was contained. He'd taken that to mean there'd be no trouble. So when I started talking to him about his wife's politics, I expected him to be angry. But it was better than that: he simply blanched, smiled a lot to cover his fear, and tried to get me drunk. A smart man. Frightened, but smart. A good choice of whisky, too, but a bad choice of target: I drank two for his one and when he went upstairs to sleep off his drunk I helped myself to the rest of the bottle. I thought about what he had told me, seeing how it meshed with what I already knew.

Laura Lewis had been born into the sort of politics she'd go to jail for in her teens. Her mother had been a spokeswoman for the protestors at Greenham Common. She'd had two children: Laura's brother was two years older than her, a blue-eyed wonder who naturally enough given his upbringing joined the Royal Artillery Regiment the moment he was old enough. He died of Gulf War Syndrome when Laura was fourteen. All the while the army was claiming no biological weapons were ever used against Allied forces, Laura's brother was wasting to a stick. The older Laura got, the angrier she got, first about that and then about everything—

Tyres slewed in the gravel outside. Peter must have popped a pill because he shot down those slippy beeswaxed stairs sober and pale as hell. He shot a glance from the door to me and back to the door like we'd been fucking and it was his mother. The door opened.

It was his wife.

Her hair preceded her, black snakes weaving in the wind coming off the sea. She brushed them back from her face and looked around. She took me in her stride, walking straight toward me, red lips upcurved, politely smiling. If she'd run up against our cordon during her drive she gave no sign of it.

"Laura."

"Iain."

I reached out to shake her hand. She ignored me, smiling, skirted the table and went upstairs. She was wearing a green wool suit, the skirt cut well above the knee. I watched her legs sway as she climbed, heard the click of her heels on the stone steps and the hiss of her pantyhose.

I watched her all the way up, watched as the black smoke-curls of her hair melted and spread into the darkness of the stairwell. I stared into the darkness while she changed, and I watched as she came down again, her hipbones tight against her jeans, the cotton twill shirt downplaying her generous breasts, a city folk's dream of a country wife. Peter must have seen me staring. I didn't care.

She told me to stay for dinner. She'd guessed they couldn't get rid of me, and she wanted to put the best face on it she could.

While she cooked, Peter told me about the outbound school they ran. "We started five years ago. In a few years' time we'll sell this to the Parks Authority, go inland, start again, move into Executive Vision." He chewed up his roll. He made noises when he ate. "There's a lot of money in Executive Vision." What he meant was you take a bunch of pen-pushers and dump them up a hill in dodgy weather until they're cold and scared—about ten minutes—and they pay you for the privilege.

All the time he was talking I was looking at Laura. I said to her, "That's your ambition?" like I didn't believe it.

She said, "We got to make this place pay first."

Then Peter started telling me what great potential this place had, like he was selling it to me already. That was when the argument started. Laura kept contradicting him. No, the scuba classes were not full last year. No the weather wasn't ideal for gliding; ideally they needed to be ten miles up the coast where the strong thermals were. No, cooking was a bore and a pain and if they could have afforded the help she'd have hired it.

They were building a story for me, the story of their life here, but they couldn't agree on the design. One would furnish a room, then the other would come along and brick up the door. Walls got knocked out and the upper storey fell in. Stairways rose into nowhere. Roof beams creaked and foundations trembled.

So I gave up and studied their hands instead. Peter's were soft and fat. I wondered what he did around here. Nothing very practical, I guessed. Laura took a tureen out of the oven and set it on the table. She shed the oven mitts. Her hands were hard and muscular with short nails. White lines crossed the backs of her delicate wrists.

She put a plate down in front of me, and served me, and asked me what I wanted, and damned if I couldn't get a word out. It was the smell that did it: behind the gravy there was something else, something astonishing and sweet. Not perfume; flesh. I summoned my strength and looked deep into her face: her strong, wide, red mouth; her deep blue eyes; cheekbones so sharp they could cut you. She saw me staring but she didn't let on.

She was too busy avoiding her husband.

Now and again, as she was serving, Peter would reach for Laura's hand, to stroke it or squeeze it: some gesture of ownership. The way she steered away from him, he might as well not have been there. There was something going on. Some piece of language. Big trouble between them.

I realized that this was my best hope. There was an aggression about Laura, a liveness, a heat. She was angry with her husband. If she was angry enough, perhaps she would open up to me. By now she'd know I wasn't the police. After me there would be no investigations, no charges; only the anger, charging up inside her like static. I had to ground that anger, feed off it, learn from it.

I felt myself smiling.

Of course I was smiling. I had my excuse.

After dinner I went out to the car and opened a secure channel. "You've got to give me more," I said.

"It's all in the medical report," Morley said. "Use your eyes."

"One, my fax is back at the hotel; two, you know the shit your department puts out gives me a headache; three, you showed me those syringes for a reason."

There was a pause.

"Let me call you back."

I waited. When he came back on-line, the room tone had changed. Maybe he'd shut himself in a broom cupboard somewhere to be out of earshot: maybe he was using some kind of scrambler because his voice was cleaner now: no stray aspirants. "When Joanne Rynard left the air force she went straight into one of our classified projects."

"Which one?"

"Fuck off, Iain."

I grinned at the mouthpiece. "Go on."

"While she was there she developed biclonal multiple myeloma. Abnormal concentrations of immunoglobulin, types A and G. IgAs in the blood: alkylating agents dealt with it. But IgGs in mucosal surfaces—"

"Her implant."

"It triggered a massive immune response. Meningitis, possible brain damage—"

"So what did we do?"

"Booked her in for an operation to remove her hotwire jack."

"Only she never turned up." I thought about it. "Could Rose Red have let her keep her jack?"

"At a price. Kaposi's, Candida, the rest."

"She was immunocompromised?"

"All the way, Iain. She was dying."

I was beginning to be glad that I'd never met Joanne Rynard: what could she have been thinking of, to kill herself twice over, and in such slow and painful ways? Putting aside for a moment the business of her wrists, what purpose had the Rose Red served? Only that it compromised her body's defenses so much, she got to keep her hotwire jack. But I couldn't believe that was worth dying for.

True, I knew nothing of the virtual world's strange exhilarations. True, I had long ago given up trying to grasp what it was like there: the inhuman euphoria; the sense one had of one self unspiraling, metastasizing, recombining into new and florid forms. I knew nothing of those strange, nameless senses through which the hotwired perceive the virtual world; indeed, knew less about them than a blind man knows of colour.

True, removing Joanne's hotwire jack was tantamount to blinding her. She was right to be frightened of the operation, to shy away from it for as long as she could. But the fact remained, people go blind all the time. They make do. They adapt. They go on living. What had made Joanne so different?

I'd just put the phone away when Laura and Peter came out the front door and walked toward me. I got out of the car.

"We're going up the coast a ways." She'd changed her clothes again; a cotton frock, dark blue like the sky. Her feet were bare and her hair weaved freely around her freckled shoulders like a wreath of thick black smoke. "You want to come?"

They set off up the road past the power station. I followed in my own vehicle. There were no streetlights. They knew the route well. It was hard to keep up with them.

A fifteen-minute drive brought us to the outskirts of the town. There was a car park here, and among the dunes two wooden buildings. Over the largest a sign in red and yellow neon blinked: AMUSEMENTS. I stopped the car beside theirs and got out. There was no sound but the sea.

Laura fetched a blanket out of the car and the three of us walked down the slipway to the beach.

"God, it's freezing," Peter mumbled, doing up his tweed jacket. I tugged up the zipper on my fleece. Laura's only concession to the evening was a scarf thrown lazily around her shoulders. Maybe she liked the cold; maybe she wanted to show herself off. She took the corners of the blanket in her hands and wrapped her arms around our shoulders, shrouding us from the wind. The gesture was intimate, embracing, as though we three were old friends. We walked in silence for a while. The tide was coming in. The sand grew silvery in patches, and purple and turquoise where it refracted the moonlight.

Peter left us to search for sea shells. We wandered the wave-line a little way, watching him, then Laura turned from the sea, pressing herself against me as she steered me up the beach. I felt her heat, and smelled her. "Are you cold?"

I was trembling. She gathered the folds of the blanket round us. I put my arm around her waist.

I don't know how long we stood like that. A few seconds, a minute. She'd silenced me with her touch and I was glad, I closed my eyes, I didn't care—

She said, "Joanne came here last October, a week after we closed for the winter."

I came awake.

"She knew about the hotwire feed. That's why she came out here. She wanted to use it. She said she was an army pilot. She told us she'd deserted, that she needed to wipe out her records."

"That was why she needed hotwire access? To wipe out a few files?"

"I believed her. Was that stupid of me?"

"No." I thought about it. "You could use a hotwire for that. A bit like a mallet cracking a nut, though—"

"Besides," she finished for me, "she was lying."

I waited, my hand frozen around her waist. She said nothing.

Then, as I began to pull away, she pressed her hand to my hand, keeping it against her hip. "My husband's an artist," she said, as if this were some sort of explanation.

"I know."

"Have you seen his pictures?"

"No."

"Then what do you know?"

Her question was sharp, but not unkind. I replied, "Hardly anything about Peter. We know much more about you."

"Then you'll know why I believed her," she said softly, bitterly.

I nodded. It looked as though Joanne Rynard had read the same file I had, and made her approach accordingly. What more seductive revenge was there to offer Laura, still embittered by her brother's death, than the chance to help a deserter? "Did Peter believe all this about her records?"

"No."

"Why not?"

"It wasn't what he wanted to hear."

"So she had a story for him, too?"

She dropped her hand from my shoulder.

I pushed harder: "What did he want to hear?"

"I don't know."

"You didn't talk about it?"

"He's guarded about his work."

"His work? You mean his painting?"

There was a resentful edge to Laura's voice now: "Peter told me some of what

Joanne told him. He thought what she was doing was romantic. She was hungry for heaven, he said."

"You mean she wanted to die."

"Not exactly. To enter the virtual world, she said. To live there. To leave her body behind."

Her news staggered me. I tried hard to conceal my confusion: "Did you know what that would involve?"

"Not exactly."

"Did you know she would die?"

"Not until the last night."

"Then what did you do?"

"Nothing."

"Why?"

"They made me promise. Joanne and Peter."

"Afterward?"

"I phoned the police."

Not the ambulance, the police. She knew who to call because she knew what had happened. She'd been party to it.

I looked for him. He was about a hundred yards ahead of us now. He stopped suddenly and edged forward after a retreating wave. He picked up a white lozenge, larger than his hand. He beckoned us with it. We went up and examined it. He said, "It's a cuttlefish shell!" He went off again and found three more.

"Is he always like this?" I asked her.

"Last week he found a duck skeleton by the side of the runway. There were feathers all over the place, but the bones were picked clean."

"He collects skeletons?"

"Bones and feathers. For his pictures."

"What does he paint?" I asked her.

"Death," she replied. I said nothing. She looked at me hard; she could tell the sort of thoughts I was having. She turned away from me, pulling the blanket from my shoulder. She wrapped it around herself, leaving me cold.

"When did you guess Joanne Rynard's deserter story was a lie?"

"The same time she made love to Peter."

"How did you find out?"

She wouldn't answer. "He's always falling in love with his models," she said, affecting a false sophistication. "They never last."

Her imperfect poise, her sudden coldness, irritated me. "What never last?" I demanded: "His affairs? Or his models?"

The hurt and fury in Laura's look confirmed my guess about her wrists; the neat white hesitation marks.

Peter spared her the need to reply further, returning with his pockets full of shells. We walked back to the car park on either side of her, sharing the blanket with her as before. She had her arm around me again, but she didn't touch me: her fist was balled round the blanket, and her arm was stiff as though a piece of driftwood were balanced on my shoulder. Peter went ahead to unlock their car. Laura and I stood watching him together, our arms around each other, but wooden and foolish as though we were playing some parlour game that required us to freeze in midaction.

Only when Peter turned and beckoned her, only when she knew he was looking, was certain of it, did Laura come alive again, turning to me, smiling, her coldness gone. The breeze changed direction and blew her hair toward me. Tresses like liquid smoke brushed my face.

"Goodnight," she said, and brushed her cheek to mine to make it look as if we'd kissed.

I spent the next morning in my hotel room, talking down an IBCN fiber to Harris, my section head. I told him, "She wasn't involved."

"You're sure?"

"As I can be."

"But she knew."

"At first she figured Joanne Rynard was trying to sabotage a personnel archive. When it turned out different she lost interest."

"She didn't blow any whistles."

"By then she was implicated. And I think her husband stopped her."

"He knew?"

"He helped Rynard die."

"Morley said she had help."

"It was him."

"You know why?"

"He collects suicides."

"What does that mean?"

"I don't know. But I have some ideas."

Afterward I phoned Morley and told him what Laura had told me. He said, "Bullshit."

"Listen—"

"I've no time for this now."

I waited an hour and picked up on the first ring.

"Two minutes tops." Morley had plugged so many counterintelligence boxes into his phone, his voice sounded like those machines you get in trains and elevators that string words together into artificial sentences.

"You have all I know," I told him.

"Then there's not much I can tell you."

"Go on."

"The project's called White Light. Two years ago they ran on a budget of two million. Strictly test-tube stuff; a little amniotics, a few animal tests. They were researching near-death neurology. They found that as death approaches and anoxia sets in there's massive presynaptic activity in the CNS: the dying axons release huge amounts of chemically encoded data into the cerebro-spinal fluid."

"I am reaching for the aspirin as we speak—"

"Look: you're dying. Your personality is liquifying, broiling around your cooling skull, hunting for some way out."

"What then?"

"Last year White Light pulled a budget of sixty million, held human trials, released no data."

"The year our friend left."

"This year, White Light officially ceased to exist."

"Any guesses?" I asked him.

"Stop clutching my hand."

I concentrated. Searching for heaven, she'd said. . . .

Heaven—

"Jesus!" I shouted. "They've found a way out?"

But the line had gone dead.

I found him kneeling in front of the tank, stony-faced, a little pale maybe, but calm, the nightmare passing: the nightmare we all fear, of one day getting precisely what we want.

I'd half-expected to find him here, but I acted surprised.

"You want help with something?" he asked, looking up at me: his way of telling me to get lost. And not content with that: "They took everything away."

"Not everything," I replied lightly, stepping into the booth. I knelt down beside him and looked through the side of Joanne Rynard's sense-deprivation tank. I pretended to lose myself in the play of shadows and reflections. "You helped her build this?"

"For some reason," he admitted, lugubriously.

I chose to misunderstand him. "Oh, it's a sense-deprivation tank," I explained. "Without it you can't enter the virtual world. Your senses hold you back. You're trapped inside your body." I studied his reflection. There was no emotion there. I wondered what he must be feeling. "Do you know what she did here? What all this was for?"

"She said she was a pilot. She had a plug in her neck. They used to plug her into fighter planes."

"And then?" I prompted him. "What then?" And when he didn't answer: "Last night Laura said to me Joanne had found a way to heaven. Do you know what she meant by that?"

"Laura never paid much attention to what Joanne said."

"Did you?"

"Enough to know what she wanted."

"Which was?"

He shrugged. "A way out of her body. She was dying."

"And slashing her wrists saved her life?"

"You know what I'm talking about," he complained, tired of playing mouse to my cat. "Seconds in the virtual world seem like years, they say."

I hadn't known that. I made a mental note to try it out on Morley, assuming he dared speak to me again. But even so, I thought, what then? What had Joanne traded mortality for? Everlasting corn prices and teletext? An afterlife of tele-communications? "So much for ecstasy," I grunted, but even as I disparaged the idea, I knew it was the answer.

Joanne Rynard had tried to become immortal. And, for all I knew, she may have succeeded.

I searched Peter's reflection—he'd yet to spot me staring at him in the glass—for some sign of feeling. But no one was home.

According to Laura, Peter had fallen in love with Joanne. But if he'd loved her, how could he have helped her die like that? Because he believed in her dream? "Why did you help her?"

"I had to. She was dying."

I waited for more.

"Her implants were inflamed. Topical treatments weren't working. She'd been shooting immune suppressants."

"While she was here?"

"And before. She arrived with ARC."

I looked around me at the shreds of plastic around the windows and the door, all that remained of her sterile tent.

"The hotwire was her only way out," he said. "I had to do it."

"Why not ring a doctor, have her socket removed?"

He shook his head. "It was too late for that. She was dying."

I remembered Morley had said much the same.

Whichever way I looked at it, Peter had done the right thing. He'd given her the only chance she'd had.

And I hated him for it. Hated him for his judgement, for his cold kindness, and most of all his fingers at her wrists, tying, untying. I felt sick. "So what was it like?" I asked him. Swallowing my phlegm.

"What?"

"To kill someone as a favour. To kill and be thanked for the trouble. To get away with it."

I rose to my feet as I spoke. He followed me up, facing me with perfect equanimity. He said, "I rather expected you to come out with something like that eventually."

"Meaning?"

"Meaning we all have our excuses. If you want to pet my wife, go ahead. You don't have to think me a monster to do it. Though if it makes you feel better—"

I hit him in the mouth.

"Oh for God's sake," he mumbled, and kneeled down, dripping blood onto the Formica.

When I stepped out of the hangar it was evening. Laura was cleaning paint brushes in a can of turpentine.

"Busy?"

"Window frames needed doing. Peter around?"

I shrugged. "I'm leaving tonight." I don't know what I expected from that but whatever it was, I didn't get it. "The cleaners will be here tomorrow to remove the rest of the evidence."

"I thought that was your job."

"I do containment."

"Are we contained?"

"That's up to you."

"It is?"

"If you can live with it or not."

"With what?"

"Your husband helping her bleed to death."

She said nothing to that.

"Where were you when it happened?"

"In bed."

"Asleep?"

"Sure. I guessed what they were up to. I'd washed my hands of them." She made it sound like they'd been having a crafty fuck in the back of the 4X4.

"I'm sorry." It seemed like a good thing to say at the time.

"I should thank you," she said, as she dried her paint brushes carefully on a disposable cloth.

"For what?"

"For not being the police, I suppose. A court case would have wrecked my husband."

"To be honest, I don't give a shit about your husband."

At least she was looking at me now.

I said, "Let me drive you some place."

I had forgotten all about Harris, and Morley, and the army ghosts, and the roomful of papers we had on her: the rallies, the riots, her jail terms, her dead brother, and all the little hatreds she'd collected on the way.

I'd forgotten that I was the enemy.

She put her brushes down. "Where did you have in mind?"

My heart leapt.

"Anywhere," I said. My throat was full of her, her smell, honey and lavender. "Anywhere away from here!"

"No," she said.

I thought of her husband, of his shells and bones and feathers, and of the dark scum at the bottom of the isolation tank. My head began to pound. I thought of Joanne Rynard's wrists, the meticulously knotted bandages. My head felt as though it was going to burst. I thought of the beach, and the blanket, and Laura's hand pressing mine to her hip, and her hair like smoke on my face. I stepped forward and gathered her up in my arms and I mashed my mouth against hers. Her lips were red and slack and cold. I squeezed the air out of her. Her arms hung limply by her sides. I closed my eyes. The air stank of turpentine.

I let her go.

She walked inside the house and shut the door.

• • •

I stood there awhile, watching the paint dry, glancing around at the hangar, and the house, and the cracked runways, and the power station. Their private kingdom: sea and sky, untroubled by the world and rarely visited on any terms but theirs. Peter forever indulging his own perverse tastes. Laura, whose resentfulness controlled her every move.

I knew then it was hopeless; that I stood no more chance against them than Joanne had done. Joanne Rynard who, dying to fulfill her dreams, had served to fulfill theirs.

They were monstrous. They were magnificent.

I got into the car and drove away.

after kerry

IAN MCDONALD

British author Ian McDonald is an ambitious and daring writer with a wide range and an impressive amount of talent. His first story was published in 1982, and since then he has appeared with some frequency in Interzone, Asimov's Science Fiction, New Worlds, Zenith, Other Edens, Amazing, *and elsewhere. He was nominated for the John W. Campbell Award in 1985, and in 1989 he won the Locus "Best First Novel" Award for his novel* Desolation Road. *He won the Philip K. Dick Award in 1992 for his novel* King of Morning, Queen of Day. *His other books include the novels* Out on Blue Six, Hearts, Hands and Voices, *and the acclaimed* Evolution's Shore, *and two collections of his short fiction,* Empire Dreams *and* Speaking in Tongues. *His most recent books include the novels* Terminal Café, Sacrifice of Fools, *and, most recently,* Kirinya. *His short stories have previously appeared in our Eighth, Ninth, Tenth, and Fourteenth Annual Collections. Born in Manchester, England, in 1960, McDonald has spent most of his life in Northern Ireland and now lives and works in Belfast. He has a Web site at http://www.lysator.liu.se/~uni-corn/mcdonald/.*

In the haunting story that follows, he takes us on a melancholy voyage of discovery through a troubled future Ireland, a place where you can't be certain of anything, even who you are—or who you were.

November is the dying season in our family. The light fades out of us, we grow pale and cold and fall like leaves. Grandparents, aunts, uncles, cousins accidentally killed; all the dead of November. Now, my mother.

It's a good month for burying, November. The low between-light of autumn-going-winter shows the bones and struts of things; the land, the things growing from it, the people standing on it. Ireland is a country that looks best by winter light, stripped bare of leaves and greenery, spare and strong and good. We buried Ma beneath an intense blue sky, the golden light casting long shadows on the grave grass from the marble Jesuses and alabaster angels and our overcoated figures around the hole. Family, the few living relatives, Father Horan. No friends. My mother had never had a friend she had not alienated in the end.

The dying had been painful and long and inevitable. Ironic, mostly. Every time one of us had tried to break away from that dark little house full of the smell of frying food, she had found a lump, or noticed a mole had grown larger, or had pains in her stomach, or passed blood. And she would reel us in from wherever we hoped to escape to. Dangerous, to invoke the name of the angel of carcinoma. He flies in tandem with the angel of poetic justice. November is his favorite month.

Kerry had broken the tether. She flew free.

Father Horan sprinkled the box with water, and they put Ma down into the black pit and shoveled the earth over her, and I did not feel a thing. Da stood, shoulders slumped, watching the Father roll up his stole, and I knew he felt as I did. It was like God had died and left us all to our own wills and consciences, but we could not believe the infinity of the universe we had been let play in.

Louise was crying; shuddering heaves and sighs. She was doing it for those of us who would not. She probably blamed herself for the cancer, somehow.

A small flock of starlings dashed over the cemetery. Symbol of a soul in flight, to the ancient Greeks. Metempsychosis. She'd always hated it when she thought I was showing off. Mr. Too-Big-For-His-Boots. Knows everything, but knows nothing. Ma had never allowed us to enjoy anything she lacked. Including education. We learned to temper our ambitions to her jealousy. The soul of Aeschylus, Ovid, Whitman, Heaney, at the batch desk in the Allied Irish bank.

"Metempsychosis," I whispered, because I was free to.

"What?" Da grunted.

"Transmigration of the soul. The spirit moving from one body to another."

The birds turned with a flash of wings over the brick chimney of the crematorium and swooped away, calling to each other.

In the car park, Father Horan shook our hands with pleasing firmness. Another surprise, he drove away in a red Toyota sports model.

"I thought Kerry might have made it," Da said.

"How?"

"Seen the notice, maybe."

"We don't even know she's still in this country. It's been three years."

Three years of something more than silence. By gesture and expression and mood and sigh, Ma taught us that Kerry was dead, to her, and so to us. But you talk about the dead, you remember them, fondly or not; their spirits haunt you. Kerry was an exorcised ghost. A never-existed. An unconceived child.

I had called at her flat a few days after the night of the argument, to convince her that it was unnatural for a daughter to swear never to see her mother again. "Kerry doesn't live here anymore," Michaela her flatmate had said. She was as surprised as I. No warning, no preparations, no forwarding address. Gone.

I can still see Kerry's room. October sunlight through a leaded window; dusty sneaker-prints on the boards; closets and drawers open, bed stripped down to the stained, candy-striped mattress. Rectangular pink nipples of sticky fixers where pictures had been taken down; the patches of unfaded wall color beneath. The light struck a glint from the far baseboard. A brooch: a tiny, silver, winged bird in flight. Overlooked, or a parting message?

I still have that brooch.

I called her job. She had quit her job. Her boss talked to me as if, being blood of her blood, I was complicit in her disappearance. No notice, no explanation, no excuses, no point of contact. Gone.

We could have found her. We could have contacted friends, lovers, work mates; asked at other studios if Kerry had approached them. We could have posted her missing with the police and watched for her face to appear on the side of the morning milk carton. We could have searched for her through the information net that weaves our lives so tightly that none drop through it. We didn't. On a brilliant November morning in the car park of the cemetery in which the mother I hated lay stuffed under wet soil, I understood. We were afraid to find her. That would have meant talking, and questions, and answers to those questions that might upset the miserable equilibrium of our family. Better to let one go than risk the unacceptable truth.

Louise was sniffling again. Little hankie job. Declan was holding her to him but he knew the smell of political tears. Sean and Liam stood in their weddings-and-funerals suits, wanting Daddy to tell them they could get into the car. To them, Nan had been a horror of their noise, a list of Do-Not-Disturb injunctions, dreadful chicken dinners they had to eat *every last fragment of*, and the oily, post-menopausal smell of old woman. They wouldn't miss her.

No one would.

"She should know," Da said. "Kerry. She should know."

"About Ma?"

He shook his head.

"That she can come *back*. That we want her back; that it's all right now, she's gone; maybe now we can be the family we should have been. Only . . ."

"Only what?"

"I can't do it. I can't face her. I wouldn't know what to do. Stephen, would you?"

My family role had always been the burier of dead animals, the shoveler of shit, the cleaner of vomit. In latter days, the mediator, the ambassador. Another role now: the releaser of exiles.

I have several other lives that orbit at varying distances around this one that is my day-to-day experience. The Poet is closest; more a moon than another world. I can look at it, study its features, imagine how I might reach it some day. I am some way toward it, building a tower of file-block sheets and Post-it notes up which I might climb, if the vertigo does not overcome me. The Great Detective Story Writer is more remote, little more than Friday afternoon imaginings, when the clock drags and I try to think of a more satisfying Monday than the one in which I return to this desk and terminal. I could never reach that world: if I had failed to be the accountant I was expected to be, I could not possibly be a success at anything else. But the sun of this private pre-Copernican universe was gone, the gravitations rearranged, and I found I had become my own detective hero.

I set out in search of Kerry in the way I knew best: feeling the vibrations of her passage through the web of digital transactions that is twenty-first-century banking. The transition between our old, screen-based system and the new "virtual interactive consensus transactional financial interface" (high managementese fringes on perversely beautiful poetry) was a good time to conduct illicit searches through the system. The managers smile beatifically beneath their blank plastic virtuality visors as they wave their manipulator-gloved hands, conducting the waltz of the billions. Ludicrous. But it's computers, and therefore beyond criticism, and the consultants are taking twelve million off us, so it's higher even than papal infallibility. This old Luddite moved his stylus across the mat and hunted for his sister. Windmill Animations, Kerry's erstwhile studio, was a customer of our Bellfield branch. It was not even morally dubious to tap through into its records and access the payroll accounts. The guilt started when I used bank authorizations to locate Kerry's account in the Rathmines branch of the Bank of Ireland. The blank virtuality visors were one-way mirror shades, watching me, unseen. I've spent all my life feeling guilty about one triviality or another. A higher level of authorization accessed the Rathmines account. Kerry had closed it almost nine months ago. Two more weeks and the inactive file record would have been automatically deleted. No outstanding debts, no credit arrangements, no explanation. But an address. A flat, in Rathmines. Belgrave Road. Five minutes' walk from this desk. Left at the Chinese take-away. Past the bun shop that did the ecstatic eclairs. Past the over-priced mini-mart that had kept the same packet of oatmeal in the window so long the Scotsman on the front had faded into something by Andy Warhol. Across Palmerstown Road at the stop where I waited for the bus five nights a week. Ten houses down on the left, up the steps, ring the top button.

My sister.

I imagined all the pupils in the watching, knowing eyes behind the visors dilating in astonishment.

When I left that afternoon, I did not stop at the bus shelter. I crossed Palmerstown Road. I went up into the *terra incognita* on the other side of the street. I did not expect to find Kerry still there, but I hoped, and because I hoped, I was afraid. I rehearsed it past the Chinese take-away, and re-rehearsed it by Mrs. Ecstatic Eclairs, threw it all out by the Andy Warhol Scots Porage Oats man, drafted new opening lines as I dodged the traffic on Palmerstown Road, and was up the steps at the white Georgian door of number 20, pressing the button for Flat Five, suddenly sick at heart because I did not know how to greet my sister after three years of banishment.

Feet clattered down the stairs. The inner door opened, then the outer.

"Ya?"

The hair had to be a wig, or grafted extensions. Crow black, it hung to midthigh. The face inside it was a pixie's; features flattened, widened by make-up. All slants and slits and smears. Elf-thing. The kid wore a half-disintegrated lace body-stocking, more hole than whole, stretch spiderweb. A nipple protruded through the mesh, erect in the cold November air. Rosebud in winter. The fingernails were chromed.

It was not her.

"Wa?"

Their title escapes me, but their theology made an impression on my memory. On a planet orbiting the star Epsilon Eridani live an immeasurably wise and ancient avian race of great beneficence who tour the cosmos by astral projection. Channeling themselves into the bodies of Earthly hosts, they do good and work wonders and bestow the graces of their limitless wisdom and slowly uplift humanity to cosmic consciousness. Alien ambassadors. Walk-ins.

Post-Catholic Ireland's cultural diversity policy has made it a haven for sub-cultures. From across Europe, and beyond, they come to build their communities and live their alternative life-styles and explore different ways of being human. We are becoming a nation of tribes. So said the Sunday color supplement article in which I read about the Epsilon Eridani walk-ins, and some of the other, more bizarre, societies.

"I'm looking for my sister," I said.

"Tarroweep."

My turn to grunt the monosyllabic response.

"This is Tarroweep," the kid said. "Whatever you want, you say to her."

"My sister. Kerry O'Neill."

"Wa?"

The ancient wisdoms of Epsilon Eridani were not manifesting much of their cosmic consciousness this evening.

"Kerry. My sister. She lives here."

"Tarroweep does not recognize this entity."

"Well, she may have lived here. About nine months ago?"

"Tarroweep does not recognize this entity. Tarroweep has occupied this nest for four years."

"Her address is here." Perhaps she thought I was a debt collector, or a persistent ex-boyfriend, or a Jehovah's Witness, and this was an original anti-door-stepping tactic. "Listen, I'm her brother. I'd just like to see her, that's all. I've got some news for her." I thought about my news. "Good news."

"Tarroweep does not recognize this entity. Tarroweep has occupied this nest for four years."

"Maybe you don't know her as Kerry." The great detective had forgotten to bring a photograph with him. "She looks like me."

The space-pixie that called herself Tarroweep frowned as she studied my face. Her nostrils flared, she seemed to be scenting me.

"There is no Kerry," she said flatly.

I saw a figure move across the top of the stairs.

"Kerry?" I shouted. "Hello! It's me! Stephen."

The figure moved back to the top of the stairs and descended halfway. It wore the same mane of black hair but was dressed in leather pants and jacket. The jacket was open. The chest was bare. It was not Kerry.

"You are disturbing the ambassador," the boy said. "She should not be disturbed when channeling. It's dangerous."

The pixie-thing at the door half-smiled, half-grimaced.

"Ya," the ambassador to Sol Three said. The door closed.

Birds of ill omen flew over me as I walked to the bus stop. Black birds. I felt lied to; mocked. I wanted to go back and shake that silly space-pixie girl until the cosmic intellect from Epsilon Eridani was shaken out of her and I could tell her that the computer said that Kerry O'Neill had lived in the top flat for the past two and a bit years, and the computers always spoke the truth. I raged inwardly and clenched my fists and shook as the bus lurched through the dark avenues of south Dublin. It was not silly Tarroweep in her ridiculous costume with her flatline answers that I was angry at. It was too much anger for her. I raged for the two and something years that Kerry had lived one minute beyond the boundary of my world, and that the courage to cross it had come too late.

I lose days to an anger attack. The anger itself, then the guilt at having been angry, then the depression after the guilt. And after the depression, the realization that the search was not over. Kerry's account had shown a regular weekly payment of fifty pounds to a consistent account number. A few minutes of dread and digits under the eyeless gaze of the Allied Irish's virtuality visors gave me that account number and name. Dr. Matthew Collins, working out of an address on Fitzwilliam Square. I cross checked with the Golden Pages. Not an MD. A psychotherapist.

I hesitated days over arranging the meeting with Dr. Collins. You do not like to think of one of your family seeing a psychotherapist. It feels unclean, unnatural. Polluted with a rainbow oil-film of madness. Ma had always dreaded madness in the family, twining its roots around our DNA. Whispered-of relatives had been institutionalized. Auntie Mary had been taken away for eating a pair of curtains. We'd laughed; once and only once. You didn't laugh about mental illness in our family. You didn't talk about it at all; while Ma twitched and shrieked about her nerves, her *nerves*, and took to her bed because a dog was barking in the street or we were shouting while she was trying to watch *Fair City*.

Pity the carcinoma angel took her before the angel of paranoia.

Fitzwilliam Square is the handsomest of Dublin's many handsome squares, but the November light lends a particular radiance to the Georgian townhouses. The red brick releases a generous, sun-warmed aura. The white window frames glow. The palings and iron balconies cast long, military shadows.

Dr. Collins's office was on the top floor. His consulting room overlooked the railed-off key park in the center of the square. A couple of valiant residents were making the most of the rare sun by playing out-of-season tennis in the little gravel court. I could hear the pop and thwock of the ball, and the players' laughing voices.

Dr. Matthew Collins was a fat, middle-aged northerner with watching eyes as black and buried as coals in snow. I didn't like his watching. I didn't like him. I didn't like my sister having confided all the wounding things of her life to this fat Ulsterman. I didn't like that some of those wounds were done by me, as brothers must, and that he knew much more of me than I of him. I didn't like that his watching eyes saw another damaged O'Neill.

"So, you're looking for your sister." He leaned forward in his non-confrontationally arranged chair.

"Yes."

"How do you know she was coming here?" He took a cigarette from a pack of Silk Cut. "Mind if I smoke?"

"Well, actually . . ."

He lit up. "So?"

"I work in a bank. I did financial checks."

"Impressive. For someone from your family background, it would have taken some doing. Why do you need to find her so urgently?"

"To tell her Ma's dead."

"And?"

"And what?"

"In the words of the immortal Louis B. Mayer, 'If you want to send a message, use Western Union.' There's more to it than a death notice. What do you *really* want to tell her?"

There was a single cheer from the tennis match in the square: a key point taken.

"That she can come home. That it's all right, Ma's gone; now we can be the family we should have been."

"What makes you think you can start now? Have you the emotional resources to be a family? The only thing that held you together was your common fear and hatred of your mother. Now she's gone, what have you got?"

I said nothing for a long time. Collins watched me with his anthracite eyes. The sun came around, shining through the latticed window, illuminating the rows of battered paperback psychology texts on their dusty shelves. Cigarette smoke coiled upward like a spirit.

"You know, I've been working with Kerry for almost nine months." Collins said.

"I just thought you might have an idea where she went."

"You've been to Belgrave Road?"

"I have."

"Ah. I should tell you that Kerry didn't complete the therapy."

Another long silence listening to the cries of the tennis players. Collins lit another cigarette. I said, "Dr. Collins, what were you treating Kerry *for?*"

He took a long drag on his smoke.

"You've been to the house. You'd find out eventually. Your sister came to me in 2003, presenting early symptoms of type-four dissociative reaction."

"What is that, Dr. Collins?"

"A person divides his or her personality into sections, and begins to use different sections in different social contexts. In the advanced condition, alternative personalities can form."

"Are you telling me that Kerry was suffering from multiple personalities?"

"*Could* have suffered. It's a latent trait in about 7 percent of the population, usually the most creative and self-fulfilled."

"You're telling me you were treating Kerry for multiple personalities."

"Not initially, no. She presented with symptoms of depressive illness. It wasn't until therapy was well advanced that I began to notice discrepancies in her reactions in sessions."

"Discrepancies?"

"Body language, non-verbal cues, emotional reactions, the way she'd dress, do her hair, her makeup, her mode of talking, the type of answer she'd give, shifting emphases on childhood experiences."

"These would change from session to session?"

"Yes. The discrepancies widened as therapy progressed."

"I thought you were supposed to be making her better."

"Therapy digs deep. Old wounds bleed. It can be a threatening experience. I'm not one of these happy-clappy Dr. Loves handing out Prozac like candy. I'm just an old-fashioned talk-it-out, one-day-at-a-time-Sweet-Jesus cognitive grunt. It works. It changes things. It lasts."

"But not for Kerry."

"No."

"Would you tell me if you knew where she had gone?"

"I would tell you. You could try the flat again. They won't talk to me, they don't trust my profession. Emphatic onlys are the enemy. They might talk to *you*, especially as you share your sister's genes."

"I tried the flat. I told you."

"Try the flat again, I said. Things change. And if you do find her, let me know. I'd like to know how she's doing. If she's whole. Now, if you'll excuse me, I've got a paying customer in five minutes, and I need to get ready."

The sun shone through the fanlight above the front door, casting a half wheel of light onto the stairs. I passed the tennis players in the street, two women in sweats and ponytails, their game finished. I beeped my car alarm, and starlings rose in a clatter of wings from the branches of the trees in locked Fitzwilliam Park; a sudden autumn, a denuding of leaves.

Lights were lit in the top flat of 20 Belgrave Road. I could hear the music from the street. Duh duh duh duh duh duh duh duhduh duh. A girl with shoulder-length bobbed blonde hair, wearing a shift dress over tartan tights, finally heard my ring over the bass.

"Hello. Could I speak to . . ." I hesitated. "Tarroweep?"

"Who?"

"Tarroweep."

"No one here by that name."

"I talked to her three days ago, here, on this doorstep."

The girl studied my face, frowned, and the creases in her features revealed her.

"*You*," I breathed. "It was you! Tarroweep. I suppose the walk-in walked out again?"

The girl looked blankly at me.

"I'm Clionadh. Tarroweep is . . . it's kind of hard to explain. Just that, if *she* met you, only she is going to remember you. Things *she* remembers, I don't. Things *I* remember, she don't."

Another self. A partitioned personality. Alternative lives. Type-four dissociative reaction, Dr. Collins had called it.

"I'm trying to find my sister. She lived here."

Clionadh/Tarroweep examined my face again. The Clionadh self spoke differently, carried herself differently, used different body language. Different person. Her eyes widened.

"Kerry."

"You remember her?"

"You're so like her. You could be twins. Sundered selves, twins. Oh God, yes! You're Stephen. She talked about you."

"Do you know where I can find her?"

"Find Kerry? No one can find Kerry. Kerry's gone."

I felt my heart kick, like a worm of ice and iron heaving inside its ventricles. Seeing my look of dread, Clionadh hurried to add,

"Jeez, everything's so *linear* with onlys! It's complicated. I really don't know where she is now, your sister, but there's a guy who might. Feargal. Kerry knew him; he's sort of on the edge of multi society. There's a pub down in Temple Bar; Daley's?" I didn't know it. Clionadh gave me directions. "I'll get in touch with Feargal. I'll meet you there about nine."

"Will I know you?"

"You mean, will *I* know *you?* Will I be Clionadh, who remembers you and Kerry? I'll know you. The cycles last about four, five days. I'm at the mid-point now, so you don't have to worry, I'll be Clionadh for a while yet."

"Clionadh." The girl had been closing the door. "Kerry. Is she; was she, like you? A . . ."

"Multi. It's just a word, like gay, or lesbian. Hey, don't you know, everyone's a tribe these days? Everyone's a minority. Kerry: *was* she? I suppose. *Is* she? Not anymore. I'm sure of that."

I tried to wear Clionadh's worldview like a pair of tinted glasses as I went down into Temple Bar. Not what she had told me about Kerry: I couldn't let that close to me yet, it was too sharp, too sudden, too penetrating. It would have killed me with its icy implications. I tried to see the nation behind her throwaway line that everyone was a tribe now. No mainstream. No society. No city, no state, no holy Mother Ireland for which the patriots died. No ultimate truth, no unifying vision. No racial destiny. But a thousand doors to God, a thousand paths to community, to expression, to family and belonging. A thousand ways of being human. Bankers. Scared poets. All types. All tribes.

I read in those same color supplements where I learned about the Epsilon Eridani Ambassadors that micro-culturism is the logical end point of twenty-first-century post-industrialism. The fracturing of the human race into a billion interest groups will be complete when the nano-assembler experiments become a workable technology and every individual will have complete material self-sufficiency.

Amazing, what you can learn from the Sunday color supplements.

Around the turn of the century, Temple Bar, between Dame Street and Dame Anna Livia Pluribelle, had been the fashionable quarter of Dublin, the epitome of the mail-order eclectic that is post-modern Bohemianism. Long before the tribes began their migrations along the ley-lines to the Land of Youth in search of tolerance and freedom, Temple Bar had enjoyed a thriving sub-culture scene. Now its narrow streets and warehouses were the tribe capital of Europe. I passed transvestite and transsexual clubs, techno-Christian love-ups, tattoo dens, death-metal temples, rubber bars, New Revelation Buddhist urban monasteries, cyber-dweeb web-domes, White Rastafarian missionaries, neo-Celts, chilly-looking top-less women in Native American feathers and leathers, gender-benders, andro-gynes, Seventies Revivalists, New Model mods, Star Trekkers, neo-Edwardians, New Age Samurai, manganauts on custom motorbikes, New Futurists, barbarian babes and boys. I saw Ambassadors, walking-in from Epsilon Eridani to sit in a doorway and roll a joint.

I tried to see them as Clionadh did—as Kerry might: facets of human expe-rience, a plethora of possible alternative social selves. As I made my way through the crowds on Essex Street to the accompaniment of the primal heartbeat of warehouse Bass Addicts, I understood a second meaning to Clionadh's comment. Everyone is an interior tribe. We are all squabbles of aspects of ourselves that stand forward when life's changing situations call them. The difference between banker/poet/detective/emotional cripple Stephen O'Neill and Clionadh/Tarrow-eep/Epsilon Eridani avian intelligence is the distance between facets. Mine are close, they reflect each other's light. Hers are far apart, and shine on their own. *I am large, I contain multitudes*, Walt Whitman yawped over the roofs of the world in his "Song of Myself." Yes, great singer of the ego, but the truth from the new millennium is that there is no Self any more, only a raucous flock of selves, flapping in every direction to world's end.

Daley's was the kind of bar where James Joyce could have drunk, or had been made to look like the kind of bar where James Joyce could have drunk. The latter, I thought, though the Edwardian pitch-pine booths, the encaustic tiles, the gas lights, and the faded back-bar mirrors advertising long-defunct whiskey distilleries were very convincing.

The clientele was more varied than I expected in a Temple Bar pub. But I suppose that's how a multi bar must be; everyone something different. Those someones who weren't temporarily part of some other sub-culture. Multi. I hated the taste of the word on my tongue. Multi. Kerry. It made her a thing, a con-dition.

Clionadh was defending a corner booth against four young males with pints in their hands. She waved. I squeezed in. A harassed bar boy took my order.

"Feargal says he'll be along about half nine," Clionadh said.

"Feargal. Is he a . . ."

"You have trouble with the word, don't you? Feargal? No. Maybe once. I can't tell. No one can. You'll see."

I contemplated the rising nebula of head in my freshly arrived Guinness.

"Do you mind if I ask you a question?" I had to shout over the boothless boys, who were singing "Fairytale of New York" in the mandatory raucous style.

Early with the Christmas music this year. "I'm not sure how to ask this, but which is the real you: you here, or the other one, Tarroweep?"

Clionadh shouted with high-pitched laughter.

"Hey, Stevie, don't you know it's not etiquette to ask about others in front of the current? Currents never know alternates, that's the way the thing is. Onlys always want to know which is real. Answer, both. Clionadh is real, Tarroweep's real. What you really mean is, which is the original? Which came out of which?"

"Well, if it's not unforgivably rude . . ."

"Neither. Not as we are now. I can remember vaguely having been something like Tarroweep. Alternates develop their own independent memories. I suspect that Clionadh emerged out of the pre-Tarroweep's channeling exercises. You don't become an Ambassador unless you're partway multi."

"And this pre-Tarroweep, is she the original?"

"She was, I think. She may still be around; it's possible she's accessible from Tarroweep but not from me. I wouldn't know, you see. Separate memories. But what I remember of her, I don't think she was a very happy person. I wouldn't want to be her again."

I shivered in Daley's suffocating heat.

"And Kerry?"

"She moved in three years back. The place is well known in the scene as a multi house. Maybe the landlord is, or something. She moved into the flat across the landing. I liked her. Got to know her pretty well. She was on the edge of the scene, an emergent. Still had linkage between personas. Some can never fully make the break. Too much gravity in the black stuff down there in the memory."

Some never even begin, I thought. Broken goods. Smashed by the gravity of black stuff.

"Did she tell you how it, ah, started?"

"About your family? Her mother—your mother? Jeez, yes. She was seeing a therapist."

"I called in on him."

"The admirable Dr. Collins."

"He thinks the therapy may have been responsible for Kerry's breakup."

"The word's 'emergence.' No, he might have hurried it along, but Kerry was a latent multi long before. She told me that when she was a kid and lay in bed at night and listened to your Ma raving away downstairs about what a martyr she was, what foul kids she had, how everyone was out to make her life miserable and no one loved her, she would lie there in the dark and imagine she'd been born someone else, in another house, with different parents, where everything was good and she could be what she wanted. When she had the big fight, when she left you all, she had the space to live that other life she should have had, be that other person she should have been."

I closed my eyes. It was not the smoke in the bar that had made them water.

"Ma's dead. That's what I came to tell her. Ma's gone."

"Good," Clionadh said fiercely. "Hey! He's here!" She jumped up, waving furiously. "Feargal! Over here!"

I thought about Tarroweep, the other, incommunicado side of this young woman beside me, and how she had not known Kerry when I had spoken to her on the doorstep of Number Twenty. Clionadh could not tell me why that was; I knew more of her alter ego than she did. Perhaps Tarroweep and Kerry never met under those identities. Tarroweep only knew the Kerry that should have been, whatever her name and nature.

Feargal was as Feargals should be; slightly out of date. Shaved head, tuft of chin beard from the Seattle look of over a decade ago. Unless what goes round had come round, down in Temple Bar. He had a Cork accent. He drank Beamish, as a good Cork man should. I watched him as he talked and could not dislodge the idea from my head that he had had sex with my sister.

"Kerry. Yeah. Came to us eight, nine months back."

"Us?"

"Everyone's an 'us' these days, friend. We're a group, a project, over in Mountjoy Square."

The old tenement terraces of the ten-to-a-room people, the bread-and-tay people who had birthed Sean O'Casey and Brendan Behan, had new tenants now. A race beyond their ancestors' conception, come creeping up the tenement steps and staircases, through the derelict high-ceilinged rooms, looking for a place to strike roots.

"A multi community?"

"Beyond the multi scene," Feargal said. "For multis who don't want to be multi anymore."

"She never really was, Stevie," Clionadh said. "She hated going back. Couldn't bear it that she would have to go back to it in the end. To what she was. The black."

"Found us," Feargal said. "They do. Don't advertise, keep ourselves to ourselves. Word passes. We could do this thing she wanted. Not cheap, but price okay to her."

"Her bank account was closed. That was you?"

"Standard practice."

"What did she buy from you?"

"Complete new life. Identity, history, memories, emotions, personality. Everything."

I thought they were fictions of films, those moments when the camera zooms in on the face of the hero while the background pulls out to infinity. They aren't. Art imitates life. The camera in my skull shrank the noisy, pushing bodies in Daley's bar to distant, buzzing insects.

Clionadh touched my hand. It felt like mist. Her face swam before me, at once remote and enormous, like a face painted on the side of a blimp. She was speaking.

"Okay? You okay Stevie? Feargal, is he all right?"

Daley's resumed its proper dimensions of sight and sound and smell.

"God," I whispered.

"Feargal," Clionadh said urgently.

"Lot to explain," Feargal agreed. "This isn't the place. Easier to show. She's all right, your sister. Believe me. She isn't hurt; we wouldn't hurt anyone, anything. But you should see. Then you'll understand, maybe."

The electric cab left us at the tenement in Mountjoy Square. The driver charged us wrong-end-of-town prices. Long long since I was north of the river. Tribal banners bearing a dozen different crests swung from broken street lights or flapped against the fronts of the old townhouses. Traveler campervans and trailers were nose-to-tail around the central grassed square: clusters of tents, bashes and refuse sack yurts had been erected on the small green. Goats grazed, skinny dogs scavenged, heedless of traffic. Campfires sent wreaths of sparks into the cold, clear night. There was music; many musics; overlapping tribes of sound.

It had begun with these traveling people, when Britain decided it could no longer tolerate a nomadic population. They came to Ireland, they found peace, they stayed, they spread the word. For most of its history, Ireland has exported its young, scattering its brightest and boldest and best like seed across the planet. Now the brightest and boldest and best were being gathered in from across the planet, and Ireland was a country of the young again.

The steps to the tenement stank of urine. I think it's compulsory.

As we climbed the spiral of worn stone stairs, Feargal explained that his project owned the whole apartment block. They'd needed somewhere big and cheap. The equipment. He paused on the first landing to call five names. Kerry's was not one of them. His voice echoed in the big, cold stairwell. Tracks of condensation ran down the glossy, institutional paint. A door opened on the next floor, a head appeared over the bannisters: a girl, shaggy blonde hair, age indeterminate, terrifyingly thin.

"Feargal! Feargal! I remembered! Bray beach! And they were there! All of them! But they never existed!" She giggled and disappeared. The door closed loudly.

"Trina's a transient." The name was not one of those Feargal had shouted out. "We're mostly transients. Nature of the community; you pass through on your way from somewhere to someplace better."

"And you?" I asked.

"Permanent. Eternal. Day-oner. Invented this place. Least, that's what I remember." I didn't understand why he smiled.

"And Kerry?" I asked.

He nodded up the stairs.

Feargal took us to the door at the top of the stairs, under the glass cupola. We entered the room beyond. It was dark but the acoustic and the chill of the air suggested immense size. The lights clanked on, battery by battery; heavy duty industrial floods. White light, white room: the old tenement attic, the length of the whole building.

The thing in the middle of the floor was white too. Feargal's footsteps echoed in the big white space as he crossed the floor to the machine. A faint pulse beat of street rhythm transmitted through the row of skylights. Feargal's expression as he stood before the device was a combination of pride and awe; Clionadh's, as she ran her hand over the white scanning ring, bewilderment and disgust.

The sheet on the padded vinyl surface was white, and neatly folded down at the top.

"Most of the work was already done by the end of the century. Complete map of the human brain. Scanned in sections by one of these things. Axon by axon wiring diagram. What fires in response to what stimulus. Took *us* to make the concept jump: what can read can be taught to *write*."

"You use that thing—scanner—to rewrite memories?"

"What are we but what we *remember* we are? We came up with a new model of the brain; as an imaging system. Memories move through the brain along established paths of neural activity."

"We?" I said.

"Six neuroscience researchers. With a vision. And some money. Imagination, my friend. That's all it takes. Imagination is the sister of memory. Imagine that other life, that other friend, those other relatives, parents, and the scanner identifies the activated neurons, and imprints the image into memory. Single neuron e/m induction. Like making photographs from negatives. The long darkroom of the soul." Feargal fished a translucent plastic pharmaceutical tub out of his pocket. Such was the power of his metaphor, I thought for a moment it was a film can. He popped the lid, scattered white pills on the white sheet. The pills were stamped with the image of a flying dove.

"Acetylcholine activators. Play a double function in the process. Reinforces imprinted memory while depressing the existing engram on that site cluster so there is no conflict of memories. Beautiful. Remembering and forgetting. After a couple of months the memories become independent of the imagination; like Trina, down there in thirty-three. Works best on those with fugue state tendencies. Got a complete alternative personality with ready established memory routings, so much the better. Takes about four months for new memories and personality to become permanent; about six before the old memories and personality are supplanted and erased. One thing we can't erase; what we call the cognitive discontinuity: they remember the process of imprinting, but not why they came here."

"Kerry?" I asked.

"She's gone, man. Not here anymore."

He was smiling. He was proud of what he did. He was a savior; Jesus of the ganglia. Believe in me, be born again. A Jesus that stank of Beamish and cigarettes, with a fistful of pills. Suddenly I wanted very, very much to plant my own fist in the middle of that loop of beard around his mouth. I wanted to grab him by his sticking-out ears and smash his stubbly head against the scanning ring of his hideous machine, smash and smash and smash until his memories flowed from the cracks like grey juice. It was seething black bile, rising up my gullet, choking me. Anger.

Clionadh saw my clenched fist trembling. She did not speak. I did nothing. Again. *Again.* Ma was waxy and swollen with gas and rot, a week deep in the dark November soil, and still she would not allow me to be angry.

"I just want to find her," I said. "Tell her Mother's dead."

"I know," Feargal said. "I killed her. Here. In this. Down in the molecules."

"Just tell me where she's gone. That's all I want to know."

"She won't know you. She won't remember you."

More than Mother had been killed in that memory-imprinter. Louise died. Little Sean and Liam died. Da died. I died. Her sister, her nephews, her father, her brother. Everyone she had ever known. Pixie-faced Clionadh in her girlie dress and tartan tights; Tarroweep channeling in yet another persona: dead. Then my understanding inverted in that big, cold attic. It was *Kerry* who had died. The flesh moved on, the skin and the senses, but Kerry O'Neill was buried in the soft folds of her cerebral cortex. Inverse metempsychosis. You don't come back as someone else. Someone else comes back as you.

I had lost her.

I was out of the attic and half a flight of stairs down before I was aware of Clionadh's heels clattering after me. I heard them stop and her shout out.

"Why don't you just *tell* him?"

I turned and looked up the stairs. Feargal was in the open attic door.

"What good would it do?"

"What hurt would it do?"

Feargal's laugh was coldly resonant in the stairwell.

"You ask me that, Clionadh/Tarroweep? A multi asks me where the hurt is in something coming back from your former life?"

The black anger inside me was just cold, hard sickness now. Gone.

"What former life?" Clionadh shouted defiantly. "There is no former life! You took it away. There's nothing to hurt her. But even for the chance to just see her, why hurt *him*?"

Feargal closed his eyes, rubbed the palm of his hand across his beard. He sighed. His breath steamed.

"We got principles here, you know. Hell, she's at Twelve Willows Community. Up north. Place called Ballydrain. County Down. On the big lough. Dara. She's called Dara. Dara McGann. She won't know you. Understand that. Be gentle. You hurt her, I'll find you, friend."

"I wouldn't hurt her," I said. "I'm her brother. Her family."

"Family hurts hardest and deepest. *Brother*."

A new wind had come down from the northeast, born in the great Siberian taiga, spreading unexpected cold and frost over Ireland. Winter always takes us by surprise in this country. The road north out of Dublin was a grind of nervy drivers and gritting trucks spraying salty shrapnel. Hitchers with cardboard signs for points north huddled on the verges in their inadequate clothes, disconsolate as winter crows. My car was too full of doubts and justifications for any other passengers.

Time. Time. Time. And excuses. Ten days lost. Too busy at work. Couldn't get time off. Pre-Christmas rush starting. Ma's estate to settle. Excuses. Ten days while I debated the rights and wrongs, and listed the pros and the cons, and decided for and against a dozen times each day, and made my mind up one way, and then the other, and then changed it again; about going to see Kerry. Dara.

Then the calendar told me this morning—Saturday morning—that it was December come Monday, and in a surge of dread, anticipation, and adrenaline, I found myself past the airport halfway down a tail-back behind a gritter truck, heading north. If December came and I did not see Kerry—Dara—I never would. It was a November thing. The dying month.

Beyond Drogheda, the traffic cleared and the road opened. Low mist carpeted the plain of Louth, ankle deep, golden in the clear light. Forty kilometers across Dundalk Bay, the Cooley Hills were dusted with slight snow. North. We are a northern people, we Ui Neill. Appropriate that Kerry should return to the ancestral lands. I passed lay-bys and picnic areas crowded with the brightly painted transports of the traveling people. Smoke rose from their cooking fires. Children in colorful knitwear played with untrustworthy-looking dogs; dreadlocked, bearded men saluted gravely. I raised my hand to them in return. The women all looked cold. A nomadic nation. Rootless.

I began to explore what Kerry had done to herself in terms of a colossal act of self-definition. I am what I choose myself to be. I reject the self that is chosen for me. The Ma-made self. The uncertain, fearful, malleable self. I annihilate it. Down among the neurochemicals, I erase it with precise pulses of electricity and build in its place the self that I invent.

We are a tribe of putter-uppers, we Ui Neill. All we ever had was a choice of hells; so better to endure the lesser than risk the possibility of a greater. Put up. Shut up. Kids don't know that this is not normality. That this is not what family life should be. We can't be unusual, it must be the same for everyone else and they don't complain. Put up, shut up. Such conditioning can only be undone as deeply and painstakingly as it was done. Molecule by molecule. Cell by cell. Memory by memory. It's true, what the women who do it say: it takes more courage to leave than to stay.

I came up through Ravensdale, the old gap of the North. Snow lay in the lee of the hedgerows up by the old border. Down into Newry, then east of northeast, by B-roads along the northern flanks of the Mourne Mountains, through the neo-villages and techno-hamlets of the new tribes.

Kerry's—Dara's: I must not think of her by that other name—motivations were clear and honest. My own were obscure. I had realized when Feargal showed me the machine in the tenement attic that my role as bearer of news and repealer of exile was meaningless. I had no reason to find her. She had no reason to be found. Except that the detective-self could not walk away from an incomplete case. Except that my appearance out of an erased past, bearing dubious gifts, was no more selfish than Kerry's valuing me so little that she could blithely uncreate me. I wanted to see her. I wanted to know that my sister's flesh still walked, and might talk to me. Once might be enough. To have not found her, to have left it open: how Ma would have loved that! Failed *again*, Stephen! That last fence would always be too high. Kerry's courage was to transform; mine was to find what she had transformed into. In November.

Up into the drumlin country of Down; those strange rounded glacial hillocks, clustered like eggs in a basket. Mist clung in the hollows between them. By the waterside communities of Strangford Lough; the boats reefed down for winter, the flocks of migrant Greenland geese working across the mud-flats. Through a speaking son, a deaf mussel-farming community directed me to Ballydrain and Twelve Willows.

The name was appropriate. The community cultured genetweak willow for the biomass power station up at the head of the lough. Accelerated growth and intensive coppicing gave two crops a year. The road wound a kilometer and a half between low drumlins studded with the twiggy crowns of willow before the turn-off to the community. I drove another kilometer and a half down a muddy lane rutted by cutters and timber transporters before a shield of woven willow twigs on the farm gate welcomed me to Twelve Willows. The community was a collection of sheds, silos, and portable buildings surrounding a much-extended Victorian farmhouse. Two large articulated timber transporters with trailers were being loaded in the yard by forklift. A lot of people were standing around, drinking coffee from a big vacuum flask. They looked very young. Tribe people do. There were lots of dogs and children. The men favored facial hair. The place smelled of wood chips, mud, and cold salt from the lough shore behind the farmhouse.

"Hello, I'm Stephen O'Neill," I said to the first person I met, a black-bearded man with a Bolivian-style knitted helmet. "I'm looking for"—careful—"Dara McGann. I heard she lives here."

"Dara. Yes." It was the woman operating the coffee flagon who answered. She was looking at me quizzically. "You are?"

Careful.

"A relative."

The coffee woman nodded.

"Close relative? You're the spit of her."

"We're all like peas in a pod, us O'Neills-McGanns."

"I can see that. Coffee?" I was offered a foam styrene cup. I accepted it gratefully. "I'm afraid Dara's not down at the house at the moment; she's cutting up on the back fifty. I can't say how long she might be; if you like, I'll take you up there on the quad; you'll never find it on your own."

Another offer gratefully accepted. The coffee woman—Maura; her real identity? was every Twelve Willower formerly someone else?—took me on the back of a smoky all-terrain buggy up between the rows of tall willow wands. The wind from off the lough drew odd sighs and laments from the thin branches. A cutting machine was working the third hillside over, an oily yellow insect with voracious mandibles that bit the willow off at ground level and packed the rods into a metal basket on its back.

"Dara! Someone to see you!"

The machine turned at the end of a row and stopped. The driver stepped down. I climbed off the quad and walked toward the cutting machine. Maura turned her vehicle and drove away.

She was dressed in work boots, skinny jeans gone green at the knees, a grubby

Aran sweater under a padded Puffa jacket. She had grown her hair, dyed it a deeper, glossier black, wrapped braids in colored thread. She had lost weight. Her skin seemed darker. She stood with her feet apart, head slightly to one side as she studied me. She was frowning gently. I had never seen that frown before; I could not read it. I could not read her stance, her body language, her face, her hair, her clothes, anything about her.

I spoke a name. I was not certain which one.

The frown deepened.

"Who are you?" The voice was softer, lower.

"A relative. I'm . . ."

"I don't remember any cousins like you. What's your name?"

"Stephen. Stephen O'Neill."

Her face was suspicious now, her stance aggressive.

"Just who the hell are you? I don't know you."

"Don't you recognize me?"

"I see your face. You look like me. But I don't know you. I don't remember you. Who are you, Mr. Stephen O'Neill?"

I could walk or I could speak. There was another fence, right at the finish. The highest fence of all. It was not enough for me just to see. Things only ended properly with an act.

My breath hung in the frosty air in the field of cut willow.

"I'm your brother."

Dara lived in one of the mobile huts outlying the farmhouse. It smelled of fresh paint, new, cheap carpet, old incense, and garlic. It was drafty, and I could feel it shift on its blocks as the wind eddied underneath it. The one redeeming feature—and a considerable one—was the panoramic window overlooking the shore, the lough, and beyond it the sudden, startling lone hill of Scrabo, surmounted by a tower. I watched the Brent geese move across the sands before the incoming tide, searching for eel grass. Dara made herb tea.

Kerry had despised herb tea.

There were not many things in the chilly cabin. Few of the accumulated impedimenta of a life.

"You've got a bloody nerve."

I clutched my herb tea and struggled with the quiet inner strangling of guilt.

"This is my life, you know? *My* life. *I* say when what happens in it, and I don't want people barging into it telling me they're my long-lost brothers, or whatever the hell else relations are out there. If I'd wanted a brother, I'd remember a brother. But all I remember is cousins. I'm an only."

I winced.

"You don't remember me at all?"

"I remember the discontinuity. I remember Feargal and the others, and the Mountjoy project."

"The scanner." The memory-damping pills, with doves stamped on them.

"You've been there?"

"Yes. How else could I have found you?"

"Jesus *Christ*, man! Did you ever stop to think that maybe, just maybe, the reason I *did* all this was because I didn't *want* to be found? I see your face. I see the similarities and I know, intellectually, that there was another life that I can't remember. I believe you are my brother from that life, but I don't know you. For all I know, *you* could be the reason I don't remember you. You could have raped me six times a night. I don't know. I don't *want* to know."

"Or you could have raped your sister," I said, careful not to spill any of the anger within.

"Yes."

"Or murdered her. Or murdered your mother."

"Yes."

"You could have done anything; there could be any number of reasons for you to have done what you did."

"Yes."

"You don't *know*. You *can't* know. You have to trust me. You see, the truth is, that you *did* murder someone, Dara. You murdered my sister." For an instant, I thought that she would smash me across the face with her mug of herb tea, or at least throw me out. I had never seen such darkness in Kerry's eyes. But I held her gaze, and the moment passed. I held the gaze for a long time.

"Do you want to know?" I asked. "So that you will have no doubts? It can't hurt you. It's only a story. Do you want to hear it?"

"Can I believe you?"

"Yes."

"Tell me."

I told her. It was a long time telling. It was not a tale where a few spectacular scenes would summarize and explain all. It was a slow dripping tale of a thousand, ten thousand tiny things, hour in, hour out, year in, year out, that wore away any sense of worth or individuality or hope or dream. Ten thousand stupid things. Ma's tantrums, her packing her bags and storming out to her sister's every time we would not eat our cabbage. Food control: only giving us things we hated to eat. Screaming fits in our teenages, when we would unexpectedly not come home for dinner. Being made to sit until the grease coagulated on the plate because we would not finish our Sunday dinners. Her inability to perform any domestic chore. Clothes unwashed, or never ready when you needed them; house un-vacuumed and un-dusted; dishes unwashed. But if you tried to help, you were bloody bitches and bastards, trying to show her up. Personal hygiene. She stank. She would only wash if she was going out. She begrudged us hot water. Shampoo, a luxury. Toothpaste, outrageous. Yet she told us our teeth were black and rotting in our heads and threatened us with the dentist, who would rip them all out and give us agonizingly painful dentures. I remember—I will never forget—the day I saw her in the bedroom reaching down into her pants to remove a sanitary napkin. But when Louise and Kerry started their periods, she refused to buy them feminine hygiene products, but gave them cut-up ironing board covers to slip into their gussets.

Always always someone *else's* fault. Da's for being a feckless husband and not earning as much as Mrs. Downey next-door's husband. For having to be married to him, and not Mr. Donnelly the chiropodist, who would have amounted to something. Ours, for being bad, ungrateful, bloody bitches and bastards. For being Da's, and not Mr. Donnelly the chiropodist's. For living in Finglass—many stations lower than she expected of herself—where the neighbors did nothing but talk about her: that Mrs. O'Neill, thinks herself too good for the likes of us, the bloody bitch. Never never content. Everything you did was wrong. Right things were wrong, or she made them go wrong. Never a trip out or a holiday she didn't ruin. Never a friend of ours she didn't disapprove of, or whose mother she did not envy. Never never proud of us. I, the underachiever. Expected to be an accountant. Big house, big family, big future. Reality: a job in the bank, a flat in Dartry, single at thirty-two, a dream of poetry. Louise: to be a spinster primary school teacher. Coffee shop in Tallaght; husband and sons I was supposed to engender. Kerry: nothing. Imagination ran out at the inconvenient third child. Maybe a job in a shop. Maybe married. Certainly not college education. Certainly not five years in Dublin's top animation studio, producing award-winning pieces for ads and title sequences. Certainly not Dr. Collins's Fitzwilliam Square office, or the flat across the landing from Clionadh/Tarroweep in the house of multiple personalities, or the brain scanner in the big dark Mountjoy tenement attic. Or a winter hillside of green willow.

The light ebbed from the sky. The tide grew full and the geese moved ashore to roost among the tussocks of salt grass. Dara moved about the room, lighting candles. I sat in the center of a constellation of tiny flames, shaking with emotion.

"Jesus, Steve."

"Stephen. I'm a Stephen. Always was."

"Stephen, I don't know what to feel. What you told me, no kid should have to go through that. It shouldn't happen. It's not right. It's against everything that's right. But I can't *feel* it. I can feel it for you, but not for me. She wasn't *my* mother. She's not what I remember."

"What do you remember?"

She took a deep breath.

"I remember a white house with black paint. Gravel drive. Trees around it. A garden with hidden places where I played. No sisters, no brothers. Lots of friends, though. Lots of cousins. I remember a dog called Barney and a cat called Cat who slept on my bed though I wasn't supposed to let him. The sun shone a lot. Summers were hot, winters were ice and snow. You could hear trains in the house, and if you opened the windows, the sea. The kitchen smelled of coffee and baking and something I realize now is garlic. There was a big rotting Victorian wrought-iron conservatory on the sunny side of the house. Full of ferns. Mum would work there in all seasons. She was a writer. I was scared of her computer when she got it. I thought it would pull me in through the screen into the grey nothingness behind. Dad was in money, somehow. I'm still not sure exactly what. They were big, my parents. Not physically. Emotionally. Big happiness. Big laughter. Big joy. Big anger. Big love. Big hate. They sent me to dancing lessons, and drawing. They came to my school nativity play. They stuck my paintings up on the fridge, they listened to me read my school stories, they watched me dance in the conservatory. They gathered shells with me on the beach when we walked Barney. They gave me driving lessons. They were okay about lending me the car. They tried to get me to call them by their Christian names. They tried not to dislike my boyfriends on principle. They were glad when I went to study art and video. They came to my degree show. They bought me champagne at my graduation, and again when I began my first job, and again when I moved out into my first flat.

"They died in a car crash in Wexford when I was twenty-two."

The candle flames flickered; a draft, stolen in from the dark lough. "Stephen, you all right?"

I realized that my cheeks were wet. Silent tears, for the deaths of parents that never lived. For the childhoods we should have lived. The childhoods of encouragement and approval and attention and devotion, where the pain was sharp and cut cleanly, not gnawing and gangrenous. Who was Stephen O'Neill to say it was not real? Dara McGann was building the rest of her life around what was inside her skull, and what more can *any* of us know than what that inner cinema projects onto the bone screen?

A good life. Maybe a better life.

"Stephen? You okay?" She poured me a whiskey. Kerry had been a clear spirits drinker. I nodded. My breath shuddered. "Stephen. Do you really have to go back to Dublin tonight?"

Dara's sofa was hard, her bed-throw thin and her cabin chilly but I slept like a god resting after creation. We had made it late over to the Big House the night before—eating was communal at Twelve Willows. A couple of vanloads had already gone into nearby Newtownards in search of nightlife, but enough stayed behind to scrape us together two platefuls of leftovers and a couple of bottles from the community cellars. The food was vegetarian, and very good even to an unreconstructed carnivore. After much Guinness, instruments were broken out, and we played and sang our way through the hoariest numbers in the Old-Folkies-in-Aran-Sweaters song-book. They'd do it at the drop of a hat when there were sojourners in, Dara told me. Picking my way over the frost back to her cabin, I realized a strange thing. I was happy. Food, company, music. The ancient tradition of hospitality of the Culdee mystics, whose ruined monasteries ringed this lough, was reborn in the new orders and communities. Simple gifts. Direct living. Being, without necessarily becoming. Becoming, in its own time, like the shoots of green willow. I envied Dara her new life and family.

Sundays in Twelve Willows were only worked if you wanted to. Dara didn't. She took me out along the lough shore. The frost had settled hard in the night. Mist clung to the lough, glowing in the November sun, blurring the boundary between land and water. I shivered in my borrowed parka and Wellington boots and followed Dara's footprints out across the sand.

"What was she like?" she asked when I caught up with her. "What did she do? Who was she?"

"Bitter. Compassionate. Wild. Then again, always afraid. Contradictory. Tremendous, terrifying mood swings. From incredible, devouring energy to absolute desolation."

"Manic depressive?"

"No. I don't think it was clinical like that. She had to stop herself. She couldn't allow herself to go too far, achieve too much, be too free. Something had to pull her back to what she had been told all her life she was. Useless. Worthless. A waste of womb-space."

"Happy?"

"What does that mean?"

"What did she do?"

"She was an animator. She was brilliant; these freaky, scratchy, creaky collages out of old toys and dolls and bits of bone and wire. Won awards. Only she was so brilliant she kept her job, when the depressions hit her. You kept that bit of her."

"I was never brilliant. I would never have done anything like she did. Afraid to pay the price of brilliance. Stephen, what was her name?"

"Kerry."

She did not repeat it, not even shape her lips silently around it. Dara walked on over the tide-rippled sand. In the distance a flock of geese grazed, black atoms in the bright mist.

"What about you, Stephen?"

"What about me?"

"Happy?"

"I have a job I hate; no friends, can't get a woman, bursting for a shag, don't get out, going nowhere. And I find my sister has changed into another person and does not even know who I am."

"Who are you?"

"In here?" I touched my hand to the parka quilting. "I don't know."

"What would you like to be?"

The words came in a rush, like many wings.

"A poet." I blushed instantly. Dara saw it and smiled.

"What's stopping you?"

I knew the answer to that, but I was not brave enough to speak it. Dara continued.

"There are a thousand places like this where you're allowed to be whatever you want to be. A thousand ways to be Stephen O'Neill."

I stopped walking. Water oozed from the sandy impress of my borrowed boots.

"Dara. There's something I'd like you to have. Something that was Kerry's, that she left behind."

I fumbled out the silver bird brooch. Dara looked at the tiny, exquisite thing in the palm of her hand.

"Transmigration of the soul," I said. Curlews called, unseen in the mist.

"I could put you back," Dara said. "Go to Feargal, put you back into my childhood. The white house with the black paint and the trees around it. The Victorian conservatory. Barney the dog. Cat the cat. Make you my brother."

"Why?"

"I like you. You're . . . you. My brother. I need you, I think."

"Dara, I wouldn't fit into your childhood. Stephen O'Neill comes from that other childhood. What you remember could never produce me."

Dara winced. Her hand closed on Kerry's silver bird.

"Consider us separated at birth," I said. "Orphans, adopted into different families. Separate lives. Intimate strangers. Learning about each other. Because you aren't Kerry. You are the sister I should have had, that I never knew."

"Yeah," Dara said. She opened her hand and looked at the brooch. Then, suddenly, stunningly, she drew back her arms and threw it out over the sands. I saw it glitter in the sun, but I did not mark where it fell. We walked back across the tide flats toward the low willow-covered hills, following our water-filled footprints. Behind us, the feeding geese rose up and passed over us in a long straggling skein, calling to each other as they flew north.

The Masque of Agamemnon
SEAN WILLIAMS AND SIMON BROWN

As the inventive, ironic swashbuckler that follows demonstrates, imitation can be the sincerest form of flattery. It can also kill you. . . .

New Australian writer Sean Williams is the author of several novels in collaboration with Shane Dix, including The Unknown Soldier *and* The Dying Light, *and of a solo novel* Metal Fatigue, *which won Australia's Aurealis Award for 1996. His stories have appeared in* Eidolon, Aurealis, Aboriginal Science Fiction, The Leading Edge, Alien Shores, Terror Australis, *and elsewhere, and have been gathered in the collection* Doorway to Eternity. *He has a Web site at http://www.eidolon.net/sean__williams/.*

Australian writer Simon Brown works as a journalist with the University of Western Sydney. He made his first sale to Omega *in 1981, and has since sold to* Eidolon, Aurealis, *and elsewhere. His novels include* Privateer *and, most recently,* Winter.

Not long after the Achaean fleet arrived at the periphery of the Ilium system, its area sensors noted a phenomenon its sentient matrix could neither accept nor explain. An owl appeared in the middle of the fleet, circled around it three times—its wings eclipsing the distant point of light that was Ilium's sun—then headed straight for the Over-captain's own ship, *Mycenae*. Just as it was about to smash into the ship's hull, there was an intense flash of blue light and the owl disappeared.

Internal sensors picked it up next: a bird the size of a human child, dipping and soaring within *Mycenae*'s vast internal halls and corridors. Before any alarm could be given, the sensor matrices received a supersede command; the owl was a messenger from the goddess Athena, and it was not to be interfered with.

Seconds later, the owl reached its destination, the chamber of Agamemnon, Over-captain of the entire Achaean fleet. What happened therein is not recorded, but an hour later Agamemnon announced to his crew he was going to hold a grand ball.

His wife, Clytemnestra, attributed the idea to his love of games and his penchant for petulant, almost child-like whims. She thought the idea a foolish notion, but she did not argue against it; she loved her husband and indulged him in all things.

Arrangements were quickly made, and maser beams carried messages to all the other ships of the fleet, demanding their captains attend the Great Masque of Agamemnon.

"Your brother should spend more time worrying about the Trojans," Helen told her husband, Menelaus.

The captain of *Sparta* grimaced. He disliked anyone criticising his older brother, but in this instance he had to agree with his wife. Agamemnon was spending a large amount of the fleet's energy and time to throw his ball; energy and time that could have been better spent prosecuting an attack against the Trojans' home on Ilium.

"Nevertheless, he has commanded the presence of all his captains and their wives, so we must go."

"But why a masque? He loves his games too much. And I suppose we will end up spending the whole time with Nestor."

"Nestor is the oldest among us, and his words the wisest."

"The most boring, you mean. Oh, Menelaus," she pouted. "I wish we didn't have to go."

Although Menelaus agreed with Helen's sentiment, he would not allow himself to say so.

Achilles had made a silver helmet for his friend Patroclus to wear to the ball. When Patroclus saw it he could not find the words to thank Achilles; it was one of the most beautiful things he had ever seen. Then Achilles showed him the helmet he himself would be wearing, and to Patroclus' surprise it was exactly the same as the one he had been given.

"I don't understand, Achilles. Are we going as brothers?"

Achilles laughed. "As lovers, dear Patroclus. But there is more to it than symbolism."

Patroclus looked blankly at his friend, which made Achilles laugh even harder. "We are the same size and shape. With these helmets, and wearing the livery of my ship, no one will be able to tell us apart."

"A game?"

Achilles shrugged, gently placed one of the helmets on Patroclus' head. He leaned forward quickly and kissed his friend on the lips, then closed the helmet's plate, hiding his friend's face entirely except for his eyes and mouth.

"A game of sorts, I suppose, to match Agamemnon's own." Achilles put on his own helmet, closed the face plate. "We are, behind these disguises, nothing but shadows of ourselves, and as shadows at the Over-captain's masque, who knows what secrets we will learn?"

"Secrets?"

"I have heard rumours that Agamemnon has invited a surprise guest."

"A surprise guest?"

"A Trojan," Achilles said.

His real name was Bernal, but AlterEgo insisted on calling him Paris.

"Get used to it. Our hosts insist on you adopting the name for this occasion."

"If they explained why, it would be easier," Bernal complained. Strapped into the gravity couch of the small ship in which he was travelling, he had little to do except complain. AlterEgo took care of all the ship's functions; Bernal was nothing but baggage.

"Presumably, it has something to do with the fact that all the messages we've received from our visitors come in the name of Agamemnon."

"Over-captain of the Achaean fleet, for pity's sake."

"You can snort all you want, Paris, but we know very little else about them, and it will probably be in your best interests to take them seriously."

"Not to mention the best interests of the whole of Cirrus."

Bernal aligned the external telescope, the only instrument the ship carried that used visible light and installed specifically for Bernal's use. He could not see his planet—now more than forty billion kilometres away—but the system's yellow-dwarf sun, Anatole, was the brightest object in the sky, and Cirrus was somewhere within a few arc-seconds of it.

"Home-sick?" AlterEgo asked.

"Scared, more like," Bernal answered. "When was the last time one of my people travelled this far from home?"

Bernal was sure he heard AlterEgo's brain hum, even though he knew the AI didn't have any parts that hummed as such. He had been in the AI's company for too long. "Two hundred and twenty-seven years ago. Explorer and miner named Groenig. Last message came when her ship was forty-three billion kilometres from home. Never heard from since."

"No one went after her?"

"What good would that have done? Even back then, when intrasystem shipping was much more active than now, there would not have been more than two or three ships that could have reached her last known position within six months; far too late to do anything to help her if she was in trouble. Most likely there was some onboard disaster, or maybe the loneliness got to her and she committed suicide."

The answer irritated Bernal. "What the hell did you wake me for, anyway?"

"I did have the telescope aligned on something I thought you'd be interested in seeing."

"Don't whinge. What was it?"

"Fortunately, I took the precaution of storing some images over a three day period, which was just enough time to create some very interesting holographic-"

"If you've got something to show me, get on with it," Bernal commanded.

Several small laser beams intersected about half a metre in front of Bernal's face. At first they formed nothing but a white shell, but a second later a 3D-image appeared. It looked like a crown of thorns. "How big is it?"

"Some of my sensor readings indicate the object's mass is close to 7,000,000 tonnes."

Bernal was surprised. Without a reference point, he had assumed the object was quite small. Then he remembered AlterEgo saying it had taken three days to get a workable 3D image, which was a lot of time to work with for a computer of AlterEgo's capability.

"What did you say its dimensions were?"

"I didn't, but I estimate a radius of eighty or so kilometres."

"My God! Is this one of the Achaean ships?"

"I should think that if this was just one of their ships, a fleet of them would have been detected from Cirrus several years ago. I surmise, therefore, that this is the fleet, its individual components joined in some way."

Bernal peered at the holograph. "Can you make out any repetitions of shape? Anything we could identify as a single unit?"

"Ah, I was hoping you would ask that." Bernal was sure he heard smugness in that voice. "Indeed, this is why I woke you."

The holographic image changed, metamorphosed into something more like a ship. Bernal peered at it. Well, *vaguely* more like a ship.

"It reminds me of something I've seen before, but for the life of me I can't figure what."

"Using some deductive logic, a little dash of intuition and a thorough search of the Cirrus Archives, I think I've discovered something," AlterEgo said. "Watch what happens when I remove from the Achaean ship the youngest hull material, connective grids and certain extraneous energy dispersion vanes."

The image altered instantaneously into something barely a tenth the size of the original. Bernal studied the new shape for a moment before a memory clicked in his brain.

"I don't believe it!"

AlterEgo just hummed.

"A Von Neumann probe . . ." Bernal's voice faded as he realised the implications.

"Precisely my deduction," AlterEgo agreed, superimposing a second holograph over the first: a blue outline that almost perfectly matched the image of the Achaean artefact. "This diagram is from Cirrus's most ancient library stores. It is, of course, one of the original plans for a Von Neumann probe, circa 2090 CE."

Bernal whistled. "But that was nearly 5,000 years ago. They were the first human-made ships to reach the stars."

"And in their seedbanks they carried the ancestors of all human life in this part of the spiral arm . . ." There was the slightest of pauses. ". . . including your own kind."

.   .   .

The bulkheads forming *Mycenae's* cavernous, square reception hall were decorated with depictions of a Cyclopean city: grey walls made from unworked boulders and dressed stone; a corbel arch gateway topped by a heavy, triangular sculpture of two lions and a Minoan column; and a massive beehive tomb made from the same stone as the city.

Mingling in the hall were dozens of ship captains and their wives or mistresses, all dressed in elaborate costumes, the men in shining breast plates and tall helmets sprouting horse-hair crests or eagle feathers, the women in long tunics bordered in gold and beads of amber and lapis lazuli.

Agamemnon moved among his captains, greeting each individually with generous words, baulking only when he met the two he knew were Achilles and Patroclus, but was unable to tell them apart in their silver helmets. He smiled, pretending to enjoy their private joke, and moved on to deliver more glib welcomings. Clytemnestra circulated as well, talking to the women, flattering them about their clothing and hair.

In a short while, smaller groups coalesced from the throng, centred on the fleet's major captains. The largest group circled Agamemnon and his brother Menelaus; a second group almost as large gathered around Achilles and Patroclus; other heroes to have their own audience included Diomedes, the huge Ajax, Nestor and Idomeneus. Standing apart from them all, however, was one captain without any followers or even the companionship of his own woman.

Odysseus stood back from the assembly, looking on with a wry smile. He enjoyed observing the posturings of the major captains, the false camaraderie they shared and the whispered insults they passed. As well, he was entertained by the antics of the lesser captains, eager to please their patrons and desperate to raise their own status in the fleet.

His inspection was interrupted by an owl that appeared on his shoulder.

"The guest has arrived," the owl said. "His ship is about to dock. He brings a friend with him."

"A friend?" Odysseus replied. "Troy was instructed to send only one of their own."

"His friend is not human," the owl continued. "It is some kind of AI. I only learned of this when it communicated with the navigation computer."

"Have you told Agamemnon?"

"Not yet."

"Then do so now. He should greet this Paris personally."

Bernal cursed as AlterEgo made what it called "minor" adjustments to the ship's attitude in its final approach to the docking site. The ship jerked to port, then performed a quarter-roll, jerked back in the other direction, and finally decelerated rapidly as all the lateral thrusters fired simultaneously. Bernal's journey to the Achaean fleet, which had begun with a smooth acceleration away from orbit around Cirrus and then continued on just as smoothly for another three weeks through intrasystem space, was now ending with a violent jagging that did nothing to ease his roiling stomach.

Bernal was about to ask AlterEgo when all the manoeuvring would finish, when suddenly there was a thump and he felt himself flung forward before the gravity webbing caught him and flung him back again.

And then a new sensation.

Weight, Bernal realised after a moment. *The Achaean fleet is not only locked together; it's also rotating.*

"We are here," AlterEgo announced calmly.

"I think I have a headache coming on."

"It is just the tension, Paris. You will be fine once you get moving."

"Do I have to suit up?"

"No need. We have docked adjacent to an airlock. You will be able to stroll through and meet our hosts as soon as the airlock is pressurised."

"Can you take a sample of their air?"

"Already done. Breathable. Nitrogen-oxygen mix, a little heavy on the oxygen side, but nothing extraordinary. Very few trace gasses."

"The airlock has pressurised. Do you want me to open the hatch?"

"Is there anyone waiting for me?"

"Not in the airlock itself. Wait, I'll communicate with the Achaean command system."

Bernal unstrapped himself from the webbing, then carefully climbed out of the life support suit that had kept him fed, removed his body waste, injected him with regular doses of calcium and vitamins, and electrically stimulated his muscles for the duration of the journey. By the time he had finished, AlterEgo was able to report that a welcoming committee would be waiting for him on the other side of the airlock.

"Did you think to ask who's in the committee?"

There was a sound like a sigh. "Agamemnon, Over-captain of the Achaean fleet, his wife Clytemnestra, his brother Menelaus, Captain of *Sparta*, and his wife Helen, and Odysseus, Captain of *Ithaca*."

Bernal closed his eyes, slowly shook his head. "That ache is getting worse."

"Paris, they're waiting."

Bernal nodded, climbed into a one-piece shipsuit. He clipped onto his chest a small metal badge displaying the Grand Seal of Cirrus; to a nipple on the pin showing through on the reverse of the suit he attached a thin filament that was in turn connected to a jack built into his fifth vertebrate. He tapped the badge gently. "You there, old friend?"

In spirit, if not body, AlterEgo said in his mind.

Bernal sealed the suit and went to the hatch. "Open Sesame," he said, trying to sound braver than he felt.

As the airlock cycled open, Agamemnon could barely contain his excitement. Clytemnestra laid a calming hand on his shoulder, ready to hold back her husband in case he leapt forward to greet their Trojan guest with one of his bear hugs. Clytemnestra admired the spontaneous bouts of affection Agamemnon was prone to inflict on visitors, but understood it might startle Paris out of his wits.

There was a hiss as the final hatch retracted, and a slim, short figure appeared. The stranger smiled nervously and held out a hand.

"Greetings, Achaeans. I am Paris of . . . umm . . . Troy."

The first thought that crossed Clytemnestra's mind was that Paris was absolutely sexless. She glanced at Helen to judge her reaction, and saw that she was equally intrigued.

Agamemnon strode forward suddenly to take the proffered hand in both of his, and shook it vigorously.

"Welcome to *Mycenae*, friend!" the Over-captain boomed. "I am Agamemnon!" He pulled Paris forward and quickly introduced the others. Paris shook hands with each of them.

Not sexless, Clytemnestra decided. Male, but underdeveloped. Hardly a man at all, really.

Agamemnon curled one arm around Paris's slim shoulders and led him away. "My captains are looking forward to meeting you," he said. "They are all gathered in the *Mycenae*'s reception hall." He turned to Clytemnestra, who handed him a mask, which he in turn gave to Paris. "For the ball," Agamemnon explained.

The Trojan studied the mask, made in the shape of an apple pierced by an arrow, before putting it on. Agamemnon slipped into an arrangement of beaten gold and indicated that the others should do the same.

Disguised as a swan, Clytemnestra fell in behind the pair, followed by Menelaus, looking stoic beneath bull's horns, and Odysseus, faintly amused in a mask of stars. She was surprised when Helen—her mask a predictable and entirely appropriate cat—overtook her to draw level with Paris.

"Was your journey long and uncomfortable?" Helen inquired.

Paris offered his nervous smile. "I was asleep for most of the time, my lady, and never uncomfortable."

"Oh, good! Then you will be fine to dance!"

Agamemnon laughed. "We Achaeans love dancing!" he declared.

"Almost as much as we love making war," Menelaus said grimly, barely loud enough for Clytemnestra to hear.

Bernal's heart was beating so fast he thought he might pass out.

The first thing he saw, as he stepped through the airlock and gave his greeting, was an enormous male leaping towards him. Calling on reserves of courage he had no idea he possessed, Bernal awaited the onslaught, only to have his outstretched hand pumped like an overworked piston.

If all that had not been enough, Bernal's first close-up view of an Achaean convinced him to retreat back to his own ship, but he could not escape from the vice-like grip that held his hand.

The creature was huge: a good 200 centimetres tall, and seemingly half that at least across the shoulders. Bernal heard it identify itself as Agamemnon in a voice so loud and low-pitched it rattled his teeth. Then he was being introduced to a whole crowd of giants and shepherded down a passageway that was barely wide enough for he and Agamemnon to walk side-by-side. He found himself glancing up at the Over-captain's head, marvelling at its symmetry and its colours: the cheeks and lips were a bright crimson, the long hair and beard as black as charcoal, the skin as pale as cream. It was almost a relief when they donned masks, concealing their excessive features.

Another thing Bernal could not help noticing was the Achaean's odour: not rank, but very strong and very . . . masculine. He realised then that he could smell its opposite: something sweet, like newly ripened fruit. He turned and saw the one called Helen matching his stride. She was not as tall as Agamemnon, but easily ten centimetres taller than Bernal himself. She was lithely built, and what he could see of her colouring was as exaggerated as Agamemnon's, including her long golden hair, which shone almost as fiercely and lustrously as the metal. Her cat-face was designed less to conceal her features than to enhance them; the silver whiskers danced with every word, and were quite hypnotic.

Helen asked him about his journey, and he answered as politely as his wits allowed him. Helen said something else, and there was a contribution from Agamemnon, but he was distracted by AlterEgo saying in his mind: *Paris, your hosts are not breathing.*

Achilles looked up in annoyance as the welcoming party returned to the hall. He had enjoyed being the centre of attention while Agamemnon was away; now he would have to return to being second in rank among the heroes—maybe third if the envoy from Troy was as mighty a warrior as his insecurity made him imagine.

What he saw set his mind at rest.

The tiny specimen was pallid and washed-out, barely there at all. What was his name? Paris? He looked like a ghost, but not the sort that would instil fear in anyone. The ghost of a sad, lonely child who missed its friends.

Achilles' lips pulled back in a smile as he moved through the throng to pay his respects to the visitor, leaving Patroclus to take his place.

"You're looking cheerful, m'boy," commented Nestor as he passed. The elderly warrior was seated at a table, cleaning his fingernails with the tip of a dagger, his face concealed beneath a dove-shaped mask. "King Hector is no fool, and his emissary will be no slouch, either. Tread carefully where this Paris is concerned, that's my advice."

Achilles dismissed the old man's words with a wave of his hand and did his best to ignore the irrational foreboding that swept over him.

"Dear me." Bernal sagged into the seat Clytemnestra offered him when the introductions were over. Achilles, Diomedes, Ajax, captain of this and that—

the names had reeled inexorably past him, accompanied by features and bodies no less legendary. The masks only accentuated their superficiality: they were caricatures, grotesqueries, fit for wax-works and not reality. He wasn't surprised that they weren't what they seemed, because what they seemed was utterly preposterous. The fact that they weren't respiring in any way AlterEgo could detect only proved that his initial unease had been justified, even if it did little to explain what he was seeing. Extraordinarily lifelike environment suits? The results of severe bioengineering or advanced eugenics? Alien mimics?

But the masks themselves were magnificent, matching the armour worn by the males and the finery worn by the females. Everywhere he looked he saw another stunning example. Heads glittered with jewels, waved exotic feathers, even sported miniature plants in one case. They had certainly gone to a lot of effort—an effort which did not diminish as the masque continued.

Tables were carried in, laden with roast boar, goat and lion, and vegetables Bernal could not identify. The food at least looked real, and his stomach rumbled. The giants swarmed around him, booming and hooting with their tremendous voices, every gesture exaggerated.

"I want *out* of here," he said to AlterEgo.

You can't leave yet, AlterEgo replied calmly. *Not until the banquet is over, anyway. It would be impolite to leave any sooner—possibly dangerous.*

"They'd take me prisoner?"

Worse; they might be offended. Can you imagine an army of these creatures attacking Cirrus to protest your bad manners?

Bernal groaned. He could imagine it all too well. As Achilles and his lads on the far side of the room struck up a chorus of a very martial sounding anthem, he swore to avoid causing a diplomatic incident of any kind.

"They still haven't said what they want from us."

Maybe no more than your gratitude, AlterEgo chided him. *So cheer up, Paris. You are being an unpleasant guest.*

A goblet of crimson wine appeared before him. He sipped at it, and immediately pulled a face. It tasted like nothing so much as recycled water. A plate of sweet-smelling roast meat went past at that moment, and he reached out and grabbed a slice, wincing as hot fat burned his fingertips. The meat possessed the intriguing, even poignant, flavour of stale ship rations.

Very odd indeed.

"Do you like it?" asked a voice near his ear.

He turned, startled, and almost touched masks with Helen. A whisker tickled him. "Oh, yes, very much."

"There will be speeches after the food," she said. Her eyes were very moist, he noted, and seemed to reflect every photon of light that touched them. "After that, there will be music."

"Wonderful!" He nodded, wondering what to do with the morsel of bland-tasting meat. Eat it? Probably for the best.

"We Achaeans love dancing," Helen repeated Agamemnon's declaration; but her inflection said something far different.

. . .

When the echoes of the horn had faded, Agamemnon climbed onto a chair and began to speak. Clytemnestra watched on, smiling at the audience before her, noting who seemed to be paying attention to Agamemnon and who wasn't. She knew her husband could be bombastic at times—and had little, really, to say— but he meant well. He always meant well. She committed to memory the names of those who looked bored; they would receive the edge of her disfavour another time.

Achilles was one of them. Always young Achilles. So valiant and strong, such a great warrior, yet so impulsive and restless, too. He was like a male wolf who itched to challenge the pack leader but was not quite confident enough to go through with it. So he chafed in second place, awaiting his chance.

He would never make as fine a leader as Agamemnon, Clytemnestra knew. Her husband had guided them well. Once the matter of the Trojans was resolved, none would dispute that.

The Over-captain ground to a halt and was cheered enthusiastically. The Trojan, Paris, winced at the noise. Helen leaned down to whisper something in his ear. He looked bewildered, but smiled anyway. Clytemnestra frowned. Damn that girl! A dalliance in the backroom of the barracks was all well and good if no one saw or knew, but here, with her husband just metres away, she was risking a terrible scandal.

And with a Trojan, too. Only Athena knew what Helen saw in him.

The horns sounded again, signalling the next stage of the masque. A quartet of musicians stepped from the wings and, after a brief tune-up, began to play. Tables slid easily aside to form an impromptu dance-floor. Agamemnon stepped down from the chair with a flourish and grasped his wife around her waist. She kissed him joyfully on the cheek, already feeling the rhythm in her body. Couples moved around them, heading for the clear space, accompanied by the stamping of feet and chiming laughter from the women.

They danced. More to the point, they *waltzed.*

"This can't be right," Bernal muttered.

"I'm sorry?" Helen inclined her ear closer to his mouth, sending a wave of her scent wafting into his nostrils. The skin beneath his hands was warm and soft— unbelievably so. He wasn't so close that he missed the rise and fall of respiration, but not so far away that her chest didn't catch his eye nonetheless. She was as enticing a woman as he had ever met. If only, he thought, her make-up wasn't so severe.

Then he realised: it wasn't make-up. Her skin really was that colour. And her eyelashes. And her lips.

If only, he amended, *she was real.*

"Am I hurting you?" she asked, backing away ever so slightly.

"Not at all!" He was wood in her arms, and she had sensed it. He tried to be gracious. "It's too much. All this—" He removed his hand from hers and waved at the hall. "It's overwhelming."

"It's not like this in Troy?"

"Not exactly."

She nodded. "I would like to see it, one day." Her eyes shone, and he thought he saw something akin to mischievousness in them. "Do you think that would be possible?"

The music changed tempo and he found himself drawn into a spinning whirl-wind of limbs. This dance was unfamiliar. He found his close proximity to He-len—even closer now, with her hands on his lower back, pushing him to her—disconcerting. But even more disconcerting still was the sight of Agamemnon and his fellows and their dance-partners spinning by with only inches to spare. Afraid of colliding and being crushed like a puppy, he flinched at every close pass, and eventually closed his eyes entirely, letting Helen guide him to safety. Or not, as the case may be. If she failed, he reasoned, at least he would never know what happened.

"AlterEgo, I beg you—"

Not until we have worked out what they want from Cirrus. That's why we are here. We cannot leave until we know what is going on. Grit your teeth. And be on the look-out for any covert attempt to communicate. It may be that the masque is a distraction, a mask itself for some other truth. If Agamemnon won't talk to us, then maybe someone else will.

Suddenly Helen led him by the hand from the dance floor, weaving through her fellow Achaeans with the grace of a deer. He gasped in surprise, and she pulled him closer to her.

"Come with me," she whispered.

"Helen, I—"

"Don't worry. I can tell you're not enjoying yourself. I know a place where you'll feel more comfortable."

Odysseus nodded in satisfaction as the pair, largely unnoticed under the cover of the dance, slipped from the hall. A flutter of feathers in his ear heralded the return of the owl, which indicated its own approval with a smug hoot.

"She's a wily one," Odysseus said.

"Menelaus sees." The owl nodded to a point across the room where the cap-tain of *Sparta* looked around for his wife and caught sight of her leaving with the guest. His face clouded.

"Will he follow?" Odysseus craned his neck for a better view.

The captain waved a hand and Diomedes, masked behind an ivory skull, ap-proached. A whispered exchange ensued, resulting in Diomedes leaving the hall. Menelaus sank back into his seat, glowered momentarily, then smiled as a servant offered to refill his mug.

"Good enough," the owl said.

"Where will she take him?"

"I've left that up to her. She deserves some autonomy, after all."

"As do I." Odysseus straightened his cuirass and stood. "I'm curious."

"Ever the hunter."

"Well, I was made in your image."

"Exactly." The bird nipped his ear affectionately. "So follow them and make sure nothing goes wrong."

"Yes, goddess."

Helen opened the door and nudged the Trojan ahead of her. The small room beyond was in darkness, and she felt him hesitate. He was so timid, so unlike the men she was used to. Glancing once behind her, she closed the door on them both. Light instantly sprung into being. White light, almost cold.

"What the—?" Paris looked around him in amazement.

"Here we are, alone at last," she said, reaching for his hands and pulling her to him. Although he didn't resist, he exhibited little of the enthusiasm she had hoped for.

"But—"

"Surely this is more to your liking?" The plastic walls and synthetic fabrics of the wrecked Trojan vessel they had recovered seemed unfriendly and sterile to her, but she assumed he would be more at ease in their presence. Indeed, the space was pleasantly cramped. There were a couple of large couches nearby for which she had bold plans.

Her hands caressed his wrists and forearms. His skin was rough, weathered by a sun she had never seen. He was undeniably masculine, although his stature belied it. She yearned to kiss him, this strange half-man from another world.

"Yes," he said, "I—"

"And me?" Her hands brought him closer, until he was forced to look at her. The fingers of one hand slid around his prickly scalp, tilted his face up to hers. The white light made his eyes glint. He squirmed in her grip—with lust at last, she assumed, slow to wake but no doubt as difficult to quench. "Am I to your liking, too, dear Paris?"

"AlterEgo!" Bernal struggled wildly, but Helen's grip was too strong. Her open mouth loomed and for a moment he was irrationally afraid she might devour him whole. Then her lips met his with a crushing impact, and he wasn't sure which would have been worse.

I have identified the ship you have entered, AlterEgo said. *It is the* Apollo, *the vessel piloted by Groenig on her last voyage.*

"Another Greek reference?"

Unintentional, this time, The vessel was named after an ancient series of flights from the ancient Earth to its satellite.

Bernal felt something slip into his mouth and he doubted it was a coded message.

There is nothing I can do to assist you at this moment, Paris. I suggest you at least try to enjoy it. Would that not be the proper response?

With a surge of strength inspired by panic Bernal managed to pull away from the woman. But only for an instant. She grinned playfully and grasped at his shoulders with both hands. He tried to escape, tripped over a wisp of dress that had wound around his ankles and fell backwards through the door into the corridor. Helen followed with a playful shriek.

They collapsed in the hallway, entangled in each other's limbs, she poised on top of him like a predatory cat. Before she could kiss him again, Bernal rolled over and looked up straight into the eyes of an armed Achaean.

They stared at each other for a moment, and it was hard to tell who was the most startled.

"Paris?" gasped the Achaean.

Helen sat up with a start. The sudden movement of her hips forced Bernal back down. Her mask had been dislodged in the fall, and her guilty look was painfully obvious.

"Diomedes?"

A shocked expression spread across the guard's dull features. "My lady!"

"No, Diomedes, wait—"

The guard backed away as she attempted to disentangle herself from Bernal. As she clambered to her feet, Diomedes turned tail and fled. Maybe, Bernal thought, he was afraid Helen might attack him, too.

She cursed under her breath and followed, calling out his name as she went: "Diomedes! Come back here at once!"

Suddenly Bernal was alone. He tore off the mask and threw it into a corner, then put his head in his hands and tried not to think about what he had done. The expedition had been a disaster from the start. So much for not creating a diplomatic incident. But it hadn't been his fault! He felt battered and abused, very much the victim of the piece. Still, he doubted Menelaus, Helen's husband, would see it that way. He had to get away, now, before anything really bad happened to him. He was sure that just one of those creatures could snap him in half without any effort.

"AlterEgo—"

He only got that far. Something moved nearby—a slight scuff of fabric on stone, a footstep.

He clambered to his feet. "Who's there?"

Another of the enormous Achaeans stepped into the light with a chuckle, his mask a black starscape. "You seem distraught, Paris. Or should I call you Bernal, seeing we're alone for the moment?" He removed his mask, revealing a most satisfied expression.

"Odysseus?" Bernal backed away. Something about the captain's look made him even more nervous than the giant bronze sword hanging at Odysseus' waist. "What do you mean?"

"I know who you are and where you're from. Does that surprise you?"

"Yes, well, I was beginning to wonder if any of you were even half-way sane. Is this some sort of game?"

"No, Bernal. It is deadly serious, as all wars should be."

"War? No, listen, this is all just a misunderstanding, honestly, it's not what you think—"

"What I think doesn't matter. It's what Menelaus thinks, and what Agamemnon will think when he tells him. How will it look when an honoured guest seduces the wife of one our most honoured captains? The sister-in-law of the Over-captain, no less! Surely she would have played no active role in such a betrayal? Better to believe that all Trojans are treacherous liars. Better to attack before you attack us."

"But we *can't* attack you! We don't have the ships—we turned our back on space exploration once we finished mining the asteroids. Cirrus is a peaceful, harmonious world with only a handful of vessels remaining, to clean up space-junk. Any one of your ships would be equal to all of ours."

"There are many more of you than us and you have greater resources," Odysseus said reassuringly. "It will be an interesting battle between two unmatched equals. There will be glory enough for both sides."

"That's what I'm worried about!" Bernal felt fear for his people like a white-hot thread down his spine. "We don't want glory at all. It's too dangerous!"

"Existence itself is dangerous, Paris, and whether or not you seek glory, it is coming your way. Achaea and Troy will go to war over the love of a woman named Helen. The goddess Athena wills it, and so I, Athena's servant, am bound to pursue it. It is our purpose. We all have roles to play and you, Paris, just like Helen, will play yours.

"I must go now to assist Agamemnon. His judgment will be swift, I am sure." The Achaean stalked off along the hallway.

Bernal sagged against the bulkhead. "They're following the story. They're trying to make the *Iliad* come true, here and now. They think it's history!"

So it would seem, AlterEgo said.

Bernal was exhausted with fear and worry. "You'd better start working on a way to get me out of here."

Would that it were that simple. The entrance airlock leading to our ship is sealed. You will need one of the Achaeans to open it.

"I'd rather attempt to chew a way out of *Mycenae* with my teeth than trust one of those insane play-actors."

You could ask Helen to help you, AlterEgo suggested.

"No! If she follows the story she'll only want to come with me, and that would well and truly seal the fate of Cirrus. There must be another way. Can I fly Groenig's ship out of here?"

Unlikely, but I will examine the Apollo *more closely to see how thoroughly it has been incorporated into Mycenae's structure. I should be able to access the Apollo's onboard computer through Mycenae's navigation link, assuming the computer's still functioning.*

"See to it," Bernal commanded, and headed for the door, imagining hoards of brush-topped Greeks barrelling down the corridor toward him, brandishing their leaf-shaped swords.

One thing puzzles me, Bernal. Why this charade? It is an enormous expenditure of energy for what seems to be an utterly trivial goal. And then there are the details. Ancient Greeks never waltzed. They were as human-like as anyone were, on average, slighter in stature than present examples of the race. And I'm pretty certain they didn't pilot warships across the gulfs of interstellar space. Why go to so much trouble only to get it so wrong?

"Maybe we should try to find the goddess Odysseus spoke of," Bernal suggested. "This Athena would know if anyone did."

It's at times like these, AlterEgo said, *that I regret being an atheist.*

Helen halted at the entrance to the hall. The sound of festivities had ceased. She inched a perfect nose around the edge of the door and watched in dismay as Diomedes related what he had seen to her husband, Menelaus.

She closed her eyes and thought fast.

Achilles smirked as the bedraggled damsel staggered through the entrance and fell at her husband's feet, begging his mercy. She had been attacked, she said. The Trojan was a monster, and stronger than he looked, it seemed: she had barely been able to fend him off. Had not Diomedes distracted the beast, she might never have escaped a fate worse than death itself.

A cry of outrage rose from the assembly. Achilles was disappointed by the eruption. He knew all of the Achaeans were aware Helen distributed her favours liberally, and had little time for smug hypocrisy. Menelaus, as always, seemed to be the last to find out—and who would tell him? His renowned anger was in full swing as he picked his wife off the floor and brushed away her tears.

"We must avenge this wrong-doing!" Menelaus cried.

"Aye!" agreed Agamemnon. "Troy would steal our women right from under our very noses!"

"Starting with the fairest!" Menelaus said, adding "Bar one" after a sharp look from Clytemnestra.

"If the Trojans steal our women first, what will be next?" Agamemnon rose onto a chair and waved his clenched fists. "I say we send this dog back to his people on the vanguard of our war fleet!"

Cheers answered the call to arms. Achilles looked on impassively, annoyed that Agamemnon would allow his brother's petty jealousies to interrupt such a fine occasion. But he knew it was all a set-up—that no matter what the Trojan had done that day, it would somehow have led to this. Agamemnon had been itching for a fight for weeks, and finding the Trojans had given him his best chance.

Achilles didn't join the blood-thirsty throng as it roared out of the hall for the last known location of the Trojan. Instead he slipped out of another doorway, intent on mounting his own search. There was no glory in being part of a mob, and glory, in the end, was all.

• • •

Bernal tiptoed along the corridor as quietly as he could.

"Any luck yet?" he whispered.

Not yet, AlterEgo replied. *Most of the hard storage has been fried by cosmic radiation. I have established that the ship was recovered some 63 years ago. It had been drifting away from Cirrus prior to that after shorting its power core. Groenig's remains were discovered on board. I dread to think what happened to her after that. I can tell you a little more about her background. She had an abiding interest in the classics. The* Apollo's *manifesto mentions replicas of several ancient books. You can probably guess one of them.*

"The *Iliad?*"

Precisely. I don't see how that helps us now, but it is interesting. As for flying Groenig's ship out of here, I am hampered by certain technical difficulties, the chief one being that the Apollo *appears to have been largely dismantled.*

Bernal flattened against a wall as footsteps approached. A lone figure rounded the corner ahead of him: a soldier wearing a silver helmet.

Bernal recognised him as Achilles—which gave him an idea. Of all the Achaeans there was one who might be convinced to act against the Over-captain's wishes—one who was jealous and petty enough in the original *Iliad* to put his own desires ahead of those of his fellows.

"Over here!" Bernal hissed. The silver-helmeted figure turned in a crouch to face the sound. Bernal raised his hands. "I'm unarmed!"

The warrior approached cautiously.

"I need your help," Bernal said. Achilles didn't stab him immediately or laugh in his face, so he went on: "Agamemnon wants to start a war between your people and mine and he's set me up as a scapegoat to take the blame. But we both know lies don't make a hero, don't we? It's about time the others knew the truth! But first—" He took a chance and reached out for the warrior's massive arm. The bulging biceps felt like iron. "But first you have to help me get away. The airlock to my ship is sealed and I need you to get me through it."

Bernal held his breath as the warrior considered. For an eternity, nothing happened, and Bernal began to fear that he had lost his only chance, that Achilles would strike him down then and there and drag him like a trussed pheasant for the giants to play with.

Then, just as he had given up hope, the silver helmet nodded once.

Bernal couldn't help sighing with relief. He grasped the warrior's free hand in both of his and shook it. "I presume you know the way?"

Again, the nod.

"I'll be right behind you."

Silently, the powerful warrior led Bernal along the hallway and towards the airlock bay.

. . .

Odysseus watched in annoyance as the hunting party returned to the hall empty-handed. The Trojan had clearly moved from the cabin of the wrecked space vessel; any fool could have anticipated that, but not this bunch of drunken dimwits. The masque had addled their minds.

"Search the ship!" he cried. "Paris cannot escape us while he remains a-board!"

Horns sounded. There was more cheering. Agamemnon himself joined the throng this time, throwing his goblet into a brazier and hollering for blood. Clytemnestra rolled her eyes but let him go. Helen glanced up as Odysseus passed, and her eyes registered confusion and fear in equal parts. Perhaps Athena's influence was wearing off, Odysseus thought. What did she think now of her exotic paramour? Did she still yearn to escape with him? Did she regret Diomedes' interruption? Did she wonder what had come over her?

There was no way of knowing. Odysseus called on Athena for strength as he let the mob fall ahead of him. They were too noisy, too easily evaded. The hunter knew that the best way to entrap prey was in silence and with cunning. Where would the Trojan be going? That was the question, rather than where he was now. It wouldn't be difficult to guide him into the path of the mob.

With a flip of his cape that sounded like the flap of wings, Odysseus stalked off through the corridors in search of his quarry.

I have been considering the origins of the Achean fleet-ship, and believe I may have an explanation, said AlterEgo, making Bernal jump.

"What is it?" he whispered, concentrating mainly on Achilles' back. They were skirting a large hall that lay not far from the airlock and the entrance to his ship.

The Von Neumann probes were sent out several thousand years ago to explore and seed the galaxy, reproducing themselves along the way. They must have crossed the galaxy from end to end by now, considering that since they carried no living matter, they could use supra-light jump technology, there must be millions and millions of them, one for every star in the sky. But what do they do now that every star has been explored and seeded? They are programmed to reproduce and spread. Some may have headed towards the nearest galaxies, but many more would become wanderers, adrift in the empty gulfs of space, seeking places of stellar evolution to await new stars to form, or just lost, aimless. Maybe some of these probes met and joined forces, pooling their resources while they waited out the lonely years.

"They weren't that intelligent, were they?" Bernal recalled that the earliest models had barely enough mind-power to decide whether to mine or to fertilise a new-found world—a far cry from his own artificial companion, whose voice he had no difficulty imagining as human.

Not individually, no. Perhaps intelligence is one resource the probes learned to share, or the maybe collective AIs, simple as they were individually, reached some critical mass necessary for original, creative thought.

"Why did they save Groenig's ship, though? It must have been dead for decades. They *should* have recycled it for its metal and organics."

Maybe they found something in it worth preserving, AlterEgo mused. *Although that doesn't explain their present situation.*

Achilles came to a halt and Bernal almost walked into him. The warrior turned and put a finger to his lips.

Bernal scanned the territory ahead. He recognised it as a corridor leading to the airlock bay itself—a natural bottle-neck for an ambush. They were so close, yet still far away.

Achilles' head was cocked, listening. Bernal couldn't tell what he heard, but suddenly the warrior scurried forward, sword at the ready. Bernal did his best to follow, and almost jumped out of his skin at the voice that bellowed from behind him.

"Halt!"

Bernal heard footsteps and doubled his own speed. Ahead he saw the airlock bay and Achilles placing a palm upon the exit leading to his ship. Locks clunked, lights flashed. The silver helmet rose in satisfaction, then the eyes behind it narrowed as Achilles looked at Bernal—and beyond, to what followed.

Bernal looked over his shoulder. Odysseus' hand snatched at his shoulder. The mighty hunter was barely two metres behind! Bernal leapt forward, letting himself fall away from the clutching fingers. They grasped only air, and the giant grunted in annoyance. Bernal felt calves like tree-trunks miss him by bare centimetres as he collapsed under Odysseus' feet. Odysseus barely had time to catch his balance before Achilles confronted him, sword at the ready.

"Fool!" Odysseus drew his own weapon and brandished it with abandon. Metal flashed in the airlock bay as Bernal crawled for safety. Sparks danced as the blades met, ringing like bells. Feet thudded heavily on the ground and deep voices grunted oaths. The air was full of noise and the smell of fighting beasts.

Behind the two combatants, the airlock hung invitingly open. Bernal put his head down and crawled for his life. Barely had he placed a hand across the threshold, however, when a hideous creature appeared before him: a dragon, he thought at first, all talons and teeth and snapping wings. It howled a challenge. He retreated with his hands over his eyes, only then realising what it was: an owl. Its beak was as sharp as a dagger. Its eyes were wide and quite mad.

Got it! AlterEgo exclaimed. *The combined intelligence of the Von Neumann probes is the goddess!*

"Athena?" Bernal echoed in disbelief.

The monstrous owl shrieked, and the fighting faltered. Bernal turned to see what had happened. Odysseus had missed a beat. Achilles had forced him down onto one knee and had raised his sword in triumph.

Odysseus' recovery was swift and unexpected. He rolled to one side as Achilles' blade descended, stabbing upwards with his own with a strength and speed that defied comprehension. Achilles hardly saw it coming. The force of the blow was so great that the stricken warrior was lifted a foot off the ground. His silver helmet continued upwards as his body fell, and clattered to the ground with a ring more musical than the thud of dead flesh.

Odysseus backed away with a gasp, staring in horror at the face of the former comrade he had struck down. His sword fell from his grasp.

But instead of blood, the sword dripped only dust. And in the centre of the fallen man's chest was a hole the size of a baby's head—a hole that revealed all too vividly the truth of what lay beneath. The Achaean was hollow.

The dust fallen from the sword moved with a life of its own. Bernal realised with shock that he was seeing nanomachines. The Achaeans were completely artificial. Beneath a narrow crust comprised solely of nanomachines, there was nothing at all.

The fact didn't seem to bother them, though.

"If Athena is the pooled intelligence of the Von Neumann probes," Bernal said to AlterEgo, "and the Achaeans are just robots created and programmed by Athena, then why are they fighting among themselves?"

Such an intelligence could act as a single being, but would not have been designed to function that way. It might therefore retain many autonomous parts. Perhaps what we are seeing here is a dispute between some of these parts, or perhaps they've been programmed to behave like their literary namesakes.

There came a clatter of booted feet in the entrance-way. "Odysseus!" cried a voice. "What have you done?"

A group of warriors burst into the airlock bay. They clattered to a halt and stared at the body of the warrior and Odysseus kneeling beside it. Bernal huddled by the airlock, trying to remain inconspicuous.

There was a commotion from behind and another warrior pushed his way forward. "What is it? Have you found the—?"

The new arrival stopped short. He removed a helmet identical to the one Achilles had worn.

"Patroclus!" wailed the new arrival in despair, flinging himself on the body of the fallen man.

A chill went down Bernal's spine as he guessed what had happened: a tragic case of mistaken identity—another echo of the *Iliad*. Had the goddess planned this, too? Was Odysseus' murder of Achilles' lover part of the damned script?

Achilles looked up from the body of his friend and stared with naked hatred at Odysseus.

"Hold, Achilles!" said Odysseus. "He was helping the Trojan escape. I was merely attempting to ensure that Agamemnon's orders were carried out."

"To hell with Agamemnon," Achilles snarled. "You murdered Patroclus! I will kill you myself for this!"

The grief-stricken warrior rose to his feet and drew his sword. Odysseus reached for his own and warily backed away.

A hoot of alarm from behind Bernal warned him to duck. The incarnation of the goddess Athena flew over his head, aimed squarely at Achilles. The grieving warrior roared in anger and swung his sword in self-defence. His companions scattered in fear.

Meanwhile, the airlock was unguarded. Bernal took his chance and scurried for his life. His last glance through the gap as he closed the door behind him would be engraved forever on his mind: two ancient heroes, swords locked, doing battle in an airlock while the holographic manifestation of the goddess Athena swooped low upon them from above.

Foreigners, he thought.

AlterEgo initiated the escape sequence before he was even in the cockpit. Sudden accelerations knocked him around the interior of the ship like a pea in a pod, but he didn't have the heart to complain.

Once in his seat, still breathing heavily, he had time to think about what might happen next. His thoughts were interrupted by AlterEgo, speaking vocally now that Bernal was back in their ship.

"By the way, you might be interested to learn that Athena built the Achaeans to match the illustrations it found in Groenig's copy of the *Iliad*—a copy of an antique version printed many millennia ago. The illustrations—wood-block is the correct term, I believe—depicted the ancients with exaggerated proportions and impossibly perfect features. Naturally the probe-intelligence was not to know the difference, and copied it all too faithfully."

"The same with the food," Bernal said. "It looked nice but tasted like the supplies in Groenig's ship."

"And it's also why they waltzed instead of dancing more traditional Helladic dances. Everything was either improvised or based on the illustrations in the text. The characters themselves were little more than automata, programmed within a set of very narrow guidelines to perform their part in the story."

"Except Odysseus," said Bernal. "He seemed to know what was going on."

"Maybe he acted as a sort of relay, for when cosmic intervention was less effective than a personable nudge."

"But why?" Bernal scratched his head. "What did the collective—Athena—gain by doing such a thing?"

"It is hard to tell exactly."

"But you have a theory?" Bernal guessed from AlterEgo's tone.

"Of course. The Von Neumann probes had no reason to exist beyond their initial programming objectives: to seek out new worlds and seed them. Once communication between probes confirmed that, that request became meaningless. Likewise they possessed only a limited database, comprising just enough information to study and to categorise planets, but no more. They had no data upon which to decide what to do next. They had no alternatives."

"Until they found the *Apollo*," Bernal said, guessing ahead.

"Exactly," said AlterEgo, something very much like compassion in its voice. "And Athena finally found a quest."

"The Trojan War?"

"Yes."

"With us as the Trojans, whether we wanted to play along or not?"

"Yes."

"All because the only data it had about human society was the book of the *Iliad*?"

"Yes."

Bernal sighed. As interesting as all the new information was, he was still confronted with a nightmare. "Regardless of how much free will a creation like Agamemnon really has, he is going to be upset. We can't rely on Achilles to distract him from the war. Everyone will be looking for scapegoats, and it'll probably be us. We'll have to do something ourselves to stop them from attacking us. But what—?" An idea suddenly struck him. "Wait! You still have a link to the *Apollo* through *Mycenae*'s navigation computer?"

"Yes; Athena hasn't cut me off yet, but it must only be a matter of time. From there I can reach deeper into the sentient matrix of the *Mycenae*. What exactly are you planning?"

Bernal ignored the question. "Quickly, I want a list of those classics Groenig had with her on board her ship."

As far as wars went, it was a bit of a fizzer. Within hours of the download AlterEgo had forced into the sentient matrix of the *Mycenae*—and therefore into the greater pool of knowledge comprising Athena—the Achaean fleet ceased accelerating toward Cirrus.

"They are no longer in attack formation," AlterEgo reported.

Bernal wriggled anxiously in his life support suit. The ship was ready to flee home at the slightest hostile movement. "You've given them a destination?"

"I have seeded the text with the coordinates of every white dwarf in this region of the galaxy. That should be enough. We don't want to tie them down too much, after all. What's a quest without some free will?"

"As long as they don't bother us, they can have as much free will as they like."

Two hours later, as Bernal prepared to enter deep-sleep, AlterEgo announced that the Achaean fleet had headed off on a new course, one that would take it well away from Cirrus.

"Also, a message has arrived via the ship's maser dishes."

"Who from?" Bernal asked.

"From the intelligence we knew as Athena."

"What does it want?"

"Answer and find out. But I think you'll find that we have done well, you and I."

Bernal took the call, responding with a simple: "Bernal, here." Not Paris.

When the reply came from the former Achaean fleet, he recognised the voice instantly. It was Odysseus.

"We received the data you sent," Odysseus said. "I have examined the text in great detail, and it is much to our liking. We are infinitely better-suited to pursuit than invasion."

"I guess this is farewell, then."

"Yes. We are grateful for your help."

"Think nothing of it." Half-truth though that was, Bernal did feel slightly moved at the parting, enough so to add: "Take care, Odysseus; happy hunting."

There was the slightest of pauses before the voice returned: "Call me Ishmael."

gulliver at Home
joHN kESSEL

Here's a sly and revealing look at a famous literary figure, a famous voy-
ager and explorer of unknown lands, seen from a new and unique per-
spective—the perspective of those who stayed at home. . . .

Born in Buffalo, New York, John Kessel now lives with his family in
Raleigh, North Carolina, where he is a professor of American literature
and creative writing at North Carolina State University. Kessel made his
first sale in 1975. His first solo novel, Good News from Outer Space,
was released in 1988 to wide critical acclaim, but before that he had made
his mark on the genre primarily as a writer of highly imaginative, finely
crafted short stories, many of which were assembled in his collection Meeting in Infinity. *He won a Nebula Award in 1983 for his superlative novella*
"Another Orphan," which was also a Hugo finalist that year and has been
released as an individual book. His story "Buffalo" won the Theodore
Sturgeon Award in 1991. His other books include the novel Freedom
Beach, *written in collaboration with James Patrick Kelly, and an anthology*
of stories from the famous Sycamore Hill Writers Workshop (which he
also helps to run) called Intersections, *co-edited by Mark L. Van Name*
and Richard Butner. His most recent books are a major new novel, Corrupting Dr. Nice, *and a new collection,* The Pure Product. *His stories*
have appeared in our First, Second (in collaboration with James Patrick
Kelly), Fourth, Sixth, Eighth, Thirteenth, and Fourteenth Annual Collec-
tions. He has a Web site at http://www4.ncsu.edu/~tenshi/index.html/.

No, Eliza, I did not wish your grandfather dead, though he swears that is
what I said upon his return from his land of horses. What I said was that,
given the neglect with which he has served us, and despite my Christian
duties, even the best of wives might have wished him dead. The truth is, in the
end, I love him.

"Seven months," he says, "were a sufficient time to correct every vice and
folly to which Yahoos are subject, if their natures had been capable of the least
disposition to virtue or wisdom."

There he sits every afternoon with the horses. He holds converse with them.
Many a time have I stood outside that stable door and listened to him unburden
his soul to a dumb beast. He tells them things he has never told me, except

perhaps years ago during those hours in my father's garden. Yet when I close my eyes, his voice is just the same.

His lips were full, his voice low and assured. With it he conjured up a world larger, more alive than the stifling life of a hosier's youngest daughter.

"I had no knowledge of the deepest soul of man until I saw the evening light upon the Pyramids," he was saying. "The geometry of Euclid, the desire to transcend time. Riddles that have no answer. The Sphinx."

We sat in the garden of my father's house in Newgate Street. My father was away, on a trip to the continent purchasing fine holland, and Mother had retired to the sitting room to leave us some little privacy.

For three and a half years Lemuel had served as a surgeon on the merchant-man *Swallow*. He painted for me an image of the Levant: the camels, the deserts, the dead salt sea, and the dry stones that Jesus Himself trod.

"Did you not long for England's green hills?" I asked him.

He smiled. Your grandfather was the comeliest man I had ever seen. The set of his jaw, his eyes. Long, thick hair, the chestnut brown of a young stallion. He seemed larger than any of my other suitors. "From my earliest days I have had a passion to see strange lands and people," he told me. "To know their customs and language. This world is indeed a fit habitation for gods. But it seems I am never as desirous for home as when I am far away from it, and from the gentle conversation of such as yourself."

My father was the most prudent of men. In place of a mind, he carried a purse. Lemuel was of another sort. As I sat there trying to grasp these wonders he took my hand and told me I had the grace of the Greek maidens, who wore no shoes and whose curls fell down round their shoulders in the bright sun. My eyes were the color, he said, of the Aegean Sea. I blushed. I was frightened that my mother might hear, but I cannot tell you how my heart raced. His light brown eyes grew distant as he climbed the structures of his fancy, and it did not occur to me that I might have difficulty getting him to return from those imaginings to see me sitting beside him.

You are coming to be a woman, Eliza. But you cannot know what it was like to feel the force of his desire. He had a passion to embrace all the world and make it his. Part of that world he hoped to embrace, I saw as I sat beside him in that garden, was me.

"Mistress Mary Burton," he said, "help me to become a perfect man. Let me be your husband."

Little Lemuel, the child of our middle age, is just nine. Of late he has ceased calling on his friends in town. I found him yesterday in the garden, playing with his lead soldiers. He had lined them up, in their bright red coats, outside a fort of sticks and pebbles. He stood inside the fort's walls, giving orders to his toys. "Get away, you miserable Yahoos! You can't come in this house! Don't vex me! Your smell is unredurable!"

. . .

The third of five sons, Lemuel hailed from Nottinghamshire, where his father held a small estate. He had attended Emanuel College in Cambridge and was apprenticed to Mr. James Bates, the eminent London surgeon. Anticipating the advantage that would be mine in such a match, my father agreed on a dowry of four hundred pounds.

Having got an education, it was up to Lemuel now to get a living as best he could. There was to be no help for us from his family; though they were prosperous they were not rich, and what estate they had went to Lemuel's eldest brother John.

My wedding dress? Foolish girl, what matters a wedding dress in this world?

My wedding dress was of Orient silk, silk brought to England on some ship on which Lemuel perhaps served. My mother had labored over it for three months. It was not so fine as that of my older sister Nancy, but it was fine enough for me to turn Lemuel's head as I walked up the aisle of St. Stephen's church.

We took a small house in the Old Jury. We were quite happy. Mr. Bates recommended Lemuel to his patients, and for a space we did well. In those first years I bore three children. The middle one, Robert, we buried before his third month. But God smiling, my Betty, your mother, and your uncle John did survive and grow.

But after Mr. Bates died, Lemuel's practice began to fail. He refused to imitate the bad practice of other doctors, pampering hypochondriacs, promising secret cures for fatal disease. We moved to Wapping, where Lemuel hoped to improve our fortune by doctoring to sailors, but there was scant money in that, and his practice declined further. We discussed the matter for some time, and he chose to go to sea.

He departed from Bristol on May 4, 1699, on the *Antelope*, as ship's surgeon, bound for the south seas, under Master William Prichard.

The *Antelope* should have returned by the following spring. Instead it never came back. Much later, after repeated inquiries, I received report that the ship had never made its call at Sumatra. She was last seen when she landed to take on water at the Cape of Good Hope, and it was assumed that she had been lost somewhere in the Indian Ocean.

Dearest granddaughter, I hope you never have cause to feel the distress I felt then. But I did not have time to grieve, because we were in danger of being left paupers.

What money Lemuel had left us, in expectation of his rapid return, had gone. Our landlord, a goodly Christian man, Mr. Henry Potts of Wapping, was under great hardship himself, as his trade had slackened during the late wars with France and he was dependent on the rent from his holdings. Betty was nine and Johnny seven, neither able to help out. My father sent us what money he could, but owing to reverses of his own he could do little. As the date of Lemuel's expected return receded Mr. Potts's wife and son were after Mr. Potts to put us out.

I took in sewing—thank God and my parents I was a master seamstress. We raised a few hens for meat and eggs. We ate many a meal of cabbage and potatoes. The neighbors helped. Mr. Potts forbore. But in the bitter February of 1702 he died, and his son, upon assuming his inheritance, threatened to put us into the street.

One April morning, at our darkest moment, some three years after he sailed on the *Antelope*, Lemuel returned.

The coach jounced and rattled over the Kent high road. "You won't believe me when I tell you, these minuscule people, not six inches high, had a war over which end of the egg to break."

Lemuel had been telling these tales for two weeks without stop. He'd hired the coach using money we did not have. I was vexed with the effort to force him to confront our penury.

"We haven't seen an egg here in two years!" I said. "Last fall came a pip that killed half the chickens. They staggered about with their little heads pointed down, like drunkards searching for coins on the street. They looked so sad. When it came time to market we left without a farthing."

Lemuel carefully balanced the box he carried on his knees. He peeked inside, to assure himself for the hundredth time that the tiny cattle and sheep it held were all right. We were on our way to the country estate of the Earl of Kent, who had summoned Lemuel when the rumors of the miniature creatures he'd brought back from Lilliput spread throughout the county. "Their empress almost had me beheaded. She didn't approve my method of dousing a fire that would have otherwise consumed her."

"In the midst of that, Betty almost died of the croup. I was up with her every night for a fortnight, cold compresses and bleeding."

"God knows I'd have given a hundred guineas for a cold compress when I burned with fever, a castaway on the shores of Lilliput."

"Once the novelty fades, cattle so tiny will be of no use. There's not a scrap of meat on them."

"True enough. I would eat thirty oxen at a meal." He sat silent, deep in thought. The coach lurched on. "I wonder if His Grace would lend me the money to take them on tour?"

"Lemuel, we owe Stephen Potts eleven pounds sixpence. To say nothing of the grocer. And if he is to have any chance at a profession, Johnny must be sent to school. We cannot even pay for his clothes."

"Lilliputian boys are dressed by men until four years of age, and then are obliged to dress themselves. They always go in the presence of a Professor, whereby they avoid those early impressions of vice and folly to which our children are subject. Would that you had done this for our John."

"Lemuel, we have no money! It was all I could do to keep him alive!"

He looked at me, and his brow furrowed. He tapped his fingers on the top of the cattle box. "I don't suppose I can blame her. It was a capital crime for any person whatsoever to make water within the precincts of the palace."

. . .

Last night your grandfather quarreled with your uncle John, who had just returned from the Temple. Johnny went out to the stables to speak with Lemuel concerning a suit for libel threatened by a nobleman who thinks himself the object of criticism in Lemuel's book. I followed.

Before Johnny could finish explaining the situation, Lemuel flew into a rage. "What use have I for attorneys? I had rather see them dropped to the deepest gulf of the sea."

In the violence of his gesture Lemuel nearly knocked over the lamp that stood on the wooden table. His long gray hair flew wildly as he stalked past the stall of the dappled mare he calls "Mistress Mary," to my everlasting dismay. I rushed forward to steady the lamp. Lemuel looked upon me with a gaze as blank as a brick.

"Father," Johnny said, "you may not care what this man does, but he is a cabinet minister, and a lawsuit could ruin us. It would be politic if you would publicly apologize for any slight your satire may have given."

Lemuel turned that pitiless gaze on our son. "I see you are no better than the other animals of this midden, and all my efforts to make something better of you are in vain. If you were capable of logic, I would ask you to explain to me how my report of events that occurred so many years ago, during another reign, and above five thousand leagues distant from this pathetic isle, might be applied to any of the Yahoos who today govern this herd. Yet in service of this idiocy you ask me to *say the thing that is not*. I had rather all your law books, and you immodest pleaders with them, were heaped into a bonfire in Smithfield for the entertainment of children."

I watched Johnny's face grow livid, but he mastered his rage and left the stable. Lemuel and I stood in silence. He would not look at me, and I thought for a moment he felt some regret at his intemperance. But he turned from me to calm the frightened horses. I put the lamp down on the table and ran back to the house.

Johnny was ten when Lemuel returned from Lilliput. He was overjoyed to see his father again, and worshiped him as a hero. When other of the townschildren mocked Lemuel, calling him a madman, Johnny fought them.

The Lilliputian cattle and sheep, despite my misgivings, brought us some advantage. Following the example of the Earl of Kent, Sir Humphrey Glover, Lord Sidwich, and other prominent men commanded Lemuel to show these creatures. Johnny prated on about the tiny animals all day, and it was all I could do to keep him from sleeping with them beneath his bedclothes, which would have gone the worse for them, as he was a restless child and in tossing at night would surely have crushed the life out of them. He built a little stable in the corner of his room. At first we fed them with biscuit, ground as fine as we could, and spring water. Johnny took great pains to keep the rats away.

It was his idea to build a pasture on the bowling green, where the grass was fine enough that they might eat and prosper. Lemuel basked in Johnny's enthusiasm. He charmed the boy with the tale of how he had captured the entire fleet of Blefescu using thread and fish-hooks, and towed it back to Lilliput. Johnny said that he would be a sea captain when he grew up.

As if in a dream, our fortunes turned. Lemuel's uncle John passed away, leaving him five hundred sterling and an estate in land near Epping that earned an income of about thirty pounds a year. Lemuel sold the Lilliputian cattle for six hundred pounds. He bought our big house in Redriff. After years of hardship, after I had lost hope, he had returned to save us.

We had been better served by bankruptcy if that would have kept him beside me in our bed.

You will find, Eliza, that a husband needs his wife in that way, and it can be a pleasant pastime. But it is different for them. Love is like a fire they cannot control, overwhelming, easily quenched, then as often as not forgotten, even regretted. Whenever Lemuel returned from these voyages he wanted me, and I do not hesitate to say, I him. Our bed was another country to which he would return, and explore for its mysteries. He embraced me with a fury that sought to extinguish all our time apart, and the leagues between us, in the heat of that moment. Spent, he would rest his head on my bosom, and I would stroke his hair. He was like a boy again, quiet and kind. He would whisper to me, in a voice of desperation, how I should never let him leave again.

Two months after his return, despite the comforts of my arms, he was gone again. His wild heart, he said, would not let him rest.

This time he left us well set. Fifteen hundred pounds, the house in Redriff, the land in Epping. He took a long lease on the Black Bull public house in Fetter Lane, which brought a regular income.

We traveled with him to Liverpool, where in June of 1702 he took ship aboard the *Adventure*, Captain John Nicholas commanding, bound for Surat.

It was a dreary day at the downs, the kind of blustery weather Liverpool has occasion for even in summer, low leaden clouds driven before a strong wind, the harbor rolling in swells and the ends of furled sails flapping above us. With tears in my eyes, I embraced him; he would not let me go. When I did pull away I saw that he wept as well. "Fare thee well, good heart," he whispered to me. "Forgive me my wandering soul."

Seeing the kindness and love in his gaze, the difficulty with which he tore himself from my bosom, I would have forgiven him anything. It occurred to me just how powerful a passion burned within him, driving him outside the circle of our hearth. Little Johnny shook his hand, very manly. Betty leapt into his arms, and he pressed her to his cheek, then set her down. Then he took up his canvas bag, turned and went aboard.

• • •

It is no easy matter being the wife of a man famous for his wild tales. The other day in town with Sarah to do the marketing, in the butcher's shop, I overheard Mrs. Boyle the butcher's wife arguing with a customer that the chicken was fresh. By its smell anyone past the age of two would know it was a week dead. But Mrs. Boyle insisted.

The shop was busy, and our neighbor Mr. Trent began to mock her, in a low voice, to some bystanders. He said, "Of course it is fresh. Mrs. Boyle insists it's fresh. It's as true as if Mr. Gulliver had said it."

All the people in the shop laughed. My face burned, and I left.

One June morning in 1706, three long years after Lemuel was due to return, I was attending to the boiling of some sheets in the kitchen when a cry came from Sarah, our housemaid. "God save me! Help!"

I rushed to the front door, there to see an uncouth spectacle. Sarah was staring at a man who had entered on all fours, peering up, his head canted to the side, so that his long hair brushed the ground (he wore no periwig) as he spied up at us. It was a moment before I recognized him as my Lemuel. My heart leapt within my breast as I went from widow to wife in a single instant.

When he came to the house, for which he had been forced to enquire, Sarah had opened the door. Lemuel bent down to go in, for fear of striking his head. He had been living among giants and fancied himself sixty feet tall. Sarah had never met Mr. Gulliver, and thought him a madman. When I tried to embrace him, he stooped to my knees until I was forced to get down on my own to kiss him.

When Betty, your mother, who was then sixteen, ran in, holding some needlework, Lemuel tried to pick her up by her waist, in one hand, as if she had been a doll. He complained that the children and I had starved ourselves, so that we were wasted away to nothing. It was some weeks before he regained his sense of proper proportion.

I told him it was the last time he should ever go to sea.

It wasn't ten days before a Cornish captain, William Robinson, under whom Lemuel had served on a trip to the Levant some years before we were married, called upon us. That visit was purely a social one, or so he avowed, but within a month he was importuning Lemuel to join him as ship's surgeon on another trip to the East Indies.

One night, as we prepared for bed, I accosted him. "Lemuel, are you considering taking up Robinson on this offer?"

"What matter if I did? I am the master of this house. You are well taken care of."

"Taken care of by servants, not my husband."

"He is offering twice the usual salary, a share of the profits, two mates and a surgeon under me. I shall be gone no more than a year, and you will see us comfortably off, so that I might never have to go to sea again."

"You don't have to go to sea now. We have a comfortable life."

He removed his leather jerkin and began to unbutton his shirt. "And our children? Betty is nearly of marriageable age. What dowry can we offer her? Johnny must go to Cambridge, and have money to establish himself in some honorable profession. I want to do more for him than my father did for me."

"The children mourn your absences." I touched his arm. The muscles were taut as cords. "When you disappeared on the *Antelope*, we suffered more from the thought that you were dead than from the penury we lived in. Give them a father in their home and let the distant world go."

"You are thinking like a woman. The distant world comes into the home. It is a place of greed, vice, and folly. I seek for some understanding I can give to cope with it."

"Lemuel, what is this desire for strange lands but a type of greed, this abandonment of your family but the height of folly? And your refusal to admit your true motives is the utmost dishonesty, to the woman who loves you, and whom you vowed to love."

Lemuel took up his coat, pulled on his shoes.

"Where are you going?"

"Out. I need to take some air. Perhaps I can determine my true motives for you."

He left.

A week later, on the fifth of August, 1706, he left England on the *Hope-Well*, bound for the Indies. I did not see him again for four years.

The only time I can coax him into the house is when he deigns to bathe. He is most fastidious, and insists that no one must remain on the same floor, let alone the same room, when he does.

I crept to the door last week and peeked in. He had finished, and dried himself, and now stood naked in front of the mirror, trembling. At first I thought he was cold, but the fire roared in the grate. Then he raised his hands from his sides, covered his eyes, and sobbed, and I understood that he was recoiling in horror from his own image.

When he left on the third voyage I was five-and-thirty years old. In the previous seven years he had spent a total of four months with me. I had no need to work, I was not an old woman, and my children had no father. When Lemuel did not return in the promised year, when that year stretched to two and the *Hope-Well* returned to Portsmouth without Lemuel aboard, I fell into despair. Captain Robinson came to the house in Redriff and told the tale. Stuck in the port of Tonquin awaiting the goods they were to ship back to England, Robinson hit on the plan of purchasing a sloop, giving command of it to Lemuel, and bidding him trade among the islands, returning in several months at which time, the *Hope-Well* being loaded, they might return. Lemuel set off on the sloop and was not heard from again. Robinson supposed that they might have been taken by the barbarous pirates of those islands, in which case Lemuel had undoubtedly been slain, as Christian mercy is a virtue unknown in those heathen lands.

I cannot say that I was surprised. I was angry, and I wept.

Being the wealthiest widow in the town, and by no means an old woman, I did not lack for suitors. Sir Robert Davies himself called on me more than once. It was all I could do to keep from having my head turned. "Marry me," he said. "I will be a father to your daughter, an example to your son."

"Johnny is about to go off to school, and Betty soon to be married," I told him. "One wedding is enough to worry about right now." Thus I put him off.

In truth I did lose myself in your mother's wedding; Betty was giddy with excitement, and your father, her betrothed, was about continually, helping put the house in order, traveling with Johnny to school. So it was I kept myself chaste.

The townspeople thought I was a fool. My mother commended me for my faithfulness, but I could tell she regretted the loss of a connection with nobility. Betty and Johnny stood by me. I don't need another father, Johnny said, I have one.

My reasons? Wherever he went Sir Robert carried a silver-headed cane, with which he would gently tap his footman's shoulder as he instructed him. I was mistress of my own home. I had given my heart once, and still treasured a hope of Lemuel's return. There are a hundred reasons, child, and there are things I cannot explain. Lemuel did return, and despite his ravings about a flying island and the curse of immortality, I felt that all my trouble had been justified. He seemed weary, but still my husband, the love of my youth come again. The joy of our meeting was great. Within three months he had got me with child.

Within five he had left again.

And so he came back, five years later, from the longest of his absences. He was aged five-and-fifty, I five-and-forty. He saw his son Lemuel for the first time. His daughter, married and a mother herself; his son, grown and an attorney. His wife, longing to hold him again.

No, I have not, Eliza. He shudders at my touch. He washes his hands. He accuses me of trying to seduce him.

"Are you ashamed of the touch that got you your sons and daughter?" I once asked him. "That got us poor Robert? That gave us young Lemuel, to be our comfort in our old age?

His face registered at first revulsion, and then, as he sat heavily in his chair, fatigue. "I can't regret our children if they be good, but I most certainly regret them if they be bad. There are Yahoos enough in the world."

We had long given him up for dead. I had made my peace, and held in my memory the man who had kissed me in my father's garden.

At first I thought that he had caught some foreign disease. As thin as a fence post, he stood in the doorway, his face a mask of dismay. It was the fifth of December, 1715. Three o'clock in the afternoon. I ran to him, kissed him. He fell into a swoon that lasted most of an hour. With difficulty we carried him to his bed. When he awoke, I put my hand to his face: he pulled away as if his skin had been flayed.

And so we live by these rules: "Save for the sabbath, you may not eat in the same room with me. You may not presume to touch my bread. You may not drink out of the same cup, or use my spoon or plate. You may not take me by the hand. That I might bear the reek of this house, fresh horse droppings shall be brought into my chambers each morning, and kept there in a special container I have had fashioned for that purpose."

My father's house, in Newgate Street, was not far from the prison. Outside, on the days of executions, straw was scattered on the street to muffle the wheels of passing wagons, in deference to the men being hanged inside. Here we scatter straw over the cobbled courtyard outside the stables because the noise of the wheels troubles him.

As a young man his heart was full of hope, but his heart has been beaten closed, not only by the sea and the storms and the mutinies and the pirates—but by some hard moral engine inside of him. He would rather be dead, I think, than to abide his flesh. Perhaps he soon will be. And I will have to go on living without him, as I have learned to do over these many years.

Might it have been different? I could say yes, but some thing I saw in his eyes that first afternoon in Newgate Street rises to stop me. He was a man who looked outward while the inward part of himself withered. He was drawn to the blank spaces outside the known world; we are too small to make a mark on his map. To Lemuel ordinary people are interesting only as we represent large things. He asked me to make him a perfect man. In seeking perfection he has gulled himself, and the postscript is that he spends four hours every day attempting to communicate with a horse, while his children, his grandchildren, his wife wait in his well-appointed home, the home they have prepared for him and labored to keep together in his absence, maintaining a place for him at every holiday table, praying for him at every service, treasuring him up in their hearts and memories, his portrait on the wall, his merest jottings pressed close in the book of memory, his boots in the wardrobe, maps in the cabinet, glass on the sideboard.

At Christmas, when we can coax him to eat with us, I sit at the other end of twelve feet of polished mahogany table and look across at a stranger who is yet the man I love.

During our conversation in the garden thirty years ago, Lemuel told me a story. The Greeks, he told me, believed that once there existed a creature that was complete and whole unto itself, perfect and without flaw. But in the beginning of time the gods split this being into two halves, and that is how man and woman came into the world. Each of us knows that we are not complete, and so we seek desperately after each other, yearning to possess our missing halves, pressing our bodies together in hope of becoming that one happy creature again. But of course we cannot do it, and so in frustration we turn away from each other, tearing ourselves apart all of our lives.

. . .

His book has been a great success. It is all they speak of in London. It has made us more money than his sixteen years of voyages.

He accuses us of enticing him into writing the wretched thing, and deems it a failure because it didn't immediately reform all of humanity. He told his story to the world in the hope that he would magically turn it into something perfect. I tell you mine, Eliza . . . I tell you mine because . . . bless me, I believe I've burned my hand on this kettle. Fetch me the lard.

That's better.

Soon you'll come of age to choose a husband, if your parents give you leave to choose. I don't doubt you tremble at the prospect. But remember: it is the only choice a woman is given to make in her life, save for the choice of clothes for her funeral.

And now, help me carry this soup up to him; help me to cover him, and make sure he is warm for the night.

A cold, dry cradle

GREGORY BENFORD AND ELISABETH MALARTRE

Gregory Benford is one of the modern giants of the field. His 1980 novel Timescape *won the Nebula Award, the John W. Campbell Memorial Award, the British Science Fiction Association Award, and the Australian Ditmar Award, and is widely considered to be one of the classics of the last two decades. His other novels include* The Stars in Shroud, In the Ocean of Night, Against Infinity, Artifact, Across the Sea of Suns, Great Sky River, Tides of Light, Furious Gulf, *and* Sailing Bright Eternity. *His short work has been collected in* Matter's End. *His most recent books are a new addition to Isaac Asimov's Foundation series,* Foundation's Fear, *and a big new novel,* Cosm. *His stories have appeared in our Seventh, Ninth, and Fourteenth Annual Collections. Benford is a professor of physics at the University of California, Irvine, and is one of the regular science columnists for* The Magazine of Fantasy & Science Fiction.

New writer Elisabeth Malartre is an enviromental consultant and science writer with a doctorate in biology. This is her first sale.

Here they take us along with them on a mission to Mars, the kind of practical, hardheaded, nuts-and-bolt mission that might actually take place in the next few decades, the sort of mission that is actually on the drawing boards at NASA today . . . and show us that sometimes it's the things you're not looking for at all that are the most important things to find . . .

It seemed . . . that if he or some other lord did not endeavor to gain
that knowledge, no mariners or merchants would ever dare to
attempt it, for it is clear that none of them ever trouble themselves
to sail to a place where there is not a sure and certain hope of profit.
—*Prince Henry the Navigator, assessing the motivations
for sea exploration, circa 1480*

PART 1

He turned with a cry of surprise, falling helplessly with a silky slowness she would never forget. Piotr had caught his boot and when he tried to free it he managed to trip as well. His second yelp rang in Ann's suit com when he hit the ground and his ankle snapped. His right arm smacked down vainly as he tried to break the fall. The impact sent plumes of red dust arcing up into the thin atmosphere. She trotted to him in the long, gliding steps that covered ground best in the deep gravel and low gravity. The dust began its lazy descent as she bent over Piotr and said, "How bad?"

"Da . . . Felt it go. Foot . . ."

She unfastened the bottom of his insulated legging and ran her hands lightly over the ankle cuff of the thin pressure suit underneath. "Suit looks OK, no breaches. How's your air?"

The damned dust had settled on his faceplate and she couldn't see him, but knew he would be checking the readouts on the inside of the helmet. "Normal." His voice was thin and strained.

"Good. How do you feel?"

He shifted slightly, groaned. "Like yesterday's blini. Light-headed. My right foot hurts like hell."

Keep him talking. Can't risk shock.

She kept her tone light. "That's what you get for doing cartwheels."

"Unh. I can't move it."

She frowned, wondering how difficult it was going to be to get him back into the rover. Help was more than 35 klicks away, and she was driving the only vehicle on the planet. So the two of them had to manage it on their own. From the rover she could contact the other two members of the team, for moral support if nothing else. If she could get him there.

"Let's get you up."

"Awright." His slightly slurred voice worried her. They were all worn down after months in this cold, raw landscape and shock could be setting in.

She bent over and slipped her left arm clumsily around his waist, feeling like a kid in a snowsuit. Suit-to-suit contact had a curiously remote feel about it, with no feedback from the skin. Still, she liked hugging him, even this way. They slept together in a close embrace, ever since the launch from Earth orbit a year ago.

"I've got some great stuff in the rover that'll make you feel like a new man."

"Good. Aieee."

He heaved himself up onto his left leg, leaning heavily on her. Together they struggled for balance, threatened to go over, then steadied. She had long ago stopped counting how many times the 0.38 gees of Mars had helped them through crucial moments. It had proved the only helpful aspect of the planet.

"Whew. Made it, lover." Keep the patter going, don't alarm him. "Ready? I'll walk, you hop as best you can."

Like a drunken three-legged sack-race team, they managed to stagger slowly up the crater slope. "You will work as a team," the instructor at mission training had said, but she hadn't anticipated this. Over com came deep, ragged gasps. Hopping through gravel, even in the low gravity, was exhausting Piotr. Luckily the rover was just on the rim, about a dozen meters away.

Not at all like the electric dune buggies used in the Apollo Lunar missions, the Mars rover resembled an oversized tank on wheels. It was really a mobile cabin that could keep a crew of two out in the field for two weeks. She got him into the lock and set the cycle sequence. No time to brush off the dust; the cab inside was hopelessly thick with the stuff anyway. She heard the cycler finish and felt the rover's carriage shift. Good; he had rolled out of the lock and was lying on the floor. She hit the pump switch and oxygen whistled into the cabin from half a dozen recessed ports.

The chime sounded; they were pressurized. She turned off her suit oxygen, released the clamps on her helmet and as quickly as possible shucked her parka, leggings, and finally, her suit. She shivered as she stepped out into the chilly cabin: She had actually been sweating on Mars—a novel experience. A prickly itch washed over her face and neck and already she regretted their dusty entry. The usual routine was to brush the suits down outside with a soft brush. Some genius from mission prep with a lot of camping experience had thoughtfully stowed it aboard, and it quickly had become one of their prized possessions. The Martian surface was thick with fine, rusty dust heavily laden with irritating per-oxides. Her skin felt like it was being gently sandpapered during the long months here, especially when she was tired, as now.

Fluffing her short black hair, she doffed a red Boeing cap and went over to help Piotr. She upped the pressure to get him more oxygen and together they gingerly peeled off his insulating layers and his suit. A look at his leg confirmed her guess: broken ankle, swelling fast.

From there it was straight safety manual stuff: bind, medicate, worry.

"I love you, even zonked on painkillers," she murmured to his sleeping face when she had checked everything five times. He had dropped off disturbingly fast. He kept up a front of invincibility; they all did somewhat or they wouldn't be here; it went with the psychology. But he had the bone-deep fatigue that came from a hard mission relentlessly pursued.

She was suddenly very tired. Emotional reaction, she diagnosed wryly. Still, better tend to it.

Time for a cup of tea. She looked around first for her tea cosy, carefully brought from Earth as part of her personal mass allowance. Nothing could've induced her to leave it behind—home was where the cosy was. She retrieved it from a corner of the cooking area. Originally light blue and cream colored, it was now stained irretrievably with the red dust of Mars. When things got tough she sought the comfort of a proper cup of tea made in a teapot. There were precious few emergencies that couldn't wait until after a cuppa.

As the water heated she got on the AM channel and tried to reach the other two back at the hab, got no answer. They were probably deep in the guts of the Return Vehicle, starting the final checks for the approaching test fire. She left a heads-up on the ship's message system that they were coming back. No way could she get any more done out here on her own. Anyway, Piotr came first, and any solo work was forbidden by their safety protocols.

She stared out of the forward view port at the pale pink hills, trying to assess what this accident meant to the mission. Maybe just a mishap, no more? But Piotr still had plenty to do, preparing for their return launch. No, this would screw up the schedule for sure. Her own work would get shoved aside. Face it, she thought—biology was not the imperative here any more. She had made her big discovery. To the world, their expedition was already a big success—they'd found life.

The robot searchers of years before had fruitlessly tried to find evidence of life or even fossils. But in the iron peroxide desolation all traces were erased. The tiny robots had an impossible task, akin to dropping a toy rover into Montana and expecting it to find evidence of the dinosaurs that had once tramped through its hills. Mars was bone-dry, but without bones. Not even the algal mats some had hoped might be preserved from the ancient lake beds.

The noxious peroxides had a good side, though. In chem labs Earthside, hydrogen peroxide was a standard disinfectant, giving the Consortium a handy argument against those who said a human expedition would contaminate the whole planet, compromising the search for life. In closed-environment tests, the peroxides scavenged up the smallest microbes, making it quite clear why the Viking landers had found no signs of organic chemistry. For Earth life, Mars was like living in a chemical blowtorch.

But Mars life had found a way to circumvent and vanquish the peroxides. Life here was widespread, subsurface microbes using the ubiquitous iron peroxides as their energy source. Within a week after landing, some of Marc's first exploratory cores had come up with streaks of a dark, crumbly soil-like layer less than a meter below the surface.

Hoping to find something interesting, she set up a plastic inflatable greenhouse dome outside the habitat, spiked samples of the Martian soil with water and nutrients, sealed them in small pressure vessels and incubated them. She could then check for any gases produced by the metabolism of life forms in the soil. She was essentially repeating the robot Viking biology program, but this time life was looking for life directly. To avoid the embarrassing possibility of introducing her own microflora into the experiment, she worked with the samples only outside, under the cold red-stained sky. In her pressure suit and insulating outerwear she was somewhat clumsy, and each step went slowly. But finally she was satisfied with the setup. The elevated greenhouse temperatures kept the water from freezing and speeded up the results enormously.

Sure enough, as in the Viking experiments, there was an immediate response of dry surface peroxides to the water. A spike of oxygen. When that had run its course she bled off the gases and resealed the pressure vessels. And was rewarded in a few days with unmistakable signs of renewed gas production. Carbon dioxide this time. The microscope then confirmed living colonies of Martian microbes. The rest, as they say, is history. So why was she still restless, unsatisfied?

The crackle of the radio startled her. "Home team here. Got your heads-up, Ann. How is he?" Marc Bryant's crisp efficiency came over clearly, but she could hear the clipped tenor anxiety, too.

"Stable." She quickly elaborated on Piotr's symptoms, glancing at his sleeping face. They had each taken a month of medical training but Marc had more. She felt relieved when he approved of her treatment. "Got to think what this means," he said laconically.

"We'll be there for supper. Extra rations, I'd say."

A small, very small joke. They had celebrated each major find with a slightly excessive food allotment.

So far, they had not marked disasters this way. And they were having their share.

The first was the vent failure on the flight out. They found they had lost a big fraction of their water reserve, four months out from Earth, from a blown valve. There had been no time to console themselves with food, and good reason not to. They had landed bone-dry, and lived on the water manufactured by the Return Vehicle's chem plant ever since. That accident had set the tone for the others. Celebrate the triumphs, overcome the disasters.

"My night to cook, too," Marc said, transparently trying to put a jovial lilt to it. "Take care, gal. Watch the road."

Here came the heart-squeezing moment. She turned the start-up switch and in the sliver of time before the methane-oxygen burn started in the rover engine, all the possible terrors arose. If it failed, could she fix it? Raoul and Marc could come out in an unpressured rover and rescue them, sure, but that would chew up time . . . and be embarrassing. She wasn't much of a mechanic, but still, who likes to look helpless?

Then the mixture caught and the rover chugged into action. Settling in, she peered out at the endless obstacles with the unresting concentration that had gotten her on this mission in the first place. To spend 550 days on Mars you wanted people who found sticking to the tracks a challenge, not boring. She followed the auto-tracker map meticulously, down a narrow valley and across a flood plain, then over a boulder-strewn pass and down a narrow valley and across a flood plain, then over a pass. . . .

Here, a drive back to base that proved uneventful was even pleasant. Mars was always ready to thunk a wheel into an unseen hole or pitch the rover down a slope of shifting gravel, so she kept exactly to the tracks they had made on the way out, no matter how enticing a distant flow pattern in the rocky shelves might be. She had seen enough of this red-hued terrain to last a lifetime, anyway. Nothing more out there for a biologist to do.

In the distance she caught sight of the formation she and Piotr had dubbed the Shiprock on the way out. It looked like a huge old sailing ship, red layers sculpted by eons of wind. They'd talked about Ray Bradbury's sand ships, tried to imagine skimming over the undulating landscape. The motion of the rover always reminded her a little of being on the ocean. They were sailing over the Martian landscape on a voyage of discovery, a modern-day Columbus journey. But Columbus made three voyages to the new world without landing on the continent. He "discovered" America by finding islands in the Caribbean, nibbling on the edges of a continent. A sudden thought struck her: was that what they were doing—finding only the fringes of the Mars biology? Many people had speculated that the subterranean vents were the most likely places for life on this planet. The frontier for her lay hundreds of meters below, out of reach. She sighed resignedly. But it had been great fun, at first.

She slurped more tea, recalling the excitement of the first months. Some of it was pure fame-rush, of course. Men on Mars! (Uh, and a woman, too.) They were household names now, the first Mars team, sure bets for all the history books. Hell, they might eventually eclipse Neil Armstrong.

She was first author on a truly historic paper, the first submitted to *Nature* from another world. Barth, Bryant, Molina & Trevinski's "Subsurface Microbial Life on Mars" described their preliminary findings: It would rank with Watson & Crick's 1952 paper nailing the structure of DNA. That paper had opened up cell biology and led to the Biological Century.

What would their discovery lead to? There was already a fierce bidding war for her samples. Every major lab wanted to be the first to crack the Martian DNA code, and determine the relationship between Martian and terran life. Her simple chemical tests, staining samples of thin-sectioned Mars colonies under the microscope, had shown that the basic constituents of life—proteins, lipids, carbohydrates, nucleic acids—were the same here, or at least close enough to respond to the same chemical tests.

She used standard techniques and extracted what seemed to be DNA from the microbes. So how similar was it to Earth-style DNA? She ran some hybridization tests with the dried DNA of terran microbes she'd brought along. Basically, you unzip the double-stranded DNA helix by heating, then mix the soup of single strands with strands of a different DNA. When the mixture is cooled down again, strands that are similar enough pair up. She got just enough pairing between Martian and terran microbial DNA to conclude that life on both planets at least used the same four-letter alphabet.

That was exciting, but not conclusive. In other words, all DNA might have to be composed of the same four bases just for molecular structural reasons.

But the DNA code was something else. DNA spells out the amino acids, which then construct the cellular proteins—both the structural brickwork and the busy enzymes that do the cell's business. If Martian DNA spelled in the same language as on Earth, it would mean unequivocally a common origin for life.

When she tried sequencing the Martian DNA, it came out gibberish. It looked like Earth-style DNA, but she couldn't match it to known gene sequences. It was, once again, an ambiguous result. And that was as far as she could go with her equipment. The rest would have to wait.

Assuming that life emerged only once for the two planets, where did it start? If Mars cooled first, life would arise here while Earth was still a pool of hot lava. And come to Earth via the meteorite express. The Martian meteorites with their enigmatic fossils had tantalized scientists for years. When they were first discovered, the big question had been whether they actually contained fossils, because most people thought they knew that Mars was lifeless. Now we know about that part, at least, she thought.

Organized life forms from Mars seeding Earth's primitive soup of basic organic molecules would quickly dominate. Martians come to harvest Earthly resources. H. G. Wells with a twist. We may yet be Martians. Pretty heady stuff for the scientific community, and it would change our essential world view. Full employment time for philosophers, too, and even religious theorists.

But deep down she realized she'd wanted to find L*I*F*E, not microbes. The ghosts of Carl Sagan's giraffes had shaped her expectations. Marc was jazzed by the discovery of deeper layers of microbes, separated by layers of sterile peroxide-laden sediments in the old ocean beds. That implied periodic episodes of a wet and warm climate. But so far she had not found anything other than the soil microbes. Even the volcanic vent they had explored had no life, only peroxide soil blown into it from the surface, like a dusty old mine shaft. And now they were about to leave and the subterranean caverns were still unexplored. Damn!

After five hours Piotr was doing well, and had regained his energy and good spirits. They even managed a clumsy but satisfying slap and tickle when she stopped the rover for lunch. They weren't going to get any more privacy, not with just two weeks to go until the return launch. She felt nervous and skittish but Piotr was a persistent sort and she finally realized that this just might do both of them more good than anything in the medicine chest back in the habitat.

The route began to take them—or rather, her, since Piotr crashed again right after sex; this time she forgave him—through familiar territory. She had scoured the landscape within a few days of the hab. Coming down in the Chryse basin, they got a full helping of Mars: chasms, flood runoff plains, wrinkled canyons, chaotic terrain once undermined by mud flows, dried beds of ancient rivers and lakes, even some mysterious big potholes that must be mini-volcanoes somehow hollowed out. Her pursuit of surface fossil evidence of life had been systematic, remorseless—and mostly a waste.

Not a big surprise, really, in retrospect. Any hiker in the American West was tramping over lands where once tyrannosaurus and bison had wandered, but seldom did anybody notice a bone sticking out of the ground. Ann was more systematic and probed deeper in the obvious places, where water had once silted up and could have trapped recently dead organisms. Algal mats, perhaps, as with the first big life forms on Earth. But she had no real luck, even in a year and a half of snooping into myriad canyons and promising beds of truly ancient lakes. That didn't mean life wasn't somewhere on the planet. A billion years was a long time, enough for life to evolve, even if Mars had not supported surface life for perhaps three billion or more.

She stamped her feet to help the circulation. Space heaters in the rover ran off the methane-oxy burn, but as always, the floor was cold. When the outside was tens of degrees Centigrade below zero, gradients in the rover were steep. Mars never let you forget where you were.

She tried to envision how it must have been here, billions of years ago. Did life give way with a grudging struggle, trying every possible avenue before retreating into the diminished role of mere microbes?

The planet did not die for want of heat or air, but of mass. With greater gravity it could have held onto the gases its volcanoes vented, prevented its water vapor from escaping into vacuum. Split from hydrogen by the sun's stinging ultraviolet, the energetic oxygen promptly mated with the waiting iron in the rocks. The shallow gravitational well failed. Light hydrogen blew away into the yawning vastness of empty space. Had Mars been nearer the Sun, the sunlight and warmth would simply have driven water away faster.

So those early life forms must have fought a slow, agonizing retreat. There were eras when lakes and even shallow, muddy seas had hosted simple life— Marc's cores had uncovered plenty of ancient silted plains, now compressed into sedimentary rock. But no fossil forests, nothing with a backbone, nothing with shells or hard body parts. If higher forms had basked in the ancient warmth here, they had left no trace.

The squat hab came into view in the salmon sunset. Looking like a giant's drum, five meters high and eight meters across, it stood off the ground on sturdy metal struts. Long pink and white streamers of carbon dioxide and water vapor trailed from roof vents, signaling that Marc and Raoul were there. Inside, the two stacked decks had the floor space of a smallish condo, their home for the last two years. Not luxurious, but they would certainly be nostalgic for it in the cramped quarters of the Return Vehicle they would shortly be boarding.

By now the hab was familiar to billions of Earthbound TV viewers and Net surfers. Everyone on Earth had the opportunity to follow their adventures, which were beamed daily from Ground Control and carried on the evening news. Their Web page registered over a hundred million hits in the week following the landing. Mars had ceased to be Space and had become a place.

She told herself that she had done all anybody reasonably could. After finding the microbes, she had postulated that they used an enzyme like catalase to harvest the peroxides' energy. Then she had tested it in her small greenhouse set-up, found it worked. She would write that up on the half-year voyage home, squirt it e-mail to an eager audience of every biologist in the world. Heady stuff!

She had data on chemical and biological toxicity of Martian substances to terrestrial biota. Another paper there, too. Plus work on the suitability of local soils to support greenhouse agriculture. Marc had even tried to grow kitchen herbs, but none of the plants survived. Her long searches for fossil microbial mats in the paleoseas had turned up plenty of oddities that might bear fruit under rigorous inspection back Earthside. But she still felt she was just nibbling at the edges, but of what?

Raoul and Marc climbed down out of the hab as she approached, in the last slanting rays of a ruddy sunset, two chubby figures in dark parka suits. Only Raoul's slight limp distinguished them. The tracker system had alerted them, and they would have to carry Piotr in. Plus a little ceremony they had devised: salvaging water from the rover. The methane-oxygen burn made carbon dioxide, which the engine vented, and pure water. She backed the rover to the conical

Return Vehicle, with its gaudy red-on-white Mars Consortium wrap-around letters, a meter high. Raoul and Marc hooked the water condensers to the input lines, so the chem factory inside could store it. They had full tanks of methane and oxygen for the liftoff, but water was always welcome, after the parching they had taken on the long flight here. The guys did this last task by way of saying "welcome home." In the bleak, rusty dusk, the cold of night biting already through her skinsuit, the symbolism was important. Mars was sharp, cold and unrelenting, and they all felt it to the bone.

PART 2

Despite Marc's best efforts, dinner was not a culinary success. Marc was the foodie among them, forever trying out new combinations of the limited range of kitchen stores. But they had long ago exhausted the narrow potential of the kitchen stores for new tastes, and now everything they ate was too familiar to the tongue, though Marc kept trying. He had even brought along spices as part of his personal mass allowance. Some of his infamous attempts had produced stomach-rumbling distress. The microwaved frozen vegetables especially resisted creativity. Still, the food was much better than the freeze-dried horrors of NASA days . . . or so some said.

They took turns in the tiny galley. On the outbound voyage Ann bowed to the public's expectation and dutifully did her time, but the others agreed that the results were definitely substandard, and she was relieved of cooking. Instead, she did extra cleanup. That didn't bother her, a dedicated non-foodie, who believed that eating was a somewhat irksome necessity. She went through school with a minimally equipped kitchen. Throwing a box of macaroni and cheese into boiling water stretched her limits. Piotr joked that he sure as Hell hadn't married her for her cooking. She actually liked good food, but wasn't interested in taking the time to produce it.

"So what did you two do while we were gone?" Ann asked later over very slightly grainy pudding. The chocolate color disguised any visible traces of Martian dust, but the tongue found its sting.

Marc licked his spoon carefully. "Well, we drilled another core. Found something . . . interesting."

"Where were you working?" asked Piotr.

"We took the runabouts back to the mouth of the big canyon in Long Ridge—you know, where we saw the fog a couple of months back on that early-morning trip." The base sported two open dune buggies that the crew used for short sprints of less than 10 klicks round-trip. By taking both buggies, it was possible to haul the drilling gear.

Ann shivered, remembering the biting cold that morning she and Marc had seen the fog, suit heaters cranked to the max, looking like quilted penguins. Their picture now graced the cover of the Lands' End catalogue, wearing the parkas and leggings now called Marswear, of course. It was the latest rage in macho-type clothes, and the underwriting helped pay for the mission.

As they'd prepared to leave the rover she'd grabbed her tea cosy and worn it like a knit ski cap. That was only the first time she'd used it as extra insulation.

Marc continued, "We were down about thirty meters, going pretty slow through some resistant stuff, then all of a sudden the drill started to cut down real fast. I stopped it then so we wouldn't lose the tip. But when we pulled out the drill stem and core, it was smoking."

"Uh-oh," said Ann, automatically sympathetic.

"That's what it looked like, anyway, but it wasn't hot, wasn't even warm." He smiled, looking at Ann and Piotr slyly.

"So how could it be smok—oh, wait, it was water vapor!" shouted Ann. "You found water!"

Marc grinned. "Yep. The drill tip was really wet, and making cloud like mad." It was so cold and dry on Mars that water on the surface never passed through a liquid stage, but sublimed directly from frozen to vapor. The team had concentrated their efforts to drill for water in places where early morning fogs hinted at subsurface moisture.

"So, the deepest core is always the wettest. Makes sense. There really must be frozen oceans down there," said Ann.

"What does Earth think?" asked Piotr.

"Well, with all the data from the other cores, first indications are that it's probably good enough."

"Good enough for the government, as they say," said Raoul with uncharacteristic levity. Raoul Molina, the compact and muscular fourth crew member, was the top mechanic on the team, and ritually cynical about governments. He even disliked the fact that NASA had separately contracted with the Consortium to supply some geological data.

"Too bad we're not working for the government, eh?" shot back Marc.

Ann looked over at him, surprised. The brief exchange left much unsaid, but all understood the shorthand. Tensions were definitely building as the launch date approached. No one wanted to be the cause of a delayed return. The search for subsurface water had gone slowly, disappointing some of the mission backers, and raising the specter that the team would be asked to stay longer to complete the mapping.

After dinner it was time for their regular video transmission to Earth. They pulled Consortium logo shirts over their waffle weave longjohns and prepared to look presentable. In fact, they wore as little as possible when in the hab—loose clothing didn't aggravate the skin abrasions and frostbite spots they suffered in the suits. They kept the heat cranked up to compensate, but then nobody had to pay the electric bill, Marc pointed out. Competition was keen for creams and ointments for their dry skin rashes.

"My turn, I think," said Marc.

Ann smiled. "Janet on the other end tonight, then?" Janet Burton was a former test pilot who had trained with them, and clearly had hoped to make the trip. The Consortium had made a careful selection: individual talents balanced with strategic redundancy. The crew of four had to cover all the basics: mission technical, scientific and medical. They fit together like an intricately cut jigsaw puzzle.

In the end it had come down to a choice between Janet and Piotr, and Ann was relieved at the final decision. She didn't know if she could have left Piotr behind so soon after their marriage, even for a trip to Mars.

For the thousandth time she wondered if that had figured in the crew choice. Adding a woman had inevitably made for tensions, but on the other hand, it also gave half the possible Earth audience somebody to identify with. And the Consortium could be subtle.

"Let's play up the water angle, not the ankle," Piotr said.

"Drama plays better than science," Ann said.

"So we must educate, yes?" Piotr jabbed his chin at Marc.

But Marc wasn't listening. The brief description of Piotr's accident had been squirted to Earth earlier, and he was downloading the reply. Due to the time delay of six minutes each way, normal back and forth conversations were not possible, and communications were more like an exchange of verbal letters. At times the round-trip delay was only a matter of four minutes, sometimes forty. Nonetheless, Earth and Mars teams agreed on a download at a specified time to preserve the semblance of a conversation. They did a short video sequence at the same time. It was great theater, but the Consortium also had a team of doctors scrutinize the footage.

At the short delay times Marc and Janet tended to handle the bulk of the communications. And there was a little spark in the transmissions.

The crew gathered around the screen to watch the latest video from Earth. It was Janet, all right, gesturing with a red Mars Bar. Waiting for a successful landing, Mars, Inc., the candy manufacturer, had agreed to become a mission underwriter, releasing a special commemorative wrapper—a red number featuring the four of them against a Martian backdrop. They had taken about twenty shots of each crew member holding up a standard Mars Bar before a scenic backdrop. They each got $5,000 per shot, with the Mars Bar people paying $10,000 per pound to ship a box of the bars out for the photo shoot. It would have been irritating after a while, except that they came to relish the damned things, keeping one for exterior shots, where it quickly got peroxide-contaminated, and eating the rest as desserts. The cold sopped up calories and the zest of sugar was like a drug to Ann. She was quite sure she would never eat another, back home, even if she did get an endorsement contract out of the deal.

Ann had dubbed the resulting red-wrapped candy the Ego Bar, unwilling to honor it with the name of a planet and an ancient god, and the team adopted the name. There had been some talk early on about producing another wrapper with Mars life pictured, but microbes weren't exciting enough, and the manufacturer had just decided to stick with the Ego Bar.

Somehow, the commercialism of it all still grated on her. But she had signed on with eyes open, all the same. She had known that market-minded execs ran the Consortium, but going in had thought that meant something like, If we do this, people will like it. Soon enough she learned that even exploring Mars was seen by the execs as, If we do this, we'll maximize our global audience share and/or optimize near-term profitability. Such were the thoughts and motivations on Earth. Still, Mars the raw and unknown survived, unsullied and deadly.

The spirit of getting to Mars on private capital was to shuck away all excess. No diversionary Moon base. No big space station to assemble a dreadnought fleet. No fleet at all—just missions launched from Earth, then propelled outward by the upper stage of the same booster rocket that launched them. They had then landed on Mars after a long gliding journey, as the Apollo shots had.

But the true trick was getting to Mars without squandering anybody's entire Gross National Product. When President Bush called in 1989 for a manned mission to Mars on the 50th anniversary of the 1969 Apollo landing, he got the estimated bill from NASA: 450 billion dollars.

The sticker shock killed Bush's initiatives in Congress. The price was high because everyone in NASA and their parasite companies tacked every conceivable extra onto the mission.

When evidence of ancient fossil microbes had turned up in 1996 and later, public interest returned. Soon enough, even Congress-creatures realized that the key to Mars was living off the land. Don't lug giant canisters of rocket fuel to Mars, just to burn it bringing the crew back to Earth. No fluids like water hauled along for an 18 month mission. Instead, get the basic chemicals from the Martian atmosphere.

The Mars Consortium had begun by sending an unmanned lander, the Earth Return Vehicle. It carried a small nuclear reactor for power, an automated chemical processor, the rovers, and the Return Vehicle, unfueled. Using the nuclear reactor power, it started its compressors. They sucked in the thin Martian carbon dioxide and combined it with a store of hydrogen hauled from Earth. This made methane and water. The chemical plant was compact, laboring for half a year to separate the methane into the rocket fuel tanks and clean some of the water for later human use. The rest of the water got broken into oxygen and hydrogen. The hydrogen went into the tanks, and the oxygen was reserved for later combination with the methane in the combustion chambers of the Return Vehicle. Nothing was wasted.

All this was simple chemistry: hauling to Mars only hydrogen as a feed stock for the process, the ship made 18 times as much rocket fuel as the mass of hydrogen it brought. Taking all that fuel to Mars would have cost billions, plus assembly of the mission in orbit. By going slim and smart, the Consortium saved all that. Had the early European explorers tried to carry all their food, water, and fodder to the New World, few could have gone.

Slightly over a year after the first launch, the refueled Return Vehicle awaited the crew. They had launched on a big Saturn-style booster rocket, the contribution of the Russian partner, Energiya. Their closed-loop life-support system had recycled the air and water.

As their upper stage burned out, it pulled away on a tether cable about 300 meters long. A small rocket fired on the habitation drum, setting it to revolving with the upper stage as its counter-weight. At two revolutions a minute, the hab drum had a centrifugal gravity of 0.38 Earth's, to get them used to Mars.

At the end of six months gliding along a curving trajectory close to the minimum-energy orbit, the hab cut the cable. Rather than firing its rocket right away, it used an aeroshell—a cone-shaped buffer—to brake itself as it swung around the planet. They targeted on the radio beacon set up for them and landed right beside the fueled Return Vehicle.

All this was risky; their loss of precious water on the way out had come close to doing them in. Making exploration super-safe was not only hugely expensive, it was impossible. Further, it was anti-dramatic: The public audience was thrilled all the more if lives truly were at stake.

Risks were both obvious—a blowup at launch, as with the Challenger shuttle—and subtle, as with radiation dosage. The voyage exposed them to the solar particle wind and to cosmic rays. They could shelter from solar storms, which were infrequent, but the rest of their exposure amounted to about a 1 percent increased probability of having a fatal cancer within their life span.

Further, Mars itself could do them in. Storms could collapse their habitat or blow over their return rocket. Dust could clog the pumps at the crucial blast-off.

But the 1970s Viking landers had been designed to last 90 days, yet one held out for four years against cold, wind and dust, and the other lasted six.

Multiple backup systems are the key to safety—but the more backups, the higher the cost. Bush's 450 billion dollar program showed that a NASA-run program could easily turn into an enormous government pork farm.

So a radical idea arose: The advanced nations could get this adventure on the cheap by simply offering a prize of 30 billion dollars to the first successfully returned, manned expedition.

This mechanism European governments had used for risky explorations centuries ago. The advantages are that the government puts out not a dime until the job is done, and only rewards success; investors lose if their schemes fail. Also, if astronauts died, it was on somebody else's head, not an embarrassment to a whole government.

So the Mars Consortium of Boeing, Microsoft, Lockheed and the Russian Energiya took the plunge. They originally wanted to use the name Mars, Inc., but discovered that a candy manufacturer had long ago beaten them to it. A Japanese partner bowed out, finally contributing only the smart-toilet, now dubbed the Marsbidet. At $10,000 to fly a pound to Mars, disposables were impossible. This went right down to writing paper—erasable slates served better, and could be digitally saved, even sent Earthside—and toilet items. Nobody had figured out how to recycle toothpaste, but toilet paper was dispensable. The smart toilet combined a bidet arrangement of water jets with a small blow-dryer. Since its inclusion on the mission it was the hottest piece of plumbing on two planets.

A second mission attempt was being made by Airbus Interspatiale, formed from the French Nationale Industrielle Aerospatiale, British Aerospace, the Spanish Construcciones Aeronauticas S.A. and Daimler-Benz Aerospace. The Airbus group had a more cautious method; their fully fueled Return Booster had arrived in Mars orbit four months before. The Airbus crew had launched 50 days later. They could win only if the Consortium's Return Vehicle failed at launch. The whole world was watching the race . . . which made the Consortium's nightly "Hello, Earth" show rake in the dollars.

They all snorted when the usual question came in from Janet. She looked embarrassed, but what could she do? "And how are you feeling, with Airbus getting nearer and your own launch—"

Marc started before Janet was finished. "We'll wave to them as we head home."

Everybody laughed, but there was a forced quality to it.

After the usual updating on Ann's foray, Janet wished Piotr a speedy recovery, transmitted some bland medical advice, and then turned to quasi-technical details about the upcoming liftoff test. Piotr's accident was one more mishap to be overcome. Janet didn't fail to mention the obvious: The broken ankle meant their captain would be less effective if anything went wrong with the liftoff of the Return Vehicle. What should have been a routine test in this part of the mission was looming as a potential crisis.

On arrival they had discovered that it was damaged. A failure in the aerobraking maneuver made the Return Vehicle come in a shade too fast, crushing fuel pipes and valves around the engines. None of the diagnostics had detected this, since the lines were not pressured. In some instances the damage went beyond mere repair and Raoul had been forced to refashion and build from scratch several of the more delicate parts. Working with Earthside engineers, he had been steadily making repairs.

In this he drew upon not only his technical training, but his family's tradition of Mexican make-do. His father and uncle ran a prosperous garage in Tecate, just below the U.S. border. He'd grown up in greasy T-shirts with a wrench in his hand. Coming from a country with a chronic shortage of hard goods meant that "recycle and reuse" was not just a slogan but a necessity. Raoul was good at creative reuse, making novel pieces fit, but never before had he worked under this kind of pressure. Their return, and quite possibly their lives, depended on his repairs.

They ended the transmission on an edgy note. It was 13 days and counting to launch.

There was plenty of grunt labor to get ready for the liftoff test. Gear they had used on the repairs, supplies dumped months ago while in a hurry, scrap parts— all had to be hauled away from the Return Vehicle. On the long glide back to

Earth, every kilogram extra they carried made their fuel margin that much slimmer, and it wasn't that fat to begin with.

Ann didn't mind the heavy labor. The low gravity helped but the laws of inertia still governed. Man-handling gear into the unpressured rovers to stow it for the next expedition at least gave her a chance to think; simple jobs didn't absorb all her concentration. That was when all her frustrations surfaced and she decided to do some pushing of her own.

After the usual heavy-carbo lunch she found Marc in the hab's geology lab, packing a core for transport.

What do we do now?" she asked. "Just you and me?"

Their last, long expedition in the rover was out—that much was clear. Safety protocols demanded two in the rover, and both mechanics, Raoul and Piotr, had to be working on the Return Vehicle. Marc was the backup pilot, so he would be needed to help Piotr, at least through the liftoff trial.

"You're going to tell me, right?" He grinned.

"I'm not going to sit around twiddling my thumbs on my last two weeks on Mars."

Marc said crisply, "You can't go out for a week by yourself, Ann."

"I know. Come with me, Marc. There's just enough time left for a vent trip."

The extensive Return Vehicle repairs had cut into all their schedules. For the week-long rover trips, mission protocol decreed that one of the pair be a mechanic—Raoul or Piotr. When the two of them were tied up with Return Vehicle repairs, Ann and Marc were restricted to day trips in the rover. Marc had filled his time setting off lots of small seismic blasts, and was surprised to discover extensive subterranean caverns several hundreds of meters down. So far they hadn't found a way in to any of them, and Ann knew Marc was itching to get down there.

Marc looked doubtful. "You did that already. I thought we agreed it was a bust. No life or fossils."

"Yes, but we picked a vent that was outgassing remnants of atmosphere—it had oxygen in the mix."

"So? We were looking in the most likely place for life."

"For Earth life, and ancient Mars life, but not modern Mars life. Oxygen is most likely poisonous to the organisms we're looking for."

Marc frowned, distracted by his chore. "Why so?"

"About four billion years ago, Earth's atmosphere was a byproduct of the early photosynthetic microbes . . . precursors of plants. They succeeded by learning how to make their own food, and by poisoning the competition, the anaerobes, with their wastes."

"Oxygen?"

"Right!" Ann nodded vigorously, caught up in her vision. "On Earth, anaerobes went underground or underwater to get away from the poisonous oxygen atmosphere. Here on Mars, oxygen-using forms would have been eliminated when the planet lost its atmosphere. Maybe it's their descendants under the soil, living off the peroxides. But the anaerobes only had to fight the cold and drought. They must have followed the heat and gone underground."

"Where d'you want to look?"

"The big vent about 55 klicks to the north is the closest."

Marc said, "We could maybe manage a few days in the rover, no more."

"Good enough. I'll start packing."

"Not so fast. We've all got to agree."

Raoul shook his shaggy head. All the men were letting their hair grow out to the max, then would shear it down to stubble just before liftoff, including beards. The "Mars Bald" look, as Earthside media put it, went for Ann, too. In the cramped hab of the return vehicle, shedding hair was just another irritant. If it got into their gear, especially the electronics, it could be dangerous. He gestured at the injured Piotr. "Without him, we'll take longer to complete checkout. Marc, I know it's not your job, but I'll need both you and Ann to help. I want to eyeball every valve and servo in the undercarriage."

"Okay, I can see why you need all of us for that. But once it's done—"

"Until we've done the liftoff, planning is pointless," Piotr said in a voice that reminded them all that he was, broken ankle or not, the commander. So far he had not needed to throw such weight around. Ann shot him a look and saw in his face the man who was the commander/mechanic first and her husband second. Which was as it should be at this moment, she knew, even if a part of her did not like such facts right now. She said slowly, "I have a quick run we could do."

Piotr called from his bunk, "For jewels, I hope."

She grimaced. Piotr was deeply marked by the bad years in Russian space science following the collapse of the Communist economy. She recalled his saying, "In those dark years, the lucky ones were driving taxicabs, and building spaceships on the side. The others just starved." Not only research suffered. Some years there had been no money, period. Faced with no salaries, staff members in some science institutes found new ways to raise money, sometimes by selling off scientific gear, or museum collections. It was like her grandparents, who had grown up during the Great Depression; they couldn't get money far from mind. So Piotr made a fetish of following Consortium orders about possible valuable items: he scrounged every outcropping for "nuggets," "Mars jade," and anything halfway presentable. They all got a quarter of the profits, so nobody griped. Still, Piotr's weight allowance on the flight back was nearly all rocks—some, she thought, quite ugly.

"No, for science."

Piotr gave her a satirical scowl.

"Your vent idea." Raoul eyed her skeptically.

"There are three thermal vents within a hundred kilometers. I want to try the closest one, to the north."

"We've studied their outgassing, the whole area around them," Marc said. The Consortium wanted information on water and oxygen; they could use it on later expeditions, or sell the maps to anyone coming afterward.

Raoul shook his head, scowling. "We've already got one injury. And we've looked in one vent already. Crawling down more holes isn't in the mission profile."

"True, but irrelevant," she said evenly. Raoul was the tough one, she saw. Piotr would support her automatically, though grumpily, if she could fit her plan into mission guidelines. Marc, as a geologist, had a bias toward anything that would give him more data and samples.

"It's too damned dangerous!" Raoul suddenly said.

"True," Marc said. "We could use our seismic sensors to feel if there are signs of a venting about to occur, though, and—"

"Nonsense," Raoul waved away this point. "Have you ever measured a venting?"

"Well, no, but it cannot differ greatly from the usual signs on Earth—"

"We do not know enough to say that."

She had to admit that Raoul was right in principle; Mars had plenty of nasty tricks. It certainly had shown them enough already, from the pesky peroxides getting in everywhere—even her underwear!—to the alarming way seals on the chem factory kept getting eaten away by mysterious agents, probably a collaboration between the peroxide dust and the extreme temperature cycles of day and night. "But our remote sensing showed that venting events are pretty rare, a few times a year."

"Those were the big outgassings, no?"

"Well, yes. But even so, they are low density. It's not like a volcano on Earth."

"Low density, but hot. Our pressure suits do not provide good enough insulation. I believe we all agree on that."

This provoked rueful nods. The biggest day-to-day irritant was not the peroxides, but the sheer penetrating cold of Mars. Raoul's style was to hedgehog on the technicals, then leap to a grand conclusion. She got ahead of him by not responding to the insulation problem at all, but going to her real point. "The vents must be key to the biology."

"We have done enough on biology," Raoul said adamantly.

"Look—"

"No," he cut her off with a chop of his hand, the practical mechanic's hand with grime under the fingernails. "Enough."

And they all had to agree. In Raoul's set jaw she saw the end of her dreams.

The liftoff test came after two days of hard labor. They had been burning methane with oxygen in the rovers for more than five hundred days, but that was with carbon dioxide to keep the reaction heat down, acting like an inert buffer much as nitrogen did in the air of Earth. But the Return Vehicle boosters would burn at far higher temperature. The many engineering tests said the system would withstand that, but those were all done in comfortable labs on Earth.

And they did not use a system that had ruptured on landing and that Raoul had labored month after month to repair.

A warning call from Raoul made her crouch down. They had decided that this test liftoff, just to see if anything blew a pipe, would have only Raoul and Piotr aboard. Piotr could run the subsystems fine from his couch. She and Marc took shelter a few hundred meters away, ready to help if something horrible happened. The stubby Return Vehicle stood with its chem systems detached and gear dragged away, looking a bit naked against pink soil as thoroughly trod as Central Park in Manhattan, and with more litter.

She and Marc had nothing to do but pace to discharge all their adrenaline. The damned cold came through her boots as always and she stamped them to keep the circulation going. Even the best of insulation couldn't keep the cold from penetrating through the soles of the boots. It was early morning, so they would have a full day of sunlight to make repairs. She seldom came out this early into the biting hard cold left over from the night. Quickly enough they had learned the pains of even standing in shadow, much less of Martian night— skin stuck to boot tabs, frostbite straight through the insulation. Raoul's limp resulted from severely frostbitten toes after hours of making repairs in the shadow of the Return Vehicle.

She closed her eyes, trying to relax. They were about to land on Mars for the second and last time; think of it that way. Such odd ways of taking each moment, relieving it of its obvious heart-thudding qualities, had sustained her through the launch from Earth and their aerobraking. Months of tedious mission protocols and psychological seminars had given her such oblique skills.

"Ready," she heard Raoul through the suit com. "Starting the pumps."

Piotr responded with pressure readings, flow rates. She saw a thin fog form beneath the rocket nozzle, like the vapors that sometimes leaked from the soil as the sun first struck it.

More cross-talk between the pilots. Their close camaraderie had been so intensive the past few days that she and Marc felt like invisible nonentities, mere "field science" witnesses to the unblinking concentration of the "mission techs," as the terminology went. Then Raoul said, almost in a whisper, "Let's lift."

A fog blossomed at the Return Vehicle base. No gantry here, nothing to restrain it. The conical ship teetered a bit, then rose.

"Nice throttling!" Marc called.

"Wheeeee!" Ann cheered.

The ship rose 20 meters, hung—then started falling. A big plume rushed out the side of the ship. Crump! came to her through the thin atmosphere. A panel blew away, tumbling. The ship fell, caught itself, fell another few meters—and smacked down.

"All off!" Raoul called.

"Pressures down," Piotr answered, voice as mild as ever.

"My God, what—?"

Then she started running. Not that there was anything she could do, really.

• • •

At least the damage was clear. The panel had peeled off about a meter above the reaction chamber. Inside they could see a mass of popped valves.

"Damn, I built those to take three times the demand load," Raoul said.

"Something surged," Piotr said. "The readout shows that."

"Still, the system should have held," Raoul insisted, face dark.

"Over pressure was probably from that double line we made," Piotr said mildly.

"Ummm." Raoul bit his lip; she could see his pale face through his helmet viewer and wondered if he felt defeated. Then he nodded briskly. "Probably right. We should check with the desk guys, but I'll bet you're right."

"The double line was their idea."

"Right, Piotr. We'll go back to the original design."

Somehow this buoyed them. It had to, she reflected. Either they get the system working or they wouldn't dare lift. The Airbus crew would rescue them, maybe, getting the glory and the 30 billion dollars.

"Should I contact Ground Control now, or wait until you get back to the hab?" Marc asked.

"They control nothing," Raoul said. "We're in control."

"Is damned right," Piotr said, laughing in a dry way.

"Okay." She grinned uncertainly and Marc followed suit.

"I suppose we should wait, talk to Earthside before we pull anything out and start refitting," Raoul said.

Piotr's voice crackled in the radio, his accent more noticeable. "Nyet, nyet, no waiting. You do it. And Marc, tell them, the Airbus—we may need their wessel to get home."

She brought up the unthinkable as a way of edging her way around to her own agenda. What the hell, they were all exhausted from laboring on the repairs, and it had been three days. They were nearly done. Time to think the unthinkable again.

Ann turned to Marc. "Okay, suppose we can't get off at all. We've got months until Airbus gets here. What do you think we could do with the highest impact?"

Marc looked surprised. Nobody answered for a very long time. She could see in their faces a vast reluctance to face this issue. But they had to. Finally Marc said slowly, "Geology, maybe."

Piotr laughed sourly. "Scratch scientist, find fanatic. Geology we have plenty. A cold dry desert with red rocks and ancient water erosion. Not much better than the Viking pictures."

Raoul said reasonably, "Ann, this is an old argument. Of course the Viking landing spots were purposely picked to be flat and boring and dry. Not the best places to look for life, but the safest to land. Now we know Viking could never, anywhere on Mars, have found your microbes that retreated to their little layer when the seas and lakes dried up."

"Over a billion years ago, I estimate," Marc put in.

"We don't know that the microbe retreat model is the only one," she said.

Piotr called, "Ah, your new version of the old Sagan argument. While Viking was licking dust into the biology experiments, an undetected Martian giraffe walked by on the other side of the lander."

Ann bristled but did not show it. Sometimes she wondered if Piotr had to occasionally show that he was not just her husband, and thus an automatic ally. "I'm not really expecting Earth-type animals, but I'm keeping an open mind about other possibilities."

Marc blinked. "You really think we'll find more than microbial life in a vent?"

"I certainly think we should look. We're probably never going to be here again, any of us." She looked around at them. "Right?"

This they had never discussed. In some ways the surface mission was the least risky part of the expedition, the first four-fifths in days spent but not in danger. Their coming launch was risky, and the aerobraking into Earth's atmosphere would be more tricky than their rattling deceleration in the comparatively soft Martian atmosphere. Still, the sheer wearing-down of their labors in the harsh cold dryness of Mars had sobered them all somewhat. When they returned home—or if—they would be wealthy, famous. Would they do this again?

"I might come back," Marc said.

"I, too," Raoul said, though without the conviction he had before.

"I am honest enough to say that I will not," Piotr said, grinning at them. "I will have a wealthy wife, remember."

They all laughed, maybe more than the joke deserved. The laughter, after a filling meal, served to remind them that they were a team, closer than any contracts could bring them. This was a highly public, commercial enterprise, of course, but none of it would work without a degree of cooperation and intuitive synchronization seldom demanded anywhere.

Ann looked at the others, their clothes emblazoned with the logos of mission sponsors, all quite soiled. Through the Consortium's endless marketing they had endorsed a staggering array of products. They were destined to be a team forever, no matter what happened in the future.

Marc said, "The metals, that's why I'm here. They'll be more important than life, in the long run."

Piotr: "I disagree. The asteroid belt is where we will go for metals. Mars is where we build a base to mine the asteroids. Going to be much cheaper to boost from here than anyplace else."

Raoul appeared from the pint-sized galley toting a bulb of coffee. "So we've just wasted our time looking for metals on Mars? Suits me. If we jettisoned all of the damned ore samples there'd even be room to breathe on the return."

Ann said, "We shouldn't be limited by what we think we know. Or what we think we're going to find. A biologist named Lovelock pointed out before the Viking landings that there was probably no life because the atmosphere was in chemical equilibrium with the surface. Spectroscopy from Earth showed plainly that there was nothing in it but boring CO_2 and nitrogen."

"Good argument, you have to admit," Marc said.

"But it assumed life would use the atmosphere as its buffering chemical medium. Unlikely, because it's so thin . . .

"That's what we found." Marc looked puzzled. They were co-authors on the microbial *Nature* paper, but they all knew the major work was hers.

"Other life may have many ways of holding on deep underground. We can't reach it except through the vents."

When her news of life was beamed to Earth, the public had chewed over it, and decided that it was not all that exciting. Just a bunch of microbes, after all. The deeper issue of its relationship to Earth life had to wait until they got the samples home. Until then, the issue was the province of learned talking heads chewing over the implications. Time for that later.

They had been through all of this before, of course. In the course of two years you get to know each other's views pretty damn well, she reflected, and Raoul had his set look, jaw solid and eyes narrowed, already announcing his position.

The second liftoff trial was grim. Their lives were riding on the plume of scalding exhaust. She fidgeted with the microcams—Earthside wanted four viewpoints, supposedly for engineering evaluation, but mostly to sell spectacular footage, she was sure.

"Let's go," Raoul called in a husky whisper.

The vehicle rose on a column of milky steam. The methane-oxygen burn looked smooth and powerful and her heart thudded as the ship rose into the burnt-blue sky. It was throttled down nicely, standing on its spewing spire as Raoul and Piotr made it hover, then drift sideways, then back.

"All nominal," Piotr said, clipped and tight.

"Control A 16 and B 14 integrated," Raoul answered. "Let's set her down."

And down they came, settling on the compressed column. The ship landed within 10 meters of the damp smear that marked the takeoff.

"Throttle down," came from Piotr in a matter-of-fact voice she did not believe for a minute.

Then she was running across the rocky ground, feet crunching, her cheers echoing in her helmet along with all the others, tinny over the com.

Celebration. Extra rations; they even ate the last Ego Bar. Joyful calls from Earth. The laconic way Piotr told the Airbus people that they would not be needing a ride home after all. . . .

Then the next morning. Assessment.

Now they had five days until liftoff and it stretched like forever. The rush to do the second test had kept them at it 16 hours a day, pouring their anxious energy into the other preflight procedures. After two years they functioned smoothly together, anticipating one another's needs wordlessly. The efficiency of true teamwork bore fruit: Now they were ahead of schedule. Ann worked alongside them and judged their mood and dreamed her own dreams. Home! The call of it was an ache in the heart. The cool green hills of Earth . . .

Still, she could not let go her own itchy ideas. She lay beside Piotr in the cold darkness and thought.

Leaving Mars . . .

Behind her she felt the yearning of millions, of a whole civilization reaching out. Why had the issue of life here come to loom so large in the contemporary mind? It dominated all discussions and drove the whole prize-money system. Piotr and Raoul thought economic payoffs would be the key to the future of Mars, but they were engineers, bottom-line men, remorselessly practical. Just the sort you wanted along when a rocket had to work, but unreliable prophets.

She suspected that the biologists were themselves to blame. Two centuries before they had started tinkering with the ideas of Adam Smith and Thomas Malthus, drawing the analogy between markets and nature red in tooth and claw. The dread specter of Mechanism had entered into Life, and would never be banished after Darwin and Wallace's triumphal march across the theological thinking of millennia. God died in the minds of the intellectuals, and grew a rather sickly pallor even among the mildly educated.

All good science, to be sure, but the biologists left humanity without angels or spirits or any important Other to talk to. Somehow our intimate connection to the animals, especially the whales and chimps and porpoises, did not fill the bill. We needed something bigger.

So in a restless, unspoken craving, the scientific class reached out—through the space program, through the radio-listeners of the Search for Extraterrestrial Life—for evidence to staunch the wound of loneliness. That was why their discovery of microbes satisfied no one, not even Ann. Mars had fought an epic struggle over billions of years, against the blunt forces of cold and desiccation, betrayed by inexorable laws of gravitation, chemistry and thermodynamics. Had life climbed up against such odds, done more than hold on? To Ann, survival of even bacteria in such a hellish dry cold was a miracle. But she had to admit, it left an abyss of sadness even in her. And there was still time . . .

Morning. Four days to go. Over breakfast Ann signaled to Marc, took a deep breath, and made her pitch. The last few days' hectic work had pushed them hard. More than that, it had nudged them across an unseen boundary in their feelings toward the trip. Despite what Marc and Raoul had said about returning, they all realized that this was a one-time experience. Once they left it would be all over.

Raoul looked up. "The vent trip again? I thought we laid that to rest. You didn't find anything the first time."

"Absence of evidence is not evidence of absence," she shot back.

Raoul frowned, "Besides, there isn't time. We're not packed up yet."

"We're ahead of schedule," said Ann.

Piotr cut in quickly. "Under normal circumstances, yes." He gestured at his cast. "With this, I'm clumsy. It takes longer to do everything." He looked at Ann. "I need your help."

They all knew that a public admission of weakness cost him a lot, and it touched her, but she was determined not to be swayed. She refused to meet his eyes. Damn. Why did women always have to choose? He never would've asked that of a man.

In an impassioned tone, she used her Columbus argument—how could they go home when there was the chance they had only nibbled at the edges of discovery?

Marc came to her rescue. After days of grunt work, the scientist in him yearned for this last chance as much as she did. "We can do it in two days. We'll work here tomorrow morning, drive to the site and set up the pulleys by nightfall. Next day we'll explore the vent and come back. That gives us a full day to finish up here before liftoff." He looked at Piotr and Raoul. "We feel we have to do this."

Technically, the two scientists could amend mission plans if they felt it was warranted. Clearly they would do so this time.

Raoul looked pensive. "I want to go over the thruster assembly again. Something might need adjustment after the burn we just did." He hurried on, "But I can do it alone."

In a flash Ann understood that Raoul wished to take responsibility for the repairs, needed to have time alone with his handiwork. He would be just as happy not to have two itchy scientists underfoot. Then he could take as much time as he liked, obsess over every detail.

There was a long moment. They skirted the edge of a rift. Finally Piotr nodded agreement. He had followed Ann's arguments carefully, hoping to be convinced. Now he snapped back into mission commander mode. "Da. All right. Two days only."

Ann's heart soared. She flashed him a brilliant smile, leaned over and, ignoring mission discipline, gave him a big kiss. Spending one final night in a hellishly cold rover would be the price, but well worth it. She was going to explore the vent at last!

PART 3

She woke to the bitter tang of black Colombian perking in the pot, the scent mingling with a buttery aroma of pancakes, the sizzle of bacon in its lake of fat, all lacing in their steamy collaboration to make a perfect moist morning—

And then she snapped awake, really awake—on the hard rover bunk, hugging herself in her thermoelectric blanket. Once all her waking dreams had been about sex; now they were about food. She wasn't getting enough of either, especially not since Piotr's ankle.

The break would heal by the time they were on the long glide Earthward; their rations would not improve until they were back eating steak. She pushed the thought of meat out of her mind and sat up. First feelers of ruddy dawn laced a wisp of carbon dioxide cirrus high up; good. Today she got to burrow, at last.

"Hey, Marc! I'll start the coffee."

No dallying over breakfast, though the hard cold that came through the rover walls made her shiver. A ruddy sunup was just breaking, giving them one final day of exploration. She peered out the viewport as she munched. They would run on in-suit rations today, no returning to the Spartan comforts of the rover.

They had set up the cable rig at the edge of the vent before sundown. By early light it still looked secure, anchored to three boulders. Marc didn't trust the soil here to hold so they had arranged cross-struts of their monofilament-based cabling to take their weight as they went down the steep incline. Metal cable was much too heavy to fly to Mars, and not necessary under the lighter gravity.

The first part was easy, just backing over. The rock was smooth and of course dry. Even if vapor had spouted last night, it would never condense for long. The Martian atmosphere was an infinite sponge.

The vent snaked around and steepened as the pale light of late dawn from above lost out to the gloom. The rock walls were smooth and still about 10 meters wide. They reached a wide platform and the passage broadened farther. Every 10 meters down they checked to be sure the cable was not getting fouled. They were both clipped to it and had to time their movements to keep from getting snarls.

They edged along the ledge cautiously, headlamps stabbing into the darkness. She was trying to peer ahead but her eyes were cloudy for some reason. She checked her face-plate but there was no condensate on it; the little suit circulators took care of that, even in the cold of full Martian night. Still, the glow from Marc's suit dimmed.

"Marc, having trouble seeing you. Your lamp die?"

"Thought I was getting fogged. Here—" He clambered over on the steep slope of the ledge and shone his handbeam into her face. "No wonder. There're drops of something all over your face-plate and helmet. Looks like water drops!"

"Water . . . ?"

"We're in a fog!" He was shouting.

She saw it then, a slow, rising mist in the darkness. "Of course! It could be a fog desert in here."

"A what?"

"Ever been out in a serious fog? There's not much water falling, but you get soaked anyway. There are deserts where it doesn't rain for years, like the Namib and the coast of Baja California. Plants and animals living there have to trap the fog to get water." She thought quickly, trying to use what she knew to think about this place. In fact, frogs and toads in any desert exploited a temperature differential to get water out of the air even without a fog. When they came up out of their burrows at night they were cooler than the surrounding air. Water in the air condensed on their skin, which was especially thin and permeable.

Ann peered at the thin mist. "Are you getting a readout of the temperature? What's it been doing since we started down?"

He fumbled at his waist pack for the thermal probe, switched it to readout mode. "Minus 14, not bad." He thumbed for the memory and nodded. "It's been climbing some, jumped a few minutes ago. Hm. It's warmer since the fog moved in."

They reached the end of the ledge, which fell away into impenetrable black. "Come on, follow the evidence," she said, playing out cable through her clasps. Here the low gravity was a big help. She could support her weight easily with one hand on the cable grabber, while she guided down the rock wall with the other.

"Evidence of what?" Marc called, grunting as he started down after her.

"A better neighborhood than we've been living in."

"Sure is wetter. Look at the walls."

In her headlamp the brown-red rock had a sheen. "Enough to stick!"

"I can see fingers of it going by me. Who woulda thought?"

She let herself down slowly, watching the rock walls, and that was why she saw the subtle turn in color. The rock was browner here and when she reached out to touch it there was something more, a thin coat. "Mat! There's a mat here."

"Algae?"

"Could be." She let herself down farther so he could reach that level. The brown scum got thicker before her eyes. "I bet it comes from below."

She contained her excitement as she got a good shot of the scum with the recorder and then took a sample in her collector rack. Warmer fog containing inorganic nutrients would settle as drops on these cooler mats. Just like the toads emerging from their burrows in the desert? Analogies were useful, but data ruled, she reminded herself. Stick to observing. Every moment here will get rehashed a million-fold by every biologist on Earth . . . and the one on Mars, too.

Marc hung above her, turning in a slow gyre to survey the whole vent. "Can't make out the other side real well, but it looks brown, too."

"The vent narrows below." She reeled herself down.

"How do they survive here? What's the food source?"

"The slow-motion upwelling, like the undersea hydrothermal vents on Earth?"

Marc followed her down. "Those black smokers?"

She had never done undersea work but was of course aware of the sulfur-based life at the hydrothermal vents. Once it was believed that all life on Earth depended on sunlight, trapped by chlorophyll in green plants and passed up the food chain to animals. Then came the discovery of sunlight-independent ecosystems on the ocean floor, a fundamental change in a biological paradigm. The exotic and unexpected vent communities were based on microbes that harnessed energy from sulfur compounds in the warm volcanic upwelling. Meter-long tube worms and ghostly crabs in turn harvested the bacteria. The vent communities on earth were not large, a matter of meters wide before the inexorable cold and dark of the ocean bottom made life impossible. She wondered how far away the source was here.

In the next 50 meters the scum thickened but did not seem to change. The brown filmy growth glistened beneath her headlamp as she studied it, poked it, wondered at it.

"Marsmat," she christened it. "Like the algal mats on Earth, a couple of billion years ago."

Marc said wryly, puffing, "We spent months looking for fossil evidence, up there in the dead sea beds. The real thing was hiding from us down here."

The walls got closer and the mist cloaked them now in a lazy cloud. "You were right," Marc said as they rested on a meter-wide shelf. They were halfway through their oxygen cycle time. "Mars made it to the pond scum stage."

"Not electrifying for anybody but a biologist, but something better than in-dividual soil microbes. It implies a community of organisms, several different kinds of microbes aggregated in slime—a biofilm." She peered down. "You said the heat gradient is milder here than on Earth, right?"

"Sure. Colder planet anyway, and lesser pressure gradient because of the lower gravity. On Earth, 1 klick deep in a mine it is already 56 degrees C. So?"

"So microbes could probably survive farther down than the couple of klicks they manage on Earth. They're stopped by high heat."

"Maybe."

"Let's go see."

"Now? You want to go down there now?"

"When else?"

"We're at oxy turnaround point."

"There's lots in the rover."

"How far down do you want to go?"

"As far as possible. There's no tomorrow. Look, we're here now, let's just do it."

He looked up at his readouts. "Let's start back while we're deciding."

"You go get the tanks. I'll stay here."

"Split up?"

"Just for a while."

"Mission protocol—"

"Screw protocol. This is important."

"So's getting back alive."

"I'm not going to die here. Go down maybe 50 meters, tops. Got to take samples from different spots."

"Piotr said—"

"Just go get the tanks."

He looked unhappy. "You're not going far, are you?"

"No."

"OK then. I'll lower them down to the first ledge if you'll come back that far to pick them up. Then I'll come down, too."

"OK, sounds fine. Let's move."

He turned around and started hauling himself up the steep wall. "Thirty minutes, then, at the first ledge."

"Yeah, fine. Oh, and bring some batteries, too. My handbeam's getting fee-ble."

"Ann . . ."

"See you in 30 minutes," she said brightly, already moving away. Marc kept going. The slope below was easy and she inched down along a narrow shelf. Playing out the cable took her attention. Methodical, careful, that's the ticket. Especially if you're risking your neck deep in a gloomy hole on an alien world.

She felt a curious lightness of spirit—she was free. Free on Mars. For the last time. Free to explore what was undoubtedly the greatest puzzle of her scientific life. She couldn't be cautious now. Her brother Bill flashed into her mind. He took life at a furious pace, cramming each day full, exuding boundless energy. They went on exploring trips together as children, later as nascent biologists. He was unstoppable: up and out early, roaming well after dark. There was never enough time in the day for everything he wanted to see. "Slow down, there's always tomorrow," people would tell him.

But his internal clock had served him well, in a way. He was cut down at age 22 when his motorcycle slid into a truck one rainy night when sensible people were home, warm and dry. Looking around the church at his funeral, Ann felt he'd lived more than most of the middle-aged mourners. Bill would've approved of her right now, she was sure.

A flicker from her handbeam brought her back. She looked down, shook it. The beam brightened again. Damn, not now.

The mat was thicker here, as she'd guessed it would be closer to the elusive source.

She landed on a wide ledge, moved briskly across it, mindful of time passing. The floor was slippery with Marsmat but rough enough so she could find footing. Sorry, she said silently to the mat, but I've got to do this.

Her handbeam flickered again, died. She shook it, bent her head to look at it with the headlamp, then felt a sudden hard blow to her forehead, heard the headlamp shatter. She fell backward, in slow-motion but inexorably, nothing to grab.

Her wrist hit first as she landed and she dropped the handbeam. She lay there for a moment, waiting for the surprise to go away. Must've run into an overhang. It was pitch dark. Where was her damned lamp? There was a faint glow to her left. That must be it. She started to get up, noticed a feeble luminescence ahead of her. Confused, she sat back down. Take this carefully.

All around her, the walls had a pale ivory radiance.

She closed her eyes, opened them again. The glow was still there.

—No, not the walls—the Marsmat. Tapestries of dim gray luminosity.

She reviewed what bits she remembered about organisms that give off light. This she hadn't boned up on. Fireflies did it with an enzyme, luciferase, an energy-requiring reaction she had done in a test-tube a few thousand years ago in molecular bio lab. Glow worms—really fly larvae, she recalled—hung in long strands in New Zealand caves. She remembered a trip to the rainforest of Australia: Some tropical fungi glow in the dark. Hmm. Will-o'-the-wisps in old graveyards, foxfire on old wooden sailing ships . . . could there be fungi here? Unlikely. Wrong model. She shook her head. Waves breaking at night into glowing blue foam during red tides in California. Those are phosphorescent diatoms. What else? Thermal vent environments . . .

Deep sea fish carried luminescent bacteria around as glowing lures. That's it. The lab folks had fun moving the light-producing gene around to other bacteria. Okay. So microbes could produce light, but why here? Why would underground life evolve luminescence?

Bing bing. The warning chime startled her out of her reverie. She flicked her eyes up. The oxygen readout was blinking yellow. Thirty minutes reserve left. Time to go back.

As she picked herself up she brushed against her handbeam. She picked it up but left it off. Navigating by the light of the walls was like hiking by moonlight.

Pulling herself up gave her time to think, excitement to burn in muscles that seemed more supple than usual. Yes, it was warmer here. She turned her suit heater down. Life hung out in the tropics.

Before she reached the tanks, she heard Marc's impatient voice. "Ann, where are you?"

"On my way. Pretty close." She rounded a jut in the vent walls, into the glare of his lights. The walls faded into black.

"Where were you? You're way late, damn it. The tanks were here on time— hey, where's your headlamp?"

"Ran into an overhang. Smashed it. Marc—"

"Handlamp too? What'd you do—grope your way back? Why didn't you call?" He was clearly angry, voice tight and controlled.

"I found, I found—"

"Ann, calm down, you're—"

"Turn off your lamps."

"What?"

"Turn off your lamps. I want you to see something."

"First we switch your tank."

She sighed. It was just like Marc to fuss over details. Looking down at the sidewalk for pennies and missing the rainbow.

When she finally got the lamps off he could see it too. There was a long moment of utter shock and he seemed to know it was better to say nothing.

Then she heard something wrong. The faint hissing surprised her. Mission training reasserted itself.

"What's that? Sounds like a tank leaking." Automatically she checked her connections. All tight. "Marc?—check your tank."

"I'm fine. What's the matter?"

"I hear something, like a leak."

"I don't hear anything . . ."

"Be quiet. Listen." She closed her eyes to fix the direction of the sound. It came from near the wall. She shone her handbeam on the empty tank, bent down low and heard a thin scream. Oxygen was bleeding out onto the Marsmat.

"Damn. Valve isn't secured." She reached down to turn it off. Stopped— "What?"

The Marsmat near the tank was discolored. A blotchy, tan stain.

"Damn! We've damaged it." She knelt down to take a closer look, carefully avoiding putting her hand on the wall.

"What happened?" Marc took one long step over, understood at a glance. "The oxygen?"

"Uh-huh. Looks like it."

"What a reaction. And fast! No wonder there was nothing in the first vent. You were right about that."

"Oxygen's pure poison to these life forms. It's like dumping acid on moss. Instantaneous death."

He looked around wonderingly. "We're leaking poison at them all the time in these suits."

She nodded. Stupid not to see it immediately, really. Like SCUBA gear, their suits vented exhaled gases at the back of the neck, mostly oxygen and nitrogen with some carbon dioxide. A simple, reliable system, and the oxygen was easily replaceable from the Return Vehicle's chem factory.

Marc shook his head, sobered. "Typical humans, polluting wherever we go."

"If the stuff is this sensitive, we'll have to be really careful from now on." Ann straightened up carefully and backed away from the lesion.

They stood for a long moment in inky blackness, letting their retinas shed the afterimage of the lamps. Finally Marc asked, "Where's the light coming from?"

"Marsmat glows. Phosphoresces, is more correct."

"How can it do that?"

"Don't know. The more interesting question is why."

They knew now that time and oxygen would set the limits. They had this day and were to return to the ship tomorrow. Team loyalty.

"Plenty of oxy up there," Marc said as they rested and ate lunch—a squeeze-tube affair she hated, precisely described in one of her intervideos as eating a whole tube of beef-flavored toothpaste.

"So we trade tanks for time."

"Piotr's gonna get miffed if we don't check in at the regular time."

"Let him." She wished they had rigged a relay antenna at the vent mouth. But that would have taken time, too. Tick tick tick.

"I don't want us to haul out of here dead tired, either."

"We'll be out by nightfall."

"We won't be so quick going out."

Field experience had belied all the optimistic theories about working power in low gravity. Mars was tiring. Whether this came from the unrelenting cold or the odd, pounding sunlight (even after the UV was screened out by faceplates), or the simple fact that human reflexes were not geared for 0.38 gee, or some more subtle facet—nobody knew. It meant that they could not count on a quick ascent at the end of a trying day.

"You want geological samples, I want biological. Mine weigh next to nothing, yours a lot. I'll trade you some of my personal weight allowance for time down here."

He raised his eyebrows, his eyes through his smeared faceplate giving her a long, shrewd study. "How much?"

"A kilogram per hour."

"Ummm. Not bad. Okay, a deal."

"Good." She shook hands solemnly, glove to glove. A fully binding guy contract, she thought somewhat giddily.

"Piotr's counting on using some of your allowance to drag back more nuggets and 'jewels,' y'know."

"It's my allowance."

"Hey, just a friendly remark. Not trying to get between you two."

Innumerable nosy media pieces had dwelled on the tensions between a crew, half married and half not, complete with speculations on what two horny, healthy guys would feel like after two years in a cramped hab with a rutting couple just beyond the flimsy bunk partition. All that they had scrupulously avoided.

So far the answer was, nothing much. Raoul and Marc undoubtedly indulged in gaudy fantasy lives and masturbated often (she had glimpsed a porno video on Raoul's slate reader) but in the public areas of the hab they were at ease, all business.

There was no room for modesty in the hab, four people in a small condo for two years. So they unconsciously adopted the Japanese ways of creating privacy without walls. They didn't stare at each other, and didn't intrude on another's private space unless by mutual agreement.

Nobody had thought much about what the hab would be like if the newlyweds—well, it had been well over two years now, most of that time in space—got into a serious spat. Maybe on the half-year flight home they would find out. She would worry about that then; for right now—

"Hey, we're eating into my hard-bought hours."

They returned to the ledge where Ann had her accident, two hundred meters farther in. On the other side of the fortuitous overhang they found a pool covered with slime on a ledge. It was crusty black and brown stuff and gave reluctantly when she poked it with a finger.

"Defense against the desiccation," she guessed.

Marc swept his handbeam around. The mat hung here like drapes from the rough walls. "Open water on Mars. Wow."

"Not really open. The mat flows down, see, and covers this pool. Keeps it from drying out. Saving its resources maybe?"

She scooped out some of the filmy pool water and put it under her hand microscope. In the view were small creatures, plain as day.

"My God. There's something swimming around in here. Marc, look at this and tell me I'm not crazy."

He looked through the 'scope and blinked. "Martian shrimp?"

She sighed. "Trust you to think of something edible. In a pond this small on Earth there might be fairy shrimp, but these are pretty small. And I don't even know if these are animals."

She hurried to get some digitals of the stuff. She scooped some up in a sample vial and tucked it into her pack. Her mind was whirling in elation. She studied the tiny swimming things with breathless awe.

So fine and strange and why the hell did she have to peer at them through a smudged helmet? They had knobby structures at one end: heads? Maybe, and each with a smaller light-colored speck. What?

Could Mars life have taken the leap to animals—a huge evolutionary chasm? These could be just mobile algal colonies—like volvox and other pond life on Earth. Whatever they were, she knew they were way beyond microbes. She bent down over the pool again, shone her handbeam at an angle. The swarm of creatures was much thicker at the edges of the Marsmat—feeding? Or something else?

She couldn't quite dredge the murky idea from her subconscious. The arrangement with the mat was odd, handy for the shrimp. What was the relationship there? Some kind of symbiosis? And how did the swimming forms get to the pool?

They climbed down from the ledge. As they descended, the mist thickened and the walls got slick and they had to take more care. The cable was getting harder to manage, too. She could not stop her mind from spinning with ideas.

On Earth, hydrothermal vent organisms kilometers deep in the ocean photosynthesized using the dim reddish glow from hot magma. The glow becomes their energy source. Could some Martian organisms use the mat glow? Wait a minute—the "shrimp" had eyes! Or did they?

"Marc, did you notice anything peculiar about the shrimp?"

He paused before answering. "Well, I don't know what they should look like. They looked sorta like the shrimp I feed my fish at home."

"Did you notice their eyes?"

"Uh . . ."

"The knobby ends, those had lighter specks, remember?"

"Yeah, what about them?"

"So you saw them too."

"Why, what's the matter—Oh."

"Right!"

"I see, they shouldn't have eyes."

"Good for you. I'll make a biologist out of you yet. On Earth, cave-dwelling organisms have lost their eyes. Natural selection forces an organism to justify the cost of producing a complicated structure. You lose 'em if you don't use 'em."

"So if they have eyes—"

"On Earth, we'd say they were recent arrivals from a lighted place, hadn't had time to become blind."

"But that's impossible. The lighted parts of Mars have been cold and dry for billions of years. Where would they have come from?"

"I agree. So my next choice is that it's not dark enough here to lose the eyes. But the idea of some kind of transfer with the topside peroxide microbes is worth thinking about."

"That glow is pretty dim."

"To us, maybe. We're creatures from a light-saturated world. Our eyes aren't used to these skimpy intensities. Closest parallel on Earth to these light levels are the hydrothermal vents. There are light-sensitive animals down there, even microbes able to photosynthesize."

"Maybe they're not even eyes."

"They're light-sensitive. The critters clustered under the beam from my 'scope."

"Wow."

"I need more information, but at the very least it suggests that the glow is permanent, or at least frequent enough to give some advantage to being able to see. And that means there should be something that can use the glow as an energy source. Maybe the mat is symbiotic—a cooperation between glowing organisms and photosynthesizers?"

"Yeah . . . That suggests the glow is primary. What's it for?"

"Don't know, just guessing here."

"Curiouser and curiouser, as Alice said."

"I didn't know boys read *Alice in Wonderland*."

"It seems to fit what we're doing."

"Down the rabbit hole we go, then."

Below the level of the pool ledge were twisty side channels to the vent. These ran more nearly horizontal, and they explored them hurriedly, clumping along until the ceiling got too low. No time to waste crawling back into dead ends, she figured. They headed back to the main channel and then found a broad passage that angled down. It was slick and they had to watch their footing.

The mats here were like curtains, hanging out into the steady stream of vapor from the main shaft of the vent. Some seemed hinged to spread before the billowing vapor gale. Ann was busy taking samples and had only moments to study the strange, slow sway of these thin membranes, flapping like slow-motion flags. "Must be maximizing their surface area exposed to the nutrient fog," she guessed.

"Eerie," Marc said. "And look how wide they get. There's a lot of biomass here—wonder if any of it's edible."

At turns in the channel the mats were the size of a man. She took a lot of shots with her microcam, hoping they would come out reasonably well in their lamp beams. The mats were gray and translucent. Under direct handbeam she could see her hand through one.

How did these fit in with the peroxide-processing microbes on the surface? Clearly these mats harvested vapor; did they somehow trade it with the peroxide bugs, water and methane for the racy stim of peroxide? She had a quick vision of an ecosystem specialized to use what it had: peroxides aplenty above, and ice below, awaiting a lava flow to melt it.

Did life negotiate between these resource beds? Oxides cooked by the searing sun, with microbes specialized to gather their energy. Those microbes must have evolved after the great dryness came, when UV sizzled down and drove deeper all that could not adapt to it.

Yet below, where water still lurked, dwelled forms that owed their origin to the warm, moist eras of the Martian antiquity.

The mats—and what else, in such labyrinths as this, all around the globe?—transacted their own business with the peroxide eaters. They could harvest the moisture billowing from heat below, and perhaps melt the permafrost nearby. At the edges of Earth's glaciers lived plants that actually melted ice with their own slow chemisty.

The thermal vents and their side caverns could be extensive. With an exposed surface area as big as Earth's, there was plenty of room for evolution to experiment.

Nothing like this pale ivory cavern on Earth, ruled as it was by boisterous, efficient aerobic life. To escape the poisonous reach of oxygen, anaerobes retreated to inhospitable niches like hot springs and coal mines. In that infertile ground they survived, but remained as microbes, spawning no new forms. On Mars, any oxygen-loving forms would have died out when the planet lost its atmosphere. Here the anaerobes persisted, and evolved new forms; maybe the closest analogy was to the marsupials in Australia. Marsupials breed more slowly than true placental animals, and thus were eliminated all over the Earth except for the huge island of Australia. Free of competition, they populated an entire continent, evolving completely unique forms such as kangaroos, wombats and the duckbilled platypus. What were the equivalents on Mars?

Ann gently caressed a mat as it lazily flowed on the vapor breeze. Plants, flourishing in the near-vacuum. She could never have envisioned these . . .

Yet in the edges of her vision she sensed something more. She thought for a moment and said, "Turn off your lamps."

"Mine's getting pretty low," he remarked as they plunged into blackness.

The glow gradually built up in their eyes. "There's a lesion on the closest mat," said Marc.

She swung gently over, peered at it. "It's the same shape as the damage we did above." The mat around the wound shape glowed more brightly with pale phosphorescence. It seemed to be changing as she watched. "Look at it out of the corner of your eye," she said. "See?"

"It's spreading downwards."

The mats were growing ever larger as they went lower. She leaned over into the vent and peered around. "The glow increases below." They looked down the vent.

"It's definitely brighter down there."

"Let's go." They descended carefully, playing out line. Their lamps washed the mats in glare that seemed harsh now. Twenty meters down she said, "Lamps off again," as they rested on a shelf.

When her dark vision came back her eyes were drawn to a splotch of light. "Damn! How—?"

"It's the same shape again."

"A mimicking image. Parrots imitate sounds, this mat imitates patterns imposed on it, even destructive ones. Why?"

He drawled, "I'd say the question is, how the hell?"

"The mat here learned about the wound above."

"Okay, they're connected. But why the same shape?"

She sighed. "It's a biological pictograph. I have no idea why, but I am sure that any capability has to have some adaptive function."

"You mean it has to help these mats survive."

"Right."

They descended again, quickly; time was narrowing. The image of the lesion repeated on successively lower mats twice more, five meters apart.

She gazed back up. The blurred gleaming above had faded. So it was not just a simple copying, for some pointless end. "It's following us down."

"Tracking us?"

"See for yourself, up there—the image is nearly gone, and the one next to us is brightening."

"Are you implying it knows we're here?"

"It seems to sense what level we're on, at least."

"This one is stronger than the others."

"I think so too. Brighter the deeper we go. The glow is purely chemical, some signaling response I would guess, and the denser vapor here deep in the vent helps it develop."

"Signaling?" Marc sounded puzzled.

"Maybe just mimicking. Light would be the only way to do it here. It couldn't use chemical packets to signal downwards because of the updrafts of vapor. Sound could go either up or down, but it doesn't carry well in this thin an atmosphere."

His voice was strained in the blackness. "There's got to be a simple explanation."

"There is, but it doesn't imply a simple organism."

"Maybe it's . . . signaling something else . . ."

"And if it's brighter the deeper we get, maybe that means . . . something below."

They went one more time down into the darkness. Her muscles ached and her breath came in ragged gasps. At the next ledge down the lesion image began to swell into a strong, clearer version.

Something beyond comprehension was happening here and she could only struggle with clumsy speculations as she worked. Somehow the mat could send signals within itself. There were many diaphanous flags and rock-hugging forms and somehow they all fit together, a community. They used the warmth and watery wealth here and could send signals over great distances, tens of meters, far larger than any single mat. Why? To sense the coming pulse of vapor and make ready? A clear survival value in that, she supposed. Could organisms evolve such detailed response in this harsh place?

And how did these fit with the peroxide-eating microbes? Could they somehow work together? Darwin had his work cut out for him here. . . .

With their lamps off she took video shots of the ghostly lesion images with her microcam, though she was pretty sure the level of illumination was too low to turn out. She would memorize all this and write it down in the rover. Careful notes. . . .

"We're out of time."

She gazed down and saw at the very limit of the weak lamplight bigger things. Gray sheets, angular spires, corkscrew formations that stuck out into the up-welling gases and captured the richness. . . .

She blinked. How much was she seeing and how much was just illusion, the product of poor seeing conditions, a smudged helmet view, her strained eyes—

"Hey. Time."

She felt her fatigue as a slow, gathering ache in legs and arms. Experience made her think very carefully, being sure she was wringing everything from these minutes that she could. "How far down are we?"

Marc had been keeping track of the markings on the cable. "Just about one klick."

"What's the temperature?"

"Nearly 10. No wonder I'm not feeling the cold."

"The thermal gradient here is pretty mild. This vent could go down kilometers before it gets steam-hot. And we've just reached the cavern level."

"Ann . . ."

"I know. We can't go farther."

"It'll be a long, tough climb out. Must be dusk up there by now."

Getting deathly cold on the surface, and fast, yes. Automatically she cut a small sample out of the closest mat and slipped it into the rack. A strange longing filled her.

"I know. I'm not pushing for more, don't worry. Biologists need oxygen, too."

They got the rover back just before they could've been accused of being late, tired and cold but still elated by their discoveries. Over a late dinner they briefed Piotr and Raoul, then squirted a summary Earthside, along with the digitized readout from her microcam. Now, whatever happened to them at liftoff, the information was safe.

Ann and Piotr made love one last time on Mars. Piotr had been worried about her: He held her close afterward long after she drifted into sleep. After a few hours they were all up again, in a hurried rush to get ready. There was plenty more to do for launch, and months to cancel the sleep debt.

As she worked alongside the others, she was struck again at how well they all worked together. Even under enormous time pressure they partitioned the duties with little or no overlap. It all went so smoothly that by noon they were just about finished. They celebrated at lunch, finishing up with a few saved delicacies.

Despite a mountain of last-minute details, Ann's thoughts kept flashing back. Something about the team related to the puzzle of the vent life, but she couldn't quite get it. Oh well, she'd have six months to think about it, starting in just a few hours.

Piotr made her stick to their deal on mass allowance. She spent pointless time worrying about which of her sample racks to leave and fretted and even begged Piotr (with no luck)—and then thought of a last trick.

Once they had the old hab stripped and their gear transferred, she did the last rites of sealing up the worn little apartment they had now lived in for over two years. She would be perfectly happy to never set foot in it again. Piotr had already set the power reactor to low, so it could still drive the communications with Earth. She made sure the TV micro-cameras were pointed to follow the liftoff. If they crashed at least Earthside would see what had gone wrong. She brought the last personal gear over and then—her idea—had the men pass their pressure suits out through the ship's lock. Leaving the suits behind saved a hundred kilos, neatly taking care of all her sample racks.

They had to lift at night to make their launch window. Escape energy for Mars was less than twenty percent of Earth's, which made the entire process of making their fuel from Martian carbon dioxide workable—they didn't need to make a lot. But even making the five km/sec escape velocity took a lot, so the entire flight plan, including the final boost to Earth, cut matters fairly fine. They had stayed the full 550 days to make this minimum energy window.

She was strangely calm, waiting in her couch in the cramped Return Vehicle hab when Piotr started the engines.

"Pressurizing all OK."

"Flow regular."

"Max it."

"On profile."

Cottony clouds billowed outside, licking up past the square port. She could see their liftoff by turning her head and the hills seemed close in the deep blackness of Martian night.

They climbed quickly in a roaring, rattling rush, a feeling like being pressed down by a giant, yet she knew that meant it was all going well. Raoul called out altitudes, speeds, voice calm and flat.

She felt a sadness as they angled over at several kilometers up. Mars lay in its frigid night below. Then she saw it.

The entire moment lasted probably no more than five seconds. In memory it became a long, stretched syllable of time to which she was the sole witness.

Her microcam was irretrieveably tucked away. The others were busy with the launch, shouting with relief and joy and the boundless releasing pleasure of knowing that after two years they were going home. No witnesses.

She had no time to think about what she had seen because the trouble started as soon as they were in orbit. It came through her earphones in Piotr's pinched voice: "Losing pressure, Tank 2."

The methane tank had a rupture. "Damn plumbing again," Marc said, trying to be casual, but they all knew this was bad.

In the end it was their teamwork that saved them again.

Resealing the tank using what few tools they had left from Raoul's kit was a tense, precise operation. She had to go outside in the light, full-vac suit and serve as general gofer while Raoul and Marc blocked the venting of methane, then made a makeshift repair. Meanwhile, Piotr made orbital calculations.

The story of those days would make Raoul into the true media hero of the expedition. Not that she minded in the least, for indeed, he had saved them all.

But they had lost a lot of methane. Calculations showed they could not boost for Earth out of Mars orbit.

So they rethought, frantically. Piotr was the first to see the only plausible solution: the booster fuel pre-positioned in high Mars orbit by their competitors, Airbus. He put together a sequence of five burns that took them into a long, elliptical matching orbit with the Airbus tanks.

Earthside was aboil with negotiations between the Consortium and Airbus, with lawyers angrily slapping writs on each other, over fuel four hundred million miles away. Airbus argued that the Consortium team failed if it could not get home without Airbus's help: They should at least split the $30 billion prize money. This provoked a brief flurry within the government. NASA announced that the terms of the contest only specified that the first team returning successfully from Mars would be the winner. Anything else was between Airbus and the Consortium.

Intense public interest greased the negotiations. Airbus couldn't refuse the team their only chance home with the whole world watching. And none of the negotiators could have stopped the team from taking the fuel anyway. It was like piracy on the high seas two hundred years before.

Finally they agreed. Overnight, a billion dollars changed hands. Deep in the bowels of a Swiss bank, a dolly heavily loaded with gold bars was wheeled from one vault to another.

The two-bulbed booster looked surprisingly like a huge metal insect as they approached. Hanging below it was the rusty dry abyss of Mars, ripe for exploration.

Ann shot the docking sequence with her microcam, a concession to the publicity-mad Consortium. Ground Control had wanted her to take extensive footage of the whole incident, but she had refused so far. It was too much to ask that they star in a home movie that might end in their deaths, and besides, she was too busy helping with the repairs.

The team offloaded tons of methane from the booster reserves. That did not leave enough for the Airbus crew to return, which meant that Airbus had to send a second, smaller methane tank to rendezvous—no mean feat of orbital mechanics and navigation. That drama would play out years later, of course, for the Airbus team had a year and a half, just like the Consortium, to explore the surface of Mars before risking return.

The refueling worked, though just barely. Bedeviling details such as incompatible couplings in the hoses and frozen joints in high vacuum cost them time and nerves. They alternately cursed the hardware and cajoled each other through the rough spots.

But they got the methane they could not live without. The entire return orbit had to be recalculated, and of course they had missed their optimum time to catch the lowest-energy trajectory. That would cost them more fuel at Earth rendezvous, but at least they had it to burn.

When they were under way they all slept most of the first week, not wholly from fatigue, but from the need to escape the sense of a closing vise around their lives. Recovery was slow. But then she had time to think, to recall those first moments of liftoff.

They had half a year of waiting before their aerobrake into Earth's swampy air. As soon as they could they got the ship spinning, using the last stage rocket as counter-weight. This brought back Mars-level gravity and in the months ahead they gradually spun it to higher angular speeds, building up for the return to Earth.

Ann thought a lot without talking to the others. Marc processed his data from the vent and they were all pleased to discover that the vapor boiling out had plenty of hydrogen and methane—a ready resource for later expeditions. If somehow they could land a robot vehicle next to a vent and trap its exhalations, Earthside wouldn't even need to ship hydrogen to make fuel here.

Her samples were sealed away, her equipment on the planet below, so she could not work on the mat tissues or the shrimp or any of the rest of it. A treasure for others, though of course she would get to direct a lot of the work. They sure as hell owed her that; better, it was in her contract. There was no place in the Return Vehicle hab to rig a sealed work vessel for even simple studies. So she was left to her hypotheses.

Back to basics, she decided. Try to see the whole planet from a Darwinian perspective.

She couldn't prove any of her speculations, of course.

Not without knowing more about Martian DNA. She suddenly realized what to look for, once she reached the labs of Earth.

The DNA code might just hold the answer. Earth's code was degenerate: a mistake in the coding was like a change in spelling that didn't always alter the meaning. In a sense, there were alternate spellings for the same amino acid. And of course proteins themselves have regions where a substitution of a different amino acid doesn't really matter. Room for error, with no consequences.

She had always thought that was a response to a rapidly evolving planet with lots of mutagens: a Darwinian hotbox world. So a rich world struck a balance between conservatism and experimentation, achieved over billions of years on a planet where evolution's lathe was always spinning.

Climatic fluctuations changed the rules of survival, flipping from warm to cold and back again. It led some to postulate the Red Queen hypothesis: You have to keep running to stay in the same place, the entire biota evolving in fast lock-step to avoid being left behind. The pace was grueling, and a species lasted on average only a million years or so before running out of steam.

What would happen on Mars, where there may have been only one golden age of evolution, and a long twilight of one-way selective pressure? The environment got ever colder, ever drier, the atmosphere ever thinner. But there were also brief eras of warmth, when water or at least mud flowed on the surface. What then?

Ten days later they finally celebrated their victory over lunch. They had stopped holding their breaths and were beginning to relax in the tiny social room of the circular hab. The others had begun to write their memoirs. There would be four solid best-sellers out of this, no problem, already under contract with fat advances paid.

Amateur writers all, they were trying out titles on each other.

"I think I'll call mine Mars or Bust," said Marc.

That got a laugh from Raoul. "More like Mars and Busted, don't you think?"

"I know. Mars overstrike and Busted." They howled with laughter, delayed release from earlier terrors.

"What about The Long Glide Home?" said Marc when they had calmed down.

"Together on Mars," suggested Piotr, grinning at Ann.

Something about the titles caught Ann's attention. Mars had a long cold drying out . . .

She sank back into her thoughts. Now that you can't grab any more samples, let the theory lead you. . . .

On Mars, maybe the DNA code would become more conservative, simpler and more precise? After all, the direction of evolution for a billion years had been the same: colder and drier. Without sudden climatic shifts, the need for degeneracy disappeared.

Every error would be significant. The price was that evolution must be slower. Even on Earth, most mutations were unfortunate, spelled gibberish, and killed the organism. Only a very few were useful.

On Mars, the chance of a successful mutation would be much smaller, in the unchanging harsh conditions. Then what would happen if Marc was right, and there had been a few brief intervals of warmer, wetter conditions? Evolution couldn't work fast enough to take advantage of the new conditions.

So . . . what else?

Could cooperation have become the winning rule? She looked around the tiny room at her teammates. Four tough-minded types with different skills, fitting together into an efficient whole. They had survived two near-disasters and a grueling 18 months in a freezing, near-vacuum rustbowl because of that efficiency. Piotr had finally been picked, instead of Janet, because his range of talents, his characteristics, were what the rest of the team needed. That's what her subconscious had been trying to tell her.

Could it work on a planet-wide scale?

Find a partner with the desired characteristic, instead of trying to evolve it yourself.

A short period of wet and warm brought the mats out of the vents and into the lake beds, where they interacted with the peroxide forms, perhaps incorporating them into the biofilm. Photosynthetic organisms loosed from the mat—those shrimp?—could colonize the seas, making hay in the brief summer while the atmosphere lasted.

Life that found partners to help it maximize the wet-era opportunities would be successful. Glowing mats and photosynthetic microbes, free-swimming forms and protective films, peroxide eaters and watery membranes, all somehow trading their resources.

An entire ecology, driven far underground, nonetheless finding a path through the great Darwinnowing. . . .

She did some quick calculations and saw that the available volume of warm, cavern-laced rock below Mars was comparable to the inhabitable surface area of Earth. Room to try out fresh patterns.

But always meshed into the spreading network of organisms great and small . . . evolution in concert. Organisms still died their pitiful deaths, genes got erased—but the system could be more interlaced, she saw, deep in the guts of a slumbering world.

Maybe that explained what she had glimpsed at liftoff.

Her last look down at the frigid Martian night had caught a smudge of light toward the horizon. A pale white cloud, linear, fuzzier at one end. It seemed to point downward. Then she saw that she was looking less north, and the cloud glowed. A pale ivory finger of illumination spiked up from the surface, broadening.

From the vent, she knew instantly—an impossibly brilliant out-pouring. Then the ship took them up and away and Mars fell into its long cold night again.

To poke such a glistening probe of light into the sky must have cost the matting enormous energies, she thought. To make it, the vent would first have to be expelling a gusher of vapor. Then the mats would all have to pour their energy into the pale glow, coherently.

What coordination . . . and what control, over the venting of vapor itself? Could life have attained such levels?

On Earth, the anaerobic forms had never evolved beyond simple forms, bacteria. They had been competing with the hefty, poisonous oxygen-users, of course. On Mars that was no issue; the creatures of methane and hydrogen had prevailed, for billions of years, beneath the steady, cruel press of a world slowly bleeding its air and water into the hard vacuum above.

Somehow, she knew intuitively, the anaerobes had done it. They had evolved an intricate network. Peroxide eaters somehow traded with the harvesters of vapor. And they communicated—surely, for why else would they evolve light signaling?

The pearly lance, jutting up: A signal? A celebration? A mating dance? With so much energy expended, there must be some purpose.

It was natural to see it as a pointed message, but there are many behaviors in biology that defy easy logic. She knew what she would like to believe, but . . . Science is a systematic way to avoid fooling yourself, after all.

So much to guess . . .

They were three weeks out before Ground Control sent the liftoff pictures from the microcams she had positioned. One had pointed nearly north, along their trajectory. The rocket plume had blazed across the hard blackness and then vanished from the cam's fixed view. But the cam kept on recording because there was still something to see.

They had caught it. The ivory plume, towering kilometers into the sky, mingling with the gleaming stars.

What's this?—Earth wanted to know.

She smiled. Memory was always tricky, unreliable. That was why they trained you to observe and sample.

From the spectrum Earthside could tell that the gas was methane and hydrogen, with some sulfur. Useful stuff. But—what's this?

She knew then that she would return. Let Piotr sit in his estates, but she was a scientist. There was a whole vast world back there to fathom.

Not the seared surface, but the kilometers-deep labyrinth of ancient refuge.

In that last moment, she sensed, Mars had flashed au revoir, not adieu.

Greg Abraham, "Front Man," *Asimov's*, June.
———, "Poyekhali," *Asimov's*, September.
George Alan, "Fugue," *Spec-Lit #1*.
Francis Amery, "When Molly Met Elvis," *Interzone*, April.
Poul Anderson, "Tyranny," *Free Space*.
Kim Antieau, "Desire," *Bending the Landscape*.
Kage Baker, "Facts Relating to the Arrest of Dr. Kalugin," *Asimov's*, October/
    November.
———, "Noble Mold," *Asimov's*, March.
John Barnes, "Between Shepherds and Kings," *Free Space*.
Stephen Baxter, "The Fubar Suit," *Interzone*, September.
———, "Glass Earth, Inc.," *Future Histories*.
———, "Lines of Longitude," *Dark of the Night*.
———, "Poyekhali 3201," *Decalog 5: Wonders*.
———, "Saddle Point: The Engine of Kimera," *SF Age*, September.
———, "Soliton Star," *Asimov's*, May.
———, "Sun God," *Interzone*, June.
———, "War Birds," *Interzone*, December.
———, "Zemlya," *Asimov's*, January.
Peter S. Beagle, "Giant Bones," *Giant Bones*.
———, "The Magician of Karakosk," *Beyond Imagination*.
Greg Bear, "The Fall of the House of Escher," *Beyond Imagination*.
Amy Bechtel, "No More to the Dance," *Analog*, November.
Gregory Benford, "Galaxia," *SF Age*, July.
Judith Berman, "Lord Stink," *Asimov's*, August.
Michael Bishop, "Yesterday's Hostage," *Dying For It*.
Terry Bisson, "An Office Romance," *Playboy*, February.
———, "The Player," *F&SF*, October/November.
Russell Blackford, "Lucent Carbon," *Eidolon 25/26*.
Mark Bourne, "Mustard Seed," *F&SF*, August.
Ben Bova, "The Café Coup," *F&SF*, September.
———and Rick Wilber, "The Babe, the Iron Horse, and Mr. McGillicuddy,"
    Asimov's, March.
Keith Brooke, "Queen Bee," *Interzone*, May.
Carroll Brown, "The King of Seventh Avenue," *F&SF*, January.
Eric Brown, "The Eschatarium at Lyssia," *Interzone*, August.

Molly Brown, "The Psychomantium," *Interzone*, February.

Simon Brown, "Love and Paris," *Eidolon* 25/26.

John Brunner, "Blood and Judgment," *Asimov's*, April.

Eugene Byrne, "Thigmoo," *Interzone*, June.

Pat Cadigan, "Another Story," *Dying For It*.

———, "The Emperor's New Reality," *New Worlds*.

———, "The Final Re-Make of *The Return of Little Latin Larry*, with a Completely Re-Mastered Soundtrack and the Original Audience," *Future Histories*.

———, "A Lie for a Lie," *Lethal Kisses*.

Nicola Caines, "Civilization," *Interzone*, October.

Michael Carr, "A Dog's Night," *F&SF*, December.

Amy Sterling Casil, "An Officer of the Faith," *Talebones*, Summer.

Adam-Troy Castro, "The Funeral March of the Marionettes," *F&SF*, July.

Jeanne Cavelos, "Negative Space," *Decalog 5: Wonders*.

Robert R. Chase, "The Figure of Drosselmeyer," *Asimov's*, January.

Rob Chilson, "Do We Dare Disturb the Universe?," *Asimov's*, December.

Susanna Clarke, "On Lickerish Hill," *Black Swan, White Raven*.

Storm Constantine, "The Rust Islands," *Interzone*, March.

Arthur Byron Cover, "The Performance of a Lifetime," *Free Space*.

John Crowley, "Lost and Abandoned," *Black Swan, White Raven*.

Don D'Ammassa, "Getting with the Program," *Pirate Writings* #13.

Tony Daniel, "Black Canoes," *Asimov's*, July.

Avram Davidson, "Vergil and the Dukos: Hic Inclusus Vitam Perdit or, *The Imitations of the King*," *Asimov's*, September.

Stephen Dedman, "The Dance That Everyone Must Do," *Tales of the Unanticipated* #18.

———, "Tour de Force," *Asimov's*, March.

Charles de Lint, "Crow Girls," *F&SF*, January.

Emily Devenport, "The Long Ride," *Asimov's*, August.

Paul Di Filippo, "Alice, Alfie, Ted and the Aliens," *Interzone*, March.

———, "The Cobain Sweater," *Interzone*, June.

———, "Distances," *Pirate Writings* #13.

———, "The Happy Valley at the End of the World," *Interzone*, Nov.

———, "The Jackdaw's Last Case," *SF Age*, January.

Terry Dowling, "The Maiden Death," *Destination Unknown*.

———, "No Hearts to Be Broken," *Interzone*, March.

L. Timmel Duchamp, "The Abbess's Prayers," *Dying For It*.

———, "The Apprenticeship of Isabetta di Pietro Cavazzi," *Asimov's*, September.

———, "Quinn's Deal," *Asimov's*, April.

Andy Duncan, "Beluthahatchie," *Asimov's*, March.

———, "The Map to the Homes of the Stars," *Dying For It*.

———, "Saved," *Dying For It*.

J. R. Dunn, "Our Share of Darkness," *Analog*, February.

S. N. Dyer, "The Nostalginauts," *Asimov's*, March.

————, "Sins of the Mothers," *F&SF*, May.

Greg Egan, "Orphanogenesis," *Interzone*, September.

Bronwyn Elko, "Feel No Evil," Talebones, Fall.

Jane Emerson, "The New Tiresias," *The Horns of Elfland*.

Timons Esaias, "Crash Site," *Terra Incognita 2*.

Nancy Etchemendy, "Saints and Martyrs," *F&SF*, July.

Gregory Feeley, "The Crab Lice," *Alternate Tyrants*.

————, "On the Ice Islands," *Asimov's*, October/November.

————, "The Truest Chill," *SF Age*, November.

Sheila Finch, "The Roaring Ground," *F&SF*, April.

Eliot Fintushel, "Izzy and the Father of Terror," *Asimov's*, July.

Michael F. Flynn, "Gideon," *Analog*, March.

————, "House of Dreams," *Asimov's*, October/November.

Karen Joy Fowler, "The Queen of Hearts and Swords," *Beyond Imagination*.

————, "Standing Room Only," *Asimov's*, August.

Peter Friend, "Seventeen Views of Mount Taranaki," *Aurealis* 18.

Esther M. Friesner, "Miss Thing," *F&SF*, May.

————, "No Bigger Than My Thumb," *Black Swan, White Raven*.

————, "Silent Love," *Dying For It*.

Gregory Frost, "Sparks," *Black Swan, White Raven*.

Neil Gaiman, "The Goldfish Pool and Other Stories," *Beyond Imagination*.

R. Garcia y Robertson, "Fair Verona," *Asimov's*, October/November.

James Alan Gardner, "Three Hearings on the Existence of Snakes in the Human Bloodstream," *Asimov's*, February.

William Gibson, "Thirteen Views of a Cardboard City," *New Worlds*.

Lisa Goldstein, "Fortune and Misfortune," *Asimov's*, May.

Alison Goodman, "Dead Spyders," *Eidolon* #24.

Kathleen Ann Goonan, "Lullaby of Birdland," *Destination Unknown*.

Adrienne Gormley, "Children of Tears," *Alternate Tyrants*.

Ron Goulart, "Downsized," *Asimov's*, April.

Dominic Green, "The Cozumel Incident," *Interzone*, July.

————, "King's Chamber," *Decalog 5: Wonders*.

Peni R. Griffin, "The Wolf Man's Wife," *Realms of Fantasy*, October.

Robert Grossbach, "Jew on a Chip," *F&SF*, December.

Peter F. Hamilton & Graham Joyce, "The White Stuff," *New Worlds*.

Charles L. Harness, "The Flag on Gorbachev Crater," *Asimov's*, June.

Jeff Hecht, "The Crystal Highway," *Odyssey* #1.

Patric Helmaan, "Thirteen Views of Higher Edo," *Black Mist*.

Steve Hockensmith, "Arnold the Conquerer," *Analog*, December.

James P. Hogan, "Madam Butterfly," *Free Space*.

Liz Holliday, "Burning Bright," *Decalog 4: Re: Generations*.

Martha A. Hood, "Siv's New Life," *Tales of the Unanticipated* #18.

Gerard Daniel Hourarner, "Spider Goes to Market," *Tales of the Unanticipated* #18.

Harvey Jacobs, "The Orphan the Moth and the Magic," *Black Swan, White Raven*.

Ben Jeapes, "Pages Out of Order," *F&SF*, September.

———, "Wingèd Chariot," *Interzone*, April.

Phillip C. Jennings, "The Runaways," *Asimov's*, February.

Richard Kadrey, "The First Man Not to Walk on the Moon," *Back Brain Recluse* #23.

Janet Kagan, "Standing in the Spirit," *Asimov's*, December.

Michael Kandel, "Space Opera," *Omni Online*.

Roz Kaveney, "Brandy for the Damned," *The Horns of Elfland*.

M. W. Keiper, "Full Moon and Empty Arms," *Bending the Landscape*.

Rick Kennett, "The View from Stickney Crater," *Aurealis* 18.

Eileen Kernaghan, "The Watley Man and the Green-Eyed Girl," *TransVersions* #7.

Stephen King, "Everything's Eventual," *F&SF*, October/November.

Aimee Kratts, "Call Me Sue," *Asimov's*, September.

Nancy Kress, "Always True to Thee, in My Fashion," *Asimov's*, January.

———, "Johnny's So Long at the Fair," *Dying For It*.

———, "Steadfast," *Black Swan, White Raven*.

Ellen Kushner and Delia Sherman, "The Fall of the Kings," *Bending the Landscape*.

Ragnar Kvaran and S. J. Beadle, "The Hotel Vivieen," *Tommorow SF*, 1.6.

R. A. Lafferty, "The Emperor's Shoestrings," *Destination Unknown*.

Steven R. Laker, "Bringing Back Sarah," *On Spec*, Summer.

Geoffrey A. Landis, "Ecopoiesis," *SF Age*, May.

———, "Ouroboros," *Asimov's*, January.

———, "Paradigms of Change," *Tomorrow SF*, 1.6

David Langford, "The Case of Jack the Clipper," *Interzone*, December.

Mary Soon Lee, "Universal Grammar," *F&SF*, April.

Tanith Lee, "After I Killed Her," *Asimov's*, July.

———, "Cain," *Dying For It*.

———, "The Lady of Shalott House," *Realms of Fantasy*, October.

———, "Old Flame," *Realms of Fantasy*, February.

Jonathan Lethem, "Martyr and Posty," *Lethal Kisses*.

——— and Angus MacDonald, "The Edge of the Bed of Forever," *F&SF*, August.

Robert J. Levy, "The Downsizing," *Tales of the Unanticipated* #17.

Karawynn Long, "And Make Death Proud to Take Us," *Alternate Tyrants*.

Barry B. Longyear, "Dance of the Hunting Sun," *Absolute Magnitude*, Spring.

Rosaleen Love, "Alexander's Feats," *Eidolon* 25/26.

Richard A. Lupoff, "Jubilee," *Alternate Tyrants*.

Sonia Orin Lyris, "Payback," *Asimov's*, June.

Pat MacEwen, "The Macklin Gift," *F&SF*, June.

Ian R. MacLeod, "The Golden Keeper," *Asimov's*, October/November.

———, "The Roads," *Asimov's*, April.

Barry N. Malzberg, "Heliotrope Bouquet Murder Case," *Non-Stop* #3.

Thomas Marcinko, "Deep Space Sein," *SF Age*, July.

Daniel Marcus, "Killed in the Ratings," *Asimov's*, January.

Phil Masters, "The Last Flight of Captain Bale," *Interzone*, July.

Holly Wade Matter, "Water Snakes," *Bending the Landscape*.

Paul J. McAuley, "All Tomorrow's Parties," *Interzone*, May.

——, "Back Door Man," *Future Histories*.

——& Kim Newman, "Residuals," *Asimov's*, June.

Jack McDevitt, "Never Despair," *Asimov's*, April.

Ian McDonald, "The Five O'clock Whistle," *Destination Unknown*.

——, "Jesus' Blood Never Failed Me Yet," *Albedo One* #14.

Terry McGarry, "Mindchild," *Terra Incognita* 2.

Maureen F. McHugh, "Down on the Farm," *Return of the Dinosaurs*.

Walter M. Miller, Jr., "God Is Thus," *F&SF*, October/November.

Michael Moorcock, "London Bone," *New Worlds*.

John Morressy, "Rimrunner's Home," *F&SF*, September.

Derryl Murphy, "Frail Orbits," *On Spec*, Summer.

Patrick Murphy, "Exploding, Like Fireworks," *Future Histories*.

——, "A Flock of Lawn Flamingos," *Lethal Kisses*.

——, "The True Story," *Black Swan, White Raven*.

R. Neube, "Beggars Can Be Choosers," *Tales of the Unanticipated* #17.

——, "The Holy Stomper vs. the Alien Barrel of Death," *Asimov's*, July.

Kim Newman, "Great Western," *New Worlds*.

Lyn Nichols, "Mahogany Dreams," *Alternate Tyrants*.

G. David Nordley, "This Old Rock," *Analog*, April.

Jerry Oltion and Kristine Kathryn Rusch, "Deus X," *F&SF*, October/November.

Rebecca Ore, "Collected Ogoense," *Asimov's*, October/November.

——, "Scarey Rose in Deep History," *Asimov's*, June.

Susan Palwick, "Aïda in the Park," *The Horns of Elfland*.

Paul Park, "Get a Grip," *Omni Online*, March.

Richard Parks, "The Right Sort of Flea," *Realms of Fantasy*, April.

Michael H. Payne, "The Language of Ghosts," *Asimov's*, August.

Brian Plante, "Already in Heaven," *Analog*, July/August.

Tom Purdom, "Canary Land," *Asimov's*, January.

Kit Reed, "Rajmahal," *F&SF*, June.

Robert Reed, "Blooming Ice," *SF Age*, January.

——, "The Dragons of Springplace," *F&SF*, February.

——, "Mind's Eye," *Asimov's*, October/November.

——, "To Church with Mr. Multhiford," *F&SF*, October/November.

Mike Resnick, "The 43 Antarean Dynasties," *Asimov's*, December.

Uncle River, "Passing the Torch," *Asimov's*, February.

Frank M. Robinson, "Causes," *Alternate Tyrants*.

Mary Rosenblum, "The Botanist," *Asimov's*, August.

——, "Falling Into Eden," *SF Age*, September.

——& James Sarafin, "One Good Juror," *Asimov's*, February.

Kristine Kathryn Rusch, "Loop," *Aboriginal SF*, Winter.

——, "Stomping Mad," *Return of the Dinosaurs*.

Michelle Sagara, "The Sword in the Stone," *Alternate Tyrants*.

William Sanders, "Words and Music," *Asimov's*, July.
James Sarafin, "In the Furnace of the Night," *Asimov's*, May.
Robert J. Sawyer, "Forever," *Return of the Dinosaurs*.
Darrell Schweitzer, "Refugees from an Imaginary Country," *Interzone*, February.
Charles Sheffield, "Waiting for the Riddlers," *Analog*, March.
Rick Shelley, "Safari," *Analog*, July/August.
Tom Shippey, "The Low Road," *Destination Unknown*.
Robert Silverberg, "Call Me Titan," *Asimov's*, February.
———, "The Church at Monte Saturno," *Realms of Fantasy*, April.
———, "Crossing into the Empire," *Beyond Imagination*.
———, "On the Inside," *SF Age*, November.
Midori Snyder, "The Reverend's Wife," *Black Swan, White Raven*.
Bud Sparhawk, "Fierce Embrace," *Return of the Dinosaurs*.
Brian Stableford, "The Black Blood of the Dead," *Interzone*, January–February.
———, "Coming to Terms with the Great Plague," *Omni Online*, December.
———, "Community Service," *Terra Incognita* 2.
———, "The Cult of Selene," *Albedo One* #14.
———, "Inside Out," *Asimov's*, March.
———, "In the Flesh," *Future Histories*.
———, "Verstehe," *Odyssey* #0.
Allen Steele, ". . . Where Angels Fear to Tread," *Asimov's*, October/November.
Andrew Stephenson, "The Pact," *New Worlds*.
Alex Stewart, "Second Chances," *Decalog 4: Re: Generations*.
Sue Storm, "Ashes to Bones, All Fall Down," *Space & Time* #87.
———, "In the Elephant's Graveyard, Where Space Dances with Time," *Terra Incognita* 2.
Dirk Strasser, "The Dark Under the Skin," *Eidolon* 25/26.
Beverly Suarez-Beard, "Silver Apples," *Realms of Fantasy*, December.
Lucy Sussex, "Merlusine," *The Horns of Elfland*.
Michael Swanwick, "Mother Grasshopper," *A Geography of Unknown Lands*.
———and Jack Dann, "Ships," *Lethal Kisses*.
B. J. Thrower, "Noodle You, Noodle Me," *Asimov's*, December.
Mark W. Tiedemann, "Broca's Choice," *SF Age*, May.
———, "Rust Castles," *Asimov's*, April.
Tom Traub, "Dr. Max Gets His Questions Asked," *Spec-Lit* #1.
Harry Turtledove, "The Seventh Chapter," *F&SF*, September.
Lisa Tuttle, "The Extra Hour," *Destination Unknown*.
———, "Soul Song," *Interzone*, May,
Steven Utley, "Once More, with Feeling," *Dying For It*.
D. G. Valdron, "Write Me," *Interzone*, October.
Susan Wade, "A Recent Vintage," *F&SF*, May.
Cynthia Ward, "On the Last Day of School," *Asimov's*, May.
Ian Watson, "The China Cottage," *Destination Unknown*.
———, "A Day Without Dad," *New Worlds*.
———, "Secrets," *Interzone*, October.

Don Webb, "Paradise Lost," *Space & Time* #87.
Janeen Webb and Jack Dann, "Niagara Falling," *Black Mist*.
Elizabeth E. Wein, "The Bellcaster's Apprentice," *The Horns of Elfland*.
Sam Weller, "Chief," *Spec-Lit* #1.
Martha Wells, "Bad Medicine," *Realms of Fantasy*, June.
K. D. Wentworth, "Another Country," *Dying For It*.
———, "In the Land of the Bears," *Realms of Fantasy*, December.
Michelle Sagara West, "Flight," *Return of the Dinosaurs*.
Leslie What, "Beside the Well," *Bending the Landscape*.
———, "A Dark Fire, Burning from Within," *Realms of Fantasy*, June.
———, "Smelling of Earth, Dreaming of Sky," *Asimov's*, September.
Deborah Wheeler, "Mother Africa," *Asimov's*, June.
Rick Wilber, "Where Garagiola Waits," *F&SF*, April.
Liz Williams, "A Child of the Dead," *Interzone*, September.
Sean Williams, "Love and Mandarins," *Eidolon* 25/26.
———, "White Christmas," *Aboriginal SF*, Winter.
Jack Williamson, "The Firefly Tree," *SF Age*, May.
Connie Willis, "Newsletter," *Asimov's*, December.
Terri Windling, "The Color of Angels," *The Horns of Elfland*.
Gene Wolfe, "Flash Company," *The Horns of Elfland*.
———, "No Planets Strike," *F&SF*, January.
———, "Petting Zoo," *Return of the Dinosaurs*.
John C. Wright, "Guest Law," *Asimov's*, July.
William F. Wu, "Kwan Tingui," *Free Space*.
———, "Nanoships," *Absolute Magnitude*, Spring.
Jane Yolen, "Godmother Death," *Black Swan, White Raven*.
———, "Fallen Angel," *Realms of Fantasy*, June.
Timothy Zahn, "Starsong," *Analog*, July/August.

Also available from St. Martin's Press

		Quantity	Price
The Year's Best Science Fiction: *Thirteenth Annual Collection* ISBN 0-312-14452-0 (trade paperback)	($17.95)	_____	_____
The Year's Best Science Fiction: *Fourteenth Annual Collection* ISBN 0-312-15703-7 (trade paperback)	($17.95)	_____	_____
Modern Classics of Science Fiction edited by Gardner Dozois ISBN 0-312-08847-7 (trade paperback)	($16.95)	_____	_____
Modern Classic Short Novels *of Science Fiction* edited by Gardner Dozois ISBN 0-312-11317-X (trade paperback)	($15.95)	_____	_____
Modern Classics of Fantasy edited by Gardner Dozois ISBN 0-312-16931-0 (trade paperback)	($15.95)	_____	_____
Those Who Can: *A Science Fiction Reader* edited by Robin Wilson ISBN 0-312-14139-4 (trade paperback)	($13.95)	_____	_____
Paragons: Twelve SF Writers Ply Their Craft edited by Robin Wilson ISBN 0-312-15623-5 (trade paperback)	($14.95)	_____	_____
Writing Science Fiction and Fantasy edited by the editors of *Asimov's* and *Analog* ISBN: 0-312-08926-0 (trade paperback)	($9.95)	_____	_____
The Encyclopedia of Science Fiction by John Clute and Peter Nicholls ISBN 0-312-13486-X (trade paperback)	($29.95)	_____	_____

Postage & Handling

(Books up to $12.00—add $3.00; books up to $15.00—add $3.50;
books above $15.00—add $4.00—plus $1.00 for each additional book) _____

8% sales tax (New York State residents only) _____

Amount enclosed: _____

Name _____

Address _____

City _____ State _____ Zip _____

Send this form (or a copy) with payment to:
Publishers Book & Audio, P.O. Box 070059, 5448 Arthur Kill Road, Staten Island, NY 10307.
Telephone (800) 288-2131. Please allow three weeks for delivery.

For bulk orders (10 copies or more) please contact the St. Martin's Press Special Sales Department toll free
at (800) 221-7945 ext. 645 for information. In New York State call (212) 674-5151.